D1353610

The Ballad of Sawney Bain

The Ballad of Sawney Bain

Harry Tait

Polygon
EDINBURGH

© Harry Tait 1990
Polygon
22 George Square, Edinburgh

Set in Linotron Sabon
by Koinonia, Bury and
Printed and bound in
Great Britain by
Redwood Press, Melksham, Wiltshire

British Library Cataloguing in
Publication Data
Tait, Harry
The ballad of Sawney Bain.
I. Title
823'.914 [F]

ISBN 0 7486 6046 1

The publisher acknowledges subsidy
from the Scottish Arts Council
towards the publication of this
volume.

Historical Events, Personalities and Political
Groupings that Appear in the Novel

Political Groupings (1630–1660)

Covenanters. Those who signed the Solemn League and Covenant in 1637. The movement was very widespread; the vast majority of the Lowland population of Scotland swore to defend the Calvinist Presbyterian system, by arms if necessary, against the monarchical encroachments of Charles I. In 1642 they signed the National League and Covenant with the English Parliamentarians. The conditions of this, though they subsequently caused much argument and acrimony, were that in return for Scots military assistance against King Charles, the Parliamentarians agreed to establish Presbyterianism in England. This alliance broke down in 1646, was re-affirmed in 1648, and then finally broke down leading to war in 1650. After 1648 the Covenanters are often known as Whiggamores or Whigs.

Royalists. Supporters of Charles I. They are also known as Cavaliers; Tories; Sons of Belial. In Scotland they are broadly the old Aristocracy supported by some of the Highland Clans. They also receive support from Ireland.

Parliamentarians. English supporters of Parliament against the King. During the course of the struggle they split into many factions and sects, the main three being broadly, Radicals (Levellers); Independents (Cromwell); Presbyterians (Moderates).

Political Groupings (Post-Restoration, after 1660)

Covenanters. Different from the previous. They are now no longer a National movement, but are essentially peasant rebels fighting against the Restoration Monarchy and the repressions of Charles II and James VII and II. They maintain a sporadic and bloody guerrilla war until 1688. This is the period covered by Walter Scott in Old Mortality and known in Scottish history as The Killing Times.

Cameronians. Extreme Covenanters, Republicans, and Calvinist zealots. They believe in an armed struggle to establish an Egalitarian Theocracy and develop into a formidable military force. They eventually compromise with William of Orange in 1689.

Royalists. Government forces of Charles II and James II. They are used with extreme brutality in their attempts to suppress the Covenanters and Cameronians.

1

Alexander Leslie. Commander in Chief of the Covenant armies. Previously he had been a Field Marshal in the Swedish army of Gustavus Adolphus in the Thirty Years War (1618–1648), and was one of the most famous soldiers of his day. It was his return from Europe in 1639 with an army of Scottish veterans that enabled the Covenant army to be formed, though at the age of fifty-seven he was probably past his best.

David Leslie. Alexander Leslie's kinsman and protege. Major General of the Covenant cavalry, and after his patron the most famous Covenant soldier of the period.

Archiebald Campbell: (Macalein More). Marquis of Argyll and Chief of Clan Campbell. A staunch Covenanter, one of the greatest statesmen of the period, and for a time, arguably the most powerful man in Scotland. He is the direct antagonist of Montrose despite the imbalance in their talents, Argyll being a reluctant soldier and Montrose a reluctant politician. Executed by Charles II after the Restoration.

James Graham Marquis of Montrose. Minor poet, scholar, and outstanding soldier. At first a Covenanter, when it becomes apparent that the logic of the Covenant position is leading inevitably to revolution, he changes sides and becomes the most committed of Royalists. He raises a combined Highland and Irish army and wins a brilliant series of victories in Scotland, almost turning the tide of the Revolution in the King's favour. He is defeated in 1646 at the battle of Philiphaugh by David Leslie. Considered by contemporaries as the greatest general on either side, he was executed by the Covenanters in 1650.

Alasdair MacColla MacDonald. Also known as Colkeitach. He was the son of a Western Isles Chieftain and Montrose's lieutenant. He was a man of gigantic stature who steps into the period like some antique hero. Invaluable to Montrose as the leader of the Irish contingent in his army and as a recruiting sergeant amongst the Highlanders. A superb field captain, he was the enabling factor in Montrose's victories though his political understanding of the contemporary situation, like that of most of his clansmen, never really stretched beyond an antagonism to Argyll and Clan Campbell.

Charles I. Crowned King of England, Scotland and Ireland in 1625. His belief in the doctrine of the Divine Right of Kings, his attempts to impose Anglicanism in Scotland as an instrument of royal rule, his contempt for the parliaments of both countries, leads in the 1630s to a situation of unbearable tension and riots in the streets. This finally explodes, after several postponements and fruitless negotiations, into civil war when the Covenant army invades England and unites with the Parliament forces. Executed by Parliament in 1649.

Oliver Cromwell. Parliamentary general and eventually Lord Protector of the Republic. Makes several uneasy alliances with the Covenanters in the 1640s. Relations finally break down over differing interpretations of the National Covenant. In 1651 Cromwell invades Scotland and defeats the Covenanters at Dunbar. Dies in 1657.

2

Historical Personalities (Post-Restoration 1660-1688)

Charles II. Restored to the throne in 1660. He provokes further rebellions in the Lowlands of Scotland.

James VII and II. Crowned King in 1679. A secret Catholic, he increases the persecution in Scotland and attempts to restore the doctrine of the Divine Right of Kings generally. Forced to abdicate by parliament in 1688 in favour of William of Orange. He is subsequently defeated by William's army in Ireland. His supporters in Scotland are initially victorious but are ultimately defeated by Cameronians.

John Graham Marquis of Claverhouse and Viscount Dundee. An Arch-Royalist he was one of James's agents in Scotland during the Killing Times. Celebrated by Walter Scott as Bonny Dundee, in popular Lowland memory he is Bloody Clavers, an agent of the Devil and possessor of one of the most murderous reputations of the period. He was killed fighting for James II at the Battle of Killiekrankie 1689. Shot according to legend by a silver bullet.

William Prince of Orange. Dutch Protestant Prince. He was the son-in-law of James II and was invited by Parliament to become king in his stead. His appointment in 1688, the 'Glorious revolution', establishes the supremacy of Parliament, and marks the end of the seventeenth-century revolutionary period. The new bourgeoisie are now the ascendant class in both Scotland and England. The Presbyterian Church is recognised as the official church in Scotland.

Significant Battles that are mentioned in the text (1640-1660)

Newcastle 1640–42. Covenanters invade England, occupy Newcastle and defeat the king in a skirmish. This forces him to call the first Parliament for eleven years, known as the Long Parliament.

Marston Moor. First major battle of the Civil war in which a combined Covenant and Parliament army defeat the King.

Montrose's Victories 1644–1645. Tippermuir, Aberdeen, Inverlochy, Auldearn, Alford and Kilsythe. They force the main Covenant army in England to return to Scotland.

Philiphaugh 1646. Also known as Slain Man's Lee. Covenanters under David Leslie defeat Montrose. Montrose escapes abroad.

Preston 1648. New Royalist army invades England under Duke of Hamilton. Defeated by Cromwell.

Whiggamore Raid 1648. David Leslie leads an army of Covenanters into Edinburgh and to popular acclaim reasserts the Covenant position. Cromwell visits Edinburgh and a new treaty is signed. From this date the Covenanters are often referred to as Whigs or Whiggamores.

Carbisdale 1650. In the year following the execution of Charles I Montrose returns to Scotland with an army of foreign mercenaries. Defeated by the Covenanters, he is captured and executed in Edinburgh.

Dunbar 1651. Cromwell invades Scotland and defeats Covenanters. From 1651 to 1660 Scotland is under military occupation.

Post-Restoration Battles (1660-1689)

Drumclog 1679. Moorland battle in which Covenant rebels defeat Claverhouse.

Bothwell Brig 1679. Government forces defeat Covenanters in major battle.

Killing Times. 1666–1688. A period of guerrilla warfare, massacre, and indecisive battles between the forces of the Restoration Monarchy and Covenant peasant rebels.

Killiekrankie 1689. Highland army under Claverhouse defeats the forces of William of Orange. Claverhouse is killed.

Dunkeld 1689. The same Highland army is subsequently checked and dispersed by Cameronians, thereby assuring the Williamite succession in Scotland.

Religion

The Reformation of 1560 had been a popular affair biting deeply into the Lowland Scottish consciousness. Scotland in some ways came closer to the Calvinist ideal of a Theocracy than elsewhere in Europe with the exception of sixteenth-century Geneva. In a country where Parliament was no more than a rubber stamp for the King, the General Assembly of the Kirk composed of ministers and elders, for the time more progressive and democratic than Parliament, came to be seen, and eventually to act, as an alternative Parliament.

Religious doctrine governed all men's actions in both England and Scotland. Among the revolutionaries in the 1640s the second coming of Christ was thought to be imminent and the hand of God was directly involved in the affairs and events on earth. Atheism, while not being unknown, was hardly seen as a tenable position personally or politically, but rather a result of despair bordering on insanity.

That notwithstanding, the period is one of doctrine being stretched to justify recognisably modern political concept such as the Levellers and Diggers. It was also of course used to justify royal autocracy and the doctrine of the Divine Right of Kings. Scotland, a poorer and more backward country than England, never produced advanced political movements like the Levellers; extremism in Scotland tended to be extreme Calvinism with an ideal of a Theocratic Republic variously interpreted.

Witchcraft and Warlockry

By this the church meant renunciation of baptism, the demoniac pact, and in the case of women, sexual intercourse, and indulgence in sexual perversions, with Satan and his followers. Witchcraft was made a criminal offence in 1597 after James VI wrote a book on the subject.

There is no evidence that such witches and warlocks actually existed, but the belief in them was almost universal and witch hunts were endemic throughout the period, often coming significantly during periods of national disaster.

Plagues and Famines

These occurred with various degrees of virulence throughout the century. The worst famine was from 1693–1699 in which a quarter to a third of the Lowland population may have died. It was known in popular memory as King William's ill years.

Highlanders

In the seventeenth-century, Scotland was culturally and linguistically divided along the Highland Line. Highlanders who lived North and West of this Line spoke Gaelic and wore tartan. In many ways they lived in a semi-independent tribal state several centuries behind, and outside the Lowland political nation. That notwithstanding, they were a formidable military force and could, and did under the leadership of Montrose, intervene dramatically in national politics. The problem with them, for Montrose, was that their interventions tended to be more concerned with Highland politics i.e. an antagonism to Clan Campbell and Argyll, rather than any particular concern for King Charles.

MacGregors

Also known as the Children of the Mist. A once powerful clan, they were outlawed 'put to the horn' by James VI and I in 1603. This edict, which stated that anyone bearing the name Macgregor could be killed on sight, produced a tough and resourceful clan of outlaws.

'Sawney Bain . . . '

In the two days of interrogation the minister's voice had changed from one which demanded an answer to one which pleaded for a reply. He had changed the position of the chair on which he sat for reasons which he could not fully explain – he had wanted to avoid the blue eyes which glowed with a strange gentleness from above the iron-grey beard. This thought left him coldly dissatisfied with himself. At one point it had struck him that the huge right arm which had torn human flesh from the bone could, ancient and decayed as it now was, possibly activate itself and grasp his throat. It would not be a grasp that would be easily broken.

'Alexander Bain . . . '

They had tortured him badly – and they were men who knew their trade. But they had not succeeded in drawing a word, or a curse, or the mildest reproof from his lips. All that had come out they said was the icy breath of Satan. Again and again they had lifted that archaic body with its miserable shrunken legs on to their machines, until in the end they had fled in superstitious terror to their ale.

The minister looked down at the legs. They were withered senseless things which now looked as if they hardly belonged to the body, though when he could stand on them, and the minister had read the story of when that had been, he had been far above average height.

'Alexander Bain, I want to talk to you. I want you to tell me your history . . . your . . . '

The minister hesitated. The words had the sound of blasphemy about them, a trumpet blast of warning to his senses ' . . . wife and son have spoken at some length. Why will not you? This silence can avail you nothing.'

The head turned slightly. Framed in a mane of grey hair the eyes glowed like a heraldic lion's. Nothing on earth could now save him, the minister thought. He reeked of blood, slaughter, and vileness, and even to question him in this way was sinful prurience.

The minister clutched the bible which lay on his lap. The woman had said that Bain had read the bible daily in the old Scots tongue, and certainly the boy had been thoroughly instructed in his catechism, and had recited it with such perfection that the minister had not slept for two nights. The minister had tried to read to Bain, but it had been with terrible difficulty, nor had the words evoked any response from the cannibal. The minister had come near to dashing him in the face with it.

'Sawney Bain, I know they have tortured you badly, uselessly . . . Is there anything I can get you which might be of some comfort to you?'

There was no reply. The minister sighed. He was the progenitor, the patriarch of the clan, and his body and mind were all utterly degenerate, scarcely human, and his soul beyond any earthly prayers. The men who had tortured him were, of necessity, barbarous brutes, but the minister knew now what had frightened them. They, like him, had looked upon Satan's terrible price, but unlike them he had a duty to stand his ground before it.

'I cannot help you if you will not speak. I know the famine that wracked the land was a terrible thing. I was in Holland at the time but still I heard about it, men, women, and children dying by the roadside . . .'

The minister drew back. For nearly thirty years this man had lived underground, he and his wife, producing their vast incestuous cannibal progeny. The minister's words hesitated in his throat.

'Your son claims that you conversed daily with angels, which you must now know were devils . . .'

'A pipe and some tobacco wad be a blessing.'

The minister was startled. At first he did not understand. The man's voice was low and sweet, quite unlike anything that he had imagined.

'A pipe and some tobacco you say? Then you will speak to me?'

The cannibal did not reply. The expression on his face acknowledged nothing.

'Very well. I will get them for you.'

The minister rose to his feet and walked to the door. At first he had thought of sending a servant, but in the end he went himself. Edinburgh, he reflected, probably stank as usual, but to him the air smelled balmy and fresh. He bought a fine pipe and the best tobacco that he could find. Within minutes he was back in the cell.

'See, I have brought you what you asked.'

He reached out his right hand. They had broken his left arm so that it was now as useless as his legs.

'Ye hae my thanks Sir.'

The minister shuddered. The voice sounded as simple as a child's in its pleasure.

'I will fill it for you too.'

'I hae sufficient skill left.'

The minister placed the pipe and the tobacco in the outstretched palm, withdrawing his own swiftly. With extraordinary dexterity the long broad fingers extracted the tobacco, filled the pipe, struck a flint, and fell to a gentle puffing.

'Yer a gentleman Sir.'

The minister waited. The smell of the tobacco purified and polluted the air, the minister could not tell which.

'Will you now speak to me?'

The cannibal did not reply. It was as if, once again, this time behind the smoke of his pipe, he had sunk entirely outside the minister's world and time.

'Very well you have tricked me this once . . .'

The pipe was finished. Indifferent to the heat of the thing the fingers scooped out the black ash. His anger rising, the minister watched as it was re-filled and lit.

'It is obvious to me that your trade and your habits have robbed you of everything that is human. But I have something that I will read to you which may make you remember better things. It is the memoirs and notes of the parish of Trig written down by the Reverent Mr Mathius Pringle. I think you know of the place, and I think you know of the Godly gentleman, because he continues, with special reference to Alexander Bain, the witches Janet and Agnes Douglas, and the infamous warlock Steven Malecky. Are you that Alexander Bain?'

The minister's voice shook and burst into a roar.

'Answer me in the name of the Lord you bloody and incestuous villain! Answer me! Can you not see to what a pass you have been brought? Nothing as monstrous as you has ever walked the face of the earth since the flood or before it. The savages of Africa and the Americas would retch at the sight of you, such an insult to the creator, to humanity, to all nature.

But I will humble your pride. You will shortly be in Hell with your master, but before that I will humble you and him.'

Controlling himself with an effort the minister waited. By no visible movement did the terrible head acknowledge his words or his presence. When he spoke again his voice was cold and hard.

'Very well, I am no barbarian with instruments of torture for you to mock at. But I will read this memoir, which in the beginning at least gives you an honourable appearance. Whether you are capable of recognising that appearance, or the events it describes I do not know, but I will read it to you all the same.'

Memoirs and Notes of the Parish of Trig by Mathius Pringle, Minister of the Gospel in the Reformed Kirk of Scotland.

It was in the year 1639 in the month of September, I was travelling on the road to the parish of Trig, which is in Galloway, alone and on foot, which is my custom, deeming it baith healthful and seemly. I had been sent to inquire into some suspicions of witchcraft and warlockry in the aforesaid parish of Trig, God having been pleased to give me some small skill in the rooting out of these diabolical things.

I was also as it were, looking out for some Godly lads for our army, which by the grace of God and the Heaven-sent skill of General Leslie, looked to be the best and Godliest force in the history of the warld, and of which I was shortly to become a chaplain. The parish of Trig had not been forthcoming with the expected men, and it was strongly in my mind that the first suspicion had something to do with this laggardliness. I was about six miles from the kirktoun of Trig when I heard a horse come up behind me and turned to see who it might be.

It was a fine big horse of a grey colour, still some way off but coming at a gude brisk trot. I could see that its maister too was a muckle man, though not so big as to be a giant. There were at that time so many Scots lads new back from Germany with Leslie that there was little doubt in mind that this was another such, for I could see the sun shining on a steel breastplate, and over his shoulders a great foreign bearskin coat, forbye the weather was mild and hardly warranted it. As he drew nearer I could see that guns he had in plenty, four on his belt and two more on his saddle, alang with a nice musket, a trigger piece. All that besides, he had an honest blue bonnet on his head, forbye I later observed a steel ane amang his gear.

He had of course seen me and though I continued to walk on he reined his horse in as we drew level.

'Gude day Sir,' I said.

'Gude day yer honour.' Said he, very civilly.

He was a youngish man, but with a gude black beard and a face burnt unnaturally brown by the weather. By his side he had a muckle Hieland sword, and in his boot a dirk to match, but he did not appear to me to be a Hielandman.

After the first greeting he seemed little inclined to either talk or hurry on, and I, thinking of our army, was inclined to feel him out, so in a forthright way I asked him if he had indeed come from Germany.

'Aye,' said he, 'frae Germany.'

I suggested that he was no Hielandman, forbye the basket hilt on his sword. He laughed a bit at that, nervous seeming, and replied: 'Na, nae Hielandman. The sword was gien me by a Hielandman, a gude man but, but after the battle o Lutzen he had nae further use for it, nor the dirk, being mortally wounded. Cameron was his name, gin I should meet a kinsman o his the sword sall gang hame forbye I wad be sorry tae lose it.'

I put forward the opinion that like all Hieland Amorites he would doubtless have a lot o kinsmen. He smiled in a simple kind of way at that.

'Och,' said he, 'I sall ken wha tae gie it tae.'

I asked him if it was not at Lutzen that the King of Sweden Gustavus Adolphus himself had been killed? This of course I knew well enough, Leslie himself having been Gustavus's best general, but it was necessary to find out if he had fought for principle as well as money. He answered that it was and put forward the opinion that the army had nae gude luck since that day.

I admonished him a bit, telling him the plain truth, that the arm o flesh will aye run out o luck. He answered briskly enough that it was a Protestant army and a Protestant monarch. Which I agreed was true, though only in a manner of speaking, they being of the Lutheran confusion. He answered nothing to this, nor did I expect it, theology was not his trade.

11

We continued for some time in silence, he walking his horse and showing no desire to hurry, and me being a long-shanked man had no difficulty in keeping level with him. I told that I was travelling to Trig on Kirk business, it being plain at this stage of the road that neither of us could be ganging to any other place. He said simply that he was born there. I asked him when he went away, and he replied sixteen hundred and thirty, but he spoke now it seemed to me in a troubled way.

Indeed as we journeyed I had the strong feeling that he had something on his mind – some stain of sin or guilt doubtless. I had learn't much about soldiers since being with Leslie's men, and I ken weel that they are ignorant superstitious louns for the maist part, who when they're not fighting and killing, they're drinking and fornicating, having mair opportunity than maist folk for that – but quick to their prayers when they have a bullet in them and think they're near to death. But the Kirk needs them in this hour and the Kirk must look to their souls if the body would wield a Godly sword. He did impress me a bit by offering me his horse to ride, but I told him I walked by preference as the apostles did and he said no more.

In the end, I said in a plain way as we were passing over a burn, that on the road to Trig I aye stopped here and had a bit bread and cheese, and that he was welcome to join me. This he agreed to with what seemed to me a very gude will, lighting doun off his horse and tethering the beast.

He had on him a flask of brandy and two very elegant small cups, looted no doubt from some great house in Germany, because that class of gear is not to be found in Trig. But as my purpose in accepting was a Godly ane I did not refuse to share his brandy with him.

This seemed to please him somewhat, and indeed when I looked at him full-face he seemed a bit younger than I had at first thought. Indeed it was in many ways a simple kind of face, and underneath the honest blue of his bonnet, he seemed, forbye the martial gear, the kind of loun you would find in any kirk in Scotland with his collie dog at his heels – and having tae be instructed tae leave the beast outside.

I put it to him that most of the Scots lads had come home with General Leslie when they had heard that the Kirk had need of them.

He did not, I remember very clearly, reply at first, but I felt an eagerness in him then, which at that time I thought to be to his credit, and there was a clean weel-keepit look about him, and he followed me decently in our prayers, and he ate his food without slobbering like a pig, and lastly, for a soldier his language was quiet and respectful. I could know nothing then of what was later to become of him, and I write how he appeared to me at the time so that I can be seen to be without malice, though I ken as weel as any that Satan is aye a subtle deceiver.

Next I put forward the opinion that this king of ours seemed strongly inclined to forget that his was but a warldly position, and, as Andrew Melville had told his father, he was but God's silly vassal, but he wanted to rule over God's folk like some papistical tyrant, to such a degree that even the English were fairly vexed with him and waited eagerly for the day when our army crossed the border. He ventured the opinion that maist kings were like that, even the King of Sweden.

I was about to answer him when all at ance he looked at me firm and steady-like.

'Yer honour, I wad like very much tae seek yer opinion and advice.'

At the time it had pleased me greatly that a man after so many battles and killings should speak like that. I asked him what his name was, and he told me it was Alexander Bain, though maist folk called him Sawney, and not knowing, for it is the Lord's will that we should not know, anything of what the future held, I told him that Mathius Pringle was at his service.

He then proceeded to tell me a story, which I have written down, as far as possible in his own words, and as he told it, so that others can judge it, and my judgement on it, in the circumstances of our time the year 1639.

It seems that he had been on a scouting party with a body of horse – the place he mentioned, but it is of little importance, what followed was a skirmish not a battle. But it seems that the Scots and the Swedish ran into a party of Spanish horse and there was a fight, and in the manner of these affairs an adversary gave him a fair dunt which knocked him clean out of the saddle.

'I lay there minister, trying tae regain my feet but finding it near impossible, and I was still on my knees when I saw this Spanish rider coming towards me at the gallop. My guns war empty and my sword, minister, could hardly be grasped, and it appeared tae my een that this man was coming at me out o a mist. When awe at ance, nae mair than twelve paces awa, his horse was doun, and in sic a way that it rolled on tap o his maister pinning him helpless. I was on my feet now and my ain sword was out, but still I staggered like a man drunk. But when I reached the Spanish man, why his horse pressed on him in sic a way that he could reach neither sword nor gun, and nae doubt he was saying his prayers.

'I was at that time little inclined tae gie quarter, but maybe even less tae murder him whaur he lay. Sae I offered a truce and dragged his deid beast off him and helped him tae his feet, and bade him remember the name o Sawney the Scot in his prayers. Awe o this he thanked me for wae some gallantry afore retreating frae the field briskly, the rest o his comrades being already in a rout.

'For maybe a minute I stood staring at the horse, blessing the ball that had brought it doun, and saying a prayer, and promising tae say mair – I confess tae haeving much neglected them at that time. When awe at ance it struck me that the beast was entirely unhurt, nae sign o blude or wound. I looked it ower wae care and it was a fine, young, strang horse, and it seemed tae me that its hairt had just gien out for nae account-able reason, like an unseen hand had just struck it doun in a moment that could hardly hae been mair fortunate for me. I felt afeard minister, if it wasna miraculous it was very fortu-nate.

'That nicht I went tae our Scots chaplain and prayed lang wae him. It was about this time that mony o our Scots lads wad gang hame wae Leslie, but wae a kind o stubbornness that I canna weel explain now, I wadna gang wae them, which michtily vexed our gude chaplain.

'It was shortly after that at the battle o Nordlingen, which was a bludie and sare affair. I was riding on the left flank o a charge o horse when a volley frae some hidden musketry made a hash o us, and I felt a ball hit my horse, and there was a rush o pikes coming at us and I pulled round sharply kenning that *she was hard hit and could gang doun ony minute . . . But yer honour she galloped like she had neer galloped afore and we got weel clear afore the brave beast went doun. But yer honour Sir, the ball had gaen clean through her hairt and by awe that's natural she ought tae hae drapped whaur she was hit, and I Sir, certainly killed or captured, the former maist likely. This time, minister, it seemed tae me mair than fortunate.'*

Fortunate man, I said tae him, fortune is how the superstitious explain the warks o God.

He looked at me then, and I could see that his eyes were searching and his heart was seeking, and when he spoke his voice was low and humble like a man who had thought lang and hard, and perhaps for the first time in his life.

'Yer honour,' said he, 'dae ye think these incidents war providences?'

I told him the truth, that I knew little of the details of battles, but I knew that God never acted without a purpose, and that nothing ever happened on Earth but that he commanded it in Heaven. But I inquired of him further what he did next, and he declared, that on that very spot he resolved immediately to return to Scotland, condemning himself for his previous wilful laggardliness. I told him from my heart that in my poor judgement the Lord had indeed preserved him for that purpose.

It was apparent to me then that a muckle weight had been lifted from his shoulders, and a blessed light had descended in its place, and he wad pray and he wad weep, and it seemed a blessed thing tae see tears in the eyes of this weir-man. And why when he mounted his horse again he seemed tae me nae mair than a bairn with his blue bonnet cocked up and his bearskin coat slung ower the saddle, for he declared that it was now a fine day and he had nae further need of it.

On what remained of that journey I acquainted him with all the affairs of Scotland, and of England, and of what a poor pass they had come, and how the Kirk had a fine army to put them tae rights and spread the true word of God. I had this strong feeling then that such a brave man with such a Godly spirit about him would have a salutary effect on the laggards of Trig, and when he left to join Leslie, which he promised me he would, why many would gang with him.

Before we parted he gave me reason to have some misgivings on his account, though to be charitable I do not think he could have intended them. He said that he had some small business to attend to, and some very dear friends, ane in particular to see. I asked him who these friends might be, and he replied: 'Why yer honour, Mr Steven Malecky wha I hae kent since I was a bairn, and auld Janet Douglas and her dochter wha war aye gude neebours o mine.'

I bade him gude day and said nothing more at the time. My misgivings arose from the plain fact that Malecky was the very name of the man whose iniquities I had been called upon to investigate. The man the minister of Trig had declared was the worst warlock, sorcerer, and seducer of God's folk that had ever lived in Scotland. Aye and the two carlines he had named were the very anes that the minister of Trig had named as Malecky's associates.

☆

The minister stopped reading. For some time now the odour of the pipe mixing with the odour of the cell had almost choked him.

He looked at Sawney Bain. The man's hand still clasped his pipe stem, his eyes stared straight forward in front of him – blankly into nothing, or backward into the past, the minister could not tell which. For a moment he thought there were tears in his eyes and he felt a quiet exultation in his breast.

'You are the man of whom he speaks are you not? This brave and Godly soldier of whom he had such great hopes.'

Bain did not answer, but the minister was sure there were tears in his eyes now, more tears than his torturers had ever managed to spring.

'Who is Steven Malecky? Why, I do believe there are tears in your eyes.'

The head turned slightly towards him and it appeared to the minister that the tears dried up instantly and his features took on a ferocity which the minister had not seen before. He wanted to flee this pestilential cell but this devil was attempting to fight him now. The minister knew his strength and believed he must win the fight in the end.

16

'Very well, there is more, and I will read that more to you.'

☆

The minister of the parish of Trig, Mr William Munro, was a worthy and a Godly man, but over seventy years of age – ower auld as he confessed to me for this place.

It was he who first told me that this Malecky lived slightly out of the toun in a house on a wooded hill – a bit of land that he had got from his father, who had got it from the auld laird whose life he had ance saved in some drunken brawl. Or at least such was the story, none it seems could vouch for its truth. Some were of the opinion that auld Malecky had come from the Hielands, others said from Fife – some said that he was just travelling tink that had taken the auld laird's fancy.

None of this is of any importance now, but this Malecky it seemed had little inclination to work and had himself travelled a bit here and there, none it seemed quite knew where. On returning to the parish he had set himself up as a kind of doctor, forbye having no qualifications, or any real skill in that profession, just a bit mumbo-jumbo that he had picked up which was no doubt quite enough to beguile the folk o Trig. But kenning that he was sure to be discovered in time, he had, like so many of these gentry, turned to Satan himself for advice.

None knew when or where this had taken place, for the subtle rogue regularly attended Kirk, in William Munro's own words, a blasphemy in their midst.

He has three grey dugs, Mathius, of monstrous size and terrible aspect, gifts frae his maister, which gie him advance warning of ony move against him. And why Sir, should a man, or his wife, or his bairn, fall ill in this toun, his prayers are hardly out of his mouth afore he's awa tae Malecky wae gude money in his hand, pleading for a spell or a divination, or some charm tae cure his ills. He claims tae read a man's fortunes in the stars, to find his gear when he has lost it, to pronounce on matters that the Lord has put outside our knowledge.

There is a man in this parish, Mathius, James Robertson, a carpenter, not short o sillar but a God-fearing respectable man, wha at the age of fifty or sae married a lassie half his age and grieved somewhat that after three years she had not

17

conceived. I telt him that the Lord alane ordained these things, and that he should keep himself tae his prayers and his peace and not shout his complaints in the street which was baith unseemly and blasphemous. But what dis Jamie Robertson dae, in flat contradiction tae my instructions but tak himsel off tae see Malecky? And what dis Malecky say, but bring yer wife tae me Jamie Robertson.

This the silly loun dis, and Malecky they say gied tae him a potion and maks him tae lie doun on a bed war he falls asleep, and when he chanced tae open his een, why ane o Malecky's dugs near bit his heid off, putting him in sic a fear that he never opened his een again awe the time that he was there. But in that twinkling they say he saw his wife naked on the floor wae Malecky whispering in her lug.

It seemed to me, as I remarked at the time, that the men of Trig had as little wits as they had faith, not to mention martial valour.

'True Mathius, but Jamie Robertson's wife duly conceived, aye and has gone on conceiving. He now has three bairns and still the name of a respectable man.'

I gave the opinion that while all this was indeed deplorable, and measures would have to be taken to put an end to it, and I would myself see this Jamie Robertson, none of these claims was in any way byordnar, being the stock in trade of maist of these folk. We must be specific William, I said to him, apart from his dugs ye say he has two female associates.

'Janet Douglas, that they call Black Janet, an auld widow wife and her dochter that live near the foot o Malecky's hill hae the name o witches baith, but they hae the protection o the auld laird for his ain reasons. They say that he shares Black Janet's bed. Aye and when she got ower auld they say she stripped her ain dochter and thrust her intae the laird's bed in lieu o rent – not that the dochter wae sic a mither was unwilling tae gae – Black Agnes they call her for she's as dark as her mither. Jamie Mcleish and Walter Rankine, at separate times claim they hae seen Malecky and the Douglas carlines, dancing at midnight, naked on the muir wae Malecky's three dugs, dancing and fornicating tae Malecky's pipes, richt in the middle o a bog whaur awe folk ken that if a man put but ane foot wrang he will sink ower his heid. But they danced, awe o them, three, fower, and five feet in the air, aye and higher. And it is weel kent that if ony move against the Douglas carlines they move against Malecky, aye and maybe the auld laird tae – forbye there's nae charge against him ither than fleshly lust.'

Lairds Willie, I told him plainly, meant nothing to me, and if he is implicated, implicated he will be.

'He has some power and influence.'

'And the Kirk has an army now,' said I, for I could see clearly the route his thoughts were taking. But I resolved that I would see this Jamie Mcleish and Walter Rankine, and the Douglas women.

'They are very deceptive, Mathius, wae sic a douce and decent outward appearance that its hard tae believe that the dochter is lusted after by every man in the toun, forbye the young lads will not gang near her for they say that ane glance in anger frae either o them will freeze the seed in a man's belly – but like dugs in season they yelp at her shadow. There are witnesses tae the effect that Malecky ance raised a man frae the deid, Allan Bruin a shepherd, wha is anyway now properly deid.'

I was of the opinion at the time that most of this was of course nonsense, but it's the beliefs that matter, and if but ane tenth of it was true – and in my previous experience this was generally the case, stern measures were lang overdue. My opinion of William Munro was that he was a Godly man but sae auld that events had just overtaken him. Which was perhaps fully demonstrated when I asked him why this Malecky had not been apprehended before now.

'Steenie, Mathius, is not yer ordinary warlock, fleeching and cowering in some corner. He is an unco bauld man in his manner and they say he has fower loaded muskets at his door, forbye his three dugs. He also has the reputation o being a very clever man wae sword and gun. If I tried to lead a party against him why nane wad follow, tae my face they wad tell me that Malecky is a harmless peaceful man – pure cowardice, their true belief is that few wad return. The truth is, Mathius, he has an unco queer hold on awe o them, unco queer, as much politics as sorcery, and he's cleverer in warldly things than ony o the louns around here, sae approve or disapprove they are feart tae cross him.'

I put forward the point that he was doubtless growing rich on their superstition, and that at least should vex them.

'Na, na, he has the reputation for taking nocht in payment than what a man can easily pay, even on occasion gien his services free. Sae subtle is he that he stands charity on its heid, and even the poorest wha micht itherwise be spared are drawn intae his clutches. Nor dis he personally, by ony public utterance or word, say onything that's wrang, but leaves ithers tae dae it for him. In sic ways his power is spread leaving him tae pretend ignorance and disbelief.'

I confess that at that time I baith frowned and smiled a bit, which was unkind, but at that time I neither shared the Godly auld man's fears or his apprehensions. I would gang and see this terrible man for myself, and if he was to be apprehended then apprehended he would be, and why a file of our Covenant soldiers would soon dae that forbye his dugs and his magickings.

I retired to bed early that night spending much of it in prayer. This place I was convinced, needed a very stern hand, and though my present duties were to the army it came to me in my prayers that I was more needed here, a warning which in my earthly blindness I did not sufficiently heed. I was further troubled too, principally about Mr Bain. I had mentioned him to William Munro who had given him the name of a venturesome but not a bad lad, and forbye he was thick with Malecky before he went away, that was before Malecky had the malignant reputation that he had now, forbye Munro was of the opinion that it was going on in secret then too. That aside, that my first inspiration that Mr Bain would be just the man to captain a band of lads from Trig might now have to be revised was vexatious to me.

I rose very early the next morning and had some breakfast with Mr Munro. My plan of campaign was that I would see as many of these folk we had mentioned the previous night as was possible in the morning, and in the afternoon I would gang up to see Malecky himself, and if a Kirk service could be arranged for the evening I would have a troop of lads on their way in two or three days. This was a plan which like any gude campaigner I knew would have to be changed as circumstances arose.

They arose, as is the nature of these things, very quickly,

when William Munro, his countenance a furious thing and his tongue near speechless in its anger, took me to the door of his house and pointing with his finger cried out:

'There he is, and there is yer fine captain wae him.' Certainly there was Mr Bain, much as he had been the previous day, and with him another man that I took to be Malecky himself.

He was a little, square built man of about thirty, mounted on a fine horse and turned out like a well equipped sodger with a gude sword and three or four guns. Indeed had he been other than who he was I would have been well enough pleased with him, for though he was small he looked handy and rode his horse extremely well, and besides his other weapons he carried a lang auld shiltron spear on his shoulder. Munro ran into the street with more alacrity than I would have thought possible,

'Malecky,' he cried.

Malecky turned. He was a subtle, clever, clean looking man, and seemed not at all daunted by Munro's wrath.

'Gude day minister, and tae ye tae Sir.' He cried, doffing his bonnet as he spoke.

'Bid me not gude day Malecky, what gars ye leave yer wolf's den?'

Mr Bain himself gave me a very civil greeting which I returned.

'I'm awa now minister, and my gude friend here says he will ride wae me.'

Malecky laughed out loud at that, and addressing himself tae Munro said:

'Aye minister, it seems that what small liberty we hae is being threatened, and even Steenie Malecky wha as awe folk ken loves peace maun ficht.'

Munro was now like a cannon double-charged in his anger.

'Ye'll not gang frae this place Malecky, tis Godly men the Kirk wants.'

Malecky appeared to take no offence, and of course by this time the commotion had produced half the toun as an audience. With great coolness, Malecky turned to face them and sticking the auld shiltron in the ground before him he addressed them in a great loud voice.

'Lads,' cried he. 'Ye awe ken richt weel that Steenie Malecky is maist reluctant tae lift his hand against ony man. But it seems

21

that we hae this Stuart King, the son o the auld ane, wha in my opinion blessed Scotland by the leaving o it, wha wad tak awa the few puir liberties we hae, and hae by richt. He wants tae be a tyrant, though in my ain experience awe kings want tae be that. My opinion on kings is weel kent as ye awe ken, but if we maun hae them, let them sit upon their thrones wae their mouths shut, or keep their ravings for them that choose tae fawn about their feet, and let them not forget that a gude sword is as lang as a sceptre, and a handier weapon forbye.'

'Malecky,' Munro shouted. 'Be silent wae this, this sedition and republicanism, the Lord's battles are not fought by warlocks like ye.'

Malecky turned then, and if there was some visible anger in him it was very well controlled.

'Minister, I am nae warlock, witch, or ony sic nonsense, and my opinion on kings is as gude as ony in the bible. But I will gang, wae yer leave or without it, and I sall see if General Leslie is as scrupulous as ye about wha should ficht and wha should not.'

'Dare tae bandy words wae me Malecky?'

'In my ain defence, minister, wae ony man.'

Malecky turned again to the assembly quite unchecked by Munro's admonishing him.

'Lads, I will tell nae man what tae dae, but I think we maun ficht and that's what I will dae. I hae left my three gude dugs wae Janet Douglas and her dochter, tae keep them safe, seeing how they bide alane, and tae let the warld ken, which folk here already ken, that they are friends o mine and I winna hae them cam tae hairm. Now Sawney we maun ride.'

It was plain to me that this Malecky was certainly an impudent rogue, and I confess I shuddered to see how he was assisting me in my purpose, and indeed how impotent Munro was to check or admonish him.

I stepped forward and cried out to him, demanding that I might speak with him.

He looked straight at me, and lang have I reflected on the strang misgivings I felt at that time, for the expression on his face was unco cunning and clever.

'Na, na, I'm awa. If yer chaplain tae the army, which I've heard ye are, then nae doubt we sall hae meetings in plenty.

Until then gude-day minister.'

Without another word to me, and only a brisk salute from Mr Bain, the pair dug their heels into their horse's flanks and took off down the road Malecky waving his shiltron like a Border reiver of lang ago. Mr Munro roared after them to come back, which I thought unseemly as well as foolish, it being plain to all that this was not their intention, but the Godly auld man was justifiably angry.

I left Trig the next day. I had got my troop and while I was well enough pleased with them, I was sorely dissatisfied and troubled by this parish. I had questioned Mcleish and Rankine, and though they swore that what they had seen upon the muir they had seen, the twain had such a reputation for drunkenness, that their evidence, if not exactly worthless, hardly meant much on its own. The Douglas women appeared as Mr Munro had said they would, douce and decent, the lass too much of a beauty to have remained this long unbetrothed and a trouble to men. As for the three dugs, which, if they were not large beyond the bounds of nature they were certainly byordnar huge, were indeed true demons they made a very gude job of impersonating dugs in my presence.

But none would deny that Steven Malecky might be a warlock, but none of any repute would insist that he was, and if, as Mr Munro insisted, all were guilty of ganging up that hill at some time or another, then they were very close mouthed about it.

In the case of Allan Bruin, the shepherd supposedly raised from the dead, two men of unquestioned reputation testified to me that he had simply fallen into a ditch while drunk, cracked his head and lain there all night unconscious. The plain truth of the affair they declared, was that Malecky was the only man with wits enough to see this, and half a flagon of whisky and a bucket of cold water was all the magic he had used to resurrect him.

All that forbye, in my soul I trembled for this place. There was unfinished work here and a strong hand was needed, and I promised that if the Lord preserved me I would be back, but for the moment God's Kingdom itself was in danger and the affairs of Trig must wait.

☆

23

The minister looked up. The bones of the cannibal's face had set as hard as stone into which the eyes receded like two dark caves. The pipe had gone out and lay still in his hand, the stench pervading the cell. The minister felt as if he was standing at the mouth of these caves and peering down into the darkest soul that had ever walked the earth. For the first time he felt an absolute terror of the man. It swept over him like the icy breath his torturers claimed had issued from his throat instead of natural cries.

The Reverent Mathius Pringle's fears, he thought, held more truth than he could ever have imagined.

'Agnes Douglas, the daughter of her they called Black Janet, is her you call your wife is she not, though no religion ever blessed the union?'

The man did not reply. The minister slowly regained control over his terror. It was a battle now, a Godly battle – it was impossible that he should lose.

'Is she not, Alexander Bain?'

The minister's sharp eyes spotted the tears as silently they started to roll down the man's granite cheeks.

'There is much more that this good man says, Alexander Bain, much more, and I will read on.'

☆

I did not get back to Trig for six years, it being as everyone knows an eventful time. I had heard, though neither had ever sought me out, of some of the doings of Bain and Malecky. The former had been made a captain of horse with Malecky under him, and they had both I had heard, though sadly wrongly, been killed on the blessed field of Marston Moor.

I had pondered deeply then, and since on the lessons of that day, and how, with the Parliament army near broken the Lord had caused the great to flee the field in despair and had declared himself his own General, and had bidden the common folk to stand firm in his name and the Scottish horse to charge at his command. This they had done maist valiantly, slicing the Sons of Belial from their saddles and driving them from the field.

The English had angered us much in the aftermath of that

Heaven-sent victory by denying the Scottish army any credit for the part it had played, aye, and in murmering and whining in a maist faithless and unseemly fashion over the Covenant they had signed with us, as if they had not also signed it with the Lord and in his sight to be a blessed and a shining light to all men.

I reflected much on these things as with a heavy heart I rode to Trig – I rode now, getting auld. I had heard in a letter from William Munro that both the Douglas women had been arrested. Things had been quiet there for a while after Malecky had ridden away – or so it had seemed. But in time they had flared up again, with Janet Douglas becoming a cursing blaspheming affront to all her neighbours, casting in her auld age such an evil eye upon them that they were afraid to meet her in the street until at last the Lord had brought her to the stern test.

The auld laird had died, and his young heir, very different from his father, and by all accounts a very sober and Godly man, would have his rents, which had not been paid for a long time. The pair had it seemed tried ance again to bribe him with the daughter's body, but he could not be tempted by that and in proper payment had taken their milk cow and calf – which it was of course his legal right to do.

As he had walked away with it late ane evening Black Janet had followed him, cursing him and crying upon Satan that if he owed her ought he owed her his life. And that night, three witnesses, who if their accounts slightly differed, the end result was the same, that the cow and her calf had dragged the young laird into the bog, and he, helpless to prevent it, or let go the rope, had met his death there.

Others said that the cow went mad and knocked him in, and yet another said that it seemed to him that solid ground gave way and sank beneath their feet. But that he was dead with Janet Douglas's curses ringing in his ears none disputed, and Mr Munro had them both arrested, shooting ane of Malecky's wolf-hounds in the process, but not before it had so sorely mangled a soldier that he died the same day.

That I felt a heavy responsibility I cannot deny. The Lord six years previous had placed a burden on my heart which I had not fully acted upon, and forbye he had – as I at that time *thought - settled his own account with Malecky, I felt that burden heavy upon my spirit when I rode into main street of the toun. William Munro hearing of my arrival came out of his house to greet me. He had aged much since our last meeting, indeed it seemed to me that he was only clinging to life in order to see an end to this business which had so bedevilled his parish.*

'They hae confessed,' he said. 'Agnes Douglas has confessed, but Black Janet remains stubborn.'

'Have they confessed everything?' I asked.

'Not everything, not everything, but that Malecky was the Deevil's man there is nae langer ony doubt. Nor that he went tae the wars on his maister's instructions, and when he was awa Satan himsel took his place and their house became the scene at midnight of such monstrous pacts and ceremonies and fornicatings that hae never been heard of before, with the dugs taking on demon shape and human voice. The ane dug that was killed wad not dee untill a silver bullet had pierced its heart releasing its fleshly body.'

I saw the confessions, which were indeed horrible, and which had been extracted, not without considerable persuasion and effort from Agnes Douglas; Janet Douglas having become so witless and near to death on account of her sins that she could neither say or comprehend anything coherent.

Munro took me to them in their cell. Janet Douglas lay in her filth in a corner and neither looked up as we entered, or by any visible sign acknowledged our presence. Agnes Douglas wrapped in nothing but a grey rag of a plaid stared at the ground, and would not or could not, look into my face. I freely confess it made the soul of a Christian shudder to behold and bear witness to what a pass their master had brought them. I put this to her but for reply she snapped and snarled like a beast. 'There is more tae cam out o her yet.' said Munro, and sadly I knew this to be true, and compassion and pity, which I naturally felt, had no place in such an encounter.

I took her head in my hands and thrust it upwards so that it met mine, but her jaws slavered and her eyes closed against me.

'Dae ye no see Agnes,' I said. 'What this false allegiance o yours has done tae ye, poor bairn, ye didna ask for sic a mother

or sic a master, and ye can still be free of them baith.'

I looked for tears or signs of repentance but there was none.

Malecky was dead and could not help her, I told her – which I at that time believed. This seemed to produce from her a mingled groan and a sigh, but whether it referred to her own despair or the news I could not tell.

It is well known that witches, ance they have been discovered and are in their utmost extremity, will be visited by their master in some convenient shape or other, a rat or a mouse, a beetle or a spider, anything at all. He comes to whisper in their ear and give them false comfort, and bid them be strong in his service. It is then that ye must pounce if ye would break the hold forever. So Munro and I that night resolved to stay up watching and waiting to see if anything at all should approach them, nor should we let them sleep but with constant proddings keep them awake.

Accordingly we made preparations, and for two nights we sat up, and it was on the third night, Munro was partly asleep, but I was fully awake, when all at ance, as if out of the very element itself standing in the middle of the cell was Malecky himself with all the appearance of a fleshly creature. I know not how he had got in, but Bain was with him and baith had pistols in their hands and Malecky pointed his straight at me his eyes blazing with an unnatural fire like two hot coals. I confess I was surprised, but the Lord gave me sufficient strength not to be daunted.

'Sae ye hae cam back Malecky,' I cried out. 'Tae finish your work?'

He answered me in a voice that seemed to come from Hell itself.

Cam back Pringle? Why I hae never been awa. Ye ken but little o death minister, but cry out, or mak ony sound at awe and ye sall surely find it out.'

In that instant I knew beyond any doubt that I was staring at the highest demon of them all. I looked at Bain but could not see his face concealed as it was by darkness. Malecky rapped out a command and he too levelled his gun at us, for Munro was awake now and struck with fear in a very unseemly manner.

Malecky next went over to Agnes Douglas, and whispering

27

something in her ear he picked her up in his arms. She gave a fell scream and upon that instant, he clapped his hands across her mouth and whispering still in her ear he handed her to Bain. Then he went over to Black Janet whispering in her ear so loud that I could hear.

'Auld wife,' said he. 'I hae never done ye hairm in the past and I will not now, but ye maun trust me and tak this.'

It was as brazen a confession as ever I had heard and he followed it by taking a small flask from his pocket. In that moment I knew that he would poison her thereby capturing her soul forever. I knew my duty and crying on the Lord for assistance I threw myself upon him meaning to grapple with him, but like a serpent he turned and struck me.

I returned to consciousness with Munro bending over me, his eyes stricken with fear and apprehension. I thrust him aside and ran out of the door in time to see Agnes Douglas perched on the back of Sawney Bain's horse as naked as when she had danced for Satan, until he threw his bear coat about her shoulders, mounted himself, and all three, for Malecky was already in the saddle, galloped off into the night.

I shouted to rouse the soldiers that were billeted there. Ance mounted we pursued them at the gallop there being only ane road that they could take, the bog lying on either side of it. Or sae I reasoned, but they did not take the road but headed at a gallop flying straight across the auld bog – a bog that few dared to cross even in daylight sae narrow was the path. I turned to Munro, but he, his voice quavering said:

'Mathius, we canna pursue them there, the men will not follow, we wad lose the troop.'

I turned to the captain who was in command, but it was plain that what Munro said was true. They could ride, aye fly, across a place that we could not follow, and to hear Malecky's wild, exulting shouts my ain sin, negligence, and unworthyness, rose to near overwhelm me.

Munro reached over and touched my arm and said:

'The Lord will hae them in his ain time, Mathius. They may fly across a place whaur we canna go but there is nocht but Hell waiting on the ither side, we sall never see them again.'

Such thoughts might comfort him, but I could not so easily absolve myself, and I resolved to do all in my power to make

amends, and to see to it that no corner of Scotland should be
safe for them, for it was my firm conviction then, and subse-
quent events have proved me correct in this, that we had not
seen the last of them or their mischief.

☆

The minister looked up. Sawney Bain's eyes were open, his
pipe had fallen to the floor, his leonine head rested gently on
his massive chest. It was some time before the minister realised
that at some point while he had been reading, Sawney Bain had
died.

☆

The minister sat on the towering cliff known as the Salisbury Crag. Behind him rose the great mound of Arthur's Seat, formed by some whim of nature into the pagan outline of a sphinx. The minister smiled at his own fancy. Below him the city sloped from the medieval, but still serviceable, hulk of the castle to the Frenchified elegance of the royal palace – between them the spires of many churches. They had been placed, it seemed to the minister's eyes, almost at random; as if the Scots had given up trying to make harmonious sense out of the contours of a city that had been laid down by the necessities of another age, and had planted their places of worship in defiance of them, creating by accident a city caught on the cusp of time.

On his arrival back from Holland he had stood on the deck of his ship and thought the place presented a noble prospect. When he had disembarked on the quay at Leith it had been with a trembling elation. When he first met the Reverent Robert Carmichael, who was to be his host, he had looked with frank admiration at the sturdy white-haired old Covenanter with his cavalryman's legs and his soldier's physique, who in his youth had ridden with Leslie's army and been chaplain to the Cameronians at Dunkeld.

Edinburgh now had the odour of death about it and Carmichael himself appeared a shadowy, fading figure. Everything joyous it seemed to the minister had been eclipsed by the rock-like silence of Sawney Bain, and the subtle, bitter ferocity of Agnes Douglas. She had appeared to the minister a creature infinitely more terrible than Bain himself. When he had told her that he was to be the new minister of Trig her black eyes had flashed eagerly.

'Weel then if that is tae be the case then happily I sall dee.'

He had not fully understood what she had meant, but when he had inquired further she had merely laughed. Sometimes when she had spoken to him, for she had none of her husband's reticence, it was as if she knew that her words would be eternal barbs in the minister's flesh and she had placed them there with a galling exactness. At other times her voice had become soft, wistful, almost tender, as if she had forgotten the minister's presence and was speaking only to herself.

'Ye hae my Black Book,' she had said. 'In which awe is

written doun, awe that is of importance.'

She had given her book, which she had somehow managed to conceal about her person, only to him. It had been written during the years in the cave and neatly bound in black hide.

'Why have you given this to me and to no other?' He had asked her.

'For sae I hae chosen tae dae.'

At first the minister had simply allowed the book to lie unopened on his lap.

'Why Sir, are ye feart tae look intae it?'

'No, why should I be afraid?'

He had opened the book in her presence, almost he thought, in defiance of her. It was written in a bold, firm, scholarly hand, educated beyond her station, and if the story were true by the warlock Malecky himself. Her eyes flashed darkly, already it seemed to him from a place beyond his reach.

'Ye sall burn Black Agnes, but ye sall not burn my Black Book nor ye hae read it. Aye and it may be not even then, for I ken ye, and I sall gang wae ye whaur ere ye gang.'

At first he had tried to talk to Carmichael. The old man had regarded him sternly and with disapproval.

'Ye ken awe the abominations that took place in that pit o damnation? Brother fornicating wae sister, mither wae son, faither wae daughter, naked day and night like brute beasts, and worse, a pack o wolves conducts its business wae mair natural decency than could be found in that place. A wolf kens not what it does, but they Sir, rising frae their pit murdered and devoured Christian flesh. Ye ken Sir that yon place was visited day and night by Satan himself wha saw it truly as a corner o his kingdom, and weel did he exult that sic a place could be, a blasphemy in the midst o the Lord's people.'

'And yet,' the minister had replied. 'Bain read the bible daily, and the boy knew his catechism thoroughly.'

'And is that not horrid beyond anything that has ever been heard of before?' Carmichael's normal eloquence had failed him.

'I am afraid Sir, nor dae I ken the meaning o any o this, but I ken that them and awe memory o them should be burned frae our midst. The black witch should hae been burned lang syne.'

The minister could hardly in the circumstances deny this,

31

but the stark fear and barbarous reaction to it, as it had seemed to him, of the old man had secretly shocked him – a Christian, he thought, should have greater spiritual fortitude in the face of evil, particularly evil of such dimensions. He had looked, as Carmichael had not, upon the dark corruption of Agnes Douglas, which even in old age possessed an awesome fire all of its own. She had fought alongside men. She had slaughtered her fellow human beings like cattle – butchered and cooked them over a fire. She had fornicated with her own offspring producing a murderous brood of incestuous monsters, and now that she knew she was to be burned she laughed like a wanton girl.

The boy had disturbed the minister in a different way. Apart from Agnes Douglas and Bain himself he was the only survivor of the tribe which had inhabited the cave for nearly thirty years. He was the only one who had confessed anything about the kind of life they had led there. He was hardly more than a child whose total knowledge of the world outside the cave, a world he called Chaos, was his bible, his catechism, and the names of battles. He had always believed that this Chaos would kill him if it had the opportunity, and there could be no contradiction in his childish mind now that it was about to do so.

He had looked at the minister, this sturdy lad of fifteen or sixteen, with a passivity which the minister had at first taken for brutish indifference. And yet he had talked confidingly, volubly, and without prodding, until the minister was also forced to recognise that his acceptance was also incomprehension.

'Did you eat human flesh?' The minister had asked.

'We ate as the Lord provided, as he provides for the beasts o the field and the birds o the air, as he aye provides for them that he loves and wha love him, and wha hearken tae his words as faither did.'

'How did your father do that?'

'Faither kent the Lord very weel, aye and Jesus tae, and near awe the Heavenly Host he kent by name, for nightly they wad visit wae him and converse lang wae him about the wickedness o Chaos and how the Lord had forsaken that place sae that the Deil now ruled without restraint. Aye and whiles famine wad hae the grip, aye and then alang wad cam pestilence in its tail, and them that did not dee o ane deid o the ither, and the sword cleft asunder ony that war left, awe the while the Deil stooking his fire and waving his twa pronged lance . . . '

The minister had taken a step back then. The boy's voice only recently come to maturity seemed itself to have become a thing of Hell.

'Round and round the flames he danced, and awe his Earthly servants danced wae him, and the fire at his command wad strike doun great places like Germany and Aberdeen and Scotland and England in a day and a night. But the angels telt faither that nane o this could cam near us, and that in truth the Deil was a muckle coward and could only torment Chaos because the Lord had gien him leave tae dae sae, haeving himsel sickened o that place lang syne.'

'Did you ever see these angels to whom your father spoke?'

For a moment the boy had looked at the minister in utter perplexity.

'I myself have never seen an angel.'

'Och they dinna waste their time wae the folk o Chaos . . . Only faither saw them, for sae it was ordained, but we wad hear them talking day and nicht in a language that we kent not but which faither did. Why faither wad sleep aye at the mouth o the cave, tae receive them he said, at his front door in a proper way, forbye he couldna stand up, but the angels minded not that . . .'

'Did you lie with your sisters?'

'Did not the Lord tell faither that we should multiply and ony that should bid us cease we should ignore, for sic a command could only come frae the Deil, but we wad grow and multiply and nane should ever dee in our cave, and nane ever did for sae the Lord commanded it . . .'

The minister had felt his soul shudder then. The boy had regarded him curiously, like an imp of horror veiled by innocence.

'Do you know what is going to happen to you?'

'Killit, or hingit, or burnit.'

He had answered as if none of these fates held any meaning for him.

'Can't you understand now that these were devils who

33

spoke to your father and they spoke lies?'

'Why we aye kent that if Chaos should drag us forth we wad be killit, for sic a thing is Chaos that it kens nae ither thing, and can dae nae ither thing, as Jesus himsel kent weel enough when he cam doun frae Heaven tae try tae teach the folk o Chaos how tae live decently.'

The minister had felt suddenly and briefly overwhelmed by pity. He had reached out his hand.

'Poor child.'

Suddenly startled the boy drew himself back against the wall.

'Hingit or burnit, och I ken it weel, and woe is me that I hae neither sword nor gun tae guard me.'

The minister had taken two steps back. The boy had flattened himself against the wall, his face a hobgoblin's mask of rage and terror, the minister could not tell which, but then suddenly, almost miraculously, his features had softened.

'But I care naething, for I ken very weel wha waits on the ither side, and I ken tae wha waits for the folk o Chaos.'

The minister stared out over the city. It was a fine spring day, so clear that he could see far beyond the boats rocking at the quay of Leith to the hills beyond the Forth. He looked at the book lying on his lap. The Lord had put them in his path, the minister thought, for a purpose; and if that purpose was as yet unknown to him, it still could not be avoided, or thrust aside, or burned out of his mind by a pile of peat faggots. She had known that he would read her book, and if this fine Spring day hardly seemed the proper time and place, such things as it contained hardly had a proper time and place. He opened it and started to read.

☆

I Agnes Douglas was born in the Kirktoun of Trig around the time, or a bit before it, when Charles Stuart that they later killed, becam king. My mither was Janet Douglas and we lived at the North end o the toun. My faither I never kent, and if I was tae believe William Munro the minister afore my mither he was Satan himsel. For my mither's part he was a gentleman o the Douglas clan wha was killed in

34

some auld fight.

William Munro hated my mither, for what reason I canna say, and my mither in turn cared not a fig for him, but she wad gang tae the kirk tae hear him preach, baith out o her ain convictions and the law that said she must. Mither had protection then, the auld laird John Doig was her friend, and Steenie Malecky wha lived on a hill just outside the toun.

The auld laird was a drunken roaring skellum wha cared neither for kirk nor minister, and had enough power at that time tae defy baith, and he protected mither and mither wad let him intae her bed, which in the circumstances she had little ither choice.

Often he wad gang by on his fine horse, a fat, swearing great gentleman he seemed tae me. Mither said, -Lassie ye come o a line o folk that wad hae thought it a shame tae tether their horse in his midden yaird.

At that time her words did not mak sense tae me, gien that we had very little and lived under his protection which mither paid for wae her body. Mither used tae say that we had three friends in the toun, the laird wha wad be a friend for as lang as it suited him, and Steenie Malecky wha wad be a friend for ever and beyond, and then there was Sawney Bain wha went awa tae Germany.

I remember very weel the day he went awa. I was a bairn playing in the yaird when he cam by tae bid us fareweel. A tall handsome sodger he was then, wae a sword and a gun, wha picked me up in his airms and telt me that when he made his fortune in Germany he wad come back and marry me.

He had sold everything he had, and that was but little, tae buy his weapons and his horse, and he had tried hard tae mak Steenie gang wae him but Steenie wad not. That day he carried me on his shoulder intae our biggin, and mither had looked at him wae a gey queer eye, and said that this Germany maun be a mighty bludie place, and a rich ane, since half the lads in Scotland seemed tae want tae gang there, either tae be killed or mak their fortunes.

Now some said that mither could see intae the future and Sawney asked her if he wad prosper, but awe she said in reply was that she hoped he wad but she could not say, but he looked brave enough, the very picture of an auld riding Douglas.

Sae he went, and nae doubt Willie Munro was glad tae see him gang, seeing he was a friend o mither's and o Steenie's. Willie Munro as weel as being the minister was also the parish dominie tae wham I went tae learn tae read and write, and in these days he was kind enough tae me, seeing as he ance said, that it was nae mair than his Godly duty tae be a Godly influence, despite my mither, but he hated Steenie mair than any man.

It happened ane day, not lang after Sawney had gone awa, when mither wad tak me up the hill tae see Steenie, whaur I had never been before. The minister, mither said, hated Steenie aboun awe men because Steenie had read far mair books than he had ever heard o, and kent mair things than any ither man in Galloway and aiblins in awe o Scotland.

We got very near the top o the hill, and we could hear Steenie's three big dugs that he had got in the Hielans baying our approach, but friendly like. The auldest ane was called Sam, and he was a muckle huge beast, and then there was Gregor and Lady Gregor, the last being my favourite forbye she was not as muckle as the ither twa. Sam had ance killed the heid wolf o a pack in single fight.

In Steenie's house there were books and maps o awe kinds, and wonderful things frae far awa places, and Steenie wad laugh and joke awe the time, and sometimes he wad play a bit tune on the small pipes at which he was very skillful, reciting some wild auld ballad as he played. Everybody in the parish respected Steenie for his wisdom and learning, only the minister wad snap his teeth in rage at the very mention o his name, nor was Steenie aye tactful about the minister.

That day he sat me doun wae a book tae read and expressed astonishment at my poor ability, and straight awa offered tae teach me himsel. This after some persuasion mither agreed tae, putting him strictly on his honour, for soon she said, I wad be nae langer a bairn, and Steenie maun mind that. Steenie just laughed at that and said,

-Och I'll mind, auld wife, I'll mind.

36

From that day forward I wad gang regularly up tae see Steenie, and he wad aye wait for me at the top o his hill playing his pipes and reciting.

> True Thomas he lay on Huntlie bank,
> When a ferlie he spied wae his ee
> And there he saw a lady bright
> Cam riding doun by the Eildon tree.

And I wad sing in reply tae him

> Her shirt was o the grass green silk,
> Her mantle o the velvet fine,
> At ilka tett o her horses mane
> Hung sixty sillar bells and nine.

I learn't awe the auld ballads frae Steenie, and whiles we wad sing them thegither, and whiles we wad sing them verse about. Steenie said that they were the last gude songs that had been made in Scotland, and laughed at how the Kirk tried tae write them ower again and mak them intae Godly hymns. But I learn't a lot mair than auld sangs frae Steenie Malecky, I learn't a muckle amount o ilka thing he kent, and when the hour o need cam he was my maist righteous saviour.

☆

The minister put down the book. What had it been about this girl and her mother that had so terrified William Munro? What had it been about Malecky? Given the outcome the validity of his fears could hardly be denied him – and yet.

The eyes of the aged Agnes Douglas had been like two steel blades mercilessly pointed, neither giving nor asking quarter. They had taunted him and mocked him, and yet at other times they had softened, become almost gentle, as if they had wished only to yield to him.

His heart had exulted on these occasions, and in turn it had been humbled by the realisation that her memory had merely slipped away from the present into a time that did not include

37

him.

'Mony things,' she had said, 'war cried far and wide about Steenie Malecky by them that hated him, nane war true, awe war false, Steenie Malecky was a maist gallant man.'

The minister picked up the book again. Before opening it he looked down at the maze of infested streets which surrounded the castle. Further to the South, straggling down the High Street, lay the fine, elegantly faced, thick-walled houses of the merchant class, their narrow doors guarded by Christian slogans.

He opened the book. He had studied his own soul deeply and he knew himself well enough to know that apart from a direct command from Heaven he was condemned to read it.

☆

As Munro grew aulder, sae tae did his wrath grow fiercer. He wad denounce Steenie as a warlock and mither as a witch, and mysel as a Devil-born temptation tae men. And though Steenie wad say naething in order not tae provoke him further, mither wad answer him wae like words, and wad still gang tae the kirk tae hear God's word, even, she said, frae the mouth o Willie Munro.

I asked Steenie if I was indeed a temptation tae men, and he looked at me unco cunning, and said:

-Aye indeed, and I wad be sae tempted, but I hae promised yer mither, and gude faith but she intends tae keep me tae it tae my deeing day.

And then he becam solemn and said:

-But yer auld enough tae ken now that Willie Munro means mischief, and wad I think, hae tried it before now but that he kens the people o Trig are no wae him in this matter.

I asked him what kind o mischief, and he replied,

-Excummunication, aye and worse, lassie it's nae joke tae be named for a witch and hae it taen up.

Then he said.

-But this war that's coming might change many things.

There had been much talk o war that year. Women had been rioting in the streets o Edinburgh, and the swords and guns had been out in the kirk itsel, marching intae England they said, tae put an end tae the misdaens o King Charles which had angered awe folk tae sic a degree that they had signed a Godly bond against him, which they caed the Covenant. -If it curbed, aye and maybe got rid o this pestilence o kings forever it might be a worthwhile endeavour, Steenie said. -But if it did not it wad just be a wasteful business like awe wars. But they say that for ance even the English are ready tae welcome us.

It was about this time that Sawney cam back. Quietly he cam, but ane fine day in late Summer there was this muckle man at the door wae a great sword at his belt and a musket on his shoulder. I mind very weel just staring at him, sae much aulder and bigger he seemed than I could remember. He laughed out loud and sang an auld bit sang,

Cam I early or cam I late,
I found Black Agnes at the gate.

Mither cam out and looked at him. -I am glad tae see that ye hae no been killed, she said.

-Nearly Janet, whiles it cam gey near tae it.

We took him inside and mither poured him out some o her ain ale, which he drank, and whether he was on his first jug or his second I mind not, but he looked at me and said:

-Agnes Douglas, ye could be the Queen o Scotland in yer sark if appearance counted for ought.

I telt him that Willie Munro had said I was a temptation tae men, and mither telt me tae haud my tongue, but I had minded, forbye it was but a joke, that I wad marry Sawney ane day.

But Sawney had nae thoughts on that score, for awe his warlike appearance he had becam unco pious and wad gang tae join the army o the Covenant that was tae invade England and put everything tae rights there. Mither said that little gude had ever cam out o invading England, but Sawney said it was different now and the English were tae be our brithers in Christ.

-Aye weel, we sall see, mither had said. But she telt me that she doubted if even the Lord God himsel could mak the Scots and English brithers.

But sae it cam tae pass. The very next day Sawney and

Steenie wad gang off tae join General Leslie's Godly host, and Steenie left his three dugs in our keeping, and baith took me aside secretly and said they hoped I wad not gie mysel tae any man until they should return, or I should hear, and hae it confirmed, that they were deid.

I laughed at them baith, and said that I wanted nae man that wad gang sae blithely off tae a war, especially Sawney wha should hae had enough o fighting by now.

There was a great commotion in the toun the day they went awa. Steenie becam fair warlike, waving an auld spear and saying that this was ane war that had tae be fought. And auld Munro went red in the face and looked as if he wad fair hae flown at him, because every Sunday now for a month he had been trying tae get lads for the army and nane wad gang, and now when Steenie spoke they wad awe gang. And what is mair, he had another minister wae him, a fierce and powerful man o the Kirk, that we wad soon ken ower weel, that had been sent on purpose tae hae Steenie arrested as a warlock, and now Steenie was gone for a Godly sodger and there was naething he could dae.

This ither man, Mathius Pringle was his name, a very dour and stern man, went for some days about the parish trying tae get evidence that Steenie was a warlock, which nane wad gie, forbye he roared at them and threatened them wae being accomplices, but still finding naething he went awa tae be a chaplain in the army, promising that if the Lord preserved him he wad be back.

-A half-brither tae the craws, mither had said at the time. Snapping his bill for want o flesh.

Awe that forbye, that he kept his promise nane can deny him.

☆

The minister nudged his horse gently along the road, such as it was. He reflected that such a wretched track would hardly have passed for a road in Roman times – or elsewhere in Europe. He had not trusted it when he could see it. Now that the mist had come down the minister's progress had been brought almost to a halt.

On either side he knew there were dwellings, but to the minister's eyes they were such wretched places that he almost feared the inhabitants, and the many assurances that he had been given in Edinburgh that they were the most Godfearing people in Scotland did not re-assure him.

He stroked the horse's withers. They were damp. The beast was steady but uneasy, waiting for his guidance. It was a fine horse, the minister was a gentleman, and a good horse, indeed an exceptionally fine horse, was the minister considered, his one major worldly vanity. He excused himself for it. He had to travel, and he could not tolerate broken-down intractable nags.

The horse stopped and let out a long piercing whinny. It trusted neither the road nor his hand. The minister would have to dismount and lead him, and he knew the road would be ankle deep in mud. For a moment the minister sat in the saddle and prayed. He opened his eyes to the swirling mist around him and once again started to push the horse forward. It bellowed mournfully, and from out of the mist it was as if the shaggy, silent head of Sawney Bain now bellowed mockingly with him.

The minister had completely lost his way. In his heart he condemned the foolish vanity that had wanted to make the journey to Trig without a guide, but he had wanted to see the country and the people, which were after all his people and his country, on his own.

He had seen them. The country was hills and stones and crows, and the people were a surly peasantry with the marks of hunger and pride deeply engraved on their faces. Wrapped around in grey plaid and blue bonnet they appeared to his eyes like the shrouded ghosts of a stubborn race. They had saluted him as he passed, with a forwardness which mingled respect and arrogance in a way which unsettled the minister.

He took a sip from a flask of whisky. In the circumstances he felt it was justified, and indeed it seemed to attune his eyes more keenly. He pushed his horse forward with more confidence and it responded. This road, he reasoned, may not be the correct road, but it must be the road to some place.

He felt cheered by this logic. The mist was no more than a natural hazard and to master it some sensible care had to be

41

taken. There were no other dangers. The dreadful pestilence of the cannibal clan was already a thing of the past, already a terrible secret, but still, he thought, days like these would surely have been counted as blessings by them.

Suddenly a voice hailed him. Beneath the uncouth dialect to which he had not fully accustomed himself he caught the name of God. Boldly the minister answered it and a figure stepped out of the mist. At first the minister could hardly make him out so enveloped was he in his plaid, but he was a short, almost dwarfish figure, his small stature accentuated by a great breadth of shoulder. On his head was the ubiquitous blue bonnet, and underneath it a bearded face which the minister thought not so much savage, but certainly lacking in all refinement. Over his shoulder he carried a weighty staff which seemed almost too large for his frame. A few paces behind him stood a boy also wrapped in a plaid, who seemed to tower insubstantially over the man.

'Yer honour, Sir, though it may not be my business, wad seem tae be in some difficulty . . . I heard the horse Sir . . .'

The man pushed back his hood. The minister quickly mastered a sudden apprehension. The face was pitted with small pox scars, and another long scar travelled from his hair to his eyebrows.

'I am looking for the house of a gentleman of this district, Mr Andrew Gilmore.'

'Andra Gilmore, aye, ye'll hae lost the road in the mist . . . It's back a small bit, this ane gangs tae nae mair than my ain bit biggin.'

'Do you know the gentleman?'

'Aye, aye, gin I should dae, seeing that in an earthly way o speaking he's my maister.'

For a moment it seemed to the minister that the small man's mind had wandered. Quickly he said:

'If you can lead me to his house I will pay you well enough for your trouble.'

'Na, na, keep yer sillar, tis not the kind o thing tae be flinging at a Godly man for what's nae mair than a Godly service. Gang awa Samuel and tell Gudeman Gilmore we sall shortly be at his door.'

The boy briskly shouldered his staff and to the minister

seemed to just disappear. The minister noticed that the scar on the small man's face extended over his scalp, parting his hair.

'Turn this beast round Sir, we maun gang back.'

Apprehensively the minister turned his horse. For a moment it occurred to him, that to any sensible man it would be at least a possibility that this dwarfish brigand had merely sent the boy ahead to prepare a more convenient ambush. This thought was not eased when the man took hold of his horse's bridle, confidently apologising as he did so. He set off at a walk pulling the horse behind him. The minister resolved himself to trust, wherever they were going the pace of man and horse was now a steady one. The minister listened to the man's brogues squelching in the mud and felt oddly re-assured by the sound. Suddenly without looking round he said:

'For yer sillar I hae nae desire, but a drop frae yer bottle wad not gang amiss, unless ye think the thrapple o John Erskine is amiss.'

He had watched him for some time before revealing himself, the minister thought, but could make nothing further of that. But the man had a name and had given it freely. He handed him the flask and John Erskine promptly threw back his head and took a prodigious swallow.

'Take all you please, it's a cold evening and my blundering has no doubt inconvenienced you.'

'John Erskine thanks ye,' he said, taking another huge mouthful before handing the flask back. 'It's a fine beast yer riding . . . Ance I had ane nearly as gude, but it had been sare ridden by a dragoon, wha, as is the nature of these creatures, had tae be piked frae the saddle ere he becam John Erskine's. Frae that time on he prospered in God's service and wae a kindly maister.'

'I'm glad to hear it, though I wonder a bit at the occasion.'

'He caught me at my prayers Sir and the Lord guided my hand, which he has aye done.'

They came to a fork in the road which the minister should have taken, which, though it was wider was in no better condition. The minister began to feel safer and wanted to question John Erskine further, but he had either decided to fall silent, or when he spoke his language was so strange that the minister could not always follow it, till suddenly he shouted out:

43

'An here is Andra Gilmore the gentleman ye are seeking.'

The mist appeared to have drifted slightly now. The minister's eyes following John Erskine's outstretched arm could just distinguish a sturdy looking man riding towards them on a shaggy pony, the boy Samuel trotting lightly at his heels.

'Gude evening yer honour, I was about tae gang out and look for ye mysel when Samuel here turned up.'

His clothes were much the same as John Erskine's, and, if the minister was re-assured by his appearance and his greeting, he would not have marked him out in any company as a gentleman.

'The Reverent Carmichael in Edinburgh gave me your name and place and said you were a Godly man in whose house I could stay for the night, but I would have gone right past it had it not been for the kindliness of this man and his boy.'

The two men exchanged words. For a master and a servant they talked to each other with an easy familiarity, but in a language which was to the minister's ears like a foreign tongue. When the old man and his boy started to depart the minister said:

'Mr Erskine, take the rest of this flask, not in payment but in thanks. It will comfort you more than me. I am comforted enough to know that I will have a roof over my head tonight. I was entirely lost and it was a blessing to meet up with you.'

For a moment the small man looked vaguely offended, Andrew Gilmore laughed merrily.

'Tak it John and let's hae nane o yer Cameronian quibbles. A shepherd has mair need o it on the hillside than a minister by a warm fire.'

The shepherd smiled, which made the scar wrinkle hideously across his brow. He stretched out his hand for the flask.

'John Erskine thanks ye minister.'

'And I thank John Erskine much more.'

The mist, which had seemed to be clearing, had thickened up again. The shepherd and his boy disappeared into it as if it was their natural medium. The minister followed Andrew Gilmore, whom he could now barely see, in single file along the track.

'It's unco strange tae get sic a mist at this time o the year, ' was all Gilmore said.

44

'I am very grateful to your man, who at first I must confess somewhat startled me by his appearance.'

'John Erskine is naebody's man as I am naebody's maister.' The minister felt a sudden twinge of exasperation.

'He referred to you as his master.'

'Aye John will hae his wee jests. He looks after the sheep for me, and a handy man he is wae them, but he owns nae earthly maister, nor wad ony that had ony sense ever fee him.'

'How did he get that terrible cut on his head?'

'At Drumclog. Ane o Claverse's dragoons damn near split his skull. But when he turned his horse – little thinking that John could be onything but deid, John rose frae the heather presenting sic a sicht that the beast threw his rider. And forbye the sodger was on his feet quick enough wae his ain sword out, the sicht o John Erskine covered in blude and crying on Jesus maybe unnerved him a bit, for John shredded him like a corn-stook. Nor did he stop till Claverse and his bludie pack had awe ran awa. Some say his brains never quite knitted thegither after that, but he fought at Bothwell Brig, and at Dunkeld, gieing quarter tae nane, and some they say near deeing o fricht at the sicht o him, forbye he's a kindly enough man in his ain way.'

The minister felt the cold hand of this country grip him from out of the mist. Andrew Gilmore continued, the tone of his voice almost jocular.

'After Dunkeld the Hielanmen made a sang about him saying that he was nae mair than a fairy driven out of the fairy country on account o the fact that they couldna thole his bludie ways.'

Andrew Gilmore held up his hand. Through the mist the minister could see that they were at a house, which, if it was better than many the minister had seen that day in that it was built of stone, would have been considered a poor enough dwelling by any prosperous Dutch peasant. He followed Gilmore in dismounting. A boy of about ten appeared to take their horses.

'Ye can leave yer fine horse in Colin's keeping, he kens weel what's needed.'

The minister retrieved his bags and handed the reins of his horse to the boy. Andrew Gilmore beckoned him and he followed him through the door.

It took a long time for the minister's eyes to adjust from peering into the mist to the gloom of the cottage. The room was almost bare, a cabinet chest, a table and some chairs, all of plain wood, though the chest and the chairs had been varnished. The floor was of stone covered with straw, but the straw was clean and there was a fine fire in the hearth.

A handsome woman of about thirty, greeted him in a respectful way which suddenly cheered the minister. She took his bag and cloak while Gilmore motioned him to sit down by the fire. Andrew left the room and returned with two large mugs of thick beer, which looked foul to the minister's eyes, but certainly, as he admitted, warmed his insides. On the wall above the fireplace hung a musket and a fourteen foot pike, both gleaming and well cared for. They affected the minister's mind somewhat when for the first time he looked properly at Andrew Gilmore himself.

He was a stalwart, dark-haired man of about average height and forty years of age. It was an open kind of face, the minister thought, with clear grey eyes. And though there was nothing of the gentility that the minister had expected, there was nothing cloddish about it either.

'Weel minister, ' he said at length. 'And how is the Reverent Carmichael?'

'Very well, and in good health, and he sends his regards to you.'

'He was our chaplain at Dunkeld, and a rattling gude preacher, but he wad hae nae cheering after the victory, saying it was the Lord's wark and no ours which had achieved it. Which was very stern tae my way o thinking, gien that I had a musket-ball in my leg and my airm near sliced off by a Hielanman's broadsword. And I had fought canny like, while ithers looked just desperate tae bid the warld gude nicht. Nae doubt he will hae telt ye about this . . .'

'Not much, though I have heard of the battle. I have only recently returned from Holland where I have spent almost all of my life. I am to be the new minister of the parish of Trig.'

'Could ye no hae got a bit body tae gang wae ye, ane that kens the country?'

'It may appear foolish now, but I wanted to travel alone, and

I was assured that the countryside was peaceful enough now.'

'Peaceful enough, aye, beaten and starved and exhausted, but there's still a pickle o wild hameless folk in the hills, but poor and tame now.'

The minister could hardly follow the man's rambling speech, which seemed to him to be full of vague implications and questions. A bonnet-laird was how Carmichael had described him, an independent man with just enough land to keep himself and his family, and no doubt, the minister thought, his bonnet on his head.

'The Kirk and State are secure now, which surely must be a blessing to everyone.'

'Aye, the Kirk is secure an King Willie is on his throne, an nae doubt it can be said, an is said, that that is a fine end tae awe our troubles.'

Was he even contemptuous that the minister had played no part in, and had only hear-say knowledge, of their already ancient brawls? The minister did not know, and there was no time for an answer, Gilmore stated that it was time to eat and he would undoubtedly say a few words before the meal.

At the meal, which was a plain one of mutton broth and oatmeal bread, the minister met the rest of Gilmore's family, the boy who had taken his horse, and another younger son, also a comely girl of twelve.

'There were twa mair,' said Andrew Gilmore. 'Wha deed during the ill years. We aye remember them in our prayers.'

Gilmore spoke their names, they had both died in infancy, and the minister duly remembered them.

After the meal was over the minister's host drew some more beer, and, the rest of the family having gone to another room, signalled that the minister should once again join him by the fire.

The minister felt tired and irritated. Did this fellow think that the price of a bed was that he should drink half the night with him? It was not, as the minister saw it, how a Christian man should spend his evenings. Nor was the ale, which he gathered was brewed by Gilmore's wife, much to his taste, but he sat down.

'Was the famine very hard in this district?'

It seemed to the minister then as if all of Andrew Gilmore's

47

features darkened and aged.

'It hammered the life out o people as naething else could, an we suffered it better than maist. Mony hae never recovered tae this day. Mony went in search o food and never returned. Ye'll nae doubt see their graves on the hillside and by the road. Todd Grey was their last company on earth.'

'Todd Grey?'

'Todd Grey, or Grey Todd as some folk say, an auld man wha made it his unfeed profession tae bury the deid whaur ere he found them. John Erskine said it was the Lord's strang richt hand lifted in righteous wrath against the folk.'

'Surely you don't believe that kind of thing. It's sheer superstition.'

Andrew Gilmore shook his head, but it was difficult for the minister to interpret the gesture.

'Ane nicht a man turned up at this door wae the corpse o his wife on his back. He threw her doun at our feet and said, in the name o God will ye bury her, an if ye winna dae that, stick her on yer dyke whaur she'll keep the foxes frae yer hen hoose. For awe that we could dae for him he deed himsel the next day. John Erskine's boy Samuel we found by the roadside eating grass. An sae it went on, an the people ate the seed they should hae kept for next year's planting, an a pestilence hit the cattle, an mony thocht that maybe they had been ower hasty in declaring Dutch Willie as the Lord's anointed, an that we war, as auld Erskine wad insist, in Eygpt ance again.'

The minister felt the weight of an oblique rebuke in everything Andrew Gilmore said. Involuntarily he thought of the impenetrable silence of Sawney Bain, the wild and hag-like savagery of Agnes Douglas, and the youth Dugald who had eaten little but human flesh, and who knew nothing of the world except his bible and the names of battles.

'Ye see minister, an I mean nae impoliteness, mony o us thocht, that despite what Parliament said, and the gentry said, aye and the Kirk said, that maybe William of Orange was not a very satisfactory end tae awe our sufferings.'

The minister glanced up at the gleaming head of the pike. It seemed to trail a century of barbarity and confusion behind it.

'When I get to Trig it will be my duty to minister to what is there now, and what is to come in the future, not what has happened in the past.'

'I was born in that year, when as my faither said, a country that never thocht it wad see a king again, sat a new pharaoh on the throne, an cheered themsels hoarse tae see him sitting there, an within six years the swords were out on the hillside again an the dragoons war riding the glens . . . But minister, dinna mistake me, nae doubt this is a new time and yer principles and convictions dae ye credit.'

Once again the minister could not read what lay behind the man's words. Once again he felt vaguely irritated. Andrew Gilmore stood up.

'Come, ye maun be tired after sic a day, an I sall show ye tae yer bed.'

☆

The minister sat on the bed without undressing. The Black Book lay un-opened at his side. He had prayed long for guidance. Now he stared out of the tiny window, thankful that it was at least glazed, on to the naked hills still wrapped in a mist which seemed to deny them any corporeality. He thought of the green parks of Holland tilled by a decent and industrious peasantry who could love and fear God without dragging him as their standard into their primitive brawls.

'Ye sall not burn my Black Book nor ye hae read it.' She had said, and she had been right. He started to read by the light of the tallow lamp that Andrew Gilmore had provided.

☆

We heard very little o the war at that time in Trig. On occasion some lads wad return sorely wounded, or minus an arm or a leg, and some wad say that great and Godly things were being done, and ithers wad say very little. Leslie, it seemed, had joined up wae the English that were against the King, and had been their strong back-bane driving the King's men frae the field at a place called Marston Muir, though it was said that the English wad gie them nae credit for it and were likely tae behave treacherously ower the Covenant they had signed in return for Scots help.

When mither heard o this she just laughed them awe tae Hell for being brainless louns. Mither had becam very strange about this time, and wad on occasion curse folk in the street for what she said were her ain reasons, but which were beyond me. And nae doubt they were beyond ither folk tae, for they wad either avoid meeting her, or gang by her wae a swift gude day and their heid bowed.

Nor was she any langer respectful o auld Munro, and he in his auld age and rage wad hae as little restraint as she, till the hale parish said that the place was damned by a mad minister and a mad witch and the Lord could hardly be expected tae put up wae it much langer.

It was about this time that the auld laird passed on, deid drunk in his sleep they said. His son the young laird wha was at the university in Edinburgh, cam then tae Trig, first

for the funeral and then tae claim his inheritance, and folk
said how very nearly the clear opposite o his faither he was,
being sober and Godly and strang for the Kirk. That forbye,
frae mither he wanted his rents, aye and he wad raise them
tae, tae mak up, he said, for awe the years whaur mither,
because of the auld laird's favour, had paid nae rent ither
than wae her body.

I mind the day very weel when he first cam tae our
biggin. A thin man he was, dressed in black wae a fine silver
sword by his side, and for ance mither was very quiet when
she received him, though at the time I kent not exactly what
passed between them. As he left I was in the yaird and he
stared at me for a lang time wae a strange bit smile curling
about his lips, but he offered nae word o greeting before
mounting his horse and riding awa.

Mither, when I found her, looked as if awe the fire had
gone out o her. She just sat unco quiet drinking her ale, her
fingers curling and uncurling in the lang hairs on Sam's
neck, the dug watching her wae a queer look in his een.

-We are ruined lassie, she said, -plain ruined, and maun
tak tae the roads and beg, for we canna pay what we canna
pay.

She looked at me then, and she had tears in her een,
which I could not remember ever seeing before, and then
her voice grew a bit fierce again, but she spoke tae the dug
and not properly tae me.

-Why Sam, gin I had only mysel tae think about, I wad
hae snapped my fingers and ye wad hae had his throat ere
he spoke tae Janet Douglas like that. Nor wad I hae cared if
I had hung or burned for it, but I hae the lassie tae think
about.

I said that if Steenie or Sawney cam back they must
surely be able tae help in some way. My mither turned on
me then a very hard auld ee.

-Why carline they may be without God, but they are no
without wits. The new laird wants his rents, and Munro is
pushing him, and why, for they are neither o them brave
men? But news has cam that Sawney and Steenie were baith
killed at Marston Muir, the daft louns, riding against
English guns, daeing the Lord's wark, when ithers are daen

the Deevil's behind their backs. Damn them awe, this warld o men wha ever rules it, is as much a Hell as any that Willie Munro will gang tae, or yon holy ferret o a new laird wha telt me that my presence dishonoured his mither's memory, when it is weel kent that when he stuck his heid out o her she deid o fright at the sight o him.

Mither stayed indoors after that. It seemed at the time true that Steenie and Sawney were baith deid, and forbye Munro wad say that they had got their deserts, and that the Lord wad not be mocked, and that the new laird was a fine and Godfearing man, few wad agree wae him but just waited tae see what wad happen, sad nae doubt, but silent awe the same.

It was two weeks after the laird's visit. He had it seems, been tae Edinburgh. For mither and me, and for the toun that watched, it was as if time itsel was standing still, and the warld was daen likewise, except that mither got very quiet and auld.

Awe ended when the laird cam late ane night and mither wad not let him in forbye he hammered on the door, not maybe for very lang, the dugs making it plain tae him what he wad meet if he tried tae break in, but mither said never a word.

He gied ower his hammering and cam intae the shed whaur I was seeing tae the cow and her new calf. I turned tae find him standing in the door leaning on the wall, ane hand resting on his fine silver sword. For a while he just stared at me, his face sae pale and thin that it seemed tae just shine in the night. I watched him, but wae my een lowered, not kenning what tae dae or what not tae dae, frightened, for he seemed drunk, aye and mair than that.

-I hate this place, he said. -Even though I am maister here.

I didna answer him. How could I? He walked towards me, staggering a bit but his een were steady and never left staring at me. And forbye I backed awa as he advanced there was naething behind me but the wall and he was almost upon me when he stopped and sat doun on a heap o straw.

-I am worried about yer mither, Agnes. She has barred

52

the door and willna answer it, which is not at awe the way I should be received.

-Mither, I said, -has becam a bit strange in her auld age, maist folk mak allowances.

He stood up then, very close tae me, and reaching out his hand he pulled the plaid back frae my heid.

-But we are young Agnes, are we not?

His hands played wae my hair then, and certainly he felt they had every right tae dae sae.

-I ken not why ye country girls wrap yersels up like sacks o tatties.

I could feel his breath then, hot and hard, which seemed tae gang before him panting like a dug.

-Ye ken the situation here now Agnes, dae ye not? Yer mither's a whore, and she has paid for this place in what my faither was nae doubt prepared tae accept as his rents in kind. Now that is an auld custom which is deeing out, and I hae little inclination tae tak my faither's place in yer mither's bed, and forbye I am rightly vexed at the way she is treating me I can be generous and forgiving tae them that I like, and wha like me.

He gied out a bit laugh then, like a screech, and I could retreat nae further, and then his hands were tearing at my plaid and thrusting themsels inside it. I put up my hands only tae hae them grasped in his.

-Why Agnes, there is nice clean handy straw here, sae we can see how weel we like each ither, which will bode weel for the future.

There seemed nae way out that night, nae way at awe. I kent there was nae use in protesting that wad not bring doun mair trouble on our heids. And weel he kent that tae, and I could see the sureness in the weasel bit smile that crept about his lips.

-Doun Agnes, doun and on yer back, and if ye are kind and I like ye, why ye maun bide here till judgement day, but if I dae not, why ye and yer mither maun become gypsies.

Then awe at ance mither hersel was at the door o the shed.

-Damn ye Doig, she shouted, -tae the deepest dungeon o Hell.

53

She was standing there wae a muckle auld musket in her hands and Sam and Gregor at her heels. She was screaming and cursing far mair demented than I had ever seen her before.

-Are ye no feart man? When Black Janet Douglas curses Heaven and Hell baith listen.

Many ither things she cried mair terrible than flesh could stand. The young laird got tae his feet, his pale face turning red, his hand on his sword.

-Haud yer tongue auld woman, haud yer tongue.

Mither's screams rose tae an awful wildness then.

-Why should I? Why should I haud the tongue that's sending ye tae Hell this night?

The auld gun waved wildly in the air but it was plain tae see the laird was less afraid o that than he was o the dugs.

-I hae my legal rights, and if ye will not pay my rents, or even answer the door, why I sall tak this cow and calf and yer daughter's attempts tae play the whore wae me will not stop me. I hae a pistol which will soon put an end tae that hound o yers, and if ye try tae shoot that gun ye are as likely tae hit the girl as me.

-Ye hae but ane ball in yer pistol, ye dung beetle's bastard and I hae three gude dugs, the least o them worth mair than yer corpse.

-Ye sall hang for it auld wife, ye and yer daughter, if they dae not burn ye first.

Unless mither went completely mad and shot him, or set the dugs on him, he had the upper hand and he kent it, and I went ower tae mither and telt her tae pit the gun up. She looked at me then her een blazing mad, but awe she said was,

-Cover yersel lassie, the een o a beast like thon will shrivel yer guts.

I telt her tae haud the dugs, and the laird seeing that he had won, and of course thinking tae that this was by nae means the end o the business, took the cow and her calf, and swaggering and staggering he pulled them out o the door after him, the beasts very laith tae gae but he was a brave jockie now, and wae a pistol in his hand. If he turned a bit pale at the sight o Sam and Gregor wae their hair up

54

just desperate for his throat, he kent very weel that I had a
firm grip on baith and dared not let them gae.

-These beasts are a very small part o what ye owe me,
but I will tak them just tae let ye ken that I'm no the fool
my faither was, nor am I tae be played like ane. When I cam
back again, which will be soon, I expect tae meet wae some
sense.

He staggered doun the road dragging the beasts after
him, when mither, as if awe restraint had deserted her, was
running after him, raging at him wae sic curses that it was
later said the hale toun could hear, curses that were sae
terrible that the laird could neither say his prayers, shoot his
gun, nor find his way hame, but mither followed him awe
the way, hounding him intae the auld bog whaur they
found him the next morning, the cow and her calf quietly
chewing by the side o it.

Some said that they had dragged him in, and then of
course being witched had quietly walked out again. Ithers
said that on mither's instructions the cow had gone mad
and knocked him in, and still ithers said, but very quietly,
that the beasts had simply had mair sense than the laird and
kent weel when firm ground was under their feet and when
it was not.

Munro had nae doubts on the matter. A Godly man had
been done tae death by witchcraft and mither and I maun
burn for it.

Wae this purpose he cam tae our door wae a file o sodgers awe shivering in their breeks, and Sam tore the throat
out o ane o them before a sodger shot him, and forbye they
tried tae shoot the ither twa, mither telt them tae be gane
and tae breed whelps tae plague the parish o Trig till the
day o judgement.

But in sic fashion they took us, and dragged us through
the toun and stripped us naked, and stuck a needle intae
awe parts o us sparing nane, looking for what they caed
Satan's mark. Awe this auld Munro wad watch, his red face
glowering and his een triumphant.

-When did ye last see the Deil, Agnes? When did ye last
tak him tae yer bed? He canna help ye now Agnes and sae
ye maun confess.

55

On and on his voice ranted and I could see the blude running ower my flesh, and he could see it, and it may be that made his ain blude boil the faster, and I could hear mither's banes cracking under their instruments, and her screaming and cursing at them, and they left nae part unmolested sae sure were they that the Deil had not.

At night they wad leave ye tae lie in yer ain muck, but watching ye awe the time in case the Deil himsel should pay a visit. This did not of course happen, but still ye wad lie there listening tae mither moaning, and kenning, aye and praying, that she was deeing fast, hearing yersel howling, kenning that sometimes it was yersel, an at ither times it was like a beast far awa in the hills. Aye and whiles ye kent the Deil was there for ye wad see this beast, muckle, black, and wolf-like, wae blude running frae its jaws, and at ither times it wad be like a serpent o silver and gold wae een like red moons, and at ither times ye wad see naething at awe, just the darkness that fell about ye, and then the darkness itsel wad becam fiery red and colours and shapes o awe things wad race through it, and aye ye couldna sleep, for should ye close yer een they wad prod ye awake, and ye kent that in the morning their hands wad seize ye ance again and hoist ye on tae their ropes, murdering ye bit by bit, and telling ye aye that the Kirk had a duty, and it was a sare duty, wae a lang hard road tae gang ere a witch could be snatched back frae the jaws o Satan.

In the morning of the second or third day auld Munro cam in and I looked up at him and cried out tae him. -Look weel on yer wark Willie Munro look weel on it . . :

He roared at me then in a terrible voice tae be silent and not tae further compound my iniquities wae resistance. He had a confession for me tae sign which might save mither and me further torment, if I wad but confess tae awe that he kent tae be the truth, word and deed.

And what was I tae confess tae? That I had renounced my baptism at Satan's command, that mysel, mither, Steenie, and the three dugs in demon shape had danced wae the Deevil himsel, ten feet in the air aboun the auld bog whaur the laird had drouned, awe tae the screeching o Steenie's pipes, dancing and fornicating, baith wae the Deil and wae Steenie, aye and on occasion wae the dugs. Aye and what was mair he wad hae the demon names o the dugs, for without them they could not hunt the twa that got awa doun, and surely I maun ken them.

I was tae confess tae that awe his life Steenie had been a great warlock and mither and I were his servants, which is why I never married, and that often we had conspired thegither tae witch auld Munro himsel, but we had aye failed sae strang was he in righteousness.

There was nae end. Even when the Covenant wad gaither its army for its Godly wark we had witched the men o Trig sae that they wad not gang when the minister asked them, but went in the end wae Steenie at their heid, a blasphemy in the sight o the Lord which had brought the hale army naething but ill.

He had looked at me then wae tears in his een.

-Poor bairn, awe my wark tae redeem ye has failed, and now yer maister Malecky has ganged tae meet his maister, and ye are awe alane, and ye maun sign, lassie, ye maun sign.

Aye and I maun sign that the auld laird was a witched man and it was witchcraft that had been the death o him. But when the young laird cam and mither finding that her powers were ower weak for sic a Godly man, and that he could not be tempted wae my flesh, she had cried upon Satan that he had promised her the life o any that should hairm her and she demanded his, and the Deevil in reply had driven him in tae the auld bog while mither flew about him cursing him as he drouned.

And sae great it seemed were our powers that the borders o Trig could not restrain them, and nae ill-deed great or small had happened recently in Galloway, aye and even in awe o Scotland, that had not started at the door of our biggin, or in Steenie's house. Ships wracked, men drouned, cows, sheep and horses struck doun, bairns born deid, ale turned sour, armies losing battles, aye and even the falseness o the English.

And sae I signed, for it seemed tae me that there was neither mercy not any possibility o escape. But ance signed Munro wad ken mair. Awe the diverse shapes that Satan

wad assume when he cam tae my bed. Did he come as a
great black bull wae a serpent's heid? Or as a dug wae
scales instead o natural hair? Or as a tall dark man wae
green een and skin like leather when he stripped off his
duds? And how cauld and comfortless was his embrace, and
how his member was like a yard o hot iron, and how he
had promised me that if I should remain true tae him he
wad gie me power ower awe the folk o Trig, and any that
should dae me hairm he wad kill, and how could I not see
that these were awe lies? And forbye he might come tae me
in the night in the shape o a mouse or a rat or a beetle tae
comfort me still, it was but another lie, and they wad prove
tae me that it was a lie, for he and Mathius Pringle, wha
had great skill in these matters, wad be watching and
waiting tae crush him under their feet, and he was sure I
wad not remain stubborn then.

And then this ither man wha had been tae Trig before
cam up tae me and put his hand gently under my chin and
lifted up my heid and said,

-Dae ye no see tae what a pass he has brought ye Agnes,
and is that not proof o awe his falseness?

Then he turned tae Munro and said:

-See there are tears in her een Willie, which is a gude
sign.

And then he looked at me again,

-Why if ye wad but fight lassie ye wad find us yer strong
right airm. But ye maun ken Agnes, that her ye call yer
mither has three teats on her, and nae doubt as a bairn ye
suckled on the third, which was placed upon her even by
Satan himsel.

He pushed his face very close tae mine then and forbye
there are many things o that time that I canna clearly mind,
or put intae words, never till my deeing day or beyond it
will I forget that lang face, cruel it seemed as nae ither face
before that time or since, wae een like ice set in a heid that
was itsel like a thing frae which flesh and mercy and awe
things belonging tae a natural man had been riven, and in
my hairt and on my lips I cursed him like I hae cursed nae
ither man on earth, and there was nae ill that could be
wished that I did not wish on him.

58

Awe that day he spoke softly in my ear, naming by name hale legions o demons and demanding that I should name any that I kent, and wha had visited me and fornicated wae me. And when I telt him that I was still a maid his softness wad gae and he wad roar in a terrible voice, and say that what persuasion could not dae ither things could, and why should the Kirk haud back until they kent awe the things that had been affected and afflicted by my devilries, and rooted them out, sae that ance again Kirk and country could prosper.

I ken little mair o what happened. That night I lay, kenning but nae langer caring that they were watching us. Now that I had signed they wad tak us tae Edinburgh or Glasgow tae stand trial as confessed enemies o Heaven. It mattered little, if I prayed for anything at awe it was that mither and I wad just dee quietly awa in the night.

Neither thing cam tae pass. At some time in the night, I ken not at what hour, I lifted up my een and there was Steenie Malecky himsel bending ower me, and I mind very clearly how I thought, here is there proof cam frae the grave itsel. And whether my heart exulted at that or whether it did not I canna mind, and it may be that I thought very little o the fact that he lifted me up in his airms and put me intae the airms o Sawney, and it may be that it mattered as little that he tae had cam frae the deid, and that he whispered in my ear,

-It's ower now lassie and ye maun gang wae us.

I kent naething at the time o how Mathius Pringle had launched himsel at Steenie tae crush him under his feet, and how Steenie had knocked him doun and cam near tae shooting him. But I could hear his voice quiet and angry, and Sawney's quiet and comforting, and how intae the night they had carried me and put me on Sawney's big horse and threw his bear coat about me, and then mounting himsel he had strapped me tae him wae a leather belt and bade me cling tae him. Awe this I did, lying in the warmth o that great beast's coat, neither kenning whether I was in Heaven or Hell, forbye I felt Sawney's horse between my legs, and his cauld armour pressing against my breasts, and Steenie crying out in a loud voice.

59

-Now man we maun ride.

They galloped that night like madness itsel. And when ance I looked ower the rim o that great coat, the night was black and Heaven was black, and I could hear the guns going off in our rear, and I clung tae the harness on Sawney's back, and maybe then I kent there was a living man beneath the steel.

We crossed the auld bog which nae ither person in the parish wad hae crossed in that darkness, but Steenie kent the way, and lighting doun off his horse he telt Sawney tae dae the same, throwing him a line tae guide him.

-Walk damn carefully man, put yer feet on the exact spot whaur I put mine, and mind for the horses.

Sawney lifted me on tae his back because he feared for the horses, and barely sensible o anything it seems, I clung on tae him, and we moved ane careful step at a time intae that dark place whaur Munro had said we danced wae Satan, and whaur the laird had drouned, and whaur there was only ane narrow strip o solid ground which twisted as it ran.

-Slowly now, I heard Steenie say. -They'll not follow. The sodgers hae ower much sense, and if Pringle drives them in he'll answer for their lives.

I could not see the ground below Sawney's feet, or tell whether it was solid or had only the appearance o it. Nor I think could he, but he wad prod it carefully wae the point o his sword ere he put his foot doun. Steenie lit a torch which gied out some light, but that forbye it seemed the place was darker than ever, and Sawney I could hear speaking tae me and tae his horse, but nane I think answered.

Only ance I looked back and the horsemen that pursued us had reached the edge o the bog, and there they stood waving their torches and shouting and firing their guns. And think ye no that I laughed then tae see how close they were and yet how far awa they seemed, and how they could neither catch us or even see us, and how Munro had made me confess tae flying across this bog, and now he and Pringle maun be watching, gnashing their teeth tae see me, not flying but moving very slowly, but still they couldna follow. Aye and it seemed tae me haeving kent maist o these folk awe my life, that like in the auld ballad I was leaving living land and living folk behind.

I heard Steenie inquire o Sawney as tae how I was, and Sawney replying that he thought I might not be conscious. I mind weel I laughed out loud then, and awe that were listening heard me laugh, and twa or three guns went off in reply, and it may be that I laughed again and cried out,

> Oh it was a mirk mirk nicht
> And there was nae starn licht
> And they waded in red blude tae the knee,
> For awe the blude that's shed on earth
> rins through the rivers o that countrie.

And then Steenie laughed tae and sang out in reply.

> Syne they cam tae a garden green
> And she pu'd an apple frae off a tree
> Tak this for thy wages True Thomas
> It will gie thee the tongue that can never lee.

-Wheesht man, Sawney said. -It serves nae purpose tae incense them that are already incensed.

But Steenie strange man wad not wheesht but wad sing quietly, and I kent him weel enough tae ken for wham it was he was singing.

> Light doun, light doun, now True Thomas.
> And lean yer head upon my knee,
> Abide and rest a little space,
> And I will show ye ferlies three.
> O see ye not yon narrow road,
> Sae thick beset wae thorns and briars?
> That is the path o righteousness.
> Though after it but few inquires.

> And see ye not that braid, braid road,
> That lies across the lily leven?
> That is the path o wickedness.
> Though some call it the road tae Heaven.

And see ye not yon bonny road
that winds about the fernie brae?
That is the road tae fair Elfland,
Whaur thou and I this night maun gae.

Sawney cried out then, -Why man in our present situation a Godly psalm wad be mair appropriate.
But Steenie laughed out loud again at that.
-Why Alexander Bain, ye are in the company o a named
witch and warlock, excummunicates baith, pursued by Kirk
and State. Whaur else maun we gang but Fairyland?
And it may be that I thought that it was indeed tae Fairyland that we were ganging, or tae anither place far below
the water itsel, for it seemed tae me that it washed ower my
heid, and I saw the light flicker and gae out, and of that
time I ken nae mair.
I woke tae the sound o the sea, and kenning not at awe
whaur I was, forbye I was swaddled still in Sawney's bear-
coat and Sawney himsel was bending ower me, and nae
doubt I asked him whaur we were for he said,
-Steenie's cave, for I ken nae ither name for it.
And then I heard him shout tae Steenie that I was awake
and Steenie himsel cam in.
-Why lass ye hae cam back tae join us.
-Whaur is this place?
-It is a very safe place that maybe only I ken about.
I had been asleep it seemed for nearly a week, and sae
much had just passed awa in that time, and now that I was
awake trying tae look back it seemed ower far, and a lot o
things had just ceased tae be, and a line o fiery men stood
between then and now, but what they truly divided I kent
not, wha was alive and wha was deid.
-What was it that ye gied tae mither?
-As we couldna tak her wae us and she being very near
tae death, something merciful tae tak her weel out o the
hands o Willie Munro.
It awe cam back tae me then. And nae doubt, as they
later telt me I did, I screamed and cried aloud at that, and
Steenie bent ower me and gied me something tae drink, and
kissed me softly on the lips and said that I wad sleep natu-

rally now, and when I woke I wad be fine and weel. This I did, and I thought before I slept that he had the face o the wisest and kindliest Scot that had ever been born.

When I woke again it was tae the sound o water playing on the rocks like a drunk piper wha has lost his notes. But the line o burning men was still there, and fierier than them awe the lang face o Mathius Pringle. I kent then that they wad aye be there, and for me there was nae returning past them, and something had gone out o me intae the water o that auld bog, nor wad it return. But Steenie and Sawney had been my salvation, and had cared for me, and had clung tae me, and wae them I wad gang whaur ere they ganged, and bide wae them whaur ere they bode, and I wad care naething for any ither thing or body.

I could see them as they sat at the entrance tae the cave smoking their pipes, Sawney sae muckle and huge, Steenie small and quick as a fox. Their armour and swords lay against the wall o the cave and they sat in the light o the sun that streamed in frae the sea.

I got tae my feet then. And forbye they had wrapped me up weel in blankets and furs I was still naked underneath, and whether I kenned not or I cared not, I canna weel mind, but very unsteady on my feet I walked ower tae them and Sawney turned his heid and said,

-God save us awe.

But Steenie just laughed and I sat doun between them and baith he and Sawney gied me a bit kiss, ane on each cheek.

True Thomas he lay on Huntlie bank,
When a ferlie he spied wae his ee,
An it was a lady bright,
Cam riding doun by the Eildon Tree.

And I replied like sae often I did when I was a bairn.

Her shirt was o the grass green silk,
Her mantle o the velvet fine,
  At ilka tett of her horse's mane,
  Hung sixty sillar bells and nine.

I looked doun at the water that lapped almost tae the door o the cave, and kent then that it was it that had been making the queer music, but I kenned not how.

-The space under us is hollow, Steenie said. -And why when the tide cams in the air in it maun gang out. And for awe the years o Scotland's history, folk hae been frightened o that, nae doubt thinking it was boggles or fairies playing their instruments.

I telt him then that mither and I had been telt that they had baith been killed.

-Na Agnes, just wounded a bit, and in the confusion o the day we ended up amang the English that were wounded. And thinking o the unforgien nature o Mathius Pringle we becam Ironsides for a time, which is what they call the English Parliament men, and fought wae Oliver Cromwell.

It still seemed tae me little short o miraculous that they should hae turned up when they did, and I asked them if it had indeed been by chance.

-Partly, but not quite. We heard frae ane John Armstrong, wha ye might weel mind had ance been a shepherd in Trig, but wha was now a sodger, that some mischief was likely being brewed up by Munro against some friends o ours. We never thought how far advanced that mischief had got, and we still curse oursels for not getting there sooner. Aye and Mathius Pringle and William Munro will never be nearer tae being shot if they live till judgement day, for I was very fond o yer mither, and indeed I am vexed about my dug Sam, and regret that he didna hae the wits tae bite out Munro's throat and no some poor sodger's, but what's done is done.

I telt him then what had happened tae Gregor and Lady Gregor and mither's pairting words tae them.

-Damn Munro, I liked my dugs, but if they run wild they'll be worse than wolves, they'll mak real mischief, worse than any demon that dwells in his heid.

He looked unco sad then, and said that we wad hae tae think what we were gaen tae dae next, for wae the Kirk and Mathius Pringle as our enemy, nae place in the Lawlands o Scotland wad be safe for us, and that some duds wad hae tae be got for me seeing that the Kirk had left me as bare as the day I cam intae the warld. Then he smiled a bit and said that as I was near as tall as himsel his ain claes wae a bit alteration could nae doubt be made tae fit me.

I looked intae mysel then. Intae that body which they had hurt, and which they still hurt, and which wad aye hurt. And I kent then that I had nae desire at awe tae leave this great cave whaur even then I thought ye could live forever and never be found, and ye could leave the warld aboun tae gang on wae its madness and its cruelty.

-And live on fish and rabbits forever? Steenie said. -Na Agnes, we wad gang mad oursels within a twelvemonth.

And Sawney was restless tae, and said that this was not what he had cam back tae Scotland for, tae dwell in a cave like a beast. And when I thought o ye lass when the fighting was done, this was not the kind o life I had thought o.

I looked at him then and asked unco quietly, -And how much did ye think o me, Sawney Bain?

He regarded me then and at first he smiled. I was wearing a suit o Steenie's claes, which, altered a bit, fitted me nicely enough, and whether that made him laugh, or whether it was some other thing, I ken not, but he laughed low and gentle.

-Och about as much as Steenie Malecky.

Then I said, neither o ye should hae ganged sae merrily off tae fight.

-It was Godly wark, or sae I thought, aye and still think. But I ken ye are nae witch, nor was Janet, and Steenie is nae warlock. But kenning that, there is now nae further place tae turn tae, except just ganging back tae being a sodger, fighting for wha ever will employ me.

Tae this Steenie said that he was nae mercenary, and wad not draw his sword again unless he could see that there was some purpose in sae daen.

-I had a purpose, and wad like tae find it again if it can be found.

Steenie was silent then, blowing on his pipe, and I ken not truly, but it may be that Sawney felt like I felt, that we were like twa bairns waiting for Steenie tae tell us what we should dae next. At length he said,

-We canna stay in the Lawlands, Pringle's anger is not

something tae be easily turned aside. In his een ye are as near damned as Agnes and mysel. He wad hae us awe burned.

Sawney turned his heid and now baith anger and despair were in his een.

-Damn them awe tae Hell. God's cause is mair than just Mathius Pringle. Aye and yet still I mind how much he impressed me the first time we met. How he clarified and instructed me on sae many things, and how he telt me that naething happened on Earth but that the Lord commanded it in Heaven. And I canna see how he did not command us back tae Trig, which tae my mind was neither gude fortune or chance, but a great providence for awe concerned, aye even Munro and Pringle, and wha kens but time will show that.

-No for auld Janet, or Agnes's suffering, or for my dug Sam.

-I ken not, yer dug is but a beast, and surely we awe maun suffer if we are tae rightly ken his mercies. Aye and wha kens but the Lord thought that it was time auld Janet should gang and bide wae him and Pringle and Munro tae be humbled and rebuked in her ganging.

In the end he just rose tae his feet and said that he could nae langer thole this beast's den, and he thought that even tae see a few ships wad be a blessing.

We watched him gae. His step was heavy at first but seeming tae get lighter the further he went awa frae us. Steenie blew on his pipe and said,

-This willna dae, this willna dae at awe. We are in a country whaur ilka man wha kens us might weel think that it is nae mair than his Godly duty tae turn his hand against us, and in awe things we maun be as ane.

I looked at him then, silent he was, just watching and waiting and thinking.

-I hae been sleeping in Sawney's coat, I said. -Maybe he has a right tae share that tae.

-Nae man has rights in sic a matter aboun what ye consent tae gie.

-Aye, I said. -But maybe Willie Munro was right in ane thing, that I hae been a maid ower lang, forbye after awe

66

that's taen place I can hardly feel like ane. But tae my mind there canna be any sin left tae ane that's counted a witch, fornicated wae the Deil, half his host, three dugs, and yersel forbye.

-When Sawney and mysel were in England we met some folk, Levellers they caed themsels, wha were as Godly in their ain way as any in Scotland, forbye they werena quite sae fierce, wha counted naething a sin that yer conscience didna tell ye was a sin, and they wad hae nae minister ruling their conscience, nor any arbitrary power ruling their bodies, and it was tae put an end tae sic things that they fought.

I said I couldna think o sin at awe in this place. When we crossed that auld bit bog I felt half mad, and then I woke up here, and here I could bide for ever. I think that this place could be Fairyland, sae little for me it has in common wae the warld. I can think that, forbye I ken very weel there is nae sic place.

-This is an earthly place by an earthly shore, a very weel hidden place, but naething mair than that. And whiles ye ken, I think that there is naething mair in the warld but what we hear and see and feel, and minister's rant is but minister's rant, and they ken nae mair what's right or wrang than ye or me, and witches and warlocks are things that dwell in their heids and not in the warld.

I looked at him then, and he had that unco wild light in his een, which I minded seeing on occasion when I was a bairn. It happened when some new idea excited him.

-Ye mean, I said, that there is nae God at awe?

-I dinna ken Agnes, but as something went out o ye at the hands o Willie Munro, something went out o me when I saw auld Janet there, and twa Christian men wae less mercy between them than a polecat in a hen house.

-And Sawney? I asked.

-Aye, something went out o Sawney tae, and I'm feart that despair has filled its place. And now he's struggling tae get it back, that thing that brought him back frae Germany, that why, Scotland and England, wad, after a few battles had been fought, be a kind o paradise. He's no alane in haeving thought that either. Why in England there are many on the Parliament side baith learned and common wha haud that Jesus himsel is shortly due tae return and awe will be equal under him, he haeving nae taste for great folk. I ken not, baith countries are in their ain way caught up wae a host o new ideas, and if the ideas themsel lack shape being new, the Kirk is speedily gien them that shape. And if I fear ought, I fear that maybe ance again auld Jock o the Commonweal will be left shaking his heid and saying, this is not what I had in mind at awe.

-Sawney ye see cam back frae Germany seeking, and he is as stubborn in his seeking as he is in a fight, and Pringle was a man wha when first met, as he himsel says, deeply impressed him. He is in need o comforting now.

-And what about ye, Steenie Malecky? Ye that are a man o sic great understanding and learning, ye maun surely ken that if ye but touched my legs they wad open for ye . . . Are ye not in need o anything?

He leaned ower quietly then and put ane airm around me and wae the ither he undid the neck o his shirt that I was wearing, and I felt his hand upon my breast which still had the marks and still hurt frae their needles.

-Aye lass, but we might lose our ither friend. For I love Sawney tae and I ken very weel what he wad dae if this despair o his taks a real haud o him. It wad be up intae the saddle wae his gun in his hand, and his sword wad gang tae the highest bidder, and he wad maist likely be killed very shortly.

He drew his hand slowly awa. I laughed at him, for what reason I ken not truly, and said, then I think I sall dae what ere I please, and ye baith maun ken that.

He smiled a bit, quiet and fox-like, and reaching ower for his pipes he blew them up and started tae play some sad auld border air, which I kent weel but at that time could not put a name tae. At ane point he stopped, leaned ower and kissed me hard on the lips, and when he released me I sang out.

Harp and carp Thomas,
Harp and carp alang wae me,
And if ye dare tae kiss my lips,
Sure o yer body I will be.

He smiled ance again and fell tae playing this new tune and singing himsel.

> Betide me weel betide me woe,
> That weird sall never daunton me,
> Syne he has kissed her rose-red lips
> All underneath the Eildon Tree.

He sang the song through, and when he had finished, I mind very clearly that it seemed that the seven years that Thomas spent in Fairyland had already cam and gane. And I asked him whaur we wad gae when we left this place?

-Tae my mind it maun be the Hielans, or England.

-England?

-England is no sic a bad place, and the English common folk are fine when they're not bedevilled by auld hatreds. But my vote is for the Hielans just now whaur I hae gude friends.

-Steenie, I said tae him then, -if we are tae leave this peaceful place, will ye teach me how tae fight?

-Fight, Agnes?

-Aye, wae sword and gun, itherwise I willna leave this place, for I canna be a helpless lassie again.

He did not laugh or mak fun o me, but just quietly got tae his feet and took his second sword out o his gear and handed it tae me. Then he took his ain.

-Now guard yersel, Agnes Douglas.

That day he showed me how tae guard, feint and cut. And he wad order me tae strike at him as hard and fierce as I could, and think ye not that I marvelled at how easily he could catch awe my blows wae his blade sae fast was he wae it. Nor did he stint in striking back wae the flat o his sword, shouting, -Jump lassie, keep yer guard up, Agnes Douglas I pronounce ye deid.

For nearly twa hours the cave rang tae the sound o us fighting, before, still a bit weak, I near collapsed intae his airms and we held each ither up laughing. But I resolved then tae mak him practice every day wae me, kenning frae when I was a bairn what a gude and firm teacher he was.

-Dae ye think I sall mak a gude sworder, Steenie?

69

-By the time I pronounce ye fully trained better than half the louns in the Scots army wha handle their swords as if they were chasing a stirk wae a broomstick. Why if Sawney had cam back he wad hae thought the cave was being invaded.

And maybe when he said that he was thinking o what was awe at ance on baith our minds.

Sawney did not cam back that night till after dark. Steenie had put a rabbit on the fire tae roast and was quietly playing his pipes when we saw him cam walking ower the sand. Steenie changed his air as if he was slowly piping him up tae the cave. His face was not angry any mair but it seemed tae me that something ither than anger had settled there. Steenie leaned ower and cut a shank frae the rabbit and handed it tae him. Sawney thanked him and started tae eat. When he had finished, Steenie still playing asked,

-What ails ye man?

-I saw some fisher-folk and some farming-folk, ganging about their wark and I wanted tae hail them, but I kept out o their sight feeling like a wolf out o its den.

-Swallow some whisky man and listen tae what I've got tae say. I hae friends in the Hielans, gude friends as awe Hielanmen are, wha put loyal friendship before King or Kirk, and laugh at witches and warlocks, and I think we can be safe there for a while.

-And run about the hills wae nae breeks?

-Aye and why not?

-They say Montrose has gane intae the Hielans.

-Weel the Hielans are a big place, and nae doubt we can avoid Jamie Graham, or mair likely some loun will hae shot the mad deevil ere we get there. But as I see it, it's either there or England, sae think on it. England is an unchancy place just now as ye weel ken, and I can trust my friends in the Hielans wae awe our lives.

-Yer friends nae doubt, but they hae a mighty swift and bludie way o dealing wae their enemies.

Steenie got tae his feet.

-It's only a thought tae think about. But for now I am awa tae look at my traps and tae see if there's no a bit fish on my lines.

It was very dark now, forbye the moon and the stars were up. Sawney had gane tae see tae the horses. I lay very quietly under his bear coat waiting, watching the water cam in, making its elf music and every now and then booming like a great drum, while at ither times it just gied a bit whistle as if out o breath.

When Sawney cam back he seemed a bit mair cheerful, being around horses had aye done that for him. I looked up as he stood ower me and he gied out an eldritch bit laugh.

-Sae he wad hae us gang tae the Hielans wad he, and becam breekless caterans?

It seemed tae me then, as it was tae seem on many anither occasion, that Sawney and mysel were like the hale country, kenning not what we desired, and desiring not what we kent. And Steenie kenning everything but being able tae change very little. But that night I glowered at the fine handsome loun and said unco shamelessly nae doubt.

-This night, Sawney Bain, I wad hae ye gang tae me and tae nae place else.

He knelt beside me his een shining.

-Draw back this muckle coat o yers, Sawney.'

He did as I bid his hand shaking a bit. And I just lay there, as naked as I had been born, and as naked as they had stolen me frae the hands o the Kirk, laughing tae see his een taking in every pairt o me, as if I had no ridden in sic a state on the back o his horse, and on his shoulders.

-I am still a maid Sawney, even if no entirely unmolested.

-And what will Steenie say? Said he unco quiet.

-Ye'll no hae me tae yersel Sawney, I'll hae ye baith or I'll hae nane. I agree wae Steenie that we three maun be as ane, for while ye and he may mak yer way alane, there is nae gate for Black Agnes alane. Sae ye maun choose Sawney, tae strip and come under this coat wae me, or tak yer coat and gang whaur ere ye please.

☆

The minister muttered a prayer. Dark eyes intercepted his words and slipped like iron points through his flesh.

She had known when she had looked at him that the

71

memory of her would never leave him. And yet, this savage matriarch had once been beautiful, and had moved upon the earth with the appearance of innocence, or real innocence that had been falsely accused and barbarously assaulted. He did not know and the anguish of his doubt howled in his soul.

> Had we twa been upon the green
> And never an eye atween
> I wat I wad hae had ye Flesh and Fell
> But yer soul sall gang wae me.

He had pitied her then, pitied her impotent fury, pitied her deranged lust, pitied her fate, pitied her eternal damnation.

'I pity you,' he had said. 'From the bottom of my heart.'

His compassion had broken against her like a mild wave against a rock. Her fury had brought him to his feet commanding her to be silent. Her voice had sung out high above his anger.

> Oh gae ye tae the Toun o Trig,
> And wait ye there for me.
> And if I cam no by the Toun o Trig,
> Then a false woman call ye me.

☆

Sawney stripped was a mighty man, and he lay beside me for a lang time running his hands ower my flesh which had sae early ganged sae many a strange and unnatural gate. He whispered in my ear bidding my legs tae open and let him in and he wad crush out awe memory o Mathius Pringle and Willie Munro, and awe their dirty fingered servants.

And sae I let him in, and sae carefully and gently he slid intae me that it hardly hurt at awe. But memories are no things that are sae easily jinked, forbye Sawney could slip in and out o them, laughing and crying and panting till he cam tae his end, and he could bury his heid in my breast sighing wae a fearful joy that kent not whether tae laugh or cry, like a muckle bairn.

I reached doun and felt his member then, and it seemed

tae me like a strange joke that the Lord had played on men, that a thing which had been sae strang and straight and sodger-like, was now small and silly and out o his command.

And then I felt the blude running doun my legs, and felt glad o that tae, and if I feared for a minute that it wad stain his coat I minded that auld coat had in its time shaken off a river o blude. Still I said I wad get tae my feet and wash mysel in the sea. He just stared at me then, his een goggling like a loun's. But I ran intae the sea at a point whaur it was shallow, and I mind very weel just staring up at the stars that were still there, and the moon that was high in the sky. And I could see Steenie in the moonlight, wae rabbits and fish under his airm walking slowly along the shore. And I kent then that what I had said tae Steenie was true. I cared naething for Kirk or State or King, nor riding men wae guns, and wad be happy if we never left this place and never met anither living soul, and I cursed them for fools and louns that they wad not.

I returned tae the cave, and Sawney was smoking his pipe and drinking some whisky. Sae I leaned ower and took his member ance again intae my hands and said,

-Why Sawney Bain, is there anither charge in this gun o yers? He laughed out loud then, a great giant o a mither naked man, and said he could never be sure.

I laughed back at him and cried out,

> Now haud thy peace the lady said,
> For as I say, sae it maun be.

And the second time was slower and sweeter than the first, and when we finished that I just lay in Sawney's airms wondering whaur Steenie was, and thinking yet again that we were just twa bairns under Steenie's guidance, leading me out o the hands o the Kirk and Sawney out o his despair, and that maybe at that moment he was sitting by himsel doun by the edge o the sea smoking his pipe.

-Steenie is teaching me how tae fight, I said. -Wae sword and gun.

-What, cried he, waking up and fair astonished, then

laughing, and then a bit mortified.

-Why lassie I sall aye protect ye.

-I need tae be able tae protect mysel, just a bit, before I will gang out o here, and ye maun teach me tae.

He laughed again, and then seeing that I wad get angry he put his heid doun on my breast and said,

-I ken not, I ken not, but it's a sad place this Scotland o ours that seemed sae full o promise, that ane that was but lately a maid in her mither's house will not now gang out without sword and gun in her hand.

☆

In the morning the mist had cleared. The minister rose from his bed, dressed and went out into the yard. It was early but Andrew Gilmore was already up. To his question as to whether or not he had slept well, the minister at first did not reply. The truth, that he had barely slept at all despite his physical weariness of the night before, he felt might offend the man, so he merely said:

'Well enough Andrew, well enough.'

Gilmore grunted cheerfully.

'Yon bit mist has cleared weel awa.'

'The truth is Andrew I am distressed by the state of the country. I had not expected such a poor, bare, and tormented place.'

Gilmore stared at him. The minister could tell nothing from his expression.

'Poor and tormented it hae been minister, which wad seem tae be the Lord's will for the folk are industrious enough, forbye maybe a bit wilful, sinful, and stubborn, as the Reverent Carmichael wad hae it, and faithless tae awe principle as auld Erskine wad hae it.'

'How would you have it Andrew?'

'I ken not, except that we're a poor place and sma stuck on tae a muckle place and rich, and hae aye been sare ridden by that fact. It wad eat us, an we maun spend awe our gear and strength in making it choke on the morsel.'

'Do you blame the English then, Andrew?'

'Only in that they are poor neighbours wha hae the strength

tae mak awe our endeavours come tae nocht if they disagree wae them . . .But that it seems has aye been the case.'

Andrew Gilmore paused.

'First they wad hae a king, an then they wad not hae a king, an then they wad hae a king again, an then a new king, an we maun just gang alang neither kenning or not kenning what we oursels want.'

The minister felt irritated. Gilmore's earthy wisdom irritated him as the thought of John Erskine's ferocious zeal irritated him. They were both men thinking and judging beyond their station or their knowledge. The problems of this country seemed as much a refusal to accept intelligent guidance as anything else.

'Minister . . .'

Andrew Gilmore was speaking to him again. The minister looked anew at the strong broadshouldered figure. He did not look like a soldier, and yet he had stood on the field with sword pike and musket, for principle, and now he could not say what that principle was. Unlike John Erskine who believed fervently that every stroke of his sword was seconded by God.

'Minister I was thinking, that maybe I'll gang alang wae ye, at least pairt o the way, for I canna see how ye will find yer road itherwise.'

The minister felt as if he had suddenly been rebuked.

'That is very kind of you Andrew, but who will look after this place?'

'I hae sent the lad up the hill tae bring in auld Erskine an ask him as a favour tae bide here a while.'

'Is he reliable for that?'

'Reliable! Och he can be relied on tae mind the place weel enough, and begging yer pardon, sanctify it wae mair psalms and prayers than hae ever been heard since we put up Kilbracken and Sawney Bain and a congregation o wild Cameronians in the barn . . .An here he is now.'

The minister felt his soul start at the casual use of that terrible name, and the fact that he was known to Andrew Gilmore. Silently he watched John Erskine come riding into the yard, a dwarfish man on a small shaggy horse. He dismounted beside the minister. In bright daylight he looked more tangibly ferocious than when he had emerged out of the mist.

'Good morning to you John, my preserver of last night.'

'It was the Lord's daen minister, wha kens weel how tae let his servant ken when his services are needed.'

'Yes indeed John.'

'If every man had nae ither maister awe wad be equal, without kings and lairds and sic like cattle, which for our sins and our falseness and our lack o principle, are bred up tae sic a power tae be a pestilence in our midst and a rod upon our backs, under which we groan and wail and gnash our teeth, but dae not the ane thing that wad put an end tae awe our woe...'

'John,' Andrew Gilmore interrupted, 'The minister I fancy wad not try tae teach ye or me our trade.'

'The word o God Andrew Gilmore is not a trade, but a prayer, that every Godly man should cairry in his hairt, and on his tongue, and in his sword airm, an I'm richt sorry tae hear yer ganging awa minister for I wad hae liked fine tae hae talked wae ye. But wha kens but I micht weel gang by Trig ane day an judge if ye war a preacher worth leading out o the mist, as I'm sure ye maun be or the Lord wad neer hae sent John Erskine tae be yer guide.'

'Thank you John for your good faith, and once I am settled in Trig you will always be welcome there.'

The little man saluted with an almost merry grace, turned and strode across the yard leading his pony, walking despite his age with the agility of a hillman. The minister watched him go, smiting himself inwardly, for he did not know how, and had hardly any desire to enter into conversation with the man.

He followed Andrew Gilmore indoors where they all break-fasted on bannocks and cheese washed down with beer. Even as the minister said grace he felt John Erskine's ears measuring every syllable, but at the amen the man seemed contented enough. Or perhaps it was simply that Andrew Gilmore had warned him about disputations at the table. When they had finished the minister stood by the door waiting for Gilmore to get ready. John Erskine he could see was still eager for an argument. The minister suddenly decided to forestall him.

'Have you ever heard of one Sawney Bain, John?'

'Sawney Bain, why dae ye ask o him?'

'It's a name I heard of in Edinburgh, and Andrew tells me he was known in these parts. He was born in Trig, which is of some interest to me.'

'I kent Sawney weel enough. A gude and Godly man, an a very gude sodger, wha's faith showed in the strength o his airm raither than the claiking o his tongue, which is the kind o man I like. He was cursed though in my opinion, by a dark Douglas Jezebel o a wife, but I sall say nae mair on that score, for it ill becames a man like me tae judge them that hae been lang judged.'

'Oh what happened to him?'

'Martyred minister, by Satan's hirelings. Him and awe Kilbracken's congregation, though Sawney they say did not gang easily slaughtering twenty dragoons and maybe mair. Nor wad it surprise me if the Douglas carline did not equal his score, for she could ficht wae sword and gun better than maist men. Och a wild carline she, an kent not her place, but I sall say nae mair.'

For all that they would tell me, the minister thought, of this country and its past, there are things I know which they do not know. He looked at the misshapen utterly fearless zealot standing before him, and wondered if the true outcome of Sawney Bain's martyrdom would frighten him.

At that point Andrew Gilmore came out of the house. He wore a stout broadsword and carried a long musket.

'Do we need arms Andrew?' Asked the minister.

'Maist unlikely by the grace o God.' Andrew replied, hooking the musket on to the horse's saddle and swinging himself gracefully on to its back. He turned to the minister.

'But ye never can ken and the gun will be handy for shooting a bit fresh meat.'

The minister mounted his own horse which gave a spirited jump as he did so.

'Tis a michty fine beast for the hills.' John Erskine commented.

'The wrong sort you think?'

'Awa John it's a very fine horse.'

John Erskine grinned diabolically. Andrew Gilmore's wife and family stood at the door to see them off. The minister blessed them and thanked them before following his guide out on to the road though the minister could still hardly bear to call it that, it being no better than the track along which he had been led the previous night, and which in many places they had to travel in single file.

As they rode it seemed to the minister that Andrew was leading him higher and higher into a wilderness of hills, a rolling sea of green and brown speckled by habitations and people clad in hodden grey and blue bonnet, who appeared as no more than growths on its surface. Many recognised Andrew Gilmore and saluted him as he passed.

The minister noted that he appeared to be a well liked man in this area, an observation which for a time allowed the minister to feel a warmth of security which he had not felt when alone, which he had not really felt since before his encounter with the cannibals. Now it seemed a fine thing to be riding, sometimes alongside, sometimes behind this stalwart christian, though Andrew seemed little inclined to conversation, for which the minister might have felt grateful if his mind had been as light as Andrew no doubt assumed it was.

They had ridden for about three hours, sometimes at a walk, mostly at a brisk canter, when Andrew Gilmore suddenly pulled up. He pointed with his hand into the distance where the road dipped steeply into the valley.

'Sodgers,' he said. 'Let's draw in a bit tae let them pass.'

The minister could see a small troop of dragoons, the sun glinting on their breastplates, coming towards them at a swift trot.

'Why Andrew you seem to be almost apprehensive of the King's soldiers.'

'Na, na, but the path is narrow an sodgers are aye unchancy deevils.'

'Surely you are thinking of the past rather than the present?'

'Och they're no as rough as they ance were, and they're kept on a very tight rein . . .but still they sall inquire as tae wha we are an whaur we are ganging.'

'On a lawful journey with a lawful purpose.'

'I hae sma liking for them, for forbye a firm hand is controlling them they're still a molestation tae the countryside, as sodgers in my opinion maun aye be. They remind us awe of sae mony oppressions and sae little redress.'

They drew off the road. The dragoons in a mobile column of steel approached them, stopping as Andrew had predicted alongside them. The captain, a stocky florid-faced man, guided his horse towards them.

'Gude day gentlemen.'

'An gude day tae ye tae Sir.' Andrew Gilmore answered.

For a moment the captain stared at them both. To the minister it was a look that was both insultingly arrogant and careless. When he spoke again it was with an affected gentility, which did not and hardly seemed intended, to disguise a coarse indifference.

'Pardon my curiosity, but might I inquire as tae wha ye are and whaur ye are ganging?'

The minister's irritation had been steadily growing and he saw little reason to conceal it.

'You might Sir, and I think I might also ask why it should concern you?'

The captain's eyes took in the minister's clothes, his speech, and his horse. His voice became subdued.   .

'Come, come Sirs, I hae my duties, and it is a civil enough question, seeing that ye are ganging somewhaur, and wae sword and gun.'

'If your duty requires you to ask the business of honest people that you happen to meet on the road then no doubt you must do it. We are, Sir, travelling to the town of Trig where I am to be the new minister of the gospel. This good gentleman is my guide seeing that I am not familiar with the country.'

'Trig is it Sir? Then ye hae a lang journey ahead o ye, and I wish ye God speed on your Godly purpose. Trig is a remote place and could nae doubt dae wae a bit of religion.'

The captain saluted, turned his horse and rode back to his troop which at a wave of his hand clattered into motion again.

'Gude-day Sirs,' he shouted back at them.

'And good day to you too Sir,' the minister replied.

They watched as the dragoons moved off down the track. The minister felt oddly compelled to examine each weather-beaten face as it passed him.

'Insolent fellow,' he said quietly.

'Aye minister, an what ye saw war his nicest manners, seeing he realised ye war a gentleman.'

The track had been badly churned up by the dragoon's horses which further added to the minister's vexation.

'Do they molest the people much?'

'Not much now, except maybe them are still a bit wild and hameless, an not as Godly as they ance war, maistly just poor folk driven out by the famine. But a sodger, minister, is a creature that maun aye be kept on a tight rein, for ance off it he will not miss any opportunity that should come his way. An sae he'll steal a bit if he can, an if he should chance tae meet a bit lassie on the hill then maybe she maun howk up her skirts for him and open her legs, for as they say, sodgering is lusty wark.'

'That's atrocious, Andrew.'

'Aye, but what else maun the carline dae. In the auld days she maun open her legs or get her throat cut, an in the end maybe baith, and forbye that is unlikely tae happen now unless she be a gypsy or a tinker, how is she tae be sure o the difference between rough persuasion and deidly threats?'

The minister was silent. For a time there was only the soft sound of their horse's hooves on the mud. Occasionally Andrew would point to clusters of gravestones on the hillside, sometimes naming the people who lay there. Some were martyrs of the Killing Times, others were Todd Grey's work and were victims of the famine. The minister felt his heart sickening.

He closed his eyes reciting quietly an old and loved prayer. For one long peaceful moment the darkness enveloped him. When he opened them again the very light which illuminated this land seemed cruel, a shining, naked, lawless land, which Andrew Gilmore peopled with ghosts.

They rode on until the light began to fade. Andrew signalling to the minister reined his horse sharply in. They were standing on a high ridge which cut abruptly down into a steep, small, tree filled valley. They had come upon it so suddenly and it looked so inaccessible and wild that if the minister had been alone he would have ridden past it, nor did there seem to be any visible route down to it. Even now, pointed out to him in the evening light, it seemed to wink with satisfaction, acknowledging the meticulous craft which had gone into its concealment.

'There's a serviceable big biggin doun there hidden in the trees whaur we maun pass the nicht, but the way doun is not frae here. Frae here we maun ride round and dismount. My bit mare might mak it at a push but yer beast wad not.'

They rode on for another half mile and the path which Andrew eventually led the minister down was itself hardly visible, and so strewn with rocks and holes that it would have presented problems to an agile man unless he knew it very well. At the bottom was a dense thicket of trees, a stream, and a cottage which seemed no worse than many others the minister had seen. Indeed to the minister's eyes the whole place had a dense and secret tranquillity about it.

'Who uses this place Andrew?'

'Shepherds in season, an in the past it was the God-given refuge of many poor hunted folk. Hidden though it is, a sharp lookout can see any approach that's made tae it, and yon bit path is baith weel hidden and not exactly the kind o hill doun which horse are inclined tae charge, forbye the fact that a tree across it maks it impassable. Na, na, a man could rest quietly here and dine every day off fresh trout while the dragoons were beating every bush on the hillside. Conventicles were held here, and tae some folk it seemed as if the psalms rose frae the very guts o the earth. Hale congregations dwelt here, why it maun be ane o the holiest places in Scotland . . .At least in recent times. Afore that ither people used it wha war maybe not quite sae Godly.'

The minister walked into the cottage. Inside it was a dark primitive place with a hearth but no proper chimney, simply an opening in the roof. What furniture there was, was rough in the extreme, a table, two benches, and a few chairs. On the table an ancient bible sat slowly mouldering into dust. The minister looked at it briefly. It was in the old Scots tongue which to his ears gave the most familiar passages a wild barbarous ring, as if the gentle words of the very gospels had been reborn here.

For a moment the minister wondered why Andrew had brought him here, and then it struck him that Andrew making this journey would simply, naturally, stop here without thinking about it. The strangeness of the place was something that affected him alone. The minister turned and walked out of the door of the cottage. Andrew Gilmore was seeing to both their horses.

'I didn't ask you to be my servant, Andrew.'

Andrew Gilmore turned round. He had unhooked his

musket from his saddle, and with it on his shoulder and his sword by his side, he looked to the minister's eyes as if he had stepped straight out of the centuries which inhabited the place. He smiled placidly.

'A fire minister, we need a fire, an I think I sall dae a bit o fishing.'

Andrew made the fire and left the minister to watch it while he went to catch some fish.

'But Andrew you have no rod or line that I can see.'

'Why minister I hae hands, which if ye slip gently under the rocks whaur the fish lie and apply a little kindly persuasion they'll shortly consent tae be our supper.'

The minister smiled wanly and fell to poking the fire with the broken rusty sword which lay in the hearth for that purpose. Within half an hour Andrew returned with four trout of between a quarter and half a pound, which he deftly prepared, grilling each over the fire on the blade of his knife. Eaten with bannocks and ale the minister had to admit that the meal wanted for nothing and the last of it eaten the minister sat quietly sipping his drink, willing his heart to be at peace. Andrew quietly filled his pipe.

'It's odd dae ye not think, that sic a spot as this should be stuck upon land fit for naething but sheep and folk wha dae not want tae be found? An there are mony ithers like it, as if the hale o the country was made for a people that wad hae mair need o places tae hide than fields tae grow grain.'

'That wad seem to imply that the Scots are a nation of outlaws.'

'Aye maybe, for ane reason or anither gude and bad.'

'Tell me about Sawney Bain.'

'What interests ye about Sawney Bain?'

'He was born in Trig, and I read about him in an old memoir of the place. I am surprised that he was still active in your day.'

'Och mony war, o them that war still alive, still fichting, still seeing a great day o salvation ahead o them, forbye kings and republics cam and went. Sawney was wae a congregation led by Joshua Kilbracken. My faither, wha forbye he thocht they war awe utterly mad, let them hae a barn an a bit field for their use, making it plain tae them that he had nae desire tae be included in ony o their daens, an wad deny them should ony trouble arise.

'I was around fourteen at the time, an I mind seeing them, poor ragged folk, singing their psalms or listening tae Kilbracken, wha was a gey fiery man as a preacher, but faither said had little sense itherwise. Sawney I met ane day on the hillside, just sitting on a bit rock smoking his pipe an reading his bible. Just an auld grey-bearded sodger he seemed tae me, wha it seems was out o favour wae Kilbracken on account that he wad mak the men drill and train, which seemed sensible gien the fact that they war being wickedly hunted by dragoons. But tae Kilbracken's mind it was nae mair than a reprobate lack o faith in the strength o the Lord. But forbye he sounded off on that point, he wad not expel Sawney, an it seemed that Sawney wad just gang alang, baith him and his wife, baith wae Kilbracken and no wae him at the same time, he declaring that as he had been elected military commander he wad dae his duty and brook nae interference wae it.'

'He was a man of some importance among them?'

'Tae my mind he himsel had but little warldly ambition, but they kent his worth and judged him the canniest and maist salted sodger amang them, a true judgement in my opinion. But now ye maun ken, Kilbracken did not wholly approve o Sawney, but he hated his wife Agnes, wham he caed a black Douglas witch, at which she wad just smile and say naething. She wad cairry her ain sword and gun, and declared that she wad not relinquish them tae ony man, aye, an maybe she made it plain that she ganged wae Sawney and no wae Kilbracken.'

'I was, weel, a bit curious when I first saw him, and nae doubt a bit cautious tae, but he just looked up at me and said: 'Aye lad.'

'I asked him what bit o the bible he was reading, and he just replied, 'I hae read it awe frae back tae front an I can find nae way out, nae sign o what we should dae frae here.'

'I thocht at the time that it was a gey queer thing tae say, gien Kilbracken's sureness about these matters, but as I kent him better I cam tae ken that he was aye like that, puzzling awe the time, only really kenning what was wanted and what was tae be done when there was a ficht tae be fought.

'He looked at me that day on the hill and said: 'Ye ken that

bit when Jesus is about tae be taen in the Garden o Gethse-
mane, an tae prevent that Peter taks a swipe at a sodger
slashing the lug off him, an Jesus in rebuke o Peter sticks the
lug back on and bids the man tae be at his ease?'

'I said that I kent it weel enough, an next he says tae me his
een twinkling wae a wild look. 'Nae doubt Peter was wrang
and Jesus was richt, but in my earthly opinion Peter was ower
delicate wae his sword airm, why if mysel had been there I wad
hae sliced his heid clean off, nae doubt occasioning an even
bigger miracle an a bigger rebuke. Now is that no reprobate,
kenning richt and daen wrang?'

'I said I didna ken, wondering at the time if faither was richt
and they war awe mad. But he just blew on his pipe and didna
look the least bit mad. 'It just seems tae me,' he said, 'that we
can never prosper if we just suffer oursel tae be dunted and
driven and hunted as they please. Which has been the case ere
since the English louns wae maist o Scotland helping them set
a throne ance again under the King's arse. Aye and hardly had
their witless cheering deed awa, and he safely seated, his spurs
war ance again in their bellies.

'Sae we maun gang through the hale business again, wae nae
backsliding, nae malignants, and nae cattle o gentry tae
confuse the issue. For that we need an army, which we sall soon
hae, and despite what Kilbracken says, I never kent the Lord
ever tae gie the victory tae an army that didna keep its guns
loaded and its blades sharp. Dunbar laddie, should hae been
a lesson no tae be forgotten, but then I am auld and few really
remember.'

I had of course heard o the battle o Dunbar and asked him
mair.

'Dunbar laddie,' he said, 'was a battle won in the pulpit and
lost on the field, which is nae doubt what Steenie wad hae said.'

'Steenie?' interrupted the minister.

'Aye, Steenie, Malecky was his ither name, a man wha it
seems had been a comrade o Sawney's in the auld days. Baith
him and his wife seemed tae haud Steenie's name in great
respect and wad often second ony point they made, saying
that's what Steenie wad hae said, or that wad hae been
Steenie's opinion. I ance heard Agnes say that ane thing Steenie
wad not hae done was trail about the hills wae a loun like

Kilbracken, an Sawney I mind clearly made nae reply tae that.

'I asked him ane day when I kent him better, if Steenie war deid. He I mind just looked at me wae an unco strange look in his een, an said that he kent not but he doubted it somehow. Agnes said in an even queerer way that Steenie wad never dee, but was sitting up on a hill somewhaur, glowering at awe o Scotland, and weeping ower the foolishness o its people, and wad certainly turn up ane day when folk had ower and enough o it.

'I thocht at the time that maybe baith their brains war a bit addled what wae suffering and the desperate life they led. But Sawney cured that when he found out that I was but a fairmer's son wae nae idea how tae use a broadsword, and he straight away proposed that he should teach me. An if I am a bit mair than just a serviceable swordsman now it was due tae Sawney then, wha for the time the congregation bided wae us wad exercise daily wae me. Nor was there anything addled about his brains or confused about his thinking when he had a broadsword in his hand. An he was a hard maister tae, dunting me mony times wae the flat o his blade and crying out, 'That wad hae been yer heid laddie.' Aye and whiles Agnes Douglas wad tak a turn, an if I was laith tae strike at a woman it was misplaced, for she wasna laith tae strike at me. Aye an I learn't why maist men war unco wary o her, forbye she was aye maist kind tae me.'

The minister stared into the ashes of the fire.

'What happened to them, Andrew?'

'Ane day they went awa. Afore he left Sawney gied me as a present this gude sword which I'm wearing now. In the end they war awe murdered by dragoons.'

'All?'

'Aye awe, men, women and bairns. My faither was in the party that went up to bury them. O they fought stiffly enough, but at the finish the dragoons had just ridden ower them. An if mony o the women warna just cut doun as they ran, in the end they wad wish they had been, for they war killed awe the same . . .'

Andrew Gilmore's voice had become low and hard. To the minister it was as if he could feel the dark anger within him.

'And yet John Erskine said that Sawney Bain had cut down

twenty dragoons before he himself was killed. Somebody must have lived to tell that tale.'

'Folk wha hae been defeated will aye hae tales tae tell, an nae doubt Sawney did not gang quietly tae the grave, but my faither said there was nane alive, an they searched very carefully.'

'It seems an entirely unnecessary barbarity.'

'Weel minister, in the wake o it I kent mony wha uncovered their lang hidden weapons, an did I not dae sae mysel?'

'Violence follows upon violence . . .'

Andrew Gilmore smiled slowly. For a brief moment it seemed to the minister that the smile transformed Andrew Gilmore's soul, and the minister realised that at that moment Andrew resented him, perhaps even hated him. It was not a mean or superficial feeling, it was something from deep within the Borderman's soul. The minister was also sure that it was not something which honest Andrew Gilmore was aware of expressing, it was a cloud which passed over his features and disappeared again.

'If ye will excuse me minister I think I sall gang tae bed now, these auld brawls can mean very little tae ye.'

'I need to know the country Andrew if I'm to minister to it.'

'Yer een will tell ye awe ye need tae ken about this country, for the rest ye'll hear stories, and few wha tell ye these stories will be able tae vouch for the truth o them.'

'How so Andrew?'

'Why in this country, at this time, tales and truth hae got very queerly entangled, the second often being nae mair than a decent garment for the first, which if it was allowed tae gang naked wad fair turn men's stomachs.'

Staring into the fire the minister's thoughts drifted away. He thought of the cannibal cave. The very knowledge of it lay like an awful unspeakable weight upon his mind. It seemed to him that it would have been so much better if they had just died as the others had died. But in some way, it had been ordained that they should survive. To torment him alone? It was a question he could hardly bear to contemplate. Andrew Gilmore was sad but contented with his memory of a brave and Godly soldier, and a kindly man, he with a depraved monster.

The cave, he thought, had become almost a clearly imagined

thing in his mind. In good weather they went naked, father, mother, brother and sister. They were locked like animals from the earliest age in incestuous fornication. They left off only to emerge like wolves from holes in the ground. They attacked, violated and murdered the world of men, dragging their corpses below ground where she-wolves dismembered them and salted down their flesh, singing psalms as they worked, with knives held in intelligent hands.

'Will you pray with me before we sleep, Andrew?'

'Why minister, richt gladly I will, forbye I doubt very much if our prayers will match the anes that hae been said before us in this place.'

The minister lit the crude tallow lamp. For a moment it flickered softly against the wall before the flame steadied itself. He could hear the gentle sounds of Andrew Gilmore sleeping. He wore a sword given to him by Sawney Bain and his soul was at peace in this cradle of fierce dreams.

☆

Sae we were tae gang intae the Hielans. For what reason I cared not, but I wad practice daily wae my sword, Steenie being a maist severe teacher.

In the beginning Sawney wad sit and watch shaking his heid wae amusement, and on occasions intervening when Steenie was showing me a new stroke, correcting him on points o style sae that the twa o them wad begin tae quarrel fiercely. Then ane day Steenie laughed and said,

-Why man the lassie has fair worn me out, sae why dinna ye, wha are sic a great swordsman, no tak a turn?

Sawney said he wad, but it was plain that he found the hale business fair amusing. Nor wad he fight wae anything like Steenie's fierceness, but wad parry my every stroke wae a simpering bit smile on his face, till in a rage I flew at him, striking and slashing till the sparks flew frae our blades and I drove him back against the wall, whaur, suddenly angered himsel he did wae a clever twist send my sword spinning frae my hand. Naething daunted I picked it up and struck at him again sae that he cried out.

-My God but we hae a right Black Douglas here and nae

mistake.

Awe this time Steenie roared wae laughter, but Sawney did not play wae me like a bairn again but wad fight wae me near as fierce as Steenie, and between them baith I learned much, for they also taught me how tae load and shoot wae musket and pistol.

I mind these days tae be gude days, sometimes fighting, sometimes singing, sometimes just sitting quietly watching the water come in.

Steenie had gien me a breastplate and a sodger's buff coat, and when dressed in them baith had proclaimed me a fine handsome sodger. Steenie said that when we travelled tae the Hielans we should travel by night and hide out by day in order tae avoid any trouble, and as I looked sae weel in it I should wear sword and armour.

As the day cam nearer in which we were tae leave, Sawney went out for the day tae try and find a horse for me tae ride. Steenie and I had been practising, mysel wae my armour on now as awe true sodgers should. And when we practised alane there was an unco fierceness in our fighting, and I wad attack him wae awe that he had taught me. Steenie, strange man, was the kind that ye could baith love and be very angry wae at the same time, and now that I lay at night wae Sawney aiblins there was a bit division between us. I kent not truly, haeving nae experience at that time tae judge sic matters, each night Steenie wad leave our company tae see tae his fishing lines, or his snares, or the horses, or just tae walk by the sea shore, and think ye not that as I lay wae Sawney I wad on occasion think o him.

This day I kent if Sawney found a horse for me we were tae leave the next evening. And if that decision had been taen, I was still maist reluctant tae leave. I was still in my heart very afraid, and that governed awe my thoughts and awe my practising, till in the end I near collapsed o fatigue, and he, knocking my sword aside caught me in his airms.

-Why Steenie Malecky, I said, -What a gallant man ye are, tae fight wae yer enemies until they drop and then tae catch them when they dae.

-Why Agnes is awe this wild weir play tae mak us enemies?

-There are times Mr Malecky, there are times when I wad stick ye sarely if I could.

-There were times when ye wad get very angry wae me when I was teaching ye yer letters, och a Black Douglas ye were then tae, accountable tae nane for yer passions.

-Aye but then ye wad laugh and toss the book aside and play a bit tune on yer pipes.

-And wad ye like me tae play a bit tune now?

-Aye Steenie, but maybe on anither pipe.

He sat doun beside me, and I still wae my sword in my hand launched mysel at him taking him by surprise and putting the point tae his throat.

Harp and carp Thomas,
Harp and carp alang wae me.
And if ye dare tae kiss my rose red lips,
Sure o yer body I sall be.

He pushed the sword aside then, and it was a strange thing tae kiss wae twa bodies covered in steel, and when he ran his hands ower my breast and met nae thing but that I laughed out loud.

-This breastplate can stop a musket-ball, he said.

-Aye and ither things tae it seems. But ye ken Steenie, if ye wad want me ye maun tak it off or in it I sall bide.

It was a thing that had tae be settled before we left the cave, for I doubted very much that it could be settled in the warld outside. For I thought, aye and I think I kent in my heart, that very little wad be settled out there. For ance there, forbye we could avoid them for a bit, its bludie laws and cruel rules wad catch us up.

And sae wae my ain hands I took the harness frae Steenie's back and he took the harness frae mine, and it may be that nae twa folk wha wanted tae be ane ever stripped in sic a fashion. And Steenie looked at me and said,

-Ye ken lassie, when ye were asleep I used tae wash this body doun sae many times wae herbs for yer hurts.

I said that I had kent awe that, and why, did he think that I had not wondered about it? And wondered what he had thought at the time.

-Maistly that ye might dee.

I telt him then, and it might weel be that it was in a way that I could not hae telt Sawney, awe that had happened, and awe that I had felt at the hands o Munro and Pringle. And how I had tae say that I had renounced my baptism at Satan's request, and how he had handed me the confession tae sign, and how I had cursed Mathius Pringle, and how it had seemed like madness itsel had broken loose and taen ower the warld. And if learned men like Pringle and Munro could in gude faith believe sic things, then there was naething tae stop that madness eating us awe up, and if we were ready tae suppress awe that our reason, and awe that our senses telt us, how could it no just devour us?

-Steenie's hands stroked my flesh then, cunning and gentle, as if they had nae desire tae hurry on.

-If we hae a God, then surely we hae a Deil, and if there is a Deil then surely there maun be witches and warlocks? And dis not the bible, Leviticus verse twenty, say that we maun kill these witches and warlocks? Why the auld King James wrote a great book on the subject, and awe Christian folk throughout the warld forbye they disagree on every point o doctrine there is, are as ane on the question o witches, that they are the Deil's servants and God's enemies, and when caught they maun be burnit or hingit.

-And what dae ye say Steenie?

-I ken that I am nae warlock and that ye are nae witch, and when I think o awe the burnings and hingings o witches that hae taen place, I think that if there are any sic creatures in the warld they are no the folk that priest's and minister's catch, wha are for the maist part poor defenceless folk wae ken naething o what they're accused, or how tae defend themsels against the charge. Aye, and in my experience it is a charge against which there is nae rational defence, which tae my mind is a madness. But as they see it, belief in witches and warlocks is a necessary rampart tae their beliefs, and if they forfeit that the castle falls. But I hae never seen or met a witch or a warlock, or God or Satan, but I hae met many honest men and madmen alike wha think they hae.

His member was now firm in my hand, and I looked doun at it, stroking it, feeling strangely pleased wae it sae that I bent doun and kissed it. I looked up at him then, and why for ance it seemed tae me that Steenie's face had lost its cleverness and his mouth its gift for words.

-Why Steenie this is ane o they things that Mathius Pringle wad hae me confess tae, ane o the things that the Deil aye demands o his servants.

-Aye and dis he not dae this in return?

He bent doun ower me then and thrust his lips against me and his tongue deep inside me. And still I lay, thinking o Mathius Pringle and kenning right weel that the Deil did exist, and that he was riding high aboun the warld on a great black horse wae eagle's wings and feet o fire. And in ane hand he carried a great twa-pronged lance, and in the ither a whip that was a living serpent. And aye the lance wad flash and the whip wad crack, driving folk mad like cattle before a storm, wha kent not why they ran or whaur. The Deil had a member a yaird lang which ripped out the guts o his servants and planted his seed whaur their hearts should be, but Steenie cam in wae awe the lightness o a fairy, and I kent then that I was nae langer a bairn tae him, and that he was in truth nae great warlock but just a man, and that this cave belanged tae him and was the only corner o the earth the Deil could not find, forbye he dinged doun the warld in the anger o his searching.

And sae I pulled him tight tae me sae that he wad not draw awa, and strange it was tae lie there wae awe pairts o our bodies touching, like brither and sister, whimpering and simpering in a silly way.

Sawney cam back late that night wae a fine big horse he had bought off a fairmer. Whether he kent or whether he guessed what had taen place I ken not. At that time he just sat doun hungry tae eat and pleased wae the horse he had got. Or sae it had seemed, when awe at ance he declared that there was a reeking plague in Edinburgh and that they were burying corpses by the hundred, and awe that could get out had got out.

-Which way is the plague moving? Steenie asked him.

-I ken not, and wha can tell which way a plague will gang next. I got the news frae the man wha sold me the horse, and he was a sober enough man, but he kent little mair than I hae telt ye. But the Kirk says that the cause is sae plain that a brainless loun wad ken it, which is that there is muckle evil in our midst and the plague canna be expected tae lift until it is caught and burned out.

-I ken not how the plague comes or how it gaes, but I am sure it is not driven out by burnings.

-Och yer name has been mentioned in Edinburgh, as a worse affliction than wars or plagues, and Agnes and mysel as yer ser-vants and inferior associates. That honest fairmer kent not at awe tae wham he was talking, or wha wad sit on his gude horse.

-Why Sawney if the hinging o me wad cleanse a city o the plague I might mak the bargain mysel, but it will not, as ye and I ken very weel.

Sawney was in an unco troubled mood that night. He lay wae his heid resting on my breast wae it seems little desire tae talk or anything else. And forbye I kent weel enough that it was not the best time, I kent tae that it was not something that should lie lang untelt, and said that I had lain wae Steenie.

He said naething at first, and then he sighed a bit, and then it was a bit later he said,

-I ken not the reason why, but this country o ours seems certainly damned. Them that are supposed tae govern us ken nae langer why or for wham or for what we are fighting. The English hae broken faith wae us, and, I hae it on gude authority that Jamie Graham is in the Hielans wae an army o wild Hielanmen, and now the plague is devouring Edinburgh and the Kirk says there is evil and abomination in our midst, and until it is rooted out the Lord's wrath against us will not be lifted and naething that we can dae can hope tae prosper. I ken not what tae think, but I canna laugh and sing and mock as Steenie dis without thinking it a deidly sin.

I said naething tae him in reply. But I minded when they had first ridden off tae fight, nor was Steenie slow tae gae, and mither had said that when men's brains were no between their legs they were either in their sword hilts or their tongues.

Sae I lay silent, and Sawney nae doubt thinking that I

was asleep got quietly up, and I watched him put on his breeks and wrap his plaid about his back and gae out o the mouth o the cave. I looked tae see whaur he had gone, but he had not gone, but was there sitting on a bit rock around which the water whirled for the tide was about half in.

For a time I just watched him sitting there, and when I looked up Steenie was standing ower me haeving himsel been disturbed.

Should we no gang ower tae him? I asked, for it seemed unkind tae just leave him there.

Steenie said tae just let him bide, and he wad bide up tae see that he cam tae nae hairm.

Sae we watched and sae we waited, and it seemed tae me then that he took as little notice o us as he did o the water that was rising about his feet.

In time it may be I fell asleep, for I remember very clearly waking up tae the sound o a very loud voice that seemed tae hae awe things in it, anger and despair, and a kind o fierce wildness that I canna weel describe. Steenie was sitting quietly by my side smoking his pipe while Sawney was standing on the sand below the cave dressed only in his breeks wae a flagon o whisky in his hand. He was gey drunk leaning on a muckle stick he had found.

-Damn them awe, he shouted. -Damn them awe. I cam back as a gude sodger tae help tae deliver this place which at that time seemed sarely in need o deliverance. And them that wad be our leaders in this great wark did murder my friends and neighbours behind my back, and now wad murder me and awe that is mine, and mak awe things tae be the opposite o what they should be, and instead o a blessed light falling on the land we hae a plague roaring through it. I ken nae mair. Let the Lord deliver us himsel if it sae pleases him, for we canna deliver oursels. Or let him damn us awe tae Hell if sic be his will. For nae doubt it is awe written doun and we maun just gang alang like the heretic Musselman says, bowing tae his will and proclaiming his mercy in ignorance o whaur they are tae be found.

He ranted on, his voice breaking and cracking like a madman's. And Steenie went doun and put his airm round him and dragged him back up tae the cave whaur he looked at me lying there and said,

-Now there Steenie lies something that can be grasped.

Steenie telt him tae be steady, but it was hard for him tae hold up sic a big man and he just fell doun at my side, and I took his heid and laid it on my breast, and he looked up at me his een rolling in his heid.

-I ken not the whaur-for nor the why-for, but ye are tae be a witch and Steenie is tae be a warlock and mysel some ither class o Deevil-damned man, and we awe maun gang through the warld like whigmaleeries, while the rest o the country just bangs it out bravely for a purpose that is hidden frae us. Sae tae the Hielans we maun gang and live in the wilderness amang the breekless heathen as my gude friend Steenie says we maun, for our brithers in Christ hae excummunicated us and put us tae the horn, declared us tae be wolf's heids and when caught are tae be hingit or burnit, whatever taks their fancy. Sae open yer legs lassie and let me gang in, for I hae nae sic wisdom tae gang elsewhaur, and ye Steenie maun come and lie beside us for there is nane left in the warld tae love us but oursels.

But he just fell asleep then, and I held his heid cradled on my breast and listened tae him simpering sadly in his sleep. And when I looked up Steenie was just standing there staring out at the water. And it seemed tae me then that the cave which had been sic a peaceful place was now itsel filled wae the madness o the warld.

☆

The minister, paralysed by his own silence, rode like a man who felt himself to be a shadow, and the world through which he passed no more than a barbarous dream.

Whether Andrew Gilmore noticed anything at all of this the minister did not know. Sometimes it appeared to him that the other man was scrutinising him closely at all times. On other occasions his indifference seemed to the minister almost a rejection. And yet, he thought wearily, none of these suspicions could be said to be detectable in the man's behavior which was always courteous and cheerful. I am simply not the kind of clergyman he is accustomed to. He is accustomed to fire-eating warhorses like Robert Carmichael.

The minister reasoned thus, and yet he suspected that Andrew did not have a very high opinion of Carmichael. Indeed there were times when the minister suspected that Andrew did not have a very high opinion of anyone above his own station, and that he often simply fell quiet to avoid a quarrel. Most galling of all was the feeling that Andrew thought him a kind of simpleton, and was even secretly undertaking his education.

They were riding side by side when the minister noticed a covered cart on the road ahead coming towards them. As it drew nearer the minister could see that it contained a family. The minister's heart sank. The appearance of all of them was utterly wretched, to the minister's eyes, human beings in the last stages of decline. The minister knew in his soul that he did not know how to pass them. He felt that a gesture was called for, indifference would be unchristian, and yet any ostentation had to be avoided.

He had of course seen beggars before, myriads of them, crowding the towns and cities of Europe, and he had given to them often. Out here on the road among these wild hills, this ragged hunger-scourged crew clinging to a wagon pulled by a dreadful skeleton of a horse seemed like an affront to nature. They filled the minister with loathing. He watched their eyes taking in what to them could only be the approach of two prosperous gentlemen, with dull curiosity, dull hope, and dull greed.

He looked at Andrew but could read nothing in his countenance, and dared not ask him how they should behave, or if he should offer money to them. As they drew level they made neither by word or gesture any sign that they were begging other than by the pitifulness of their appearance. They did not however draw back off the road as the minister had somehow expected they would. Indeed it was Andrew Gilmore who did this, moving his horse before the minister's into single file.

'Gude day Sir,' Andrew said.

'An gude day tae ye tae.'

They spoke in very broad dialect which as yet the minister could not always follow, but there was no trace of condescension in Andrew Gilmore's manner or speech, and when he reached into his saddle-bag and pulled out a hare that he had shot earlier that day, it was easily accepted and disappeared instantly into the back of the wagon. He scribbled out a note and handed it to the man.

'That should satisfy auld Erskine.'

The man took it and pocketed it without looking at it. He was about to continue on his way when the minister leaned down from his horse and handed him a sovereign.

For a moment the man looked at it, astonishment crawling over his features. Their eyes met and the minister felt the sharp harsh stab of the man's pride, fearful in its magnitude and ridiculous in its expression.

'In the name of our Lord ye hae my blessing minister.'

'And you and your family have mine.'

There was a movement and the woman thrust forward a child of about three years. The minister felt now the fearful judgement of all their eyes. He reached out his hand and blessed the child and the woman. There were five other children who were all presented to him, and in turn the minister blessed them all, saying an audible prayer for each as he did so. It seemed to him that for a brief moment each face was infused with light and then both parties were on their way.

They rode in silence. When the family was out of sight the minister asked:

'Do you know them Andrew?'

'Och aye, them and thousands like them. The man fought at Bothwell Brig when the Stuart Pharaoh's troopers drank their fill o the Godliest blude in the West.'

'What did you put in that note?'

'Just a bit word tae auld Erskine that if they should come by him they were tae hae twa gude milk ewes. The bairns looked as if they needed them.'

'That was a charitable act Andrew.'

'Charity, minister, is a word that aye sticks in my throat, and nae doubt it sticks in his tae . . . Nae doubt it had a fine meaning in the Bible but it has very little in the present day. And wae five bairns tae feed, why it wad hae made mair sense whatever if he had just stuck a gun at our breasts and taen awe we had . . .'

'That would be robbery, Andrew.'

'An nae doubt if caught he wad be hingit for it. As if he

himsel hasna been robbed, an I'm maist reluctant tae believe onybody is hinging for that.'

The silence resumed itself. The minister felt his dissatisfaction growing. Agnes Douglas, he thought, would not have waited in proud humility for alms and a blessing, bloody murder without warning would have been her course. For a moment a vision of the hideous pack swarming from the ground, half naked and bristling with weapons, tortured his imagination. He turned to Andrew Gilmore.

'Andrew, do you find my company distasteful in any way?'

The Borderman looked at him in frank astonishment.

'In the name o God minister what on earth maks ye ask that?'

'I don't know Andrew, I don't know, but to be plain I did not know what was expected back there, or what was acceptable, or what would hurt his feelings.'

'Och his feelings are tough enough by now, an nae doubt they were hurt. In the circumstances they could hardly be flattered. But the lang and the short o it, which he understands better than ye or I, is that for a time they will be fed and we hae nae power tae dae mair.'

'It's just that you seem to be angry.'

'If I'm angry it's maybe because when we did seem tae hae some power we misplaced it, an I'm weary o the story we get frae on high, and frae the pulpit, that Orange Willie's arse is warm on his throne and we won a victory, which is still, against awe the evidence tae the contrary, mouthed by every loun ye meet.'

'Robert Carmichael seemed to believe sincerely that it was a victory.'

'Nae doubt it is, he nae langer needs tae run about the hills dodging dragoons but can preach doucely and safely frae his pulpit in the Tron Kirk.'

The minister felt strongly that he ought to be offended, and yet he could summon neither passion nor reason for a reply. He had nevertheless resolved to ride in stiff silence when Andrew's countenance suddenly cleared.

'I like yer company fine minister, I ken not what gars ye think itherwise, an yer feelings an actions on awe matters dae ye credit.'

With that the minister had to be satisfied. Andrew quickly became talkative again returning to his old habit of pointing out landmarks and mentioning the events they commemorated. As evening fell he led the minister to another bothy in the hills.

☆

We left the cave the following night. I dressed like a sodger in Steenie's armour. It was Steenie's plan tae which we awe agreed, that we should journey through the night and rest in some hidden place by day. Steenie himsel laid out the route. Haeving made the journey many times before he kent many quiet roads tae the North.

Sae we went, some nights we rade three abreast if the road wad allow it, at ither times Steenie wad lead wae mysel in the middle and Sawney bringing up the rear.

It was an unco strange thing tae ride through the night like that, like we were hardly living folk at awe, but as Sawney had said the previous night just spirits passing through, seeing houses and bits o biggins in the distance, some wae their fires still burning, maist in darkness. And when I looked round at Sawney's face in the moonlight, it wad seem tae me that it was set very hard, as if, forbye the material night, he was riding intae darkness itsel.

He had said nae word about his wildness o the night before, and indeed at the beginning o our march had seemed very cheerful tae be ganging. But now it was as if the previous night had just o'ertaen him as he rade, and I kent in my heart, that it was as if awe the warld that he had believed in and loved had forsaken him, and it may be that he felt tae that the warld we were riding through had forsaken itsel.

I mysel rade feeling naething at awe that I can put intae words, except that the Agnes Douglas that had ance been was now nae mair, and the body that had ance been hers was now a different thing, and had a steel harness clasped about its breast and back and a sword by its side, and was discovering that the Scotland that had ance seemed sae small now seemed very large, and awe things in it were like the hours we kept, the reverse o natural, and being out o control had nae power tae right itsel, but maun gang forward intae darkness.

The first day we camped in a bit wood and had for our supper bannocks and oatmeal like sodgers o lang ago. After we had finished Steenie went intae the wood tae see if he could shoot a bit meat, and I lay wae Sawney feeling awe the despair and confusion draining out o him, and he for a time returning tae his former self, laughing and crying, kind and gentle.

And then he wad change very quickly, and say that the warld that had ance been wad never be again, and that for awe that he had kent it had truly deed in Germany, and that the Germany that he had left behind had just reached out tae follow him, and the thing that had destroyed Germany was now driving on Scotland, and now the plague was driving tae.

The news o the plague had much affected him forbye he had encountered it often before. But now he said, that at this time and in this place, it seemed tae run counter tae awe the prophecies that had been made, and could only mean that the Lord's judgement was hard at hand and was something ither than what minister's thought it was, and what he had believed it was, and he had near gien up awe hope o ever kenning what was required o him.

Then he wad laugh and say wha could truly ken anything and ken that it was true, and that it might weel be that the Bible itsel was nae mair than tales o wild auld folk? Then anither self that had been his before I had properly kent him wad declare that he cared for naething in this warld, and for naebody, for he was but a sodger wha's living was in his weapons, and wha maun expect tae dee any day that being the conditions o his trade.

I asked him if he cared naething for Steenie or for me, and he wad laugh and say, -why should I? For are we not awe but dust and dirt and doubt that a strang wind can tumble whaur it pleases.

Then he wad repent quickly and say that he cared sae much that he thought it was maybe a sin, for unless ye loved the Lord aboun awe things then folk were of nae mair account than beasts ye skinned for yer supper.

Steenie on the ither hand wad get mair and mair blithe the further we travelled frae Galloway, and wad say that was because there was less chance o us being apprehended.

Ane day we sat on the brow of a high hill in the early morning, I canna mind whaur Sawney was at the time, and we watched an army o sodgers gang past in the glen beneath us. Steenie said that it was not a full army just a few troops o horse and foot marching tae join up somewhaur. But tae me, never haeving seen an army before, it was the largest body o men I had ever set eyes upon at any ane time, and the crash o their feet and the singing o their voices rang in my ears like a sound that was louder than anything natural that I had ever previously heard and the sun shone on their steel bonnets and waving spears as if it tae was dumbfounded and kent not intae what kind o warld it had risen.

-Wha are they? I asked.

-Covenant sodgers, Steenie answered. -Freshwater anes by their appearance, but not being in touch wae recent events I ken not whaur they are ganging.

By freshwater sodgers Steenie meant anes that were newly raised and lacked experience. But tae me at that time, they looked as if they could just hae marched ower anything that was in their path. Steenie just laughed at that, and said that if the thing that was in their path had spears and guns tae, and looked as fierce, then it wasna sic an easy matter.

I asked Steenie then what a battle was like. In reply he just gied a grim bit smile, and said that a battle, for awe what great captains did and said, was maistly confusion tae a sodger.

-Often ye can see neither tae yer left or yer right sae thick is the air wae smoke frae guns, and the noise. Why the very air is as thick wae noise as wae smoke. And some lads are yelling tae stand firm and ithers are running awa, and ithers are just deeing awa. If ye are standing in line wae a pike ye are just standing guarding the muskets, waiting tae strike at the first body that ye can see and that comes within yer reach. And when ye get the order tae gang forward, then forward ye gang, stabbing and slashing at anything in yer path, and wondering why ye hae no sae far been shot, for ye can see many around ye wha hae.

-If ye are on a horse, which Sawney and I were, ye just gallop, trying tae slash the heid off the pike that's trying tae pike ye, or if ye hae a ball in yer gun trying tae shoot the lad that's handling it. And if it is anither horseman ye are faced wae ye maun try and meet him wae a bit sword-play, killing him or knocking him frae the saddle if ye can. And if ye get through, why ye maun turn as a body and charge in again. Aye and sometimes a confusion sets in and horses and riders just keep on galloping, only realising when the smoke and the noise has deed awa that they hae left the battle far behind them in a maist unsodgerly fashion.

It seemed impossible tae me that any should come alive out o sic an affair, and he explained tae me how he and Sawney wad aye ride side by side, which was a cunning way tae fight, and how on many occasions they had saved each ither frae being killed. Sawney, he said, had been in far mair battles than him and was a very skillful sodger, brave enough without being mad, sae that the men that he captained trusted him, and he in turn kent weel just the time tae rally them and bid them be cheerful and brave, and not tae run awa, which was often mair dangerous than fighting. He telt me how at Marston Muir when the battle was at a very desperate turn wae many sodgers on baith sides running awa, and the Generals themsels haeving fled the field in despair, Sawney and he had charged in wae David Leslie's Scottish horse, and how Sawney had made the heids o the King's cavaliers tae just dance in the air.

And then Steenie had got himsel wounded, and Sawney had got himsel wounded while killing the man that had wounded Steenie, which is how the news o their deaths got out. But the truth was that baith had been commended by David Leslie for their brave example, forbye at the time it seems he tae thought they were deid.

We watched the sodgers as they marched out o sight singing their Godly psalms, awe of which I kent weel though queer and strange they sounded against the thundering o their feet.

When Sawney cam up tae us, and of course he had seen them tae, and he said that he had felt a great desire tae just

101

step intae the road and speak tae them, sic a brave and Godly troop they had looked, forbye he agreed wae Steenie that they were new raised sodgers. Which set them baith tae wondering why new raised sodgers should be marching Northwards.

I asked them how they kent they were new raised, and Sawney just laughed and said,

-They march and sing wae ower much alacrity, as if they kent not at awe intae what they are ganging, but that forbye, I wad hae liked fine tae hae talked tae them and discovered if there were any new events that were taking them tae the North.

Steenie had sat quietly for a bit, and then he said,

-Events will gang their ain gate whether we ken about them or no.

-I mind the day when ye thought that the struggles o men were mair than just events but had something tae dae wae liberties.

For aboun a minute Steenie made nae reply, and then he just gied a bit sigh.

-Aye weel, that sang has not sung itsel out yet.

-Maybe Montrose is indeed in the Hielans, but ye said ye didna think the Hielanmen wad rise for him.

-Some might, forbye there wad be nae sense in it. But the Gordon horse might, they being aye King's men.

-I envy them their sang, aye and whiles I think we're just ducking out o our duties.

-Then maybe ye should just gallop after them. They will nae doubt welcome ye till some kirkman recognises wha ye are.

-Dae ye think that awe is already lost then, forbye the fighting gangs on?

I could feel the despair in Sawney's questions then, like he was without hardly kenning it looking for a quarrel because he couldna find an answer. Weel Steenie kent it tae, and wishing tae avoid it said,

-Wha kens, there are many lang verses still tae be played. But they hae cast us out, and for the present I can see nae sense in just riding tae our deaths on a point o honour and duty. I might weel think differently if circumstances were different, but haeving murdered auld Janet and excummunicated us maks me think differently o them.

There was nae mair said at that time on that subject. The next night we rade on and cam tae a wide river called the Forth which we crossed quietly at a place Steenie kent, and the morning saw us safely in a range o hills called the Ochils, frae whaur we could look back on the sweet carse o Stirling laid out before us.

I mind this place weel, forbye I could not then ken that it wad be a lang time ere I looked on sic peaceful rich fields again. But I mind Steenie sitting drawing on his pipe and saying that there were times when he thought folk were little better than brainless beasts, for wad it not be a simple and easy thing tae just gie each man an equal share and portion o awe this fine land, mair than sufficient for him and his family? And what need wad sic folk hae for wasteful cattle o kings, nobles and gentry? Wad they not hae in their ain hands awe the skill needed tae mak the land prosper? Aye and tae defend it should any try tae tak it frae them, forbye he thought it wad be a bold man indeed wha wad try tae steal frae sic free folk.

He said little mair at that time, but I ken that the idea that he formed there remained aye wae him, forbye however simple and easy it sounded in words there was nae way o achieving it in the warld in which we lived. And as he himsel said at the time, if the sensibleness o it was apparent tae us sitting on a hillside, it was as little apparent tae maist o the louns in the country as it wad be tae Steenie's ain horse.

I said I thought it was a fine idea, which is an opinion I still haud despite awe.

-Aye Agnes, he replied, -Ane that might weel be worth drawing a sword for, and if the folk wanted a kirk . . .

-How could folk no want a kirk? Sawney inquired, his voice baith quiet and demanding.

-Weel let them build ane, and bid some minister body tae preach in it on Sundays and leave the folk in peace the rest o the time.

-The Lord is not just for Sundays, but for every day o the week and hour o the day.

Sawney's voice had risen a bit then, and it grieved me deeply, as it had done before, and was tae dae again, tae see how near they could be tae a quarrel. This time Steenie just laughed, chaffing him a bit, and saying that it was only an idea he had found in his pipe. And anyway he could live easily enough wae the Lord, it was ministers and priests he couldna thole. Sawney himsel laughed a bit at that, forbye he said he could wish it itherwise, and Steenie said nae mair.

From there we started tae climb high intae the Hielan hills, which seemed tae me at that time tae be a truly terrible place o mountains and water, and the route we took and the roads we travelled wad hardly hae appeared roads at awe tae them that did not ken them. And though we rade by daylight now the forests through which we rade were sae dark that there were times when it seemed tae mak little difference.

It was Steenie wha said we should ride by day now, being out o the immediate sight o the kirk, and there being little point in trying tae hide frae Hielanmen in their ain country either by day or night it was safer tae be seen moving openly and plainly.

Ance or twice Sawney wad ask him if he knew certainly whaur we were ganging, and Steenie wad just smile and say that he had travelled the route often enough before. There was a way when he spoke then that ye could think that it was possible that Steenie himsel was lost, not in his physical direction, but in ither ways. As if he tae, as Sawney had hinted, felt that we were just riding out o our time and place.

We were in a place called Argyll which Steenie said was the country o a folk called the Campbells, when awe at ance there was a man standing in front o us.

Tae my een at that time, he looked the wildest man I had ever seen, wrapped around in a muckle tartan plaid sae different frae our grey anes, and under it his legs were naked. He was armed tae, a great sword at his side and twa pistols sticking in his belt, but he showed little inclination tae draw either.

As we drew nearer I could see that in truth he was a gey

auld man wae a thick grey beard. Behind him stood a tall
young man dressed in the same wild way but wae a musket
on his shoulder. Neither made any move forward or back
but just seemed tae be waiting.

-Dae they mean us any hairm dae ye think? Sawney
asked.

-If they had meant us hairm I think we would hae experienced the hairm lang ere we caught a glimpse o them. We
are in his country and nae doubt he just wants tae exchange
a civil word. Dae naething tae show that ye hae any misgiens.

Steenie moved his horse forward and shouted out something in a wild foreign tongue, which was the Hielanman's
natural language, which at that time I had nae idea o. The
auld man shouted back and started walking towards us.
When we drew level wae Steenie they started to talk, and
while the speech seemed friendly enough I understood nane
o it and Sawney only a little. Then awe at ance the auld
man raised his hand and on either side o us twa men rose
frae the ground, almost it seemed tae me, frae beneath our
feet. Twa had guns in their hands while the ither twa had
longbows, and if they had them levelled at us when they
were lying doun they lifted them up when they stood up.

-Lord save us, Sawney said quietly. -It's Amorites we are
amang.

But Steenie called us forward and introduced us tae the
auld man and said his name was Iain Glas Campbell and
that he was a gude friend. The auld man then shook our
hands in a maist friendly fashion, though it seemed his
knowledge o the Scottish tongue stretched tae nae mair than
gude day and God be wae ye. His son wha was the young
man wha stood behind him, and was called Iain Oig, also
pressed forward tae shake our hands, and the four men wha
had been concealed now strode forward as if they were
right glad tae see us, and it seemed very strange tae me that
this was still Scotland, and how on a small misunderstand-
ing they could hae shot us.

The auld man next said a few quick words and ane o the
Hielanmen just seemed tae just disappear intae the forest
again. Steenie turned tae us his een twinkling slightly at our

unease.

-Grey John, for that was the man's name in our language. -Wad not hae us riding through his country and by his house without stopping in for a bit meat and some refreshment.

We accepted gladly and started tae follow the auld man as he directed us, the Hielanmen trotting lightly at our sides, we looking at them and they looking at us, mair than was polite, though nae doubt in the circumstances it could be forgien. They were awe very fine young men, but at that time strange tae me. Weapons they had enough o, but they seemed tae hae nae armour apart frae a round shield which the carried on their backs, alang wae a pouch for arrows wae lang steel heids.

Frae time tae time they wad try tae speak tae us but apart frae a few words that Sawney kent, we had nae language in common. For my part I felt sure that they were not taen in by my disguise for they looked in their ain way like very keen men. But if that was the case they gied nae sign o it.

They took us off the track that we were on tae their biggin, which was ane o a number alang the banks o a burn, and there open tae the air they had a table spread waiting for us. There were women and bairns there now, the women wrapped in tartan plaids, and the bairns in anything that cam tae hand, and sometimes in naething at awe. And whisky they poured for us in plenty awe the time talking in their ain language wae here and there bits and pieces o Scots.

I discovered frae Steenie that they belanged tae a great clan that was for the Covenant, and some had been in the army that Leslie had taen South intae England, whaur their wild appearance and their bows and arrows and great pipes had gien the English cavaliers a fright, though nae doubt they had laughed a bit tae.

After we had eaten a great meal o venison, Steenie in thanks tae our hosts, wad play them a bit tune o his small pipes which set them tae dancing and singing and shouting, which at that time seemed very fierce tae me. And ane o auld Iain's sons wha was called Allan cam out wae a set o great pipes, and forbye they made a dreadful screeching as he blew them up, made very fine and sad music ance they were gaen, which brought loud applause frae awe o us, and Steenie saying that his pipes were nae mair than a bit whistle in comparison.

We had not intended it, but we stayed wae them that night, they haeving got us sae drunk that it hardly seemed wise tae move. And think ye no that it was strange for me trying tae be a man in this company, and not really kenning how men behaved, nor haeving a heid tae haud the muckle amount that they drank? But not kenning their language was helpful tae me in this, and if they guessed they said naething. Steenie said it was not the Hielan way tae inquire too deeply intae yer guest's business ance ye had taen them under yer roof. That forbye, I think the auld man kent for his een twinkled in a strange way at me.

We left them in the morning weel fed and weel supplied, and some o the Hielan folk cam wae us tae the end o their glen and stood waving tae us as we left.

We had ridden on a bit when Sawney said,

-Weel if we meet nae worse folk in the Hielans I'll be contented.

-Steenie wha had been talking lang and close wae auld Iain Glas, said that there was already trouble, and that Montrose was indeed in the Hielans, burning and looting in the King's name wae an army o wild Hielanmen and Macdonalds frae the West, and even some frae Ireland.

-Iain Glas said that the hale clan is just waiting for the day when their chief should cam back frae Edinburgh tae lead the people out against Montrose tae put an end tae his mischievings. For they ken weel that if Montrose's ambition is tae put the King back on his throne, his Hielanmen's ane was tae roup Argyll.

When I asked him why this was, awe he said was,

-Hielan brawls, Agnes, are very obscure things. But ye see these folk wha were our kindly hosts are o the Clan Campbell, which is a very powerful clan, mair powerful than any ither in the Hielans, and their chief that they call Macalein-More, but wham the rest of the country kens as the Marquis o Argyll, is a stern man o the Covenant, and it may be that at the present time he is the maist powerful man in Scotland, and has but tae whistle quietly tae hae six thousand broadswords at his back.

-Weel a great clan like that has been pressing hard on the small clans around its edge, aye and further afield. The Campbells ye maun ken hae a clever way o winning land by the sword and keeping it wae legal parchment. Some folk just get swallowed up by them, change their name and wear a Campbell badge in their bonnet, while ithers tak tae the hills wae a sword in their hand, landless and swearing revenge.

-Why these Macdonalds that hae cam frae Ireland are for the maist part but the sons o men driven out o Argyll by the Campbell sword and forced tae flee tae their kinsmen in Antrim, and if Montrose will lead them against the Campbells, why then they will follow Montrose, forbye they care little wha sits on the royal throne. And Jamie Graham ye see if he loves the King aboun awe men might weel hate Argyll a bit mair. The Graham ye see was ance very strang for the Covenant but has now turned traitor tae it, and some say it was because the Kirk sided wae the Parliament men in England, and ithers that he dis indeed love the King, and then again it may be that it was out o his ain proud and ambitious heart which near broke in twa when the Kirk favoured Argyll ower him.

I said at the time that it seemed tae me a wild and confused business, and Steenie said that while Argyll was a great man in the Government and the Kirk he was nae military man tae be the chief o a great Hielan clan. And while Iain Glas and his sons were waiting for him tae come back and raise the standard, Argyll dallied in Edinburgh attending tae great affairs o state, which tae his people seemed o little importance when their auld enemies were gathering against them.

☆

There was nothing unusual about the travelling family the minister discovered. In the wilder and more barren parts of the hills large camps of them congregated. Andrew kept to the road, giving them, it appeared to the minister, a wide berth.

'They hae nae desire at awe for our company,' he said. 'And why should it be itherwise, for there is naething we can dae or say which wad profit them in ony way, but could only be irksome, and they hae persecutors enough.'

'Who persecutes them?'

'Maist everybody, few caring tae hae sic a great number o hungry folk at their door.'

If the minister and his guide met any of them there was a brief salutation, which was almost an acknowledgement on both sides that they were no longer the same brethren with little left in common. Beneath their rags the minister saw disease and despair, and the occasional sword and gun. The wreckage of the century they seemed to him, a banditti of beggars without purpose or spirit. Charity and compassion which could be exercised on one family was entirely over-whelmed by this army. He felt relieved to be past them.

'Were do they come from?' He asked Andrew.

'Frae awe places and frae nane. Some are sodgers wha hae lost limbs, some are folk wha hae lost their bit land, driven out nae doubt by some fine laird. Ithers are folk wha hae never recovered frae the famine, some wha hae been wandering since the auld days, maybe still praying and singing, maybe not. There are ithers wha's memories couldna gie them an answer if they asked it. Why minister there hae aye been sic folk.'

'Are they completely outside of all civil society and religion?'

'Aye unless they should fall foul o it, and nae doubt they war awe Godly folk at ane time, and nae doubt there are still a few mad auld preachers amang them, though maybe little o what the Kirk wad now call true religion.

'They will gaither thegither in a barren place like this ane and bide for a time and tak tae the road at ither times, begging a bit here and there, not stealing much for folk are gey wary, forbye they will gie a bit charity provided them that receive it gang on. Folk ken very weel that in the years that hae gone it took very little bad luck tae thrust a man and his family out of the warld intae yon pit.

To the minister it seemed impossible that they could survive at all. He thought of that other pit and how they had survived. He thought of the boy Dugald Bain and felt his soul trembling within him. Indeed he often thought of him before he slept, and the image remained with him throughout his fitful slumbers, greeting him as he woke. Nor could his logical mind escape the terrible contradictions of his existence, born into a situation which put him from his conception beyond the possibility of redemption. The minister remembered his strong yet childish hands clinging to his gown, his eyes, dark like his mother's, regarding him with fear and wonder and loathing.

'*Ane night,*' he had told the minister. '*Ane night when awe the people were asleep but I was not, mither cam up tae see me and said, I sall gang out this night and ye can gang wae me if ye are not ower tired.*

'*Mither we kent, often went out for lang walks in the night by hersel, tae see, she said, if ought had changed in Chaos, but aye she had returned tae say that the place was as mad as ever it had been wae corpses o the deid and deeing lying about in ilka place. But never before this time had she asked me tae gang wae her, sae this night I felt properly honoured and not a bit tired, and just asked her if I should bring my gun? She said, aye, and yer dirk tae. This was just a wise precaution in case we should meet ony o the folk o Chaos, and mither hersel put twa pistols under her plaid as weel as her dirk.*

'*Afore we went mither went and whispered in faither's ear, forbye he seemed tae me tae be asleep, but mither said he slept very lightly haeving trained himsel that way when he was a sodger and might at ony moment be called tae his arms because o an alarm. Then she took me by the hand and we slipped out o the hole that led frae our cave intae Chaos.*

'*For a time I just stood there at a place whaur twa roads met sae astonished was I at the hugeness o Chaos which seemed tae stretch further and further and hae nae end at awe. I asked mither if there was an end tae it? She just laughed at that and said nane that she had ever seen. But forbye it was big, it was neither a pleasant nor a warm place, and for years now, ever since she was a bairn, the folk in it had been killing and murdering each ither, which I kent very weel haeving been telt it often enough, and about the plagues and famines which tormented the place. She said that at this time it was her opinion that famine had the grip.*

'I kent not what famine could look like, but after walking for a bit we cam tae this auld bit cart, and when we looked inside awe the folk were deid, and sae deid that there was hardly ony meat on them at awe. Very still they lay, a man and a woman and twa or three bairns, covered in rags and wae their een and tongues hinging out, and in some they had been pecked by gulls and craws and awe stinking maist awful. Mither said that they should hae been buried, which was what folk did wae deid folk in Chaos, but famine had sic a grip that there was few tae dae even that.

'Mither looked about and telt me tae dae the same, saying that sometimes there were folk wha were still alive, though on this occasion she thought they war ower lang deid for that. We did find anither a bit frae the cairt, but he was deid tae. He was about my age but very thin and sma, and looked as if he had been trying tae eat leaves and grass and sic like rubbish. I looked at him a bit an ye could see in the moonlight whaur his hands had been tearing at the ground, and mither bent doun and closed his een which the craws had pecked and telt me tae come awa.

'We walked on a bit but there was naething at awe tae see. Mither said that awe the land tae either side o us was ance full o grain and cattle and sheep which the folk o Chaos wad eat, but by now they war already awe lang deid and eaten.

'Mither put her airm round me and I asked her if awe o Chaos was like this? She replied that it might weel be for awe she kent. Chaos was aye in the grip o suffering.

'I asked her if suffering had a worse grip than famine or war or pestilence. She just gied out a grim bit laugh at that and said that whiles they cam in each ither's wake and whiles they cam on their ain. She telt me tae that it had not aye been like that, and when she was a bairn it had been a happy enough place, but that I kent was before the Lord got angry and smote it.

'We cam tae a row o strange things that mither caed biggins in which the folk o Chaos lived, for they did not live in a great cave like us but had tae build places, and mither said that she had been born in and had lived for mony years in sic a place. That was in the time before the folk o Chaos dragged her awa and hung her up and stuck pins intae her and wad hae killed her if faither and Steenie had not saved her.

111

'There war nae folk living in these biggins now, and mither sat doun and looked around her, and I asked her if she war tired and she said aye in manner o speaking she was. And sae we sat there for a while but there was naething at awe tae see, and I asked her if we could look inside the biggins, and she said she didna want tae but there might be something still alive.

'We walked intae awe the biggins and maist war just empty, except for bit things that mither caed tables and chairs, and occasionally a bit sword or knife, which of course I kent about. In ane biggin we found a row o deid folk that warna lang deid, and mither said they maun hae bided behind for reasons o their ain, ither folk haeving taen tae the road tae try and find meat.

'I went intae ane biggin on my ane, and sitting in the middle o it eating the dirt frae the ground was a bairn, or maybe not quite a bairn but a bit aulder, around the same age as my sister Leezie, wha is a gude bit younger than me. She had nae claes on bar a bit rag and she just stared at me, her een popping out o her heid and did not try tae run awa or dae onything at awe. Ance when she tried tae stand up she fell ower again and I shouted for mither.

'When mither cam in and saw her she ran and picked her up in her airms wae a great shout o joy, at which the lassie burst out crying, and mither telt me tae gang and search carefully for there might be mair. I briskly did as I was bid, but forbye I searched in awe the biggins and found twa mair deid folk I found naething living. When I cam back mither was sitting whaur we had first sat and had opened her plaid tae let the bairn feed, which it was daen maist greedily an she was singing it a wee sang. We sall tak it back Dugald, she said, and it will be a wee sister tae ye as soon as it is weel and strang for naething ever dees in our cave.

'Mither had done this often before, ganging out and bringing back bairns and I had never kent and had aye wondered whaur she had got them.

'We sat for a bit watching the bairn, which looked better and better the mair milk it got. And then mither said we maun be awa because she couldna thole this place ony langer and the bairn shouldna hae ower much at ance after being hungry for sae lang, and sae I carried it on my back, it weighing hardly onything at awe, and we started off hame.

112

'As we war nearly hame, but no quite, we saw twa men on very big horses riding towards us singing at the tops o their voices. Mither very quickly, forbye I needed nae bidding, thrust me doun behind a bank and telt me tae put my hand ower the bairn's mouth sae that she could mak nae squeak.

'I did as I was telt feeling baith the bairn's heart and mine ganging near daft, but still I held her very tight while mither took out baith her guns and laid them at her side.

'The twa men drew nearer, and haeving stopped singing they war talking in very loud voices and war passing a bottle ane tae the ither, and seemed tae be already gey drunk, sae that ane that I could see when he passed the bottle very nearly fell off his horse, except that the ither had tae lean ower and steady him.

'Mither of course was not gaen tae shoot them unless she had nae ither choice. But as they cam nearer I could see that they wad very nearly trip ower us, and could hardly no hae seen us if they looked doun. But they didna, which was just as weel because mither wad hae had tae shoot them, or being folk o Chaos they wad certainly hae shot us.

'But they passed us, and just as they war passing they started tae sing again and went on singing till they war near out o sicht and mither said I could let the lassie gae. She then asked me if I had been feart and when I said that I had, she telt me that I had been brave awe the same, and the men on horses war sodgers, caming back nae doubt frae some late night mischief and drunk as the Deil.

'I asked her if they war sodgers just like faither had been, and did he ride about in the middle o the night daen mischief and getting drunk? She laughed at that, and said it was doubtless no uncommon, but faither had been a Godly sodger, at least maist o the time.

'We picked oursels up, and I took the lassie wha now looked frightened near tae death ance mair on my back, and we went on our way hame.

'As soon as we reached hame mither set about tending tae the bairn, and when faither wha slept very lightly, woke up she handed it tae him, and he looked at it and took it intae his airms and blessed it and said, praise the Lord but ye hae got this ane just in time. And mither said that it wad be awe right now for

113

nane had ever deed in our cave, and faither said that the Lord should be thankit for that, and that he thought the bairn should be caed Rebecca, which it was, and as mither had prophesied it got better in a very short time and becam a new sister tae us awe.'

The minister sighed. What power had it been that had preserved that child whom Bain had blessed and re-named Rebecca? What power had plucked her still living from the community of the Christian dead, damning her infant soul with an act of seeming mercy?

He glanced at Andrew Gilmore and wondered, as he had often wondered, how the story would affect him. The Borderman, as if suddenly aware of the minister's scrutiny, turned his head. He smiled gently at what he no doubt thought of as the minister's physical weariness.

'Sax or seven mair miles and we can rest for the nicht.'

☆

We passed out o the land o the Campbells, and rade higher and higher intae a country that tae me then seemed hardly like a possible place, a place that had neither roads or touns or kirks, but just great lochs and forests, and mountains higher than anything I had previously kent. Nor did I ken anymair, and neither I think did Sawney, whaur Steenie was taking us or why, but tae me it was as if he was leading us out o the warld itsel.

An unco strange mood had taen Sawney ower, as if he had resolved certain things in his heid, or had just put them aside, or it may be that he had decided that the Lord was leading him and had arranged things in this way, and ane day the purpose o it awe wad be revealed, or not be revealed as the Lord chose. But now he never quarrelled wae Steenie, or expressed any misgiens at awe but wad simply follow whatever route Steenie suggested we should tak.

In the evenings he had taen ance again tae reading his bible, screwing up his een and reading wae difficulty by the light o a fine little lamp which he carried and which he had got in Germany. Steenie had said tae him in a joke that if he

114

was gaen tae bide up awe the night he might as weel stand guard. Sawney did not laugh but just stared back at him wae een that were red wae strain, and said that reading the bible comforted him in a way that natural sleep did not, and that if he read lang enough he might find some key tae the wildness and disorder that he saw awe about him, and which he had experienced awe his life, and which plagued him in his dreams when he slept.

Some nights Steenie wad sit up tae and talk wae him, and I wad lie listening tae their conversation but haeving nae desire tae join in. I remembered weel what Steenie had said about the warld, and I kent that deep in his heart that thought had grown stranger and stranger till he himsel was mair confused about the truth o things than at any time previously in his life, and when he talked tae Sawney it was tae comfort him, but he dared not tell Sawney the unco strange notions that were really in his heid.

It was these notions that made it nigh impossible for him tae tak part wae any gude will in fighting and battles, which he said should only ever be undertaen in a spirit o truth and righteousness, and if that could not be assured, at least tae the satisfaction o a man's conscience, then awe that remained was tae live quietly in some quiet place. It may be that it was for that reason he had brought us tae the Hielans, forbye tae my mind it seemed an unco strange place tae choose, full o folk wha wore weapons at awe times, and cared as little for the Bible as they did for breeks.

I ken not truly, for the first time that I could remember since haeving kent Steenie, which seemed awe my life, there were questions that I could put tae him tae which he wad not venture an answer or an opinion, but wad just say that awe things that had previously thought tae be true now seemed tae him tae be quite deid, and it was the emptiness that they had ance covered that was now revealed and wad drive folk mad.

There was nae sign o madness about Sawney, but I hae heard it said that a body can gang mad without gien any sign. I ken not, but ane night I lay under his coat watching him reading, sitting by his lamp and showing nae desire tae move. Steenie wha had sat up wae him for a time had by now gone tae sleep.

I got tae my feet and wrapped in naething but his bear-coat I walked ower tae whaur he sat, coming up behind him in sic a fashion that it seemed tae me he maun hae kent I was there. He gied nae sign o acknowledgement, sae then I bent doun and quietly put out his light, at which point he turned his heid sharply, his een suddenly dark and mad staring at me.

-Damn ye, he said.

-Yer ower late for that Sawney, for them that hae mair authority than ye in sic matters hae already pronounced that judgement.

-Awa tae yer bed woman and leave me be.

I reached out and touched his heid then, and whether there was something about the nearness o me which affected him I ken not truly, but awe at ance he turned wae sic muckle force that he knocked me tae the ground whaur for a time I lay watching him, but he made nae further move.

For a minute or sae nae sound at awe passed between us, and he seemed at ane point tae be just about tae light his lamp again, and then at anither tae be hardly able tae move at awe. In the end he got tae his feet and bending ower me he lifted me up and carried me back tae the place whaur we slept and laid me doun, stripping himsel and slipping in beside me.

That night he clung tae me like some fierce beast wha's enemies are pressing him hard and wha kens not whether tae fight or flee. In the end he slept and I lay listening tae the sounds in that wild place, and I heard wolves howling and deer barking, and here and there a cat yelling, and I thought then that this warld o men was a fierce and bludie dream or it was a warld o despair, and there was nae route out o it except in death, and it was the warld itsel which set the conditions in which men had tae live, and there was nae altering o these conditions forbye they rade here and there and made a brave show o principle and certainty, as if this warld which had not been made by a sword could be altered by ane.

I slept that night in a troubled way tae wake in the morning tae a hand shaking me like a dog on a rabbit. I opened my een and looked up intae a face that was like nae earthly face I had previously seen wae green cat's een and a great mane o red hair.

As soon as I turned, it just seemed tae spring back, and now Sawney himsel was up, naked and wae his sword in his hand, ane foot planted firmly on either side o me, and awe around were men o a wildness I canna weel describe, clad in tartan plaids wae feathers in their bonnets. And while I was used tae Hielanmen by now these folk seemed wilder and mair heathen-like than any that I had seen before. Awe carried sword and shield and some had guns and longbows. The red-haired man wha was as tall as Sawney carried a great axe wae a shaft as lang as himsel on his shoulder.

In a second Steenie tae was at my side and addressing the red-haired Hielanman in his ain language. Sawney wha's anger was near tae bursting, and nae doubt wad hae burst if discretion had not made him cautious said,

-Ye ken their language, weel then, tell breekless Donald tae keep his hands for his ain business.

Steenie's conversation however was very quiet, and the red-haired man's ain voice, angry at first, becam itsel quieter. And when Steenie turned tae us his een were full o caution.

-Him wham ye call Breekless Donald, gangs by the name o Red Hector o the Axe, which is barbarous enough, but I dinna think he got it by twiddling his thumbs. They are Montrose's men, and Jamie Graham it seems is very near here. I think we maun gang wae them.

-Gang wae them?

-Or be taen prisnor by them. I hae telt Hector Roy that we are gude King's men, seeing that he just might be inclined tae hing or shoot awe ithers.

Sawney lowered his sword point fixing baith Steenie and the Hielanman wae a look o cauld mistrust. But if he was angry he was ower much o a sodger and man o experience not tae see that there was little point in any resistance. I had counted the Hielanmen and there was about twelve o them, some standing, some sitting, some just leaning on their weapons. The man called Hector Roy, Red Hector in our language, drew them back, turning his ain back on us while we dressed. I mind Sawney staring lang at that back and the great blade that curved ower it.

-I never saw sic a pack o Amalekites in awe my life, and I hae fought alangside Transylvanians.

-They are determined tae tak us tae Montrose and I think in the circumstances we maun behave wae some cunning.

-Damn Jamie Graham, Sawney said quietly. -And damn them. Dae ye no think that ance mounted and them on foot?

-In this country? Why these Hielanmen wad just run ye doun and think it poorer sport than chasing deer. Further-mair I hae gien Hector my word and I think he will behave civily enough as lang as I am seen tae keep it.

As aye it was Steenie's voice we followed, forbye I could feel that Sawney was cursing him quietly for our predica-ment. But we dressed, and I buckled on my armour feeling baith safer inside it and a bit mad, and we led our horses up tae the Hielanmen sae as not tae arouse suspicion by mounting.

At our approach they turned, and Hector Roy alang wae awe his weir men regarded me wae a queer astonishment in their faces, which made them awe look a bit bairn-like. And then Hector spoke tae Steenie and Steenie turned tae me, and if his een were twinkling a bit his face was very solemn.

-Our friend here wad like tae apologise for disturbing ye in sic a fashion this morning, but he didna realise ye were a woman. But he wad not like ye tae think that Hector Roy Maclean disna ken how tae behave properly.

In truth he did look damn sheepish, and as nae doubt it was wise tae keep on gude terms wae him I smiled and forgied him.

From then on it seemed that Hector Roy Maclean wad indeed play the gentleman, holding my horse for me while I mounted, which neither Sawney or Steenie had ever done. Then we rade at the trot wae the Hielanmen running at our sides like men wha had nae need o horses.

We rade for about a mile before Hector stopped us in a very quiet and sheltered place. He could talk only tae Steenie but it seemed that he wanted us tae bide there wae his Hielanmen and that he wad gang on and shortly return.

-He's gone tae fetch Jamie Graham himsel, Steenie said. -Or ane like him, and we maun just wait.

-If what they say about the Graham is true, Sawney said. -I think we wad be daen this country and its people a muckle favour if we just shot him and deed for it.

I looked round at the Hielanmen, wha were neither friendly nor unfriendly, and though they watched us, it was a careless kind o watching, secure nae doubt in their ability tae catch us if we ran awa. Ane aulder than the rest cam up tae us wae a flask o whisky and handed it tae Steenie wae much proud smiling. We passed it round each taking a drink and then we handed it back, but he waved his hand tae indicate that we were tae keep it.

-Weel, Sawney said. -Unless they hae poisoned the drink they seemed little inclined for the present tae murder us. And ye ken, in a professional kind o way I'm curious about their auld artillery.

Steenie wha had tried tae keep up a friendly conversation mentioned this tae the auld man, and he, wae a bit laugh called out the name o ane o them wha stepped forward wae a bow in his hand. He was a tall handsome young man, mightily pleased wae himsel he seemed tae me, and he explained tae us through Steenie that his mark was a fork in a birk tree about seventy paces awa.

He stood for a minute staring at it, and then wae a lang swift movement he sent an arrow straight intae it, and then, as if not wholly satisfied sent in a blink o an ee twa mair tae follow. We awe heartily applauded his skill and Steenie rade up tae retrieve his arrows for him. Sawney said that the accuracy and rate o fire was something modern sodgers underestimated, nor wad they be inconvenienced by rainy days which sae bedevilled musketeers.

In this way we passed the time, and as Steenie said, wad keep them weel disposed tae us. And anyway for the maist part he liked Hielanmen, and it grieved him tae see sic wild simple folk fighting for a king they could hae nae notion o, or he o them, except that Argyll that they hated was the Kirk's man. It ended when the auld Hielanman made a sign and we turned tae see Hector Roy, mounted now and wae anither man cam riding through the trees.

This man was like nane I had ever seen before. About middle-height and dressed completely in black armour, he rade towards us his slender body very straight in the saddle, his handsome face held high, and when he cam up tae us the manners o a fairy prince sic as I had never before beheld. He was like a man wham in awe his life nane had ever stopped or checked in anything, and his graciousness was just an acknowledgement o that.

-Jamie Graham, Steenie said quietly. -The first man in awe Scotland tae sign the Covenant, and the first o any worth tae turn traitor tae it, and wad now bleed the country for a king.

He stopped a few feet frae us, his een smiling gently, haeving already telt him it seemed tae me, everything there was tae ken about us.

-Gude day gentlemen, and tae ye tae madam, wha maun be, incomparably the bonniest sodger I hae ever set my een upon.

Nae doubt I smiled, and wha could not hae smiled, he seemed hardly a mortal man. And if Sawney kept a stiff and sodgerly face I admired Steenie at that moment aboun awe men, for he faced him wae nae sign o deference, ither than a short bow tae indicate that he kent that this was James Graham, Marquis o Montrose, the King's Lieutenant in Scotland, wha carried King Charles royal commission signed by his ain hand in his pocket.

-These are hard times my Lord, as doubtless ye ken, and it seemed mair convenient.

Montrose nodded his heid, his lips smiling unco gently.

-As ye say, gentlemen, these are troubled times. and if by the grace of God they will soon be ower, they are not ower yet, and ye will nae doubt understand that I can hardly pass sic gude sodgers as yersels on the road without some inquiry as tae wha ye are and whaur ye are ganging.

-My name is Steven Malecky and my experience as a sodger starts frae these troubles. My friend and comrade Mr Alexander Bain on the ither hand was for many years a captain o horse in the army o the great Gustavus, and the lady wae us is his wife Agnes Douglas. We hae baith fought at Marston Muir wae the army o the Covenant, which is perhaps less tae our liking now than it was then. We were on our way tae pay a visit tae my very gude friend Ewan Cameron o Lochiel, and tae see if the state o Scotland looked any fairer frae these high hills.

-Lochiel is a great and true friend o mine, and of King Charles. If ye are a friend o his I hardly feel I hae any leave tae question yer principles.

-And if our principles were not tae yer Lordship's liking?

Steenie's words were sharp then and Montrose's hale face just seemed tae cloud ower wae a look o sic gracious sorrow that it seemed tae me that had he prolonged it, tears wad surely hae followed.

-Come Sirs, ye ken the rules o war, ye wad leave me in a very unhappy position. Either I wad hae tae tak ye prisnor, which I can hardly afford, or should I just let ye ride on, possibly tae join up wae the King's enemies, as ye freely admit tae haeving done before, which could hardly be appreciated by my ain men?

-We are Presbyterians my Lord.

-And am I not? Did I not sign the Covenant and petition the king until his gracious majesty agreed tae the justice o awe our requests? Aye Sirs, but that did not satisfy those wha wad rule and ruin the country in his stead, and frae a pulpit. Religion Sirs is ane thing and I think those wha ken me will tell ye that I revere it as much as any man. But sedition, rebellion, and revolution, are quite anither. Against the Lord himsel they wad deprive the Lord's anointed o his throne. In their insufferable pride they wad mak ane that cannot be commanded ither than by God, tae sign a paper saying that henceforth he will be content tae be king in name only, wae nae mair real power than it taks tae twirl a sceptre. The road they tak is Satan's road tae republicanism, ruination and Hell, and if I love this land better than my ain heart's blude, I will see it in flames ere I see it gang that gate.

-I speak plainly Sirs, I hae the king's commission tae raise an army in Scotland for the salvation o his majesty and the scourging o awe rebellion. My army is at present composed of wild fellows like these, and the loyal Irish, all brave and

121

skillful men. If the tactics that we are for the present forced tae use wad appear somewhat ancient tae the great Gustavus, they are not tae be despised for awe that, as the rebels at Tippermuir discovered. But we are I freely confess in need o gude sodgers wha ken their trade, sic as I believe I see before me. Tae be plain gentlemen, if ye will earn my gratitude and the gratitude o ane higher than me, and eternal honour for yersels . . .

It made my blude run cauld tae ken that beneath the fine words and fine manners o this bright lord and awe his plain speaking, there lay an aulder and a plainer truth, if we refused his honour he was as like as not tae shoot us on the spot.

This was like a truth beyond fine words that even the Hielanmen wha had nae Scottish could understand. And Steenie understood it weel enough when he answered, forbye he telt me later that apart frae a certain mischief he felt in lying tae a turncoat traitor, the words baith stuck in his throat and cam out smooth enough.

-As I hae said my Lord, we hae cam tae the Hielans tae see if there was a fairer view o Scotland tae be had. It is my belief that we hae found it, and in a better condition than I could hae hoped. Ye hae awe our swords as yers tae command.

At these words Jamie Graham himsel looked mightily relieved, and nae doubt he didna exactly relish the idea o hinging us.

-Keep yer swords gentlemen and gie me yer hands.

They awe then clasped hands Sawney looking stiffer than he ought. But the Hielanmen let out a great roar as if they tae were relieved that they had not the job o killing us. And then Jamie Graham rade up tae me and wae great gallantry took me by the hand and said,

-And dae I hae yer sword tae, though by the grace o God it will never be needed?

Following Steenie's lead I assured him that he had and the Hielanmen cheered again wae sheer delight. And it was easy for me tae see that this man had a way wae awe men, and he could mak awe men's hearts beat for him while his beat only for a king, wha, as Steenie was later tae say, wad not hae kicked the best part o any o his Hielanmen.

That forbye, as we trotted through the woods tae his camp it seemed tae me that his hale soul was on fire wae passion for his cause, though he was not of course speaking tae me. But he spoke wae great eagerness tae Sawney and Steenie of his army which was just lying off the toun o Aberdeen, and of how he had sent word tae that toun that it maun surrender or be attacked. and if he had great reluctance tae dae this, still the toun had tae be secured and his people had tae be fed, and he was offering them very honourable terms which stubbornly they had sae far refused.

When we reached his camp and I looked around me, I could truly never hae imagined sic an army o Amalekites. Men, women, and bairns, huddled ower their cooking pots their tartans drawn about them, just waiting it seemed, watching as we cam in, but ance having observed us taking nae further interest. Montrose had billeted his officers in a row o biggins frae which the folk had the sense tae flee, and his men slept in the field.

We were gien a bit biggin whaur we were left tae hae our breakfast after which Montrose had requested Steenie and Sawney's attendance on him.

While we ate I chided Steenie a bit, I ken not rightly why, things had taen a very strange turn which at that time I baith feared and did not fully understand, but I said tae him that it seemed tae me that he could be very gude company tae the highest in the land when he had a mind.

I mind very weel the look he gied me in reply, as if ance mair in his een I was naething but a bairn.

-This is not the time for jests Agnes, I ken not what we should dae.

-It seems tae me that ye hae won him ower.

-Lord lassie but ye ken naething. He kens not whether we are Covenant spies, or King's men, or just mercenaries looking for pay. The last twa wad suit him fine but he will not believe it until he has seen us fight, aye and maybe not even then, and he means tae sack the toun.

-The toun should surrender, Sawney said quietly. -His principles may be wrang but he's an honourable man and a great captain.

123

-Lord save us awe, what are ye saying? I care naething for Jamie Graham's honour or his sodgerly skill. Scotland, aye and England tae will burn for his honour and his king, as ye heard him say. And ye ken better than me what will happen when ye pack a hungry army sic as this ane outside a rich toun like Aberdeen, and awe this talk o treaty is but the frills o civility in which he's pleased tae indulge, and might even believe for awe I ken or care. That toun will be sacked Sir, and we hae three choices, tae shoot the Graham and be hingit, tae try and run awa and be hingit, or tae fight in the King's army.

Sawney had gone strange and quiet beyond what at that time I could fathom. And it may be that the truth o it, and what had aroused Steenie's anger, was that Montrose had affected him deeply, and that, I hae found by experience ower the years was something in Sawney's nature. Suspicious o maist men and their motives, some men could affect him in sic a way that he wad follow them, and see in them a way out o the confusion o his spirit. Mathius Pringle had affected him in sic a way, as did Steenie himsel. But now he spoke unco soft as if his heart was breaking.

-Ye hae brought us here, Steenie, when I warned against it. Montrose wad be deid ye said. Jamie Graham was but a foolish boy and it was pure fancy tae pour intae a daft king's ear that he could get an army in the Hielans tae follow him. What did wild Hielanmen care about kings? Weel look out o that window Sir and ye will see wild Hielanmen and even wilder Irish sharpening their swords, sae tell me nae further what tae dae.

Steenie was silent then, aware as he telt me later, o the narrow truth o Sawney's words. But when we had finished our bit breakfast he got tae his feet and said,

-Weel Sawney, nae doubt but what ye say is true, still we should not keep the great marquis waiting or he might get tae thinking that our loyalty is not hale hearted.

They left and I sat there staring out o the window trying tae understand the position we were in, baith understanding it and not understanding it, being at that time a stranger tae war and hardly able tae believe that sic a fine gentleman could snap his fingers and hae us hingit frae the nearest

tree. He was not just a bit laird like John Doig, or a powerful man o the Kirk like Pringle, he was very nearly the King
himsel. For a time even the thought o Steenie shooting him
seemed impossible, impossible that sic a man could be
struck doun by twa bit sodgers out o Galloway.

And then I looked at the army that this man led, and they
seemed tae me far awa frae anything that I had kent, and
different frae the fright that Hector had gien me that morning. This was a hale army o Hectors as fierce as the enemies
o Israel in the Bible. Women wae bairns at their breasts and
dirks and guns at their girdles, and here and there great
gentlemen armed like Montrose himsel wad ride past, and
before them awe was the city o Aberdeen, o which at that
time I could mak nae sense at awe.

They were a lang time wae Montrose, and think ye not
that I grew afraid that he had hung them after awe. And did
not I then curse Steenie for bringing us here, him that was
sae wise. And I thought tae that I kent but little o Sawney's
true mind, and could think it possible that he wad like a
gude sodger throw himsel in wae the maist convenient host,
and seeing that he could not fight for the Covenant it
haeving declared us enemies, then it could come tae pass
that the Covenant's enemies wad be our friends.

When they cam back there was a sternness in baith their
faces. I could see that they had quarrelled and Steenie wad
say naething tae further that quarrel, or it may be that a
feeling o guilt at his ain responsibilty kept him silent.

-And what dis our great man say now? I asked.

-Why he has sent a final messenger wae a wee drummer
boy under a flag o truce tae demand the toun's surrender.
And if it will not, why then we attack it, and ye are now
looking at Captain Alexander Bain o what pitiful horse the
King has here, for Jamie Graham, was ye can be sure sae
greatly impressed by his new captain's great knowledge o
taking cities that he sat like a school bairn at his feet.

-Haud yer tongue, ye flattered him enough, I merely followed yer lead.

-I played wae him a bit because our necks are at stake.
Jamie Graham might weel be the greatest gallant on earth,
but he kens weel enough, as ye ken weel enough, that while

we are on the battlefield Agnes is a hostage and we are awe prisnors.

-I can see his point, nae general in the present circumstances wad just let us gang, it wad be little mair than military madness. It is my belief that the toun will surrender, and if it disna and decides tae fight, weel there is an auld law o war that they ought tae ken about.

-Och I ken weel that auld law by which sodgers are pleased tae justify their deeds. If a place resists mair than they think is reasonable and puts them tae the trouble o storming it, then awe can be killed, man, woman and bairn, for being sae inconveniently stubborn. Now that may be yer trade but it's not mine.

I looked at Sawney then and he was just standing there wae a face as black as a mirk night, as if he could neither speak nor think, as if there was a rage he could neither understand or grapple was burning deep inside him.

-Aye it is my trade as ye say, and I hae returned tae Scotland tae put it at the Covenant's service, and ye ken the story o that, and ye ken how the English that were tae be our brithers in Christ will use us, and jouk us, and twist us at every turn, and ye ken how the Kirk wad lick the arse o the King if he wad but mak them the power in the land, and ye ken weel wha ever wins wha's spurs will be in wha's belly. Ye that ken sae much ken awe these things, and maybe the Lord is wae Jamie Graham, for he wasna wae the Kirk at Tippermuir, and they had odds o three tae ane wae every pulpit in the land promising them victory.

Steenie just got tae his feet and went tae the door o the biggin. He turned there his een flashing darkly.

-Nae doubt as soon as I gang out I sall hae six Hielanmen for company, and doubtless they will thole my company better than ye.

When he had left, I walked ower tae Sawney and put my airm round him. He looked at me out o the great silent sadness o his een. It was aye tae be like that wae him, as if the Lord had set a burning question in his heid and supplied nae answer. He took my heid queerly and tenderly and there were now tears in his een, and his voice when he spoke was like a man saying a prayer.

-Montrose is a great captain and a Godly man, and it can be nae dishonour tae fight under him, and wha kens but that the Lord has sent him, which he himsel sincerely believes. I ken not, but the Kirk has excummunicated us, and wad hing and burn us if it could but lay its hands upon us, and it might weel be that it has sae mired its cause wae its lust tae be a power ower awe men that the Lord's hand is lifted against them, forbye they themsels ken it not, but I canna think it impossible that we are awe here in this place for a purpose. Or dae ye doubt that even God almighty could lead a great warlock like Steenie Malecky by the nose?

I telt him plainly that I wad not hae him speak like that. He just laughed, a harsh rough laugh.

-Aye why then should I be sae elevated aboun Red Hector o the Axe, and hae scruples that wad never enter his heid? Damn Mr Malecky, damn them awe, and as ye hae been named my wife by nane ither than Mr Malecky why should I not hae some obedience?

He looked at me then his een suddenly blazing.

-Sae strip yer body out o these men's claes for I hae need o it, and frae here on I forbid ye tae wear them.

He launched himsel at me then, and I, suddenly feart o him, for it seemed that something in him had broke and just gone mad, jumped tae my feet, and he losing his balance found himsel staring at the point o my sword.

-Then man, ye maun whistle tae the wind for yer supper, and for ither things.

Wae a great roar he tried tae knock the blade aside wae his airm, but I kent the thing better now and managed tae avoid him. He jumped tae his feet then, and if his hand went tae his sword handle he did not draw it, but just stood there like a man wha was senseless o everything. Outside the biggin some Hielanman was playing some wild rant on his pipes, which I weel remember as a brainless bludie sound, and I cursed the ignorant loun for it, and at that point Steenie cam through the door.

His een took in the situation for a second, and then he strode between us knocking my blade aside and Sawney's hand frae his hilt.

127

-God save us awe, he said.

Sawney, hardly it seemed, noticing his presence raised his hand towards me.

-Hear this Agnes Douglas, I hae nae further need o ye and ye are free tae gang whaur ere ye please.

Out o patience and unco angry I looked back very hard at him.

-I sall gang whaur ere I please and ask nae leave o ye.

Steenie looked at us baith and nae doubt his patience was running thin.

-Naebody is ganging anywhaur at this precise moment without the leave o Jamie Graham.

-And why should he dae itherwise? Hae we no baith signed up wae him?

-Aye Sir, weel hear this. Ye ken that wee drummer lad that was sent wae the Graham's messenger? Weel some man has shot him while under a flag o truce, and the Graham's honour, which awe the warld kens is a maist delicate thing, has been sarely offended, and we march on the toun at dawn.

It was the first I had ever seen Sawney look anything like afraid but it was as if his hale soul was about tae cough itsel up.

-Wha shot him?

-The Lord alane kens. Some say, why on this side they awe say, that it was a musketeer frae the toun walls, but perhaps I just hae a suspicion that it was a convenient plot tae provide a convenient excuse. Some folk in this army are getting gey impatient wae the preciseness o the Graham's honour, and aiblins they thought it could dae wae a bit jolt.

I looked at them baith then, kenning I think, a truth that I had never truly kent before. Then battles had been far awa things that ye heard news o, but tomorrow they could baith be killed. Sawney had ance telt me that surviving in a battle was half skill and maistly luck, and doubtless that was on their minds tae for Steenie just said,

-Sae whatever private fight we may be in the middle o I suggest that if we canna mak peace then a truce wad be appropriate, for dammit awe if I hae never been happy about deeing, I am maist unhappy about deeing fighting folk that are daen nae mair than defending their ain toun wae a less than sensible stubbornness.

Sawney just nodded at us baith. He bent doun and picked his bible out o his gear and taking his little lamp he walked intae the ither room, his mind it seemed now quite set on ither matters.

I watched him gae then, and I felt that everything that was now happening had been clearly in my mind as I lay in the cave, clearly in my mind but still only dimly kent, as if things o which ye hae nae experience ye can never truly ken, and this ignorance gies us leave tae think we can ride the warld when awe the time it is riding us running its knees ower wae blude and confusion.

It was perhaps then that Steenie, wha had been very quiet, said that while he had been out walking looking ower this army o which he was now a part, that Jamie Graham himsel cam up tae him and spoke tae him in a very friendly way, saying that he recognised that he was learned far aboun a sodger's station, and nae doubt amang that wild rude army Jamie Graham himsel was lonely for sic company.

-He's despite awe no sic a bad man Agnes. And he kent weel enough that we wad hae gien his army the go by if luck had been wae us. But he's besotted wae the king tae a degree that is damned near idolatry, and he kens the king weel tae. How any man wae his wits can be sae fond o sic a weasel-faced wee dissembler like Charles Stuart is damned hard tae understand. But it's mair than that. He's besotted tae wae a dream o restoring a Scotland that never was, wae the King secure on his throne, wae nane but God aboun him, and below him awe folk happy in their station, and wae the Lord smiling on them awa. He dreams o conquering Scotland, aye and then England, wae his Hielanmen and his Irish, frae Dan tae Beersheba he said, and handing them tae the king like David tae Saul.

-I telt him that I had fought wae Cromwell and that his army wad not be ane that was easily brushed aside. He just smiled a bit at that, and said that Cromwell had won awe his fights wae the odds high in his favour, while he had won his wae the odds against, and Cromwell had never seen his

Hielanmen fight.

-Properly handled, he said. By ane wha kens their unorthodoxy in battle as I dae, they can break any foot in Europe, even if in certain matters o discipline they are hardly like sodgers at awe.

-I wad hae said mair but there was a kind o wild light in his een. I wad hae said that aiblins his Hielanmen wad hae little inclination tae leave the Hielans, for what did they care about the rest o Scotland? Even less o England, or wha sat on its throne? Charles Stuart's faither had treated these Irish that are now sae fierce on his son's behalf as nae mair than cattle tae be driven out and slaughtered, and the Hielanmen as wild beasts tae be tamed or killed. They are baith in this business because the Graham will lead them against Argyll and Clan Campbell, and after that accomplished, or no accomplished, they will I fancy find there ain business tae attend tae and a river o blude wad droon his dreams.

-I like ye Steenie, he said. -And I ken ye hae misgiens, but cleave tae me and ye will not regret it, for there is I believe a great destiny waiting for us awe. And then he hesitated a bit and smiled a bit, and said, and if there is not and only a bludie end, I think ye are a man that can come tae terms wae that.

-I looked at him Agnes and felt mair than ever that here was a man that needed tae be shot. Sic a dreaming man, and sic a great captain, is a damn dangerous man, and will certainly burn us awe in Hell if we dinna bow the knee tae his dreams.

-And what about tomorrow Steenie?

-If there's a fight, which seems likely, then we maun gae. Montrose is everything I say and mair, but he's not the kind o man tae just let us ride out on the eve o a battle.

-And what if ye are baith killed?

-Then ye maun say a prayer for Sawney, but nane for me. I hae got very sick o prayers o late and I fancy the Lord has tae.

I telt him then tae hush, and that whatever he thought in an idle moment this was nae time for sic terrible talk and could dae him nae gude at awe, and was not Sawney himsel at his prayers?

-Sawney is a man wha aye needs a plain clear light tae follow ere he can be happy. He ance thought he had sic a light, while, wha really kens, the truth might be that sic lights hardly exist in the warld. But now he sees darkness and confusion awe around him, and still, there is a desperate part o him that thinks that it could be that the Graham is that light. They are queerly alike they twa in their needs, and why at the present time half the country wad seem tae hae sic needs, and the ither half maun just fight or flee, except that they press in on ye sae thick that ye can dae neither.

And yet he tae had his dreams did he not? And I minded him o what he had said on the hill as we looked doun on the carse o Stirling. He just looked back slyly at me.

-Why Agnes I still hae them, but between the king and the Kirk there is damned little space.

I said between him and Sawney there was damn little space for me, aye and it seemed tae me that baith him and Sawney had just becam prisnors in Jamie Graham's dream, and I just a worthless thing that had been thrown awa as Sawney had done.

He leaned ower and kissed me warmly and said that could never be sae as lang as he lived, and he had lived through battles before. For a time after that we just sat quietly hauding each ither's hands, listening tae the wild sounds o the army, and I wondered if they had any fears at awe for the morning, for I kent not how sic people wad think? And then Steenie just took out his pipes, blew them up and started tae sing about anither sad silly auld fight.

> Late at e'en drinking the wine,
> And ere they paid the lawin,
> They set them a combat atween
> Tae fight it at the dawin.
>
> O stay at hame my noble Lord
> O stay at hame my marrow
> My cruel brother will you betray
> On the dowie houms o Yarrow.

O fare ye weel my lady gay
O fare ye weel my Sarah
For I maun gae though I neer return
Frae the dowie banks o Yarrow.

She kissed his cheek she cambed his hair.
As she had done afore o
She buckled on his noble brand,
And he's awa tae Yarrow.

Halfway through the sang Sawney cam in very quietly and sat doun in the corner smoking his pipe. I looked ower at him but could not tell whether or not we were friends. Steenie just went on wae his sang.

O he's gane up yon high high hill
I wat he gaed wae sorrow,
An in a den he spied nine armed men
On the dowie houms o Yarrow.

O are ye cam tae drink the wine,
As ye hae done afore o?
Or are ye cam tae wield the brand
On the dowie houms o Yarrow?

I am no cam tae drink the wine,
As I hae done afore o,
But I am cam tae wield the brand
On the dowie houms o Yarrow.

If I see awe ye're nine tae ane
An that's an unequal marrow.
Yet I will fight while lasts my brand,
On the bonny banks o Yarrow.

When the sang was finished Sawney cam ower tae us wae a flask o whisky. The same that the auld Hielanman had gien us, and we just passed it round and round, and Sawney said what mair were we, and what mair should we be, but three drunk Scots on the eve o a battle?

And as awe Europe kens, the Scots sword is as saleable as
it is serviceable.

I minded then the last verse o Steenie's sang and cursed
them awe.King and Kirk and Jamie Graham, and the witless
louns that ran at their arses.

> Tak hame yer oxen, tak hame yer kye,
> For they hae bred awe our sorrow
> I wish that they had awe gane mad
> When they first cam tae Yarrow.

☆

I hae heard it said, though I mysel did not observe it, that
the sun that night sank blude red intae the sea and the
moon rose the same colour. I ken not, but I kent that morning what a terrible weir man was Sawney, wae his steel
bonnet and his steel gloves and awe his war gear on, and his
horse not at awe like the horse that I had sae often ridden
and kent as a gentle beast, but now baith were like things
that rade on fire.

The army tae was up wae swords and axes waving in the
air, singing and dancing wae their pipes playing and wae
Jamie Graham himsel riding amang them in his black
armour, and at his side a Hielanman wha was a giant far
beyond natural size, and wha Steenie said was Alasdair
MacColla Macdonald, that was also called Colkeitach. He
was Montrose's lieutenant wha handled the Macdonalds
and their Irish kinsmen for the Graham.

He was aye wae Montrose, and every time the Graham
wad slice his sword through the air, this Alasdair wad
smash his broadsword against his targe and gie a great
shout, and the Hielanmen wad gie a great shout, and the
Irish wad gie a great shout, and they awe stood like something born o fire that had not been there the previous night
but that Hell's gate had opened tae let out.

Ance Montrose looked ower at Sawney and waved his
sword at him, and Sawney drew his sword and waved it
back, but Steenie just gied a quiet bit bow. Steenie it seemed
tae me forbye he was armoured like Sawney, hardly part o

anything, but just sat on his horse wae a grim bit smile on his face. Even when Montrose rade ower tae them he could not bring himsel tae dae mair than return his salute. And the Graham almost as if he kent what was in their minds said,

-Barbarous and wild gentlemen, but brave and bonny fighters as ye sall soon see.

Steenie replied that he had nae doubt at awe about that, and Montrose commended them baith on their appearance, and said that if he had a few thousand horse wha looked as brave and weel turned out as them he thought that the King's troubles wad soon be ower.

I kissed them baith, and then they were awa, and think ye not that my heart did not gie a queer jump at the idea that it could be for the last time. And the sight o them riding wae the Graham's horse could be my last sight o them alive. The Graham had very few horse at that time, around seventy or eighty in awe, which is of course why he wanted Sawney and Steenie wha were better armoured than maist o them. But the Hielanmen wore very little armour, and seemed tae care naething for it, but wad fight wae their plaids tucked up around their shanks sae that they looked near naked as they ran doun the hillside, waving their swords in the air and leaping like deer, wae awe their womenfolk cheering after them.

Tae me they appeared as savage as their men, and had brought their bairns, baith them that were at the breast and them that could walk, out tae watch the fight frae the hill, nae doubt reasoning that the sight wad impress itsel on their minds and be a fair example tae them in their maturity.

They saw me, and while they greeted me in a friendly enough way we could not speak haeving nae language in which we could converse. And perhaps there wad hae been naething tae say, nor any room tae say it in, for the boom o the great guns frae the city's defences went up and we could see them as they ploughed intae the Hielanmen, and the women wad gie out queer shouts at that. I watched because there was nae way out o watching. Sawney had left me his lang glass and through it I saw a troop o horse charging at the gallop and my ain heart near gaed out, but I kent not wha's it was.

On the top o the hill awa frae the women stood a man that Steenie had said was a poet, wha did not fight himsel but watched the battle in order tae mak a song about it sae that people should not forget wha lived and wha deid, and wha was brave and wha ran awa.

It was strange tae me that he could see anything at awe now sae loud was the noise frae the guns and the field itsel covered in smoke. At ane point, tired o holding the thing I turned awa and ane o the women grabbing my airm cried out, -Look look, they gae.

She meant I think that the Hielanmen were gaen intae the charge but had nae words tae say mair. But I lent her the glass, and when she looked through it she gied out an eldritch scream which was maybe joyful and maybe was not, for I could see naething now but a storm o folk. Nor could I ken what it could be like.

But the Hielanwomen kent about sic things and were now gaen near mad themsels waving dirks in the air alang wae a few auld swords, and even here and there a gun. And them that couldna lift a weapon wad lift high their bairns as if tae mak them see better. And if they looked at me they nae doubt decided that I was worth naething that I wad not cheer. It was then, as I later learned, that their Hielanmen and Irish had just cut their way clean through the city's defenders and were driving them back intae the toun slaughtering any they could catch.

The women themsels now went fair mad and ran doun the hillside wae their plaids tucked up under their arses and their legs caring naething for thorns and thistles. But any sodger wha was deid they wad fall upon and strip o his duds, and if he wasna quite deid they wad stab him or cut his throat, or strip him first sae as not tae spoil his claes wae his blude.

I looked through Sawney's glass and saw them close in on ane man wha was standing on a single leg, the ither haeving been cut off, and he was using his musket for a crutch and cutting at them wae his sword. I looked at his face and the madness tears and blude that were there, and

135

aye he kept cutting and hacking, but he being crippled and the women being nimble they just skipped out o his reach, till ane jumped on his back and anither sliced his belly open frae his belt tae his breast, he haeving on nae real armour. Ance doun they set tae stripping him quickly, cursing nae doubt the spoilation o his duds, which seemed tae be their greatest concern.

I lowered the glass. The hale army it seemed had now stormed the city while the women foraged like wolves on what was left outside. I looked at the auld poet still standing on top o his hill, his white hair and beard blowing in the wind his hands clasped in front o him. I ken not whether he kent I was watching him, but he turned his heid towards me and his een seemed tae be shining wae sic a fierce joy that the tears rolled doun his cheeks. He wad ken, forbye at that time I did not, that the toun was being murdered before us.

He started tae walk slowly towards me his een closed and his lips moving, forbye they produced nae sound, and nae doubt he was quietly turning ower his verses in his heid. When he was about ten paces frae me he stopped and bowed maist graciously and declared that their prayers had been answered and the true hearted had prevailed. He pointed out across the field, and riding across it coming towards us, was a body o horse.

-See the Graham returns.

I mind very weel what I thought then, of awe the poor folk that lay deid under that great gentleman's feet, naked and gutted, less than corpses, less than deid, less in value than gude meat. Jamie Graham looked neither tae the left or tae the right as he rade through them. When he drew level wae us he bowed tae the auld man wha seemed quite beside himsel wae pleasure, and then he bowed tae me. And nae doubt divining clearly what was in my mind said,

-Yer husband and his comrade are baith unhurt, and indeed I am very weel pleased wae them, their conduct being steady and brave throughout.

I thanked him warmly feeling very relieved and he bowed again. He looked tired but slid lightly enough off his horse, and wad hae gone I think intae his quarters, had not ane o his companions touched his airm and pointed back across the field. Riding across it at a very hard gallop was anither man, and before I had put the glass tae my een I had recognised Steenie's black horse. He was level wae us before I could even steady the glass, and he was in a great anger, shouting directly at Jamie Graham himsel.

-Damn it my Lord ye maun stop this.

The twa gentleman standing wae Montrose looked straight at him their een near popping frae their heids.

-The fight's ower my Lord and ye hae won, but yer Hielanmen and Irish are devouring yon toun like beasts, which ye maun ken, and ken that only ye can check them.

Ane o the gentlemen laughed then, a high weel born laugh.

-This tenderness Sir, hardly becomes a mercenary sword.

-Laugh wad ye? Aye indeed yer liver might becam it mair.

Awe at ance the affair looked tae be clean out o control and Steenie shouted tae me tae mount up. We had arranged before hand that I wad be ready tae ride in any eventuality, and Steenie was now beside himsel wae a terrible anger sic as I had never seen in him before. Struggling tae get a grip o himsel he ignored the ither twa and spoke directly tae Montrose .

-My Lord this is hardly the action o a kindly Scot, tae stand here playing wae yer bonnet while yon toun is rouped frae North tae South, sae that ye canna ride the street but ye ride through blude and murder, and folk dragged frae their houses and lassies driven through the streets for sport. Ye ken weel the game, ye ken it my gude lord and ye hae ridden awa frae it.

The Graham looked up at Steenie then. Baith had the marks o blude and battle on them, and whether Jamie Graham's een were sad, or whether they were not, was mair than I could tell.

-I lead wolves Sir and wolves maun be fed.

Montrose's voice was soft when he spoke but it grew harder. Steenie's when he replied was as cauld as death.

-Sae yer wolves maun be gien leave tae devour the country and its people in order that the King's arse can ance mair find its royal seat?

-Be silent in the King's name Sir, I command ye. I regret what has happened in that place, but three times I offered them terms and the third time they shot my drummer boy, a lad of thirteen.

-Nane kens truly wha shot that lad or why. But some say, for I ken their language weel, that ye promised yon outsize Hielanman the sack o the toun as a reward for awe his troubles in the King's service, for certain it is that win or lose he'll get little ither thanks frae the King.

Something seemed tae just snap in them awe then. But in a blink o an ee Steenie had a gun in each hand levelled at them, and each o the gentlemen had a pistol levelled at him. Montrose was unco calm wae an air that just seemed tae lift him right out o the warld as if he was responsible for nane o it.

-In ither circumstances this is an affair I wad settle right now, but I hae an army that needs me and the king's business tae attend tae, and I will hae nane in my army that will not put the king's rights first.

For a lang time it semed that he and Steenie wad just stare at each ither. I kent not what was gaen tae happen and laid my hand quietly on my ain gun, which of course being a woman nane o them wad notice. In the end Montrose put out his hands and lowered his ain men's guns, asking Steenie in his unco soft voice if he meant tae desert them.

-It seems sae my Lord, for I willna murder a country for the sake o a king, nor will I dae it anymair for the sake o a kirk.

Montrose then without any further word just turned his back, forbye the gentlemen wha were wae him did not. Steenie signalled tae me and the twa o us just rade out o their camp, Steenie never taking his een off them or his guns out o his hand until we were weel clear and out o range, then we rade as fast as we could Steenie's horse being tired.

I did not speak tae him. The look on his face seemed tae be language enough about how he felt, and it was only when we slowed doun that he spoke tae me.

-It was strongly in my mind tae just shoot Jamie Graham.

-I think if ye had we wad hae baith been killed.

He said that aye he thought we wad hae, and then said naething mair, leaving me for a time tae my ain thoughts and my ain heart which was galloping like a mad thing, for I did not ken truly what I wad hae done. And what wad it hae mattered sae litle value bodies seemed tae hae now, living or deid? I asked him about Sawney, minding that Montrose had said that he was alive, but thinking how easy it could be itherwise.

-He was weel enough when I left him.

And then the story cam out. The defenders o the toun had resisted stoutly enough at first, but in the end apprentice boys and toun burghers, and a few troops o freshwater sodgers, forbye they outnumbered their enemies, had stood nae chance against Hielanmen wha are born wae swords in their hands. But the worst part had cam when they had stormed the toun and they had just charged through the streets, smashing doun the doors o houses, killing or driving out every body that was inside and feasting their een on riches that were far aboun their hungry imaginings. In the end they had stripped baith the houses and the folk o awe that they could carry sae that there was hardly a virgin intact or a soul unhurt in the hale toun, as the Hielanmen wae their Irish kinsfolk dragged them frae holes they were hiding in, some tae be slaughtered, some tae be driven naked through the streets, some tae be carried off tae their camp as it pleased them, till it had seemed as if the toun itsel was crumbling under the blude and horror o it awe.

And Steenie telt me how when the Graham had ridden awa he had kent that there was tae be nae check on the army, and that it was true that he had promised the sack o the toun tae Colkeitach and wad not gae back on that promise for fear the Macdonald wad just tak his folk and desert him.

At that point he and Sawney had just changed sides. And he telt me how they had just cut their way out through a pack o blude mad Hielanmen tae try and rescue some folk that were near witless wae fear, and how they had succeeded in getting out o the toun, and how he had ridden back tae get me and tae try and find Montrose.

-I had thought better o the Graham, whatever his principles, I had thought better o him. But Argyll is on his tail, and he will maybe prove a bludier man than the Graham, and I ken not what will happen tae the folk o this country caught between the hammer o ane and the anvil o the ither.

These were his words then, and yet, as he telt me at the time, what had happened was in nae way unusual in war, and the Hielanmen had nae reason at awe tae love the folk o Aberdeen wha in the past had harried them like wolves, and wad dae sae again gin they had the chance.

I listened tae his talk and the unco queer anger in his voice. The Scots, he had said then, were aye ower cruel in their fighting. I did not fully ken what he meant, till in a dark part o the wood we met up wae Sawney himsel and the people he was wae.

They were folk frae the toun, men, women and bairns, some as naked as the day they were born, ithers wrapped in nae mair than a bit plaid, and many wae great bludie wounds and the blude just pumping out o them as they lay on the ground, and awe looking sae desperate that it seemed tae me that they cared naething for any o these things but just lay on the earth, some moaning, some howling, some silent like creatures divested o their senses.

Sawney stood a bit tae the rear, a dozen or sae sodgers standing wae him, and tae my een it was as if he had just washed himsel in blude sae terrible did he look, and facing him was this minister wae his finger pointing at him, roaring like a bull, and shouting that it was him that had brought this tragedy on God's folk, and as lang as his presence was tolerated amang them, God's strang and righteous hand wad be lifted heavily against them.

Sae great was this man's anger that he neither heard nor saw Steenie and mysel draw up. Sae great and loud was it that it seemed tae me that that the rest o the people had becam like folk in a terrible picture wae his rage the only truly living thing amang them.

It wad hae been better by far, he cried, -That ye had deed whaur ye were struck and been safely in the arms o the Lord than that ye should hae been saved by this man. For ye ken not wha he is, or wha he serves, and intae what perdition his assistance wad hae led ye had I not been here

140

tae check him.

When ane women cried out that it was better than in the hands o a Hielanman, this minister cried on her tae be silent for she kent naething o what she spoke. And that however much o a Hell-hound or an Amalekite a Hielanman might be he was but a fleshly being, while Sawney was mair than that, and had saved their bodies only tae damn their souls.

When he saw Steenie and mysel it seemed that his wrath could only increase for he turned and strode towards us his voice rising,

-See, they hae cam, they hae cam. If this man here is nae mair than Satan's minion, here cams the highest ane o awe tae laugh and gloat ower his wark.

In a day o storms it seemed as if his anger wad be the greatest storm o awe, and awe maun shrink before it, and I mysel shrank before it. And I looked at ane woman wha lay on the ground at my feet wae naething but a shawl around her, and her hands between her legs and her knees drawn up tae her breasts, and her body turning this way and that on the grass, and her een turning this way and that in her heid, and any that tried tae help her she wad shake off wae a wild cry, and I wanted tae tak her in my airms and comfort her but I could not, and if I thought anything at awe then it was that the warld itsel stood at the crossroads o madness.

-I ken wha ye are Malecky, I ken weel, aye weel I ken, and I ken wha that is wae ye, and I ken now why this day has turned out as it has.

Steenie whispered tae me that damn it awe if he kent a way tae rid the country o baith the Graham and this corbie craw, and it took blude tae dae it he wad prove a bludier man than either.

He spoke these words softly, but still that minister heard them.

-Ye hear, ye hear. He sees our wretchedness and taks it for weakness, and cries his triumph in our ear sae bauld is he and sae little he recks o us. Know weel what ye see and ken the truth. How else could it be that Godly men strang in the strength o the Lord could be overthrown by naked Hielan Amalekites and Irish Papists but that they allowed a pestilence tae grow in their midst, allowed it tae ride the country frae the South tae the North daen the Devil's wark o destruction? Why sae great if ye will not oppose it, is this man's power that he has damned the armies o Scotland and England and brought the holy wark o Godly men tae nought.

By now Steenie himsel had lost his temper and was shouting back at him.

-Damn ye man, will ye not be silent, I hae had enough madness shouted in my lug this day, nor are we sae far frae the toun that some Hielanman might not be by.

-And wad that not be a blessing if they wad but put an end tae ye? But nae doubt ye wad hae the power tae stop that, or doubtless ye wad, just as ye hae done before, join them in their wark.

Afraid that he could not control himsel further Steenie louped frae his horse tae see, as he telt me later, if there was any help he could gie, and resolving tae just ignore the minister. But this minister, wha was a tall stout man, wad not be ignored, but stepped in front o him barring his way.

For a lang minute they just stared at each ither. Sawney had ance telt me that while Steenie was very slow tae quarrel, and unlike ither man wad just laugh and walk awa frae fights in a way that ither men wad hae called dishonourable, few thought o him as a coward, and very few could face him when he was really angry, sic a queer way he had o looking at folk that it just unnerved them. But this minister just blocked his path as if he had nae fear at awe, shouting tae the sodgers tae come tae his aid.

I watched them closely but they just stood dumbfounded, some seeming tae move but not moving, and Sawney himsel just stood watching, like a man that had nae langer a part tae play in the warld.

And then Steenie hit that minister that wad not let him pass, a great clout on the jaw, which forbye he was bigger than Steenie knocked him flat on his back. At that point it was as if the hale mad picture broke open and four o the sodgers rushed forward wae their swords drawn.

Steenie turned and making nae move tae draw his ain sword faced them very calmly, and if they had looked dangerous enough when they approached it was plain enough tae me that they were indeed freshwater sodgers, apprentice lads frae the toun, their faces showing clearly that the shock o the day was still upon them, and while ane helped the minister tae his feet, beyond that they kent not at awe what tae dae. And Steenie asked ane stoutly built lad, wha was the maist forward, how many battles he had been in, and the lad confessed that today had been his first.

-But ye rallied frae the defeat and fought yer way out, is that not true?

The sodger looked at Steenie then, and there was plain tae see, tears o bitter despair and confusion in his een, and he said how that was not quite the hale truth, and how they had been rallied by yonder bludie man wha it now seemed was nae mair than a demon in human form.

At this the minister, wha had recovered himsel, cried upon them for laggards that they did not immediately arrest us. But Steenie just continued tae talk calmly.

-Now listen tae me my lad, I hae been in a few fights and yon man has been in many mair, and if it had not been for him ye wad surely be deid now. He is nae deevil, and we are nae deevils, and while on my reckoning there maun be enough ale and spirits in the toun o Aberdeen tae keep the Hielanmen there for a while, we are certainly still in some danger should we hit upon a party o them. Now my proposal is this, that we should get these folk gaithered, carrying them that canna walk, and march in as gude order and wae as gude speed as we can tae the next toun whaur there will be Godly folk tae help us. Now will ye accept that comand under us, bearing in mind that I can see little chance o salvation itherwise?

That the sodgers were eager tae put themsels under Steenie's command I could easily perceive, but at that point that minister just thrust them aside, and if some o the fire had gone out o him a cauld determination had taen its place.

-Salvation Malecky? Dare ye tempt us wae salvation that are the maister o our damnation? Dare ye?

Steenie looked directly at him, wae an effort mastering his anger. At the same time he glanced ower at Sawney, and

143

while that man was on his feet watching, he looked still like a man that was hardly amang the living, and forbye I had beckoned tae him many times he had neither moved nor acknowledged us.

When Steenie spoke again his voice was quiet.

-Can ye no see that this is madness, tae hae sic a quarrel in sic a place, and in sic a predicament as we are in? Look about ye man, in the name o God look about ye. The people are deeing o their wounds, they're deeing o the cauld, and they're deeing o fright. Wad ye hae them dee o foolishness as weel?

The minister said not a word in reply but just strode forward as if he wad seize Steenie himsel. But Steenie wae a clever movement stepped back, and now his sword was out and he gied out an eldritch laugh.

-Sae folk maun fight on earth and burn in Hell and God's wark gangs bonnily on. But for now, minister, it stops and ye maun step aside till I see what can be done for these folk.

That minister moved not an inch but just stood, his ain chest near thrusting itsel on the point o Steenie's sword.

-Nae mair words ye imp o ruin, I bar yer way.

I felt a black hatred for them awe then that they could still play sic a game at sic a time, as besotted wae their prides as the Graham was wae his king sae that it carried them aboun awe suffering. I hae little doubt that the young sodger felt the same for, suddenly resolute, he stepped forward putting himsel between the minister and Steenie.

-Sir, I canna bear this. Ye hae done much for us this day, ye and yer friend, but I canna hae ye murdering Maister Dalyrimple. Sae put up yer sword Sir and we sall gang as best we can without ye, for I hae nae skill tae judge the truth o any o this.

Steenie just gied out a great sigh that seemed tae carry fear and pity as weel as anger in it. But he put awa his sword forbye the look on his face telt me plainly that never in his life had he felt sae helpless. He grasped the sodger by the shoulders, as much, he telt me later tae stop himsel frae falling doun in despair as tae put some resolution intae him.

-Keep the women and the bairns and them that hae wounds in the centre. Ye hae a dozen sodgers, put three on each flank and keep a body o six horse in yer rear. Share out the powder and mak sure that every gun has a ball in it, and march as quietly and as fast as ye can.

The young sodger nodded and immediately began tae bark out orders, which nane questioned, but awe that could move, wae a kind o relief jumped tae obey. Awe except for Maister Dalyrimple wha never budged but just stood there as if he alane was standing in awe o Satan's host and had nae doubts at awe about the rightness o his duty. Steenie louped back on his horse and looked doun at him.

-May the Lord reward ye weel, Maister Dalyrimple.

-Nae words Malecky. I canna apprehend ye now but apprehendit ye sall be and there will be words enough then.

-Aye Dalyrimple, I ken weel the words and how they will be got.

I left them and rade ower tae Sawney wha awe this time had neither moved or done anything at awe. And as I approached him my heart near gaed out sae strange did he appear.

-Are ye hurt? I asked him. He just turned his heid awa frae me and said,

-Ye see how they hate us, Agnes. They hae cast us out intae darkness, nor is there any returning. I ken not what tae dae. We might hae taen them tae safety and yon Dalyrimple wad finish Pringle's wark and burn us awe for our fee. Aye and nae doubt awe these poor folk wad themsels be damned for turning tae the Deil.

I looked at whaur he looked. The young sodger and his comrades were getting the people gaithered as Steenie had instructed, and pitiful they looked, clasping their bit rags about them like folk wha had lost their way in a dark dream o nonsense. I looked at Sawney and there were tears streaming doun his face which was still black wae the blude and sweat o the battle, and I put my airms round him and could feel his heart sobbing out just like a great mountain o a bairn.

-I had thought that after this day's wark they wad hae relented, but now I ken they will not.

I looked doun at his broadsword which seemed tae hae cleft sae much flesh that even its pouch was black wae blude. And he telt me that while they had waited there he had telt Dalyrimple awe our history which had as I weel kent, weighed heavily on his heart. He had done this because in his soul he had believed that the outcome o this day was a sign frae the Lord that he had led us intae the Hielans, and tae this battlefield, forbye we kent it not, tae be of service tae him, and Dalyrimple had seemed a douce, kind, and Godly man, wha had himsel behaved very bravely, and at that time had naething but praise for Sawney.

But when Dalyrimple had heard he had let out a great cry, for did he not ken Mathius Pringle very weel, and kent our story very weel?

He kent, and was horrified at the company he and his people were keeping, and as he could not apprehend him, wad maybe hae led them awe back the way they had cam tae avoid him. Being powerless tae dae either o these things he had twisted Sawney's heart and soul right round inside him, for Sawney could not stand against him as Steenie could.

-If they willna hae me, then why should I not just gang back tae Jamie Graham, wha at leasts speaks fair and straight, and is a gude and skillful captain?

-That bludie King's man, wad ye gang back tae him? I asked.

He just looked at me then as if he was pulling himsel out o some dark pit intae which he had fallen.

-It was a battle lassie, and no byordnar bludie for awe that. And the Graham is a Godly man in his ain way, but will hae nae minister twisting his soul till it becams his ain deidliest enemy. And he wad hae Scotland as it ance was, and no damned as it is now wae awe our hopes in ruins, and the English that were tae be our brithers playing us false at every turn, and the Kirk that was tae free us now wants tae rule us in awe things, and be a rod upon our backs as sair as any in the past has ever been.

We watched the people moving out wae Maister Dalyrimple stalking in their rear. The sodgers, in defiance o him, stopping tae say fareweel tae Sawney, timidly like, sae that I could see plainly that in their een he was a terrible

weir man and they kent not whether he had led them out o
Hell or intae it. Awe he said tae them was,

-Gang quietly lads ye're salted sodgers now. But when
they were out o sight he said tae me. -If they are attacked by
any number they will hae nae chance at awe.

It was then, in plain defiance o Steenie's instructions and
Sawney's last words, we heard Dalyrimple's great voice
bursting out intae a psalm that for noise wad hae rivalled a
Hielanman's pipes. Tae my mind it seemed plain that sic
foolishness was below a brute beast's, but Sawney just said,

-Dae ye no think that aboun awe the Kirk is aiblins right,
and the proper duty o God's people is just tae struggle and
suffer and praise his name and trust in him, and not in
muskets and swords, their earthly sense, or any ither weak
things? And tae dae this until he chooses tae help us and
scatter our enemies wae a wave o his hand?

-I ken not, but if awe our hopes, and awe our futures, are
out o our hands, then I am nought but a silly sodger wha
thought in his pride tae be o some Godly service. But if that
is not possible, still I canna skulk like a wolf in the hills
while the country is in sic a state. I am not Steenie wha has
never really been a sodger, but only when it pleased him.

Steenie had by now cam up behind us forbye Sawney had
paid him nae heed. Now awe he said was,

-Let's awa frae here.

Sawney then turned on him a look that wad hae shaken
the faith o Moses.

-Tae whaur? Tae whaur sall we gang now, Mr Malecky?

-Why I thought we could just follow alang behind these
daft singing folk tae see that they got safely out, no for any
ither purpose.

It was unco strange the way Sawney just silently agreed
swinging himsel on tae the back o his horse. We could still
hear them singing, and in my heid I noted every psalm as
they sang it, kenning them awe weel. I tried tae think what
maun be in their hearts, and how like the folk o Israel in the
Bible they were, and how if there was foolishness in it there
was also courage, and if the Lord let them be killed I wad
never turn tae him mair. I telt Steenie this and he just
looked grim.

-If they meet any o the Graham's men wha hae still got murder in their hearts they can sing themsels hoarse but it will change naething.

Then Sawney spoke. In plain contradiction it seemed tae me o his previous words.

-What are ye saying man?

-I am saying what ye yersel ken very weel.

Sawney said naething after that and we rade in silence, listening tae their singing until we kent they were weel clear and we oursels found a quiet place whaur we could rest, being unco weary.

That night a great quarrel broke out between them baith. Sawney said that he wad indeed gang back tae join Montrose, and Steenie said that he wad not, nor could he agree wae sic a move. And Sawney asked him what else he wad hae us dae seeing that maist o his previous advice had brought us naething but disaster. Steenie replied that he honestly did not ken, but he kent that Montrose wad bring disaster tae the country, and if he hoped for anything at awe it was that David Leslie wad bring the army back frae England and put an end tae him, for he was the only captain on the Covenant side wae the strength and skill tae dae it.

Sawney sneered bitterly at that, and said that however brave Leslie's army was the Kirk had a hold upon its throat, as they had a hold upon the hale country sae that nane could breathe freely, but they could only breathe wae their leave, and that it might weel be that the Lord had sent Jamie Graham tae break that hold, and humble the pride o them that wad set themsels up tae be our liberators but were now a rod upon our backs as heavy as any king's.

It was then that Steenie went very quiet. And at first he wad not answer, and then he said that he nae langer thought that anything was the Lord's wark, but awe was just the haverings o foolish men, and if anything grieved his heart it was the greeting and murdering o the people that were being led by them. But they were still the people, and the people's cause man aye be right ower against the king's.

And then Sawney stood up and said in a voice which seemed tae come frae some dark place o despair, that he couldna thole the fact that Steenie wad not pray for guidance, wad not try tae understand what it was the Lord wanted o them, and wad deny God's warks upon the earth, and the abundant signs o his pleasure and displeasure, and his abundant providences, but wad just ride the country like a heidless hen in a midden yaird.

Aye and perhaps the Kirk was right, and he was that warlock in their midst turning awe things intae the opposite o what they intended, and that he Sawney wad be wise tae be free o him, for he wished mair than anything else tae dae the Lord's wark, and tae discover what it was the Lord wanted o him, for the Lord had saved him in Germany for a purpose and he wad never deny that, and while Steenie had seemed tae him tae be a true friend, now he thought that perhaps it was for a false purpose and tae mak him blind, and that the flesh o Agnes Douglas was but a trap sent tae ensnare him, for he kent that Steenie had shared it tae.

Aye he kent that, and perhaps he had not minded it as he should hae, and that now he found himsel surrounded by perdition, and his soul raging tae be out o him, kenning him weel for a Deevil damned man.

Sawney spoke as if the words themsel had just got him by the throat and were fairly choking him. And in listening tae his words a great fear cam ower me that I had lain sae lang wae this man, wha was now anither man, a terrible weir man burning wae an awful zeal and an awful despair, and hardly an ounce o gude sense tae guide him. Steenie just looked at the ground between his feet. Nor could I see anything at awe in his face, and awe he said in reply was,

-That canting auld raven Dalyrimple maun be a damned fine preacher for he has fairly sunk his talons intae ye. But I will argue nae mair and ye maun gang yer ain gate.

-Maister Dalyrimple asked me when I had last seen ye pray, and I had tae confess Steenie Malecky, that forbye the kirk when we were bairns I hae never seen ye pray.

-How often hae ye seen me shit? Or let my thoughts and deeds be governed by a Dalyrimple, or any ither corbie craw?

-Damn ye man, that's a blasphemy and near enough a confession.

In a Dalyrimple's lug it wad stand for a confession many times ower.

Then Sawney put his hand tae his sword hilt, and said unco quietly that aiblins an end should be made o it awe right now.

Steenie made nae kind o move at awe, but just said, his voice neither quiet nor loud, but unco calm, that he had not lived through a battle he didna want tae fight tae be cut tae pieces in a quarrel he didna want tae hae, and that Sawney could mak an end o what ere he pleased but he, Steenie, wad just bide whaur he was.

I had heard enough o their wild nonsense, and I was very afraid now o the outcome, sae I walked ower and put mysel between them and pulled Sawney's hand awa frae his sword. I looked up intae his face when I did this and his een were rolling in his heid like a moonstruck man's, and it was in my mind tae just tak him awa and mak him lie doun and pray mysel for baith o them, and that by tomorrow this day wad be ower. But he shook himsel free then and said in the same voice as before,

-Agnes Douglas, I release ye frae awe obligations tae me, unsanctified as they hae been, and I release yon man frae awe obligations o friendship.

He turned his back on us baith and without anither word swung himsel on tae the back o his horse. I shouted tae him, but putting spurs tae the beast he was awa. And then Steenie tae was mounted and chasing him at a gallop that was as mad as their words.

-I'll fetch him back Agnes, he cried, -I'll bring back the daft loun.

I could hear the sound o their horses in the forest. I could hear the sound o Steenie shouting, and nae doubt I waited tae hear the sounds o a fight that I neither wanted tae hear or see or tak part in. I ken not, I mind not clearly and canna weel describe the time, and it may hae been that time itsel was unco still, but Steenie cam riding back alane and still I didna move but just stood there waiting as he lighted doun frae his horse and walked ower tae me.

-He's awa, was awe he said.

That night we just sat for a lang time, drinking a bit

whisky and he smoking his pipe. He said naething and I said naething, as if we baith agreed that ower much had already been said and awe tae an ill end. I watched the moon as it passed, playing ower the shadows on his face and on intae the trees. And think ye not that I blessed the silence thinking o the tumult that had raged that day, and I thought o Sawney riding through the night and it seemed tae me that his madness was but anither side o that madness that afflicted awe, and that Steenie's face was the only quiet spot on earth. I said tae him that I kent not how Sawney could gang back tae Montrose after seeing sae many folk murdered.

Steenie just took his pipe frae his mouth and said,

-Agnes, Sawney has seen many great battles, and great cities sacked and burned, besides which what happened at Aberdeen was nae mair than a wild Hielan foray.

Then why, I asked him, was his blude sae hot wae the Graham?

He answered that like Sawney said, he was nae real sodger, nor had he ever wanted tae be, haeving nae taste for the profession, and wad only fight willingly if he could see a clear path and a purpose beyond the battle.

I asked him if he had spoken tae Sawney out there in the forest, and he said, aye that he had, forbye it had been short and sad, and nae doubt Jamie Graham wad be very glad tae see his fine captain returning tae him, his army being very short o horse.

He stopped for a bit and took a drink frae his whisky and handed the flask tae me.

-I wish this day was ower, Agnes. It was yon Dalyrimple wha did it. That hard and canny man kent weel the soul he was fishing for, and put it straight tae Sawney, which Sawney put tae me, that if we were sae guiltless o awe charges did we not trust the Kirk and the law tae find us sae? For the Kirk was surely mair than the spleen o Willie Munro, aye or Mathius Pringle, wha could awe be guilty o earthly errors. But the Kirk as a body was the airm o the Lord on earth and if we wad not trust it, surely that was a sign o guilt before Heaven?

-It was that which started the quarrel between us, for I

151

telt him plainly that he kent weel enough whaur that argument wad lead us. But I had a feeling then, and while it has in nae way been confirmed I feel unco sure about it, that Dalyrimple telt him that the Kirk and nae doubt God in Heaven wad look very kindly on his misguided confusion if he could bring it the heid o Steenie Malecky, either on his shoulders or off them. They wad prefer the first but wad be contented wae the second. When we parted in the wood he said that aiblins he wad tak the Kirk the heid o Jamie Graham which wad be at least a heid wae some purpose in it.

Steenie didna ken for certain. But I minded that Sawney had indeed put his hand on his sword. And I minded that despair in his een like a fish caught in a net. And it seemed tae me that awe folk at that time, the ignorant and wise alike, were caught in a net like fish, a net that spread the breadth o the land and clutched ye tightest whaur it could not be seen.

-Dae ye think that he means tae kill Montrose?

-Wha kens what he means tae dae. Jamie Graham is canny about minding his heid, and Sawney is nae murderer, and ower gude a sodger tae kill his ain captain, and nae doubt the Graham will just march him frae ane fight tae the next.

Until he's killed I thought, but did not say it, forbye Steenie kent weel enough what I was thinking. And I thought how that day I had seen my first plain o deid men, and Montrose riding through it in black armour and mounted on a great horse, deeming nae doubt that what lay on either side o him was wark that had been weel done and was now finished. And still I thought o Sawney wae his een rolling in his heid and his soul twisting in his guts, and him that was sic a gude man in sae many things had but little sense in ithers.

-What sall we dae now Steenie? I asked him. -Whaur are we now tae gang?

He looked at me then, his een squinting, and they had that thing in them that I had seen before, forbye it seemed stronger now that Steenie himsel was lost, in his ain way as lost as Sawney.

-Are ye still inclined tae gang wae me? My guidance sae far hasna exactly been wise or advantageous.

152

It seemed tae me then that there was nae place in Scotland that was a wise place tae gae, or advantageous tae be in. And I minded how he had guided me out o that ither place, and the memory o it cam back as it often did like a dark crash o thunder on a mirk night, and out o it Munro's face glowed like an auld moon clouded ower, and how Agnes Douglas's body had hung naked and bleeding before his een like a pig that had been stuck and stuck again, crueller than any Christian man wad behave tae a beast, and how I kent not whether his auld heart was trembling or whether it was not.

-Why wad ye leave me alane in the wilderness?

He looked ower at me then his een tired and quiet, and the earth upon which we sat seemed itsel tired and quiet, as if the drumming o horses feet and the marching o sodgers were things that it had just shrugged off, declining tae carry the burden o men's deeds upon its back.

-Is it true Steenie that ye dinna pray? I hae never seen ye pray except in the auld days at Trig.

-Oh I prayed then. But na I dinna pray now, and hae not done sae for a lang time. Not through forgetfulness but just maybe I hae lost the art, aye and aiblins the belief. And whiles I think that there are enough prayers at present ganging up frae this land tae deafen the Lord, and awe his angelic host, for deaf they seem tae be.

I said then that I couldna thole that. I couldna thole sic a warld at awe, tae be nae mair than a bit o dust. And then I remembered again that plain o deid men, and deeing men, wae the women cutting their throats and stripping them o their duds, and the auld poet noting it awe doun in his heid. And I thought tae o that ither ane, riding through the night wae his heart broke and his horse tired, but wae the living Deevil on his tail.

-Agnes Douglas, Steenie said. -I am a very poor guide for ane that is nae langer a bairn.

I just laughed then tae see him sae humble, and telt him that I wanted him tae haud me tight which wad assure me that we were not just creatures o dust and nae account, but living things how sae ever forsaken.

☆

153

Andrew Gilmore reigned in his horse and pointed to a faint track which forked off the main route. It seemed to the minister to be seldom used.

'It's a bit inn, minister whaur we can stay for the night, run by an auld widow wife and her niece, and slightly hidden as ye might say. Very much used in the auld days but now only by travellers and local folk wha ken it. But ye will be very comfortable there for the night and I will come back for ye in the morning, begging yer pardon, but I hae a bit business tae attend tae wae a fairmer in this district.'

'I'm glad the journey won't be entirely without some profit for you.'

'Och what earthly profit there is will hae tae wait on this bit fairmer, he is no the man tae gie it lichtly. But ye'll be fine wae Martha while I am at the haggling. I like tae gie her my custom when I pass by this way, her being very worthy, if a bit fierce and Cameronian in her worthiness.'

They turned on to the track which led over the brow of a hill, curving round sharply so that it ran parallel to the road but was hidden from it.

The inn itself was so situated under a tremendous overhang of rock with which it just seemed to blend, that the minister felt sure that without his guide he would certainly have ridden past it. As they approached, a stout, grey-haired old woman came out to meet them. She roared a greeting at Andrew Gilmore in a hearty, almost masculine voice.

'And gude evening tae ye tae Martha,' Andrew replied. 'I wad like ye tae meet this friend o mine wha is a a Godly minister new back frae his studies in Holland, and will be taking ower the parish o Trig tae which place I am guiding him, seeing that forbye he is as Scottish as ye or I, he is something of a stranger here.'

For a moment the minister felt the old woman's eyes appraising him with a boldness which in other societies might have been almost bad-mannered. But she simply said,

'Awe folk that walk in fear o the Lord and nane ither whether they be laird or loun are welcome here. Sae ye may baith light doun an cam inside. The lassie will see tae yer horses.'

A girl who had been standing in the doorway stepped

forward. She was tall and slender, and if the minister could make out wisps of red hair he could make out nothing more of her features so wrapped around in a shawl was she. She held his horse for him while he dismounted, which the minister felt was unnecessary; Andrew simply leapt off his. The girl gathered up the reins of both and led them away without a word.

The minister followed the old woman and his guide inside. They were left to choose a table to which Martha, without being requested brought three mugs of ale one of which she placed in front of herself.

'Supper will no be lang,' she said.

The minister thanked her. She acknowledged the thanks looking keenly back at him. Her eyes were light grey and it appeared to the minister that they no longer belonged to her face, which was consumed by old age to such a degree that what she might have looked like at any other age was impossible for the minister to imagine.

'And how hae things been wae ye Martha?' Andrew Gilmore asked.

'The Lord looks after his servants, and if not sae mony cam by here now, we hae friends and we hae sufficient.'

A wisp of white hair clung to her chin and upper lip. Her remaining teeth were few and isolated, her skin reminding the minister unpleasantly of stone crumbling to dust, and yet there was an animation in her eyes which seemed to deny everything else about her.

'Sae ye hae cam frae Holland hae ye Sir? But ye are Scots are ye not?'

'I am, but as my childhood and maturity were all spent out of this country, my ignorance of it is so great that I am almost ashamed to admit it.'

'Aye,' she said.

'I am studying hard to get to know it.'

'The Lord will teach ye awe ye need tae ken about this land if ye but ask him. Awe our trials and awe our sufferings are inscribed in his hand on tablets o gold. Nor is there ony man or woman, saint, sinner or bairn that he will leave out o his account. Awe their deeds and misdeeds, foolishnesses and prides, written doun lang afore they war born and merely confirmed in the present time. Aye and will be further confirmed when they sall appear roaring and greeting at his feet, and they sall ken then how pitiful hae been their daens, and how lang the account o them will be, and naething in that account can be denied, earthly lies haeving lang since crumbled intae earthly clay. But the few wha hae been a shining licht upon the earth will ance mair be a shining licht in Heaven, and for the rest, the darkness that hae been theirs will be darkness ance again.'

The old woman intoned her speech, a fierce joy manifesting itself in her features.

'God is merciful and we must believe in his mercy.'

'Aye tae them wha he has chosen, and that hae loved him, and hae loved their sufferings in his name.'

'Martha,' Andrew interjected, and it seemed to the minister that he winked as he did so, 'thinks that ower much mercy tae some folk might be a bit misplaced.'

The old woman turned towards Andrew her voice escaping from her throat in a hiss of hot air.

'Haud yer tongue Andra Gilmore, and speak not lightly o the Lord's mercy, which ane day ye sall hae need o, nor can it be bought like a pint o ale, or bargained for like a cow in the market.'

'God save me auld wife, wad ye affront me afore the minister?'

'Affront ye, Andra? How could a middling gude man like ye be affronted? And nae doubt the minister will be sufficiently educated in the wisdom o the warld not tae be affronted.'

'Andrew has been an exceedingly kind and resolute guide to me at a great inconvenience to himself.'

'Andra was aye a true friend, and aye a gude guide, forbye he himsel ganged not aye whaur he guided.'

'Auld wife, auld wife, we hae cam a lang way.'

'And there is a langer yet still tae gang, as weel ye ken. But I sall awa and get ye some supper tae gie ye fleshly strength, which is awe I can gie.'

She rose to her feet, surprisingly lightly, the minister thought, for someone of her age. He turned his head, partly to avoid Andrew's discomfiture. As he did so his eyes fell on an old spear with a twelve foot shaft which hung on the wall.

'Martha ance put a hale body o dragoons tae flight wae that

auld shiltron, did ye not, Martha?'

Martha, already half way from the table to the kitchen, turned round on her heels.

'The Lord, Andrew Gilmore, put them tae flight, I merely thrust the point whaur he bade me.'

'And there are ither things that ye ance put whaur he nae doubt bade ye.'

The old woman suddenly burst into uproarious laughter which swept her garrulous solemnity away.

'The Lord kens that I will aye dae as he instructs and gies me the strength.' Her laughter died with the suddenness with which it had begun, and she, with a sudden resumption of dignity, stalked out of the room. Andrew Gilmore turned to the minister.

'If Martha appears a bit strange minister ye maun mak allowances, aiblins it's true her wits are not what they war, but they war sharp enough ance.'

'Why did she suddenly laugh like that?'

'An auld memory she has, which in its way is amusing enough. Ance, mony years ago when I was a bit halfling boy and Martha was a bold handsome woman, a body o dragoons cam by here, maurading, beating the glens, looking for poor folk that they might molest. And finding nane worth hinging, why did they not cam in here demanding ale and information. Martha had nae information for them but she had ale, and in true sodger fashion they set themsels tae drinking it wae a right gude will, seeing that they had nae intention o paying for it. Sae what dis Martha dae, but match the dragoons drink for drink, and in the way o nature what gangs in maun gang out again, and as Martha is in the next room pouring out their ale for them it is a simple matter tae just lift her skirts, and ye see, tap up each ane as it passes. Why Sir, in the next morning ye ne'er saw sic a griping o the guts and sliding frae the saddle, and sic behavior that even the horses they war riding war fair disgusted, and their sergeant ower ill himsel tae curse them for not being able tae haud their ale. It was a story, minister, that awe the country kent, forbye Martha hersel wad never vouch for the truth or falseness o it.'

'It would seem,' the minister said, 'that I will have to regard this woman in a new light.'

157

'Aye, but as I say minister, whiles, sometimes her brains are mair addled than at ithers and she thinks the auld days are back, and the dragoons . . .'

'She is not likely I hope to mistake us for dragoons.'

'Na, na minister, but that auld spear o hers . . .'

At that moment the girl came into the room and Andrew Gilmore, breaking off the conversation hailed her over. He introduced her to the minister who rose from his bench to greet her.

'And how are ye yersel, Helen?'

The girl pushed back her shawl revealing a mass of red hair.

'Weel enough, Mr Gilmore, weel enough.'

'And is there not some young lad on the hillside ye hae yer een on? For unless lads hae changed greatly there maun be mony wha hae their een on ye.'

The girl smiled gently. To the minister it appeared that she both accepted and resented Andrew Gilmore's remark.

'Why Mr Gilmore I ken not whaur lads hae their een if they are not in their heids.'

'Aye indeed, Helen, the dochter o John Melville is not the kind o lass tae be throwing hersel at the first bit drover loun wha comes through the door. But tell me Helen, how is auld Martha these days? Dis she still gang abroad?'

'No for some time Mr Gilmore, since the last time she near froze tae death afore we could fetch her in. Tam Laidlaw and his wife helped me then, but she scared the life out o awe three o us, and Tam was ance a sodger. When she has that auld spear in her hand it's as if she's mair than half mad, and far stranger than ony auld woman ought tae be.'

Andrew Gilmore looked at the girl and then over at the spear.

'For awe its Godly history maybe it wad be as weel tae remove the thing.'

'She winna hae it. Naething maks her fly intae a rage mair quickly than ony suggestion that it might be removed. A sermon on the subject is likely tae be her least reply, awe about how without that auld shiltron she and mony ithers wad not be able tae call themsels honest women, and might weel be deid anes, and it is there as a reminder o the Lord's wark.'

The girl excused herself and went to help the old woman

158

prepare the meal. When they were eating alone the minister asked:

'Well Andrew, I am in the dark. What is the significance of that spear?'

Andrew looked up from his meal.

'It is a weel kent story. It happened after the defeat at Bothwell Brig, when the dragoons war out and about in earnest, and war intae a great deal mair mischief than stealing a carline's ale. Weel a party o women and bairns war sheltering in this place when a bunch o loose maurading sodgers and a sargeant cam by, and Martha kenning right weel that they wad not be satisfied wae ale took the women and bairns out the back way on tae the crag aboun.

'Ye maun ken minister that this house is auld, and was built wae certain things in mind, it had far fewer windows then and them awe higher up. And the back door which was a secret, and sae small that a bairn could not walk through it standing up, is the only route up tae the crag behind it, which is a high rocky and steep place wae a convenient and pleasant spring in it, and there maybe the women and bairns could be safe.

'Weel the sodgers o course quickly rouped the place, getting themsels swiftly drunk, and bludier and angrier that there seemed tae be nae way that they could get at the women. And if awe the women and the bairns war terrified at the prospect o them finding the door and the path, Martha just sat on the crag wae a musket across her knees and the auld shiltron in her hand, staring doun at them, listening tae their insults and their threats, and never heeding the occasional bullet they sent in her direction, but never saying a word tae them in reply.

'Now there was ane o their number, undoubtedly wae mair whisky in him than sense, volunteered tae climb the face o the crag, which can be done by a skillful man. His reasoning nae doubt was that ance up there it wad be but a simple matter for an armed sodger tae subdue a dozen women and bairns and let his comrades up.

'Weel, slowly and carefully this man climbed, while his comrades covered him frae below, ready tae shoot if ony should try tae hit him wae a stane. Nane did, tae their een it seemed that even Martha had gane frae the ridge. But when that sodger stuck his heid ower the edge, there she was, crouched doun low, and way ane stab o that auld shiltron she speared him clean through the throat, and wae strength that I canna weel imagine, she grabbed him by the hair and brought a sword doun on his neck cutting his heid frae off his shoulders leaving the body tae clatter at the feet o them below. And then, taking that heid, she swung it round her and flung it straight intae their midst crying out: 'Whaur is the man that will follow this ane.'

'It is said that she raged at them then, waving her spear and cursing them in sic terrible language that nane wha heard it will ever really repeat it. And forbye they tried tae shoot her she wad not move, nor could they hit her, and when she put a musket ball clean through their sergeant the hale drunken pack o them took tae their horses, near killing the beasts before drawing rein.

'That is the story as it's telt, and if maist o it is true, it was still I think a mair terrible night when it happened than could be thought possible now. What wae the countryside being in a panic and a rout, the women could hae hoped for naething in the way o mercy, and Martha's actions war sae bludie and her language sae wild . . . I ken not, it taks a lot tae spook drunk sodgers wha hae won a fight and are looking for some entertainment, but it is said that tae their een, Jesus himsel was standing next tae Martha, guiding her aim and brushing bullets awa like flies. Sae mad and drunken was the sodger's gallop that ane was found haeving fallen frae his horse and broken his neck, and twa mair war lost, horses and riders baith in an auld bit bog.

'Weel, forbye there was nae appearance o it at the time, Martha continuing as a pillar of strength throughout the nicht. In her auld age the memory has maybe addled her brains a bit, and she has been kent on occasions tae gang abroad at nicht wae that auld spear in her hand, sometimes out on tae the muir, maistly up tae the crag. And Helen, wha has tae bear the full weight o things has tae gang after her, or get some neighbours tae help her, because they say that it is a damned unchancy thing tae approach her in that state, and sae they maun watch and wait until sleep and exhaustion tak her ower.'

Andrew Gilmore left after supper. The minister continued to sit in his place. He thought it might be considered impolite

160

to go immediately to his room, and yet, he did not know what kind of company these people expected from him. The girl moved about him like a wraith. It was clear that she did almost all the work that was to be done about the place. The old woman sat quietly in her corner fortifying herself with her ale and her bible, or as the minister observed, she appeared to be sleeping with it open on her lap.

Occasionally other customers came in. They were always introduced to the minister. They were always courteous.

'Is it tae Trig that ye are ganging? Och it's a fine place Trig, but doubtless no sae fine as Holland.'

Then the grey clad figures would turn aside, exchange a few words with Martha and take their ale off to a corner. As far as was polite the minister scrutinised each hard leathered face, each with his stout staff, each with his collie dog at his heels.

They told him nothing at all about these people. The fact that some left quickly after consuming only one jug of ale made the minister wonder if his presence had made them uncomfortable and disturbed their evening. He could not tell, they sat huddled at their tables talking low in a language he could not follow, drinking their ale with the methodical steadiness of men who are tired.

He looked at the great spear with its long barbarous point. It seemed an utterly alien thing to these peaceful men. And yet they undoubtedly knew the story, and it was more likely than not that at some time in their lives, for they were all men of mature years and over, their hands had grasped a similar shaft. If Andrew Gilmore had been there he would have talked to them familiarly, sharing the past, and perhaps too, beneath their humble appearance they shared Andrew's judgement on the present. The minister could not tell, and yet, in a very short time he would be ministering to just such people as these, and if he could not judge them, he feared their judgement on him. Had they known or heard of Sawney Bain? It was more than likely, as was the memory they would have of him as a brave and Godly soldier with a difficult wife, one of their heroes who had died a martyr. The minister felt the truth like an adamantine chain which bound his soul alone.

He called to the girl. She turned and smiled a quite brilliant smile which disconcerted the minister by its forwardness.

161

Almost at once he rebuked himself for his judgement, her smile was merely a smile of untutored curiosity which could not disguise itself.

'I think I will go to my room now.'

'Aye Sir, I will tell Martha that ye are awa.'

The old woman opened her eyes before she was told.

'God bless ye, minister and may yer sleep be peaceful.'

'Bless you, Martha and your hospitality.'

He followed the girl upstairs. She pushed open the door of his room holding it with her hand.

'It's a poor enough bed for a gentleman, forbye in the past mony hae used it.'

'If I started on this journey a tender gentleman, a few nights on the road with Andrew have cured me. Still I find this room and this bed a great relief.'

He turned to thank her. She held out the lamp with which she had guided him up the stairs. For one bewildering moment it seemed to the minister that its flame and her countenance framed by her hair had formed one fiery unity. He quickly took the lamp from her and she stepped back fading into darkness

'Is there onything else ye might be wanting Sir?'

'No, nothing, thank you.'

She smiled again and the minister held up the lamp to give her light while she descended the stairs.

He closed the door behind him and lay down on the bed. The noise downstairs he felt had increased since he left. He would get on easier with them, he thought, when he was secure in a respected position and a relationship with them that both he and they understood.

☆

We waited anither day and night in that place thinking that there was some chance o Sawney returning, but he did not, and the next morning we rade awa.

The roads south o Aberdeen we discovered were awe full o people fleeing that place, and awe in a pitiful state, for Montrose's army had not left the city but were still making free wae it. Nor had the Graham made any attempt tae tak them out, for fear, it was said tae his discredit, of angering

162

Colkeitach.

We did not gang by the roads oursels but as previously stuck tae the routes that Steenie kent. But we went very cannily now for we had heard, forbye nane that we spoke wae kent exactly whaur they were, that Argyll and his Campbells had taen tae the field tae find the Graham. Steenie wha kent Argyll said that he thought that gentlemen wad not be in too great a hurry tae catch Montrose, which some said was cunning and some said was cowardliness. Steenie said it could be construed either way, or baith ways, and not amount tae much, for if cunning was nae doubt a gude policy in Edinburgh, cowardliness was a poor ane in the Hielans. But for mysel I cared naething for any o these things but only tae keep out o the way o either party.

We wad ride through the day and sleep in some weel hidden place at night, and if we did not ken truly whaur we were ganging our situation differed little that I could see frae the lave o folk in that unchancy time. Awe Steenie wad say was that nae doubt some friends o his wad be about.

We cam at last tae a very deep and narrow glen. On each side great mountains climbed tae vanish in mist, while lower doun it was partly forest and partly bare, and whaur it was bare it was either hard rock or bog. I said at the time that even in my inexperience it seemed the wrang place tae meet folk that didna like us. Steenie pointed up ahead and there was an auld man just sitting all alane on a great rock.

-Is that ane tae be feared then dae ye think?

I answered that it seemed unlikely tae me for he was a gey auld man wae a great white beard and hair that rolled doun his back. And if the plaid on that back was not quite a rag it had seen finer days, as aiblins he himsel had seen. For awe that I could see he had nae weapons apart frae a muckle staff he leaned on watching our approach.

When we drew alangside Steenie bade him gude day, and, as if in reply he skipped tae his feet. He was a tall man when he stood up, and he started tae babble in his ain language, dancing around us in a fashion o his ain, awe the time shaking his heid and cackling like an auld cockeril, wae every here and there an eldritch bit screech.

I asked Steenie what in God's name was he saying, at

which, forbye I spoke quietly, the auld man seemed tae just cock up his lugs.

-Sae ye hae not got the tongue hae ye not? Why then auld Coll sall speak tae yer noble honours in the Saxon tongue gin that sall be tae yer pleasure. For what auld Coll wad like tae ken o yer honours is whether tae yer mind this is indeed a gude day, or nae mair than just a way o speaking? For tae my mind, if the truth be not jinked, the words that say they carry it bear little resemblance tae it. For this day I hae heard has been, and the days before it hae been, unco bad days for some. For hae I not heard that the Graham has put Aberdeen tae the sword, and the Presbyterian craws after haeving fled before him are now wheeling high in the air and beating their breasts in Godly rage, and some say they will light doun on him and some say they will not, or aiblins they will rend their garments in their pulpits or aiblins they will not, and aiblins while the Graham beats the mountain tops Macalein More sall beat the glens, for I hae heard that Campbell blude is up and the Campbell sword is shaking in its pouch, on account o some Macdonald man declaring that the Pope o Rome, wham nane has ever seen, is a greater man than their ain chief Macalein More himsel, wham awe folk ken, some for gude and some for ill. And time they say sall tell what Macalein More sall dae, for I feel a storm brewing up yer honours on this day that men call gude, and great folk and small, and false folk and honest, will be at the slaying and the bones breaking, and only the True People wae kind hearts wha are sae despised and spat upon and hunted like wolves can see, what them that wad be great canna see, blinded as they are by the dazzle o their ain greatness, that the black birds o Lochaber tak not tae the air without purpose, nae mair than dis the Badenoch wolf leave his den, but that they ken the gate that many a bonny man sall gang, be it for right or be it for wrang.

The auld man was surely mad I thought, and much o his speech I couldna catch, slipping as he did intae his ain tongue. But Steenie listened tae him, and the auld man seemed tae cock his heid first tae the left and then tae the right, and then he wad lift it high intae the air snatching his bonnet frae his pate, which was near bald, and tossing it before him.

-Doun, doun, doun, they sall fall, kenning not whaur they fall or whaur they lie. But whaur else should they lie but at the True People's feet? The True People wha hae waited through generations o suffering, man, woman, faither, mither, son, dochter and bairn, that they in times past hae cam for in the stealth o the night, kenning not that the Children o the Mist hae friends far aboun their understanding, and beyond the reach o their swords and their sillar, wha hae hearts and wills tae bedevil awe their mischievings.

I asked Steenie what he meant and Steenie just said, forbye I mind he didna laugh when he said it.

-Why Agnes, before ye stands ane o the True People. Auld Coll, half-brither tae the mist. And he asks us tae look kindly upon him, and not ower closely at his appearance, for great has been his misfortune. But that we should look beneath the rags and the ravings and think that here is a man o undoubted worth and reputation, and is certainly deserving o a bit meat, or a bit drink, or a bit sillar, and wad gie these things blithely, and not mak the mistake o thinking that white-haired Coll o the Mist is naething but a beggar.

A beggar I certainly thought, and an entertaining ane. But I did not say this for there was caution in Steenie's voice, and auld Coll seemed tae be ower watchful in his daftness. Sae I smiled and said that we should gie sic a bonny man ought o what we had tae spare.

Steenie then turned tae Coll wha was now just standing, leaning on his staff, as if he had done wae dancing and talking.

-The friends o the People o the Mist as ye weel ken hae but little in the way o sillar, but ye sall hae a little o what little we hae.

Wae that he put a coin intae the auld man's hand, at which Coll made a great show o near bairnish delight, looking at it and tossing it intae the air, and catching it on his bonnet and clapping his bonnet on his heid and then removing it, pretending surprise that the coin had not just flown awa.

Steenie next handed him our whisky.

-O that ye may drink and not stint.

The auld man took the bottle then and lifting it tae the sky let out a great oath which he quickly followed by a great swallow. Steenie turned tae me,

-Awe the enemies o the Children o the Mist, which is damned near awe o Scotland, hae just had awe their hopes and endeavors damned tae perdition.

Coll handed the bottle back. Steenie then said something mair in his language, and Coll, wha it seemed had been entirely cured o his madness by the whisky, waved his staff ance around his heid, and then anither time in the air, and wae something very like magic anither man was standing at his side, also a Hielanman, but very different in appearance, this ane being young and bold wae a sword by his side and a targe on his back.

He saluted us wae a sharp bow, and auld Coll, commanding now it seemed without a hint o silliness in him, gied him instructions in their ain tongue and the man took off doun the glen, his plaid howked and his red shanks flying.

Coll now led us doun the glen marching bonnily wae his staff on his shoulder. And while he kept up his conversation wae Steenie it seemed, though I could understand but little o it, a very sober conversation now. And while he still tossed the coin in the air as if he was weel pleased wae it, in the end he presented it tae an auld wife wha's biggin we passed, and wha looked as if she could dae wae it. But her, seeming tae ken frae wham it had cam, bowed graciously tae us and cursed auld Coll tae Hell, which gied birth tae the first natural smile I had seen on his face since we met.

In truth I kent not at the time whaur we were, or wha these folk were. Steenie telt me that at the place whaur we had met auld Coll there were six or mair Hielanmen hiding in the heather, for their chief wha was called Patrick Roy o the Mist, and was Steenie's friend, liked tae ken the nature o sic visitors as he got. In particular he liked tae ken if they were generous and kindly, or if they were tight fisted, as weel as ither things about them, sic as whether or not they kent the pass as Steenie did. Nor it seems was it just as simple as kenning the pass, it was about kenning the order o the words and responses, and it was for auld, white haired Coll tae weigh awe this up, and on his judgement many things lay, for the young men hidden in the heather were not just there tae warm their arses in the sun.

The glen widened out at a certain point and there were bit biggins in ilka place, and Hielanfolk stopped their business tae look at us, forbye nane spoke. I was of course mair used tae Hielanfolk by then and they nae langer looked as savage as they had at first, but still very wild, for it seemed that in peace or in war they put their weapons on wae their duds.

Next we heard the sound o pipes, and looking ahead there was a man coming tae meet us riding a Hielan pony at the walk, his legs sticking out o the stirrups in a queer Hielan fashion. By his side marched twa pipers blawing fit tae burst on their great pipes.

-How dae ye ken this man? I asked Steenie. He replied unco quietly.

-I ance lang ago took an arrow frae his arse. An arrow that damn near put an end tae a line which as he'll never tire o telling ye, stretches awe the way back tae Kenneth Macalpine, King o the Scots. That forbye, it was a painful operation, and not ane a man could easily be dignifiedly brave about. Tae Patrick Roy's mind the man wha performed it wad either hae tae be paid very weel, made a brither for life, or killed on the spot, and he being neither a rich man, or a particularly bludie ane, chose the middle course.

I could see the man clearly now, a large, lang-shanked man of about fifty. He wore a fine plaid and a pair o tartan breeks, and a bonnet wae twa eagle feathers in it. When he drew close tae Steenie he greeted him in a maist friendly fashion, embracing him baith wae great affection and great grandness. And when he cam ower tae me it seemed as if his pride wad swell even mair, and he telt me that as a friend o Steenie Malecky's he and his people were mine tae command.

He looked at me very closely as he said this, and I kent

weel enough that my gear hadna fooled him, forbye he said naething tae question it, nae doubt thinking that it wad not be polite, or it might weel hae been that he was sae used tae seeing folk in disguise that he thought naething o it.

I thanked him for his offer looking round at his people as I did sae, wondering what it wad be like tae command sic folk, for they looked as wild as any that followed the Graham, and they gied out a great cheer when they saw that their chief was pleased.

They were, Steenie telt me, nameless folk. What was left o the ance great and powerful clan o Macgregor. They had ance, lang ago, fallen out wae auld King James, the faither o the pre-sent ane, and he had put them tae the horn and declared them wolf's heids tae be hunted on awe sides, and they had only kept themsels thegither by making sic hunting an unchancy sport.

Patrick Roy led us wae great style tae his ain front door which was of a fine enough house, though not big. Why I learnt later that some o his ain family were turned out tae mak room for us, which of course was never mentioned, then or since then. But Steenie and mysel were gien a room tae oursels and fine Hielan claes tae wear. I was gien a gown by Catriona, Patrick Roy's dochter, wha was a red haired woman o my ain age.

Here it was that I kent for certain that Patrick Roy had kent awe alang that I was nae man, though if he wad not hae moved in any way tae embarrass or expose me had not Steenie said that it wad be fine, now he expressed great delight and declared that he waited tae be presented.

-Secrets, Agnes, Steenie said, -are best kept amang the People o the Mist by letting awe folk ken them, and ken that they are secrets and are tae be kept.

Catriona helped me out o my armour, and only when it was off did she look at me and properly smile, and mysel burst out laughing.

-She is a fine woman, she said, and indeed if that is what she thought she was a fine enough woman hersel wae a great mane o red hair and grey een. But it seemed then, and for her ain reasons she was maybe deceitful in this, that we could hardly talk, and awe she wad say was,

-She has cam a lang way and she is tired, and aiblins she has been at the fighting, and as she kent not how tae speak ither than the Saxon tongue Catriona wad teach her.

I telt her that I had little enough tae dae wae fighting, and the little that I had seen was mair than I could thole. She smiled a bit mair, but the effort o speaking and understanding exhausted us baith and perhaps I wanted tae be alane and kent that I could not be, for it was plain that she felt that she had a duty tae bide wae me and attend tae me in whatever I did, neither kenning wha I was, or how unused I was tae sic things.

Why, even when I looked out o the window at the great mountains that were awe around us, and the nameless Folk o theMist wha went about their business below them, she cam up behind me and started tae comb out my hair which had been lang tied back under a bonnet. That I was surprised I canna deny, but still I stood there for an unco lang time for the touch o her hands was very fine and gentle, and she had gien up trying tae speak Scots and sang very softly in her ain tongue.

It felt tae me then that she wad be happy tae dae this forever, but at last I turned round, and for a bit we just stared at each ither, mysel watching the light o the sun as it went doun shining on her face and neck and shoulders, and her grey een that were like the secrets o their ain mist in which they trusted aboun awe things. I thought then that I had spent ower much o my life in the company o fierce men and horses and dugs and sic like beasts, and I felt weary and had little inclination tae meet mair, and yet I kent they were preparing a feast in our honour.

That she kent much o what I was feeling I now ken weel enough, but at the time it seemed tae me that she had a way o inquiring wae her een that had naething o the canting busy body about it, but was bold and forward and made nae secret o her interest and took nae offence at it not being satisfied.

At ane point she just stood, regarding me for what seemed like a lang while, and then wae a movement o her hands she drew me close tae her and kissed me on baith cheeks and on the mouth, which astonished me, forbye it delighted me tae, making up for awe the words that could not be spoken. And then I let her dress me entirely in her ain claes. And though she was nae doubt ignorant o the fact, never in her life had Black Agnes Douglas looked sae fine, and why I thought, that for persecuted nameless folk wha lived by their swords, they had some fine things.

She took me by the hand and we went doun stairs, and there was Steenie, himsel looking the very picture o a fine Hielan gentleman. And he in turn took me by the hand and presented me, rolling out my name like a herald, tae Patrick Roy and his wife Morag and his four sons, Neil, Patrick, Calum, and Donald wha was but a bairn, but the ithers were awe fine young men wae perhaps twenty gallant words in Scots between them.

That night was a very wild night o feasting and dancing and drunkenness. And for awe that I was tired and kent nane o their dances, I danced wae Patrick Roy and awe his sons in turn for I can dance weel enough. And Steenie played his small pipes and sang for them, sometimes in their ain tongue and sometimes in Scots. Then not tae be out-done, their ain poet wad recite his verses, and I asked Steenie what they meant for they sounded very grand tae me.

He answered that forbye they sounded grand enough, in truth they were a gey wearisome tale o battles and routs, and raidings and forayings, and laments for awe the folk that had got killed daen these things, for the last thousand years and mair.

I minded weel the auld poet at Aberdeen and kent how verses like that cam tae be made. And I thought how far awa this place was frae Trig and the peaceful folk that lived there. My mither had telt me when I was a bairn, that baith my ain faither, wham I had never kent, and his faither before him had ganged a foraying themsels, winning awa wae what they could wae their spears, or getting themsels killed like my ain faither.

That of course was lang lang ago when the Douglases themsels were powerful folk. That, I remember clearly, was how the glen seemed tae me on that first night, like a place frae which time had just lifted its hand, and the folk sang their thousand year auld sangs in acknowledgement o this.

Awe that night Catriona was aye by my side, and when in the end we parted tae gae tae bed she kissed me again and said that she kent very weel that I wad arrive in their glen lang before I did, but at that time I kent not at awe what she could mean. When I asked Steenie he said that amang the Hielanfolk Catriona had the reputation o haeving the sight, but that he had little faith in sic things himsel.

I said nae mair on that subject then, I ken not why, but I said I wanted Steenie tae teach me their language, which he promised me he wad.

I wanted ither things tae. I was standing at the time looking out o the window o the room that they had gien us watching the sun begin tae come up, and I remembered that this was the first time since the kirk had dragged me frae my mither's house that I had worn women's claes, or lain in a proper bed. I mind tae him looking at me then, and his een were like a warm blanket drawn ower nakedness and confusion, and I minded o the time when I thought o mysel as a bairn in his hands, and Sawney tae. Sawney was awa now, and I kent not whether that time was past or whether it was not, and it might weel be, I thought, that nae time is ever past but is just biding quietly still within ye, and will ane day rise and tak ye unawares.

I ken not truly. I stood very still on that spot whaur Catriona had combed my hair and I felt Steenie's hands stripping me o my claes, and I minded her hands, and I minded the hands o that ither that was awa. Aye and I minded the hands o awe them in that dark place whaur it seemed Hell had broke loose. And when I looked out o the window and doun on tae the fire that was deeing below and around it some o the People o the Mist, some still sitting, some sleeping curled up in their plaids on the ground.

For them that were still awake the merriment it seemed had gone out o them now, and while there was still a bit moon it was darkness that lay ower awe o them, and it may be that made them seem wilder and mair different than at any ither time, and haeving seen them, or anes like them, being cruel, and them being kind, I kent not at awe what

171

tae think o them.

-And wha are these folk for? Are they for the Kirk or the King?

-For nane, Agnes. Their swords are their ain. But the rod o Argyll lies heavy on their backs, as dae many ither rods. Sae they bide under the Campbell's wing, clipping it a bit here and a bit there, gin they hae the chance, but no ower much, Patrick Roy has around four hundred gude men, Macalein More has mair than six thousand. Sae Patrick will not waste his people in this affair, unless he can spot a side that's winning and can see a clear sign o profit in it for them. He has some lads wae the Graham, and he keeps them there for the news they bring him, and he has some wae the Campbell for the same reason, but the mass o his people bide quietly and await the outcome. Nane has sae far offered tae gie them their name back.

I said that I kent not how folk could hae nae name, and why they seemed tae hae nae kirk either. And yet it might weel be that we hae much in common, for we hae nae kirk tae gang tae, and nae name that could be safely spoken. Tae my mind then it seemed that we were even less than they, haeving nae great glen in which tae bide and gude friends tae guard us, and aiblins that was what Sawney couldna thole.

☆

When the minister came down in the morning it seemed to him as if nothing in the inn had changed. The old woman bid him a cheerful good morning and inquired if he had slept well. It would have been impossible for the minister to answer in anything other than the affirmative, which he did and felt the lie smite him as the turmoil of the night had smote him.

Nothing of this showed in his face, he felt sure. The girl Helen had already set breakfast for him. She also smiled at him her eyes subdued and impudently flashing. For one fierce moment the minister resented them all, resented their very existence, their complacent pride and semi-barbarous theology. The moment passed quickly and left the minister feeling tired, penitent and wretched.

He must set himself to love them, he thought, as he ate his bannocks, cheese and ale. He had almost finished when he heard the sound of a horse. He looked out of the window to see Andrew Gilmore come riding into the yard at a good spanking canter. For a moment he almost forget everything in admiration of the man's agile horsemanship and the way in which he reined in his mount and slid off her back in one smooth movement. He walked in through the door, displaying the open, refreshed countenance of a man with a clear conscience who has slept well, and, thought the minister, probably drunk well, haggling garrulously with one of his own kind.

'Gude morning minister.'

'And good morning to you Andrew . . . How did your business go?'

'Wae the kind o man I had tae deal wae, a certain Jamie Scobie, the best ane can aye say is that if I haena bin skinned the profit I hae made is not ane that ony Christian man need be ashamed o.'

'I am glad to hear it Andrew.'

The minister laughed. The sight of Andrew Gilmore cheered him considerably. It was interrupted by Martha striding across the room with two mugs of ale, one for herself and one she set down in front of the Borderman.

'Sae the Lord has preserved ye still Andra Gilmore?'

'Aye mistress, and I trust ye will pray that he sall continue tae dae sae for mony a year tae come.'

'Prayers, Andra, will neither affect nor deflect what is already the Lord's will. Is that no sae minister? Only the ignorant and the superstitious and the ambitious think ye can alter God's will by whispering and whining in his lug. As if he did not already ken what was the needs and wants o awe folk, and what is their right and proper due, and has already laid it doun wae wisdom far aboun our understanding and unchangeable tae the end o time, and tae which we maun bow our heids in righteous acceptance o his glory, kenning weel that we are but dirt uplifted by his word.'

She glared at them both as if waiting for one or the other to dispute with her. Neither did. Andrew Gilmore buried his lips in his beer while the minister's shame at his previous feelings renewed itself. He felt humbled by the fierce doctrine which had kept this woman safe through more turbulence than his own life had ever known. Martha cheerfully seized upon their silence.

'Trig is not far frae here and the lassie and mysel will certainly gang tae hear ye preach, minister. Why I'll be maist interested tae find out what style they hae taught ye in Holland, and whether it be the true word or some Arminian confusion.'

'Why, Martha, you and Helen will both be very welcome, though I hope as a new preacher I can crave some forbearance.'

'Martha Liddel, minister, forbears wae awe folk that hae the truth in them, kenning weel the limitations o her judgement. Even folk that in her earthly opinion dinna shine wae as bricht a licht as they micht.'

Her brilliant eyes settled for a moment on Andrew, who, as if suddenly exasperated reached over and tweaked her nose with his fingers.

'Auld wife, I hae bin up this morning wae the cock. I hae galloped awe the way here and yer ale has hardly dried on my lips. Why I sall ride awe day wae the minister and no be sermonized in sic a fashion. Sae if ye will clap yer tongue tae my lug I wad thank ye for some mair ale tae soothe it.'

The minister watched the laughter lines crease up the old woman's face. It was a game, he thought, and felt irritated and alienated by it. Martha appeared almost to skip as she went to fill up Andrew's mug.

'The minister kens ye not for the loun that I ken ye, wha hae kent ye since ye war a bairn.'

When they left both Martha and Helen cam to see them off. The minister gave them both his blessing and felt their eyes following them as they rode away. When they were out of hearing Andrew Gilmore suddenly laughed merrily.

'What wae John Erskine and Martha Liddel, if ye cairry on in this fashion ye'll hae half the Cameronians in the country at yer kirk door.'

'They would be welcome Andrew.'

'Ye haena seen them awe yet. Why minister they wad deprive ye o the preaching pairt o yer living.'

For a time they rode in silence, obliged by the road to ride in single file. The minister felt glad, the brilliant sunlight refreshed him much more than his troubled sleep had. When

174

they were once more abreast he turned to Andrew.

'Is the girl Helen really the old woman's niece?'

'Why minister it's strange ye should ask that, but ye hae guessed richt, niece is only a convenient term seeing that she has nae ither kin that she kens about. Na, she was the dochter o John Melville, a gude man o whom I had a very high opinion. They lived in Galloway and war awe struck doun in the famine, awe except for Helen.'

For a second Andrew appeared to hesitate.

'I kent naething o it at the time, for awe I had kent John Melville in the auld days. Todd Grey wham I hae mentioned, brought Helen tae Martha's door kenning she was a warm hearted woman wha wad tak her in, and Todd Grey buried John Melville and his wife as he did mony anither. I ken not minister, I found it hard tae thole that sic a man should dee in sic a way, and mair than likely the lassie wad hae deed if Todd had not cam by, and I wad hae liked it fine if Todd had brought her tae our house. But he kent not me as I kent not him.

'It was a very Christian act. This Todd Grey does seem a Godly if strange figure. Does Martha know him well?'

'Aye, enough, she'll not often speak o him, and I ken not how weel she really kens him, but he might weel be some auld Cameronian body, forbye nane can vouch for that onymair than they can vouch for onything else about him. He just seemed tae be there in the bad years and then no there. Mony thocht o him as nae mair than a sorrowful story in a sorrowful time, but Helen is living proof that's no the case for she minds him very weel, and kens what she owes tae him.'

'What happened to him?'

'The Lord alane kens that. He was auld and aiblins he himsel just deed awa in the hills. But nane kens that I ken about.'

'I feel the hand of the Lord in all of this Andrew.'

'Aye minister, when ye look at Helen Melville now ye canna think itherwise, or that Todd Grey was his gude servamt, however much o a mystery he chose tae be tae his fellow men.'

☆

Amang the People o the Mist, Catriona had the sight. And if on occasion Patrick Roy wad mak a joke o it, it was in truth nae joke tae him, and Steenie said that he rarely embarked on any enterprise concerning his people without talking it through wae her, and that faither and dochter wad sit weel up intae the night weighing likely and unlikely outcomes. Steenie laughed, and said that it served ane gude purpose o keeping the True People frae rash undertakings. For ane that was named as a great warlock he had but little time for prophecies.

But this day I was riding alane wae Catriona high aboun the mist. Talking was easier now, I had some o her tongue, and she I discovered had mair o mine than she had at first revealed. And she wad talk sometimes in Scots and sometimes in Hielan, and whiles I wad understand and whiles I wad not, and aiblins awe she was telling me was how her folk had no aye been landless sworders, but ance awe Loch Lomondside had been theirs, and lang lang ago their ain chief the King o Scotland, and how treachery and guile had brought them tae this state, for was it not the way o the warld that the false hearted should be many and the true hearted few, and sae it wad gang on.

I asked her then about the sight and she just glanced at me her grey een shining through the mist which near covered us baith, and intae which the wolf hound that had followed us had disappeared, and awe she said was,

-Let us gang whaur the grey dug has ganged.

She said nae mair except tae point whaur the dug had gone, and in silence we followed it, and at the end o the trail it had taen the mist itsel had cleared and we lighted doun near a deep pool at which the dug was quietly drinking, and Catriona hersel lay doun and drank bringing some water tae me in her clasped hands. I remember very weel how it tasted, like nae water that I had previously drank, forbye I canna now say what the taste was like for there is naething wae which tae compare it. But I mind it weel, alang wae Catriona's grey een and her laughter as she gied it, and then the bit change in her voice as she said,

-Winter sall come and ye sall gang.

I said then, what was the plain truth, that I kent not whaur we were tae gang, and had never kent. She looked at me again in her queer way, and the mist which had come doun a bit curled ance again about her as if its ain birth-place was in the very heart o her.

-Ye ask about the sight for ye hae heard them talk about it nae doubt, my faither and Steenie, and nae doubt they had a bit smile upon their lips as they did sae.

There was a smile on her lips tae, but she had a way o smiling on occasion which had nae hint o merriment about it. As I kent her better I cam tae ken it weel, but at that time on the hillside it might weel hae been that I smiled a bit mysel, for forbye I had grown tae like them, whiles they seemed tae me tae be a folk that had an opinion o themsels sae high as tae be near a blasphemy.

-The men ken naething o the sight. What it can be asked and what it canna be asked. What it will tell without asking and what it will never tell if ye ask it a thousand times. My faither wad like it tae tell him whether this or that endeavor will be fruitful, will this foray be successful, will the Graham beat the Campbell? As if the sight concerned itsel at awe wae sic things. The sight, Agnes Douglas, tells ye when a thing is perhaps about tae happen, and aiblins it will tell ye whether that thing is a gude thing or a bad thing, and aiblins it will not. But it will tell ye tae prepare for it and tae see that ye are ready and waiting for it, for it will then tell ye what tae dae, and if ye but listen will lead ye safely in the daen o it.

I telt her that my ain mither, folk said, had possessed the gift o prophecy and it might weel hae been that she hersel had half believed it. And forbye the fact that I mysel had seen nae evidence o it the Kirk had found plenty, and the reputation had done her nae gude at awe.

Catriona just smiled at that and said that evidence was aye in the heart o the hearer and no for ithers tae affirm or deny.

-Ye see Agnes Dhu, I kent that ye wad come that day. I kent not how or why, or wha ye wad be, but I kent that a dark stranger frae far awa in the South country wad come, wha wad be dressed in sodger's gear, but wad not be a sodger, and wad not hae come tae fight. Nor did it say that ye wad be a woman, only that I was not tae think that ye wad be a man. Sae think on how I thought when I saw ye come riding intae our glen frae the hill aboun our house. I thought then that I wad wait on ye, but in sic a way that ye wad think I was nae mair than a bit girl.

-Awe this I thought, and was telt, that the tongue should be silent, for at a first meeting it is apt in its pride tae be a deceiver, but that the hands and een should speak boldly, as should the heart and lips, trusting without stint.

Hielan havering I thought, and it might weel hae been that I had not liked tae be played wae in sic a way. But I said nought, and Catriona, kenning I think what was in my mind took my heid in her hands and drew me towards her, and not for the first time I wondered at the strange colour o her hair, like fire, and skin that never seemed tae hae kent the sun.

-Dinna be angry. I dae aye as I'm instructed. And it has instructed me and telt me these days past that ye tae hae the sight, and forbye it hammers on yer door ye will not let it in.

-I hae been taen for a witch ance, I said. Awe she said in reply was that sic behaviour was but the nonsense o foolish folk.

-Nonsense it might weel be, but it was deidly nonsense awe the same.

-Awe nonsense is deidly, which is why the True People dwell as they dae.

We sat for a lang time for the mist cleared and the day was hot, and aiblins I talked then as I had not talked before, while she wad listen. And if I ance stopped speaking she wad sing very gently in her ain language, singing I thought as ye wad sing tae a bairn, but it was an auld lament she sang wae a memory as lang as time itsel. Bursting, she said, wae awe the evil that swelled in the breasts o the false hearted and foretelling their eventual rout. Towards the end she just said,

-They hae hurt ye. Aye and if they should catch ye they will hurt ye again. But in daen sae they hae let loose a storm upon themsels that sall droun awe their endeavours in the unnatural black bile that sall rise frae within their ain bellies tae owerwhelm them, sae that they will dance a reel o madness on their graves and bellow frae their pulpits in their Godly rage. And seeing their false hearts about tae burst the people sall flee frae them covering their faces in their plaids. This I ken, but kenning is never enough, for there is never enough o kenning tae be mair than a poor, silly, ragged thing testing the wind, and for awe its claim tae reason being less sure o its direction than a hunting wolf.

Much o what Catriona said at that time I couldna understand, either her words or their meanings, and whiles her Scots had a queer foreign ring tae it as if she was still in her ain tongue. She had been taught tae speak it, she telt me, by a Presbyterian minister her faither had employed in quieter times, wha being out o favour in Edinburgh was content tae live for a time amang the People o the Mist, and not tae comment ower much on their daens. But when he had left anither had cam, a dour corbie craw o a man, mair a spy for the King it seemed than any ither thing, and Patrick Roy had driven him frae the glen.

At ither times her language wad slip for lang periods intae Hielan, and for awe I kent some o it by now she wad quickly leave me behind till I imagined that I was listening tae awe manner o wild things. And then ance mair she wad be in Scots again but it wad seem tae my ears as if the web o words had taen her clean ower. And if she ance caught a look in my een which maybe said there was misgiens there she wad grasp me lightly be the shoulders and kiss me on the lips.

-Agnes Dhu, she said, for that was my name in her language.

-Dark woman in the steel coat, for that is how I first saw ye. And when I had taen off that coat and saw ye standing naked, I kent that the blindness o this warld had struck ye, which is when I kent that the sight had been true. and that I wad bring ye here far aboun their blindness.

Her hands like gentle nimble things clasped themsels about my heid, stroking my hair, while her een it seemed tae me searched in awe places at ance, and aiblins I thought there was a hint o madness in them tae.

-Agnes Dhu, it may appear strange, and yet it is not sae strange, but I ken ye very weel, and ye are ane wha in the hour o necessity will aye ken the truth o this warld. And if

179

ye but listen tae that truth ye will aye ken what ye are tae dae, mair than Steenie, wha is a clever man, but nae mair than that. And it may be that he will ane day out o necessity, or some ither reason, be content tae be guided by ye as ye are now guided by him.

Perhaps I wad hae laughed then, but there was nae laughing at Catriona until she hersel showed that she was inclined tae laughter, which was much o the time. But that day we just lay by the pool feeling the quiet secret peace o the place, and Hielanfolk I found, wha could be very garrulous much o the time, could be very quiet at ithers.

I asked her if there was now nae kirk and nae minister in her glen that she went tae? She just said that after the last minister had been driven out, the kirk the people had built tae please him had been burnt doun by some marauding Campbells, and as nae ither minister had cam by then the people had little inclination tae build anither.

She laughed a bit when she said this, and in truth she kent very little o her bible or her catechism, and cared less for what she did ken. Her ain folk, she said, had suffered as much and as lang, and had as many stories gude and bad tae tell as any in the Bible.

I looked awa. The sun I mind was ganging doun at this time and made their mountains stand out mair terrible than before. And at a distance I saw some Hielanmen driving their cattle at the trot urging the beasts on wae the flats o their swords. Wearing them doun I wad hae thought, but doubtless they had some strange Hielan purpose in sae daen, for in truth they were very different frae ither folk.

☆

Andrew Gilmore reined in his horse.

'There is the heid toun o yer new parish, minister.'

The minister looked down the long shallow glen to the clutter of cottages that stood at the end of it. The largest building he reasoned was of course the kirk. The minister felt an odd surge of apprehension. It was little different from the other villages of its kind that the minister had passed through on his journey.

His eyes took in the broad sweep of the fields around it, and to his untutored gaze they seemed well enough, with Spring grain bursting through the soil, sheep and cattle on the hillside, and the occasional human figures who looked like all the other grey clad figures he had become accustomed to. Except that these must be different, these had a right to demand a place in his concerns above all other earthly things.

The minister's apprehension changed to elation. It was not the pleasant hamlet he had imagined in Holland. It was not even the place he had imagined in Edinburgh. And on his journey here his imagination, obsessed with other things and another time had made any image of how Trig might look in the present impossible. He blessed the humble reality of it which was a solace to his soul.

They were on the road, he thought, where Mathius Pringle had first met Sawney Bain. A road along which a dark and furious past had thundered, but praise God it was the past and thundered no more, and the town had survived, and the people had survived, and he would now be part of their future. He looked at Andrew Gilmore and felt a sudden boundless affection for him.

'Will you join me in a short prayer, Andrew?'

'Surely, minister.'

The minister prayed for the past and the future, publicly, and privately that the dark shadow should be lifted from his heart, or that he should be given the strength to face it.

When he opened his eyes it appeared to the minister that the fields were greener and the hills less sombre, and he smiled at his own imagination.

'Andrew, do you think it would be thought unseemly for a new minister to gallop into his new parish?'

'Unseemly, minister? Why awa wae ye, the folk here-abouts hae a fine eye for a gude horseman.'

'Then Andrew let us go.'

The minister dug his heels into his horse which gave a sudden whinny and took off down the glen with the Border-man's mare at his heels. The minister's horse was much the faster but was hampered by the rough ground to a much greater extent than Andrew's, and Andrew, the minister had to admit, was a very fine horseman. When they drew rein they were almost neck and neck, and in that fashion they trotted up the main street of the village.

The people came out into the street to stare at them. The men doffed their bonnets and the minister in turn doffed his hat, suddenly embarrassed by his wild gallop. The minister whom he was to replace was standing at the door of the house that was soon to be his. He dismounted and walked up to him.

'Good day, Sir.'

'And gude day tae ye tae.'

The Reverent Marten Gilmarten was a small, narrow faced man in late middle age. He stared at the minister with steady, inquisitive eyes in which there was a pronounced squint.

'Come awa in, for until ye dae the louns will not gang back tae their business and idleness is not tae be encouraged.'

The Reverent Gilmarten's gaze swept through the crowd which slowly dispersed, shuffling, it appeared to the minister, outside the range of the obliquely squinting eyes. For a moment they rested on his and then Gilmarten stepped aside to allow him to enter.

The minister looked at Andrew Gilmore feeling a sudden need for his support, and was unpleasantly struck by the extent to which Andrew seemed to have distanced himself. He leant on his horse a sardonic smile on his face.

'This gentleman is Mr Andrew Gilmore who has been my good guide and mentor on the journey here. I think that without him I might still be wandering in the hills.'

'If the Lord intended ye tae be here, here nae doubt he wad hae brought ye, and Mr Gilmore and I are known tae each other.'

They followed Gilmarten into his house where he offered them chairs, but before he allowed them to sit, or any conversation could begin he offered up a prayer on the minister's safe arrival. No sooner had he finished when he turned to Andrew and said:

'Dae ye intend tae bide in Trig for lang, Mr Gilmore?'

'I hae a bit business that I might as weel attend tae, but then it's quickly back as I hae a house and a farm tae see tae. At the moment it's been watched ower by auld John Erskine.'

'Sae Mr Erskine is still wae us.'

'Aye indeed he is, and looks tae be wae us for a lang time yet.

182

Whiles I think that for awe his devotion the Lord is no ower keen tae meet his gude servant at close quarters, sae often has he preserved him when ither men . . .'

'I dinna allow levity wae the Lord's name or purpose in my parish, even less in my house.'

Gilmarten's voice was sharp. The minister watched Andrew Gilmore's countenance. The aloofness which had disconcerted him suddenly dissolved into swift anger. The minister could feel the rebuke poised on his lips, and then it was gone, discarded the minister thought, entirely for his benefit. He felt irritated. If Andrew had been guilty of mild levity, Gilmarten had been guilty of boorish discourtesy. Neither seemed inclined to make the slightest amends. The minister was suddenly and grimly conscious that his enthusiasm of half an hour ago had once again enmeshed itself in something beyond his knowledge. The Borderman rose to his feet. The expression on his face was now almost sarcastically cheerful.

'Weel, I'll awa now and see that the horses are comfortable, and look up the pickle gude friends that I hae in Trig.'

The Reverent Gilmarten gave out a brusque 'hem!' as if he had achieved his aim in making Andrew leave and had no inclination to conceal it.

'As you please, Andrew. I will see you later . . ?'

'Why certainly minister. I am not about tae vanish and Trig is not a very large place. Ye will find me, or news o me, in Mither Bruin's pleasant howf, which ilka body kens. And now I bid ye gude day gentlemen.'

He bowed slightly as he spoke, which the minister had never seen him do before, and strode to the door, nor did Gilmarten make any move to show him out.

When the door closed behind him the minister turned again to look at Marten Gilmarten. The man's eyes twinkled fiercely from the pale narrow face.

'Perhaps there is some reason for it but I wonder a bit, you seem not to much like Andrew.'

Marten Gilmarten looked utterly unconcerned.

'Some folk,' he said. 'Will not leave the past tae the past, but will still ride the countryside wae a sword by their side, and I hae little doubt, ideas in their heads, beyond their proper concerns.'

'I confess I am still new here and cannot properly judge these matters . . .'

'The folk of this land have had sixty and mair years of fighting and brawling, and twice as many wind swept notions have passed through their heids in that time. Weel Sir, we now have the victory that the Lord has decreed we should have, and he has lifted his right hand against all these extravagant and mischievous fancies, republicanisms and schismatisms and sectarianisms. Aye and in some cases so wild as to be little better than atheism and anarchy, that abounded throughout Scotland and England.

'We now have a Godly king to rule us and the Kirk is the power in the land that it should be. But we now, Sir, have to answer for this folk, for their Godliness, peacefulness, and industry, and they are as stubborn as any folk on earth. Why Sir, the lave o them ken mair about handling pikes and shooting guns now than they dae about their rightful business of tending to their fields and caring for their beasts, and paying their rents. Some, and your friend Mr Gilmore is not guiltless o this, are as likely as not when admonished to shout the Lord's name in your lug in defence o their stubbornness, which I'm sure you'll agree, is not the kind of thing that can or should be borne.

'Perhaps they feel entitled, having fought and struggled so long . . .'

'The victory is the Lord's, and they set themsels aboun themsels in claiming it as theirs. But do not mistake me Sir, do not mistake me, they are gude folk and nae mair misguided than the majority o mankind. But they must learn to be contented now, and it is the Kirk's duty to guide them in that, and no business of theirs to make it harder than it need be. Your friend Mr Gilmore is no doubt a very honest man, but he kens weel enough that it offends me tae see him riding the countryside wae a sword by his side, and saying, as on occasion he has said, that the folk have become nae mair than sheep tae be sheared, and sneering at the laird who is a strong supporter of the Kirk and its ministers, and asks no more of the Kirk than it supports him in his rightful position and sees tae it that the people respect it, for they have not always respected it in the past.'

'The famine perhaps has made many of them bitter.'

'And is that not a blasphemy in itself? To feel bitter and to rail in this bitterness of theirs? For against whom are they railing but the Lord himself? And why? Because his strong hand smote them from the high position in which their pride, arrogance, and fancy, had set them. That they were chastized sorely Sir I dinna deny, but as a sign Sir, a sign that the Lord wad hae them think mair o their duties than their rights. The Kirk and its ministers shall look tae their proper rights.'

The minister stood silently, his head slightly bowed. A host of images crept through his head. Not in any order, but juxtaposing themselves in horrid confusion, their very anarchy forcing him to resolve them in the shape of the small stern figure opposite him.

'Forgive me Sir,' Gilmarten said, his voice suddenly softening. 'I had nae intention o speaking in sic a way, but ye asked and it came out, as it should. I have nothing against your honest Mr Gilmore apart from a willfull stubbornness, which is nae mair than a common quality which bedevils a good half o this people. But it is my belief that this poor country of ours stands upon the threshold of great things, from which it will benefit, provided the Kirk maintains a firm as well as a Christian hand, and auld affrays are like auld dreams, best forgotten. Now would you care for some refreshment, though I normally eat at six every evening?'

'If you don't mind I think I would like to walk about the place for a bit, as I am an utter stranger here, and return perhaps between five and six. Indeed I think I should look for Mr Gilmore.'

'Mither Bruin's is where he said he'll be, and nae doubt he kens his ain inclinations best. It's an alehouse run by an auld widow wife, decent enough as these places go, though I would not go there myself, nor advise you to go. But if you would find Mr Gilmore . . . I will expect you back at six.'

'With Mr Gilmore?'

'Of course, of course. If I hae my divisions wae Andrew Gilmore, ane thing he will not be able tae say is that I ken not how tae be hospitable.'

The minister walked through the main street of the village of Trig. It was strange how often he had imagined this place. So much indeed that he had irrationally felt that he would in some way recognise it. There was nothing in this jumble of cottages clustered round a church and a number of farm steadings, the whole connected by a spidery network of tracks, that he could have recognised.

The church alone was new and built of good red granite in the Scottish style whose simplicity he did not find unpleasing. Indeed its harmonious proportions seemed at once to defy, pity, and frown, on the chaos around it. For a time he stood in its lee and stared at the dwellings around him. Mostly they were of clay, and some, obviously more prosperous, were of stone and had glazed windows.

The people who passed him saluted him but showed no inclination to stop and speak. They knew who he was. Undoubtedly, he thought, they were slyly scrutinising him, admitting to themselves perhaps the unknown quality of him who was to play the most absolutely fundamental role in their lives.

He watched as a sturdy elderly peasant rode towards him on a small shaggy horse. They had a right to expect love and guidance and teaching from him, and he had no right to expect anything from them. Gilmarten demanded obedience; he could only pray for acceptance.

The horseman drew level with him.

'Gude afternoon minister,' he said.

He would have ridden on, his pony ambling, his lean old frame rolling with its gait, neither hurrying nor hesitant. The minister stepped forward his hand slightly raised. The man's eye caught the movement and checked his horse.

'Good afternoon to you Mr . . .'

'Robert Glen, minister.'

For a moment the minister found himself intimidated by the primitive directness of the old man, which at the same time lacked any simplicity or charm.

Mr Gilmarten, he thought, in his heart despises these people. Gilmarten he felt, quite possibly despised him. Gilmarten judged without hesitation or fear of contradiction. For a moment the visage of the squint eyed pastor appeared to merge

186

with that of the old man.

It passed. Robert Glen was waiting, simply waiting, eyes stolid and patient beneath his blue bonnet, waiting to hear what this new alien-sounding minister would say next.

The minister felt something akin to despair well up inside him. In a moment of near hysteria Agnes Douglas had pointed her finger at him as if it had been a weapon striving to reach him. Twelve inches had separated him from the tip of that finger, and still, he who had resolved to stand his ground had drawn back. She had given vent to her delight then with a savage cackle.

'Hech! Hech! Sirrah!' She had cried. 'Ye are neither sae brave or sae bauld a man as ye wad hae the warld think, for what gars ye flinch? Why Sirrah, there are things still in Trig, aye and in Scotland, which lang after I am deid and gane sall parr yer white flesh frae yer bones and mak ye weep bitter tears. Mark my words weel that ye may be the better prepared, for they are things that can be neither jinked nor jouked.'

'I am of course a stranger here, Mr Glen, and you seem to be a man of some age and standing. How are things here?'

'The Lord bids us tae be content and we strive tae dae his will. They hae been better and they hae been worse.'

'Yes, so I have heard.'

To the minister it appeared as if Robert Glen's features managed a primitive superciliousness without visibly changing expression.

'I was just admiring this fine new church, which does the parish credit.'

'Aye, aye, it's fine enough, the Hielanmen burned the auld ane doun in eighty-five, ye'll hae heard o that?'

'Not all the details, though I daresay I will in time.'

The superciliousness in the old man's expression appeared to increase. He is incredulous, the minister thought, that this event is not engraved in my memory.

'Godless louns, drunk as the deil, and wae the brains o bairns. Nae doubt they did it tae warm their backsides haeving little ither protection for them.'

'Was anyone hurt?'

'Na, na, just bairnish mischief which sensible folk kept clear o.'

187

'Well I suppose it could be said that this fine new kirk is some recompense.'

'Aye, aye, it could be said, though for mysel I liked the auld ane fine.'

The minister hesitated. The old man waited, docile he seemed as his pony.

'Actually I'm looking for a friend of mine, Mr Andrew Gilmore who made the journey here with me.'

'Andra, aye, I spoke wae him earlier in the day, a weel respectit man. He'll likely as no be in Mither Bruin's, whaur he aye bides when he's in Trig.'

'The inn?'

'Aye, aye, ye could ca it that, forbye it sounds a muckle grand kind o name. I'll tak ye there if yer seeking Andra.'

'Is it a respectable place?'

'Elspeth Bruin, Sir, is maist respectable and much respectit, an will allow neither singing nor swearing, and drinking only in moderation.'

'Then as I presume it's close by I'll be most grateful . . .'

The old man appeared grateful to be able to avert his eyes. He nudged his pony into a walk and the minister followed him for the fifty yards which separated them from the inn.

It gave no sign of being an inn. Indeed it gave no sign of being anything other than a clay cottage. As they reached it, Andrew Gilmore himself appeared at the door. He and Robert Glen saluted each other with that intimate easy grace which the minister knew he would never be able to emulate. Robert Glen turned to the minister and raised his bonnet, remarking unnecessarily, that as he had now found him that he sought he would be on his way.

The minister thanked him and he kicked his pony into a trot, hurrying now, the minister thought, probably resenting the appropriation of his time. The minister felt an odd relief at being with Andrew once again.

'A kindly old man, I think,' he said.

'Dour enough, there are merrier folk in Trig, but as ye say kindly. But come awa in and let us hae a bit talk. I bide here whenever I'm in Trig, for, as ye'll hae nae doubt noticed, I am not the Reverent Gilmarten's favourite Christian.'

'When you next come to Trig, Andrew, I hope you will stay

with me.'

The minister followed Andrew inside. He took him into a small private apartment, avoiding the main room of the cottage where the other men sat. A large stout old woman appeared with two mugs of ale. Andrew introduced the minister. For a moment the woman's face seemed utterly confused, and then, as if resolving herself she said:

'I keep a very respectable house here minister, which the Lord has granted tae me in my auld age sae I will not be a burden on the parish, and whaur Godly men can get moderate refreshment.'

'I do not doubt it,'

'The Reverent Gilmarten has cast a few doubts frae time tae time.'

'I am not the Reverent Gilmarten.'

Andrew Gilmore's eyes twinkled.

'As ye can surely see, Elspeth, he is a far bonnier man, and in my humble judgement a truer Christian.'

The woman looked reproachfully at Andrew. The minister concealed the irritation he felt. There was, he thought, no middle way with these people, either he was an inhabitant from another plane or he was Andrew Gilmore's boon companion.

The old woman bowed slightly and retreated. The Borderer turned to face the minister. The merriment had gone out of his eyes.

He has divined, the minister thought, my embarrassment, and despises it. His pride has been pricked, and he is also slightly drunk, and he is accusing me of forsaking our camaraderie of the hills now that I am in what is soon to be my own parish.

'Well, Andrew, I cannot apologise for the Reverent Gilmarten, can I? Nor have I any wish to; his attitudes are his own. He has invited you to supper.'

'Nae doubt wae a bit jolt he has, for I doubt if he wad hae me ower his doorstep itherwise. But as a free christian I think I'll insist on haeving my supper here amang folk that like me.'

'What is it between you?'

'Little enough, or sae I hae thought, and that tae dae wae the past. Marten Gilmarten ye might weel ken, was very weel thought o by them that had authority ower us then, and by a certain adroitness he is in these changed times still very weel thought o.'

'Perhaps he acted for the best as he saw it. You yourself have told me that not everything that happened in the past was wise.'

'Wad the Lord hae us aye be wise? Why auld Erskine wad insist that it is earthly wisdom that has damned this place, while ithers wad insist that it was Godly madness. Weel minister, some nae doubt war mad, and some war richt according tae their ain lichts, and wrang according tae the authorities, and nae doubt that drove the King and the gentry mad. But maist, minister, war just poor desperate folk driven out o their biggins by oppression.' The minister drank his ale slowly. There was no point at which he could dispute with Andrew. No point at which he could disentangle his spider's web of history. For a moment he thought of Sawney Bain's bloody and tormented pilgrimage with an awful compassion, as if the Devil himself had run amok in this land and its ignorant people could only be blamed for having failed to recognise him. Andrew sat back and slowly started to refill his pipe. The minister remembered the subtle and terrifying hand of Bain.

'That oppression, minister, is still here, and aiblins it will aye bide wae us, and the Reverent Gilmarten will aye say that ye ought tae submit tae it in God's name, kenning yer betters like he has done and ye will prosper like he has done. And he has tae, him and the present Doig being very close, and gien Doig's influence in Edinburgh that can dae him nae hairm at awe. And of course under Gilmarten's influence Doig built a new kirk when the Hielanmen burnt the auld ane doun, and nae doubt ilka body maun bless him for that.'

'That was a praiseworthy act surely?'

'Och nae doubt it was, seeing that it was his ain king and his ain government, as it was at that time, that brought the Hielanmen doun in the first instance on purpose tae chastise us, which Doig welcomed, and in truth even the Hielanmen had little taste for.'

The minister knew that he feared their judgement, and he knew that they would still give it. In these times it would be silent, or rising only to a murmur, but it would be as relentless as ever for all that – and utterly circumscribed by the primitive narrowness of their beliefs. And yet, it was the church which had made these people what they were now, stamping its doctrines with an iron purpose on their primitive peasant minds, on their barbarous, riding, raiding past, and it was the church that was ultimately responsible for what they were now.

The minister glanced across at Andrew. The man's features appeared suddenly subdued.

'Pardon me, minister, I am ranting a bit, and as we will pairt the morn it's a poor way tae pairt.'

He had kept silent, the minister thought, in the face of Gilmarten's discourtesy in order not to embarrass him, and he had kept silent in the face of an insult to his friend because it was politic to do so.

'Andrew, I have never been an enemy to plain speaking but I am apprehensive. Do you think I will be of any use here?'

'Och minister, I hae telt awe that I hae met that yer a gude and Godly man, and they replied : "Sae ye sae Andra sae ye sae, and that is very fine, but we sall wait and see." '

☆

The Reverent Gilmarten ate well. Duck and wine graced his table, and if he drank his wine in moderation it was still very good wine. The Reverent Carmichael had eaten plainly and drank ale with his meals – a tough soldierly frugality it had appeared to the minister then and he had found it admirable. Now the minister was reliving the pleasure of a very good dinner such as he had not had since leaving Holland. When he offered his congratulations, Marten Gilmarten's eyes registered a modest squinting delight.

'Do not think that I feast like this every day Sir, but knowing that your journey had been moderately arduous, and the fare along the way mutton, oats, and potatoes, the laird was kind enough to lend me his cook and make me a present of a few seasonable birds.'

'You must thank the laird for me.'

'I have already done that Sir, and no doubt you will have

191

ample opportunity to do it yourself in the future. The laird, Sir, is not the man to see the Kirk or its servants starve.'

Three generations of Doigs passed through the minister's mind. The family had prospered. The present Sir John Doig was a member of parliament and a man of business, who, as well as his lands in Trig owned part shares in a number of trading ships. He thought of Andrew Gilmore's bitterness. There was more than one reason why Andrew preferred to eat among his own people.

When he had arrived for dinner without Andrew, the expression on Marten Gilmarten's face was such that the minister became acutely aware that he had confidently anticapated this outcome, and would have been more surprised by his presence than his absence.

'So the bold reiver does not condescend to eat with us?'

For a moment the minister was astounded. He had meant to formally apologise for Andrew, now he felt he was the custodian of that man's honour, and yet, he had not been able to say anything to defend it. The Reverent Gilmarten, as if both aware and entirely unconcerned by his discomfiture, became almost merry, slipping as he could, and the minister had observed he did frequently, from his scholarly English into the language of the countryside.

'Weel, nae doubt he's happier in an alehouse making mischief amang his ain kind.'

The minister had felt trounced.

'I hardly think Andrew is a mischief maker. Indeed I am impressed by how well he is respected throughout the countryside. And apart from his generous service to me, I have seen him on a number of occasions behave in a true and unostentatious Christian way.'

'Why Sir, dinna mistake me, dinna mistake me.' Gilmarten's eyes danced with a malicious glee. 'I hae nae doubt, nae doubt at awe, that Mr Gilmore is a maist worthy man, but as I hae intimated previously, he has his ain lichts, and it's my belief that for the health and prosperity of our nation and its people there should be but ane licht in the land, the true and loyal licht o the Reformed Kirk, recognised by the blessed King William. And that Kirk has a duty Sir, tae shine forth baith kindly and stern, and tae rebuke misguided opinion which has sarely plagued this land in the past, and if not rebuked will nae doubt dae sae again. I think my meaning will become plainer tae ye when ye are mair familiar wae the place and its unhappy history, which is weel worthy o study. Now let us praise the Lord and eat, and hae nae mair on the subject o our worthy moss-trooper.'

Marten Gilmarten had taken him by the hand as if he was a schoolboy and thrust him towards the table. The minister's defences collapsed before the squint-eyed pastor's unexpected gaiety, which could be switched off in the presence of the maid or the cook and bubble up again as soon as they had gone. Indeed as soon as the minister himself had relaxed into it Gilmarten changed.

'And now Sir, tell me your opinion of this town of Trig?'

'I can have formed no opinion as yet. The people that I have met with so far have behaved very civilly, a Mr Robert Glen in particular. But as you advise, I should, and intend to study them and their history. Andrew has taught me much . . .'

'Sir, there was tae be nae mair on the subject of Mr Gilmore, wha nae doubt has a hundred stories tae tell. But ye see Sir, the Kirk must set aside these tales as bairnish things, whose constant re-telling can only keep the people in ignorance and hamper its work.'

Gilmarten raised his hand as if anticipating an interruption. When there was none he lowered it, his eyes squinting cheerfully.

'The point I am trying to make Sir, is that it is not only a reforming mission the Kirk has, but a civilising one. In my opinion they gang hand in hand. It will not be many years now before there is a complete union between Scotland and England – of which I approve. It will strengthen the Reformed Kirk, and there will be many fine opportunities for a Christian, industrious and quiet folk. But nae place at awe for mad auld brawls, or the memory o them, which are in maist cases mair tales than truth, stoked by folk wha's recollection o them is, if not dishonest, I wad never say that, but unsound and fanciful, as indeed some o their religious and political tenets hae been. Religion Sir, will not, cannot, allow itself to be a cloak ever again for seditious politics, but must lift its strong right hand against them.'

Marten Gilmarten's voice softened. He lowered his eyes.

'I hae written a book on the subject, Sir. Not out of vanity or pride ye understand, but in humble, aye fearful recognition o the tasks and duties that lie ahead, and the burdens that have to be borne, and tae while awa my time in Trig. Its subject is the duties o the Kirk and the duties o the people in this new Scotland o ours. It has had some small recognition in Edinburgh, the laird's efforts not mine, which would be unseemly. I am contented that it is done and may serve as a small bricht licht o guidance. I hae left a copy in the library here which I hope might be o some interest, and some usefulness tae ye.'

'I am honoured Sir, and grateful.'

'Na na, nae honour and even less gratitude, I am an auld man and ye are a young ane, but we share the same tasks and the same burdens.'

'As I am new and ill-informed about the country, and somewhat ashamed of that fact and anxious to correct it . . .'

The minister hesitated. A vision of the depthless despair of what he did know rose before him. It seemed to him then that the stench of that could not be driven out by any number of books and theories. Marten Gilmarten's slight frame appeared to quiver before his eyes.

'What would you say is the state of the Highlands at the present time, seeing as they do form a part of the country?'

'That is a very pertinent question, Sir. Which in my book I deal with at some length, for it is true as you say that, somewhat to our disgrace, the Highlands are part of Scotland. They are, for the most part, as barbarous as King James observed they were a century ago, a land of Canaan in our midst, which must and will be subdued. There are Papists there, and Prelatists, and these are the more civilised parts, for the greater part the most sacred oath they know they swear upon the blade of a dirk. Oh Sir, there is a great and Godly work to be done there, and a cloak of darkness to be lifted, and a stern mercy to be visited upon them. Aye, and nae doubt there will be an Amalekite sword tae be beaten doun before that benighted, Godless, breekless, shirtless, pestilential race can by the grace of our Lord be translated into something you or I would recognise as civilised. They make us a laughing stock among our neighbours, whose own ignorance is considerable,

194

and who can hardly understand the difference between bare-arsed Donald with his broadsword and Christian Scots in broadcloth and hodden grey. But until we are rid of them Sir, or hae clothed them decently, the civilised world can hardly be expected to respect us.'

'But has this good work been started?'

'Barely Sir, barely. It has begun, but it will be a long work. The commonality for the most part speak no English. The only trades they know are murder and rapine and the driving of cattle. The only freedom they know is to be at the beck and call of some swaggering chieftain, while they, and he, snap their fingers at the law of the land, the majesty of the king, and ocht that disna tak their fancy, aye even at the Kirk itself. To these clannit folk Sir, the Kirk must and will be, an Israel in their midst.

'Education Sir, as befits their station in life. Instruction in the tenets of true religion. Respect for the law and those that are set in lawful authority over them. Decency in dress and the habits of industry. And for them that will not acquire these habits, why let them gang sodgering in the King's army.

'That Sir, is the policy which I set out in my book, and if it is carried out with vigour, and Christian charity, and such Christian sternness as may be required, in your lifetime, aye and perhaps with God's help in my own, the Highlands will be as the rest of Scotland, a quiet and a profitable place.'

The minister went to bed early pleading tiredness. The room he had been given was the best he had slept in since leaving Edinburgh. He stood at the window looking out across the fields to the treeless hills where wolves could still be found. He felt utterly alone. Gilmarten had prayed with him and left him, his features glowing with an inordinate satisfaction. He had enlightened the minister on all aspects of the country and the parish and cheerfully claimed him as his disciple.

The minister thought of Andrew Gilmore's contempt, justified perhaps, according to his own ideas, but at least Marten Gilmarten had a vision of a prosperous, orderly, and peaceful future, a vision in which he had faith.

He glanced at Agnes Douglas's book nestling innocently in his saddle-bags. She had promised him, her ancient frame quivering with tormented fury, that she would come again to

195

Trig. Now that he had seen Trig it hardly seemed a significant enough birth place for such a storm. And yet, as surely as Gilmarten had assumed the power to negate the past in his conversation she had assumed a greater power to resurrect it in the minister's mind.

☆

We bided wae the People o the Mist for some time, and for a while it was a perhaps a gude time, for I mind it as gude, and I learned much about them and their language. When we heard news o the rest o the country it seemed tae be much as before wae Montrose winning great victories, and nane it seemed in the Hielans or the Lawlands being able tae stop him.

When I heard o these things I thought o Sawney and wad talk wae Steenie about him, and he found ane o Patrick Roy's folk that was ganging back tae join the Graham, and charged him tae inquire as tae whether or not Sawney was still about and tae gie him a message.

I telt Catriona about this but awe she said was,

-Dae ye believe that he is alive and weel?

I said that I did, but for nae better reason than that I could not imagine him deid. She said that was reason enough for the deid had ways o letting their friends ken that they were deid, and nae doubt haeving not done sae, he was alive.

It was only on occasion that she wad speak like this, and aye wae a sureness that was baith beyond contradiction and understanding, and aiblins it was beyond sense tae, but at that time I said naething mair tae her on that subject.

It was some time after that when we were riding doun, as we often did, frae Catriona's well, when awe at ance out o a lang silence she said,

-I think the glen will soon not be sae peaceful.

I asked her what she meant, but she just said that she was not yet sure, but that she had spoken tae Patrick Roy and telt him tae bring the people in and he had sent out runners that very morn.

I asked her, and I mind I spoke unco quietly when I did

196

sae, if she thought that we were tae be attacked.

She answered that aye aiblins she did, for she had seen armed men and men on horses and it might weel be that they concerned us.

She said nae mair for a time, but when we parted she looked at me unco closely and said,

-Agnes Dhu, I maun gang and see my faither, but if ye sleep this night, as I am yer gude friend keep yer steel coat and yer weapons by ye, but say naething tae any bar Steenie o what I hae said. I may be wrang in what I hae seen and I may be right, but it is for Patrick Roy tae dae what he thinks best.

She hugged me close tae her then and said that whatever cam tae pass I was not tae be afraid, for they had lived through these things before, and wad dae sae again, and she wad bide wae me.

Her warning, and her conviction in it, were sae great that I think few wha heard it could discount it entirely. Indeed when I telt Steenie he didna scoff as I thought he might, but just said quietly,

-It's true that Patrick Roy has been calling in his people. No wae any great urgency, but quietly, and awe armed.

-Dae ye think then, I asked him, laughing a bit, -that Catriona o the Mist can indeed see things that are yet tae happen?

-Och I ken not, but if swords and guns are Patrick Roy's orders tae the clan, I think we maun keep ours close by.

While we had lived in the glen Steenie had occupied himsel tending tae folk's hurts, and here and there delivering a bairn, which was a strange thing for a man tae dae but he had an unco skill at it, and the Hielanfolk had a great faith in him, and love o him for it, sae that baith they and their chief wad hae been weel pleased if we had settled amang them forever, but Steenie wad say naething tae that.

But that night Patrick Roy himsel cam tae visit us, tae consult he said, wae the wisest man he kent. And for awe he made that small joke there was little doubt as tae how earnestly he meant it, and indeed much o the grandness had gone out o his manner and a seriousness had cam ower him, and he was, as Steenie said later, now a Hielan chief wae his people tae think about. Even when Steenie poured him out some whisky as was proper, he seemed little inclined tae that either.

-I ken not, he said. -That Catriona has the sight has been proved on many previous occasions, and she is a careful, canny lass wae her gift, and in her speech.

Steenie asked him if awe the things that Catriona predicted cam tae pass?

-No they dae not, but she hersel never claims that they dae. But in my experience a gude half o them are true, and if every warning o danger she gies dis not come tae pass, nae serious danger has ever struck that she has not warned about. And this time she thinks that it is mair than just a bit foray, horse and foot she has seen.

-Argyll maybe, Steenie said.

Patrick Roy shook his heid.

-Why should Macalein More attack me now when he might need me as a friend later, and for the time, apart frae a few lads on either side as prudence dictates, I hae kept my people quietly at hame. But wha can truly ken what a Campbell will dae, bar that it will aye be for his ain advantage. But I hae heard that Colkeitach is awa recruiting amang his ain kinsmen and the clans o the West, and they want the Graham tae lead them intae the heart o Argyll itsel, right tae Macalein More's front door.

-Jamie Graham on the ither hand, nae doubt tired o running about the hills winning victories that bring him nae real advantage, wants tae lead the army South, aye and intae England. Sae aiblins there is a bit division there, and my kinsman says that Colkeitach and his people will not follow him tae help King Charles unless he strikes King Campbell first.

-Jamie Graham, Steenie said, -may be a gude captain, but Argyll is a damned big place. It is Macalein More's boast that he alane has the keys tae his mountains.

-There are ways intae Argyll, why I hae taen them mysel, but tae tak an army wad I think be taking it on its last march.

Steenie said he thought sae tae, and nae doubt if Macalein More heard about it he wad smile a bit, which was not a thing he did often. But he thought that Montrose's hale army, bonny fighters as they were, maun be a sare trial tae him, not obeying orders and marching whaur they were telt like proper sodgers.

-But what Patrick, he asked, -dae ye intend tae dae, about these ither sodgers, whaever they might be, wha might or might not be marching towards us?

-I hae scouts out, and men enough in the passes, and the rest are in quiet readiness. If they come upon us this night or the next they will not catch us in our beds.

Steenie right awa said that if that was the nature o affairs there wad be nae sleep for him that night. Patrick Roy thanked him saying that he had expected naething less, but that we were not tae worry. The Gregorach kent how tae keep their glen.

When Patrick Roy had left I looked at Steenie and asked him if he really thought there was gaen tae be a fight. He just smiled and said that it wad hae been very impolite tae cast aspersions on Catriona's prophesying. Still, we should arm oursels and show oursels willing, for in the Hielans if ye slept under a man's roof ye fought the enemies wha cam tae his door wha ever they might be.

They did not come that night, or the next, but Catriona wad not say that she had been mistaken, and Patrick Roy wad not lift the alert, nor did his people slacken their watching, and tae me their conviction just seemed tae grow. Steenie said that was perhaps nae mair than the effect o the situation, and Catriona saying openly now that she hoped she was wrang but felt that she was not. Privately she telt me that the sound o battle thundered day and night in her ears, and before her een, sae that she dared not say that she was wrang.

It was on the fifth or sixth night, some time after midnight, that Catriona rushed intae our room dressed in a man's plaid wae a sword and dirk by her side and a musket in her hand.

-They hae cam, she said quietly. -They hae cam as I said they wad come. Four hundred Campbells and Southern sodgers, and twa hundred horsemen as I said there wad be. They are being checked at the pass but soon they will be here.

She spoke these words wae a fierce light dancing in her een and her red hair tied back under her bonnet, and aiblins kenning all alang that we had gien but little credit tae her prophecies. But now there was nae time for praise or blame, why there was little time for any thoughts at awe but just tae snatch up our weapons.

I had thought lang in the time we waited on the possibility of this hour coming tae pass. And while only half believing that it wad I had resolved mysel tae neither hesitate or be feart in any actions that it was necessary tae tak, forbye haeving nae real idea o what these actions might be, but now Steenie just said,

-Gang wae Catriona and be guided by her in awe things.

And Catriona tossed her heid in the air and said, aye, we had wark tae dae.

We ran out o the door o the house, and tae be sure there was little doubt about anything now, as men wae weapons rushed tae their positions, and Steenie gied us baith a quick kiss, and the sudden thought that we might never kiss again, seemed baith a real thing and an impossible thing in a way that I canna weel describe. And aiblins the blude was running in my heid in a way that it had never run before, for I kent about battles now, forbye that at the time what I kent seemed of little purpose. But Catriona took me by the airm and we ran tae whaur a host o women and bairns were gaithered, many o the women themsels armed wae swords and muskets and bows and arrows.

Catriona shouted tae them, and flanked by twa sturdy Hielanmen wha had been detailed tae guard us, we set off up the narrow pass which rose out o the glen.

We could hear weel enough that the fight was in earnest now, and we could see fire frae muskets blazing out in the dark. As we ran I mind thinking o the numbers, and the fact that the People o the Mist were less than their enemies, and they had horse as weel. But I also discovered why these folk loved the mist, for intae it and the night we just disappeared, auld and young and bairns, just leaping ower the rocks like goats.

It was at a bend in the pass that Catriona shouted out

that we were pursued, and frae our rear we could hear the shouts o men wha had broken through the line, or out-flanked it, or crept ower the hills by stealth. I ken not which, but that they were now on our tail there was nae doubt, and at a very narrow part o the pass which had sheer rock on ane side and dropped sharp doun intae the glen on the ither, Ranald and Donald, which were the names o the twa Hielanmen, got ready tae mak a stand while we ran on. At a certain point Catriona made awe the folk tae lie doun, and them that had guns and longbows were tae mak them ready, and she drew her sword and I drew mine, and I mind weel how we looked, ane untae the ither.

-There are not many, she said. -About six or seven.

There was aiblins a bit mair than that, I canna say for certain, but they crashed against Donald and Ranald wha fired their guns and roared out their battle slogans, and wae their targes held high in front o them and their broadswords whirling round their heids sae that they flashed in the moonlight like the flames o a fire, they threw themsels upon their enemies, and for awe that these enemies could dae they wad not tak ane backward step.

Never hae I seen twa men wha fought sae fiercely. Some wha cam on had their heids split tae their chins and were pitched ower the pass, some tae scream their last as they fell, while ithers were silent haeving already screamed their last. And then Donald, wha was fighting, it seemed tae me, against twa or three at ance, had his body run clean through wae a lance sae that the point thrust itsel out o his back, and he himsel went ower the edge taking the spear that had killed him wae him.

And now the man wha had thrust it was drawing his sword tae charge through the gap he had made. I saw him very clearly in the moonlight, nae Hielanman, but a Lawland sodger in hodden grey wae a Godly slogan on his lips, and aiblins at that moment I thought o naething at awe, but I raised my pistol and pulled the trigger when he was right in the line o it, and the ball caught him straight in the face and just blew his heid clean awa.

At that Catriona gied out a wild fierce yellach, and I kent

now that this was a real fight as anither man, a Hielanman leapt intae the spearman's place wae a great shout, and Ranald wha was now fighting like a man demented made a cut at him wae his broadsword which caused him tae jump, and Catriona fired at him wae her musket. The ball caught him but did not kill him and on he cam, and forbye she met him wae her ain sword his weight was sae great that it just carried her doun under him, himsel bleeding badly, and I looked for a spot tae lunge at, feeling like a loun for I dared not cut in the dark.

Then awe at ance Catriona jumped like a cat out frae under him, and grabbing him by the beard she sunk her teeth intae his throat, hanging like a wolf upon a stag as he tore at her wae his hands, and she tore at his face wae her hands. And whether he wad hae torn the teeth frae her heid or she wad hae torn the flesh frae his throat, I ken not, but I saw my chance then, and caring nought for anything on earth I took my broadsword in baith my hands and brought it doun on his heid, and his hale body gied a terrible jump beneath the blade, and Catriona tore hersel free wae a great lump o his flesh between her teeth, and I cut and hacked at any part o him that I could see until at last he fell.

Catriona jumped tae her feet then, and spitting out his flesh, yelled tae Ranald that it was now time tae run. And that man wha's body and sword baith seemed tae be running wae blude, cut doun the man that was attacking him, and then awe three o us were running hard doun the track.

At first it seemed tae me that we were running intae naething but blackness and that we wad certainly be cut doun frae behind, when Catriona pulled me tae ane side, and there kneeling in the heather were awe the women wae their guns ready, twa lines o them, and when them that were pursuing us cam upon them it was ower late, for they were barely three strides awa when the guns roared as ane, and tae my een it was as if a great tongue o fire had just picked them up and tossed them intae the air, and when it cleared awa only twa were alive, a Lawland sodger wae his legs broken, and a Hielanman wae an airm, and it seemed half his chest shot awa.

These twa Ranald killed, mercifully I thought, wae twa

strokes o his sword, and then awe let out a great yellach which was the battle slogan o their folk, and Catriona cried tae load up the guns for there might be mair.

There was nae mair. When we looked doun intae the glen Patrick Roy's fine house in which we slept was awe on fire and horsemen were riding about it, and Ranald unslung his longbow and started shooting at them, but Catriona telt the women not tae fire their muskets, which at that range wad dae little damage and leave them defenceless.

It seemed that the horsemen, forbye they were at the door o Patrick Roy's burning house, were in a panic and kent not whaur tae gallop next, and Ranald said that he thought the foot had been driven back and now the riders were alane, and kenning naething o the country they galloped off doun the glen, and Catriona cried out that the bones of their ancestors wad curse them if they ever returned.

It was clear tae me now what a mistake they had made, and in their confusion were riding awa frae their ain side, but nae doubt they thought that there maun be anither way out and a hard gallop wad mak it.

In the early light o that morning I could see clearly that nane o these things wad wark, and they were caught, first in a storm o bullets and arrows, and as their horses tripped on the bogs and the rocks I could see the horsemen just chopped frae the saddle by great swinging axes, and the four or five that I saw wha managed tae cut themsels free, still kent not whaur they were, but now they turned and raced back doun the glen wae the Hielanmen running after them, near as fleet as their horses, and shooting their arrows as they ran. Twa they brought doun in this fashion, but I could not see what happened tae the lave and it may be that they got out.

But now a queer quietness descended ower awe, wae just here and there a gun gaen off, and soon there was nae mair o that, and only Patrick Roy's gude house burned and cracked in the wind o a fire that was now worth naebody's strength tae put out.

-Five times that house has burned since I was a bairn, Catriona said. -And now this is the sixth time.

203

-Weel, it is ower now for this night I think, Ranald said, and for the first time I looked properly at this man wha had fought wae sic fierceness, and I could see that he had many cuts on him, and the front o his shield was studded wae pike heids that he had caught there and then chopped off wae his sword, and he was just a blackbearded Hielan kern o about thirty-five years of age, and there seemed about him now a great peacefulness, and Catriona turned tae him and embraced him and kissed him.

-Ranald Macgregor, ye are a very bonny fighter.

I tae kissed him, and felt, I mind very clearly, a great relief cam ower me as I did sae, but he just smiled dourly and said that he maun gae and find the body o his kinsman Donald.

It was truly ower now it seemed. We could see Patrick Roy waving tae us in the light frae his burning house. Catriona spoke tae the women wha were lying in the heather wae their muskets ance again primed, and they let out a cheer as they rose tae their feet. And still tae me they were a strange sight as they marched past us stepping ower awe the bodies o them that had been slain, some wae their muskets on their shoulders, ithers wae pistols and dirks in their hands, and for awe that I could see there was hardly a bairn wha could stand upright wha did not hae a weapon o some kind even if it was nae mair than a bit cudgel. I looked at Catriona as she stood wae her sword held high saluting them as they went past, and tae my een it was as if her hale body had swelled up wae pride.

-The Campbell, she cried out, -thinks we are nought but skinned wolves. Weel let him think sae, skinned we might be, but we are not without teeth tae bite.

I looked ower at the body o the man wha's throat she had bitten and thought that a wolf wad not hae been dis-pleased wae the job she had done. She, nae doubt following my een, reached out and took my hand in hers, and I said that forbye Steenie and Sawney had taught me a bit about how tae use my weapons I had never had need tae test them before now.

-Agnes Dhu, she said quietly, -henceforth ye and I sall be as ane, what ere befalls, or whaur ere the parts o that ane chance tae be, and the friends o Catriona o the Mist wha are poor and few but loyal and brave, will aye be your friends, and as lang as the True People hold this glen, which sall be forever, ye sall hae a hame here.

I thanked her and said that I could offer nae great things in return haeving nae hame, and nae friends apart frae Steenie, and about Sawney I could say nought. She just clasped my hand tighter at that and said that she liked that fine for aiblins I wad be tempted tae bide here.

I said nought then, and we walked back doun the track tae meet Patrick Roy wha embraced us wae tears o anger and joy, I kent not which was foremaist, in his een, and I could see that he tae had been hard fighting.

He telt me first that Steenie was weel and unhurt, and then he said that in awe the years that he had lived, and awe the men that he had kent, he had kent few that equalled Steenie, for not only had he fought bravely in the fight, but he was now tending tae the hurts o them that had been wounded.

Catriona asked him how many there were. He replied that sae far he had lost eleven men but the ither side had lost many mair. Catriona then telt him that Donald wha had been wae us had also been killed, and he said that sadly that added anither tae the number, and he damned the Campbells tae Hell for it had been a maist unfair attack, and wae Lawland sodgers tae, and forbye they had stolen thirty cows, he had captured a dozen or sae gude horses, but he cared naething for any o these things, or for his burned house, but only for his people that had been lost.

Catriona then telt him awe that had happened tae us, saying muckle mair o what I had done than strict truth wad hae allowed. But he embraced us ower and ower again, and there were tears in his een, and he said that frae this day he wad think that he had twa dochters, for the True People kent weel how tae cleave tae them that loved them, few though they might be.

There was an auld weariness in his voice when he spoke then, and aiblins he was thinking that he had cam a lang way, and awe o it dounhill, frae his great ancestor wha had been King o the Scots a thousand years ago. He gaithered

himsel it seemed tae me wae a sigh and said tae come awa
for he had anither house, not sae big but fine enough, and a
prisoner in it that he had gien quarter tae, and that he
hoped wad tell him the meaning o this affair.

It was at this point that Steenie himsel cam running up,
and ignoring awe else he took me intae his airms and gied
me a great kiss. When we broke awa I looked carefully at
him and his gude buff coat was cut tae ribbons, and there
was a dent in his breastplate frae a musketball, but nae ither
sign o deidly wound.

-But damn it awe, he said, -Hielanmen fight wae a stubbornness that is beyond awe reason.

He then telt Patrick Roy that a man had deed as he was
tending him, an auldish man by the name o Neil Ban.

It was as if Patrick Roy had been struck again and had
nae desire tae conceal his grief or his anger.

-Let the bard sing o them awe, he cried. -Let him sing o
Donald o the Mist, and now bid him sing o Neil Ban, wha
was born in the very year that I was born, and was ower
gude a man tae be cut doun in the night by a Campbell
sword.

We walked then ower tae Patrick Roy's second house
which lay at the far end o the glen. On the way we saw the
people gaithering themsels ance mair intae their biggins,
some making shift in their neighbours', for Patrick Roy's
house was not the only ane that had been burned. And
whiles some o the heid men o the clan wad come up and
report on this and that, and Patrick Roy wad embrace them
awe and tell them tae mak sure that the women and the
bairns awe had roofs under which tae lie, and they wad
start tae rebuild in the morning.

They were a fell brisk folk, some o them still up on the
hill harrying their enemies and guarding against any surprise return. Steenie said that he thought there was very
little chance o that, and put forward the opinion tae Patrick
Roy that the attack had not been meant as a serious battle,
but just a bit warning.

The auld chief just shook his heid then.

-Mr Malecky, if ye will pardon me for being a man that
is slightly at a loss, what wae haeving a dochter wae the

sight, and a friend wae a deep and unco knowledge o ither men's motives.

-I hae been thinking, Steenie said, -and it gaes like this. Argyll wae the support o the army, Government, and Kirk, is harrying Jamie Graham. But he is not ower keen tae bring that man tae battle, kenning himsel that the Graham is by far the better captain and a defeat wad be a disaster frae which it wad not be easy tae recover. Sae he contents himsel wae letting Montrose win victories which bring him nae real advantage, however much they enrich wae plunder and keep up the spirits o his men.

-But Argyll also kens that there are many in the Hielans wha might just be tempted tae throw in their sword wae the Graham, and he reasons that a quick night visit tae their glens will keep his ain clansmen frae grumbling ower much, and will also let them that he visits ken what might happen should they leave their houses and their lands unguarded. Last night's affair, Patrick, was aiblins just a hint that the best and safest policy for ye wad be tae bide quietly at hame.

-Damn it man, I hae bided at hame, and I hae men wae Argyll. Is that not proof enough for him?

-And ye hae men wae Jamie Graham tae.

-I am a prudent man, that's awe, I hae my people tae mind and nane kens how this game will play itsel out.

-Weel that is my opinion. Yon foray last night was tae run off some cattle, burn yer house and nae doubt kill a few folk, a tap on the shoulder frae the lang airm o Macalein More. But the fight they got was I think a bit mair than they had sought.

-Damn his lang airm, he has spent ower lang in Edinburgh wae some damn queer folk if he thinks that killing my kinsmen and burning my house will incline me tae friendship and his Party.

-Och man, what dis he care for yer friendship, only for yer quietness.

I could see the annoyance warking in Patrick Roy's face, but he was in charge o himsel and listening tae Steenie. In the end he just nodded his heid.

-Ye may be right Mr Malecky, ye may be right.

-Fabius Maximus Patrick, nae doubt Macalein More kens his latin.

Fabius Maximus, Steenie said, was a Roman captain wha won wars without fighting, and Patrick Roy said that nae doubt Argyll was a half-brither tae him.

-But this sodger lad I have captured will maybe shed some further light.

In Patrick Roy's second house, which was a smaller and poorer place, we found the sodger, a cornet o horse, Steenie said, wha stood up as we entered. He was a tall young man wae a hurt airm which they had bound up for him, and his countenance, forbye it was white frae loss o blude, was resolute enough as he regarded us.

That I felt pity for him was nae mair than natural, for I kent right awa that here was a poor young man frae my ain country, wha kent not at awe what his wild enemies wad dae tae him, and was nae doubt saying his prayers and preparing tae face it bravely. But Patrick Roy just waved his hand at him in a manner, which if it was a bit ower grand, was generous tae.

-Sit doun Sir, sit doun. I ken weel that ye are hurt being mysel the man wha fairly beat ye and hae fairly gien ye quarter, and wham Patrick Roy has gien quarter tae is safe in Patrick Roy's house and amang Patrick Roy's people. But I wad ken yer name, Sir.

The sodger bowed slightly, and his face smiled and seemed tae relax a bit. He gied his name as Andrew Cleland, and when he spoke ye could see how weary and hurt he looked, and Patrick Roy called for whisky and ale, and wae his ain hands he poured it out and handed it tae him.

-Mr Cleland, I canna entertain ye as I might wish in happier times, seeing that ye hae burnt my gude house and driven me and my friends intae this cowshed, which is not tae my mind a fair thing tae dae.

-I am a sodger, Sir.

Steenie all this time had been tending tae his airm, at which task I helped him. It had been roughly bound tae stop the bleeding, and under the claith there was a muckle sword cut.

-I turned the edge Sir, turned the edge, or ye might weel

hae lost an airm, because I liked the look o ye, but ye maun pay mair attention tae yer guard.

-Why Sir, ye were weel enough protected by that door ye carry.

-Weel enough Sir, weel enough, but why should an auld man like me cam out frae behind this targe tae be killed?

If Patrick Roy's conversation had reassured the sodger, he had started a bit at hearing our voices. And when we telt him, which he could not fail tae ken, that we were indeed frae the South, and that Steenie had ance fought in the Covenant army, he turned on us, forbye the fact that we were tending him, a look o hatred sic as he had never turned on Patrick Roy.

-I am nae King's man, Steenie said, noticing this, -and far less am I the Graham's man. I was just paying my gude friend here a visit when his house was attacked, and it wad hae been a very poor man that wad just run awa, wad it not?

He held himsel very stiffly at that, drinking the whisky that Patrick Roy never stinted, and which nae doubt dulled his pain. But he hated us still, nae doubt thinking that whatever were our reasons, or whatever were our principles, we had damned strange friends that we visited. But Steenie spoke nae further by way o explanation, just saying,

-Yer airm will be fine man, and ye hae I think Patrick Roy's kindness and gude swording tae thank for it.

Andrew Cleland bowed again, but only tae Patrick Roy, and that chieftain wae perhaps a subtle change o tone said,

-Weel Sir, ye can thank me by telling me why my people hae been killed and my house burned? It canna be for just thirty cows, Argyll has men enough tae just quietly run off cows.

The sodger glanced around him as if suddenly alert and ance mair wary o his fate. Patrick Roy raised his hand tae assure him.

-Speak Sir, or dinna speak, as ye please, but it seems tae me that ye are a sodger and nae cattle lifter, and wad not hae cam here without orders.

-I ken not Sir, but as ye hae gien me leave tae speak I sall speak. Our troop o horse was sent frae Edinburgh tae assist and be commanded by the great Marquis of Argyll in his campaign tae apprehend and bring tae God's justice the cursed malignant James Graham. Baith him and his wolf pack o an army wha's hands are at this very minute reeking wae Godly blude, sparing nane that crosses his path and will not bow doun tae him.

Patrick Roy lifted himsel up maist loftily at that point, but now it seemed that the sodger himsel was in a rage, forbye he curbed it when Steenie gied him a look.

-That disna answer my question Sir. I hae done nane o these things, but could wae fair justice claim that they hae been done tae me, and awe I hae done is defend wife and bairns and house, the last being unsuccessful as ye ken. And I tae hae gude men wae Argyll, and it seems tae me that they might think it poor recompense for their services that their glen should be burned behind their backs.

The sodger ance again looked as if he thought his quarter was about tae be lifted, but Patrick Roy just poured him out some mair whisky.

-Then I ken not, he said after a bit hesitation. -I neither ken this country or wha dwells in it, but we were under Argyll's command, and if I believed ought I believed that ye were o the Graham's Party or were likely tae be sae.

-I am of nae man's Party but am chief o these folk and care only for them, and I hae gien evidence that I am nae murderer whatever Argyll says, and I ask o ye only that ye should speak this evidence whaur ever ye hear words tae the contrary.

-And now Sir, I think we should awa tae what beds are left tae us, and ye Sir, being hurt, sall hae the best bed there is, and when ye are fit tae ride yer horse and gear sall be returned tae ye, and ye sall ride frae this glen escorted by enough o my people tae see ye safely. And Sir, should ye ever choose tae return ye sall be the welcome guest o Patrick Roy Macgregor wha bears a King's name, forbye at the present time it is a very much maligned and slandered name, the very sound o it haeving been declared unlawful. But ye Sir, I trust will testify differently, and I sall thank God that I did not cut yer airm off. But my advice tae ye as an auld man tae a young is that ye should develop a better

210

style o guard, or get yersel a wooden door like mine.

Patrick Roy had laughed heartily when he said these last words, and it was very strange tae me tae see them laughing and joking and drinking wha had but lately been sic deidly enemies. I kent that Patrick was being cheerful in order tae assure the sodger lad that he wad not be killed, and the sodger was responding in like manner nae doubt grateful for that fact. And still when I thought of awe the folk that had deed that night it seemed tae me tae be without any sense.

When I lay in bed wae Steenie in what was now nearly the morning I said this tae him. He answered that sadly he maistly agreed, and what had started as a war tae free folk, had been turned on its heid, and aiblins was now nae mair than an auld Hielan brawl which he had nae desire tae fight in or be killed in.

I said then that it seemed tae me that he had fought willingly enough. Awe he said in justification was that Patrick Roy was his friend, and our host, and in an age o rash and ambitious chieftains and great folk he was a gude and canny chief tae his people.

-Ye canna blame him Agnes for fighting sae fiercely, for it is only by sic measures that these people survive at awe, and I think Argyll has made a mistake by harrying this glen and turning an indifferent man intae an enemy. The Gregorach are angry now, and Patrick himsel is very angry and bitter, and if this is tae be Argyll's policy in the Hielans there are gaen tae be very many bitter and angry folk, and for every ane that he frightens intae submission twa will run tae the Graham in defiance, and for gude or ill aiblins hard fighting sall end what principle began.

-If we werna excummunicates and could gang and dae what we pleased, dae ye ken what ye wad dae?

-If that witchery business had never happpened, then as like or not Sawney and mysel wad just hae ganged back tae the army o the Covenant, on the principle that a fight like this ane, ance started has tae be fought out for weel or woe. Forbye I confess I wad hae little taste for trooping alang behind Argyll in the harrying o folk's glens. Aye and aiblins I wad in truth hae little taste for the present policy o the

211

Kirk and State, which wants tae mak awe folk in Scotland, aye and in England, and nae doubt the hale warld, say their prayers according tae the Presbyterian light. Aiblins tae, I still think that Jamie Graham is the biggest danger tae the country just now and will hae tae be killed by somebody.

I thought then o Sawney that was wae the Graham and could mak nae sense o that thought. I thought o Catriona wae her grey een riding high aboun the mist, and I thought o her wae her teeth in yon man's throat, and I minded how his heid had split under my sword like a bullock under an axe. And I thought if in awe places it was the case that men drove against men in the name o principle, and religion, and King, and Kirk, then we might as weel bide here amang these wild folk wha cared for nane o these things and drove only for their meat.

-The war has cam here Agnes, and will not now gang awa.

These were Steenie's words at the time, and I remember very clearly looking at him as he spoke them, and perhaps I kent, as Sawney had kent, that his days o being a guiding light o reason were fading, blawn awa by the tempest o the times in which we lived. Forbye what he said then was true.

☆

The library of the manse of Trig contained the parish record, the parish register, the first and second books of discipline, an assortment of bibles, treatises and religious works. It had about it an odour of the past mouldering into dust which Marten Gilmarten swept aside.

'It is much as I found it Sir, and if some of it is of course essential, the most of it might excite the historian or the idly curious, though not I think for any great length of time. My own library, which might have interested you, is already on its way to Edinburgh.'

The minister smiled. Gilmarten's own work lay on the desk handsomely and simply bound in bright new leather. On the inside was inscribed in Gilmarten's elegant hand: 'To my successor to whom it may be of some small interest.'

'I think I will have some need to be curious, though I hope

it will not be construed as idle.'

'Anything new that interests you, the laird, seeing that he gangs often tae Edinburgh is only too happy to procure for you.'

'That is kind of him and I shall certainly take him up on it.'

'He is a learned man himself Sir, and he believes with great conviction in an educated Kirk. And indeed while he is in Trig he thirsts for learned company, as ye nae doubt will ance ye hae been here a bit. Cows and sheep and the husbandry and sheering o them, which are proper tae those wha hae a care o them, and vital tae the country's wellbeing, hae limits as subjects o discourse.'

'Who was the minister before you, Sir?'

'A Mr Thomas Seaton who died in the year 1681. A Godly man by all acounts though I never met him. And before that another Thomas, Stevenson I think was his name, but his time was short, coming in 1656 and dying in 1664.'

'Was there a Mathius Pringle that you know of, some time before that?'

Marten Gilmarten's eyes were suddenly, almost impudently alert.

'And what Sir, gars ye ask about him?'

'I read a short memoir of his in Edinburgh, concerning this place, my first introduction to it one might say.'

'An interesting introduction I imagine. He died in 1656, and indeed is buried in Trig kirkyard. He appears to have been a Godly man, and indeed in his time many said a great one, but deeply troubled, over much some might say by the affairs of his time. He wrote much and seemed strangely taken by an auld case of witchcraft and sorcery such as afflicts these places from time to time.

'He had political opinions too Sir, which he clung to with great resolution, which might have been fine in earlier days but were not so popular at his death, and were quite out of fashion by 1660. Indeed it may have been a blessing that he died when he did, for the broad and narrow opinion of him was that he was not the kind of man to rescind them, and in my opinion we had martyrs enough.'

'What happened to his writings?'

'Oh I think for the most part they were just quietly carted

awa. I cannot vouch for the fact, but it seems to me maist likely given the times. Indeed towards the end of his life he was in the opinion of some, not of quite sound mind, not mad of course, just mair affected by wordly events than he ought tae hae been.'

'The piece I read was of some interest.'

'Aye but to whom? In his time the land was in a state of rebellion, which may or may not have been wise. For myself I am inclined to believe that very few rebellions are wise.'

'Even against a wicked and ungodly king who obliges his subjects to behave in ways contrary to their conscience?'

'Och I see the gate and the path your ganging, sae dinna mistake me, there are extremities as our ain history shows, and I honour that history. But there is a price tae be paid for it, which is perhaps mair apparent tae us now than it was then.'

'Surely there must always be a cost incurred when right is obliged to arm itself against wrong?'

'Indeed sae Sir, but in my opinion the cost need not hae ower-run the cause in the way it did if it had been tempered wae a bit mair wisdom and restraint. Revolution by its very nature needs tae arm the people. It needs tae put swords intae the hands o people wha in a proper way o living wad hae nae need o swords, and in these circumstances ideas get intae their heids tae, which they hae nae proper skill in understanding. Perhaps, let us not be ower prideful, the Kirk itsel should hae taen mair heed o that, for baith these things are hard tae ding out again. Sae however necessary it was then, I pray and believe it will never be necessary again.'

'Having seen the countryside, and from my own conviction, I cannot agree more.'

'Aye Sir, praise God it is ower and the Lord has delivered us, a great mercy on a stubborn people wha hae sinned, aye and continue tae sin, against his licht.'

Gilmarten smiled grimly, his squint accentuating the appearance of a wading bird whose prey was seditious ideas. Suddenly his smile brightened and became almost satyrical.

'Here in Trig nowadays we have only the common sins of the creature to be dealt with, fornication, adultery, drinking, swearing, idleness, sabbath-breaking and non-attendance, are the lave o them, wae here and there a bit witchifying that has tae be looked intae, though sic mischief is rare now, Satan nae doubt kenning that the Kirk is truly in charge and is a fortress against him, muckle coward that he is.'

Gilmarten shepherded the minister down the stairs, his countenance gleaming with an elation which to the minister appeared very close to triumph.

'But having mentioned these iniquitous things ye will nae doubt ken how tae deal wae them, sternly, as I dae, for they can ding doun a Christian nation mair resolutely than a sword. To assist in this work the Kirk has its faithful eyes and ears in its elders, for it's a wee bit unbecoming for gentlemen like us tae gang a skulking in hedgerow and hillside inquiring which ploughboy has got his hand, as weel as ither things, inside which lassie's gown.

'They are all gude men, strang for the Kirk and weel tried by me, and indeed will be here shortly, being as anxious tae meet their new minister as ye nae doubt are tae meet them.'

Four elders were standing at the manse door. Gilmarten had spied them though the window. The minister watched the sly contentment spread across his features. He was proud of the discipline and order he had imposed on these once anarchic people. He strode purposefully and without haste to let them in. When he opened the door the four elders doffed their bonnets and Gilmarten slipped effortlessly into dialect.

'Come awa ben gentlemen, come awa ben and meet your new shepherd.'

The minister shook each hand as it was offered to him. He felt that old sensation of having no clear idea how to behave. He wanted to present unostentatious Christian gentleness, charity and duty, and yet he knew that respect tinged with fear was also necessary.

The most senior elder was Mathew Elliot, a short sturdy man with an iron-grey beard, and it appeared to the minister an iron-grey skin, out of whose elderly folds protruded two grey challenging eyes. A peasant, and by the standards of the area a prosperous one. The texture of his hand against the minister's was like parchment against silk.

The second was Walter Hyslop, the school dominie. A lean decayed man of perhaps fifty-five who confronted the minister with a menacing stoop and a zealot's eyes. Unlike his fellows he was formally and neatly attired in worn, black cloth. The third, James Hunter was bailiff to the laird, a man just past the prime of life with a round ruddy face and a well fleshed body. His hand was firm and confident. The fourth, William Noble, was also the laird's man.

All men of substance in their own way, the minister thought. And of course the laird himsel was an elder, though he spent most of his time in Edinburgh. They all eyed the minister with a docile inquisitiveness. Marten Gilmarten rubbed his hands together his eyes twinkling, like a man, the minister thought, who throve cheerfully on his neighbour's confusion.

'Weel gentlemen, I will not detain ye lang, seeing that this meeting was just as it were by way of introduction. Unless there is anything further ye hae tae tell me, anything further on Elizabeth Adams?'

The dominie's mournful body seemed to wend its way from a cadaverous stoop to a preposterous height.

'Fornication, minister, and the result is what the result aye is.'

'And the rascal fornicator wha is he?'

'Young William Black.'

'And what has he got tae say on the matter?'

'He is willing enough, and contrite enough, but Michael Adams the girl's father will neither let the girl out or see him, and cursed him in the street wae foul and blasphemous words.'

'Weel I think Michael Adams can be forgiven, if not excused. As for the culprits, let them come tae me before I leave, and Michael tae. Or on second thoughts I sall gang and see Michael mysel, for he must ken that what is done . . . Weel nae doubt he kens that himsel.'

☆

It was a day or sae after the fight in the glen that Catriona cam tae me and we rade up ower the hill tae her pool. And aiblins we were very quiet that day, each kenning without words what the ither thought. I kent that the shock o the fight was still wae me, sae that the very thought o it made my hale body shake queerly, and that many o the desperate things that had taen place in the darkness o that night could hardly be clearly recalled in the day. She had just embraced me and said that we baith had need o quietness and a quiet place.

We rade, I remember very clearly, on a warm bright morning past the People o the Mist, wha were ance again, for it was nae new thing tae them, building their biggins that had been burned. When we cam tae the water's edge she ance mair put her airms around me and kissed me, and I could see whaur her neck and shoulders were black wae the marks that the Hielanman had left on her in his frenzy when she had a grip on his throat.

-He has hurt ye?

She tossed her heid full high at that and dropped her gown tae her waist, and I could see that the marks reached tae below her breasts.

-When folk fight, she said, -ye ken very weel that they are nae mair than half-brithers tae fierce beasts for awe their brave appearance and song-making, which they dae tae keep their spirits up and their true thoughts hidden, for they ken very weel that in the extremity o the situation a wolf's thoughts will dae them, aye and might weel preserve them, when ither mair human things might desert them.

She looked at me then her grey een unco strange. And I minded again her wild Hielan yellach and the blude that ran frae her jaws.

-For now it is ower, and I hae brought ye here whaur the dirt and madness o the warld can be washed off, this being the only water that I ken that can dae this, it haeving been blessed lang ago by ane wha was o my name.

I felt little inclined tae laugh or smile then as I might hae done in the past. Catriona stripped off her gown and her plaid and stood naked, except for a silver dirk that she kept strapped tae her leg under her gown at awe times. But now she took that off tae and said that she wad swim in the pool and that I should join her.

I said that I had nae skill in swimming, but awe she said tae that was,

-Och and what does that matter, for cannot Catriona teach ye and see tae it that ye dinna droun?

I said nae mair then but just let her strip me and comb

217

out my hair, kenning and liking the gentleness o her hands.
And then she led me intae the pool and we lay doun in a
shallow part whaur she washed me, discovering as she did
sae, that I had a muckle bruize on my left side and breast
which I had got at some time in the fight. And then I
washed her for I was naething laith now. And if the water
had been cauld at first, it was a warm day and a warm
spring frae below nourished the pool. And Catriona wad
swim across it and back again, and indeed she was very
skillful at the swimming, sae that I wad allow her tae swim
across wae me in her airms, finding it pleasant and kenning
weel that she wad not let me droun.

In sic ways did we spend the hale day till it seemed that
the night that had been was now very far awa, and I
thought as I lay there feeling our flesh touching, that
woman's flesh was very different frae man's, as was the
touch o a woman's hand. And I thought tae that this was
the first peaceful place that I had lain in since leaving
Steenie's cave. And I kent then that I had a yearning for
peaceful places, nor did I care whether or not they were
poor in warldly things, for I had aye been poor in these
things.

Catriona said that awe the true-hearted wanted these
things. But when the false-hearted heard about them, they
snapped their teeth and their hands jumped tae their sword
hilts, and their loud voices declared that the warld should
gang on as it had aye ganged on, for only in sic a warld
could they prosper and profit. For wad not the True People
be a peaceful people if their enemies wad leave them in
peace, and gie back tae them awe that had been stolen frae
them.

I asked her then how her people had cam tae lose sae
much even tae their name. She just looked at me her een
shining ance again wae an auld passion..

-Why Agnes Dhu, she said, her fingers running themsels
ower my breasts as they liked tae dae. -Ye are ane o us now,
forbye that ye hae cam frae far awa, and ye maun ken. It
was a time, no sae lang ago, and we had been at the fighting
wae a very false folk called Colquhoun, and we had agreed
tae meet them at a place called Glen Fruin, and there a

218

treaty wad be made which wad end this fighting. And tae this treaty we took only enough men as was seemly and proper, and that in spite o a woman wae the sight wha warned that they wad play us false and bring a great host tae destroy us.

-Weel, her sight turned out, as sae often it dis, tae be speaking nae mair than the truth. But their treachery did them nae gude at awe, for awe their great host we routed them. And what did they then dae, them that were still living? Why did they not gang tae auld King James and whine and fawn about his feet, till he, being a very false-hearted man, declared them awe tae be his true friends, and their enemies wad be his enemies, and he wad deprive them o their ancient name, which was far mair royal than his ain, and he wad put them tae the horn and hae them hunted like wolves and not rest until awe were deid.

-Weel it turned out not as he wanted, but many he killed, and many he drove frae their lands, but still we are here and he is lang deid, nor hae I heard it said that his bairn is a happy man. Aye James Stuart's flesh is but dust but his curse gangs on and the ancient name o the Gregorach, which is our proper name, can now only be spoken amang friends, or at the point o a sword.

She clasped my hands tightly then, and her een were inquiring intae mine, and aiblins she thought I was thinking that there were aye twa sides tae every story, and aiblins I was thinking that, but my heart had gane out tae her in sic a way that I wad hae her side and be content.

-We sall aye be here, till the water in that pool runs dry, and that sall not happen till the earth itsel runs dry and nane sall care mair. That is our story Agnes Dhu. And whaur ere ye gang in the warld we sall aye be here, and sall want ye here, but treat nane that is called Colquhoun as yer friend.

I said that I had not sae far met any o that name, which was nae doubt fortunate. She laughed and said that was indeed sae.

I was very laith tae leave that place, as was Catriona. Sae much sae that we lingered weel intae the evening and watched the deer cam doun ower the hill. Before we left

Catriona pointed tae her breast.

-See Agnes Dhu, the marks are nearly gone now that were sae red and bludie this morning.

She declared that I had been as responsible for their healing as the water, and whether it was true or whether it was not I canna say, but I was becoming very Hielan-like and was just content that it was thought tae be sae.

☆

Marten Gilmarten went about his pastoral duties with energy and zeal. Yet the minister had not been with him two days when he found himself detecting another quality, a kind of glee in the chiding and scolding of his flock, or his bairns as he would frequently call them.

The minister had gone round all the cottages in the village with him, and occasionally the sight of some grey clad, hunger bitten figure, being lectured by the squint eyed pastor, produced an anguish within the minister that he could hardly contain. It was as if he saw beneath the reverently bowed head and acquiescing eyes, a contempt slinking behind the fear. A contempt of Gilmarten, he thought, but also a contempt that stretched far beyond him, that was almost infinite in its embrace, a kind of stoical malice that effectively erased any spiritual message, and indeed the spirit itself.

The Reverent Gilmarten was unaware of it. The people were unaware of it. Of that the minister was almost sure. It was a lonely revelation which had pierced only his soul, but having done so, it would neither retreat or submit to reason, but would grow with each new encounter, each new household, until the rigorously concealed horror of it was all the minister felt. Marten Gilmarten considered it his greatest achievement amongst these people that he had rendered them quiet and he could now return to Edinburgh and the greater duties that awaited him there.

'I never allow them to dispute with me Sir, on points of doctrine, and even less of politics. They have neither the learning nor the understanding for such matters.'

The minister now realised why Andrew Gilmore offended him so much. When Andrew had stopped by the manse to say goodbye, looking his usual stalwart self, it had amused him to see the almost uncontrollable irritation in Marten Gilmarten's eyes. And when the minister had urged Andrew to stay with him whenever he was in the area, and, quite conscious of the offence he was giving, said that he hoped it would not be too long, he could feel the depth of Gilmarten's silent wrath.

And yet he knew that Gilmarten was no fool. He was an adroit manager of his world. He could condescend to an elderly peasant with an earthy good humour one minute, and swell himself out with majestic sternness the next. His grasp of theology and the tenets of the Presbyterian religion was masterly, and he would employ them as firmly and as flexibly as he chose.

It was through Gilmarten's relationship with Sir John Doig, whom he manipulated and advised, and under whose patronage he thrived, that the minister first realised the full extent of the man's skills. 'Playing the laird,' Andrew Gilmore had called it. He supported the laird in everything, defended him in everything, and guided him with a discourse which he pretended not to observe, left the laird behind while flattering him in the process. If this served his flock in anything it was in stopping the man short of behaving like a total tyrant.

The laird had gripped the minister's hand in his own large soft one.

'This is a poor place Sir, but a gude and Christian ane. Is that not sae Master Gilmarten?'

'Indeed I believe it is, with its earthly shortcomings certainly, but nae mair than maist and less than many.'

The minister had looked into the small moist eyes, powdered complexion and great cascading wig, and thought of his antecedents as chronicled by Agnes Douglas. If he had told the man what he knew, would it have mattered? The minister had thought not, almost anything could lose itself in that fleshy bulk, and the stench of his perfume would drive out any stench from the past.

'But it's a stubborn place tae Sir, och it can be very stubborn, and perhaps it has aye been, with a perversity o will which needs a vigilant eye and a stern ane. Why the louns wad wish ye gude day in the morning and beggar ye in the afternoon wae sic a tale o woe that wad boggle the mind o Job himself. As if the sorrow of this world were not the common lot of mankind but dwelt in physical form in a cowshed in Trig.'

He had laughed then, like a man who is used to having the company he keeps laugh with him.

'Sae I hae nae truck wae sic nonsense, seeing it as false charity, which, if ye tak the lang and the short view wad only confirm a false belief. But do not misunderstand me Sir, I tak nae pleasure in thinking of myself as a mean man, and indeed I surely do not think I could be called that eh? What dae ye say Marten? '

'Och John, the new kirk itself is the greatest, noblest, and visiblest testament tae that, mair eloquent than any that I could mak.'

John Doig had grunted appreciatively, dismissively waving his hand.

'I am a firm believer in all the principles of the Reformed Kirk, as my faither was and his faither before him, and if these principles ganged a bit aglaikit a while back, faith, courage, and reason, won through in the end, as pray God they always will. As for the new kirk, it is tae my mind a poor spirited man that canna dig intae his pocket tae restore his ain kirk when it has been burned doun by a rascally pack o bare-arsed jockies. For far mair than just a few stones and mortar are being restored, the potent point is that religion, reason, and author-ity, are being restored, and that the days of dinging doun these things are past. Dae ye not agree, Sir?'

The minister had nodded in the affirmative, and he had watched the laird measuring that affirmative. If it lacked something Marten Gilmarten supplied it.

'John provided the money and the congregation provided the labour, and it now stands as a shining light and example, there is a whole chapter in my book devoted to it.'

'Ye are not acquainted wae his book Sir?'

'I have been most generously given a copy, but as it was only yesterday . . .'

'Read it Sir, read it. It is a work of great penetration much admired in the capital. It was my firm belief when I gave it my blessing that its merits would outlast our lifetimes, aye, and perhaps the lifetimes of those who come after.

☆

We stayed wae the People o the Mist for sae lang that it seemed tae me that we oursels becam almost Hielanfolk. And yet it was aye like being in a place that was on the edge o time itsel, a time that was consuming itsel wae fire and sword.

Nane o this seemed tae affect the Hielanfolk. Or if it did it just seemed tae mak them grip tighter tae their weapons, seeing it as the natural order o things which had aye been, and did they not hae many sad songs tae prove it? Indeed if our glen had not been attacked again we heard o many that had, and the news was aye that the Graham was invincible and in battle after battle he had won when it seemed impossible that he should. And Argyll it seemed was content tae dae nae mair than snap at his heels and be gien the dodge by him. And it was now said that he wad soon be maister o awe Scotland, and ready tae march intae England tae save the King, wha was being sarely beaten there.

We had word frae ane o Patrick Roy's folk that Sawney was alive and weel, and had made a great and terrible name for himsel, but had nae desire at awe tae ken us. When we were telt this Steenie had looked straight at the ground his hale face clouding ower.

'Weel then he sall be troubled by me nae mair.'

I put my hand on his shoulder then and said that I minded Sawney in my prayers and wad aye mind him. He just smiled at that, and forbye it was true that I did, I also thought o him as a man far awa, a different man, and sae far awa that the auld ane could never return. The Hielanman wha brought the news said that Jamie Graham himsel loved him like a brither, sic a reputation he had for skill and bravery in battle.

-Aye, nae doubt, Steenie said. -And if I ken ought about these gentry he will hae made many jealous enemies amang Jamie Graham's high born cavaliers.

This the Hielanman said was true, for they saw Sawney as nae mair than a poor bred Galloway loun turned mercenary. Awe that forbye the Hielanmen kent a bonny fighter when they saw ane, and sae did Jamie Graham, sae they maun just whistle through their teeth.

Some they said had left the army on account o it, while

ithers, mair honourably on account o the army itsel being ower bludie. Frae the news we heard it seemed that his army was a sare trial tae the Graham, the Hielanmen winning battle after battle in grand style, wad then just gang off hame wae their weir-booty as was their custom, and wad perhaps return and wad perhaps not, as it pleased them, thinking mair o their ain affairs than the King's, and only the Irish bided aye wae him haeving nae hames tae run awa tae.

I telt Catriona about Sawney and she said that if Sawney was not killed then she had little doubt that we had not seen the last o him, for it was plain tae see that we loved him very dearly, and while there was life, aye and even in death, sic love was not a thing tae be jouked.

I asked her if the sight had telt her this, and ance again, sae weel I kent it now, her white skin seemed tae just fold ower her mist grey een.

-Not mine Agnes Dhu, but yer ain, which ye neglect, asking me the questions ye should ask o it.

I said that I had misgiens about meeting up again wae sic a bludie handed captain o horse. For had I not heard that the Graham's army was like a sword o fire and destruction whaur ere it went, which was why many folk left it, and many, even them that were for the King, wadna join it. She just replied tae that fierce and Hielanlike.

-Hae they not burned and destroyed us, even while ye hae been here, and awe that I hae telt ye?

Aye she had telt me, and aiblins it had aye been sae, and aiblins it wad aye be sae, an eternity o riding and marching and cutting and cleaving, but I dreamed o a time when it wad not be sae.

She looked at me unco strangely then, and said that she tae dreamt o sic a time. But since the day when she had ceased tae be a bairn she had kent that there was aye a storm beating itsel up somewhaur, either tae yer left or tae yer right, or in yer rear, or up ahead, intae which folk wad gang as blithely as the People o the Mist were even now preparing themsels tae dae.

This I kent tae be true. The anger they had felt about their glen being burned had never left them but had smoul-

224

dered awa in their breasts. And if Patrick Roy was angry
tae, he had checked this desire, and Catriona had counselled
against it, and Steenie had counselled against it, and Catriona had said tae me that they didna aye heed her words,
and if it was waiting for an opportunity they were, nae
doubt that opportunity was not far awa.

It was the next night, or perhaps the next, when the full
meaning o her words becam plain when Patrick Roy cam
tae visit us. His ain house that had been burned had been
built again, and he had gien Steenie and mysel his small
house, wanting as he himsel declared, that we should bide
forever in the glen, but we wad say naething definite on
that.

But we watched him as he cam tae our door, and ye aye
kent when Patrick Roy was on serious business for his hale
manner wad change, and still being civil, it wad lack that
grandness o manner which he had when he was merry and
at his ease. Sae Steenie welcomed him in, pouring out some
whisky for him as was proper, and we just waited tae hear
what was on his mind.

-I hae news, he said, -that the Graham is preparing tae
march straight intae the heart o Argyll itsel, right tae
Macalein More's front door.

-Wae Winter coming on hard, Steenie said, -why that
should mak the Campbell smile.

-His Hielanmen insist on it, and Colkeitach insists on it.
They say they will not follow the Graham South unless he
leads them against the Campbell first.

-Ding King Campbell doun ere ye raise King Charles up.
Poor Jamie Graham, forbye he hates Argyll aboun awe men
he maun be fair weary o Hielan priorities.

It seemed tae me that Patrick Roy's ain pride bristled at
that for he spoke suddenly very sharply.

-Colkeitach has been out recruiting amang his ain folk,
bringing in awe the Western clans for what they say will be
the greatest foray o them awe, and against ane wha has
oppressed us sarely, and in yer ain memory burned my
house and killed thirteen o my kinsmen without cause or
warning.

-Aye Patrick I mind, how could I forget?

225

-Weel tae my mind, and my people's mind, if the Graham intends tae march on Argyll it wad be a shame and a dishonour if we were not there tae help strike this burden frae our backs.

-Ye ken my thoughts on that, och ye ken them weel. I care naething for Macalein More, but the Graham is a pestilence upon this country and it will be a gude day when he is beaten and a bad day when he is not. And aiblins he will win again in Argyll, or maybe ance in Macalein More will just snap the trap shut on him, for Campbells as ye weel ken are no fresh bit sodger lads, and gin that should happen I think very few wad cam back. Aye, and gin Jamie Graham wins, after that it will be the Lawlands and then England. Why man he'll drag ye awe behind Charlie Stuart's coat tails, and aiblins tae disaster if Cromwell has ought tae say about it.

Patrick Roy it seemed was now sae fair astonished that he needed tae tak a lang drop o his drink before he replied.

-Och man, I hae nae intention o ganging intae the Lawlands, and even less intae England. But the truth is, as ye maun ken, that many o my lads will gang whether I gie them leave or not, and the Deevil alane kens whaur the louns might end up without their chief tae guide them. Aye, and what will they then say? Is the standard of the Gregorach tae be raised and Patrick Roy not under it? If Macalein More had not harried the glen it might hae made some small difference.

Steenie said naething. He later telt me that he had kent very weel that there was nae words that could be said that wad change anything, and Patrick Roy's next words confirmed that.

-I'm getting auld Sir, and wha kens whether or not this will be my last fight, but tae dee at the Campbell's front door as sae often he has deed at mine, now wad that not mak a song worth the singing? If I tak eighty men, or nae mair than a hundred, that will leave this place weel enough guarded. I will leave Neil Roy behind and he has been weel taught, and kens what tae dae in any eventuality, and Catriona will be here.

He stopped then, I remember very clearly, as if his words

were failing him, or he was haeving difficulty finding them, and yet his auld een shone wae sic cunning that a bairn could hae divined them.

-But ye Steenie, now I ken yer politics, and ye ken that I say tae Hell wae awe politics that come between true friends, but will ye, or will ye not, bide here for the Winter? Ye hae a house hae ye not? And it is the wrang season for the road, forbye yer friends in principle as ye call them wad hing ye on sight. Tae bide here wad be sensible as weel as friendly.

Steenie said tae me later that he kent how he was caught. It wad indeed not be sensible tae tak tae the road, and in a land o enemies the friendship o Patrick Roy was a necessary thing tae retain, and he kent that Patrick wanted him tae bide in the glen as Neil's friend and adviser without appearing tae ruffle that young man's pride. And yet, looking at it baith braid and narrow, we wad be helping the Graham by allowing Patrick Roy tae lead his clan off wae a blithe heart.

-Patrick Roy Macgregor, he said, -I am against this enterprise. Either way it ends will seem to me an ill end. If Jamie Graham wins it will perhaps be for the hale o Scotland, if he loses the anger of Argyll will fall on my friends here.

-Tae be plain Sir, Patrick Roy said, his voice rising a bit - nane o these outcomes wad change whether I went or not. Man ye ken our history. Ye ken how great we were ance and how poor we are now. Hae we nae right tae tak it back frae them that took it frae us? The Gregorach ye ken hae lived when awe wad hae them deid, by loving their friends few as they are, and sometimes fighting, sometimes fleeing frae their enemies as chance wad hae it. If awe the clans o the West, and a host o ithers will march intae Argyll whatever the risk, wad it not be remarked upon if we were not there?

-I will bide here until the Spring, but mair than that I will not promise.

Patrick Roy was greatly pleased at this and said that he had never doubted Steenie for a minute, and kent that he wad be sure tae keep a wise ee on the people, not that he doubted Neil Roy's ability, but the lad was young.

227

When he had left us Steenie turned tae me and said,

-Lassie, it seems that in awe but name I hae been made for a time the captain o a Hielan clan. Now I wonder what Catriona's sight has tae say about this and that?

I said that I thought her sight was being very quiet on this business.

-Then, her sight is damn bit wiser than maist men's words and deeds.

☆

The minister looked at the young man. He was about middle height and of slender build, dressed in what appeared to be his best clothes, or at least his cleanest. He stood with his head bowed, his blue bonnet clutched in his hands, his face set in a cast which he no doubt imagined expressed contrition.

To the minister's eyes it appeared sullen, almost brutish, his eyes shifting furtively between the two clerics while trying to maintain the impression of stillness. He was waiting for blows to descend, knowing that they could neither be repelled or deflected.

The Reverent Gilmarten circled him like a small cat judging the correct distance from which to strike, his eyes set hard in their squint, his narrow chest heaving. When he eventually spoke his voice was low and appeared to groan with intensity as if sorrow and outrage were mixed in equal proportions.

'Now here we hae a merry youth. Ane that cares nought for the laws of God, ane that cares nought for the bloody sacrifice of our Lord and maister, ane that cares not for his kirk, its ministers or its elders, but wad gang like some beast on the hillside, as if like them he was answerable tae nane in Heaven or on Earth, or in Hell for the wantonness o his lust.

'Blindly he gangs, blindly upon perdition's path, thinking that the Lord wha sees all things has nae eyes tae see him. Thinking that the Kirk has nae eyes tae see him, thinking in the reprobate hardness of his heart that in some dark beast's den, some hidden, or sae he thinks, bush, he can slink tae lie, his breeks about his heels, his hands ganging whaur nane but a reprobate's hands wad gang.'

Marten Gilmarten's hands rose into the air. The timbre of

his voice climbed to a shrill mockery.

'Och, and thinks he not this fleshly lust is sweet? Och and thinks he not that this poor body under him which he has charmed and wiled and seduced, is like untae Heaven itsel? Oh horrid, blaspheming, fornicating wretch! Fie, fie, says he, awa wae ye! Awa wae awe the Kirk has taught. The Kirk that has been a shining light tae guide him awe his days, that has nourished him and cherished him wae awe its might, armouring him wae its righteousness, and asks nae mair o him except that he keeps its Covenants and walks all his days in the kindly light of its blessings, a cause for sic exaltation that an honest man wad lift up his hands and praise Heaven that he should be sae chosen.

'But what does he dae? But cast his eyes doun, doun, doun, tae whaur they see naething but flesh and lust. Blind as a beast he sees not the Serpent there, that foul monster laughing in its glee, smells not its noisome stink sae foul is his ain, why in its impunity it can now dance before his very een and he will think his een enriched.'

Gilmarten's voice rose to crack like a whip, and then descended with the soft thud of a cudgel. However resolute the flesh had been in its sinning, it melted like butter now.

'But other eyes watched him too, Godly eyes, eyes that wept in sorrow at what they beheld. Eyes that hae plucked ye frae the black pit where in ye were like tae wallow tae awe eternity, gnashing your teeth, pleading in that place whaur ye canna weep, only that ye might weep . . .'

The girl had been a pleasant, winning, commonplace creature beside herself with grief and shame. The minister thought of the saturnine countenance of the dominie prowling the hillside and the wood. Had his eyes glittered covetously on Elizabeth Adam's flesh? For a brief moment it was as if the minister's senses were overwhelmed by the triviality of his fellow creatures. Sawney Bain's religion was a bloodbath of confusion, Malecky's warlockry no more than a shoddy and self-serving rationalism without moral courage. Gilmarten's lecture so wildly outweighed the sensibilities at which it was aimed that it was a blasphemous vanity. Sir John Doig ran true to his blood and oozed more sensuality and corruption in half an hour than the whole parish of Trig could manage in a year.

229

And there, above and below, overwhelming them all, the awful figure of Agnes Douglas rose to assault him.

Oh gae ye tae the toun o Trig
And wait ye there for me,
And if I cam no by the toun o Trig
A false witness call ye me.

The minister shuddered and felt violently sick. Mastering himself he swallowed fiercely. Still her voice cackled incoherently in his ear. Her voice drowned out Gilmarten's harangue. Her voice transformed all his words into their opposites. It was she, not he, who was shrieking in his ear. He imagined Elizabeth Adams lying on her back with her legs in the air, her gown thrust up over her waist and young Black merrily rutting away. Grinding the flesh and despair of their lives into dust as Black Agnes ground the flesh of her fellow creatures into pottage, while calling her offspring cheerfully to her bed, straining her thighs to produce an incestuous and immortal brood who now seemed to frolic in their dreadful rebellion directly below Gilmarten's feet, mining the earth from under them, mining everything from below.

'Tae yer deeing day,' she had hissed at him, 'Black Agnes sall never leave ye, for she kens what ye are, and what ye aye will be, an eagle in yer pride and a raven in yer wrath. And Black Agnes's book ye sall never burn nor ye hae read it.'

No, the minister had thought at the time, feeling the passionate pride of his outrage. Not until I have read it, for some things had to be fought, some things had to be conquered. Agnes Douglas was an enemy of Heaven, nurtured and guided by Malecky, and then turned loose to be a subterranean pestilence in God's Kingdom.

On summer nights they had sat naked round their fire gnawing at their neighbour's flesh, staring out across the flames to a world of which they had inherited a grossly corrupted knowledge, a grossly corrupted knowledge of God and of themselves, and of anything that could be called goodness by any who walked upon the Earth's surface.

The minister felt his soul groaning. They had been nurtured in a place of darkness beyond redemption, a world into which no light entered. And yet they believed themselves to be, alone, visited by angels and blessed above all the peoples on the Earth, and that they would never die, and they praised God regularly and correctly according to all the principles of the Reformed Kirk.

The minister looked at Marten Gilmarten's proud face. Did he know what iniquity was that he thought it should dwell in such proportions in the carnal frolickings of a ploughboy and his lass?

The squint-eyed pastor's lecture had by now become horribly obscene. Before the minister's eyes he was dismembering the bodies of Elizabeth Adams and William Black, rending limb from body, splitting flesh apart, grinding bones into powder. Under all this they were noiseless, and the minister could tell nothing of what they felt.

☆

'I kent I was nae langer a bairn when my sister Jean nae langer slept wae me for warmth and friendship's sake, and tae avoid Patrick wham she didna much like. Patrick was the auldest and strangest amang us and about that time had begun tae vex mither sarely by wanting tae be chief, which he wad declare was his right seeing that mither was auld and faither was a cripple. This point he wad pursue without restraint, and it wad bring forth a sermon frae faither on how much, aye maist, oh awe the woe and pestilence that had sae wracked Chaos had cam about through folk that wanted tae be kings and lairds and chiefs, and wax pridefully aboun their fellow folk. And he read a passage frae the Bible that telt how this wad happen, tae which the folk o Chaos wadna listen which had provoked God intae a mighty wrath against them, and how he could see that Patrick was aiblins ane o they folk and out o place amang the Godly.

'And sae Patrick maun learn tae behave himsel or ere lang he wad be dreaming that it was God's will that he should be chief amang them, which the Kings o Chaos had aye in their pride insisted on, and which had brought about mair destruction and disaster and war in Chaos than ony ither thing, and if he had learnt anything at awe in Chaos it was that Godly folk needed nae king ither than God himsel,

231

and ony that they set up, or wha set themsels up, wad bring naething but disaster upon them.

'Ane day faither said, forbye he kent not when that day wad come, awe the folk o Chaos wad hae routed themsels frae the Earth and the Lord wad call us forth frae this place whaur he had preserved us, tae be a new people that wad live peacefully and love him as he liked tae be loved. And did Patrick in his foolishness think the Lord wad dae this if he Patrick declared himsel chief asking leave o naething but his ain pride?

After faither's rebuke Patrick was quiet for a time, but Jean said that he wad whisper darkly and secretly, and gaither folk about him intae what faither called factions and divisions, which was anither cause o pestilence near as bad as kings. And Patrick, forbye he was very big and strang, was still feart o faither, and aiblins o mither, and sae wad remain quiet humbling himsel. But he aye wanted Jean tae lie wae him, and had promised her that ane day he wad be King and she wad be Queen, but Jean said that she wad lie wae me or wae ony that she fancied, and Patrick for awe he murmered darkly declaring that I was but a bairn, could say nought tae that, kenning weel that Jean could dae as she pleased and ask nae leave o him.

'Then ane day Jean declared tae awe that I was nae langer a bairn and there might weel be anither bairn on its way as proof o that.

'Awe war pleased at that, for sic an event was aye a great joy and blessing amang us, and even Patrick made a great show o being pleased and broke open a cask o whisky he had captured while hunting. But I was maist happy o awe, for now we had our ain bit corner o the cave intae which nane could come but we permitted them, which we did on mony occasions when the nights war cauld, and baith my sisters Margaret and Leezie wha are younger than me, wad join us, and Rebecca wham mither and mysel had found in the biggin.'

☆

When Gilmarten finally harried the couple from the manse it

seemed to the minister that he merely flung flesh and bones from his door into the road. When he turned to the minister his eyes danced with energetic zeal.

'Weel Sir, four weeks public penance in the Kirk whaur ye sall hae the scolding o them, and then decently marry them for the lass is already twa months gone.'

The minister nodded, bracing himself to meet Gilmarten's inquisitorial stare.

'A word of advice tae ye Sir, if I may as an auld man tae a young. Be not afraid tae show your wrath. I suspect that there is an over tender heart beating beneath that broad chest of yours. Now that nae doubt is a gude thing, tae be a kindly shepherd tae the people. But indulgence Sir, is quite another thing, and a false mercy when a righteous sword is mair appropriate. For they are a persistent folk in their sin, and if the eyes and ears of the Kirk were no aye on them, and the wrath of the Kirk no ower their heids, the lave o them wad backslide intae iniquity in six months.'

☆

Winter cam early tae the glen that year the Hielanfolk said. I for ane, kenning that we were tae bide there did not mind that, for it seemed tae just cut the glen off frae living land and the confusion that ruled there. We heard naething at awe about it after Patrick Roy and a hundred o his people marched awa wae their standards flying and their pipes playing, awe weel busked and keen for fighting, and the poets stoking them weel wae memories o thousand year auld wrangs, for they Hielan poets had memories that wad hae addled the brains o maist folk. But the men wha were ganging awa said that they wad right these wrangs a hundred times and bring back gear and cows tae prove it.

-Aye if they win, Steenie said, but he said it quietly, for the thing was now fixed and sic words uttered out loud could perhaps bring bad luck. But he never relented in his disapproval o the venture, and he telt me how the march they wad hae tae mak was itsel sae terrible, that aiblins the Campbells wad just sit quietly by their fires and let the snow and their mountains mind their enemies.

After they had gone, the People o the Mist that remained behind just settled doun for the Winter, biding tightly in their biggins, but not sae much that they were no aye mindful o their cattle and were soon afoot if there was any sign o threat tae them. On a few occasions Catriona warned that there just might be and Neil Roy and Steenie himsel wad lead the men out tae scout. Steenie wae a responsibility on him now nae langer poking fun at Catriona's warnings but just said that right or wrang he was taking nae risk o the glen being caught asleep.

But nae trouble cam tae us that Winter and I mind it as a gude time, kenning as I now did the Hielanfolk's tongue near perfect, and baith Steenie and mysel being maist respectit amang them, and Catriona being as gude a friend as it was possible tae hae, aye, and aiblins if I telt awe she was a bit mair than that.

Steenie wad talk a bit about the war, but his words nae langer had the courage or confidence they ance had, which he freely admitted, saying there was nae cure for the madness o the warld in his heid alane. And whiles I listened, feeling the sorrow o his words, perhaps I cared very little, for it seemed tae me that if there was a bludie gate tae be ganged men wad hasten tae gang it, and only weariness or death wad stop them. And Sawney, whatever ither qualities he might hae, was naught but a loun tae be driven this way and that as if he was the left hand o God's wrath and Jamie Graham the right. And if they were indeed daen the Lord's will, and the Kirk was daen the Lord's will, then whatever side he chose the Lord himsel was an ower angry man.

I kent not of course at that time what was tae follow, and how they had indeed marched straight across the Hielans near deeing o cauld and hunger, and how they had cam doun on the Campbell's in the heart o their ain country, and forbye they were supported by government sodgers, beat them at a place called Inverlochy.

This we kent, when as the Winter was ganging frae the glen Patrick Roy and his men cam marching back, driving as they said they wad, a great herd o black cattle, and still wae their pipes playing, and the hale glen that had news o them rushing out tae meet them, and Catriona wae her

234

sword raised in salute, kissing each man as he passed and shouting out his name, and nae doubt congratulating him for no being deid. For as is the way o these affairs, some were deid, and these the poet wad tak notice o in his verses, for now that the slaughtering o men was ower, they fell tae singing and feasting and the slaughtering o cows.

Many were the presents they had brought back frae the rich lands o Argyll. Patrick Roy gied me a fine silk gown far aboun anything that I had ever previously worn, and he gied Steenie a very fine Hielan broadsword and a dirk wae a bonny carved handle, and there was a pair o silver candlesticks which he gied tae his wife, and silks and satins which he gied tae Catriona.

I said tae him that they maun hae been fighting wae very rich folk, and Catriona said that awe this gear wad be like a snowball in Winter laid alangside awe that had been stolen frae them.

It was when Patrick Roy cam later tae our house that he seemed somewhat less blithe than when he had first cam up the glen, and I kent not why, but tae my een he looked aulder than I could remember forbye I could not say in what way. Steenie made tae pour him out some whisky but Patrick telt him tae put it awa for had he not a fine cask o brandy. When he had poured that out Steenie said tae him,

-Weel Patrick sae ye hae been tae Macalein More's front door?

Patrick Roy looked very solemn then when he nodded his heid, and Steenie's een had that queer smile in them which Sawney had ance said aye made maist men nervous. But he said naething, and after a time Patrick Roy spoke again.

-I think we will not be hearing sae much about the great Clan Campbell for a while.

Still Steenie said naething. Nor was it possible tae ken by any sign what he was thinking. And whether Patrick was looking for sic a sign or whether he was not, I ken not, but he was silent for a bit before speaking further.

-They had nae idea that it was possible for us tae march whaur we did, through snow that was arse high, and glens sae narrow that fifty cunning men could hae checked us, and we cam doun on them in sic numbers that they could

235

never hae dreamed o, and the cauld footed, cauld boned
Southern sodgers broke at our first charge, and were less
help tae the Campbells than if they had never been there,
for we now had them on baith flanks wae only the loch at
their backs. They, as ye might expect, banged it out at
sword point till damn near half their host was deid, and
that the better half.

-And nae quarter?

-Quarter Sir? The Graham kens not the meaning o the
word, and Colkeitach kens it not, and weel, the Campbells
themsels are not quarter gien folk. What was left o them
dived intae the loch and swam for their lives, and the foot
and horse were hackit doun as they ran. Seven miles frae
the field Sir some still ran and some still harried them, and
awe the way the blude and the deid froze red on the
ground, and the snow that fell and covered it was the only
merciful thing that day.

-Aye Sir, the poor folk o the Hielans feasted very weel
that day, as did every wolf and corbie craw in Argyll. And
the Graham, as ye hae said weel and often, exulting how
like that captain in the Bible he wad conquer frae Dan tae
Beersheba.

For a time after that Patrick Roy was ance again silent,
and when he spoke again it was as if his tongue had grown
weary in that time.

-I ken not. He sees awe Scotland before him, and England tae, and he was sarely displeased when I said that for
the present I wad march back hame. And ye ken Sir, when
he's being persuasive he's a man o subtle persuasion. I hae
beaten Argyll for ye, he said tae me, and now ye wad leave
me when I hae maist need o ye and the King's cause itsel is
desperate?

-Nae doubt there was some justice in his words, and
aiblins I thought his path was ower bludie, and aiblins he
sneered at that, for yon man can smile and sneer and be
kindly and fierce like nae man on earth, but whaur his bit
king is concerned he will gang the bludiest gate tae be by his
side.

-And what o Argyll himsel?

-Archiebald Campbell? Why that princely chief and

Kirk's lackey took nae part in the fight, but watched the slaughter o his clan frae his black boat on the loch, and sailed awa when it awe got ower much for him. Nae doubt that great man saw little sense in risking his neck in a Hielan brawl. Aye Sir, Argyll may tell in Edinburgh what Argyll will tell, but if any chief o my name had behaved in sic a fashion I think the dirk o the least o our people wad hae found him before the day was out.

It may be that I minded then the Campbells wha had been kind tae us when we first cam tae the Hielans, and wha had been very little different in awe things frae Patrick Roy's ain folk, and aiblins they were now deid and their rooftrees burned.

It was then that Steenie asked.

-Did ye see ought o Sawney?

-Aye I saw him, and he was alive and weel when I left him, but he cut me damnably short when I talked tae him about my twa gude friends wha were his gude friends. Aye and I wad hae got angry wae him about it, but it seemed that ane half o him was angry without reason, while the ither half was mad, like a man wha had nae sensible idea o his actions and his words. And for a man wha has every appearance o a sensible, steady sodger, he has a reputation near as wild as Colkeitach's, and is very valuable tae the Graham. And yet he laughs at awe principle and purpose, and is like a man that only the Deil or fortune keeps alive.

He stopped speaking then and ance again was unco quiet, speaking only when he saw that we waited tae hear mair.

-I ken not properly how tae speak about him. He cam up tae me later and apologised for his manner. But he telt me plainly that I was not tae speak tae him o either o ye again if I wanted us tae remain friends, for he was damned tired o Hielanmen bringing him tales o folk that were tae him nae mair.

-I said naething mair tae him at that time. If his manner was gentler it was still damned sharp. And frae that time and throughout the campaign he did not seek out my company nor I his. And I telt my people tae leave him be, as maist folk did, for Sir, he was like a man wha if left alane

237

wad pick a quarrel wae his horse, though tae be plain, that was the only creature he seemed tae treat wae any kindness.

☆

If the Parish of Trig liked their new minister they gave very little outward sign of it. If they disliked him they did that very secretly. They listened to his first two sermons with a perfect attentiveness, and then, their curiosity assuaged, notorious sleepers slept and habitual absentees contrived to be absent. All to be shaken awake or hunted down by the ever vigilant Walter Hyslop who would summon them before the Kirk Session to be fined and lectured for their sins. Indeed the only hint of criticism came from Hyslop himself who remarked when alone with the minister.

'There is a whiff of Arminianism in the air.'

At the time the minister had regarded the tall, gangling dominie almost with amusement. Yet, as he admitted to himself, there was nothing amusing about Hyslop. There was none of the robust if narrow convictions of a John Erskine or a Martha Liddel. Hyslop's mind seemed to be constructed of overwhelming despair held in check by an indomitable will to faith. The outward visible sign of this were his eyes which gave the impression of being poised permanently on the brink of madness. Or as Mathew Elliot put it, 'ane surveys Heaven and the ither Hell.'

Walter was the greatest hunter of sinners the parish had. A man who seemed to have never known love, he knew every lover's neuk in the area and would prowl hillside and muir in search of fornicators, haunt the streets in search of drunkards and brawlers, and could spot the beginnings of an illicit pregnancy with a certainty that the women could not match. Of the simple lives of the villagers he knew everything that there was to know.

Mathew Elliot had told the minister a story of how once his brother, Robert Elliot, had become so annoyed at Hyslop's prurience that he had given him a thorough if gentle cudgelling, knocking the elder to the ground, only to have the man spring instantly to his feet and resolutely continue to bar his way. Three times Robert Elliot had knocked him down only to find the man still blocking his path, as if his zeal for accusations doubled as his blood flowed.

Robert Elliot, realising that short of breaking the man's head, he could neither daunt him or get rid of him, had turned on his heels and walked in the other direction. Walter had dauntlessly sped after him calling down the wrath of Heaven on his head to such effect that to be quit of him, Robert Elliot had broken into a run, and the village was treated to the spectacle of a brawny shepherd armed with a cudgel being pursued along the road by the bloody figure of the dominie.

Robert Elliot had stayed in the hills with his sheep for a week before coming down and appearing before Hyslop and the Kirk Session, declaring that he knew he would have no peace otherwise.

'I preach that God's grace is boundless,' said the minister, 'which is what I believe.'

'And has not the book o life already been lang writ?' Hyslop had asked.

'Of course, but neither you or I can presume to know who is, and who is not in it.'

Hyslop's skeletal frame quivered like an ancient tree bracing itself against a hurricane.

'The Lord has ways o letting his people ken, aye and guiding them. Aye and trying them tae, morning and e'en, day and nicht, his presence is afore them, and weel they ken it, them that acknowledge it and them that blind themsels tae it.'

Hyslop bowed, managing to infect even that gesture with a grim portent before walking purposefully away.

For a moment the minister had watched him striding down the street. A strange pass, he had thought, for a man to come to, loved by God and hated by his neighbours. And yet these same neighbours all acknowledged, that if Hyslop was stern with the children of the parish, he was by no means unkind or brutal, and until they reached a certain age when as he himself put it, 'ye could smell Satan on their tracks', he was well enough liked by them.

Since Marten Gilmarten had left for Edinburgh the minister had spent a considerable amount of his time riding round his parish. He would talk to his flock if he saw them in their fields or in their yards. In doing this, he tried to convince himself he was getting to know them. The conversations he had on these excursions, generally resolved themselves around the weather, the crops, the cattle, and the excellence of his horse. It came as a shock, which no one else in the parish could have imagined, when he learned quite casually that the prominent hill at the North end of the town was known throughout Trig as Steenie's Hill.

Suddenly burdened with this incontrovertible evidence of continuity he had asked his housekeeper why.

'Och how should I ken, it has aye had that name.'

'It would seem to me, ' he had replied, 'that some person called Steenie must have had some connection with the place.'

'Aye, nae doubt ye could be richt, but what gars ye ask? It was caed Steenie's Hill afore I was born, and maist likely lang afore that.'

The minister felt once again quite alone. To others the hill simply existed, to him alone it beckoned. He took to asking his parishioners for the source of the name, and all, old and young gave him the same blunt answer, they had no idea, he might as well have asked them why Galloway was called Galloway, or Scotland, Scotland. He asked Mathew Elliot whom he had found an intelligent man and the most amiable of his elders.

'Nae doubt ye are richt and a man caed Steenie did live there ance, but I think it was a lang time ago.'

'How long have you lived here, Mathew?'

'Near forty year. I was not born here, but cam here wae a bit money got through sodgering, as ye ken.'

'It puzzles me Mathew. Have you ever heard, perhaps while you were a soldier, of one called Sawney Bain who was also born in Trig?'

'What puzzles ye minister? Sawney Bain, forbye I didna ken he was born here, was weel kent as a gude stout sodger, and a Godly ane tae, wha was thocht tae hae been killed at Dunbar, but was not, for the last time I heard o him was wae some Cameronian folk wha were awe killed in a bludie massacre.'

'Did you know him well?'

'No not weel, but by sicht and reputation, which was o a man wha kent his bible better than his sword, which maun hae made him a very Christian man for he kent his sword weel enough. But it was said that he was a bit strange as weel.'

'In what way?'

'Och I ken not. It was what folk said, and not kenning him weel mysel, and him now being deid, I will say nae mair. They say he was saddled wae a grim bit carline o a wife, but I canna vouch for that, I only saw her about three times and she seemed very fine tae me. But they say he ance taught her how tae use a sword, which aiblins was a bit strange. But they say she was near as gude as himsel wae it which made her unco difficult tae handle. But if he was born in Trig, weel Trig has kept very quiet about it, for in his time, in a small bit way, he was a man o some fame.'

For a time Mathew seemed to have slipped away as if musing on the past, and then suddenly his grey eyes focused on the minister's, quick and alert.

'But what puzzles ye minister?'

'In Edinburgh I read a memoir of this place by a Mathius Pringle who was for a time minister here, you may have heard of him, in which he said that Sawney Bain and his wife Agnes Douglas both came from Trig, and were in fact friends of this man Steenie, whose second name was Malecky. I am sure from his direction the Steenie of Steenie's Hill.'

'I hae heard, wha at that time had not, even as a bairn, o Mathius Pringle, and if that is what he wrote then nae doubt he wrote the truth. But as I ken it, Steenie's Hill was aye just Steenie's Hill, and whaever gied it its name I never thocht o as a man o my time. There is nae sign o occupation or dwelling on that place.'

'Who is the oldest inhabitant in the parish, do you know?'

'Och the auldest wad nae doubt be, if addled brains are ocht tae gae by, Tam Mathieson, but ye will get little sense out o him.'

'I am new to this country, Mathew. And I am interested in the history of Trig, curious about all that has gone before.'

☆

When we left the glen it seemed tae me that a lang, lang time had passed and that perhaps the warld wad be a different place. Sic was the feeling in my heart, and aiblins my heid kent weel enough that it was a foolish feeling. For had we not heard that the Graham was now roaring like a tempest through the Lawlands, driving awe before him tae sic a degree that if God was not on his side then he was surely bent on sarely trying his people.

Now we were nae langer tae travel as sodgers, it being now a dangerous way tae gang about in a country that had nae langer any love o sodgers, and wae armies that wad press any they found intae service. Sae now it was like poor travelling folk o little account that we went, and if Patrick Roy hooted in his pride that his gude friends should leave him in sic a fashion, the canny man kent that it was wise, forbye he thought it wad be wiser not tae leave at awe. But he had gien us a a bit cart and twa stout ponies, for we had left our horses wae him, it being plain that sic folk as we were now tae be wad not own sic gude horses, which many wad hae shot us just tae possess. But our weapons and our armour we took wae us, hidden in the cart, for these were not the kind o things we wanted tae be without.

The day before we left I rade wae Catriona up tae her high pool, baith feeling a queer sorrow at this parting. And she took off her fine silver dirk which had never previously left her, and tied it tae my leg under my gown in her ain fashion. And before she did this she blessed it, for awe the blessing was hardly a Christian ane, for she telt it in her ain language that it should preserve me and keep me and aye be there if I should need it. And she telt me that I was aye tae wear it, and mind that it was there, for it wad preserve me as on several occasions it had preserved her. Nor did I any langer laugh at what had ance seemed like Hielan nonsense, and in truth, there were tae be ane or twa occasions, which at that time I could hae nae knowledge o, when I was tae be very glad that it was there.

She telt me tae, as she had often done in the past, that in moments when the confusion and disaster o the warld was awe about me, and like tae fall upon me, I was tae dae as my heart bade and no tae jouk its orders, for she had recognised in me a sister wha had the sight as she had. I thought then, as I had thought often before, how her words wad hae gladdened the heart o Willie Munro, confirming as they did, awe that he had aye believed.

We had promised when we first resolved tae leave that

ane day we wad return. On that last day by the pool she had stroked my flesh and combed out my hair, awe the time singing gently, and she had said,

-Och Agnes Dhu, I ken very weel that ye sall return, for awe things that are loved return tae them that love them. But whether ye sall return in the fleshly shape in which ye leave, or in anither form I canna say, and aiblins the form in which ye return will be the ane in which ye sall never truly leave.

I nae langer smiled at her when she spoke in this way, haeving learnt much frae her that was secret, and that nae ither living person kent.

Sae we travelled quietly, and indeed we were very little noticed for there were many poor folk travelling about in like fashion at that time. Some wha had fled frae the plague which was again raging in Edinburgh and ither places. Some because their house and land had been burned by sodgers, or because it had gone barren through lack o care. There were some wha had bit carts like ours but maist were on foot haeving nae gear at awe but the duds in which they walked. Aye and there were ithers wha had hardly even that but were near naked, and near tae madness wae cauld, hunger and suffering, sae that they just sat by the roadside their een sick wae despair, and in sic a state that if they had been beasts ye wad hae shot them out o kindness.

Steenie said that it was a poor pass for a land that had prayed sae fervently and fought sae hard for its salvation, and had thought itsel tae be Covenanted wae God, that it could now only wail in its misery, which was nae doubt a sign o the Lord's displeasure.

Steenie's heart had become very hard at the sight o awe these things, and his tongue sae blasphemous that it nae langer cared what it said, but wad curse the Lord himself in a way that was terrible for me tae hear, and I telt him that it couldna be ither than courting disaster tae speak in sic a way.

He just laughed at that, and said what mair mischief could a blasphemous tongue dae that a Godly tongue and a Godly sword had no already done? And indeed it was a mystery tae me that there could be sae many folk in the warld, and wae sae many deid and deeing, armies could still be weel stocked wae sodgers.

We avoided large touns for fear o being apprehended, or catching the plague, for tae the Kirk's mind, faced wae sic chaos, they wad think the need tae apprehend us even greater than before. Steenie pointed them out tae me as we passed, but as they meant naething tae me then I hae little recollection o them now. But we had lang passed out o the Hielans and were in a country which he called Fife, which was a blasted place, forbye Steenie said it had been fine enough ance.

It was on the road there that we saw a man walking a bit ahead o us, dressed in hodden grey and carrying a muckle staff on his shoulder. He had nae ither weapons that I could see, but Steenie said that he was, or had been, a sodger, which he kent by the lang knife he wore at his belt, which he said many Scots sodgers carried.

-But we'll say naething about that unless he himsel mentions it.

As we drew near tae him the man turned about tae face us, and Steenie greeted him wae a gude day. Tae this the man replied sae dourly that I minded auld Coll's words on gude days, and it seemed tae me that it had been some time before this man could truly say that he had seen ane. He looked, and he was a sturdy enough man, baith hungry and tired, wae hair and beard that had neither been cut nor trimmed for many a lang day. But there was mair than that, which I canna weel describe, but his een just looked like deid things in his heid, and he swung his muckle staff on tae his shoulder as if guarding himsel against our approach, but mair weary than resolute.

-Wad ye care tae rest yer legs, Sir? Steenie said, clearly inviting him on tae our cart.

For a minute the man seemed uncertain what tae dae, and Steenie tossed him a flagon o our whisky, for maybe alane o folk that were on the road at that time Patrick Roy had plentifully supplied us wae it.

The man took a bit mouthful, his een ower watchful as if he thought it was a trick. When Steenie urged him tae tak mair, he said,

-Ye maun be a damn sight richer than ye seem.

-I am what ye see me tae be.

The man took anither mouthful which seemed tae mightily refresh him.

-Then I'll no inquire as tae whaur ye got it but be grateful that ye hae it.

Steenie laughed a bit and ance again invited him on tae our cart. Still he seemed tae hesitate before weariness clean owercam his apprehensions and he climbed up, oursels making a space for him.

He gied his name as William Leckie but said little mair about himsel. Indeed for a time he just sat there his een staring out intae the fields, and nae doubt he minded them as different tae how they appeared now. But naething further was said, just the whisky passing between the three o us. And if I had thought I was used tae sic things by now it was still unco strange that gude folk could meet on the road like this, offering nae mair than Christian assistance in a Christian land, and yet be afraid tae ask each ither anything lest they should arouse suspicion. In time, weary o it himsel, Steenie asked him if he was ganging far, and he mentioned a place called Pittenweem, which Steenie said he kent.

-A fishing place is it not?

-Aye, said the man, but the plain truth is, that damn little fishing will be done there now. I was ance captain o my ain gude boat, the Covenant I called her.

I gied the man some bread and cheese at this point, for which he thanked me, saying that we were Christian folk and tae his een nae gypsies.

Steenie said naething tae this but just asked him if the fishing was bad?

At first he didna answer. Indeed he was like a man wha had forgotten the use o words, and if the whisky had livened him up a bit it now seemed tae hae just cast him doun deeper than before. Even when in the end he spoke he was like ane that spoke only tae himsel.

-There is naething wrong wae the fishing, but wha is now tae tak the boats out? I ken not, wae a hundred or mair fisher captains dinged doun by the Deevil himsel in the

245

shape o the bludie Graham and his bludie handed Hielanmen.

It seemed tae me that we were ance again hearing a story
that we already kent, and Steenie I mind clearly, hesitated a
bit before asking him unco gently whaur it had taen place.
He did not answer directly but just said,

-I think ye hae been a sodger Sir?

-Aye, for a while wae Leslie.

-And nae doubt lost everything in that trade, for its a
damn poor ane for an honest man. My trade, and what I
ken best, was the boat and the sea and the fish, like awe my
neighbours wha are now I fear maistly deid. The Kirk ye see
wad hae us carry pikes and gang against Montrose, promising us fairly that now he was in the Lawlands and his
Hielan stotes awa frae their hills the Lord wad deliver him
tae us as he had lang promised, and wad we hang back frae
this Godly wark?

-Weel we did not hang back, but it turned out not as it
had been promised, and them that ken mair about sodgering than me said that the army ought tae hae won but had
been badly mishandled wae the Kirk's committee over-
ruling General Baillie wha was our captain. And whether he
kent his trade or whether he did not, I hae nae skill tae
judge but the Hielanmen cut us tae pieces Sir, roaring like
beasts out o Hell as they did sae.

The man stopped, and it seemed tae me that he was clean
overwhelmed by his memories and the bitterness o them,
for if he had been silent before, his voice was loud and
bitter now.

-It was at Kilsythe Sir, a place I'll be damned before I
gang back tae.

We had not heard o this particular fight, and Steenie said
later that it had shaken him a bit that the Graham was sae
far South. But at that time he just said,

-I ken Baillie, he's a canny enough captain, if no ower
brilliant.

William Leckie just shook his heid. He was a man, I
thought, wha wanted tae be quiet, but had been sae lang
alane that he was just desperate tae speak, and perhaps the
whisky had solved that division for him.

-I ken not, I ken not. I am nae judge o captains, but he had far mair horse and foot than the Graham, and many weel seasoned sodgers amang them. But they say the Kirk's committee just took charge o the army clean awa frae him, and whether they thought he was ower canny, and they sae firm in their Godly convictions that they had nae need o canniness, I canna say, but the day ended wae the Hielan stotes laughing and singing in their glee their swords reeking wae Christian blude. Tae hae seen them Sir ye wad never hae thought that sic creatures dwelt in Scotland.

-I stood as lang as our line stood. But the position we were in was just plain foolish, and they cared nought for musket or pike, but wad just knock the first aside and slice the heid off the ither, running and jumping and killing men sae fast that ye could hardly keep yer legs wae the blude that was about yer feet. I killed ane sir, and forbye I had mortally piked him, his soul, if he had ane, was damned reluctant tae gang frae him. But when my pike broke, and the line broke, I trusted tae my legs, as did many anither. Aye, and it can be said, that my legs might weel hae been better than maist, for they cut doun the lave as they ran, sparing nane, and I ken nane that I marched awa wae that I ken for certain are still alive, but many I saw deid. ·

He looked at us baith, and there were tears o awe things in his een, and it was plain tae me that haeving started on what was nae less than a confession he maun gang on. And aiblins he wanted us tae understand, and aiblins he didna care a fig whether we did or not.

-Nane kens whaur I am now, sae let them put me doun for deid, or put me doun for a coward, I care nought, for I hae done wae sodgering.

Steenie's face was kind, but his heart I kent was baith grim and near tae breaking. But he comforted Willie Leckie as ane that kent a bit about battles, and he further telt him that nae fault rested wae him, for nae sodger could be expected tae stand firm when captained by fools. Later he telt me how wicked it was tae send fisherfolk, wha were bold enough upon the sea but had nae experience o battle, against Hielanmen. But it showed how desperate the Covenant side was getting, for now Jamie Graham had damn near awe o Scotland in his grasp, and the proper army still sitting on their arses in England, as if the English could not fight their ain fight, and was not the Graham a deidlier danger that any captain the King had there? And ance he had Scotland, weel they wad ken his name, and he damned the Kirk's grand politics that kept the army there.

As we approached Willie Leckie's toun, I could see that he was near owercome wae fear and trembling, and he telt us plainly, that he kent not what he wad say, and that the thought o his hour had tormented him awe the time he was on the road. When we did at last draw up there a great crowd o fisherwomen cam out tae meet us, and certain it was that they had not heard the news, and Willie Leckie said his heart was damned near stopped for he could see aboun fifty o them that he kent were widows. And they themsels it seemed had been put intae a panic o fear by a band o marauding horse which had ridden through, nane kent frae whaur, but they had lifted anything that they could find, and molested any lassie that they could catch, and the women had only saved themsels frae much worse by taking tae their boats, but they had been forced tae watch while their gear was rouped and their biggins burned.

Now when they saw Willie Leckie there was nae doubt but that they were joyful tae see him thinking that this was the first o their men returning, and his ain wife rushed out tae meet him and tae tell him that his ain biggin had been burned in his absence.

He looked at Steenie then, and he looked at me, and there were baith tears and anger in his een, and he said that he regret-ted that he had nae roof tae offer us in return for our kindness.

It was, it seemed tae me, a strange regret tae hae in sic a situation, and the way he said it was sae distracted that it was a bit daftlike. And the fisherwomen were now looking at him wae a muckle horror in their een, and aiblins he looked naething at awe like the bold fisherman wha had marched awa.

For what seemed a lang time nane said anything, and Willie Leckie baith leaned against Steenie and put his airm round his wife, and then he shook them baith off, and ower ilka thing hung the reek o fish, which was like a hamely honest reek that had misplaced itsel. Then the minister o the place, a stern looking man wae lang black hair and a beard, called out in a loud voice,

-And what is the meaning o this, Willie Leckie?

That man was now baith bracing himsel and swaying on his feet, but he answered near as loud as the question.

-I ken not what ye hae heard, but the battle has been fought at Kilsythe and we hae lost, and many are deid, mair than I can count, I ken nane frae here that I ken for certain are alive.

A wailing went up frae them then, like an awful sound which just rose and rose as if it kent not whaur tae gang. And for a lang and terrible minute it looked as if they wad fall on Willie Leckie and oursels wae their filleting knives in their hands. But then it seemed that they had nae strength for that, or for anything else, but just stood there like people out o which awe things human had been struck. Only the minister pushed himsel tae the front his ain face as pale as an auld corpse.

-What dae ye mean man? He cried. -What are ye saying?

-I'm saying what I ken minister. Aye, and it might weel be worse than I ken.

The minister shook his heid as if it was stuck somewhaur between wrath and disbelief.

-Yer drunk man, drunk and hae run awa tae come wae sic a tale as this.

Willie Leckie had nae heart tae answer further, but wae the minister standing in front o him and the women around him he couldna move, and I think he kent, what was plain tae me, that the women wad hate him forever for no being deid and for bringing the news that he brought. And Steenie wha could bear nae mair o this, said,

. -It's the truth he's telling ye minister, and I hae gien him the drink, for wae sic a truth he had need o it.

The minister turned his een on Steenie then, and blasted, frightened, fearful things they were, as if the warld was turning tae dust before them, and perhaps he wad hae liked tae hae blamed Steenie for that.

-And wha might ye be Sir?

-Just a poor bit travelling man and his wife.

-Even a poor bit travelling man nae doubt has a name.

He was looking very hard at Steenie and mysel. And Willie Leckie said that we were just folk that had been kind tae him. But he said it very quietly as if his brain after resolving itsel tae deliver the news had now itsel becam a silly thing. I kent what was in my ain mind, and I kent it was in Steenie's tae, that there was naething that we could dae, and had nae right tae be there, and sae he just turned and climbed back on tae the cart. And as we took the cart out o that place I thought they wad aye remember us wae hatred, if they remembered anything at awe, and if the minister ever found out about us a pitiful sang wad hae anither verse.

Not a word was spoken as we moved out, but I mind awe the faces as we passed them, like things in which awe faith has been destroyed. Some had fallen doun in a faint and nane had stooped tae help them. Ane women was striking at her ain flesh wae her knife and forbye the blude poured out o it nane tried tae stop her.

Steenie said tae me later, for we were baith unco quiet for a time, that the toun itsel was perhaps finished, because if the women could dae many things, ane thing they could not dae was sail fishing boats, and the living o the place depended on fishing, for they had little land for growing things, and perhaps grief and ruin whaur awe that was left tae it.

I thought that if the Lord had any justice he wad hae stripped Jamie Graham o his armour and pitched him intae the midst o the women wae their fillet knives. A bitter fancy nae doubt, for if God has the power tae dae sic things he seems tae hae little inclination tae use it, and for a time I thought as Steenie thought.

☆

We continued South, and if we kent not rightly whaur we were ganging, we were little different from a great many o the Scots folk at that time, wha it seemed had nae destinations tae gang tae, and little left tae protect them on the road, bar the fact that they were nae langer worth pillaging or molesting, and aiblins that was a damned thin armour.

Some wad clan thegither in the hills, landless folk and runaway sodgers alike, and wad threaten tae shoot any armed man o either party wha cam near them. Wae some o these we on occasion stayed. But we did not bide lang haeving little desire tae linger amidst sae much despair and desperation, whaur some wad lament day and night that the Lord had forsaken them, while ithers said that they wad now be sodgers for themsels, their being little profit in being sodgers for the Lord, and they wad look tae their ain spears and guns for their livelihood, for awe that the countryside was in sic a ruinous state that this wad maybe prove as poor a profession as they had found the first.

In ilka place the talk was o the Graham wha it now seemed held awe o Scotland in his grasp and wad gie his Hielanmen the sack o Glasgow as a reward for their services. Steenie said he wad be mad tae dae that after the black name he had got at Aberdeen.

We crossed the Forth, which some folk said was madness for the plague was raging there, and in Edinburgh folk were just deeing in the streets, and awe that had money and sense had fled the place. Ithers said that the plague had now left Edinburgh and was pursuing them that had fled. Nor was there any place tae which they could flee that they wad not be met wae guns, and many deed in the hills, some o the plague, and ithers o madness, murder, and hunger.

We kent not what news was reliable, and were little inclined tae believe that any was, sae we gied the toun o Edinburgh a wide pass and went South intae what was very nearly our ain country, which if it was in better condition than some we had passed through, was still ruinious enough, wae awe its doors shut and its hands turned against any strangers.

We found a bit biggin high up on a hillside that had nae doubt ance been a shepherd's dwelling, forbye neither shepherd nor sheep had been there for a lang time. It was set high and hidden sae that nane could approach it without difficulty, and without being seen, which was a necessity now.

251

Nane cam by us, which was itsel sad and strange, surrounded as we were by gude land that the times had emptied o its folk. On a number o occasions we could see people in the distance through Steenie's lang glass, but whether or not they could see us I couldna tell. Steenie said he had little doubt but that they kent we were there, but fearful they had nae desire tae come closer.

Sae we bade very quietly there in the hills for a time, and at night I wad lie by Steenie listening tae him playing his pipes lowly, and thinking o them as strange, and like a sound frae lang ago, and thinking o awe the things that had happened, and wondering if the land wad ever be itsel again, or if, contrary tae awe that had been promised, we had becam like a limb o Hell and wad remain that way.

Steenie himsel had little tae say about that now, and it seemed tae me that much had gone out o him. That auld sureness and laughter at things he considered nonsense had gone, and how could it not hae gone, when that same nonsense, alang wae anger and confusion, rumbled across the country like a storm.

I telt him that I couldna help but believe that I had seen awe o this when we were in the cave, and which if he minded I had not wanted tae leave and indeed I wad be willing tae gang back tae it.

He just answered that we wad starve on naething but rabbits, and was I now in the midst o chaos tae be taking tae the prophesying? I tossed my heid at him then and said that Catriona had at least said some true things that cam tae pass, and I had met few ithers in my wanderings wha could dae that. He just sighed at that, a queer lang sigh.

-Aye I hae led ye many a strange gate. But the country itsel has ganged a stranger ane, and ye are alive still, and no burned, or murdered, or molested yet, and in a country sic as this ane has become that maun be counted a blessing.

I said nought, for on the road we had heard o awe these things happening. Why they were like the common stock o tales that folk now telt, of women that had been violated at sword point, their bellies cut open if they resisted. Of ithers wha had been carried awa by sodgers tae be little mair than slaves, of horsemen wha served baith sides and maistly themsels, wha just rade the countryside thriving by their weapons, and wha thought as little of lifting a woman for their sport as they did of lifting a cow for their supper.

Sic things were now sae unremarkable as tae be the common stock o folk's experiences, tales, and laments, and through it awe we had passed, and if we kent not frae whaur we cam or tae whaur we were ganging, and our hands were never far frae our guns, still we had passed cannily enough, and perhaps his bit rebuke was justified, and aiblins I thought tae, that in sic a warld as this, nae man, not even Steenie Malecky, was entirely free frae awe blame.

And I thought then of that ither man of wham we now nae langer spoke. Three nights, that were sae close they seemed as ane, I had dreamed o him in my sleep, or ane tae wham I gied his name. Ance as a great loun o a lad in Trig, and ance as blude red man clad in grey steel and mounted on a pale grey horse, and ance in sic a confused way as tae mak nae sense at awe.

And when I woke I kent very certainly that he was deid, forbye I ken now that he was not. But that night I clung tae Steenie and telt him that I wad be happier tae ken that he was deid than riding the country tae its destruction and his ain.

I mind Steenie said nought then, but I mind the fierce force o his hands turning this way and that in my flesh, gripping and holding as if he wad mould the hale shape anew and was angry at its stubbornness. Or aiblins there was anither anger that I could hardly understand, for in the end he just lay beside me very quietly as if he had nae urge tae gang on. And tae me it was as if the warld itsel had becam very still and quiet, listening like a hunted beast that kens not whether tae fight or flee. The first was Sawney's choice, and whiles it seemed a mad choice, perhaps Steenie himsel was distracted wae haeving made nae choice at awe, and seeing nane that he could in gude faith mak, he was like a man wha could neither live in the warld as it was, or change it as he wad wish, he just watched it and waited.

When in the end he released me that night, I remember clearly how my flesh sprang back frae his, for his body tae touch was like a thing on fire, burning, trembling and shivering awe at ance. And how could I no think that he was ill, aye and that the plague itsel had cam tae us at last. But he just laughed at that, and there was something unco wild about his laugh that made it hardly a laugh at awe, and then he just strode out o the biggin, naked as he was, stooping only tae pick up his pipes.

I watched him gang then, neither kenning or not kenning, what I should dae, or whether I should gang after him, for I was naked tae, and it seemed tae my senses that the night just folded ower Steenie then, as if it had waited through awe the nights since time began for this ane.

And then I heard his pipes playing, some wild auld rant that he'd learn't in the Hielans which changed midway intae something soft and gentle. I threw my plaid ower my back and started tae climb tae the sound o it, but it seemed tae my ears that the sound itsel was moving. Nor was it moving in a rational way but sometimes seemed tae be high in the sky and at ithers far below the earth, and at ithers just a fleeting, flyting sound that flew like a bird about the hill-side.

I shouted tae him that he had chosen a fine time tae play Willie Munro's warlock. But he gied nae reply ither than tae pipe awe the wilder sae that the sound hardly appeared tae be in the warld at awe.

At last I found him, for he did not by any signal or word gie any sign as tae whaur he was, as sarkless as the day he'd been born, his pipes in his hand, looking like a bit fairy, but grinning like a muckle black imp o the night.

-Why Steenie Malecky, I cried tae him. -If Willie Munro or Mathius Pringle could see ye now they wad think awe their beliefs confirmed beyond awe contradiction.

He louped doun off the rock and put his airm around me, and for a time we just stood there watching the night crawling ower the hills. There seemed nae end tae either, and oursels the only things o substance in a warld o darkness.

-What ails ye man? I asked.

He shook his heid slowly frae side tae side.

-I dinna really ken Agnes. I was just sitting here thinking

o awe the ill-living and ill-daen that we hae seen while we travelled, and aye the Kirk crying sin in ilka man's lug but its ain, and I thought, yer a Christless man Steenie Malecky.

-Ye hae been that for a while wae yer cursing and yer damning.

-Na, na Agnes, cursing and damning is in its ain way a bit like praying. No very respectful praying I grant ye. But the thought that struck me was mair than that, it was that it was awe nonsense, there was naething either tae pray tae or tae curse, and this hale country, and England tae, was riding in tae madness and disaster for naething, naething at awe.

-It hardly seemed possible, I said tae him. -Awe people believed in the Lord, except them that were ower ignorant tae ken his name. But them that kent it could doubt many things, but they could hardly doubt that without being mad or owerwhelmed by despair.

-Aye, he said, -aiblins it was madness and despair that brought me running up here. Just a madness that wanted tae blaw ane last blast in his lug, and let him strike me doun if he sae desired, or greet me wae a gude night Steenie Malecky, if it pleased him. But if he did nane o these things, weel nae mair, nae mair o him and his Covenants.

I kent not what tae think then. I wrapped him in the plaid that I had brought and we lay doun on the hillside in the night. And it was strange tae lie there looking up at the sky, whirling and swirling, whether in anger, or whether in foolishness I kent not, but I felt the cauldness o the ground that was beneath us, and the cauldness o the wind that whistled aboun us, and I minded how very recently it had been a warm night.

-There are Agnes, he said, -mysteries in the warld, far mair than the Bible teaches, and whiles I think that the earth itsel is far aulder than the Bible says, and hale warlds could hae cam and gane before this ane, and there was a time when great beasts lived the like o which we canna imagine, and they belang not tae daft auld tales, for there are places I hae heard whaur learned men hae found the bones o sic beasts buried deep in the earth, and aiblins awe things that hae passed awa are buried there, and we are but bairns in the things we dinna ken.

-I ken not truly, and it may be that we live in a time when it is nae langer possible tae ken anything truly, even oursels, and the Bible is nae mair than a tale o wandering folk that kent nae mair whaur they were ganging, or why, than the Scots folk ken now, but like a Hielan poet they just made a brave and bludie tale tae cover their confusion.

I kent not how Steenie could ken or think sic things, and it might weel be, I thought then, that in truth Steenie was a great and secret warlock, greater and mair secret than Willie Munro had ever dreamed, or that perhaps he was the Deil himsel. The Deil had a member o hot iron a yaird lang wae which he stole awa the hearts o living folk and kept them chained in Hell while their bodies wandered on the earth powerless tae dae anything ither than his bidding, which was tae torment the warld day and night.

I looked at Steenie then and kent that he was nane o these things, but still he was an unco strange man and the warld was a tormented place. But wae my ain eyes I had seen the hands that did the tormenting, and whether their hearts were in Hell, or whether they were not I canna say, but their hands went blithely enough about their wark, and Steenie was the only man I had kent wha wept for it awe.

We rose tae our feet baith feeling like the only folk on earth, and hardly sure if we were folk and this was the earth. I clung tae Steenie then, awe at ance very feart, feart o awe the things that had passed awa, and awe the things that were still tae cam tae pass. Steenie gripped my hand firmly and sang softly in my ear.

> O they rade on, and further on,
> And they waded through rivers aboun the knee,
> And they saw neither sun nor moon,
> But they heard the roaring o the sea.
>
> It was a mirk mirk night, and there was nae starn light
> And they waded through red blude tae the knee.
> For awe the blude that's shed on earth,
> Runs through the rivers o that country.

☆

It was sometime after that that we saw the sodgers. We had lived in that time strangely and indolently there being naething tae occupy our time but the catching o a bit rabbit or hare and lying in the heather. And there were times tae when I wad look through Steenie's glass at the folk in their fields, and think ye no that I thought it wad be a fine thing tae hae a bit field.

I said this tae Steenie, but he just replied that now was hardly the time, and the only bit field that we wad receive wad be a burial lair.

He had becam unco strange since that wild night, had Steenie. Like a man indifferent tae the fate o things, free, as he himsel said o baith power and faith, and it may be that left him without hope tae, for he could nae langer weep for a warld that he now believed wad thunder tae its ain destruction, or merciful exhaustion, but naething else could stop it, nae act or deed o his.

Then the day cam when we saw the sodgers. He had gone abroad tae look for a bit rabbit and seen them frae the top o a hill and cam running back his een flashing in a way they had not flashed for a while. He clasped my hand in great excitement, and in this fashion we climbed the hill and watched them as they marched past in the glen below.

Sic sodgers I had never before seen. Some that Steenie called cuirassiers were clad frae head tae foot in steel and mounted on great horses. Ithers marched by their sides wae great lances on their shoulders, and by them musketeers, and mair horsemen wae steel bonnets and waving spears, awe singing their psalms and crashing their feet in order sae that their armour rang out like the cracking of a great bell, and their singing was unlike the singing of any congregation that I had ever heard, but was low and beastlike, and rolled like thunder ower the hills, and ower their heids flew the flag o the Covenant, and after them rumbled great cannon.

When they saw us they waved tae us, and shouted that they had cam back tae free Scotland frae the tyranny of Montrose, and while they marched at a brisk pace they seemed tae tak a lang time tae pass us sae many o them were there.

-Leslie's men, Steenie said, -cam back frae England tae be

our salvation, and if they canna beat Jamie Graham naething can.

I minded o awe the young sodger lads that I had sae far
seen, and in comparison these hardly looked like mortal
men, salted sodgers frae the German wars, and ithers that
had been weel salted in England.

Steenie looked at them through his glass and said there
were many faces amang them that he and Sawney had kent,
and that the man riding at their heid was David Leslie
himsel, wha had ance commanded them, and wha was the
kinsman o auld Alexander Leslie, and the best captain the
Covenant had.

He looked at me in an unco odd way then and said that
they were the last card the Kirk had tae throw, and if they
were beaten, Jamie Graham wad truly be maister o the
country. I said that it was what he had aye hoped for, nor
could I see how sic a host o weir men could be beaten. At
that he just handed me his glass still way a gey queer look
in his een.

-Look at wha is riding wae Leslie?

I looked then, and kent full weel wha that lang-faced,
lang-shanked man in the black gown was, and that if he
looked my way his een wad still hae the power tae choke
the breath in my throat, for it was nane ither than Mathius
Pringle himsel.

He looked neither tae the left or the right, and if the very
sight o him made me gae cauld wae fear, I laughed aloud
tae that he kent not at awe I was on the hillside staring
doun at him, and I marvelled that it should come tae pass,
that he of awe men should come at the heid o sic a terrible
host tae be our salvation.

As they passed out o sight in the great cloud o dust their
heels kicked up, I thought, I remember very clearly, that
whatever the Kirk said, there was not, and never would be,
any salvation while that man lived and had power, for I saw
ance again his een bearing doun on me wrathful and bludie,
and why should I hie him on tae beat Jamie Graham, even if
the Graham was a bludie man, for there was nae man on
earth wanted me deid mair than that man?

And Steenie might say, as he did, that the principle o the

business was mair than just ane man. And that sae soon after telling me that principle and purpose was itsel awe but deid, and if it was now tae rise again in the form o Mathius Pringle, wad we then hae tae skulk in the hills forever? And if I could not see how that great army could be beaten, neither could I see how wae him at its heid could it set us free.

I looked at Steenie hardly kenning him, and I demanded o him whether he wad not hae liked fine tae be wae that great army amang awe his auld comrades? And wad he, wha was now sae Christless, sing Godly psalms again as they sang them? And wad he pray wae them, that could not pray without cursing? Or wad he be truly a blasphemy in their midst?

He just smiled a grey bit smile in reply.

-Na, na Agnes, what they hae tae dae they can dae without me, or fail tae dae. But it's just that in his heart a body maun ken what he is against, even if he's little or nae faith in what he's for.

He took my hand again as we walked doun frae the brow o that hill, and he talked lang about how he felt, very little inclined tae draw his sword in any cause, and if he wanted tae see the Graham beat it was for nae mair reason than if the Kirk was a pestilence upon the land, it was a pestilence that in time the people might rid themsels o, but Jamie Graham and his King wad turn awe things back.

☆

It was early in the morning when the minister first walked up the mound they called Steenie's Hill. There was nothing unusual about it, nor was it particularly high, it merely seemed so in relation to the rest of the village. To the left of the path stood a pleasant sparse birchwood, at this time in the morning alive with birds. To the right towered the sheer wall of the cliff. A haughty eyrie, the minister thought as he climbed, from which Malecky could survey his neighbours.

He had gone to see Thomas Mathieson the previous evening, and certainly he remembered Sawney Bain who had been born in Trig and who had ridden off to the German wars, and whom Thomas had met when he himself was a soldier. And certainly he remembered Janet Douglas and her daughter Agnes who had been accused of witchcraft, but had never been brought to trial, but had been plucked from the hands of the Kirk and spirited away by Satan himself. And certainly he remembered the laird who had been drowned in the bog by a cow; or perhaps by the Devil; or perhaps by Janet Douglas whom he had angered, and who had seized him by the scruff of the neck and pitched him in with an unnatural strength that could only be the result of witchcraft.

The minister had watched Thomas Mathieson's ancient countenance, wrinkling, first in surprise at the new minister's visit, and then again as it ransacked the recesses of a decayed mind.

'Some there war wha said it was Janet's dugs that drove the laird in, not without her command. But I canna weel say, for nane really kent then and less they ken now. That he was fished frae the bog in the morning, and that the toun was rouped frae its sleep the nicht afore by a deevilish and wild commotion is weel enough kent. But whether Malecky bided on this hill or that I canna weel say, and forbye the ane caed Steenie's Hill wad seem tae fit, there hae been mony Steenie's dwelt in Trig. But that he rade awa tae the wars wae Sawney Bain I ken tae be true for my faither was a sodger wae them. Aye and my faither had an opinion . . .'

Thomas Mathieson had leaned back in his chair at that point his fingers playing with the hairs on the necks of his two collie dogs. They had risen to intercept the minister when he first entered, but had returned to their original positions at a word from Thomas Mathieson. Now after his initial bewilderment he was rising to the role the minister had ascribed to him, that of chronicler of Trig.

'My faither had an opinion, aye he wad ca it a fact, that it was Steenie himsel wha had pitched the laird intae the bog, for he didna believe that Janet could hae done it, nor the Deil, but he thocht it might weel hae been God almighty, forbye the ane that cam after was nae better . . . Na, in his opinion it was Steenie, for at the time o the incident, nane o Steenie's comrades kent exactly whaur he was, and the common opinion held that he had heard news o what was afoot and had just

260

slipped quietly awa frae the ranks tae put an end tae it.

'My mither had anither opinion which was nae mair than that the laird had ended up in the bog in exactly the way that louns end up in bogs, ower much tae drink, and she thocht it was a shame and a disgrace tae hound a mad auld widow wife and her dochter for sic a cause.'

The minister reached the top of the hill, which was flat, and would certainly have been a perfect spot to build a house with the best view in Trig. There was nothing there, nor was there the slightest sign that anything had ever been there.

For a time the minister just sat on a rock looking out over the tops of the birches. As an excommunicated man they would have burned Malecky's house to the ground, buried the remains and allowed the grass to grow over the spot.

'Did you know her?' He had asked Thomas Mathieson.

'Aye, aye, I kent her weel enough, twa or three years aulder than me, aiblins a bit mair.'

'What was she like?'

'What was she like?' Thomas had answered, as if the question had quite overtaxed his powers of recall.

'A carline . . .' He had said at length. ' . . . Just a bit carline that wad hae naething tae dae wae lads and wadna get mairrit, that's what I mind . . .'

'That was before the witchcraft accusation?'

'Aye, aye, afore it . . . Her mither they said was a witch, but they took her tae, and nae doubt they thought she was as weel. I mind the sodgers hieing them alang the road and my mither saying it was a fell shame and disgrace. Many folk war o that mind . . . But in the end the Deil took them baith, or sae Willie Munro said. Or aiblins it was Steenie, or Sawney, or awe three. My faither said that unlike the lave o folk they warna the kind tae just let their friends be molested in sic a way, and if they thocht that Steenie was deid then they thocht wrang. They war aye fell close, like sister and brithers, which after the affair some said they war . . . But onything could be said about them, onything at awe, and was said, and my faither said the pulpit wad hae matched the alehouse for the things that war said.'

'You mean that some implied that Malecky and Agnes Douglas were actually brother and sister?'

'Some said that. Aye, some maintained it strangly, aye and

261

Sawney tae. Awe Black Janet's bairns, at different times and wae different earthly faithers, the Deil being the real faither o awe three . . . My faither said it was nonsense, and my mither said that sic tongues had mair tae dae wae the Deil than ever had Black Janet.'

'You think there is no truth in it?'

The minister had felt his soul start at this new and terrible possibility. Thomas Mathieson's lips had moved noiselessly together, as if for the moment they had lost the power of speech.

'Wha kens? Wha can ken? Nae doubt the Lord kens, and the Deil kens, and nae doubt Janet hersel kent, but I sall say nae mair o them that are awa.'

The minister's mind could not accept the Satanic paternity, and yet the knowledge of the incestuous horror of the cave rose to confound his reason, there was no horror that could be discounted in such a case. Even that such a damned nativity, hidden from the eyes of William Munro and Mathius Pringle, could be the beginning of the route that led to that infernal place produced a dark symmetry that the minister could hardly bear to contemplate.

'For mysel I think it maist unlikely.'

Thomas had spoken out of a long silence, almost in rebuke, before his eyes had turned away from the minister's, his hands absorbing themselves with hunting burrs in his dog's coat. He had that quality, the minister thought, that they all had, of a simple people whose history in its old shape of war and hardship, and its new one of revolution, had robbed of their simplicity without granting them understanding or enlightenment. Did they feel the loss? The minister did not know. It was not something they could articulate, or that could be articulated for them.

And yet, when Thomas had turned his head again towards him, the expression on his face was one of surprise, as if he was astonished, even irritated to find him still there. To the minister's eyes it was as if the man's features had taken on a certain soldierly stiffness.

'There war some said that baith the women, mither and dochter, had deed during the questioning, which ye maun ken was not a gentle affair, an what had been spirited awa was a scandal. My faither doubted that, saying that baith Steenie and Sawney war alive, and wadna be ower keen tae hae their friends spirited awa, or tae be named as parties tae ony spiriting awa. That was my faither's opinion, but Steenie was never seen again, at least no by me, or ony that I hae kent.'

'But it seems from what I have heard that Sawney Bain was well known.'

'Sawney I next saw in the army which he joined just afore Philiphaugh. I ken not whaur he had been afore that.'

'The battle of Philiphaugh?' He had asked. 'Where General Leslie defeated Montrose? Sawney Bain was there?'

The minister had regretted speaking, and for a moment Thomas Mathieson had almost seemed inclined not to answer. The minister's eyes had surveyed yet again the wretched habitation, the two suspicious dogs, and the antique man. He too had once been one of these steel clad crusaders for the Covenant.

'Aye that ane, Sawney was there. If I mind he cam quietly riding intae camp ane nicht. We had cam up frae England haeving got little gude out o being there, and because we had heard that awe o Scotland was being held at the point o Jamie Graham's sword. As I hae telt ye, I ken not whaur Sawney had cam frae, but he had this minister body riding wae him, and he just signed up there and then wae Leslie wha kent him weel and was nae doubt glad tae hae him. He gied me a bit sign that he kent me and wished me weel, but when I talked tae him he was little inclined tae say mair.

'I spoke tae him o Trig ance or twice, and if he didna quite get angry he was gey short, and said that he had left Trig when a lad and neither regretted leaving nor had ony desire tae gang back, for he had little affection for the place or the lave o its folk. Weel, I said, that was just fine by me, and nae doubt he had his reasons, and I wad remind him nae mair o what gied him sae little pleasure.'

The minister had waited silently, unsure of what to do. His previous interruption had been resented, though the reason for that resentment was obscure to him.

At length he asked:

'Was he an ill-tempered man?'

'Och no not at awe . . . On certain subjects he was tetchy.

I asked him wha the minister was wha had rade in wae him, and he just said a gude man, but wad say naething further. After Philiphaugh Fight, he just rade frae the field saying that the ending was ower bludie, and aiblins it was an ower bludie ending, an nae doubt it was the Lord's will as the Kirk said it was, and tae desist frae that wark wad only anger him ance again . . .'

The minister remembered Thomas Mathieson's voice recalling Philiphaugh, tremulous it had sounded, with ancient horror, ancient joy, and ancient confusion. Sawney Bain had ridden from the field while the Kirk had driven its soldiers to slaughter the women and children who followed Montrose's army.

'Living bairns filleted frae living guts, pikit, chopit, and hackit intae pieces sma . . .Praise Jesus and nae quarter they cried. And when David Leslie had gien them quarter the ministers countermanded that order, and at the end o the day the only quarter they got was when the sodgers themsels rade frae the field demanding o their ministers had they not yet got their fill o blude, and Sawney himsel had cried out that aiblins awe the Hielans wadna suffice tae mak them choke.

The minister looked out over the fields with their tiny figures of men, women, and beasts, their heads bowed, their chests set against the wind.

'Hip and thigh we smote them, and they war the stiffest foot that ever we fought.'

Thomas Mathieson's eyes had seared their way back through the decades to that steaming carcass of a battlefield, and then abruptly they had become blank things, cutting the minister out of their thoughts, hardly even registering the minister's parting blessing. The minister prodded the turf with his stick. Under it, like an excavation into a dead past, there would most likely be some charred evidence that Malecky had indeed lived there. But that was all. The memory of the man who had possessed such a fine conceit of himself, and who had raised such a fury in the minds of William Munro and Mathius Pringle, the people of Trig had shrugged off in a generation. Steven Malecky, the great warlock. In reality, a wretched outcast from religion, society, history, and even his own people's memories. The minister thought of him running naked on the hillside baying at the moon, imagining in his despair past worlds of monsters. Even to his last surviving contemporary he was little more than the stuff of legend.

And yet, as the minister had looked into the dully alert eyes and crumbling countenance of Thomas Mathieson, he had felt that all their history was but a legend, and it was as if he had been compelled to ride back along the twisted path of their passions, his judgment suspended, conscious of his contempt, dimly aware of the damped down fire which smouldered around him.

Riding along that path coming towards him he had imagined Agnes Douglas. The vision, if that is what it was, for at the time it had seemed to the minister almost too mundane and expected, was neither old nor young, but in her prime, wearing black body armour and carrying weapons, all partly concealed by a hodden grey plaid which left her head uncovered.

She had written her tale, he thought, not without guile, telling only that which she chose to tell, and leaving gaps when she chose to be silent. She flattered Malecky as if he was indeed an oracle, while hinting at dark rites and secret knowledge imparted by the savage Catriona, who it was now quite clear to the minister was more than half mad. He felt ashamed of the degree to which they had troubled his mind.

The road ended here, where it had began. He thought of a barefoot girl, lithe and young, singing merrily as she climbed up to where he now sat, romping with the huge dogs that William Munro's century old mind had sincerely believed to be demons, demons who could mimic dogs to a perfect degree.

The peasant memory he thought, is like the peasant mind, a childish thing, unguided it drifts helplessly in a tale composed of superstition and blood, passion, hardship, and despair.

☆

Leslie's Covenant army had hit upon Montrose at a place called Philiphaugh, and there they had cut them tae pieces in a very fierce fight. Much were we tae hear about how bludie that fight had been and how neither quarter nor restraint had been shown. We had taen tae the road again, and the road and the country was alive wae the news o how

265

the women and the bairns that followed the Graham's Hielanmen had awe been slaughtered in the fierce rising o the Kirk's fury.

It was about that time that we oursels cam upon a scene, which, forbye we could not ken it at the time was tae be o some significance.

We had driven alang by the bank o a river called the Avon, and here and there alang the bank were the bodies o deid folk, men, women, and bairns, some drounit, ithers wae their bodies cut and hacked in dreadful fashion sae that the guts spilled out o heidless and limbless corpses. And if they had been thrown intae the river, aiblins the river itsel couldna thole sic things, for it tossed them out on tae its banks and nae doubt the craws were blithe at that. And if Steenie and maist o Scotland had wished for nae ither thing than that the Graham should be defeated, weel now that thing had happened, and perhaps it was indeed a miracle, and the great day o deliverance was at hand, as awe folk that we met said it was, and the place o its coming wad for ever mair be kent as Slain Man's Lee, and wha ever it was wha gied it that name minded but little o the women and bairns that had been killed there.

I ken not, and Steenie himsel said very little, and we made tae leave that river bank being little able tae thole the sight o it.

It was then that the thing happened. A man was swimming in the centre o the river, part swimming, and part being whisked alang by it, ane airm ploughing the water, the ither clinging on tae something that I saw tae be a woman. And whether at that time I thought I kent that man, or whether I did not, I mind not truly. But I mind weel the wild riding o horsemen, five in number, on the bank across frae us, wha shot their guns at the man, and dashed their horses intae the water tae spear at him wae lances, and he twisting and turning, whiles sinking clean out o sight only tae rise again. He was trying, it was plain tae us, tae reach our bank, but the river was ower strang for that, nor wad he let the women gae, forbye tae my een it was as if he had nae mair than a corpse in his hand.

Still wae his ane free hand he struck out bravely, and if it seemed tae me certain that the sodgers wad kill him in the end, they were haeving a bit sport first.

The horsemen had not seen us, and were unlikely in their merriment tae dae sae, or tae tak any heed o us if they did, till Steenie wha was fell angered sent a musket ball whistling ower their heids.

They pulled up then looking damned dumbfounded. And Steenie louped doun frae the cart wae his gun in his hand, and roared at them in a great loud voice that this was not the way for Godly men tae behave. Then paying them nae further heed he put doun his gun and walked intae the river as far as he dared, but managing tae catch the man by the airm he hauled him tae the bank. At that a sodger fired his gun, the ball striking the water very close by. In reply I raised my ain gun, for I was as expert wae the thing now as any, and as little laith tae use it, but Steenie shouted out that I was not tae shoot.

Whether the sodger heard him or not, I ken not, but twa mair bullets struck the water, but if they were now trying seriously tae hit a target they were damned poor shots.

-Damn ye for a tinker loun, ken ye not wha he is? Ane cried out.

Steenie had nae breath at awe tae reply but went on pulling this man, and he was a muckle man, and his carline out o the water.

I thought then, I mind clearly, that this day wad see our end. For despite what Steenie had said, I kent that if any shot him I wad endeavor tae shoot him back. Whether they kent that and were shamed, or whether they were just dumbfounded, I ken not, but they did naething further tae hinder Steenie pulling the man out alang wae the carline, forbye by that time she looked hardly anything ither than deid.

Steenie stood up then and looked at the sodgers.

-Och I ken wha he is, nae doubt ane o Jamie Graham's ignorant kerns. But frae what I hae heard the fight has been won, and is now ower, and I see little Godliness or kindliness in this bludie slaughter.

-Damn ye man, and wha are ye, and hae ye no heard o Aberdeen and Auldearn and Kilsythe, and what dis yon breekless loun ken o Godliness and quarter?

-I was at Aberdeen, aye and I hae fought in the same army as yersel, and dae ye no mind me, for I mind ye weel enough Jamie Hamilton, and aiblins my opinion o ye was better then than it is now. But if ye think ye hae a quarrel wae me then trot yer horse ower and we sall see. Itherwise gang yer ain gate for my patience is no what it ance was.

At hearing his name called out this sodger was pulled up short.

-Steenie Malecky? He cried out. -Why man, awe hae thocht ye lang deid.

-As ye can see very weel I am not deid but a living and angry man.

I ken not what the outcome wad hae been. But at that point something happened that was truly like untae a miracle. Ower the hill anither man cam riding, and forbye this ane had the front o his steel bonnet pulled doun ower his face, I kent in an instant that it was nane ither than Sawney himsel. He shouted at the horsemen harsh words o command which made them fall back, but forbye I shouted out his name till my lungs near burst, he just looked ower at us wae nae hint or sign o recognition, but just turned wae his horsemen and rade awa.

-Sawney Bain. Steenie tae cried out his name, ance, twice and three times, but the hill ower which he rade paid mair heed tae it than that man did, flinging his name back at us as he vanished frae our sight.

At that time I kent not what tae think. I looked doun at the man Steenie had saved, a great muckle naked man he was, gasping like a landed fish, and the carline that he had near met his death saving, lying aside him, naked tae, and like untae ane asleep.

I kent then that I really did ken the man, for I was un-likely ever tae forget that lion's mane o red hair and green cat's een that had ance disturbed my sleep, and in truth it was nane ither than Hector Roy Maclean wha ganged by the name o Red Hector o the Axe.

He looked at me. Whether he kent me then or not I canna say, and, as he was tae say later, he could hae been in Heaven or Hell for awe he kent. Steenie, kenning weel the urgency o the situation, had gien himsel ower tae warking on the carline, and wae sic skill that he made her bring up great buckets o water, and hersel back frae the edge o death.

Awe this Hector watched, the green cat's eyes comprehending, or just watching, exhausted maybe, but alert tae any eventuality. Steenie wrapped the carline in his ain plaid and turning tae him asked him in his ain language if he kent not at awe wha we were, and did he not think it damn near a miracle but some earthly kindnesses had earthly rewards?

I had gien him a blanket tae cover himsel, and wae this wrapped about him he sprang tae his feet looking a wild enough sight, and wae many a wild oath he embraced Steenie and declared that he wad be forever in his debt, for he could see that he was a gude man and nae corbie craw o a Presbyterian. Then, sure that he was amang friends he grew conscious o his appearance and bowed tae me, hugging his blanket about him.

We carried the woman, wha for awe she was conscious, was still a lang way frae being able tae stand, and took them intae the cart whaur Steenie made them baith tae lie doun in the back, cautioning them tae be very quiet should we meet sodgers, or any folk at awe.

We left that place, choked as it was wae the deid o the Graham's last fight and the Kirk's last card, and I kent not which was the maist unco thing, tae meet up wae Hector like that or tae meet up wae Sawney, he still, it wad seem, wae very little desire tae meet us.

-He's switched sides, Steenie said. -And at a very opportune time, whether on the basis o recovered principles or just an auld mercenary's bones telling him that Jamie Graham's run was ower, I canna say. Leslie wad hae him back quick enough, but we ken that Pringle was wae that army.

We steered the cart back tae the shepherd's biggin. It seemed the wisest course in the circumstances, Hector Roy not being the safest baggage tae be seen transporting. For himsel, that man's care, ance he had decided that we were true friends and wad not betray him, was entirely for the carline, tae wham he wad sing softly in his ain language. Observing this and minding how in the river he could hae left her tae droun and aiblins saved himsel, and minding tae his orra gallantry when he cam upon us in the Hielans, I thought that he was no sic a bad man as lang as he was amang friends.

When we arrived back at the biggin we fed them and gied them some whisky tae drink, and Steenie and Hector sat a little apart talking very close. I bided wae the carline presenting her wae some o my ain claes. While daen this I quickly realised, as she hersel confessed, that she was nae Hielanwoman at awe, but had been stolen awa frae Aberdeen by Hector Roy when that man was nae doubt playing his part tae the full in the roup o the place.

She was a fine looking woman wae lang brown hair, but thin and wild, as if food had not aye been handy when it was needed. She telt me her name was Kate, and ance clothed decently, for she had been fair affronted by her nakedness, and angry at the barbarous treatment she had received at the hands o the sodgers, for had she not been born, and before fortune changed her course, as gude a Presbyterian as any o them.

Her story was a strange ane, even in that strange time when few folks lives ran their normal gate, and she telt me that she was not the only carline cut doun or captured at Philiphaugh, wha hailed not frae some Hielan clachan but had ance walked doucely in the streets o Aberdeen. That, it seemed, counted for very little at the final outcome.

She had, she telt me, been left faitherless and mitherless at a very early age, when through the gude offices o some folk she had been taen intae the house of a very rich merchant o Aberdeen. In time this merchant also took her intae his bed. Now he being a man o great influence in the Kirk and the city this was a secret weel keepit by the four walls o his house and the darkness o the night, tae be let out only in his private prayers o repentance, which tae be sure were ane lang lament on how his Christian charity had fixed a petard tae his immortal soul, which he feared wad ane day destroy him.

She wad hear him at night, Ogilvie was his name, stealthily at his brandy, and stealthier yet wad he creep up the stairs tae her bed, admonishing her sternly tae tak care that she ended up not wae a bairn, for his reputation couldna thole that.

Ten years and mair she had lived in this way, a burden baith on his purse and on his soul, and she in mortal fear that he wad ane day keep tae his resolution and be rid o her. He had ample opportunity for this, being visited often by merchants frae ither countries and captains o trading ships, wha were awe less circumspect in their admiration.

Ane, a Dutch captain, she heard ane night bargaining for her, and Ogilvie complaining that the Presbytery o Aberdeen was less appreciative o his charity that it had ance been, and he himsel thought it was time he took a proper wife.

That night it was the Dutchman wha climbed the stairs, and if he was a prettier man and a merrier ane than Ogilvie, he was nae less canny, and was inclined tae try his goods ere he bought them. Ogilvie, it seemed, had driven a hard bargain, baith in material things, and in things o the spirit, insisting that the Dutchman gied him his solemn promise tae keep her decently and not gae selling her tae some brothel in Holland, and tae mak sure that she went tae kirk, and nae doubt she wad be a faithful comfort tae him in his retirement.

Awe this she learnt by making gude use o her ears, for not a word on the matter was ever spoken tae her directly. Indeed very little was ever spoken tae her directly, Ogilvie coming and ganging frae her bed in sic silence that, apart frae his grunting and girning, he might weel hae been a ghost.

But she kent it weel enough, and ance when she asked him plainly if he meant tae sell her, he choked as if the Deil had him by the throat, and declared that what he did he did for the best, and God was his witness tae that. And did she in her childishness think that the streets o Aberdeen were a finer place than a gude house in Holland, for his new wife could hardly be expected tae thole sic things.

Awe this ended on that day when Hector's Lochaber axe crashed through her merchant's fine new door, brought frae Holland, and part o the price that had been paid for her. Ogilvie passed clean awa at the sight o him, and the Dutchman relinquished in an instant any pretensions that he had tae her, and on his knees beseeched Hector no tae kill a man that was but a visitor tae his country and had nae part in its quarrels.

Hector it seemed, did not, but he scooped up baith her and anything else that took his fancy in his airms.

For awe that, and for awe his rough wooing, he had treated her wae kindness there-after, not forcing her in anything, but biding his time quietly. She was much surprised at this, and telt me that at the time she had only been saved frae deeing o fright by the thought that she might meet Ogilvie in eternity. But in the end his kindness won her, and she resolved tae follow the Hielanman, wha was a man o note in his ain country.

Since that time she had done sae, ganging wae him on awe Jamie Graham's terrible marches, and swore tae dae sae as lang as there was breath left in either o them, and she cared not a fig if she never saw a kirk again.

Sic was her story, and forbye it nearly cam tae a bludie end on Slain Man's Lee, it was a happier story than many in the land could tell at that time.

I liked her fine, and despite awe I mind these as being gude days, as if a great storm had broken ower our heids and then passed on its way. Awe that aside, we still had the problem of how they were tae be returned tae Hector's ain island o Mull, for here they could not bide without the risk o being hung if captured.

This was much on Steenie's mind, for we had but twa horses which wad inconvenience us much tae part wae.

The matter was resolved when ane night, late at e'en, Hector just disappeared saying neither whaur he was ganging, or when he wad return. Kate, wha had becam half-Hielan hersel by now just said that, och she kent him very weel and nae doubt he had gone tae seek a way out o their difficulties.

Hector returned lang before the dawn, and aiblins there are great miracles, and aiblins there are small anes, but the man was now riding a gude horse and was leading anither. Besides that he had got a broadsword and twa or three guns.

-Ask nae questions, Steenie said. -Ask nae questions at awe.

Now it might weel be that the sodger that Hector killed in order tae get his fine new gear was the last blow struck in the Graham's bludie campaign. I ken not, according tae his ain lights he had himsel been robbed, and he and Kate near butchered in a maist dishonourable fashion, and now he, naked in a land o enemies, saw nae sin at awe in providing for himsel and his carline frae off the backs o these enemies, and nae doubt tae, that Steenie was right and it was time enough that Hector Roy Maclean should be on his way.

The next night he counselled him weel on which routes tae tak through the Lawlands. Ance in the Hielans he wad ken his ain way. He counselled him tae molest nane that did not molest him, but tae gang as swiftly as a Hielanman can. Awe of this he promised tae dae, and we gied them a bit food and drink for the journey, and baith he and Kate embraced us wae great warmth, promising us that if we ever cam tae Mull, awe that he had wad be ours, for there he was not some naked man without a name.

Sae we watched them as they set out. Dressed in hodden grey plaids they looked like Godfearing folk ganging quietly about their business, forbye the plain truth, that very few did that in these days.

-Dae ye think they sall win hame? I asked Steenie.

He said that he thought they wad, for a Hielanman can gang quieter than a cat when he has a mind, and he just prayed that nane wad hae the foolishness tae interfere wae them.

I thought at the time, how strange it was that there was Hector Roy Maclean, wha had fought and campaigned for King Charles, and was now returning defeated tae his ain island wae hardly any mair idea o that man than that man had o him. And it seemed tae me then that awe men's ideas were like that, just bit things in a storm driven this way and that, whether by God or the Deil, or their ain pride, or some ither thing, I ken not.

I looked at Steenie then, kenning in an unco strange way what was on his mind, and he shortly confirmed it when he said,

273

-Wad ye like tae gang tae Edinburgh Agnes?

I kent him, I thought, very weel. The army had gone tae Edinburgh, and maist likely Sawney wae it, and I kent this thought had been in his heid for some days.

I said that if we went tae Edinburgh it might weel be that we wad meet Sawney, but it seemed tae me that man had very little desire tae meet us, haeving passed up a fine opportunity some days ago, and aiblins I had nae langer any desire tae meet him, thinking o him now as a different man and little mair than a stranger.

-Och he'll never be that.

He spoke unco quietly, and I wondered at that, thinking o awe the times he had cursed Sawney when I had thought mair kindly on him, and why he wad not now just let the man gang his ain gate? Or was it because Steenie Malecky could not bear the thought o being rejectit, or haeving any slip out o that unco strange power o his? I ken not truly, and awe he said was,

-Times will nae doubt hae changed a bit, and aiblins folk will nae langer be as fearful as they ance were. Aye and I wad like fine tae talk wae Sawney ance again, and find out how things gang wae a three times turnabout, and tae see if the land is any happier now that it has freed itsel frae Jamie Graham, and we'll not find that out wandering in the hills like tinks.

☆

The minister stood on the brow of Steenie's Hill. He watched the light of an almost full moon filtering through the birch trees, deepening, and softening the outline of the hills. He had taken to walking up this hill in the late evening or early morning. His parishioners would watch him go, they it seemed avoided the place, as they avoided his now merely occasional questions about it.

'It's a bracing walk, and a splendid view,' the minister declared as a justification of his excursions. They merely nodded their heads, their features marked with that inscrutable dour docility which he had decided was characteristic of the majority of them when faced with something which they did not understand, or an action of his of which they disapproved. They did not climb hills for the pleasure of it, and fine views held little charm for them.

'The Scots Lowland peasant,' Gilmarten had written, 'lacks the civility and traditions of intelligent industry of his English counterpart. History has made of him an altogether more primitive creature in which primitive prides, conceits, ignorancies and superstitions, are not entirely extinguished.'

The minister smiled. He dug his walking stick into the earth of the hill. It gave him a certain satisfaction to dig it and his heels into this burial mound of dead superstition.

Even the dreadful knowledge of the cave waxed and waned in his mind as if it no longer possessed any power to injure him. They had been reduced to wretched misbegotten outcasts, Malecky a mere hobgoblin of the peasant mind. He thought of the possibility that they were all offspring of the same mother. Whether truth or tale hardly any longer affected anything, history and memory, like the earth of the hill had simply closed over them, reducing the horrors and confusions of their lives to an already ancient barbarity.

He thought of Sawney Bain himself now with some compassion as a poor dupe tossed by the events of his time from battlefield to battlefield, a simple man attempting to reason beyond his capacity. And yet he, along with Thomas Mathieson, had ridden from the field at Philiphaugh. The minister remembered with a shudder the challenge and the accusation in the ancient soldier's eyes. His brethren were ultimately at fault. The soldiers, battle hardened veterans of many wars, had shown some mercy and the Kirk had shown none, and of course they had only been Godless Highlanders and Papist Irish, themselves as savage as nature could make them. The minister felt a violent disgust for the past, whether it appeared with a Godly psalm on its lips or a Highland battle-slogan.

He thrust his walking stick into the earth of the hill, and without thinking loosened a large stone which he sent spinning into the valley below. He watched it descend, smiling at his own childishness.

He thought of Martha Liddel and her niece who had visited his church the previous Sunday. Whether Martha had enjoyed his sermon he could not tell. No doubt, he had thought, she has fiercer preachers of her own.

She had looked down at him from the cart she was driving, her own face an embattled, crumbling relic of the past. Beside her Helen Melville had sat, radiant and untainted, smiling a smile as light as thistledown which had lifted up his spirits in a way that nothing else had of late. In her he had seen redemption and renewal; preserved in childhood by the intervention of the pious wanderer Todd Grey, loved and protected by Martha's faith and courage, she was like a new Spring quietly waiting to burst forth.

The minister struck the ground vigorously with his stick, imagining playfully the possibility of Malecky's bones rattling, when suddenly he realised that he was not alone on the hill.

He turned slowly round. He could not accurately identify the source of the sound, but his expectations were of some animal which his curiosity did not want to unduly startle. His eyes fell upon the partly concealed, partly revealed, figure of Walter Hyslop, who if he was not actually hiding, was hardly inviting discovery.

'Why, Mr Hyslop, you surprise me.'

'Gude evening minister, taking the night air, Sir?'

'As a matter of fact, yes, this place intrigues me and I like the view.'

'It is a place of sin, now and in the past, aye and aiblins it will be sae forever.'

Hyslop did not physically move, but his face, suddenly furious, seemed to expand and glow in the moonlight.

'Blasphemers come here minister, aye and fornicators, strumpets, fiddlers, dancers, swearers, evil-doers and casters doun o the Kirk and its Covenants. Aye the lewd and the loud and the bold in their sin will awe foregaither here, for they ken this place, and ken as awe folk ken, that lang ago it was handfasted wae the Deevil, and Satan himsel wad visit here, and be made welcome, taking the shape o whatever beast he pleased, confident that he wad aye be kent, and waited upon, and hae his hair combed and his arse licked, and servants a-plenty tae dae his bidding. And there wad be nae uncleanness that his hairt, or the hairt o ony that served him, desired, but it wad be granted without let or stint . . .'

The elder had lurched forward, propelled it appeared by the

force of his own passion. It was either a change in proximity, or the breeze, but in that instant the minister knew what he had interrupted. The village dominie had been drinking.

The minister's senses reeled. The lonely zealot of Trig concealed in the undergrowth of Malecky's Hill at midnight, nursing his bottle. The awful comedy of that scene almost overwhelmed him. But in Walter Hyslop's eyes there was not the slightest hint of amusement, or any awareness of the minister's discovery. He continued to speak as had started, his voice a bitter, burning thing.

'Och they will not gang up here when they ken, as they aye ken, that there is a Christian man about the place. For ane Godly man Sir, is enough tae send the hale pack squealing like pigs tae their pits. Which is why I hae nae fear at awe o them, for they ken weel that Wattie Hyslop is not ane tae be frighted or dinged doun. But whiles as I sit here I might get wind o a bit o fornication here and there, which is the common run o things that I maun deal wae.'

The minister felt he could hardly be amused. More than ever Walter Hyslop appeared to him as despair held erect by an indomitable will. The minister felt helpless before it. He neither wished to take the elder to task, or to say anything to indicate that he knew that he had been drinking, but nor did he feel it was proper just to leave him. Indeed Hyslop gave every indication that he wanted the minister to stay. His voice, as if suddenly conscious of itself, lost its stridency and became quiet, almost conversational, even absurdly whimsical.

'The Deevil Sir, hates this land, for he kens that it was a land chosen by the Lord himsel, and Covenanted wae him tae be a blessed light upon the Earth. But Satan kens how easily they can be tempted, and wae what subtilties they can be beguiled, and wad be if the Lord had not set some tae watch and wait. And aiblins even then minister, dae what we can, awe sall be lost. For the people o this nation are a fallen people wha out o their ain perverseness hae hurled themsels frae the high pinnacle on which he set them, and hae hearkened tae the beguilements o awe that wad beguile them, wha, for awe they are many, wad, if a true stand was made against them, matter as little as flies on a Summer's day.'

Hyslop's body swayed as if the power that held it upright

277

was itself wavering. His eyes shone, they appeared to the minister, both baleful and beseeching, the voice alternated between anguish and anger.

'We delude oursels minister, aye and perhaps the lave o us hae aye deluded oursels, kenning not that in the days o defeat Sir, when many were slain and many were humbled, but when courage and faith was still high, were aiblins even then the hours o victory which we kent not, and this hour o seeming victory is Sir, the time when awe things end.

'I ken not, but I ken this, that I hae been sent tae guard this folk, and guard them I will, for I ken nae ither gate. And when they gang blindly doun the path o wickedness, there at its heid they sall find auld Wattie Hyslop that awe the toun laughs at, wae a burning brand in his hand, tae mak them see, and tae let them ken, that if they gang on, they will gang on kenning weel intae wha's hands they are ganging.

'Sae let Marten Gilmarten whisk himsel off tae Edinburgh tae dance a reel at the laird's coat tails. For I hae telt him tae, that whaur the laird dances ither things dance as weel, that will hae baith him and the laird by the arse o their breeks and the scruff o their necks, and a bonny jig that sall be, and a bonny tune will be played then, and hands wha had thocht tae be grasping some wee whore's cunt, sall aiblins be covering their een frae the horror o it awe, though muckle gude it sall dae them.'

'Mr Hyslop I beg you to desist. This is nonsense. I order you to desist.'

The elder's voice rose like a sudden storm over the minister's head. Awed the minister watched it rise it only appearing to become coherent when it reached its zenith.

'Desist awa, nae man maks Wattie Hyslop desist. If the Lord calls upon me tae cry out wha then dares say desist? And will then nae doubt tell me that John Doig, for awe that he has the sillar tae build fine kirks is a Godly man, wha in truth has less Godliness than the Hielanmen wha burnt the auld ane doun? Or that Marten Gilmarten wha kens weel how tae rage against some poor sinful loun in Trig, kens not also when tae haud his tongue when he is amang great folk and sees their doings. Or when some doxie is lifting her skirts in some Edinburgh den, a darker place than ony hillside in Trig, bar this ane? Oh ho,

Sir! Oh ho, fegs, ye are a but bairn, or hae the brains o ane, or hae been amang the Dutchmen ower lang if ye ken not these things . . .'

Suddenly as if losing his balance, the elder sat down on the grass. He stared up at the minister his voice sunk almost to a whisper.

'We are alane Sir, or sae nae doubt think ye, and which enables ye tae stand wae sic elegant self-assurance, firm in the conviction that yer senses are in yer heid whaur they ought tae be, while poor auld Wattie Hyslop's are aiblins elsewhaur, aiblins a lang way elsewhaur. But ye ken not wha this hill was named for?'

The minister's hand was partly raised in rebuke, and then suddenly his anger subsided. Hyslop's face was a mask of tortured malevolence. Beside him, barely concealed, was a flagon of whisky.

'But I ken ye, och I ken ye weel, ye wha hae a conceit o yersel as fine as yer gude horse. Och, but folk are easy tae ken, sinful, fleshproud louns wae a fine sark upon their backs and a feather and bonnet on their heid, and am I no a brave Jockie, tae pay sae little heed tae what lies tae the left and tae the right and up aheid.'

'In my opinion though nobody in the village appears able to confirm it, this hill was named after a Steven Malecky.'

With a speed that startled the minister, the elder was once again on his feet. A long emaciated arm with its finger outstretched pointed straight at him.

'Whaur dae ye ken that name Sir? Answer me quick for I maun ken.'

'In Edinburgh, before I came here, I read some of the writings of a Reverent Mathius Pringle, who mentions him in very unfavourable terms.'

'Unfavourable minister, unfavourable, aye indeed unfavourable, sic a dainty tongue ye hae Sir, for I kent Mathius Pringle weel and he wad hae a rougher tongue than that for ane wha has been, and might weel still be, the worst pestilence that has ever visited this land. A man Sir wha has been awe these lang years the cause o awe our woes, a man Sir wha by wiles and deceits and false kindnesses, and a tongue as subtle as the Serpent himsel could steal awa the soul, guts and hearts o awe but the Lord's elect. Och aye, twas a sure way of kenning the elect, being them that stood firm against Malecky, and could watch wae neither fear nor apprehension in their hearts, as he was forced tae first back awa and then tae flee, snapping his teeth in his rage, kenning that he had met wae sic a power against which he was nae mair than chaff in the wind. Sic a man was Mathius Pringle, wha drove him frae the parish, and wad hae apprehended him except that the men wha followed him were superstitious ignorant louns o sodgers. He was guardian and teacher, and mair than a faither tae me . . .'

The minister felt suddenly overwhelmed. It was as if the myriad strands of history, the tentacles of the dead, and the thunder of old passions had all collided simultaneously at the spot from whence they had started with an unnerving precision. And the people of Trig it appeared had lied to him. Or if they had not lied, they had simply parried his questions, or evaded them, or not understood them. 'Ye will hear stories,' Andrew Gilmore had said. 'And few wha tell ye these stories will be able tae vouch for the truth o them.' He looked at Walter Hyslop, the man was visibly swaying now, whether through the force of his passions or through whisky the minister could not tell.

'You have been drinking.'

The elder's eyes glinted savagely from a waxen face. The minister felt suddenly smitten by these eyes which with a fanatic certainty seemed to penetrate to the depths of his soul. Yet when he spoke again his voice was soft, almost subservient.

'Aye Sir, that I hae, and aiblins there are reasons, which are not very gude reasons, but we are taught forbearance are we not, and forgiveness? And aiblins a man daen tae the best o his poor abilities what he perceives tae be the Lord's wark can be allowed a bit warmth to keep the night at bay.'

'I'm sorry, I did not mean . . . forgive me . . .'

'Nae need, nae need, chastisement is nae doubt in order.'

The minister was astonished to see that the eyes were now moist with tears.

'Sae the folk o Trig hae denied tae ye that the name o this hill hauds ony meaning for them?'

'They appear to think that the man after whom it was named

lived a long time ago, and be unaware that he had any connection with them or their immediate history. All apart from Thomas Mathieson perhaps.'

'Why, minister that is but their bit evasion, near a denial o the Kirk that raised them. For they awe ken wha Malecky was, and what he did when he lived, if indeed he is now deid. And in their lies ye see a terrible proof o the pestilential nature o him wha seduced them when he bided here, and hauds on tae them still tae the second and third generation, sae that they will neither say yea or nay tae ony questions about him, but will whisper and dissemble and say they ken him not. And then they gie, and then they deny that they hae gien, his name tae the place whaur he ance bided, and smile unco innocently at the question o it.

'Och I ken, for there is little I dinna ken, that some even think it gude luck tae bairn their wives on this hill. And ithers will bairn carlines that are not yet their wives and nae doubt they think it no sae gude luck. Sic detestable superstitions and nonsense still persists even after Mathius Pringle investigated awe these things, and could prove, that ony wha ever consorted wae Malecky, and fell under his spell o charming had far mair than bad luck tae contend wae. And he prophesied that Malecky had been in the past, and wad be in the future, the sometimes visible, sometimes hidden, author o things mair horrible than ony could imagine, for he had faced him een tae een and kent him weel for what he was. Aye and he charged me afore he deed, that should I ever come upon him, and I wad surely ken it was him, I was tae kill him by what ever means was handiest, thinking neither of my ain safety or any ither thing.'

The minister's mind had divorced itself from the tirade, forced back to a dark and noisome place, the existence of which this poor demented soul could hardly have begun to imagine. A place that had once again become so hideous in his imagination that it poisoned the night and the air he breathed. He thought of them crawling naked through life, from childhood to adulthood, from birth to death, except that they believed they would never die, but would spend eternity crawling into each others beds like pigs in a sty, crawling beneath the earth, waiting for that day when they believed they would be called forth. He saw their undulating bodies that

281

could not die, pale and dreadful flesh locked in an unceasing and indiscriminate rut. Eyes that witnessed these things but were not blinded, lips that mouthed unspeakable desires but were not struck dumb. The minister began to laugh uncontrollably. They were children these fierce men of the Kirk in their knowledge of evil.

He stopped laughing abruptly when he saw the scandalised expression on Walter Hyslop's face.

'Forgive me Walter, something came over me, I don't know what it was.'

The dominie looking suddenly solemn, slowly nodded his head.

'It's this place minister, it can play queer tricks when it kens it is meeting the resistance o ane o the Lord's elect. But pay it nae heed for they can dae ye nae hairm but aiblins just tak ye unawares by a few bairnish tricks.'

To the minister's dreamlike amazement Hyslop stooped, picked up a large stone, and hurled it with great force into the undergrowth.

'Begone ye imp ye, they'll be nae gaithering this nicht, Wattie Hyslop sall see tae that.'

He turned to the minister.

'He'll no be back, they're fell cowards without their maister, and when in a rout he runs faster than ony.'

The minister waited. Walter seemed to have forgiven his laughter, or at least found a satisfactory explanation for it. Indeed having thrown the stone the elder seemed to have drained himself of any further enthusiasm.

'You talk as if Malecky was still alive, which is surely unlikely.'

'Aiblins aye minister, aiblins no. He was apprehended in Edinburgh at the time o the battle o Dunbar, but he escaped minister, how naebody rightly kens, for awe a bairn could guess, for his name was written in blood for awe tae see on Dunbar field. But he cam again minister when the Deevil was riding the land by the side o John Graham o Claverhouse. Aye, and aye his style was the same, subtle words and false kindnesses tae folk wha war in great need o kindness, and I pray the Lord will forgive them for that. I ken not, but awe Malecky's guile was tae ane purpose, and that accomplished he wad pitch them intae a ditch without prayer or blessing.'

'He murdered them?'

'Na, na Sir, he was far ower subtle tae murder their bodies, but he destroyed their minds and left their hearts and souls in sic confusion that in the end they murdered themsels out o despair.'

Hyslop's voice started to rise again, rolling like distant thunder towards the minister, his eyes peering into his as if he was a slow-witted child. The minister felt himself transfixed by them, accepting their judgement, as if all his learning, all his beliefs, were like skittles unable to withstand or contradict Hyslop's onslaught. And when the elder suddenly seemed to erupt, pouncing like a great cat to grasp the collar of the minister's coat, he felt himself shaken in a grip, that for all the man's frailty, felt fiendishly strong. He thought of Mathew Elliot's brother and knew exactly why that man had turned tail and taken to the hills. Walter breathed fire and passion, holy vengeance and battle without quarter, against which the minister's startled protests were the remonstrances of a world without substance.

'It was weakness minister, weakness and lack of faith that aye let Malecky in, weakness o the spirit and weakness o the flesh. Aye and weakness o the warld, for he was a man o great skill and knowledge in the wiles o awe these things, and kent weel that the lave o men are just composed o warldly baseness, greed, and fleshly lust. And what dis Malecky dae when he confronts sic a man? Why he just smiles upon him wae simpering cunning, and tells him no tae be feart, deevil tak his fears, for he Steeenie Malecky will just tak his fears between his finger and thumb and just toss them awa. Aye, and men's hearts open tae him, and women's legs open tae him, and their immortal souls are split asunder, and the image o God just flees out o the gap, and wae a daft bairn-like simper on their lips, they just watch it gang, and think their very een tae be blessed.

'Mr Hyslop! Malecky may be as wicked as you say, but your own speech is hardly far short of blasphemy!'

'In the famine years he cam again, wae anither name now, Todd Grey was what he cried himsel now, aye the grey fox, wolf mair like. But he was aptly named, prowling aye amang the deid and deeing like a great carrion beast bringing despair and mockery tae their last hours, rouping their biggins and molesting in unspeakable ways the bodies o the living and the corpses o the deid, exulting tae behold that this folk wha had ance been a Covenanted nation, and sae shining wae promise that it was a light upon the earth, this folk wha had dwelt through sae mony lang years o barbarous ignorance, and wha had been raised up by the hand o the Lord himsel, had ance again been delivered up tae strife, ignorance, and pestilence.

'I have heard of this Todd Grey, and sensible men have told me that he was but an old and Godly Covenanter who out of mercy buried the corpses of those who had died.'

'Sensible men, minister!' Hyslop screamed in his ear. 'A plague upon this warld o sensible men wha hang their judgements upon appearances, aye and on gude warks and fair words. Steenie Malecky or Todd Grey, whatever name ye choose, could string a sensible man by his heels frae a birk tree and he wad think he was walking doucely tae paradise, aye and aiblins was already there.'

'I think I can vouch for the good sense of my friend.'

Hyslop, as quickly as he had pounced, now released the minister and took two steps back.

'Tis the weel kent mark o a sensible man that ither sensible men will vouch for them thereby ensnaring the hale warld in their gude sense. Awe haeving sense enough tae ken which way the warld gangs – tae the court at London tae crawl about the feet o Dutch Willie – och a Solomon in his wisdom? Or tae the Parliament House in Edinburgh wae John Doig and Marten Gilmarten? A Parliament Sir, that is worth less than a herd o Galloway stirks, and indeed is soon tae be sold like ane, sensible men no being the kind tae refuse a bit sillar that gangs their way – and for awe their sensibleness it will nae doubt shortly clink in the purse o some Edinburgh whore. Sae speak not tae me o what sensible men say and what sensible men dae. Gude nicht tae ye minister.'

With a queer comic bow the elder picked up his flagon of whisky and without another word staggered off down the path.

The minister watched the long swaying figure until it was out of sight. For half an hour after that he just stood there feeling the dark derangement of the place risen anew, enclos-

284

ing, and silently testifying to a history of shrieking nonsense which Walter Hyslop bore witness to in his justified madness.

His soul felt numb. It was as if everything real and true and joyful had evaporated out of his new world. He remembered the girl Helen. She had been brought to Martha Liddel by Todd Grey. If Todd Grey was indeed Malecky, and Malecky was indeed who he was said to be, then . . . The minister felt a cool clear burning anguish for her. And yet, it was, he believed, impossible that God would allow her to be lost or tarnished in any way by an old man who had saved her life, and who might or might not be Steven Malecky.

Still, he thought, so much appeared to have been lost in this land that men went mad with the memory of it. As if each had dreamt their particular dream, and a sense of loss was all they now shared.

He walked slowly to the bottom of the hill. Walter Hyslop's words still rang in his ears. If the elder spoke the truth then his parishioners had simply lied to him; or at the very least evaded the truth; or had thought his questions hardly worth bothering their heads about; or had simply decided that there were some things they had no intention of sharing with him; or they had simply forgotten and Walter's fancies were Walter's alone.

At the bottom of the hill he was astonished to find the dominie standing in the middle of the street, ostensibly waiting for him. There was something excessive and ridiculous about that, the minister felt. He had, at least for the night, thought he had seen the last of the man, and now he did not know either how to acknowledge him or greet him, and his neck still hurt from the furious shaking it had received.

Hyslop seemed to have entirely recovered himself. He solved the minister's dilemma by speaking first, in a voice that was now placid and respectful, and indeed remarkably sober.

'Minister, as ye are tae my mind, a Godly man and a gude man, as weel as a gentle and a learned ane, I hae something here which might be of interest tae ye, and which might explain mony things which hitherto hae not been properly explained, for I am a poor man at explanations, haeving spent ower much o my time in the company o bairns and ignorant folk.'

The man was shy now, almost diffident, and in his out-stretched hand he held a leather bag.

'In this case are some o the last writings and testaments, which are like untae prophecies tae my poor self, forbye they may seem tae ye as nae mair than the farsighted words o the Lord's elect, Mathius Pringle. Nane kens that I hae them, but they war gien tae me out o his ain hand shortly before his time o struggle was ower and his never ending glory began.'

The minister stood once again transfixed. Only his discipline, his training, and his essential gentleness, kept the riot in his mind in check. Of all this Walter appeared entirely unaware. He simply stood, his head bowed, his eyes moist in the moonlight, and an extraordinarily gentle smile curving across his features. The minister realised that, if necessary, he had been prepared to wait half the night until he should choose to walk back that way.

The minister took the bag in his hands. It was an old army saddle-bag with the arms of the Covenant engraved on it.

'You will want this back some time, Mr Hyslop?'

'Indeed sae minister, though ye may mak a copy if ye wish.'

The elder bade him good night, and bowing for the second time he turned and walked briskly in the direction of his cottage.

Again the minister watched him go before himself turning and walking through the village to his house. Before entering he turned to look at the cottages that surrounded him. They were all tightly battened up for the night, with only here and there a cat to disturb the absolute silence of the place.

There were rules against allowing dogs to roam; there were rules against allowing cattle or horses to roam; there were rules against disturbing your neighbour's peace. All these rules were regularly infringed, and the fines imposed for their infringement, as were the fines imposed for fornication, adultery, drinking, swearing, and brawling, went to feed the village poor, an arrangement that had a kind of economy about it.

They had quite possibly lied to him, and yet at that moment the minister felt a deep infusion of love for this disciplined, fractious, primitive community, which kept its deepest secrets out of the reach of Christian discipline, huddled in some deep vault of their communal mind.

He remembered how Malecky himself, waving an ancient spear, had summoned the village to battle, and the village had gone when all the remonstrations of its minister had not persuaded them to go. If Munro and Pringle, and now Walter Hyslop, were right, they had gone at the Devil's bidding, thereby poisoning the whole enterprise.

Once inside he lit a candle and took the manuscript from the army saddle-bags. The minister recognised immediately the bold scholarly hand-writing. He laid it on his desk in front of him and lit his reading lamp.

☆

It was that day, I remember it well, the twentieth day of January in the year 1646, a cold hard morning in Edinburgh, when the last of the runagates taken at Philiphaugh were hingit or beheadit, each according to his station, for they are precise in such matters, binding their hearts in earthly prides even unto the brink of Hell.

There were those I remember who declared we were over bludie, speaking sincerely from a tender heart and a blindit eye. And there were others who if their courage had matched their false principles would have been hanging there too. Of them, in time, we would hear more.

I was inclined to none of these confusions. I did not gawk as the multitude did, nor did I exult overmuch, which would have been unseemly. To my mind, the Lord, after many harsh and bludie trials had brought them to his Kirk's justice at last, and it would have been foolish to imagine that he had done so in order that we should shake them by the hand and wish them well. They had been a pestilence on the land and the land was well rid of them.

If I pondered at all upon the outcome, it was that James Graham was not among them. Some there were who said that he had escaped to France, others were of the opinion that he was in Holland. I reflected only on the fact that he was alive and the meaning of his preservation was hidden from me.

Indeed as I backward cast my eye to things that I knew then, and how in a moment of weakness it had seemed to me that all our endeavors had turned into the opposite of what we had intended. And when I cast it forward to things that I could not know it was in fear and apprehension of the great trials that lay ahead. Only in casting it upwards, was I reminded, and comforted, that the Lord had not abandoned his wayward and faithless people, but with a fiery sword pointed out the lang hard road alang which they must gang.

Along that road, burning and flaming in his insolence, ready to waylay us at every turn, I could see Steven Malecky. And where I saw him I saw aye the Douglas witch at his side, his servant in all things, and though they had on many occasions come near to being apprehended, none had so far succeeded, and as a consequence I felt, and without doubt was intended to feel, the burden of their mischief and abominations lie heavy on my heart.

I first had news of them, after that mirk night when Satan's wings bore them away from the Kirk's justice, at the same time as the terrible news came from Aberdeen.

I was at that time attending to my duties with the Scots army in England. That they were sad and heavy duties I freely confess, for the English now with a fine army of their own, though riven with sectarianism and strife, were inclined to forget that this was no Earthly struggle in which we fought, but a war in God's name, and in his sight, and bound by his stern Covenants. They would treat us, their brothers in Christ, as if we were mere mercenaries, bidding us ride hither and thither at their command with neither consultation or advice, and they cursed us, when with right on our side we refused to play that part. Our soldiers, not being slow to find old hatreds burning in their hearts, would ground their pikes and refuse to march, crying aloud that the English gave them neither gunpowder or provisions, nor other things that an army needs, and to which they had previously agreed. When we won for them they gave us no credit, and when we lost we received nothing but scorn, and they hate us much that should be our brothers, and choose to forget how we left our own country to succour them in their despair.

Soldiers may be ignorant louns, but there was justice in their complaints.

In this dire time came news of Aberdeen, and from that time they cared nothing for their thankless hosts, and desired only to return to Scotland, having not the wits to see that we were in England by the Lord's command, to be a blessed light in that confused place.

I myself received the news from Aberdeen in a letter from Mr John Dalyrimple, a minister of that place. In it he told me how terrible was that day, and how the Amalekite hordes ran their naked shanks over in Godly blude, and how in the midst o this a thing happened which caused me to ponder deeply on what its meaning might be.

It seems that in the midst of this slaughter, Alexander Bain who had previously been seen riding alongside Malecky in the forefront of the Graham's horse, now appeared as a saviour in their midst, rallying what soldiers could be rallied, and in Mr Dalyrimple's own words which I have set down.

'He, setting an example which made our poor fledgling soldier's hearts to leap in their breasts, cut his way out through our barbarous enemy, seeming a David in courage and a Samson in strength so that they scattered before him.

'He saved us Mathius, that cannot be denied by any who were with me that day and who saw him, for he made our soldiers stand firm and fight, and when we retreated, as that day we had to, he made us retreat in good order, and to take with us the hurt and the wounded, women and bairns, near expiring with terror as many were. His conduct inspired each and every one and led us to safety.

'I was greatly impressed Mathius, and when we reached a place which we deemed safe I talked deeply to him inquiring who he might be.

'To be plain Mathius, he now seemed like a weeping and troubled man, and he told me all his history, vomiting it forth like a thing that had lain long in a heart that could no longer contain it. Imagine, my friend, my astonishment when it matched in every point what you had told me of events in Trig. I say the account of events tallied, his interpretation of these events differed, though I quickly perceived that good soldier though he was, he had but little skill in interpretation, and indeed his mind on many crucial points was nought but confusion.

'Indeed to be plain, he struck me as a simple man with a simple soldierly idea of loyalty which blindit him in all other matters. Malecky, whom I was shortly to confront, had known well how to use him, leading him by the nose and skelping him on the backside, tearing him with all the subtlety at his command from the Kirk's bosom, till the poor loun knew not at all where he was, until that day in the midst of battle with the Godly wailing all about him, his sight had been restored to him, and he knew, and could see, how far, and how terrible, was the road he had ganged.

'I spoke plainly to him Mathius, not without compassion, but with sternness withal, for it was plain to me that I had a duty to him.

'All this happened Mathius, before Malecky himself appeared with the Douglas witch at his side. It was perhaps only then that I myself knew the fullest extent of his diabolical nature.'

This was certainly true, for did he not come first to gloat, and then, observing how scattered and broken they were, presented himself to them as their saviour, speaking to them with gentle and beguiling words of seeming wisdom, till they, near despair, and bereft of their reason, would have fawned about his feet and counted the sight of him a blessing had not Dalyrimple placed himself between them and him, thrusting himself forward even to the point of Malecky's drawn sword, and ordered him in the name of God to gang from their sight.

He would, he wrote, have apprehended both him and the Douglas witch but he could not do it alone, and the people he was with were hardly in a condition to help him, and Mr Bain it seems, standing aside like ane transfixed, siding neither with Mr Dalyrimple or Malecky.

At that time I could do nothing. My duties kept me in England though in my heart I would have been as blithe as any in the army to return to Scotland. But I thought deeply on the letter and prayed lang for guidance. I knew Dalyrimple very well, he was a man of Godly courage and sound judgement. And perhaps I also understood how Bain had affected him, for I remembered clearly how similarly he had affected me, and perhaps too I had always believed in my heart that he was but a poor loun enmeshed by Malecky's snare, and doubtless Agnes Douglas's was a bait as sweet to his flesh as she was death to his soul, and I prayed lang that he would find the courage to break with them both, aye and to save himself by slaying them both.

Mr Dalyrimple had written that he had told him sternly before they parted, that he could, if he would, turn this day of disaster into a day of victory, for the whole purpose of it had been revealed to him, and would he now desert his plain duty? Did he think that all the trials that God sent men were but simple things like slashing the heads of runagate Hielanmen, who were but silly pawns of their masters?

I could not at that time know what the outcome of that was to be. The country at present is in a worse state than ever in England I imagined it to be. If the plague has lifted from Edinburgh it has broken out elsewhere, and famine and rapine bleed the country dry, and it is as if a tempest of lawlessness has been released in our midst. Nor do I believe any of these things will ever be overcome while that man is free.

I have heard since I have returned, that Malecky, after his vanquishment by Dalyrimple, took refuge among a Hieland clan. Them who were ance called Macgregor, but are now a nameless folk, well known as the most infamous reivers, cutthroats, and bludie men in all the Hielands. He was seen among them, advising them, and enabling them to resist a strong attack made against them, which they could never have resisted otherwise.

That the Douglas witch was there with him has been amply confirmed, but of Mr Bain himself I have had no report. I freely confess I have strong misgivings. My belief is that perhaps Bain did try to carry out his Christian duty and Malecky, divining the new temper of his mind got his stroke in first, and perhaps Mr Bain is himself now dead.

I cannot say for certain. At the present time I know nothing more, but I feel in my heart that Malecky is still alive, and a more potent danger to us than any that had been killed that day in Edinburgh. In truth a greater danger than Jamie Graham himself wherever he might now be.

Mathius Pringle, Minister of the Gospel in the Reformed Kirk. Edinburgh 1646.

☆

The minister laid the Black Book of Agnes Douglas at one end of his desk, the memoirs of Mathius Pringle at the other. In the middle he put the notes he had made while carrying out his interrogations. They were like three-quarters of an incomplete and discordant whole, flickering in the lamplight like three parts of a demoniac jig.

Above them on the shelf stood Marten Gilmarten's work, elegant and new. The minister smiled grimly. It was not the fourth part and indeed would disdain utterly any attempt to enlist it in that role, and yet, at this moment of the night, the same unstable light embraced them all.

In that light he felt a sudden renewed sympathy for Sawney Bain. At that thought a stench assailed his nostrils, the stench of a dark and noisome place and the poisoned souls who had inhabited it. A place in which all the principles of religion, humanity, and nature, had been stood on their heads, and the Heavenly light which nurtured these things had been shut out.

The minister shuddered. He remembered the boy Dugald Bain huddled in the corner of his cell, clad only in a grey plaid his eyes wide in fear and incomprehension. On one occasion he had clung to the minister's gown, and he had stroked his head, feeling a horror of his own compassion.

'Poor child, ' the minister had said then, 'poor unfortunate child.'

The soldier had looked through the door at that moment, and the boy, with a cry of terror which had been scarcely human had tried to conceal himself entirely in the minister's gown.

'I am tae be killit . . .' he had said.

Angrily the minister had waved the soldier away. The boy had been silent for a time after that, listening like an animal as the iron-clad man shuffled down the passage.

The boy, he thought, had been right to be afraid.

Eventually the boy had stood back, his features set, almost adult, they had glowed with gross passions and ferocious insight.

'Am I tae be hingit or burnit? Ane o the ither, I ken it weel enough. For this is Chaos, lost tae the Lord, whaur the Deil rides on a great black horse wae ane eye golden and the ither ane blude red, pricking men and women wae his great lang lance till each ane strives tae be wickeder and madder than his neighbour. And kings and queens and ministers and priests run

292

at his side seeing him as their shining licht on a mirk nicht. And by his licht, and at his bidding, they cut doun poor folk, and true folk, and peaceful folk, for sic things are an abomination tae their een. And if they should chance upon a bit carline, or an auld wife, her they catch and strip her naked, and thrust great pins intae her till she cries out that she is a witch, and then they hing and burn her, making merry awe the while.'

'I am a minister of the Kirk,' he had said then.

'Och I ken that weel, and woe betide me for I hae neither sword nor gun and can be killit without any apprehension, like I should hae been wae the rest o God's folk, hackit doun and killit like they were, and hae aye been.'

It was as if at that point the boy had thrust himself entirely outside the minister's compassion, ceased indeed to be a boy at all but had been transfigured into a snarling imp of Hell. They should have all been killed in the cave, he thought, and the cave itself sealed off with gunpowder. They deserved that, but they did not deserve the aberration of fate which had brought them to Edinburgh.

Silently the minister corrected himself. The Lord had preserved them and brought them into his presence, the knowledge of them into his mind, even if the purpose and meaning of that was as yet unknown to him. There had been humanity in that child, tenderness even in his short and unspeakable life, and more terrible by far that appeared than if they had been mere brute degenerates.

He thought again of Malecky. All her life it had seemed to Agnes Douglas that she and Bain had been like children held in Malecky's grasp. Now it was as if by proxy that serpentine Scot had played one last horrid trick on his age and its hopes, and conjured up a whole tribe of bestial innocents to be his instruments and his victims.

His eyes closed again on Mathius Pringle's writings. They were incomplete, which if hardly that man's fault still seemed careless and uncharacteristic of him. But it could not possibly be construed as arbitrary that the remnants should thus fall into his hands and come under the scrutiny of his eyes. It was as if from within the polished leather of the old preacher's saddle-bags, embossed with the ancient Saltire of the Covenant, they had waited to speak only to him.

☆

It was in the year 1648 when I was sent for, nay I was summoned, with some urgency to go to the town of Pittenweem, which is in Fife. We had received information that witchcraft, sorcery, and devilry, had near overwhelmed the place on a scale which previously had hardly been imagined, and though he himself was not there the hand of Malecky had been discerned.

The country had been quiet that year. The plague had long since lifted, and if the harvest was not over abundant it was sufficient. Order had been restored to the countryside and a land weary of strife seemed blessed for a time with peace.

That it could not last I had thought at the time, too many things I knew lay in wait to destroy it, and would have to be dealt with ere they did. Montrose, our intelligence informed us, was wandering through the courts of Europe. Fawning it was reported, at the court of this king and that queen, pleading for a new army to further molest his countryfolk. The English, aye vexatious as our ally, had grown insufferable in their pride, but their own country was wracked with faction and division, which it cannot be fairly said was undeserved. But faction and division were murmuring in Scotland too, and forbye the fact that James Graham was in exile, many were now eager to take his place who through jealousy, pride and cowardice, had hitherto been unco quiet.

So I rode to Pittenweem with much misgiving, thinking, for how could I not think, that things that were happening there were a divine warning of the things to come if we did not act swiftly to root them out. Earthly apprehensions, I freely confess to, but by God's grace my spirit was not daunted, for I had long resolved that wherever the hand of Malecky should be discovered there would my hand be to check him, and I made it my duty to follow up every report.

The reports I had heard from Fife did not at first seem to me to be anything byordnar, exaggerated as these accounts aye are, they concerned ships sunk, cattle killed, midnight pacts, fornications and renunciations, but widespread they said, half or more of the toun being afflicted.

When I arrived at the place, I was shocked I confess it, at the scale of things. Many had been arrested, many had confessed, and the broder had been busy at his work. I confess myself to

294

have little faith in the pricking of witches, my concerns aye being with the soul and the reason. In my opinion, it is aye the ideas that matter, and this pricking business smacks of ancient superstition, and the broders themselves often rogues who will find witches because it is their business to find witches. That notwithstanding he had been about his duties in Pittenweem and found many, and as is the nature of these folk they were busily pointing to many more.

The minister of the parish, a Mr Josiah Anderson, I found to be an intelligent, Godly man much stricken by the affair, and indeed the history of it would make a braver heart than his tremble, and his was stout enough.

It seems that until the years 1645 the parish had been a very fine place. Fishing was its trade, and the men of the toun were brave and industrious in plying it. In 1645 like gude and Godly men they had marched away to the bludie and disastrous battle of Kilsythe. Only ane had returned, for the rest, more than a hundred fisher captains and their lads had been cut down that day.

This ane, a man by the name of William Leckie, of which there will be much more to tell, had it seems, dishonourably saved himself by deserting his comrades and running away. Satan it was who had preserved him then and since then.

The place had become distracted by the thing which had befallen them, which I could easily understand. The boats rotted in their harbours having no fishermen to steer them, and as a result of this idleness, poverty and pestilence struck the place. In the midst of this despair, William Leckie had set himself up as a warlock, claiming that fish that could no longer be caught in nets could be charmed out of the sea by devilry.

At midnight he had got together great gatherings to which Satan himself was invited, and was present, demanding the renunciation of baptisms and the cursing of the cross. And he made William Leckie his servant and commanded that all should fornicate with him in his name, and he would give them power to make the fish loup of their own accord from the sea, and they would prosper and grow rich and never want again, and have no need of boats.

He had lied of course, as he aye lies, for few were the fish that louped from the sea at his bidding. But in his lies he had ensnared the people, so that now, without grace or light to guide them, having cast aside these blessings, they were his servants all.

This history, which no Christian could have heard without weeping, had another more terrible aspect still which I here relate in Mr Anderson's own words.

'We had waited in prayer and fasting for news of the conflict, little kenning, for how could we ken, or imagine, the dreadful outcome. Till ane day William Leckie alane returned, alane of all the men who marched away. Alane, but not without ither company, for he came in a cart with a man and a woman, drunk he was, pitiful in his appearance and distracted in his wits, who had previously been a douce and decent man and well respected.

'His terrible experience, and the news he had tae tell, would, tae a compassionate man have explained his appearance. But the folk he was wae, I hae nae words tae rightly explain, and there was naething outwardly untoward about their appearance, but my soul was filled with loathing at the sight of them. She a dark carline wae neither modesty or decency about her, and he, a drunken vagabond at first appearance, was muckle mair than that at the second.

'I challenged him, but he wad gie me neither his name or his place, and appeared tae hae nae ither calling in life but drunkenness and the affronting of folk in their misery. Plainly I could not apprehend them as I might have wished, and he, laughing merrily awe the while, spewed forth from his cart a much transformed William Leckie, and gien nae answer either tae civil questions or commands he rattled his cart on his way. Never since that day has William Leckie been the man he ance was.'

I questioned him closely on the appearance of the pair. I did this in order to be certain, forbye I knew full well in my heart who they were.

I questioned this William Leckie, whom they had imprisoned in the steeple of the kirk, and if he had, as I accept he had, been a decent man ance, he was that no longer, but was in his appearance wild and unkempt, near reduced to a savage, who *met my questions with impudence and curses. I asked him if he had indeed lain with nigh on a hundred women of the parish, old and young. He just grinned at me, more beast than a man.*

'Wha else should they lie wae?' He cried. 'For them that they ance lay wae are awe clapped in clay, and even an auld fishwife needs her cunt tae be tickled ance in a while, forbye she has neither milk in her teats nor food in her belly.'

I rebuked him sternly, but he was far beyond any such rebukes. When I asked him if Satan had commended him to do this he gied out an eldritch screech.

'Aye Satan bade, and a staunding prick bade, and a starving cunt bade, and the sea bade, and the fish bade, and a merrier time was had at their bidding than at onything the Kirk ever bade.'

His ravings were truly awful, and had he not been bound I would not have gone near him without a stout cudgel. I have seen many lost men before but none to equal William Leckie, apart from Malecky himself, and he was in a different class altogether. I strove on, by God's grace I am not ane to be daunted by witless haverings, however vile. 'And what of Malecky', I asked him?

'I ken nane o that name.'

'The man and the woman who brought you here in a cart,' I insisted. At first he would not answer, but when I grew angry he of course grew afraid, for it is well known that Satan puts not true courage in his servant's hearts, but just a bawling false defiance.

'A gude man, an unco gude man, wha kent how wicked and foolish it was tae send men wha had nae experience o war intae sic a fight.'

I came away after that. He returned to his screeching and there was little more to be done for him or got out of him. Indeed, to be plain, there was little to be done for any of them in that unhappy place. Some could, and were, brought to a sensible recognition of their condition, but most were utterly lost.

I felt, I cannot confess it too strongly, an awful burden upon me as I walked about that stricken place. I looked at the boats rotting at their berths, their timbers stove in, their ropes and masts and nets hanging in tatters. Nor could I with my poor

297

with my poor and earthly sight see an end of it. But that there was an end, and that end a gude and Godly ane I trusted and believed, and that it should come all unbidden when we should be worthy of it I could never in heart or head doubt. And yet I do confess that this place troubled me. Ance as pleasant and prosperous as any in the land, it was now a pit of howling madness.

They all had signed whatever confessions had been put before them. Of how they had danced naked with Leckie at their head, crying upon Satan to come to them, crying upon their men to return and the fish to leap from the sea. And because they could not put to sea themselves, crying disaster upon any other boats that came to their waters, though as Mr Anderson told me, few had the courage for that. I pondered that there might have been a time when it would have been a blessing for them, and helped the place to recover, but that time was gone.

I cursed Malecky, and I cursed James Graham. If I took pleasure in any ane thing it was that Bain was not with them, though where he could be I could not then know. At that time I certainly thought it possible that he was dead.

This turned out to be false. He was, despite all his wayward-ness, the Lord's instrument, and in time the Lord would use him, but that was still to be.

Mathius Pringle, Minister of the Gospel, Pittenweem, Fife, 1648.

☆

We started out for Edinburgh and were three days on the road before we reached it. I had never been in sic a large place before, or seen sic a great multiplication o people o awe sorts frae the highest tae the lowest, nor had I at any ither time smelled sic a stink as they raised. We entered if I mind correctly, late on a Friday at a place called the West Port under the castle hill whaur Steenie had a friend wha kept an alehouse.

I had lang ceased tae marvel that Steenie had friends in every corner o the land. This ane, a Mr William Baillie, was

298

a gey auld man wae a wooden leg wha ran a sodger's tavern called the Musketeer. He had, Steenie telt me, enlisted in Leslie's army out o enthusiasm for awe he was, even at that time, ower auld for fighting. He had, it seemed got his leg shot off in some bit skirmish, and wad maist likely hae deed had not Steenie been at hand. He was a little auld man wae his heid near completely bald but wae a great white moustache and beard.

He greeted us baith very heartily, clattering here and there on his wooden leg tae fetch us ale and meat, and crying out that he had lang since thought Steenie deed, and Steenie replying that he was likewise very glad tae find him alive, what wae plagues and famines and sic like things besetting the country.

Willie Baillie had just smiled at that, and said that he thought that the plague had ance or twice peeked through his door, but seeing sic a stubborn auld man wha had defied death on sae many occasions, only ance surrendering up a bit leg, he kent weel enough that he was wasting his time, for here was a man that wad not be killed before his appointed hour.

The word had got about then that Willie Baillie's ale wad keep the plague awa, which that man wad neither affirm, seeing it as nae mair than a Godless superstition which it wad be bad luck tae affirm, but he wad not deny it either it being very gude for trade.

We were shown tae a private room, whaur, while we ate, Willie Baillie kept us company, drinking his ain ale as if he himsel had mair than a little faith in the story. Steenie questioned him closely on affairs, but awe he wad say tae that was that affairs had awe gone mad, wae the toun itsel near mad at the news o its ain deliverance,

-At ane minute Jamie Graham was chapping at the door and there was hardly a lassie in toun, maid or whore, high or low, wha was not trembling at the thought that she might be carried awa by some Hielan cataran. And now Jamie Graham's army is nae mair, there is nane, young or auld, but thinks hersel slighted if she has not a Godly hero tae dangle on her airm, let ministers rant till they burst.

In truth the toun was running ower wae sodgers, and nae

place mair than the tavern, which rang day and night tae the drinking and laughing and dangerous quarrelling o armed men. Awe that aside, Willie Baillie was o the opinion that there were many plots o sober and silent men running through the toun looking for some ither tae step intae the Graham's breeks. For the King, his cavaliers in England haeving been beaten, was now a prisnor of the English parliament, haeving been delivered up tae them by the Scots army ere it left that country. Many it seems were displeased at that, saying that now the English had him they wad now hae nae further need o the Scots, or Covenants, and that very little had been got out o sae much hard fighting and loyal support.

This was but gossip, and doubtless Willie Baillie's ears were very close tae his heid that he should hear it, for the Kirk and Leslie's sodgers made it for the time dangerous gossip.

At length Steenie asked Willie Baillie if he had seen Sawney about the toun? For a minute or sae I mind there was a queer silence wae the auld man bowing his heid, his lang white moustache near dribbling in his ale. When he looked up he stared very keenly at us.

-Aye, he said at length. -I hae indeed seen Sawney Bain, forbye he only cam in here but ance, and I hae not seen him since that time, which I tak somewhat ill.

-And why is that? Steenie asked.

-And why should it be, for whaur else in the toun should the man drink? Especially as this place is deemed satisfactory enough by the lave o his comrades. But aiblins I haud it ower much against him, for tae be plain he was a greatly changed man. Och I asked him about ye, and he said he kent naething, whether ye be alive or whether ye be deid, and tae be plain he had little wish tae hae either thing confirmed.

-How can that be? I asked him. -For in truth, in this time, many things that were ance close hae ganged aglaikit, but friendship man, is no politics, and ought not tae be sae fickle, and if ye twa hae quarrelled it was a great pity.

-Now he had been cool enough at first, but no un-friendly, but now he just banged his joug doun on the table, and said, Willie Baillie, ye were ower auld tae be a sodger when ye were a sodger, and ye are ower Christless tae tak tae the preaching now. Nor hae I cam here tae be dinged deaf wae questions and sermons. Mr Malecky and I hae severed lang syne and it is best it should remain sae.

-Weel I said nae mair. He seemed a fiercer and mair unchancy man than the ane I had ance kent. Aye and it made me wonder if Scotland had no soured him in a way that Germany hadna, for it had done that wae many wha were aye a bit fanciful in their desires.

-And were ye no as fanciful as any? Steenie said. -Or why else should a man o sixty proclaim that he was only forty and be sae eager tae trail a pike?

-Weel I'm no sae fanciful now, laddie. But weel, Sawney grew mair cheerful as he drank mair ale, and before he left he apologised for his bit harshness, and said it had been fine tae drink wae an auld comrade, and it cheered him up tae see that I was weel despite the plague and my wooden leg. But he never cam in here again, and I ken he is still in the toun for I hae inquired after him.

Steenie I kent had been growing quietly angry awe the time he had been listening, and now he said,

-Weel I sall ask after him, and if he can be sought out I sall seek him out, for I will ken the meaning o awe o this.

-But ye will bide here meanwhile? The auld man asked, his voice a bit anxious, for it was plain tae me that while on ane hand he had made light o it, Sawney had troubled him deeply.

-Aye indeed, whaur else should we bide? And if yer trade is as brisk as ye say it is why I sall gie ye a hand at it.

They drank tae that and thereafter we awe becam quite merry, while outside in the tavern we could hear sodgers laughing and chaffing and singing, and for ance they did not sing psalms but sang their ain auld sangs.

☆

I kent weel enough that ance in Edinburgh Steenie wad begin tae ask after Sawney.

-I canna help it Agnes, I canna thole the idea o him glowering in some corner forsaking the company o honest men and auld friends.

He had asked many o the sodgers wha cam intae the Musketeer, and many kent Sawney, and awe said that he was a dour and difficult man. He drank they said in a sailor's tavern doun in Leith, a fell dangerous place full of naething but sailormen and their whores, alang wae a few tinks, cutthroats, and deserters frae the army, tae wham a man wae a purse and a hale skin was a sare temptation.

Steenie kent the place, and ane night, wae a sword at his side and twa pistols under his buff coat, he said that he wad gang and see for himsel. I said naething at first for he made it plain tae me that he wad gang alane, and I had a strange foreboding about that, and I made him promise that if he should chance tae meet wae Sawney and he quarrelled wae him he should come awa ere it cam tae blows. Auld Baillie looked as if he thought the hale business was an unchancy enterprise. But after Steenie had gone he said tae me,

-They hae been friends for many a lang year and I wad hae expected naething less.

I helped him serve ale that night, as I often did, learning tae tak the daffing o the sodgers in gude spirit, checking them if they grew ower forward. But they had their ain women, and some it seemed wha wad blithely serve any number o them, and nae doubt they thought that was nae mair than their due haeving saved the toun frae wild Hielanmen.

Some nights there wad be quarrels, but auld Baillie was strict in that awe affairs o honour and politics should be settled in some ither place, for if the Kirk wad not come doun on the army at the present time, being grateful tae them, it wad hae little hesitation about coming doun on him for keeping a corner o Hell in God's Kingdom.

But that night passed without any incidents out o the ordinary, and it was after the last sodger had departed and Willie Baillie and mysel still sitting up and sharing a bit whisky, and him inquiring a bit, but no ower much, when we heard the sound o a cart at the door. He hobbled outside wae mysel at his heels, and there atop the cart was

Steenie, and inside it like a muckle slain Goliath was
Sawney himsel.

-He's drunk, Steenie said. -And according tae the gude
folk o Leith he has been sae for many a day and night.

I looked at him, hardly kenning him frae the man that I
had ance kent, for he seemed aulder and coarser, and his
beard which he had aye kept neat and sodgerly wad now
hae rivalled his bear coat. When we tried tae move him he
opened his een.

-Damn ye, he said, his voice unco quiet like a prayer. -
Damn ye awe tae Hell.

I looked at Steenie then, but that man just looked straight
back at me. He had found Sawney, he later telt me, not in
the first place he had looked, but they had kent him. Why,
in awe the taverns o Leith, he had discovered, maist folk
kent him, and maist thought him dounright mad, and wad
nae doubt hae made great sport o him but that they thought
he was fell dangerous tae. Steenie had heard sae many wild
tales about him, and frae sae many angry folk, that he
thought it wad only tak ane o sufficient courage and he wad
surely be deid.

Sae he had brought him hame, the host o the alehouse
that he had found him in being sae weel pleased tae be rid o
him that he had gladly lent him his cart tae transport him.

-He dings out their brains wae psalms by day, and wae
his sword hilt at night, if a tithe o what they say is true.

We got him intae a bed, not without some effort, for he
could neither stand on his feet or move himsel. Auld Baillie
stood looking at him and shaking his heid, and saying that
he kent not how a man wham he had aye thought o as a
superior kind o man could cam tae this.

-He is still a very gude man Willie, Steenie said, and if
these were nae doubt kind words he himsel looked unco
jaded and weary. He later telt me how strange had been his
search for him, and the tales he had heard o him, and how
his heart had near gien out at the thought of what he might
find, and how it had baith near broke and been very relieved when he did find him.

I looked at them baith and said that they should leave me
wae him. I kent not at the time why I wanted them tae dae

this, forbye that it seemed the sensible thing. Steenie had said wae a harshness that was strange tae him, that he had ower and enough o him for ane night, but he wad thank auld Baillie for some o his ale, and I was tae shout if Sawney caused any trouble.

For a time I sat alane wae him, just watching him, not kenning what tae think or dae. A lang scar now ran doun his neck which maun hae been a bad cut when he received it. I ran my finger the length o it, frae just under his chin tae his collarbane, and his armour which Steenie and auld Baillie had taen off him had specks o rust on it, which he had never allowed tae happen before.

Haeving naething else tae dae, I stripped him o his duds and gied him a bit wash, and it was perhaps only then that I could see that this was indeed Sawney Bain, and there was anither great mark under his shoulder that had not been there when I had previously kent him. Indeed there were divers marks o cuts, big and small. Some I kent frae lang ago, but maist were new, and it seemed tae me that Scotland had indeed succeeded in wounding him mair than Germany.

I washed his face which was black wae sweat, and I wad hae liked tae cut his beard tae, for awe the things that I did seemed tae be bringing him back tae himsel. But at that point he opened his een forbye I kent not at awe if he saw me.

-Sawney Bain, I whispered tae him. -And whaur hae ye been Sawney Bain?

For a time it seemed as if he could indeed see, but then wae a kind o quietness his een closed again and his voice said,

-Whaur in Hell am I?

-No in Hell, Sawney Bain, no yet, there is a lang road tae gang ere ye reach that place.

-But cam I early, or cam I late, I'll find Black Agnes at the gate.

I laughed, I mind. But there was nae humour at awe in his voice. Indeed very little o anything that was him seemed tae be in it, or anything at awe, but just a sad auld sang.

Last night I dreamt a dreary dream,
Frae beyond the Isle o Sky,
I dreamt that a deid man won a fight
And I think that man was I.

It was like a sadness it seemed tae me frae lang lang ago.

Tak hame yer oxen tak hame yer kye
For they hae brought us nought but sorrow,
I wish that they had awe gane mad,
When they first cam tae Yarrow.

For a while it was as if he wad sae mair, and then that
voice that was hardly like a voice seemed tae just dee within
him.
    -Weel, I said tae him, -I ken not whaur ye hae been.
    -Och I hae no been far awa.
    -When did ye leave the Graham?
    He made nae answer tae my questions but just said,
    -Am I amang friends dae ye think? For I hae no been
amang friends for a very lang time.
    -Och ye are amang the best friends that ever ye had.
    His voice went on like a queer lost thing tae wham even
its ain memories were strangers. He had been sarely piked
at Kilsythe, which was the mark I had observed on his left
shoulder. On account o this he could not march wae the
army and had been left behind and taen intae the house o a
minister wha perhaps kent not tae which side he belanged,
or aiblins he was ane o them wha at that time were accom-
modating themsels tae the Graham as being the new maister
in the land. Or it might hae been that he was indeed, as
Sawney said he was, a humble and Godly man wha cast a
cauld ee on the tempest o Earthly passions. I ken not sae I
canna say, but Mr Andrew Fergusson was his name, and in
his house Sawney recovered frae his wound.
    -I was much taen wae him, for he deeved me wae neither
questions nor inquiries, and nae doubt in the end he kent I
wad tell him awe, which I did, for despite awe that had
gone before how could I not, sic a great and gentle thing his
Godliness seemed. And when he heard he did not rage or

rant but did listen and advise me quietly, and did not presume tae ken about things he could not ken, but wad fast and pray for an answer.

-But he was firm in that I had done muckle wrang in fighting for the Graham, but as there was a purpose in awe things, there was a purpose in wrang daen and the despair which follows it which humbles and instructs the mind. There was a purpose tae in the seeming chance thing that I had been brought tae his door, and if he had any advice tae gie it was that I should put awe that had happened behind me, not tae be forgotten, but tae be remembered and spurned as bairnish folly. And if I was tae be a sodger, then henceforth I wad be a sodger in the Lord's army, loving and kenning him for wham I fought, for he had not preserved me through a lang night o foolishness tae be ance again a bludie handed loun in the Devil's army.

I could imagine very weel how his words were like drops o gold in Sawney's lugs, calming and admonishing the storm that was in his soul. And it might weel hae been that this was indeed a gude man, but the outcome o his ministerings was that he took Sawney by the hand, and weel I kent how lamblike that man wad be, and led him tae David Leslie's army, assuring him that any wha questioned him wad hae him tae dispute wae. And he telt Sawney that he was tae be guided firstly by his prayers and secondly by God's Kirk, for if it was in error in some things, for he himsel kent that, it was still the wisest o earthly things, and that he should never again shirk frae daen the Lord's wark but should pray and fast tae find out what that wark was.

And think ye not that Sawney's heart rejoiced at his words. And Leslie rejoiced tae see him, for Sawney could tell him many things about the disposition and style o fighting of the Graham's army, and Leslie made him a sergeant in that army, and nane questioned him or his purpose, for Fergusson was true tae his word and was ready tae dispute wae any that disputed wae Sawney, and whether Pringle kent or did not ken, I canna say, and it might weel be that canny man saw his future instrument in Sawney and was content tae quietly bide his time.

And then the day o the battle cam, and Sawney confirmed what Hector had said, and what Steenie had aye said wad happen, that the lave o the Graham's Hielanmen and many o his Irish had gone hame tae the Hielans whaur they had wives and bairns tae feed and protect, leaving the Graham wae less than twa thousand men.

-Och they fought weel enough, but fifteen hundred foot and a few hundred horse canna stand for lang against six thousand o the best horse in the land, and Leslie himsel was unhappy, his ambition being tae beat Jamie Graham ance and for awe, and on equal terms.

It was the conclusion o the fight that had twisted his soul, and dae ye not think that was a great relief tae me, for lang had my fancies been wracked by a man that tae my mind had ridden far beyond mercy.

-We wad gie them quarter if they wad surrender, Leslie himsel commanded it. But the Kirk countermanded it, and he wad not stand against the ministers wha cursed the sodgers, and drove them on tae the slaughter, driving them mad wae their ain passions till there wad be nae peace for any until awe were deid, restraint o any kind being a rejection o the Lord's express command.

-Some, mysel amang them, rade frae the field. But ithers gied nae quarter at awe, and on and on the spears flashed and like the children o Israel in the Bible Godly Scots rade their horses tae their knees in Amalekite blude.

-I ken naething Agnes, and nae doubt I understand less, and Mr Fergusson was a rare and gude man. But as for the lave o preachers, why Agnes, the Papist priests wha cam ower wae the Irish were bludier men in their words than the wildest kern was wae his sword, and if there is great difference in awe point o doctrine between them and the Kirk's ministers, they are brithers it seems in that quality, for the Kirk that day affronted nature.

At some point Steenie himsel had cam quietly intae the room. I kent he was there, but whether Sawney kent I canna say, for forbye he had een and senses they were still, I think, on Slain Man's Lee. But Steenie himsel spoke up then.

-And sae the Lord's wark gangs bonnily on, and if it affronts nature, then let nature be damned.

-I kent sae many o the Graham's men, wha fierce enough

themsels, had been my comrades, and in awe fairness should hae been gien quarter. But there was naething I could dae, and little Leslie could dae, for wae the proper fight ower the Kirk had plucked the lave o the army clean out o his command.

-Did ye no see us that day by the river Sawney?

-Och I saw ye, but like a dread miracle. For awe I kent ye could hae been the Deil's wark.

-It was Red Hector and his wife that we saved then ye ken.

-Was it now? Now I ken not why he should be sae chosen, any mair than I ken why I hae been chosen. For I ken that I hae been, and I hae nae choice but tae gang on wae it.

His een closed then, and his speech fell intae a queer mumbling sic that nae sense could be made o it.

-Let him sleep, Steenie said. -That is the greatest mercy that we can gie.

We left him then, him haeving already left us. Auld Baillie was still up. He was unable, he said, tae just gang tae his bed, for this hale affair had troubled him deeply, and set him tae thinking in sic a way that whisky was mair comfort than sleep. I mind looking at his auld face, and despite awe that had happened, I had never seen a sadder ane.

That night I lay wae Steenie talking ower awe that had happened. He telt me that Sawney had raved much when he had first found him, and he was mair than ever convinced that what the Kirk wanted frae Sawney as the price o his salvation was baith our heids.

-He will not dae that, I said, -for I tae hae talked much wae him this night, and I ken he is not the man for that task.

-In his right mind, but aiblins religion has deprived him o that, at least part o the time.

For the rest o that night I thought o him still in my dreams, and nae doubt Steenie did tae, for despite awe the trials o the previous night we baith woke early thinking o him. But early as we were when I went tae the room whaur he had slept he was nae langer there.

That he had gone there could be nae doubt, for awe his gear had gone, and I kent weel enough in my heart that he had gone, and had left nae sign or note, but just a bed, which if it was still warm was quickly turning cauld.

-He's awa, I called out tae Steenie.

-Then let him gang, he said. -for there is a limit set on what ane can dae for anither.

We never saw him again at that time. When the sodgers left Edinburgh we saw him ance mair in the midst o them at the heid o his troop. Ance again he was a weel turned out sodger wae his armour brightly burnished and his hair and beard neatly clipped, mounted on a fine big horse o a pale colour. He looked neither tae his left or his right, but I mind his airm gaen up in command and his sodgers clattering after it, but that was the last we were tae see o him for twa lang years.

☆

If the parish noticed any change in their minister they did not remark on it. Indeed their indifference was such that the minister, aware of his own feelings towards them, wondered at their's towards him. Increasingly he began to feel that such emotions hardly existed in them, he was merely a functionary in their lives, tolerated and respected because many years ago someone had impressed very firmly on their ancestor's rough minds the existence of God and the necessity of religion. And if it was in their minds a grim necessity rather than a joyful one, there seemed very little he could do about that while their minds remained fixed in a bond with a bloody past which confirmed their interpretations to their own satisfaction, and which all the hectoring of Marten Gilmarten had not dented.

His days had become a routine. Early in the morning and last thing at night he would stride up Steenie's Hill. The village would watch him go. If any had inquired why he did so he would have cited his health. None did inquire. If the minister felt gratified at that, it also made him feel utterly alone, for he acknowledged to himself that there were other motivations for his behaviour which amounted almost to compulsions. He could neither forget nor dismiss the way the past had collided with the present, their union taking place in his presence, and presided over by the drunk and half-deranged disciple of

309

Mathius Pringle. The strangest thing of all was that it now appeared that Walter, having thrust his burden from his back to the minister's, had become himself like a man transformed.

He never saw the elder on the hill now. Nor did he see anything of the extravagant activities that Walter had given as his justification for being there. Indeed it seemed to the minister that Walter was himself avoiding him, or waiting with uncharacteristic timidity for the minister to approach him. The minister had not done so, with the result that he was smitten with a terrible pang of conscience at the thought that the man was himself ailing. The possibility of this had first been mentioned to him by Mathew Elliot whom he found one day by the door of his cottage smoking his pipe.

'Good morning, Mathew.'

'Aye and gude day tae ye tae, minister.'

The minister had always felt let down by the fact that Mathew had not been more forthcoming with him on information about Malecky's Hill which he felt he almost certainly knew. All, even honest, sturdy Mathew Elliot had gently lied to him, insultingly, as if they considered him a child subject to wild fancies. And yet, he knew he could be wrong in this. The minister often felt the man's slate grey eyes following him. Assessing him? Judging him? The minister could not tell, and he knew that if he confronted Mathew with it, he would merely smile as Andrew Gilmore had done, as if such fancies were for the minister's head alone.

They had exchanged pleasantries that day when suddenly Mathew had said:

'I fear Wattie Hyslop is no the man he ance was.'

'What do you mean Mathew?'

'Och there was a time when hardly a day wad pass on the hillside but ye wad find Wattie a prowling, ither folk's sins afflicting his een. But now he has becam sae mild and charitable that I begin tae fear for this place.'

'Perhaps he has just learnt some Christian forbearance.'

'Then Trig is a mair blessed place than I hae previously thocht, a place o miracles nae less.'

The minister felt his conscience strike him, eclipsed, as he confessed, rather too quickly by a twinge of irritation.

'Mathew, have you ever heard of one Todd Grey, sometimes

310

it would appear known as Grey Todd?'

'Awe folk hae heard o him at ane time or anither.'

'Have you ever actually met him, or have any idea who he was?'

'I hae never met him mysel, or at least nane wha was ever introduced tae me as such. But ye maun mind that Todd Grey was mair than likely just a name that he went by, or that folk gied him. As tae wha he was, why at awe times, and at that time mair than maist, there were folk wandering in the hills, and nae doubt Todd Grey was anither sic harmless soul.'

To the minister it had suddenly appeared that all of Mathew's soldierly straightforwardness was nothing but a windy dissemble. He had felt a desire to be rude, by a few sharp words to impress on the elder's mind that he was not to be toyed with in this way. He treated them with more respect than he had observed Mr Gilmarten do, and he wished that respect to be returned.

'I have heard that Todd Grey's real name was Steven Malecky, who was born in Trig, and who was in fact the Steenie of Steenie's Hill, a man who in his time was accused of being a warlock.'

'And wha hae ye heard this frae, puir Wattie Hyslop nae doubt?'

The elder's voice was so low and gentle and solid, that the minister felt he had collided with a rock.

'Yes indeed,' he answered.

'I ken not why ony o this matters, or what gars ye tak an interest in Wattie's fancies. The man ye ken is not aye as sound as he appears tae be.'

The minister had felt the sudden sharp realisation that he was in danger of making a fool of himself. Mathew's gentle manner was allowing him to extricate himself gracefully. He had bidden him good-day.

☆

We bided quietly at the Musketeer. Willie Baillie was a canty auld soul and said that he could wish for nae better company in his auld age. For our part it seemed sensible, if the countryside after the defeat o Montrose was not as warlike as it had ance been, it was still a confused and unchancy place. Nor had we any reason tae believe that the Kirk's anger against us had moderated itsel in any way, for its ain strength had grown, and alang wae that its wrath against awe them that it saw as its enemies had also grown.

It was about this time that the last o the sodgers cam back frae England, awe very hard and bitter men, hating the English that had ance been their brithers in Christ. It seems that the English, now wae a fine army o their ain and the king haeving been beaten, had nae langer any need o them and sae had felt free tae default on awe the terms o the Covenant, money tae their minds not being the least o these defaults.

The king himsel, we heard, had turned in desperation tae the Scots army, which, in its anger against the Parliament-men, wad hae been blithe enough tae help him if he wad but swear tae abide by the terms o the Covenant. This the stubborn man wad not dae, declaring the Covenant itsel tae be nae mair than treason. Sae when they had marched awa they had left him behind, and it was said, that he was now a prisnor o the English.

This had created many divisions amang the sodgers and the great men o the State. Some wha had been against the king, wad now, out o wrath against Cromwell and the English Parliament men, be for him. Ithers said tae Hell wae awe kings and they cared not a fig what befell this ane. Auld Baillie just sighed sadly, and made a point o quietly loading the twa pistols he kept hinging on hooks in the taproom, for these divisions wad on occasion bring the swords out in the alehouse itsel, and in the streets awe wad be in bands, some crying loudly for the Covenant, ithers saying that if only Jamie Graham wad return they wad march behind him intae England. Ane army, a wraggle-taggle affair, composed o them that had aye been for the king, and them that were newly for him, was led awa by the Duke of Hamilton, a bit courtier wha it seems had ambitions tae be a second Jamie Graham.

We kept oursels very private through awe this confusion, which made less sense tae me than anything that had previously happened, and o the details o these events we kent

312

naething, for awe we heard was opinion, and maistly drunk opinion. The English themsels, frae what we heard, were in nae better state, part o their ain army was itsel in mutiny against Cromwell, and Steenie maintained that the sodgers wha had mutinied, were the anes that called themsels Levellers, and were the best part o the army, and folk that he and Sawney had kent weel when they were in England, and liked fine. Gude they nae doubt were, but the news we heard was that they had been suppressed maist bludily at a place called Burford, and Hamilton's bit army beaten in a fight at Preston, and folk said that the man Cromwell, wha had aye been against the King, wad aiblins now like tae be King himsel.

It was around this time, the year I mind o forty-eight, after Hamilton had gone South, that we saw Sawney again. It was on that day when David Leslie rade intae Edinburgh at the heid o five or six thousand horse frae our ain country o Galloway. They had ridden hard through the night crying 'Whiggam' as they rade, which was the cry used in my ain country for driving cattle. And nae doubt they themsels thought it was cattle they were driving, the cattle o them wha wad engage for King Charles. And tae this purpose they drew themsels up on Edinburgh green wae their lances levelled and their muskets loaded and declared that there wad be nae engaging, and nae backsliding, and they deplored loudly that it had taen a Cromwell tae check Hamilton.

Och a brave sight they were, and there amang them at Leslie's ain side was Sawney himsel. Whether he saw us, or whether he didna, I canna say, but he did not seek us out, nor were we inclined at that time tae renew acquaintance, the Kirk being very loud in its proclamations that the Whigs were the sword o the Lord cam tae restore his rights, and awe folk should welcome them. This maist folk did, them that did not keeping very quiet. The auld rant, Steenie said, though he thought it wad hae been better for the country if Leslie had beaten Hamilton before Cromwell, for now that man himsel might think he had a grip on the country.

This turned out tae be true baith in the lang and the short term, for it was not lang after the event o the Whiggamore

Raid that the man Cromwell did himsel appear in Edinburgh, and supped and laughed and daffed wae Argyll and Warriston, and ither great men o Kirk and State, and in a twinkling o an ee it seemed, awe declared themsels brithers in Christ yet again. But the folk said, and the sodgers said, that they were nae langer as bairnlike as they had ance been and that only a brainless loun wad believe sic nonsense. That forbye, the Kirk preached it frae its pulpits, and, a secure power ance again set out tae hunt doun its enemies, and the Lord's enemies, and the man Cromwell's enemies, while the English, not tae be outdone, and nae doubt unco weary o the King's stubbornness and dissembling, beheidit him in London, which some said was an ill thing and ithers said was a gude thing, and a number fainted clean awa at the news. Auld Baillie just said that it proved that Charles Stuart was not ane o God's folk.

☆

It was the year after the English killed the King and before the man Cromwell cam tae Scotland for the second time, when they at last caught Jamie Graham. He had cam back tae fight for him some called the new King, as eager it seems as he had been tae fight for his faither. But his time was now ower, for the Hielanmen wad nae langer rise for him and awe he had were some mercenaries frae Germany and Denmark, and ither foreign places, alang wae a few fisherfolk frae Orkney wha kent naething o fighting, haeving it was said, rarely in their lives seen a man on a horse. But they were pressed intae the Graham's service by their laird, and awe were cut tae pieces by Leslie's troopers.

I mind very weel the day they brought him tae Edinburgh, and how fiercely the Kirk ranted against him, urging folk tae fling stanes at him as they dragged him in a cart through the streets o the toun. In this they were thwarted, and it might weel hae been that folk wha had ance trembled at the name o this man were now unco weary o sic things, for very few abused him wae any alacrity.

Still they hung him very high in the air aboun the Mercat Cross, after he had made a fine speech justifying awe his actions and asking tae be forgien by any that he had wranged. I mind him weel as he said his last words, dressed in fine claes that wad not hae looked amiss on the King himsel. And I minded tae the braw gallant in black armour that had kissed my hand. Aye and I minded that ither time when my hand rested on the handle o my gun. And now, stripped o awe his duds, how small he looked, hinging naked aboun the street, like a bairn's doll dangling on a string.

Some hours later they cut him doun, and, as if they couldna convince themsels that he was properly deid, they hacked off his legs and arms and heid, and stuck them on gate posts the length and breadth o the toun, which some folk said was ower barbarous, while ithers said that it was nae mair than his due, and a reminder o God's wark.

Whatever folk thought, there they remained for ten lang years, and nae doubt, if corbie craws had been creatures o reason they wad hae reasoned that it had awe been done for their greater convenience, for blithely they pecked out his een and flew awa wae his lang hair tae threak their nests.

☆

The minister rose very early. Provisions for the day had been laid out for him the previous night. He saddled his horse and rode out on to the wretched track that was the main street of Trig.

Early as he was, the majority of his flock were of course up before him, and each saluted the other as they passed, he naming each one as he did so. They watched what they undoubtedly thought of as their strange new minister, not following his usual custom of striding vigorously through the village and up Steenie's Hill to breathe the morning air, but mounted on his fine horse. The minister, they no doubt divined, was going to some other place.

The minister felt an awful pleasure when he had cleared the ridge of the hills and could look back on them. From this distance, he thought, it was possible to see them differently, and to once again love them. As he had done when he had first arrived on this ridge he offered up a prayer before continuing on his way.

He kept up a good pace, urged on by the realisation, forgotten after being confined to Trig, of how endless the hills appeared once one was truly among them. On occasions when the track barely existed, and crossed other tracks, which to the minister's straining eyes seemed to have a more marked existence, he took a wrong turning, travelling along it for a few miles until some intuition or information received from a chance meeting corrected him. He passed hillside graveyards which Andrew Gilmore had pointed out to him, and alone now he stopped once again to look.

JOHN MUNRO : BORN 1645 : KILLED 1685. WILLIAM DUNS : KILLED 1685. ELSPETH MCLEISH : BORN 1650 : KILLED 1685. JOSHUA MCLEISH BORN 1640 : KILLED 1685. JANET BRUIN : KILLED 1685. MATHEW FERGUSSON : KILLED 1685. MARY FERGUSSON : KILLED 1685. JAMES DOUGLAS : KILLED 1685. MARTYRED ON THIS SPOT FOR GOD AND COVENANT.

There were five stones here covering fifteen bodies, the remains of a small group ridden down by dragoons. To the minister it still seemed a scarcely possible barbarity, and yet, the names on these stones were no more than the common names of the countryside. Mathius Pringle, he thought, knew the beat of his people's heart, and he loved that beat, to a degree that he could no more attain than he could attain that man's cast of mind.

He found Martha Liddel's inn, but not without some difficulty. Indeed for a time it had seemed to the minister's frustrated senses that the hills had simply swallowed it up. He smiled grimly at his fancies when eventually, early in the evening, he rode into the tiny secluded yard. Martha's inn stood on the same spot as it had stood for more than two centuries, Martha herself sitting by the door, her ever present Bible open on her lap. She seemed to see the minister only slowly, and then slowly rise to her feet. Still when she walked towards him it was with that lightness of gait that had

316

previously seemed to him so incongruous. She appeared to him even older than he could remember. The hair on her chin had almost grown into a beard which had spread to her cheeks, framing the ancient passion that was her countenance.

'In the Lord's name this is indeed a surprise.'

'Why I have always promised I would make the journey and visit you.'

'Indeed sae, I mind that ye said sae, and that ye are very welcome will need tae be nae mair than mentioned tae be confirmed, for ye ken it weel enough.'

She called, and the girl Helen Melville appeared. She bowed silently to the minister her face and head almost completely concealed by her shawl. She reached out to take his horse.

'Why Helen,' the minister said. 'I will see to the beast. He serves me well, and if he could reason, he would doubtless reason that he had a right to my attention.'

Martha gave a gay toss of her head.

'Awa wae ye, gie the horse tae the lassie, I ken he will be contented enough in her hands, and come awa ben.'

'I ken horses weel enough Sir.'

For a moment the girl's eyes flashed with startling directness at the minister, and then as quickly turned away, taking up the reins of the horse as she did so. Martha took hold of his arm and impatiently and proprietorially she guided him towards the door of the inn, only releasing him when he was inside.

The room was almost empty, apart from a few shepherds and their dogs. It appeared exactly as the minister remembered it, the grim old spear still occupying its allotted place on the wall. Exactly as she had done before, Martha disappeared to return with two mugs of ale. She set them down and waited quietly for the minister to speak; she did not daff with him as she did with Andrew Gilmore.

'And how do I find you Martha? As well as you appear to be I trust?'

'My condition is in the Lord's hands for weel or woe, as it has aye been, and nae doubt at its appointed hour this auld carcase sall return tae the dust frae whence it cam, and as he has minded his servant weel in life I canna see that he will forget her in her death, let his enemies and mine howl and rage as they please.'

317

'Indeed so Martha.'

'And how are the louns and carlines o Trig behaving minister? I couldna help but observe when I was last there what I had aye kent, that the Lord has a stubborn and wayward flock in that place.'

'Oh I think they're behaving well enough, and I pray their judgement on me is a charitable one.'

'They're nae doubt awe struck dumb by haeving a gentleman tae watch ower them, fine manners and gentlemanly behavior war aye strangers there.'

'I try to be just and forbearing . . . You seem to imply that Trig has a disreputable history.'

'Och only a manner o speaking. They are nae doubt nae worse than maist folk, which is not tae say that they are unco gude.'

The deference which the minister had at first detected had quickly evaporated, vanquished by force of habit. After grace had been said and supper eaten, she, deciding the minister had come especially to see her, left Helen to see to the customers and sat with him drinking her ale in a masculine manner.

She was paying him special attention, the minister realised. Normally at this hour she would be slumbering fitfully in her chair, her Bible open on her lap. She was also divining, her curiosity aroused, for she had no idea why he had come, and in Martha's theology nothing happened without a purpose. Eventually he said:

'Tell me Martha, I have heard it said that you were once acquainted with one Todd Grey? I have heard his name mentioned, but no more than that. Andrew told me it was he who brought Helen here.'

For a moment the old woman was silent her eyes probing his intentions in that manner to which he had become accustomed.

'What gars ye ask o him?'

'Curiosity, and it would appear that you, alone of anybody I know, seems to have actually met him.'

'Aye, Todd was a quiet man, and it is true I kent him weel enough, and on occasion had reason tae be grateful tae him. Not just for Helen's sake, for awe I count that far and aboun the greatest blessing o awe. But Todd, weel, strive michtily wae him though I did, was not in his outward appearance as Christian a man as ye and I wad hae wished. But the saving o her young life, aye and the protecting o it, was a wark in which the Lord Jesus Christ stood at Todd's right hand. Sae tae my een he was a blessed man, forbye he was a rebellious ane tae, and a bitter ane. He was awe these things, and some wad sae muckle mair. Ower bad tae be ower blessit, but fell ower gude tae be hingit.'

The minister waited. This was not the kind of conversation Martha craved, and yet he watched her slowly resigning herself to it.

'He wad come by here, in the days afore he found Helen, biding a bit on his wanderings, whiles on foot, but mair often on an auld bit Hielan garron. He was aye neat and weel turned out for a wandering man, wae a gude sword and twa guns, and never leaving till the place was weel stocked wae fresh meat, far mair than his keep warranted. He was a pretty man tae, even when auld. Why I mind the nicht he pitched a drunken loun o a sodger straight out the door. Och a brisk man was Todd.'

'Do you know where he came from?'

'From this district, aye, but he had wandered about sae much that he hardly belanged here onymair. He had been a sodger a bit o the time, and aiblins a wanderer for the rest. He had come doun frae the Hielans when I first met him, but that was nae mair his hame than ony ither place.'

'I heard that he buried people who died during the famine.'

'Aye he did that, but he himsel wad say very little about it, for decency's sake . . .'

Martha's voice quickened, her blue eyes shone keenly.

'Let nane ever tell ye different minister, for I ken not what gars ye inquire, but I ken weel enough that it was a hard and bitter task which few ithers at that time had the strength, aye or the courage tae dae.'

'Why should people dispute that?'

'Och folk are superstitious louns, and some nae doubt thought that the sight o Todd on the hillside meant that their end was near, forbye the truth, that he aye did what he could for the living. I ken not richtly mysel, but he kept his wits when despair hammered at mony a door.'

'What happened to him in the end, do you know?'

'He went awa, I ken not exactly whaur. Tae the Hielans I think, he had wild friends there. Ance or twice he returned, and then for a time he did not come, but if he is still living it wad not surprise me greatly tae see him appear quietly at the door. Ye see minister it was my opinion that there were earthly powers that wad maybe hae laid their hands on him if they could hae, but I hae nae clear evidence o that. Och but he was an unco clever man, unco clever . . .'

Martha's voice grew soft. To the minister's eyes it appeared as if the mists of history itself swirled about her.

'I mind the day he cam here wae Helen, a bairn then, sae thin and sma, sitting on his horse wae him walking at its heid. Awe he said was, "Martha I think she's ower young tae be gadding about wae an auld tink like mysel".'

She laughed then, a wide broad laugh.

'For ye ken minister, he was an auld kind o man, ower carnal tae be ower blessit, and no aboun an earthly jest, but honourable in awe things, sae that ye excused him mony things ye wad hae checked in ither men.'

'I have heard that Todd Grey was not his proper name.'

'That micht weel be, forbye I kent him by nae ither. He never telt me, and it was not a time tae be prying ower deeply, mony a Godly gate haeving led gude folk intae earthly danger, which micht or micht no hae been his case. I canna say, I mind him kindly enough in my thoughts and in my prayers.'

'Did you ever know of one called Steven or Steenie Malecky, who I believe came from Trig?'

'Why minister ye are an inquiring kind o man. What can auld tales sic as that mean tae ye?'

'I hear things . . . Do you think I'm wrong in being curious?'

'Na, na, no wrang, but these are things o lang ago . . . Dae ye mean Malecky the warlock that the Kirk caught and couldna haud, but the Deil cam and whisked him awa frae under their noses?'

The minister felt his heart strangely sickening. He thought of Walter Hyslop's tormented visage. 'Yes, I think that is the very one. I read about him in an old memoir of the place.'

'My mither tell me the tale when I was a bairn. Some said that he was a warlock, some said that he was a fairy. Some said that he was a man wha could conjure the living frae the deid

320

and pluck a bairn frae its mither's belly sae that she hardly felt it passing. Some said that he supped nightly wae the Deil and ithers said that he was an angel frae Heaven. And ithers said that he had ance spent seven years in fairyland and had been the Queen o the Fairies true lover, and when times got hard for him on earth he was aye welcome back there. When the earthly powers caught him and locked him up for being sic an unco strange loun, he just cocked his snook in the air, gied out a bit laugh and flew straight out through the roof o the strang place whaur they held him, and forbye sodgers rade the hale night through they couldna catch him. It was said that he wad flee through the air when their hands reached doun tae clutch him, and then, out o range he wad drop tae the ground just tae torment them. Some say that he was nae living man at awe.'

'If he could do all of these things he most assuredly was not. But I am thinking of an altogether more earthly being.'

'An earthly being! Why minister, Steenie was nae mair than a whigmaleerie tae frighten bairns wae. Ye ken, hush ye, hush ye, or Steenie Malecky sall come and tak thee! Just a daft auld bit tale and superstition which some nae doubt will believe, but some folk will believe maist onything.

'At Halloween, and at ither times, often when a bairn was about tae be born, my mither wad tell me how some folk wad put a pint o ale on their doorstep tae ensure his gude will, for it was weel kent he liked his ale, and if the morning cam and the ale was gone, why they wad say, Steenie has been by and wishes us weel! As if there war no mortal men enough in Scotland tae drink a pint o ale . . . What hae they louns in Trig been telling ye?'

'Why nothing at all. They deny the existence of even such tales as you have told me. Indeed having heard elsewhere of him hailing from Trig, their denials make me curious.'

Martha laughed uproariously.

'Why ye maun hae shamed them minister. For ye see, if stories o Steenie greatly differ, being nae mair than auld fancies, they awe agree that if he was born at awe, he was born in Trig. My mither was very firm on that point. In Trig and nae place else, and why he ance threw the laird o Trig intae a bog sae that he drouned. But taking intae account that the laird, like awe the Doig line, was a black hearted, drunken, fornicating sinner, wha did indeed droun in a bog, Godly folk should ken weel enough whaur tae look for that righteous judgement. But the folk o Trig canna thole the thocht o Steenie, forbye the truth, that there's a hill in that place named after nane ither.'

'I know the place. I walk up it often.'

'And I'll swear ye hae seen nocht o whigmaleeries or fairies, or ony sic nonsense.'

The minister thought again of the gaunt apparition of Walter Hyslop. He decided it would be unfair to mention him.

'I have been told that Steenie Malecky and Todd Grey are one and the same man.'

Martha's eyes glinted fiercely, and then it appeared to the minister that the fierceness turned into mockery, even contempt. She thinks, he thought sadly, that I have allowed myself to be the dupe of a village prankster. I have disappointed her.

'Laddie, ye are a gude and Godly man, I ken that weel, and hae kent it weel frae the first time I clamped my een upon ye. But believe naething sic folk tell ye . . . Why wha ever telt ye that tale must hae been mad, wicked, drunk or dreaming. Todd Grey is an earthly man, nane mair sae, wha has sat mony a lang night in this very room, and drank my ain ale in my ain company . . . Now wha ever telt ye that tale? Bring me ony person that can wae his hand on the Bible say that he has done the same wae Steenie Malecky.'

She sat back as if she had said the last word on the subject. The minister felt crushed beneath the weight of her conviction. Malecky, whose one time existence he could hardly doubt, had once again metamorphosed himself into a will of the wisp out of the world, time, and history.

Suddenly from her silence Martha spoke again.

'Ye hae fair worn me out minister wae these auld tales, when I had set ye up for some Godly disputation. But ye see, I maun aye defend Todd should ony say ocht against him. For, for awe I didna aye approve o him, or his thoughts, he was gude and kind, and brought me the greatest earthly comfort in my life.'

'Indeed Martha, that cannot be denied when Helen is the living proof of it.'

'She's a fine lass is she not minister? Weel whatever the louns o Trig tell ye, mind wha was the airm o the Lord wha brocht her here.'

The old woman was lapsing. It was passed her sleeping hour. The minister reproached himself. And yet, as Martha slowly succumbed to sleep, a smile of extraordinary gentleness spread across the crumbling rock of her features. It was a smile composed of absolute conviction and absolute certainty. She had weathered great defeats without falling pray to despair, and in her appointed hour, which she knew could not be far away, she confidently looked forward to a great victory. A victory in which all her enemies would be cut down by a flaming sword, incomparably mightier than anything she, or her people, had ever been able to wield.

It was hardly, the minister thought, an ideal Christian state of mind. In contemplating her features the minister thought of John Erskine, Andrew Gilmore, Walter Hyslop, and the torrent of tormented wrath that had been Sawney Bain. He was suddenly struck horribly and forcibly with the idea that the Scots were hardly a Christian people at all. To them religion was a spear, a sword, and a gun, blessed by their tribal deity, to be used against their enemies and his, the Sir John Doigs of their own land, conveniently cast as the Godless.

It was for this reason that they had joyfully cast aside old hatreds and marched to the aid of their English brethren. 'Free the poor commons!', they had cried. 'And make what little ye can of priests and great folk!'

Religion overwhelmed by revolution, and a wild and intemperate dream which had inevitably crashed about them. If the ultimate power of the King and the great nobility had been curbed, the Godly burgesses of Edinburgh and Glasgow, the Doigs and their kind, had risen on the ruins. The people had presumed to dictate to God, and it was now the Kirk's duty to instruct them that God would not be dictated to, and the place in the world that they had always occupied was theirs still, and would be theirs until the Lord, and not they, chose to alter it.

He looked around the room and its occupants. They would grow bitter, he thought. They had borne Christ the Lamb to the battlefield, and discovered that the Lord of Heaven was not their tribal deity, or the sum of their desires.

The minister called to the girl. She was talking to a young cattle drover. Her eyes were shining, her shawl had fallen to her shoulders, her hair flew like fire about her head.

When the minister called she had been fondling the drover's dog, and to his daunted soul it was as if she took an age to turn, acknowledging him by re-arranging her shawl before striding gracefully towards him. He looked at the stalwart young drover who had himself saluted him civilly. She would one day marry a young man like that, he thought, and it would be right that she did so.

'I think Martha would be more comfortable in her bed,' he said.

'Och Sir, tis her custom. She aye has a few jougs o her ale and sleeps the evening quietly in her chair, whiles waking tae bid the folk gude nicht. She wad be maist vexed if I put her off tae her bed afore her time, like a bairn.'

'As you please Helen, undoubtedly you know her customs best. It may seem a bit ungracious but I think I will retire. I haven't really got the head to match Martha's two or three jugs.'

'Och Sir, that will be fine, ye can hae the same bed as ye had the first time, which is our best ane. I will tak ye tae it.'

He rose to his feet. He blessed Martha before he left, at which the old woman's eyes opened.

'I thank ye minister, and sall mind ye in my prayers, as I hae done since first we met, but gude nicht for now.'

Her eyes closed as quickly as they had opened. He followed the girl upstairs, the drover and the other guests bidding him good night as he passed them. He returned their civil words, feeling the strangeness in his voice like the loneliness in his soul.

At the top of the stairs he held up the lamp to allow the girl to descend safely. In the semi-darkness and confined space of the landing he had felt her presence as something pressingly close and yet impossibly remote. I am a weak soul, he thought, as he heard her once again rejoin the company below, hardly worthy of them, and if they had more understanding and less charity they would realise that.

The minister sighed. If Martha was correct, poor Todd Grey, if Walter Hyslop had been able to lay his hands on him, would have died and Malecky would still survive, reduced to a childish superstition, a hobgoblin of the peasant mind – if what Martha said was true.

324

The minister felt the cold hand of reason grip his flesh. He could hardly doubt that Malecky had existed as a flesh and blood man, with an uncanny ability to ensnare the mind and heart and passions of all who came in contact with him. Beyond that, it appeared, nothing could be known for certain. For a moment the minister felt himself faced with the profound possibility that Mathius Pringle was right and Malecky was indeed Satan.

The minister felt his soul turn to ice. Many learned and intelligent men had believed it possible, and those who had actually come face to face with him had been entirely convinced. If their convictions were true, the burden that Mathius Pringle had borne, and had bequeathed to his wretched Wattie, now rested on his shoulders.

He picked up the Black Book. It felt to his touch like a thing on fire, and from its covers the hideous countenance of Agnes Douglas sprang at him.

> Oh cam ye early or cam ye late,
> Ye'll find Black Agnes at the gate.

☆

The news that the man Cromwell was now marching North wae a great army threw the people intae a panic. We kent weel the story o how bludily he had suppressed Ireland, and forbye they had awe been runagate Papists, the English it was said made little distinction in dealing wae them they called their enemies.

Sae ance again David Leslie was in the saddle, gaithering an army, this time tae meet them that had sae lately been our brithers in Christ. And frae awe corners o the land sodgers cam in response, and it seemed nae langer tae matter, tae any ither than the Kirk, wha had been for the King or against the King, or were now for this new King. Auld fears and auld hatreds now beat the drum, and they declared they wad not hae an English army in Scotland, and there was even talk o wild Hielanmen busking themsels tae fight.

I remember the time very weel, and I mind ane day

325

clearest o awe, for forbye I did not ken it, it was tae be the last day that I wad ever see Steenie.

We were walking on the great crag that they call Arthur's Seat, high aboun the clamour that had becam the toun. Steenie had talked a bit of how if Cromwell was coming North tae mak war, it was nae doubt because he had heard how the Scots were themsels making ready tae ance again invade England and help his enemies there, for wae the King now deid, Cromwell it seemed had powerful enemies amang the Parliament men.

We sat doun on the great brow o the hill. Frae this point, it being a clear day, we could see far across the Forth tae Fife and the line o hills beyond. Below us on the green we could see sodgers drilling, practising wheeling tae the left and wheeling tae the right, and advancing at the charge. And for awe the fierce shouts they gied when they did these things they seemed creatures o nae mair purpose than ants.

Steenie had been very quiet for a time, watching them and listening tae their cries which were carried up tae us on the breeze. Despite the brave show they made they were but freshwater sodgers, for it was weel kent throughout the toun, that while awe men wanted tae fight against the English nae langer caring tae which party they had previously belanged, the Kirk wad only enlist them that it considered tae be sufficiently Godly and loyal tae the Covenant, and it had been drawing these lines very narrow, turning awa many salted sodgers and gude captains, and filling up their ranks wae freshwater sodgers, many o them ower young maybe tae hae been sinners.

It was said that even Leslie himsel had flown intae a rage at them, asking them if they wad cut his army tae pieces lang before Cromwell even reached the border? But the Kirk had demanded back o him, that wad he put his faith in the arm o flesh rather than the arm o the Lord? And they had declared that a bairn could beat the heretic Cromwell if he had the Lord at his side, but how could the Lord be expected tae fight at the heid o an army o Godless reprobates?

-It's madness Agnes, Steenie said. -Perhaps the final madness. Cromwell kens very weel the task he has before him, and the army he brings will be a very gude ane.

I asked him if he thought then, that the fight might be lost.

-Agnes, he said, -Cromwell will bring a very gude army, but there's a limit tae the number o sodgers he can supply on the march, and Leslie he kens, is as gude a captain as himsel. But ye maun ken, England is a great and rich place, greater than anything this land can dream about, and his army will be better equipped than anything this country in its present state can afford. But in numbers, aye and in experience, we might hae some advantage.

-But we oursels hae seen Hielan kerns putting aside awe their auld hatreds and coming doun ready tae fight, only tae hae some minister examining their conscience in a foreign tongue and telling them they are no Godly enough tae fight, and sae they maun gang back frae whence they cam. Hielan pride, lassie is a touchy enough thing on a quiet day.

He fell quiet then, it being plain that he did think it was the final madness, and if the Kirk thought, as it aye thought, that God was on its side, then nae doubt the heretic Cromwell had a conviction on that point as strang as their ain, and matched them prayer for prayer.

I touched his beard then, stroking it gently, feeling the mood that was in him, part anger and part despair, wae neither God nor Jesus tae guide him, and weary o the warld.

-It will be a foolish fight lassie, born out o dreams and prides and ambitions, and if I ken that it dis not need tae be fought, aiblins I ken also that Cromwell's mad pride will bring him here ane day, and it might as weel be this ane, for he is by awe accounts a greatly changed man. But I nae langer ken ought, awe things hae changed, aye and changed again, and what was ance a bright dream o paradise has becam a dark dream o nonsense.

-If ye try tae join the army ye might weel be ganging tae yer death, and no frae the English.

-I might weel be sae, but I ken Leslie weel enough, and nae doubt he wad just slip me in, and why, if the fight is lost they will hae a very fair excuse ready tae hand.

I could not ken then that nane o this talk wad mean anything. But I telt him that before he ganged mad I wad hae him gang tae me.

This he did, and for a lang time we just lay there watching the toun roaring beneath us, choking wae its dreams and its fears, and its sermons and its sodgers, and its ain fate circling aboun it like a great black bird rising high in the wind that blew in frae the sea and across the crags. Salted and cauld it tasted tae me as it ran through the ranks o the sodgers that were drilling and firing their guns, and across our ain flesh that was naked and close. And awe things it seemed tae me then did it just pick up and scatter like sae much dust, and the prayers o the people, and the fierce shouting o the sodgers, and the cracking o their guns, were nae mair than things wae which they mocked themsels.

-Folk, Steenie said, -that dream o freedom, but canna live without a king, and that canna live without God, sall aye sell themsels back intae Eygpt, and plough a bludie path tae get there.

He ran his hand doun my leg till he touched the silver dirk that Catriona had gien me, and which I aye wore, and he smiled a bit, like the smile o that auld dream that at the finish had nae power tae change anything.

-We mak not the times in which we live, he said. -But they dae seem tae mak us, and set limits on awe our endeavours.

At that time I kent not properly what he meant, and how could awe ither folk be wrang about God and Steenie Malecky be right? But he just said, that grown men that whined in the Lord's lug were like bairns greeting for their mither, a mither that had far ower many bairns and fell quarrelsome anes at that.

He laughed then an unco strange laugh, and took me in his airms and said that some things we had the power tae mak. And sae we did, for the second time that day, and it was a lang and sweet time, after it we just lay there on the the grass, and aiblins it was strange that we did not ken the things that were tae come tae pass. Nor did we ken that this wad be the last time that we wad sit in sic a fashion on a hillside, and the last time on earth that I wad see him smile in sic a way, forbye he smiled a bit when we at last walked doun frae that auld bit crag.

We walked through the toun until we cam tae the Musketeer, and there at its door was auld Baillie, and tae our great astonishment Sawney Bain, baith o them in a state o great agitation, and Sawney shouted out,

-Run ye daft loun, they are on tae ye and coming tae tak ye.

Och I mind weel how their een met. Like awe the warld was in that glance, and Sawney thrust the reins o his gude horse that was a pale grey colour intae Steenie's hands and telt him tae flee the toun, and when I said that I wad gang wae him, awe he said was,

-No this time Agnes, no this time.

Then he kissed me and louped on tae the back o the horse, and crying out that he wad be back ane day never fear he rade awa.

I ken not exactly whaur they caught him, but I saw them bring him back through the toun surrounded by a body o lancers, though it was said that he had made nae resistance at awe.

When he had ridden awa I turned tae look at Sawney, and auld Baillie looked at him, and there were tears in his een that rolled without check doun his face. But there was muckle mair than that, for despite the living tears it was like a face that was already amang the deid.

-How cam ye o this knowledge? I asked him.

-I heard o it, was awe the reply he made, but he spoke in a voice that wad hae shaken awe creation had they heard it.

-They hae looked for him for many a lang year.

Auld Baillie put his arm round me then. And he reached out his hand and gripped Sawney's airm, and turned him round sae that he faced us wae as much ease as if he had been a bit puppet, and aiblins when he looked intae Sawney's face he saw mair than flesh could thole.

-God save us awe, he said.

-Save us auld man? Sawney said unco quiet. -Why he has damned us tae Hell lang syne, and ye ken his judgements are forever and aye.

He turned about then and walked awa his feet tripping as he went, as if his heid and een could hardly steer them.

☆

The minister was still awake when he heard the knock on his door. Gentle at first, and then, receiving no response urgent in its timidity.

'Who is out there?'

A voice replied, but it was as timid as the knock had been. Irritated he rose to his feet and opened the door. The girl Helen Melville was standing at the top of the stairs with a lamp in her hand. Beneath her shyness there was an insistence, almost a wildness in her eyes. The minister stepped back.

'What is the meaning of this?'

He watched the girl recoil from his words as if from a blow. Instantly he regretted them, but the girl's eyes were now downcast, strange and fearful.

'I apologise, my words were harsh, but I was almost asleep, and you startled me.'

'It's Martha Sir, she has taen the auld spear and gane out . . . I need yer help Sir, maybe she will listen tae ye . . .'

'Gone out . . ?'

'Come Sir, ye maun see for yersel. Ye mind the story Mr Gilmore telt ye? If ye canna help I maun gang ower the hill and fetch Tam Laidlaw and his wife, they ken . . .'

'I thought it had not affected her for some time?'

'A lang time Sir, I ken not what brought it on, but she gies nae warning.'

The girl was calling on him for assistance. Quite unaware, he thought, of the turmoil in his own heart. He looked at her. She was anxious but not frightened. If he refused her request she had stout neighbours who would willingly help her, and he would be as well to abandon this country.

'Of course I will help, but you must instruct me as to what is necessary.'

'Come wae me.'

Her voice was urgent now. She ran down the stairs and out into the yard with the minister behind her. She pointed up to the towering crag which protected the rear of the inn. There, right on its pinnacle sat Martha Liddel, carved like a graven image against the night sky, the ancient spear resting on her shoulder. She gave no sign of hearing their voices, or of being in any way aware of their presence below her.

The minister called softly to her. He felt sure that she could hear him but the sound produced no perceptible reaction from her. He shouted again as loudly as his lungs could manage. For a moment it seemed that her head turned, stared blankly into the night, and then resumed its former position.

'She is mad and dangerous, tae hersel and ithers.'

'There must be a way up there, can't we simply go and fetch her down? She is after all an old woman.'

'She thinks she is in an ither time Sir, a time, as she says when the Lord gied her the strength o Samson and stood beside her and exalted her. There is but ane route up tae that crag whaur that nicht lang ago she led the women and the bairns sae that they wad be safe frae the sodgers, and whaur she killed the sodger and drove the rest awa.

'She is in that time now Sir and will recognise neither ane o us. If we try tae fetch her doun she will certainly try tae pike us. But if she bides there awe night she will certainly dee o the cauld.'

The minister glanced at her. She had her plaid drawn tightly round her now so that he could only see her eyes.

'Then what in God's name do you propose we do?'

'We hae tae wait minister. In the end she will fall properly asleep, and then we can fetch her doun.'

The minister felt suddenly exhausted by the absurdity of the situation.

'She is, I maintain, an old frail woman. I'm sure if you lead me up that path I can manage her with kindness and persuasion, despite her weapon.'

Without a word the girl surrendered herself to his authority and led him through a labyrinthine passage under the house to a tiny door concealed in the wall. She opened this, and signalling to the minister to follow her she crawled through it on her hands and knees. It led on to a path, which even when there were on it, was entirely concealed from their view by the undergrowth.

This path wound its way narrowly round the crag before it started to climb up it. The refuge at the top was almost entirely sealed off by a great rock which had been deliberately placed there. The minister at once saw that while the rock could with difficulty be squeezed past, anyone who tried to do so would be at a complete disadvantage against even a weak defender.

The girl flattened herself against the side of the crag.

'She kens we're here Sir. Dinna for the love o God put yer heid round that stane.'

This the minister was about to do when suddenly the point of the spear flashed through the gap. There was no mistaking the determination of that thrust. The minister, who had harboured some thoughts of grasping it by the shaft and wrenching it from the old woman's grasp, was thwarted by the speed with which it was withdrawn. A voice which he could hardly believe possible bellowed at him.

'Damn ye tae Hell this nicht. Ye hae drunk my ale and Deil the gude may ye hae o it, but ye sall drink fire at yer maister's feet ere ye drink the blude o God's folk.'

As if to emphasise her words, she drummed her spear fiercely against the rock.

'Back I tell ye, back tae the pit frae whence ye cam.'

'Haud back a bit minister, and tak care, if she sees a mark she will stick it.'

The minister edged his way slowly down the path. He tried to look around him. The light from the girl's lamp plunged everything but her features into total darkness.

'You have been through this before, could you not distract her in some way while I endeavor to get through that gap? I'm sure that once faced with me she would come to her senses.'

'Her senses are ower distracted in ane way tae be successfully distracted in anither. There was only ane man on earth that ever succeeded in talking her doun . . .'

The minister looked up sharply.

'What man was that?'

'Todd Grey, on twa occasions Todd talked tae her sae that she let him in, but I ken not how he did it, or what he said, but he brought her out again, which was near a miracle.'

The minister felt himself give out an audible sigh. The girl continued speaking, entirely unaware of the effect her words were having on her companion.

'Ye see she thinks we are sodgers come tae ravish and murder her, and awe that's wae her.'

'There is no one with her.'

'She is in anither time, and it may be that Todd entered that time and stood alangside her in it, sae that she kent him for a gude friend and trusted him when she wad trust nane ither.'

The minister could see her now, a dark silhouette against the sky shaking her spear above her head like a barbaric sentinel.

'They rin, they rin! See how the ill-begotten ghets rin wae the Lord Jesus Christ on their tails, cutting them frae the saddle wae a sword o fire and making them tae fa intae Hell, for nae earthly bed sall they find this nicht.'

She broke into a wild rendering of the twenty-third psalm. To the minister's ears it seemed to thunder over the hills like a tribal war-chant.

'In time she will exhaust hersel Sir and just fa quietly asleep. It's then we can gae in and get her.'

The minister sat down on the ground. He tried to examine his feelings but his mind refused to focus on anything which did not disintegrate when confronted with reason. Martha continued to sing and curse like some hideous Christian valkyrie. If at certain times it seemed to his ears that her voice was failing, at others it hurled itself through the air like a volley of musketry. He became aware of the girl bending over him.

'I'm sorry about this Sir. I didna expect it. She hasna ganged out for a lang time . . . Aiblins Mr Gilmore is richt tae say that I should bury that auld shiltron, except that she wadna hae it but wad fly intae a rage, which is unnatural for her.'

She handed him a flask of whisky.

'Drink some Sir, it will keep ye warm.'

The minister felt the tangible proximity of the girl. She was fearful. She had to stay where she was and she was fearful that he would grow impatient and leave her to cope with the old woman alone. He drank some of the whisky, more to reassure her than out of any desire he felt.

'Could I not try what Todd Grey tried? Martha, I believe, likes and trusts me.'

'Na Sir, in God's name dinna, she will be sure tae hurt or kill ye, and in the morning, when she is recovered, sic knowledge wad kill her. Ye see it is mair than just liking and trusting, Todd was an unco strange man, and had great skill in sic matters, and it was as if he himsel believed awe that Martha believed, and that the place was indeed surrounded wae sodgers, and, he had his ain gun in his hand, and wad help her shoot them. And Martha replied, 'Ye maun be a Godly man despite awe Todd

333

Grey.' But she let him in, and a while later, a lang while it seemed, he led her out as quiet as a lamb.'

The minister sat silently with his head on his knees. He started to pray. A Christian should pray, he thought, anywhere and at anytime, whatever the situation. He heard her quietly following him. When he looked up he had resolved that the present situation, and all that flowed from it, he would see through to the end. The girl pulled her shawl about her shoulders and sat down beside him.

'Are you cold?' He asked her. 'I'm cold, I wonder why Martha is not.'

'Och she's cauld enough minister, and that is the danger, when her resolution fails she will fa asleep, and if there were nane tae pick her up likely as not she'd dee.'

'You are very loyal to her.'

'And why should I not be? Her that has taen me in and fed me awe these years wae never a harsh word.'

'That was when Todd Grey brought you here?'

'Aye Sir.'

'How well do you know him?'

For a brief moment it appeared to the minister that the girl's visage changed, as if it had suddenly grown older in a way that he could not fathom. He felt the heat of her body. She was sitting far too close to him, as if she had no idea how to conduct herself.

'Och I ken him weel enough minister.'

'I am interested in him. Everyone appears to know of him, but apart from yourself and Martha, I know none who have actually met him.'

'Some folk think that he is nae mair than a bit elf.'

'Which is nonsense.'

'Aye minister.'

'Who was he? Do you know?'

'Och, only an auld bit travelling man.'

'That is how everyone describes him, and yet Martha tells me he carried arms.'

'He had been a sodger ance, but that was lang syne.'

'Tell me more about him.'

'Why minister there is little enough tae tell, for there is little enough kent. He wad ride the country during the famine years,

334

appearing here and there. Whiles wae a bit food, maist times ower late for that for there was deid and deeing in ilka place. He wad gae intae biggins whaur hale families had just deed awa in their beds, and he wad bury them maist decently, and care not whether they might hae the plague. Whiles, kenning that they were deeing, he wad sit by them till they did sae.'

'His presence comforted them?'

'Little enough maybe minister. When he cam first tae our house my faither had already gane, and my mither was sinking fast. My brither, wha was aulder than me, had gane tae try tae find something tae eat, and had returned wae twa fouls he had stolen, for ye maun ken, awe the folk in the land warna starving, and then he went awa again and never returned. Mither wad insist that I ate, but wad tak little hersel but wad only pretend tae eat.

'When Todd cam tae our door I kent not at awe wha he was, just a little grey auld man wha might weel hae been a fairy. Mither though, kent him weel enough. 'Sae ye hae cam Todd,' she said tae him. 'Now that ye are here I ken it is the end weel enough.'

'Some folk wad bless Todd. Ithers war no sae sure, saying that he was in truth nane o God's folk, and should he cam upon a body in desperate strife that body was sure tae dee.

'That was just folk havering, for he was aye maist kind. When he cam tae our door he went straight tae mither and tried wae awe his skill tae help her. And when at last he cam frae her bed there was an unco sadness in his een, and he said tae me that I was tae gae ben and see her, and that she wad tell me what tae dae.

'I kent mither was deeing when I saw her, and aiblins I had kent that for a lang time. But that time she grasped my hand and telt me hersel, and telt me tae that I was tae gang wae Todd and be guided in awe things by him.

'She deed that nicht, and Todd opened up faither's grave and laid her in and telt me tae say a bit prayer. I did not ken him then and looked at him tae see whether or not he wad pray wae me. But he just looked auld and sad, and stared up at the sky and said, 'If awe the prayers this gude auld wife has said in her life willna get her intae Heaven, I hardly think the prayers o Todd Grey sall dae it.' Ye maun ken minister, and ye can hardly

335

approve, but he was nae praying man . . .'

She looked directly at the minister, and then as quickly cast her eyes downward. He felt almost as a tangible thing his authority over her, and yet the cool strength that her voice had assumed in some way that was hardly reasonable appalled him.

'Go on, I am not one to sit in judgement on this good if strange man.'

The ghost of a smile played across her lips, changing, it appeared to the minister's eyes, her countenance into that of a worldly-wise woman. Suddenly he was almost afraid of her, assailed by the thought that he had in some way lied to her.

'Prayer is a great comfort in the midst of despair, but it is not always easy or possible.'

The smile remained. The old woman was singing again. She had been singing for some time. A gentle song now, that he could not follow.

'When I had finished my prayer he went intae the biggin and brought out faither's auld sword and musket wae which he had fought for God's cause. He said that while they war gude enough tae fight for that, they war in the end poor useless things against the foe that had struck him and his doun. But he buried them as weel, and I kept some things o my mither's, and my faither's pipe and pistol. Then we left, riding baith on his bit Hielan garron.

'He had food in his bag, dried meat, and strange things that I had never afore eaten. I said this tae him and he just laughed and said no tae be afraid, and that folk can eat maist onything when they're desperate, and these bit scraps wad dae for now.

'His voice was unco quiet and gentle, and it was only when we war far frae hame that I found the courage tae look at him properly. He didna look sae auld then, wae a sword at his side, and twa pistols under his plaid and a musket on his horse. Folk wha thocht kindly on him said that he was an auld and Godly sodger, wha had lost everything, and maybe pairt o his wits in the wars.

'He asked me what age I was and I telt him I was fifteen. Then I asked him whaur we war ganging, for I was quickly nae langer afraid o him his manners being sae kindly. "Tae an auld wife o my acquaintance," he replied. "A very kindly person, wha forbye she will deafen ye morning tae e'en wae psalm singing, will feed ye and gie ye a place tae bide I'm sure." These were his words, and after a few days on the road he brought me here.'

'Which was a true and Christian way to behave.'

The girl fell silent, her head turned away from the minister. He waited in silence, feeling that she must speak again. When she did not, he said:

'Is there any more that you can tell me about him?'

'Och but he was an unco strange man, and I think he wad refuse the title o Christian. I helped him bury some folk and wad say a prayer for them, but he wad not, and wad just say that ower many prayers had ganged up frae this land and very few blessings had cam doun on it . . . I canna lie about him minister, for he wad not want that, and ye hae asked.'

'I do not judge him; atheism when it is not simply false reasoning, is a form of despair, and no doubt he had suffered much. But I must pity him, and pray for him, and indeed his Christian behaviour is in my judgement a sign that the Lord guided his actions even in his despair.'

Like some stealthy wraith the harlot's smile returned to the girl's lips. The minister felt his soul disintegrating beneath it, and then as quickly as it had appeared it vanished.

'Sir, I think we micht be able tae get her doun now.'

The minister had felt his mind plunge into a chasm that opened to receive it. At her words he wrenched it back from the brink.

He had seen Agnes Douglas standing on that brink, and the sight of her raged like the Devil through his body. He saw her standing naked in the moonlight at the mouth of an endless cave staring out at a red and roaring sea.

The girl touched his shoulder.

'Look Sir . . .'

His flesh sprang backwards from her touch. He looked up. Martha was sitting as if crushed into a ball clutching the spear in her lap. As he watched the body rocked gently in its slumber.

'If we gang quietly now minister we can get her.'

He rose to his feet and following the girl they both edged their way up the path. The girl directed the minister to watch if the old woman stirred. Martha did not stir. Silently Helen passed through the gap. Still Martha did not move. Feeling utterly weary, the minister followed her.

Once through, the girl moved swiftly across the remaining ground to snatch away the spear. Martha opened her eyes, but to the minister it now seemed as if they registered nothing.

'It's fine now Martha, they hae awe fled awa.'

The old woman's eyes closed again, her hands clasped tightly round the Bible on her lap.

The minister stooped to pick her up, astonished at how light she was. With Helen leading they started on the tortuous descent from the crag. As they passed the sleeping woman with difficulty through the concealed door she turned fitfully like a child in their arms but gave no sign of waking. The minister following Helen's instructions carried her to her room and laid her down on her bed. She was now peacefully asleep, and suddenly, to his eyes, a tiny, utterly insignificant figure.

'I will see tae her now,' the girl said.

It had been a cruel and blasphemous thought, which the minister had hardly any strength left to rebuke. He withdrew into the kitchen of the inn, but without plotting any course he did not move from there. He no longer felt cold, but there was an utter numbness in every limb, like a cold beyond cold, like a frozen pain clutching his heart.

He picked up the shiltron spear, running his hands along the monstrous steel shod shaft. He was doing this when the girl was suddenly in the room staring at him.

'She is weel enough asleep now,' she said.

She was smiling. Her duty was done; her smile was cool and civil.

'And I think I must go to sleep now too, if I can.'

She threw back her head. Without intending it the minister found his eyes following the fine fair curve of her neck.

'It was kind o ye tae help me minister.'

'Tell me, this man Todd Grey, was that his proper name?'

The minister watched her expression change. He watched her lips hesitate. She was, he felt suddenly convinced, coolly doing what they all did, preparing some dissembling tale that they hoped would satisfy him. He felt his anger rising, justifying itself as it hardened.

'It was a name that folk gied him, or aiblins he himsel took it on. Few around here ken his real name.'

Her gaze remained steady, outrageously steady, it appeared to him as if she knew how fiercely he who said he would not judge was judging.

'Is he still alive?'

'Och aye, but gey auld now. He bides in the Hielans but comes quietly doun on a rare occasion.

'Why does he still come?'

The girl's expression changed.

'Nae doubt a body can come and gang as they please.'

She sees, he thought, that I intend to block her every evasion with a question, and she is calmly, insultingly, resolving herself into an attitude of defiance.

'I ken not what gars ye mak sic inquiries seeing that the man o wham we speak is quite unknown tae ye.'

'I have my reasons, which in my judgement are sound and proper ones.'

'Weel minister I hae a judgement o my ain, and I hae telt ye I think sufficient for ane nicht. Ony ither questions ye should ask o Todd himsel, gin ye should ever meet him. But for now I think I will gang tae my bed.'

She turned to go. The minister felt his anger starting like a fury from his lips.

'Why does he still come down here?'

To his eyes, it appeared as if her features coarsened into something repulsively insolent, as if his last question had stripped her patience of any further reticence.

'Why minister he comes maistly tae see me.'

'To see you?'

'And why should he not? And aiblins a carline that's a woman grown can be kind tae a kindly auld man that she loves aboun awe ithers, sinful though it nae doubt is. Todd wad say that there is nae sin but what yer conscience tells ye is a sin, but I canna expect ye tae thole that.'

For a moment they simply confronted each other silently.

'Ye hae forced me to speak . . .'

Yes, the minister thought bitterly, and in forcing her to speak it was as if he had thrust her outside his authority. She confronted him now like a being strangely and inexplicably transformed.

'I cannot believe what I am hearing. That he seduced you with a crude old heresy, is that what you are telling me?'

He watched her flesh flinch, her eyes flash fearfully about her. In his mind he saw her body falling, and he saw himself watching the fall.

'Is this Todd Grey properly called Steven Malecky?'

'Tae his friends he is.'

It was as if something evaporated from the minister's soul, and an agony as hard as the steel head of the spear entered him. It was as if he saw clearly for the first time where God had been leading him and why.

'When did you last see him?'

'About a year ago.'

'And you fornicated with him?'

'Aye I did.'

'You should be on your knees, woman. Do you know anything of this man's reputation? Do you know that throughout his entire life he has had the name of a warlock, sorcerer, seducer, and in his heart, and in his deeds, an enemy of our Lord and all true religion, who appears in a guise of seeming kindness? Do you know this?'

'Och I hae telt ye plainly that he is nae praying man, and I ken very weel that he's the subject o many a fanciful auld tale, and that the Kirk wad hae hung him if it could but hae held him.'

'I am not taking about ancient fancies, I am talking about real deeds that are in their outcome evil.'

'Then I ken nocht o them.'

'You know nothing of anything, I shudder at your ignorance, at your sin, at your incapacity to understand it. Can you not think of your parents . . .of this godly house? '

'My faither and mither war bitter folk ere they deed.'

'And into that despair Malecky crept like a serpent.'

'He is nae serpent, minister.'

'You are very glib in your assertions.'

'I hae nae ither answers tae gie.'

'Do you think Malecky will come here again?'

'Wha kens, he is very auld.'

'If he should come again tell him that he should visit his birthplace, for there is a new minister there who would like very much to meet him.'

Her lips curled back in a smile, which to the minister's eyes appeared a thing of depthless guile. For a moment he was struck quite speechless by it. Beneath it, as if concealed by a fine veil, lay horror, corruption, and madness, reaching out to grasp him.

'Sall I betray him minister?'

The minister strove to recover himself. When he spoke again his voice was gentler.

'You are not betraying him. Nor am I the dupe of ancient fancies. But there are some things which must be sought out if their truth is to be known. And I am appalled at what has taken place between you . . .'

He hesitated.

'I serve a higher power in this, as in all things . . . Is he afraid to meet me then do you think?'

Slowly she drew her shawl about her head.

'Och I hardly think he wad be afraid minister.'

She stood for a minute watching him as if waiting for him to say something more.

'Gude nicht minister.'

She turned to walk towards the door. As she passed through it he said:

'Remember what I have said to you.'

'Aye minister.'

He watched her go. He sank down on a chair. A noisome stench it appeared to him, now pervaded the kitchen, of the girl, of Malecky, of the past and the present. He thought of Mathius Pringle's words on the arrest of Malecky.

'We apprehended Malecky as he left the city by the Nether-bow gate. It was at the end a simple matter, as if that man knew in the depths of his black heart that the power of his master, that had so long empowered him to escape us, was now, when the Lord spoke, reduced to a whining, cringing, silly thing. For surely the Lord had spoken, and the conviction that had been growing in my heart for many a lang year, that he would appoint Alexander Bain, that confused and wayward man, to be his instrument in the appointed hour, had been proved right. And in that terrible hour of the Lord's justice, that man,*

*who for so long had seemed so invulnerable in his pride,
neither had the power to fly through the air, make himself
invisible, turn himself into a swift beast, or take any other
measure to effect his escape that warlocks are supposed to have
at their command. Why, well mounted as he was, he had not
even the power to fight or flee.*

'*Oh but boldly to the end he carried himself, no poor
damned Pittenweem fisherman he, but a true pride-glutted
demon of destruction.*'

How had Malecky escaped the clutches of the Kirk on that
occasion? How had he ever extricated himself from the iron
grip of Mathius Pringle? Had he indeed simply lifted up his
arms and flown through the roof?

The minister laughed contemptuously. And yet, he thought,
Mathius Pringle was long dead, God's instrument, Sawney
Bain had been condemned to a living Hell, and Steven Malecky
was still at large.

His eyes cast themselves feverishly around the room. Undoubtedly Malecky had stood in this very kitchen, more than
likely sat on the very chair that he was now sitting on. He
thought of the Melville girl as some hideous changeling, whose
metamorphosis, taking place before his eyes, was like an awful
sign that nothing that he had encountered so far was as it
seemed.

In a sudden anger he snatched up the ancient spear and
attempted to snap the shaft over his knee. It was beyond his
strength, the seasoned wood bent but did not break. He threw
it down and strode into the night.

He saddled his horse and threw himself on to its back. Without regarding the terrain, he whipped it into a headlong gallop,
drawing rein only when he was sure the inn was far behind
him, and the cold Border night was broken by the dawn.

☆

Whaur they took Steenie I could not ken. Auld Baillie said
that whaur ever it was we could be sure that it was some
place very strang.

He did I ken, mak some inquiries, amang the Edinburgh

342

folk that he kent, for he kent near every body in the toun. Nane it seemed could tell him anything, and nae doubt wae the thought o the English army that was soon tae be hammering at their gates they had ither things on their minds.

I mysel warned him that pressing ower much might weel bring disaster on his ain heid which Steenie wad not approve o. He looked straight in my een then, wae a look in which despair and anger were sae entwined that I could not tell which was tae the fore.

-Whether Mr Malecky approves or disapproves is his ain business, and if I should come tae an ill end through my ain actions then that maun be the Lord's will, and nae doubt his judgement.

I thanked him for these brave words, and indeed for being the only comfort I had at that time. Aye, and it seemed tae me then, forbye I could not ken what wad come tae pass, that if the Lord had not already judged us awe then that judgement was hard at hand. And the Kirk in that hour o the country's desperation continued tae drive men frae the army on account o insufficient Godliness, or past malignancy, filling their ranks wae halfling boys.

Auld Baillie showed me a map o Leslie's plan o campaign and said that it was a very skillful ane, he haeving fortified a front line frae Leith tae Edinburgh, and burnt and destroyed awe that was beyond that line, sae that Cromwell was obliged tae sit whaur his supply ships could reach him, or march intae a country whaur they could not, or throw his army against strang positions whaur they wad be sarely disadvantaged.

He telt me that some light attacks had already been made, and bludely beaten off, and it might weel be the case that Cromwell himsel was thinking that the best thing he could dae wae his ships was tae embark on them, for an army on campaign which is obliged tae sit on its arse ower lang becomes a dispirited army, which he nae doubt kent as weel as any.

I kent not truly. I wad listen tae his sodgerly opinions wae but half my ears, for ither things I heard tae, that the Kirk was raging in its pulpits that sic sodgerly manoeuvres were but a lack o faith in the strength o the Lord, wha had brought the English heretics tae our doorstep tae be chastised, and wad turn a wrathful een on any failure tae dae as he expressly commanded.

For weel or woe they got their way, as it seemed they aye did, and perhaps the army itsel thought an English pike wad be a relief frae the clamour o their tongues, for the hale army clattered out o the toun, auld Baillie casting a keen eye on it as it did sae, and declaring that at least half o it was composed o freshwater sodgers, and poorly equipped anes at that.

That notwithstanding, we heard the news that they had driven the English before them and had pinned them doun in a place near Dunbar, a pestilential place in which nae army could bide for lang. Aye, and it seemed then, and was spoken widely in the street, and proclaimed in the kirk, that the Kirk speaking the word o God had been right, while sodgerly men, full of haughty pride in their earthly skills had been wrang.

Nane it seemed could gainsay them. Auld Baillie said that if the army stuck tae its position it wad be folly for Cromwell tae attack them, and however mad that man had becam in his warldly ambitions, he was nae fool in a fight, and aiblins he wad just mak peace as he had done before, or embark and wait for a better day.

I kent not truly, but I wad walk through the toun, and a dark and strange place it wad seem tae me. And I wad look up at the spike on which was fixed Jamie Graham's heid, now little mair than a bit bone, and it wad seem tae me that awe men's destinies were fixed, forever and aye by the warld in which they lived, and there was little happiness tae be found in these destinies.

If the Scots beat the English, the Kirk's power wad be without check. And tae Mathius Pringle's mind the hinging and burning o Steenie Malecky wad be but a demonstration o that, aye and a thanksgien for our deliverance.

I thought awe this, and despite auld Baillie's opinion that providence was far aboun politics, I did not believe that Pringle wad be jouked a second time, aye and I minded that Steenie had little faith left in either thing.

☆

Sir John Doig rose to his feet and advanced to meet the minister. His gait was slow and measured. The minister watched the vast bulk swell out with the expansive patronage of a builder of churches and a pillar of the state. If anything on earth could soften his feelings for his flock it was the sight of their laird. A year of his tenant's collective rents went into clothing him, and perhaps a further six months for his wig and rouge.

'Weel minister ye hae been out riding the bounds?'

'An elderly woman of my acquaintance, though Cameronian in her persuasions.'

'Dour deevils, Cameronians. Ye wad be wasting your time I think, trying tae ding sense intae that kind of heid.'

The minister did not reply. Martha, he thought, hardly needed defending against this man's humour. The laird smiled at his own jokes, he inquired after the minister's health and the parish's spiritual well-being. The minister answered his questions, amused by the uncouth diplomacy with which the man circled closer to his true purpose in asking to see him.

'Ye'll nae doubt hae a glass of claret Sir? A fine vintage, only this week come frae France, and not tae be had by every loun I can assure ye.'

The minister accepted, the laird handed him a glass of wine, bowing slightly as he did so. He touched the minister's glass with his own.

'Tae your health Sir, and that of King, Kirk and nation, and lang may all these righteous things prosper.'

Sir John took an inordinately delicate mouthful, pursing his lips, turning slightly on his heel like a great ship in full sail suddenly finding itself obliged to tack into an unexpected wind.

'All that forbye Sir, I have been hearing some disquieting tales about my tenants.'

'Disquieting . . ?'

'Maist disquieting. My good baillie, whom you yourself ken as a Godfearing and honest man, is neither as happy or as contented as a loyal man in my service has a right tae be, which, as I hae a care for him, is disquieting.'

The minister did not give any indication that he wanted to interrupt. Had he done so, the laird of Trig's large flat hand was already raised to check him.

'Hear me out Sir . . . He is obliged to thole abuse and insults when he collects his rents, doing his duty. One dared, och it's an abomination, to shake a cudgel in his face. He did not strike him with it, Heaven nae doubt forbade that, but he shook it vigorously enough to put a very real apprehension into the man. And my servants Sir, are likewise greeted with unkind words, which grieves them, and it grieves me that such things should happen. It is not what I expect Sir, and more than I am inclined to bear.'

'They are paying their rents are they not?'

'It is the spirit with which they are paying them. Such insults to my servants I take as nae mair, and nae less, than insults to my person.'

The minister felt a blissful indifference. A weary perilous indifference to the storm that was being suppressed in the laird's breast.

'The harvest has been poor, and I think there has been some fear of a murrain among the cattle. As a result they feel pressed, and men who feel pressed are commonly short-tempered. I have not myself heard of, or witnessed, any such incidents as you describe, nor do your servants appear to me to be the kind of men likely to be overwhelmed by a few rough words. It is deplorable nevertheless.'

'If the louns are in an abusive temper then I care not a fig for it, though I believe it should be ane of your duties tae correct that temper and bid it be mair gentle. I will not stand for myself, or my people being met with cudgels and black looks. It is maist unworthy, disease amang the beasts, and poor harvests, can be combatted by proper care and gude husbandry. The louns seem not tae ken or care that the lave o them could be packed off in the morning and replaced wae mair grateful folk in the afternoon, and I would be within my rights tae dae sae. Whiles I think they hae been here sae lang that they hae forgotten that fact. Weel I will hae them reminded o it briskly, and a sermon on the subject is, minister, in my opinion lang overdue. Why Sir I am even thinking of arming my servants.'

'Arming them? That hardly seems necessary. Why on earth would they need arms?'

The laird suddenly advanced on the minister, his vast countenance thrust forward like the head of a bull. He stopped short of thrusting it into the minister's face, but for a moment the minister felt himself surveyed, stripped, and interrogated by the furiously narrowing eyes.

'I hae no been speaking about insignificant matters Sir, and I hae no I hope, been speaking tae the air. If I arm them it will be for their ain protection, and tae uphold the honour o their position when threatened by some ill-natured loun.'

The minister took two steps backwards, partly involuntarily, partly to avoid the laird's breath.

'They have a few guns themselves.'

'Och I ken weel enough that there is a bit gun here and there, and a bit o cauld steel tae. But I ken, and they ken it weel enough, that the days o grasping these things are lang past, which is why this nonsense is sae vexatious tae me. I have read Mr Gilmarten's book, and I hae been tae England. There amang the country people, religion, industry, and civilitie, rule the hearts of all, and as a consequence they prosper, and wad laugh tae see what I hae tae thole here and the ingratitude with which I am afflicted.'

The laird hesitated. He took a sip of his wine. The minister took a sip of his. Sir John raised his hand in a gesture of appeasement.

'Forgive me Sir, forgive me. But, dae ye ken, aye and perhaps this has vexed me mightily, they are sae brazen that they mak a joke out of my unfortunate forebear, wha, as ye might hae heard was drowned in the auld bog in circumstances o great suspicion, witchcraft and murder no less. Nane of which was ever properly cleared up sae that the incident is tae this day a shame and a disgrace tae my name, and ought tae be a shame and disgrace tae the parish . . . But, what dae my gude tenants say? Why they say that the only gude Doig was the ane they fished frae the bog, and believe me Sir they meant after, not before, and they drink to the memory, och it's a blasphemy in itself, of Black Janet Douglas, wha was widely believed tae have had a hand in the business, and was subsequently executed for witchcraft.

'Dae ye not think that is a deplorable state of affairs for a Godly parish? Why if Mr Gilmarten was tae get wind of such words a visitation by the devil himself wad be a blessing set alangside his wrath.'

'These are hardly proper comparisons . . .'

'Proper Sir, proper! Tell me not what is proper until you hae seen tae it that I receive my proper due.'

'That is hardly my business.'

'Of respect Sir, of respect.'

The minister watched the laird's quivering rouged cheeks. Doig, it was plain to him, was, in some recess of his soul, superstitiously afraid of his tenantry, and they knew that, and knew the cause of it, and knew how to play on it.

'The Janet Douglas story is an ancient tale surely?'

'A tale it might be, but in that tale my forebear was deid enough, and we hae a gravestone in the kirkyard which has his name on it, and I wad be very surprised if his remains were not under it. Sae that he met his death in that auld bit tale there is nae disputing, though tae my mind the devilry in it was of a very earthly kind, three or fower of his ain tenantry, and the Douglas carline just a handy mad auld beldame on which tae fix the blame.'

Another version the minister thought. Each one believes the story that best agrees with their desires, or justifies their terrors.

'I think you should hold off arming your servants. I cannot see that it would serve any purpose at all, and could lead to some regrettable incidents. I will inquire into these complaints, and if there are words to be said I will say them.'

The minister spoke gently. The laird raised his hand.

'Then I need say nae mair. If I hae your assurance on that then I crave no other security, and my mind will henceforth be as much at ease, as it has recently not been at ease.'

He dropped his hands, one falling as lightly as a feather on the minister's shoulder.

'The nation Sir, as nae doubt ye are well aware, is on the verge of new and great things in which we are all honoured with a part to play. But as a gentleman of parliament I am honoured with an especially onerous part which requires my full attention. Which is why this business has vexed me a bit, for a man must be sure that his rear and his baggage train are in gude order ere he can gang forward wae a brave heart.'

Sir John Doig's face broke into a broad smile.

'I am cheerful now Sir. I ken ye for a man o discernment and understanding, which I never for a moment doubted. Men such as yourself and Mr Gilmarten are the pride of our Scots Kirk, learned far aboun their English brethren. Mr Gilmarten's book goes frae strength tae strength, and is admired by awe men o sense. Aye indeed, tae my mind, God called him tae the capital just at the precise moment when his ideas would create the greatest impression. And he Sir, bears all the praise that is sae justifiably bestowed on him wae a humbleness sae becoming, why Sir it is a lesson in itself.'

'I am happy for him.'

'Och a timely work, for the times are rough Sir. The Edinburgh mob grows bolder and mair forward by the day. Uproar and riot, it wad mak your heart tremble minister, for they dinna hesitate in stoning the carriages of gentlemen. In particular gentlemen of parliament, an affront tae the nation which shames us at home and abroad. Their knavery and disrespect is such that the very thought o them makes me think that I hae been ower hard on my ain recalcitrant louns.'

The minister left the laird in an optimistic mood. Soon all that would be at an end, curbed by stern new laws and men to enforce them, and England, for a fine price, would be allowed to swallow the ancient irritant to her peace, Lowlands and Highlands.

The minister rode slowly homewards. Past the old bog where that other Doig had drowned. Past the spot where he imagined, though he had never had it confirmed, Janet Douglas's cottage had stood.

He stopped for a time on the summit of Malecky's Hill. Once in the midst of his frustrations he had conceived the plan of excavating this hill to prove that it was possible that the man had indeed lived there.

That was now no longer necessary. His existence had been brutally confirmed, and both he and his mischief were still alive, glowering, presumably from some Highland mountain, down on all of Scotland. The minister thought too of Helen Melville; but he could no longer think of her without his soul trembling at the thought of her seeming innocence and Malecky's corruption entwined in an awful blasphemy.

☆

The army had been defeated. Why it had been mair than defeated, it had been destroyed in a bludie rout. Nane at that time could say why or how, but awe that was left o it cam riding, them that could ride, back through the city, some in gude order, ithers in nae order at awe, while ithers had scattered far and wide intae the country.

Now the hale toun rose as ane in a panic, some barring their doors, ithers fleeing the place in the wake o the sodgers, cursing them that they had ance cheered.

Nane at that time kent what the English wad now dae but awe folk believed that they wad cam on as they had aye cam on in the past, burning and killing awe that was in their path.

Auld Baillie looked as if the end that he had aye secretly feared had now cam tae pass, and forbye the tears blint his een, he declared that if he was ower auld tae fight, he was ower auld tae flee. He tried in the confusion tae lay hands on any sodger he could catch tae find out proper news, but they awe cried out that the battle had been foolishly sold, but there wad be mair fights tae be fought, but for the present there was nae ither course but tae flee, for the toun could not be held against them.

I watched them ride past, like sae much dust that had been tumbled in the wind, and politics, and principles, and providences, had awe tumbled wae them, as some tumbled frae their saddles sae sarely hurt that they could not keep in them, and some wad stop tae pick them up, and some wad not, and some just deed as they fell.

It was then in the midst o awe this wild despair that Sawney himsel stood at our door looking like a man damned. Aye, like untae a man drenched in fire wae a countenance that had been whelped anew in Hell.

-Agnes Douglas, he cried out then. -Will ye come wae me or will ye bide here?'

I looked at him and I looked at auld Baillie, and it was plain tae my een, that he was as shocked as me at what we saw, for Sawney was mair than just a sodger fleeing frae a lost fight, but was like untae a man wha's soul had been reived frae his body, which was itsel on the point o death but just kent it not.

-Are ye hurt man?

-A bit scraitch, nae mair. But it is tae Agnes that I am speaking, awe ither things that I hae loved are deid.

Even in sic circumstances his words made nae sense. And then awe at ance he fell forward on his horse as if he could not keep upright, and he looked at me wae een that were as red as the Deevil's, and he said in a voice that was like untae a man saying a prayer, that if I had ought o mercy in my heart I should gang wae him.

Pitiful though his appearance was, my heart at that time was hard against him wha had for sae lang been a stranger tae me, and I cried out that Steenie was held in some strang place, and aiblins he kent mair than he said about that.

I ken weel enough in my heart why I said these words, and harder it seemed tae me they struck him than anything in the fight had done.

-I ken not whaur Steenie is but maybe them that hold him hae fled as awe folk hae fled.

Auld Baillie looked at me then, his een near blint wae tears.

-If ye bide here lassie I canna protect ye, and the English will be hard on their heels, sae I wad tak the horse and ride.

Sae it cam about, that ance again I grasped my weapons, for this did not seem tae be the time tae be without them, and auld Baillie thrust food and drink intae our bags, and when I looked again intae his een the tears had gone frae them and an auld and stubborn thing that I canna weel describe had taen their place.

-Mind yersel lassie, and mind that daft loun, and mak sure that ye return in anither time. If I hear or see ought o Steenie I sall let him ken.

I louped on tae the back o the horse, gathering up the reins.

-Are ye sure ye can ride? I asked him.

-Aye I can ride through this warld and frae it as weel as any ither.

Weel out o it seemed indeed whaur he might be heading, and the tempest o events was driving in sic a way that I maun gang wae him whether I wad or no, for we were awe but chaff in the wind that was now whistling, whether frae

England or frae Hell I kent not truly.

Auld Baillie asked him whaur on earth what was left o the army might itself be heading. Awe he said in reply tae that, was that the army itsel was now divided, the main part marching North tae regroup at Stirling, ithers riding West for their ain reasons. Auld Baillie just shook his heid, and ance again I kissed his cheek, and awa we rade.

We spoke nae word, nor could I ken how he kept upright in his saddle. Ance when I looked at him his een were closed, and when I spoke tae him he gied nae answer, and tae gallop tae Stirling, which we wad not reach that day, seemed tae me mair than madness.

Sae without asking his leave or advice I took the reins o his horse frae his hands and turned West, thinking there maun aye be some hidden place amang the hills, and as the English army wad be unlikely for a time tae move beyond Edinburgh, tae my mind it made little difference.

We rade for a time, and whiles Sawney wad open his een, but I kent not what he could see for he said nae word. After a number o lang miles, I mind not how many, we cam, as the night drew in upon this bit wood, and on the edge o it a drover's biggin.

It was empty, as awe things were, and if I judged it nae gude place tae hide, it maun suffice, for flesh wad gang nae further. Aye, and even then, haeving clung tae his horse sae desperately for sae lang I had some trouble in getting him tae release it and had tae haud him up as we staggered intae the biggin.

Night was weel doun now, for which I was grateful. By the light o Sawney's auld lamp, which by some miracle he still carried, I stripped him o his armour and his duds.

I ken not how much blude a man can lose and still live, but the inside o his auld bear coat was as bludie as if it had been new stripped frae the beast itsel. Twa wounds he had alang wae divers cuts, ane on his shoulder whaur a pike heid had torn a second great hole, and anither at the top o his leg whaur a ball had burned its way through the flesh but frae what I could see had broke nae bone.

I cleaned them out and bound them baith up, and on oc-casion his een wad open and I wad ask him if they hurt. He laughed at that, an auld eldritch laugh.

-Damnably, but it's a fleshly pain and I think naething o it.

-There maun hae been some hard fighting in that fight.

-It was a foolish fight. The Kirk in their pulpits took command o the battle clean out o Leslie's hands, and wad hae us advance frae a strang position tae a weak ane, for the Lord had gien them a clear sign that this was his will, and that Cromwell should be chastised and no allowed tae escape. Weel perhaps he gied them sic a sign and aiblins he did not. But the manoeuvre wad hae been difficult enough wae salted sodgers, wae freshwater anes it was plain daft, and gied the English the chance that nae doubt they had been praying for, and like gude sodgers they took it, and the best part o the foot were caught between a gude position and a poor ane, in nae position at awe.

Sodgers I ken, will aye talk lang about how battles are won and how they are lost, in auld Baillie's alehouse the lave o them hae nae ither subject o conversation. But there was mair than that in Sawney, as if in the details o the battle he just saw the outward sign o the dark end o awe things, for the defeat had dinged the Kirk and its politics doun frae the high pillar on which they had set themsels, and perhaps Leslie tae for being ower supine in his command. And if the army rallied at Stirling, they wad rally wae any that wanted tae fight, and if this new King wanted tae put himsel at their heid, Covenanted or no, then he wad be welcome.

Ithers o the Western Whigs had ridden tae their ain country, and declared that they wad never fight for the King, and if the army was now tae be the army of the king's Party, they might themsels join up wae Cromwell, faithless man though he was. Tae Sawney's mind nane o this mattered, for neither army had much in the way o supplies, and the country was as naked as the day it had been created frae chaos.

I listened tae his ramblings which were pitiful tae hear, feeding him whisky tae dull the pain o his wounds and the greater pain o his heart.

In the end, drink, mercy or despair put him tae sleep. I

sat at the door o the biggin kenning not at awe exactly whaur we were, bar at the foot o some hills tae the West o Edinburgh. That he had betrayed Steenie tae Pringle I now kent frae his ramblings, and perhaps I had aye kent it in my heart. Pringle had dinged his soul the night lang, and awe the next day, speaking as if Heaven itsel was commanding, and in the end Sawney had baith answered that command and ridden like a demented loun tae warn Steenie.

I cursed him and couldna hate him, seeing him as naught but a witless bairn in the hands o the Kirk. But my heart was bitter against them awe, aye and I rejoiced that the English had trampled intae the earth, Pringle's, aye, and Heaven's promise of victory and salvation if Steenie was apprehended.

I mind not whether I slept that night or whether I did not. It mattered little, the sun rose as it aye did, kenning naething and caring less. Sawney woke as he aye did at any sound, but sae weak frae loss o blude that he was in nae condition tae move, and wad not be, I thought for some days tae come. Sae here we maun bide I telt him, for ance ye maun be ruled by yer flesh.

I ken not how much he minded o what he had confessed the previous night, but he laughed at these words, a harsh, hard laugh that had little mirth in it.

-I had thought tae gang on tae Stirling, or tae the West, I ken not which.

-Then ye gang alane Sir, or aiblins the Deil will gang wae ye, for if I gang anywhaur, which maybe I canna dae, it wad be tae try and find Steenie whaurever he might be.

-Speak not tae me o that man if ye hae any quarter in your heart.

I looked closely at him then, but there was nae sign o anything in his face that could be read, ither than despair.

-Ye ken Sawney Bain, I said tae him. -Ye are baith a bad man, and a gude man, but aboun awe ye are a brainless ane, and while I hae liked ye fine lang syne, aiblins I now think the day yer mither bore ye was an ill day.

-Why then ye should just gang awa, and gang whaur ere ye please, and if Mr Malecky is alive and weel nae doubt ye will find him, sic a wolf's nose ye hae for sniffing out right and wrang and gude and bad, can surely sniff out him.

-Wae the countryside nae doubt crawling wae English sodgers.

-Och they'll nae doubt awe be drunk in Edinburgh beds, drinking deep o their Godly rewards, and taking their Godly ease.

-And leave ye here tae dee? I said tae him. -Aye, I might weel dae that.

-Dee, och I hae nae intention o deeing. Dae ye think I hae no been piked a bit before? Why in Germany I ance rade fourteen miles wae a bullet in my back and my collarbone cut clean through, and my airm near off. Sae dinna fash yersel that I sall dee.

-Och, I cried, for I could nae langer thole sic boastful talk. -And wha mended ye and cared for ye that time?

-A gude Swedish surgeon took out the ball and set the bone, and a fine Swedish carline wae lang yellow hair minded awe ither parts.

I bent ower him then, and put the point o his ain dirk tae his throat, and said that nae doubt the carlines o Sweden had bigger hearts in their breasts than brains in their heids. But that was not the case wae Black Agnes Douglas, and aiblins his wounds wad not kill him, but if I put this dirk in its proper place than it surely wad. Sae he maun keep a nice manner about him, and a civil tongue in his heid, for a great captain o horse he might be at ither times, he was but a bairn in strength as weel as brains for the present. Nor was he tae think that I had forgotten what he had telt me last night, or that I had forgotten how often he had cast a Godly snook at his gude friends. Aye, and he was no tae forget how his Heavenly maister had delivered him helpless untae ane the Kirk called the Deevil's whore, which nae doubt was a proper recompense for losing his battles.

He was quiet then, and telt me not tae jest about sic things, but I telt him in turn that I wad jest as blithely as I pleased.

I ken not truly what I felt at that time, bar sorrow for Steenie, and it might weel hae been that alangside that I felt naething at awe. But I mind I laughed when I thought on awe their prides and certainties, and the high elevation

355

upon which they had set themsels, and frae which their ain brithers in Christ and perhaps the Lord himsel had flung them doun and scattered them. And how could ane no laugh at that, for the truth, it seemed tae me, was that their ain pride had destroyed them lang ere the English crossed the Border.

☆

For the minister, the days that now passed were days of seclusion. Days locked within the routine of his duties, his mind and his thoughts sheltered behind a rampart of discipline.

If the parish noticed anything at all, it was the sudden and wondrous mildness which had come over Walter Hyslop. Shepherds no longer encountered that once keen hunter in unlikely places. Now if Walter was met he would be merely strolling, exercising his newly acquired collie dog, his salutation hearty and cheerful.

Deserted too, he seemed to be, by his fearsome powers of detection, so that an illicit child would have to make an illicit appearance before Walter deigned to notice it. The likelihood then was that he might simply bid it good morning. Drunkards remained unrebuked, cursers unreported, brawlers left to settle their differences in their own way. The children in his care heard him reciting ancient ballads and humming old airs. When this diverted them from their studies into laughter, Walter's reproof fell like thistledown on their heads.

Some were of the opinion that Walter himself had become a child again, and what they were witnessing was the first signs of dotage. Others declared that the dimming of that fiercely shining light was a portent of disaster. Mathew Elliot said that nae doubt some angel had whispered in Walter's ear that Heaven wadna be ower keen tae be plagued wae sic an ower zealous soul, and if hunting sinners was his only pleasure in this life, then in death they might weel send him tae a place whaur they could still be got.

The minister impatiently dismissed such speculations. He looked at the ancient polished leather of Mathius Pringle's saddle-bags and the furious writings they contained, and knew the simple truth. He now bore the dominie's burden.

From that day on, he decided, he would keep a meticulous record of his own thoughts and deeds. It was a decision he had come to when he had realised that his mind could no longer contain or combat the things that assailed it. His pen, guided by his faith and his reason, and nourished by his prayers must a Godly discourse make that would counter the Black Book, that would counter the confusion of tales and legends and appearances that men called their history, that would set it in some rational order.

He looked at what he had written that morning.

'I believe there is a purpose in all of these events and revelations which is for the moment hidden from me, but with which I believe I am charged by God to find out.

In every place I see Malecky, and yet I do not see him. He is like a monstrous wraith whose presence is experienced but never confronted. He is equipped, it would appear, with the ability to take on in the minds of men and women whatever form he chooses, and whatever most aptly suits his purpose. When I think of him, I think of a man who is a serpent, and a serpent who is a man, but who possesses the serpent's ability to so confuse his prey that it knows not what it beholds, or with what danger it is threatened, so that even Christians of good judgement and sound sense, trust him and speak well of him, while he secretly assails them. And yet, of none of this can I be sure. His atheism would appear to be a well attested thing. His elusiveness a sign surely of hidden purpose. Indeed one name he goes by, in English means the grey fox, and truly no fox could be more covert in its actions.

Alongside all of this he is credited with possessing uncanny powers which smell strongly of charming, sorcery, and witchcraft, and his lusts are without restraint from honour or conscience, devouring insatiably men's souls and women's bodies.

I think especially of Helen Melville yielding her flesh to his adulterous hands, offering everything that God has given her, to him, and seeing it as no sin. With my own eyes I beheld the corruption of her spirit that has its source in that vile sacrifice. I have seen, and still in my mind see it, seeping like poison through her flesh, and the thought of it sweeps like fire through my soul. I see her burning, as so often I have seen the Douglas woman burning. Side by side they burn, the light from that fire revealing a horrid darkness, and through it Bain and all his tribe stumbling like playthings of Hell.

I think of Bain now with a deep compassion, as some man-beast monster struggling towards Heaven while he is gripped in the jaws of Hell. He and all his brood born in incest and murder, defiance and damnation, were all in truth Malecky's offspring. Indeed the oldest inhabitant of my parish believes it possible that Malecky, Bain, and Agnes Douglas, were all children of the same mother. Whether this was true or not I have no way of knowing, for I can find no record of it elsewhere, and yet I am constrained to believe almost anything possible. And yet, I cannot believe that God would allow such a thing of horror without there being some purpose, at present hidden from me.

I believe I must wait, much has already been revealed to me, nor can it possibly be construed as mere accident. But Malecky will not I believe be simply hunted down, keener hunters than I have failed in this. But I believe he will be brought to me, or I to him, as the knowledge of him has been brought to me.

I have prayed for guidance in this matter, and I must think it possible that I have been chosen to be God's instrument, and when I am finally faced with Malecky I will know as that instrument how to act. I cannot rationally think otherwise, for to do so would be to declare that God's Kingdom is but an arbitrary place of chance, and men little more than beasts imperfectly elevated by some freak of nature, and containing in their midst unnatural monsters as a matter of course.

I now read the Black Book with purpose and determination, and the conviction in my soul that it has been deliberately placed in my hands so that I might equip myself with the knowledge that is in it, and that God having brought me so far, and allowed me to see and know so much, it is inconceivable that he will refrain from taking me further, or not reveal to me the end and purpose of all these things. I prepare myself and wait.

☆

The sodgers cam on the second or third day, I mind not which, but there were three o them, foraging as sodgers will. Sawney was asleep, being still very weak, and ance I kent that they had seen me I dared not run back intae the biggin. I was dressed in my plaid then and had nae weapons, bar a pistol, and my dirk which I aye had. They rade towards me at the trot, nae doubt thinking that I wad run awa, which I wad hae done if it had not been plain tae me that it wad be a pointless endeavor, serving nae mair purpose than tae gie them a bit sport.

The first ane, wha seemed tae be the heid ane, drew alangside me. He was a small, red faced man, very weel mounted and very weel armed. For a time he just stared at me his een regarding every part o me, insolence and amusement in them, and ither things that I kent very weel, and which he hardly chose tae disguise.

Awe at ance he flipped a bit coin at my feet.

-A groat for a Scot, he cried, and I understood him weel enough, forbye the way he spoke was like nae speech I had ever heard before, for indeed he was the first English that I had ever set my een upon.

-Will ye not pick it up? He said then. -For I hae heard the countryside and its people are starving.

I wad not, and he moved his horse twa paces forward, obliging me tae tak twa back. Then wae a quick movement he reached tae tak me by the hair, crying out that if I wad not tak it I wad at least pay him something in return for parting wae it.

I jouked his hand, for I was nae bairn tae be caught like that. His twa comrades were still a bit off making nae move tae come closer, amused nae doubt, and thinking that their turn wad come soon enough. But I, judging their distance turned and ran, and he wae a merry yell dug his heels intae his horse and cam in pursuit, louping doun frae the beast when I ran intae the cover o the wood.

He caught up wae me amang the trees, his een shining now wae a hard auld fever that said he wad hae his pleasure. He had paid his groat, he said, and I had run him a bit, which had warmed his blude, and now I should be kind tae him, and tae his comrades in turn, and nae further hairm should come tae me, and was that not a decent bargain?

I felt his hands under my plaid as he pinned me against a tree tearing at my duds like things that had nae thought o being thwarted. He found the pistol and threw it aside wae an English curse.

I made nae further move then but let him pull my gown frae my shoulders until my breasts were bare tae his een, and his hands folded ower them, pressing each ane till it hurt, which was doubtless his way o letting me ken wha was maister now. I said tae him that if it was tae be his sodger's pleasure tae force me, and that I was tae hae nae choice in the matter, then we had best lie doun like Christian folk for the ground was fine and dry, and why I wad help him off wae his breeks.

Och but he was a brave man and wasted nae further time in the gallantries o persuasion, but he threw me doun and threw his ain breeks off, and hard intae me like a man after his ain pleasure he cam, and at the very peak o that pleasure which cam fast tae him, and loun-like as awe men are at that time, he saw not Catriona's dirk which was in my hand, and aiblins he had nae thought at awe that sic a thing could be possible, but it found his heart, for I kent weel enough whaur that was, and just how it could be got at frae under a man's airm whaur he least expects it, and twelve inches o steel he got for the six inches o flesh he gied me. Nor could he speak, or cry out, or mak any sound at awe, for the blude that choked his thrapple. I laughed and watched tae see awe the things that can pass through a man's een, frae joy and anger and deeing. And him that had sae fiercely flung himsel upon me, I now flung off, and forbye his hands clutched at my throat they clutched wae nae power, and twice and thrice I struck him wae the hale length o the dirk, and I ken not what tale he telt in the next warld but nae mair astonished man parted company wae this ane.

I thought nae mair on him. He had a gude sword and twa pistols at his belt, and awe these things I took frae him.

Frae the edge o the wood I saw his twa comrades sitting quietly on their horses about fifty paces awa, biding their time like proper gentlemen, and far ower lang for a pistol shot. I waited, hidden frae their sight, biding my time till impatience wad maybe bring them a bit closer, when awe at ance a musket shot rang out, and I kent very weel the sound of Sawney's auld lang gun, and it knocked ane sodger clean out o the saddle.

The ither whirled his horse round as if he kent not at awe what tae dae, for he could see nae enemy in sight, but then seeing that his comrade was deid he spurred his horse towards the trees, nae doubt thinking that this was urgent enough business tae disturb his friend's pleasure.

He was damn near upon me when I shot him. And for awe the ball hit off his breastplate it gied him sic a dunt that he was knocked frae his horses back. His hand cam up swiftly wae a pistol in it, but he kent not properly whaur I was, and wae his deid comrades sword I took a swift cut at that hand, near slicing it frae his airm, and setting his pistol off tae nae purpose.

He screamed and tried tae find his feet, but I wad not allow that and brought the blade hard doun on his neck, and for awe he saw the blow coming and rolled on the ground tae avoid it, I still caught him, but did not kill him. His gude hand reached for his ither gun, but they never met, for I stood ower him wae sword and gun pointing till he cried out for quarter.

I telt him plainly, that quarter gien was a game played between sodgers, and I was out o patience wae sodgers just then, and aiblins this affair was not tae end in the pleasant way that it had began, but end it wad. I shot him then, the ball catching him clean through the neck, and he deed straight awa.

I looked up and Sawney was standing beside me. A great loun o a mither naked man, clad in naething but a bear coat and wae a pistol and a sword in his hand, and fresh blude pouring frae the wounds that his exertions had opened. For

361

a minute he stood like ane dumbfounded, his een burning in his heid.

-Why Sawney Bain, I said. -I am no the bairn I ance was. He shook his heid then,

-Lord save us awe, but I ken not what black auld Douglas blude runs in yer veins, but it damn near maks my ain run cauld, twa salted sodgers lassie, is nae bad score.

I laughed at him and raised my sword tae his breast, and nae doubt I was an unco sight tae his een, being near naked and covered in blude.

-Weel Mr Bain, tis weel that ye ken wae wham ye ride. But for now I maun bind up that wound ere ye ance again lose awe that blude that ye hae been at sic pains tae mak up.

He just nodded his heid quietly at that, like some great fretting dug, and said that we must quickly leave this place, and as he had managed tae get tae his feet when he heard the sodgers, he could surely ride his horse.

After sic an incident this seemed nae mair than sensible, and sae I bound up his wounds for him yet again, and he rested while I stripped the deid sodgers o their weapons and a fine flask o brandy, and taking their horses, which were very gude anes, we rade South and West, taking us intae our ain country.

In the days that followed, Sawney was an unco quiet man, forbye there were times when I kent not how he kept tae the saddle. For awe that he uttered nae word o complaint, but was like a man wha's soul was burning tae sic a degree that his fleshly wound were o little account. I gied him little comfort, tending tae his wounds and nae mair, and he in turn wad acquiesce like a dumb beast tae every order that I gied, and tae every route that I chose.

Some folk that we met said that English sodgers had been seen in the West. Some said that a battle had been fought there, but it had been a small affair, the lave of Cromwell's army marching Northwards. These were maistly auldish folk and few, for the country for the maist part was a very empty place.

Ane party o horse we met on the fourth or fifth day, said that they had cam frae them that called themsels the Western Alliance o Whigs, that had thought tae ally themsels wae Cromwell himsel, seeing him as wrang, but a lesser evil than the new king. But Cromwell, it seemed, now in his hour o victory, was in nae mood tae ally himsel wae any Scots and had routed them in a bit skirmish, they being utterly out o powder and shot. Now they were riding North tae join the main army, seeing that as being their only means o salvation.

They said awe this, but it was a miracle that they could hae any faith in anything they said. Their condition was poor, many mounted on horses that were unfit for battle, and in their ain hearts, bitterness and despair, were only just held in check by an auld stubbornness. I gied then twa o the gude horses we had taen frae the English, and ane that I had grown tae like I kept for mysel, and we passed on our way.

It was but a short time after we had left these poor bit sodgers when Sawney turned tae me,

-Agnes Douglas, as it is plain tae me that ye hae little desire or need o my company aiblins I sall just ride after these men.

-Why Mr Bain, ye wad be the sorriest sodger in a sorry company.

For a minute we just stared ane at the ither, and then he spoke unco quietly.

-I canna thole this much langer Agnes.

-Ride wae them Sir, ride tae yer Heavenly maister ye mean, for I canna believe that yer immortal soul will thole sic a silly body ower lang, and perhaps its last blessing upon ye will be tae part company wae ye.

In a sudden anger he damned me for a true witch, pulled his horse round ower fiercely, and still weak, slipped clean out o the saddle. He lay on his back as I rade ower tae him, his een closed, his face like ane waiting for Heaven's pipe tae play, and whether he heard it, and whether he did not like the tune it played, I ken not, but hanging on tae his horse he let it pull him tae his feet, which was a sodger's trick he had trained the beast in. Ance up he pulled himsel back intae the saddle. I reached ower and took the reins frae his hands.

363

-Why Sawney Bain, I ken not whether ye turned aside frae Heaven or Heaven turned aside frae ye, but as ye are still a poor being o flesh, a damned witch sall lead ye whaur she pleases.

He said nae further word at that time, but I kent we maun find a sheltered place tae rest, which I did in a bit cave high up in the hills.

That night a fever took him clean ower, and for many days he lay ranting ower lost opportunities, auld battles and auld dreams. It was unco strange how they awe passed through his heid, and it seemed, had tae be fought awe ower again, and in sic a fashion that he nae langer kent for wham or for what he was fighting, and whiles he wad be high in the Hielan hills wae Jamie Graham, and whiles again he wad be cutting his auld comrades tae pieces on Slain Man's Lee. And through it awe hope and despair thundered, and Heaven and Hell thundered, and the voice o Mathius Pringle thundered loudest o awe, and Sawney himsel seemed nae mair than a bit thing they tossed this way and that for their sport.

When that time passed, as awe things pass that end not in death, he just looked at me out o clear blue een that I think had not properly seen me for a lang time.

-What has happened, canna now be made no tae happen, and it is not tae be thought that I sall forgie or forget mysel, but if ye will not endeavor tae be mair kind, then we maun part.

At that time I kent not, in my heart I had little desire for anything, and ganged on for nae better reason than my flesh chose tae dae sae, and still it was that perhaps that same heart had softened tae him in his ravings, sae like untae a stricken soul had he been, and now in his clear blue een he looked like a man that I had ance kent, and in truth I did not want him deid, which wad surely be the case, and that very shortly, if we parted. But awe I said was that I kent whaur I was ganging, for the road I had taen led tae nae ither place than Steenie's cave, whaur I kent it wad be possible tae just lie quietly and rest, and I telt him he could gang wae me or no, as it pleased him.

☆

> Oh they rade on, and further on,
> And they waded through rivers aboun the knee,
> And they saw neither sun nor moon,
> But they heard the roaring o the sea.

The minister felt his spirit shriek. He felt his hands reaching out into the darkness that his mind could not grasp, and he felt that darkness grasp him and drag him forward into a greater darkness, which he could feel as in serpentine waves it flowed about him, dashing against his naked flesh as it did so.

> It was a mirk mirk nicht, and there was nae starn licht,
> And they waded in red blude tae the knee,
> For awe the blude that's shed on Earth,
> Rins through the rivers o that countrie.

Sawney Bain had betrayed Malecky to the Kirk, and in an awful revenge, Agnes Douglas had been instructed by all the dark powers that Malecky had at his command to incarcerate him, by whatever means, body and soul in a living Hell.

The minister woke with a cry of anguish. His housekeeper was standing over him, her eyes soft with compassion, her vast body undulating before his gaze, her eyes now darting fire.

'Why Sir, are ye no weel?'

'I'm perfectly alright Elspeth. I fell asleep at my desk and had rather a peculiar dream.'

'Ye wark ower hard minister, poring ower these auld writings, and praying for the souls o stubborn folk.'

'Do you want something, Elspeth?'

'I hae received a message frae a man wha is visiting this toun and wishes tae see ye, and wha is at present in Mither Bruin's, awaiting as he is pleased tae put it, yer convenience.'

'What kind of man Elspeth?'

'I was about to say, he's a Hielanman Sir, wha has not gien ony kind o name that I ken o.'

'A Highlander?'

'Aye minister, but that forbye, his manners seem civil and decent enough.'

'Describe him to me?'

'Weel minister, I canna richtly say, a grown man, a bit taller than maist, wearing a Hielan plaid and Hielan breeks. He said that he had ridden a lang way and seemed very sure that ye wad want tae see him, but he wad say nae mair, for apart frae being civil enough he was very close-mouthed about what his business micht be.'

The minister composed himself under Elspeth's perplexed gaze. He had troubled and distressed this simple woman who took a pride in his well-being. He felt shame at having seen fire dart from her eyes.

'This Highlandman at present in Mother Bruin's, is he comfortable?'

'Och I ken not what maks a Hielanman comfortable, but he has a joug in front of him, sae I wad say that he is as comfortable as maist men wad be.'

'And civil and decent?'

'Aye, gentlemanly even, but he has a muckle sword by his side.'

'So he is armed?'

'The only Hielanmen I hae ever seen were in seventy-nine, and I hae never yet saw ane that wasna armed.'

'Well if he has come to see me I daresay I should see him. Could you ask him to call in perhaps half an hour?'

'Aye Sir, wad ye like me tae mention it tae some o the men? Hielanmen can be unchancy deevils.'

'I hardly think he has come to murder me, Elspeth. He is most likely just a Godly man in need of advice.'

'Weel minister, that may be as ye say. He didna look tae me like a man wha's conscience troubled him ower much.'

The minister dismissed her, and almost instantly forgot her. It was as if he still slept, and out of his nightmare his soul had been presented with a shining certainty – the Highlander could only come from Malecky.

The minister felt the flesh of his skull prickle with terror. It was as if, before his mind had fully grasped the fact, his soul had felt the hand of providence and would brook no denial of it, lest it should be damned by the fire of a divinely appointed moment rejected by reason.

In the time left to him before his guest arrived the minister knelt in prayer. When he rose to his feet his mind was certainty, his soul resolution, and his body a sword. When the knock eventually came to his door the minister was entirely calm.

The minister had never seen a Highlander before, nor did this man look much like he had imagined. He wore a tartan plaid and trews, and a soldier's buff coat of the kind that was now scarcely seen. By his side hung a basket-hilted broadsword and a dirk, but the minister could see no other weapons. He was a mature, dark haired man, in whose hair streaks of grey were already visible. His speech was formal and mannered, in a way quite different from the Lowland tongue.

'Good day Sir, I am informed that you wish to see me.'

'Aye Sir, if ye be the minister of this parish.'

'Might I know your name?'

The Highlander gestured in a manner which was almost Frenchified.

'Ye might Sir, and in truth it wad be a civil enough question, were it not for some accidents that hae befallen it, but Drummond Sir, is an honourable enough name, and belonged to my mother, and will dae nicely, Mr Archiebald Drummond.'

'Well Mr Drummond, that you have taken me a bit by surprise I will not deny, but will you step inside Sir?'

'I will Sir, haeving little inclination tae blether my business on doorsteps.'

The Highlander from the first struck the minister unfavourably. There was something insufferable about his deportment, his Frenchified manners, the elastic, brazen suppleness of his movements – a savage in his Sunday dress apeing the manners of a French courtier.

If the Highlander noticed this aversion he showed no sign of it, sweeping his bonnet from his head only when the minister offered him a chair.

'Well Sir, and what did you wish to see me about?'

For a second there was a brief interlude of silence. The minister scrutinised the dark intelligent face and felt that he was offending it.

'I hae cam a lang way Sir . . .'

'I would offer you some refreshment but I keep no strong drink in the house, but I can send . . .'

'Nae mair Sir, nae mair, naething against your principles or your conscience.'

'But wait Sir, there is some brandy from the days of my predecessor.'

'Sir, naething against your inclinations . . .'

'No Sir, I assure you, I will be happy to join you. If you have come from the Highlands you have ridden far.'

The minister went to fetch the brandy feeling that all the time the eyes of this preposterous fellow were fixed on him. But when he turned round this was not the case. He smiled at his own fancies; the man, he thought, was simply uncomfortable, his whole notion of etiquette no doubt having been upset. The minister poured out the brandy and waited. The Highlandman took two gentle sips.

'I hae cam Sir, not on my ain behalf, or indeed my ain inclination, but at the request of a friend, of whom I think ye have heard.'

The minister felt suddenly once more in the grip of an awful perturbation. He saw nothing in the Highlander's eyes now but frank hostility, saw nothing but menace in the basket-hilted broad sword, and he had other weapons, the butt of a pistol dangled from his belt.

'I speak of course of Mr Malecky . . .'

'Mr Steven Malecky?'

'I think there is likely only ane in Scotland, wha's equal wad be hard tae find.'

'I have never met him, my knowledge of him is only by report.'

'It is not my business Sir, I am grateful to Mr Malecky for some small and great things, but awe in my opinion tae his credit, against which I will hear nae word. But he is an auld man now, and I am about his business for friendship's sake. He lives in my country, amang my people, and is held in great esteem by them, but if ye wish tae meet him I am at your service, and will guide ye tae whaur he can be met.'

To the minister's ears the Highlander's speech took on the air of a challenge from the Pit itself.

'You are offering to guide me to the Highlands?'

'Tae be plain Sir, he is not at all sure why ye should wish tae meet him, but he believes ye might hae some news about friends o his. But nane o this is my concern, will ye gang wae me, or will ye mak other arrangements? Though, speaking plainly, my country is not an easy place to find if ye dinna ken whaur it is.'

The minister felt his mind hesitating. The idea of spending days and nights on the road with Mr Drummond Will-Do-Nicely, gave him no pleasure at all. He was aware that he was judging the man harshly. The Highlander, unless he was dissembling, could be quite ignorant of the fact that some would regard him as an emissary of the Devil, who was coolly inviting a minister of the Kirk to dine with him.

'Mr Drummond, I must think about this. You will of course stay here tonight and I will give you my answer in the morning. I obviously have duties here that I must take care of . . .'

'Tae assist ye in your thinking Sir, I might add that Mr Malecky was maist warmly anxious tae meet ye, and assures ye that while ye are in my country ye will be entirely free from any molestation, for I think by your manner that ye hae never been in the Hielans.'

'You are the first Highlandman that I have ever knowingly set eyes on.'

'Weel Sir, gin that is the case, I will not claim to be the best, but I trust I am not the worst example.'

'I do not doubt it.'

'Ane mair thing Sir, which maun be plainly said. Mr Malecky Sir, whether ye ken it or not, has many enemies, as awe true people must hae. Sae if ye come, ye must come alane, nor let any ken precisely whaur ye hae been, for Mr Malecky is under the protection of my chief, and the least of my people wad protect him against any that wished tae dae him harm . .
This is a condition that I must hae your word on.'

'I think, Mr Drummond, I will give you my reply to this in the morning. I appreciate your plain speaking. I do know something of Mr Malecky's history, and he was originally of this parish.

☆

Sawney's wounds healed quickly in the cave, but often of a night, his dreams wad backslide intae things o the past, and a cloud o darkness wad hing ower the day that followed. That I was cauld and harsh tae him then I dinna deny. At

369

the time, forbye I wad not desert him, I had little inclination tae be itherwise, for aye my thoughts were o Steenie, and if reason wad instruct me that he might weel be deid, I minded Catriona's words, and I could not believe sic a thing.

I did not hide my thoughts on this frae Sawney, and whether this was cruel or not I canna truly say, but the very mention o Steenie's name wad bring on him dreams and passions that were akin tae madness. But that was when he was asleep, during the day he had becam a very mild mannered man, much like the ane he had ance been. And whiles of an evening, when I wad relent a bit, we wad sit at the mouth o the cave listening tae the wild elf music, which aye sounded tae me as if it had been a gude tune ance, but frae which sae many notes had been lost that it had now becam just a things o stops and starts, which a great wave wad end, only tae hae it begin again wae a desperate skirl.

I ken not truly, and I hae nae words tae properly desribe that time. Late at e'en before the sun went completely doun, mysel, or Sawney, and maistly it was Sawney, for he liked tae exercise his leg, wad gang out tae check our lines and traps. I wad watch him wae the aid o a staff making his way alang the shore gieing a bit tug here and a bit tug there, and pulling a line in if there was anything on it. On his return he wad stop intae see tae the horses, and then come intae the cave smelling a bit o them, which was a smell I aye liked, and he wad sit down by me, smoking his pipe, silent until I should choose tae speak, or tiring o my silence he wad tak tae reading his Bible.

I remember very clearly thinking at the time, how in awe his life he had read nae ither book, bar a few sodgerly books on how tae win battles, and I thought o awe the books that Steenie had read, and why, as a bairn under his teaching, I had read far mair mysel. He looked up then and caught my een smiling at him.

-Why Sawney Bain, I said, -ye are near a hale man again, and what are ye tae dae now?

He did not answer for a bit, nae doubt taken aback that I was being friendly, and then he just said,

-The Lord has preserved us Agnes when thousands he has smitten. I ken not why, and aiblins I now think that it is a sinful thing tae inquire intae, for has he not tumbled pride frae the saddle and trodden impudence intae dust, and them that he has not slain he has flung doun, and it might weel be that on the earth they should lie until his hand and his pleasure should be clearly seen tae raise them up again.

I minded then how Steenie wad rage at Heaven itsel, and whiles I wad in my heart rage wae him, and whiles I wad tremble tae hear his words.

-A Covenanted army, was destroyed at Dunbar, Agnes, and I canna now believe anything ither than that awe we had thought tae bring tae pass, will not now come tae pass, but ither things will, and in them we maun seek a meaning.

At that time I said naething in reply, but tae my mind, nae doubt the English thought they had as much right tae the Lord's gude will as ever had the Scots, and confused himsel, he had just gone tae his bed, and left cauld steel and guns tae decide the issue.

That night I lay wae Sawney again, and whether there was pleasure in it, or whether there was not I canna mind. But after it I lay thinking that the Bible and the earth, and awe that it contained was indeed just that auld dark dream o nonsense, and the tears that men shed ower it were but the tears o bairns plucked frae their mither's breast and thrust out intae a fierce warld that cared not a fig for their appetites and desires.

☆

I feel I must examine my soul and my purpose on every point. Likewise my reasons and my thoughts. All must come under the most careful scrutiny.

It is difficult. I feel myself, perhaps for the first time in my adult life, to be a stranger to myself, unable to judge the wisdom, or unwisdom, of my thoughts and intended deeds – nor can I even see clearly what I do intend.

Of Malecky's living malevolence I have material proof, and I know that I must confront this man, though with exactly what one confronts such a creature I do not rightly know, and how he will appear to me I cannot imagine. They say he is a very old man now, which would be natural, but in the depths of the night I imagine that this is only how he chooses to appear, and that when I meet him he will be a virile demon, mocking death, and reeking of ageless evil.

This I understand, is hardly rational or possible, and yet a pestilence as subtle and determined as this serpent Scot, who has so beguiled the hearts of men and women must be in himself exceptional, a sorcerer of souls far beyond the fraudulent conjuring imagined by William Munro, perhaps even beyond that discovered by Mathius Pringle.

I have resolved to go to him. I will dash the Black Book in his face. I will tell him of the final outcome, and I will demand of him in the name of God whether or not this is his work. He will lie, but I believe that I will know that he is lying.

Having made this resolution, I fear, and yet I do not fear, a deadly trap. I have decided to conceal a pistol in my baggage, though I can hardly explain my purpose in so doing.

The minister heard the Highlander's voice laughing and joking with Elspeth, and by the sound that emanated he had quite overcome that good woman's apprehension about Highlanders. He felt irritated with them both, and irritated with himself. Archiebald Drummond Will-Do-Nicely had done nothing so far, he thought, to warrant such animosity.

He walked into the drawing room, the Highlander rose to his feet his hand extended. At least, the minister reflected, he has chosen not to wear his sword and pistols for breakfast.

'Good morning Mr Drummond, I trust you slept well?'

'Never better Sir, never better. Ye hae a fine bed, and nae doubt it seemed finer still after three or four nights in the heather.'

He was being reminded, the minister thought, that Drummond's journey had been arduous. And yet the Highlander's open countenance belied any such calculation, he seemed genuinely at ease, eating his breakfast without any further comment on his business. After the meal the minister spoke privately to Elspeth.

'What do you think of our Highlandman now?'

'Och, he's aiblins a civil enough man Sir, gentlemanly even, for a Hielanman, forbye he wad reveal naething about his business.'

'Oh I know his business, it concerns an acquaintance of mine, and as a consequence I will be away for a time, but I think the parish can manage without me can it not? I do not expect to be gone long, and no doubt Walter Hyslop can read the service on Sunday?'

Elspeth's eyes opened wide. If she thought the Highlander was civil enough, it did not follow that she viewed her master riding off with him with equanimity.

'Wattie Hyslop is not the man he ance was.'

'I know that well enough, but no doubt he can still read.'

'Och he can still read I'm sure.'

The minister gave her no further room to speculate. He turned and strode back into the drawing room.

'Mr Drummond, you have come a long way to find me, and I do not think you should ride back empty handed, so I will indeed ride back with you.'

What the Highlander thought of this decision the minister did not know. He bowed gently and said that he thought his good friend Mr Malecky would be pleased to see him, and it would be his duty to guide and guard him.

'Do you think I will need guarding Mr Drummond?'

'Och Sir, nane kens when he will need tae guard himself, or his friends. But my words were to put your mind at ease, not to cause it any apprehension, my country is a safe place for my friends, and the friends of Mr Malecky.'

'I must of course make some arrangements here for this sudden departure, but I think we could leave tomorrow morning.'

'I am at your service Sir, I can amuse myself until then.'

How did such a man amuse himself, the minister wondered. He felt a sudden necessity to issue a warning.

'I am still relatively new to this country, but I gather as a result of old troubles, the people of this district are a mite touchy about Highlanders.'

A slow smile spread itself across Drummond's features.

'Och there are touchy folk in awe places, but I hae already met a few men o this toun, and they seemed douce and decent, if perhaps a bit Whiggish in their douceness.'

Once again the minister felt nettled. Once again he felt that it would take all his forbearance to put up with this fellow, but he smiled and bowed, excusing himself for the moment from any further conversation.

☆

In time, we left the cave, Sawney saying cheerfully, that however much the Lord hated the Scots he surely was ower merciful tae ordain that we should live forever on fish and rabbits.

We heard frae some folk that we met, awe that had cam tae pass, and how the man Cromwell had stormed the country far and wide, and how in a last wild throw the new king had led an army intae England tae join up wae his friends there. But at that time, it seems, he had few friends in England, and awe had been bludily beaten at a place called Worcester, and now Cromwell's hand lay unopposed ower awe. Awe that is bar the Hielans, Cromwell haeving nae mair desire than maist men wad tae lead an army intae that place.

We oursels travelled through the land like hameless country folk, of which there were many. But as a result o the times there was much empty land now tae, and in time we found a bit o that in our ain country o Galloway, which we got through the favour o a sodger friend o Sawney's. I mind weel the night we sat in his biggin drinking his ale, and Sawney asked me if he was tae become a fairmer ance again? I laughed at him then, for in truth he kent but little o that trade, but he just quietly declared that nae doubt it could be learnt.

Sae we becam fairmers, and for a time we lived quietly. There was, I remember clearly, a strange quietness throughout the land at that time, as if the Scots folk were themsels sick o fighting, and if they rankled under the English hand that lay upon them, and if here and there ye still heard tales o bit fights around the Hielan line which cam tae naething, the lave lived peacefully enough.

We oursels did weel enough on our bit land, and it seemed fine tae me tae see Sawney wae nae mair than a bit stick in his hand and twa collie dugs at his side driving his beasts before him. I mind not truly whether I kent at that time, or whether I did not, that the auld wild dreams were not deid, but just being kept for a time on a tight rein. The folk glowered at the sodgers, and the Kirk rumbled in its pulpits, but quietly, for now they were a power only by English toleration, and the English, it seemed, sick o hunting witches in their ain country, had but little patience wae it in Scotland.

I laughed lang and loud at that, and said that surely the Deevil maun indeed be a muckle coward, and his true servants fickle folk if an English decree could drive them and their wickedness frae the land. Yet sae it seemed, for nane were caught or heard o in these years, and nae doubt the Kirk snapped its teeth at that, and some said the English were themsels allied wae Satan. Tae me it was fell amusing tae think that was awe it took tae mak the Scots folk live in peace.

Ance I rade tae Edinburgh tae see auld Baillie, kenning that if there was any news o Steenie he wad hae it, but awe I discovered, was that he himsel had been deid a year, and there was nae news tae be had.

Indeed it seemed tae me, at that time, as I ance again walked through the streets o Edinburgh, and seeing the Musketeer packed wae English sodgers, as drunken louns as ever the Scots had been, and the castle itsel garrisoned by them, that the past that had made sic a din in its passing had just been blawn clean awa. Awe bar the heid o Jamie Graham which still clung tae its spike, and if the lave o folk thought the time o kings was ower then aiblins it kent better than they.

I rade back frae Edinburgh wae a heavy heart. If I thought that Steenie was indeed deid, it was not a thought I could easily thole, and if my reason insisted that it maun be likely, in my heart I hae never truly believed it, but there was nae mair tae be done.

☆

August 10th 1699.
I have spent my first day on the road with Mr Drummond Will-Do-Nicely. I no longer harbour any apprehensions of

375

him, and I am convinced that he is innocent of any design other than to do his duty as a messenger and guide. Indeed, he now strikes me as a rather simple man, who through much travel has acquired through mimicry, a certain antique gentility that is as out of fashion as his soldier's buff coat.

All this notwithstanding, and despite the civilness of his manners, the men of my parish treated him with suspicion, and not a little apprehension. The consternation in the faces of Mathew Elliot and Walter Hyslop at the thought that their new minister was about to be stolen away by a Highlandman afforded me no small amusement. Indeed Mathew offered to lend me a stout kinsman, whom he described in his own fashion as being a 'good man of his hands', to accompany me if ride with Mr Drummond I must.

I of course, declined the offer, though I was touched by it, and regretted how much I had slighted them in my thoughts. To Walter I breathed not a word as to the nature of my expedition, knowing the turmoil it was bound to raise in the soul of that much changed man.

Of Miss Melville, who has clearly been the enabling factor in all of this, I must confess, that while I strive to understand, I cannot think of her without fear and horror. I tremble for her, nor can I any longer view her as the innocent and winning maid of my first acquaintance. Now I see in her a dreadful corruption, a blasphemous masquerade without either self-knowledge or shame, who can put on the trappings of piety with as little thought as she dons her grey plaid.

I strive to keep my mind free of over harsh judgements. That she was not wholly responsible I am aware, and indeed I intend, and would be failing in my duty if I did not fling her destruction in Malecky's face when we meet.

In all that I have to consider, I am sensible that I have to strive to separate that which is real from that which has merely the appearance of it, and yet, all is so intermingled. That Bain, while he lived upon the earth's surface, was in many ways an exceptional man, I am forced to acknowledge.

I think this, and my memory is constantly assailed with the sight of the monster stubbornly silent in his cell. Was his silence due to a resurgent conscience overwhelmed with its own evil? Had he spoken I would have striven to understand and pity.

I think this, and day and night before my eyes I see hosts of murdered Christians and my heart is filled with horror.

Will Malecky tremble when I lay their unspeakable sufferings at his feet? I do not know, but answers I will have, and I believe that God will direct me and protect me in this as he sees fit.

August 11th 1699.

On the first day of our journey Mr Drummond had proved a silent companion, which indeed was so much to my taste that I made no effort to disturb it.

I think he thought of me as poor company. On the second day, after we had been some few hours in the saddle, he remarked, I think on purpose to provoke me, that it saddened him to see the people of my parish so sorely ridden by what he described as a midden yard laird, and having no longer any among them to teach him respect and good manners, for he had known them in his youth to be bold men, if a bit Whiggish for his taste.

I told him, I imagine rather testily, that times had changed, and all men of sense acknowledged that change and rejoiced in peace. He merely smiled rather dissemblingly in reply, and said that he had seen few signs of rejoicing, but much acknowledgement that he drives them hard, frittering away their rents in Edinburgh politics and pleasures.

I felt no inclination at this point to defend Sir John Doig, but simply remarked that I felt sure that the lairds in his part of the country could hardly be saints.

'Why no Sir,' came his reply. 'But my own chief, that ye will doubtless meet, kens very well, that if he is to remain chief he must have bold and well armed gentlemen to follow him, and they must love him, and they would hardly do that if he squeezed the last piece of meat out of them in a bad year, placing money in his pocket as of greater value than a loyal sword at his back, and them his own kinsmen.'

I replied that I hardly thought the laird of Trig thought of his tenants in such an antique manner, and not at all as his kinsmen.

For a time he was silent, and indeed I hoped he would remain so, but it was not to be.

'Still, I find it sad Sir, that all their wild Whiggamore rant should have brought them to this state. Why I was on the opposite side from them in eighty-nine at Dunkeld, ye might have heard of the place, when they, well positioned in the auld round tower beat us back that had just beaten a government army the previous week. But for all that we could do that day, why we could have hacked down that tower stone by stone and they would not have budged.'

I told him, somewhat wearily, that perhaps what he chose to describe as their wild Whiggamore rant of the past, had made them value quiet and Christian living in the present, and order was always preferable to disorder, even the present order which he so plainly despised.

He smiled again, this time a rather insufferably superior smile, but at last he fell silent.

This was partly determined by the road which obliged us to ride single file. But he did not bring the subject up again, no doubt deciding that I was no more than a sour Whig pastor, and the people of Trig even more unfortunate than he had previously thought. For my part, I could not forbear from reflecting, that both Andrew Gilmore and John Erskine had fought on the opposite side from him, and if the three had met they would have disagreed on every point of politics and principle, but would be as one in their dissatisfaction with the present.

☆

The time o the Republic was a peaceful time, if an uneasy ane. Some folk said that the auld sang had at last run out o breath, and right glad they were that it had, for a man and his wife and his bairns could now live peacefully. Ithers said that the Lord was merely biding his time in order tae humble his folk a bit, sae great had they grown in their pride. And as he had kept Israel in Eygpt many a lang year, sae he wad wae the Scots, but in the end he wad lead them out, scattering the mighty wae a wave o his hand.

Sawney had nae real answer tae any point, just saying that awe his life he had ridden this way and that like a bit bird in a storm, and now that the storm was a bit quiet,

378

why he himsel wad bide quietly, and nae langer try tae think on things that the Lord had put outside our wits.

Tae my mind, naething wad last that needed riding men, wha in general split their share o brains wae their horse, tae mak it last.

We had nae bairns at that time, and for awe I kent that grieved Sawney, it did not grieve me much, for I had lang decided that I was not a woman that was tae hae bairns. Nor did I love this warld wae sufficient force tae be ower sad on that account.

On some days I wad gang alane up intae the hills and just stand on a bit peak and look about me, and mind o awe the things that had taen place since they had first dragged mither and me frae our biggin in Trig, and I thought o awe the things that the tongues o men had said, and the heids o men had dreamed, and the voice o the Lord had commanded. And I minded what Steenie had said on that last day that we lay thegither, and I kent that it was a true thing that he had said, that until folk learned tae ken the warld, and the things that truly drove it, aye and learned tae live in it without a God in Heaven or a king on Earth, it wad aye be the case that the warld wad drive them and turn ilka thing intae the opposite o what they intended, and turn their ain beliefs intae a sword tae ding them doun.

I had little faith that men could ever hae sic skill, and tae my mind bairns were just things that they wanted sae that their pride should not dee, but should ance again mount that mad horse which in their auld age had pitched them tae the dust.

☆

August 14th 1699

As we ride ever Northwards it is as if the pages of the Black Book are opening before me. Even in a time when the woman calls herself happy, she neither looks for nor desires the love of God or the love of children. Her melancholy attempts to understand things that are beyond her understanding, lead to judgements that are pitiful in their childishness, that in turn lead her spirit into the despair of an endless atheistic night, in which her soul, discarded, longs for peace, and her flesh, insatiable in its desires, longs for Malecky.

I pity them as I would blind creatures stumbling between Heaven's light and Hell's fire, so blinded by the second that they cannot see the radiance of the first. She is indifferent, and no longer has the capacity, and perhaps it was always thus, to tell one from the other. He is like a man with the brain of a child, who occasionally glimpses the truth, and yearns for it, but besotted with her flesh he allows her to drag him inexorably to his doom, as Mathius Pringle prophesied she would.

My conviction that this was all Malecky's work, and they little more than foolish victims of it, grows daily stronger, as does the courage to confront him with it.

Mr Drummond finds me a wearisome companion. On occasion I have tried to engage him in conversation about Malecky, and what manner of man he finds him to be. He, despite the burden of our silences at other times, appears reluctant to do this, and merely praises his 'good friend' extravagantly while telling me nothing that I do not already know. I have decided that I do not entirely trust him on the subject, and he is rather too adroitly careful in keeping from me how much or how little he truly knows about Malecky, or my business with him.

Perhaps I misjudge him. Often, after hours of silence on the road he will burst into a song in his own tongue. He sings rather well, and his language is melodious, though I do harbour a suspicion that if I could understand the words he sings I would be forced to strongly disagree with them. That I may be doing him an injustice in this I am aware, but there is a mischievous, almost reckless smile on his countenance when he sings, which, whether he intends it or not, I find provoking, even mocking.

August 16th 1699.

I have spent most of the night in prayer, and rose from my knees wonderfully refreshed. I am convinced now that everything that has befallen me has been ordained, and could not have happened otherwise, and everything that will happen to me has already been foretold. There is no longer any place in

my heart for fear, apprehension, or doubt, and as a conse-
quence my spirit feels as light as air.

My companion has observed this change within me, and
while he knows not the cause, gives every sign of being relieved
by it.

In some ways I have judged him harshly, for he is a civil and
courteous man, not only in his dealings with me, but, I have
observed, with all others too, never passing a beggar on the
road but he gives them something. His explanation for this
open-handedness is, as he himself insists, no more than a
childish superstition that such generosity will bring him good
luck in the future, and will indeed keep his wife and children
safe in his absence.

I am, I must confess, too shocked by this admission to be
much amused. When I suggested that prayer might be a more
efficacious way of easing his soul, he made the merry reply that
he would ask the opinion of the next beggarman. I suggested
that to do both things in a Christian spirit would be much to
his credit.

In this he agreed with me, and indeed he agreed to pray with
me. Alas, I think this acquiescence is out of politeness and a
desire not to offend me, for in truth I have failed to detect any
sign of true religion in him at all, other than a formal courtesy
to my position.

I do not mean to imply by this that Mr Drummond lives in
a state of atheistical despair. It is simply that lacking the habit,
and perhaps the opportunity, religious observance has played
very little part in his life, and he is, for an intelligent man,
horribly ignorant of catechism and text.

This is perhaps the only thing, at least while he has been in
my company, in which he lives up to the savage character Mr
Gilmarten gives to all his people. Indeed, not only is he
ignorant of the blessings of religion, he clearly feels that he has
no need of them. The beliefs that he does hold, which only slip
out, as it were by chance in occasional observations he makes,
I can only describe as superstitions, undoubtedly pagan in
origin.

I am further saddened, as he is by no means an unlettered
man, and, having been for a time in his youth an officer in both
the French and the Spanish armies, he knows both languages

and countries very well, nor is he beneath an occasional, tolerably articulated, Latin phrase.

I have resolved, while I am with him, to study him, his attitudes and opinions, and his reasons for holding them, which, for I think he is a fair representative of his people, must give me some insights into the Highlands and the Highland race.

If I could arrange his opinions and views of the world as I have so far discovered them, I think they would appear something like this: a dislike of Presbyterianism, which he refers to as Whiggery. This I forgive because of his ignorance, and indeed, since we have been on friendlier terms he has taken pains to moderate this and has become quite amiably tolerant. He has a pride in, and loyalty to, his own tribe of Highlanders which is so excessive as to be almost idolatry. I believe also that he has some sentimental knowledge of the Roman Catholic religion, picked up with a careless convenience in France. That he considers himself a gentleman, and the equal of any man on earth, he leaves me in no doubt. Indeed I cannot help but be amused at the way his antique pride can bristle beneath his antique courtliness at the slightest whiff of a slight. Few knowingly do this, for he leaves no one in any doubt, that if provoked he would prove a formidable man.

I am reminded when I speak of him, of some aspects of Mr Gilmarten's book, in which he spends much ink on ways of civilising these people. Of course as regards religion I cannot be out of sympathy with him, but I think it would take preachers of infinitely more tact and sympathy than Mr Gilmarten to reach their hearts. Lastly, I think that having undertaken the duty of guiding me to Malecky he would probably, for the duration of the journey, defend me with his life if I was threatened.

The contrast between himself and Andrew Gilmore could hardly be greater, and yet, in so many things they are not unalike, and I imagine the difference in the previous century would not have been so great, which is, I believe, an excellent example of the benefits which accrue from the blessings of religion.

☆

I mind weel the day when they set up the new King upon the throne, and free ale without stint was gien out tae the people wha were then bidden tae be cheerful, and cheerful they were with a right gude will.

Sawney wad drink nae ale at awe that day, and cried them awe for witless louns baith in Scotland and in England, and wae a harsh auld laugh telt them that now they wad ken what Egypt was really like, and did they think that when they discovered this the Lord wad excuse them in their foolishness? Or that awe the folk that had been killed in awe the bludy years wad think sic a celebration a cheerful thing?

Sae it had cam tae pass. Hardly had the cheering deed doun than this new King declared that he wad right the wrangs his faither had suffered, and wad hae bishops tae rule ower God's folk and keep them in order, and tae let them ken that he had nae inclination tae gang the gate his faither had. And he had the heid o Jamie Graham taen doun frae its spike and buried maist reverently, and on that same spike he stuck the heid o Macalein More, and whether the craws thought that was a fairer heid than the first, or whether they did not, I canna say.

Weel some said this and some said that, and some wad now look back on the days o the Republic as a blessed time, and ithers said that it was a sure sign o the Lord's hand, and that this new pharaoh wad be the final scourge o a laggardly people.

For mysel I kent not, I had nae langer an ear for sic things, and many folk heard as I heard until the truth cam hammering at their door. It was then that they kent, that if they had nae ears tae hear, they had flesh tae feel, and a scourge upon their flesh this new king seemed determined tae be, his sodgers, riding it was said, frae dawn tae dusk, billeting themsels by his command on poor folk, and driving them frae their hames that wadna comply, hinging ithers by the roadside that wadna submit. Some they cut doun on the hillside whaur they now said their prayers, haeving nae langer a kirk in which tae say them.

Many sic tales we heard frae folk that cam by our biggin, which we aye fed and helped, that the new King's sodgers, riding men that they called dragoons, were ance again stacking weel the fires tae burn out any trace of what they called sedition, and the folk that wadna thole this were ance again digging up swords and guns which had lain hidden for many a lang year.

I remember very clearly that day when what was left o a hale family, four folk out o what had been seven, walked awa frae our door saying that they wad not bide, however great their need, wae folk that hesitated when the Lord ance again called, for they had nae desire tae be a burden on them that loved earthly things.

Fair mad they had seemed tae me wae grief and suffering, and crying upon Heaven for revenge, but loading their guns tae, as if they wad tak that revenge wae Heaven's blessing or without it. And Sawney wha had cried them awe tae Hell at the time o the crowning o the second Charles Stuart, was now, I could plainly see, very much affected.

☆

On Sundays, about that time, them that had been driven frae their hames and kirks wad haud services high in the hills. I wad not gang tae sic affairs, the plain reason being, that for awe I had lived wae Sawney awe these years, and in awe things they had been gude years, I had becam maist like Steenie in my ain thoughts. In the years o peace I had said little o this tae Sawney, and he naething in the way o re-buke. But now Sawney wad gang alane tae these meetings, and as secretly the word had gone out that arms were needed, for if the dragoons cam upon them they wad ride them doun, why Sawney wad tak arms, and the auld bear coat, weary it maun hae been, wad ride ance again tae the Lord's command and the Covenant's drum.

There was for a time, nae trouble at these meetings in our country, till ane day, a bit after dawn, these folk like untae a small army o men, women, and bairns, turned up at our door. Pitiful they seemed tae me, wild and ragged as gyp-sies. At their heid was a tall thin man wae a great grey beard, wha cam marching up tae me, Sawney being in some ither place at the time, asking, but mair like commanding,

384

that they should hae the shelter o our field and barn.

I looked them ower, and while I kent very weel that there was quite a bit o cauld steel and guns hidden beneath their plaids, still a poor sight they were. And then this minister, Joshua Kilbracken was his name, seeing that I hadna answered his commands, wad cry a bit mair upon the Lord for assistance, and I cried back at him, that awe we could gie we wad gie, but I wad not hae my senses deafened as weel.

He looked at me then, wae a look that said that he kent me very weel, and I looked back at him wae a look that nae doubt telt him plainly that sic a man as he was nae stranger tae me. It wad hae been mair than a miracle if that had daunted him.

-Whaur is yer gudeman, he cried out. -For I hae heard o ye.

-Och, what ye hae heard ye hae heard, I telt him. -And nae doubt Sawney will hae heard yer clamour by now.

At that point, and prudently, a young sodger-like man of about thirty stepped forward, a brisk and handsome man wae a clever face.

-Mistress, said he, -dinna be offended. Ye can see for yersel the condition o these folk, and there are many amang them hurt and wounded, and I canna think that ye wad deny them aught.

He was weel armed this man, and around him were a group that like himsel seemed tae hae a sodgerly appearance.

-I'm no offended, I said, -I hae telt ye plainly that ye are welcome.

Sawney himsel cam running up then and at ance took in the hale sight. Kilbracken he kent, haeving often ganged tae hear him preach, and out o his mouth now cam the words which aye cam out o sic men, and if Sawney gied out little sign at the time, I could see them working on him like fire on steel.

But that morning we killed three stirks for them that they might eat, and when that was done, and them that were hurt had found some shelter, and Kilbracken was working up tae a sermon tae keep their spirits up, the young sodgerly man cam up tae Sawney and me asking for a word in our ears.

385

This man, Jock Elliot was his name, wha had indeed sodgered for a time in Cromwell's army, now sat doun opposite us, his hands on his knees, a thin bit smile on his lips, and his een steady in his heid.

-I'll be plain Sir, he said. -For I wad not hae any misunderstandings. We had trouble Sir, wae a pickle o dragoons, wha by the grace o God we beat off wae the loss o three men, and the wounded ye can see for yersel. But they ken we are in the country and will likely be finding sic reinforcements as they can. Sae are we tae bide here, or are we tae gang? I maun ken seeing as I hae the military command o this company.

-They are, tae my een, in nae condition tae gang anywhaur.

-The Lord has brought us out o worse than this.

-Na, na, ye sall bide here, I ken my duty Sir and ye hae nae need tae bang it out on my heid. But these dragoons ye say?

-They are feckless louns for the maist part, but very weel armed and very weel mounted, and hunting poor folk is a great sport tae them. They might find us and they might not, but if they dae there will be a bit fight.

Sawney answered then wae a brisk twinkling o his een, that if it was some time since he had last taen out his sword it was not yet fit for naething but poking the fire.

At this the fine young man gied out a bit grin that wad not hae looked amiss on the face o a fox, and in my heart I kent very weel the gate his mind was ganging, which was mair than confirmed later that night.

-Then Sir, will ye let us bide here, and will ye fight wae my troop should any come against us?

-Why Sir, dae ye think I intend tae run awa? But if men wad be called a troop they maun learn tae march in order.

-I ken, I ken, I hae a few o some experience, but maist hae nane at awe but what the Lord gies them in their hour o need, but they stood firm enough in that last bit fight.

-Against how many horse did ye say?

-No aboun forty.

-Aye weel Sir they maun hae been very bauld and confident horse in the first instance, and when I look around me, no without reason. If ye are tae bide here, tae my mind a bit drilling wad not be amiss.

Jock had heartily agreed wae him, and indeed, I could see very clearly that he had impressed Sawney greatly,sae that when he asked personally if he could visit us that evening, Sawney said that he wad be mair than happy tae receive him.

That night he sat lang wae Sawney and talked about the history o the rebellion, and the days o the Republic, which for awe he had been ower young tae be a sodger in, he nevertheless kent very weel. He put forward the opinion wae great conviction that the hand o the Kirk had been ower mighty on the field o battle whaur it had nae skill, aye, and aiblins in the affairs o state tae. And the auld cause itself had stunk wae the cattle o gentry wha wad twist and turn it for their ain purpose, and wad change sides when it suited them.

But now, he declared, there wad be nane o that, for the gentry did very weel wae this new king, as did the lave o the ministers, wha blithely preached what ever tune he fiddled. But the people o the South-West, and in time the common folk throughout Scotland, wad write ance again in their ain blude a new Covenant. For was it not written that the Lord wad raise up the humble frae the dust and ding doun the mighty forever.

He spoke very weel and wae great enthusiasm, and if tae my mind, his enthusiasm had mair tae dae wae republican politics than religious zeal, I liked him the mair for it. And he said that throughout the country poor folk driven frae their hames by sodgers wad gaither, and wad be a great new army tae finish that auld wark.

Events, it seemed, were just picking Sawney up and thrusting him intae the saddle ance mair, and nae doubt awe his auld dreams lent a hand at that, and aiblins his heart was blithe at awe these things, and if there were folk that wad still draw a sword for them, then how could he be a laggard in drawing his? But armies, he telt Jock Elliot, win battles wae sword and gun, and horse and foot that ken their trade.

-Aye Sir, and if folk are tae learn that necessary trade

they maun be taught by them that ken it.

He looked very keenly at Sawney then, och a man o subtle understanding was he.

-Weel Sawney, as ye ken, I hae some experience, and a few ithers likewise, but if ye join us in this endeavor, I hand the command o my troop, sic as it is, ower tae ye.

That night he clung tae me like a fierce and restless beast, and he asked me if he went wae them wad I gang tae. I said that I wad, for it was clear tae me that I could hardly bide alane at sic a time. But I telt him plainly that I had little taste for wandering the hills wae a loun like Kilbracken at my heid, and that despite awe the assurances we had got frae Jock Elliot that he wad be kept in check, I had kent men like him awe my life, but I had never kent a time when they could be kept in check, and in my heart I feared for awe the people in this enterprise.

He said he kent awe that very weel, but haeving put these folk up, the dragoons wad mair than likely be at our door, ane day or anither, and if he was set tae hae anither throw, then he wad prefer tae hae it frae the back o his horse than frae his kitchen door.

Next morning he went out and telt Jock Elliot that he accepted the command. Jock smiled, and why should he not smile, for he had got what he cam for, an experienced sodger tae lead them, and if he had employed some guile tae dae it, it wad in truth hae taen less cunning than he imagined, for if the people were rising, then in the end Sawney could nae mair hae stayed out o the fight than he could hae gien up the dreams in his heart without his heart itsel ceasing tae beat.

I kent it very weel when I saw him ance again mounted on his horse and his bear coat about his shoulders. And nae doubt the very sight o him, did, as weel Jock kent it wad, put life and heart intae them that wad be sodgers. And if Kilbracken's fire had touched his heart tae, he had not forgotten times past, and he bade that man cut short his morning sermon sae that he could see just what this troop o his consisted o.

Kilbracken had turned on him then wae an auld and fiery ee, and asked him wha he was that he should dare tae dae sae much? Sawney telt him plainly that the intelligence he had was that the enemy was near at hand, and that if he was tae command then command he wad.

I could see the anger clearly in Kilbracken's een when he declared that the Lord God Almighty was nearer than any earthly enemy. On that occasion, forbye it took awe Jock Elliot's adroitness tae smooth the situation, Sawney got his way and the troop was briskly in line wae their arms present. And Sawney wad tak some weapons off ane man and gie them tae anither that was under armed, and he showed them how a pike line should be formed, and how musketeers should be drawn up, and he shared out the powder and shot, which, it haeving been used up in the previous fight, was very scarce, barely twa bullets tae a gun.

It was very little for now, as he himsel telt me, but tae mak them look like sodgers might hae some effect. Of the horse there was around fifty or sixty, but many mounted on farm beasts that wad never stand the shock o a charge, and these he kept in reserve. He himsel, kenning the land, positioned the scouts, doubling their number.

Awe this I watched. At ane point Jock Elliot turned tae me and said that he kent he had done right in coming here. Kilbracken just glowered at these words, and while he declared it was against the arrogance o the airm o flesh, tae my mind it was just between his airm and Jock Elliot's.

☆

August 17th 1699.

That Bain is now in the time described by Andrew Gilmore I am well aware; that the laws were harsh, and the men who enforced them barbarous and cruel, I must accept. But that these simple people should take up arms against a great state and its armies makes me shudder to the depths of my soul. I would tremble for them even if I didn't know the eventual outcome of their actions. And yet, I know that in my own parish, there is none among the common people who would not treat their memories with honour and pride, as indeed they keep their graves fresh on the hillside.

That they were valiant I cannot deny them. Or that Sawney

Bain was at that time a valiant and exceptional man, who was prepared to put what he conceived to be his Christian duty, before his worldy security. But still, if I can perceive a meaning in what ultimately befell them it is that already, as Agnes Douglas approvingly relates, seditious politics and earthly revolution marched alongside, and strove to march at the head of, Christian zeal.

I believe I understand Mr Gilmarten's book a great deal better now. Indeed I believe I understand fully why he felt it his duty to set his wisdom and his learning against the passions of his people, and maintain the plain truth that there can be no prosperity in a country where ignorance in the pursuit of extravagant dreams arms itself against authority. However sanctified their cause appears to them in their own hearts and minds, they will be used by subtler men for their own ends, and earthly politics and earthly passions will lead all inevitably to disaster.

August 18th 1699.

We have passed through what are called the central Lowlands, which struck me as more prosperous by the standards of the country than my own parish. If this journey had any other purpose than the one it has I would have been delighted to stop off at such places as the ancient town of Stirling. Mr Drummond however rides at a brisk pace, both because I think he finds his duty, however loyally he will perform it, tiresome, and because he feels himself uneasy in any part of the country which is not the Highlands. Indeed his dress and manners mark him out, almost as a man of a different race, and no doubt he feels the usual derision and contempt which the ignorant apply to foreigners.

Yesterday we passed over the hills at Stirling and today we are in the beginning of what are the Highlands proper.

My companion's whole demeanour changed as soon as we were across what he terms the Highland Line. This morning he cheerfully informed me that his name was no longer Mr Archiebald Drummond-Will-Do-Nicely, but was now Mr Roderick Dhu Macgregor.

I confess I was both taken aback, and not a little amused,

having grown accustomed to Mr Drummond I now find it difficult to think of him as anything else. At the same time I could not suppress a kind of apprehension. His name, which in his own language means Black Roderick, struck me as barbaric, though he gave me to understand that it is merely a physical description of his colouring. Still, its effect on me was to bring me with a sudden jolt into proximity to all that I had read, and to how close I was to fulfilling my purpose.

This was further enhanced by the countryside through which we now passed, which was wild and untamed to an extreme degree, and the routes along which my guide led me hardly visible to the untutored eye. If my mind had been otherwise than fixed on the one thing that had brought me here I would have noticed more, but as it was my senses were quite overwhelmed; nor could I see any way in which Mr Macgregor, as I must now call him, could know his way, guiding me as he did, through dense forests and narrow defiles. He, it is true, hardly faltered, though I am of the belief that he took many a circuitous route for his own reasons, principally I believe to keep to areas where he could be sure of friendship.

If this was true, it was certainly efficacious, for he hailed all that we met in his own language, and often by name. They in turn were demonstrably friendly, though all were armed in some manner, usually carrying sword, shield, and longbow, many also with muskets and pistols.

As the majority of them have no English I could not speak to them, or they to me, but I took pains to observe them closely.

The men and women are, for the most part, comely in appearance, clean-limbed and burned rather brown by the weather. Their general appearance is marred somewhat by their dress, which in the males consists of a voluminous multi-coloured plaid, which they allow to fall about their shoulders in good weather, and with which they muffle themselves in bad.

I was pleased to observe that in the country through which we now passed, Mr Macgregor was well respected and liked. We stayed now in the houses of his friends who received us with great civility and docility, offering us on arrival, whisky to drink, which they distill themselves, and which is never absent from peaceful social occasions.

391

I refer to their dwellings as houses, but indeed few of them, and these belonging to men of obvious substance qualify for that title. For the rest their dwellings are quite savage, being little more than domes of mud and wood with a hole in the roof to allow smoke to escape. In good weather they will as cheerfully sleep without a roof as with one.

Their wealth, such as it is, consists mainly of half-wild cattle of which they keep great numbers. These they seldom eat considering them of greater value in the marketplace than in their stomachs. That notwithstanding, and given their material poverty in all civilised things, which is often very great, they do not appear to be underfed, keeping goats and sheep for milk, and of venison, in which these mountains abound, they eat a great deal, bringing their quarry down cleanly with the longbow and the assistance of large swift hounds.

They take great pride in the possession of these dogs, treating them kindly and taking great care that they breed true to their type. Alas I cannot think of them as other than the breed which so horrified poor William Munro, and which he classed as demons.

In one evening I spent with some kinsmen of Mr Macgregor's, who possessed a fine – according to the standards of the country – wooden house, they regaled us all evening with songs and music, and would have plied me with strong drink to such an extent that I would certainly not have been able to move the next day had not my companion checked them.

Their music and songs are not inelegant, and I gather mostly celebrate the passing of former glories, the love of women, and the deeds of brave men, their bards, it seems, rarely choosing any other subject.

That like all primitive people they are great lovers of, and much moved by, music and poetry, is without question. Indeed, some are so disturbed by it that they will think nothing of giving vent to their emotions in wild dancing, throwing their broadswords on the ground and dancing as close to the blade as they dare without cutting their feet.

Of my function and office I think they understood very little, apart from what Mr Macgregor chose to impart, and as he did this mostly in his own language I know not what he said.

They know, I believe, something of religion, but it has been adulterated so much with their own wild superstitions that it can hardly be called religion at all. That some have been inside a church on a few occasions in their lives I gathered from a special courtesy with which they addressed me. I may be mistaken here, for once having committed themselves to receiving a guest they are all courteous and attentive, and what I at first took for a remarkable lack of curiosity on their part about myself, is merely a belief that it is bad manners to inquire too deeply into a guest's business.

They are to my eyes, a curious mixture, coming somewhere between the Dorian antique and the true savage. The pride of even the least of them in what he supposes to be his genealogy and his tribal heritage is both childish and monstrous, and is expressed as if the perimeter of any world worth inhabiting is bounded by their mountains.

Their bards constantly remind them of this, so that unlettered as most of them are, they are all historians of a peculiar kind, and are inclined to be very prickly if their account of any particular event is doubted, even if that event is already some centuries old.

The women, are on the whole, graceful in their appearance, but very bold and forward in their manner, challenging and arguing over the decisions of their men, who do not appear to think of this as unusual behavior, even if, as I often observed, they found it exasperating.

I do not believe the forwardness of the women, for they will look even a stranger such as myself in the eye, actually indicates immodesty, so much as a lack of cultivation. Marriages here are usually unsanctified, and seem to follow an ancient custom of handfasting, signifying an engagement, which if it lasts becomes marriage by repute. Nevertheless, I believe they are as firm in it as any people.

That these people can undoubtedly make as ferocious enemies when roused as Mr Gilmarten, and indeed the Douglas book, describe, I accept. I do not believe however that they are quite as beyond redemption as he often implies. Having said that, it would I believe take dedicated preachers, of their own race, or at least ones who knew their language and their customs thoroughly, to lead them out of their darkness.

☆

393

It was three days before we saw the horsemen. At first sight they just drew up some three hundred yards awa, a troop o around twa hundred or sae, wha for a time, did nae mair than just regard us, and Sawney telt the folk tae keep their weapons hidden, for he wad see for himsel how they dealt wae peaceful folk.

Och but I was proud o him then, sae calm and resolute in appearance was he, and how awe folk cheerfully followed his commands, trusting their lives tae his judgement. And when twa officers frae the dragoons rade towards us wae a white flag aboun their heids, Sawney rade towards them, stopping cannily about a pistol shot frae them, and crying out tae them what their business was and what they did here? Ane officer cried back that he had mair right tae ask that question o Sawney, than Sawney had tae ask it o him.

-This is my bit biggin, and my bit land, and these are but Godly folk in need o shelter, which a Christian man can hardly refuse.

-There is a law against sic gaithering, as surely ye maun ken.

-There are many laws on earth Sir, and but ane in Heaven, wad ye command me tae obey the former and neglect the latter?

-I command ye tae obey the King's law and tak a care o yer tongue, for nae law o the King's can contradict Heaven, and any that says that it can is a rank traitor and a rebel.

-Sae is a bit psalm and a bit prayer tae be rebellion and treason?

The captain was turning swiftly intae a very angry man, but he was as little inclined tae move forward as Sawney was tae gang any further tae meet him.

-I dae the King's wark, and hae nae intention o bandying words on that, I see faces amang these folk that I hae seen before now, and if ye are sic a Christian and hospitable man, why then ye can refresh my troop while I examine their consciences.

-And hae ye skill in examining a man's conscience? For if ye dae then ye maun be a very clever man that rides at the heid o a troop o freshwater horse.

-For the last time damn ye, I hae mair than enough

strength for baith things and will dae my duty whether it be wae my tongue or my sword.

-Tak the wiser course laddie and rest baith.

The twa officers whirled their horse in their rage and galloped back tae their ain ranks crying out that we had been gien fairer warning than we deserved. Sawney trotted quietly back tae us.

-They are coming I think, sae stand tae it and be cheerful, was awe he said.

That they were coming awe could see. First at a trot and then at a gallop, spreading out as they rade. This was tae fright us, for they could not ride through or jump ower the dyke on that ground, and just before they reached it they wheeled round and wad hae discharged their carbines, but Sawney gied the order first and our men let fly wae their guns. Now whether they were impatient wae waiting, or whether it was luck, and aiblins it was indeed the Lord's hand, but it was what sodgers call a perfect volley, roaring out like ane lang crack, emptying many saddles and making their ain volley a wild thing, still, many on our side fell deid.

Ane I got wae my musket, and anither wae my pistol. But they were hard against the wall now cutting and slashing wae their swords, and Sawney was roaring tae the men tae stand steady and pike them back, and the women threw great rocks which we had stacked in readiness, and which at close range can sarely disconcert horse, and then anither volley o musketry tore out frae our biggin whaur Sawney had hidden them catching them on the flank.

This threw many o them intae a great confusion, but ithers had ridden alang tae harder ground in order tae jump the dyke and outflank us. Sawney had kent very weel that they wad try this, and against that event he had made us dig a great ditch on the ither side, and intae it the horses crashed, flinging their riders frae the saddle.

It was at that point that Sawney gied the order for our second and last volley, and it, at barely an airm's length awa, ripped right through them, and we could see in their faces that they themsels kent that they were in a far harder and mair desperate situation than they could ever hae imagined. It was then that he put himsel at the heid o our ain horse and charged at the gallop, knee tae knee, as horse should charge, cutting off them that were on the ither side o the dyke frae them that were on ours.

Of them that were on ours, half the pikes turned on them in a body. Ane I killed, catching him on the airm wae my blade, for he used his ain sword in a wild and desperate way which did him nae gude at awe, for my stroke cut the strings o his sword airm, and my next, for he had lost his steel bonnet, split him frae crown tae chin.

Back they were driven, some trying tae climb back ower the dyke, ithers trying tae climb back on tae horses that were themsels near daft wae fear, and of the dozen or sae that got ower the wall, about half we killed, and the ithers ran awa.

The troop itsel was now in flight, and Sawney checked any pursuit, which wad hae been foolish gien our poor horse. But our hearts louped in our breasts tae see them flee, and we gied out a great cheer, which was later tae mak Kilbracken preach an angry sermon declaring that it was the Lord's wark and no ours. But Sawney telt them awe that he was very proud o them, but they were not tae forget that this had been an easier fight than maist wad be, for the dragoons had nae notion at awe intae what they were riding, and had they kent wad never hae charged sae foolishly.

Eight men we lost that day, and three women. Mair were wounded, some tae dee in the days that followed when we took tae the hills, kenning weel that there we could nae langer bide, for we could hardly think itherwise than that they wad be back.

Sae we marched awa in gude order haeving collected guns and bullets frae the deid sodgers, seventeen haeving been killed and nine gude battle-horses captured. And aiblins it was as Kilbracken wad hae it, that we were like untae a new Israel marching tae a promised place. But for mysel I minded how often that promise had been broken in the past, and wad be again in the future, and think ye no that I was sad tae think how the dragoons wad burn our biggin in their rage.

Frae that brave beginning our life becam that o a hunted beasts, sleeping wae weapons in our hands and hunger in our bellies, and dreams and psalms and prayers louping in our heids. And some wad sicken and some wad dee, and some wad leave tae gang they kent not whaur, and ithers driven frae whaur they could not return wad join up wae us. Aye, and there were some wha wad bide quietly in their biggins and let the sodgers drive them whaur they pleased, while ithers wad fall intae madness and railing at Heaven, and yet ithers wad sink intae an eternity o quietness like untae death. And aye the King's horse rade the glens, and when met there was neither quarter gien or taen, and Kilbracken's great voice wad thunder like a senseless thing, and Jock Elliot wad ride this way and that drumming up men and weapons and food, and Sawney wad drill and train as if a forest o pikes could hold back Hell and shake Heaven frae its slumber.

☆

August 22nd 1699.

I awoke this morning in the midst of a hideous dream. A figure of a man mounted on a great black horse stood on top of a hill beckoning to me, and even as he stood the horse became a beast of fire, the flames consuming its body, until both it and its rider stood, entirely unaffected it appeared, in the midst of a conflagration born of their own flesh.

The apparition moved slowly down the hill towards me. I made no attempt to move towards it or to flee from it, but to my horror a great company of men, women, and children, some mounted, some on foot, advanced towards it, seemingly quite unaware that it was there, and now another figure, a female, also mounted, stood by his side. She appeared to be quite naked, and carried a long lance in her hand.

If I am certain of nothing else, I am certain that the woman could be none other than Agnes Douglas, and when the multitude had vanished over the brow of the hill and the fiery man had gone to I know not where, she alone stood, her lance pointing directly at me as if she was aware of me.

I awoke, and the horror that I felt must have been engraved deeply on my countenance, for my companion was bending over me a deep and touching concern in his features.

He told me that he had heard me cry out and I do not doubt that he speaks the truth. I looked up into his manly honest visage, both moved by his concern, and aware alas, of the chasm that yawns between us, and how impossible it would be for me to divulge anything to him of what lay in my heart. Even when I explain to him that my crying out was merely the result of an unsettling dream he nods his head with an air of superstitious wisdom and declares that there is in his glen a kinswoman of his who sets great store by dreams, whether good or bad, or merely unsettling, and has great skill in divining their meaning.

I confess I am too disturbed to be amused, and cannot think otherwise than that the multitude of people were Sawney Bain and his band of Cameronian zealots whose fate is already known to me. And though the full meaning of that fate is at present hidden from me, I cannot believe otherwise than that it will be in time revealed.

Heavy rains held us up for the rest of that day in the house of Mr Macgregor's kinsman. I was left alone, the Highlanders divining civilly that such was my wish. For many hours I sat watching the storm roll itself across these dreadful mountains. I am filled with an awful trepidation. I will not call it fear but it is certainly akin to it. I realise that I am very near Malecky.

In listening to the conversation of the Highlanders, and trying to pick up the nuances of their speech, Malecky's name is frequently mentioned. Mr Macgregor's kinsman assures me that as a friend of Mr Macgregor's I am very welcome, but as a friend of Mr Malecky's I am doubly and trebly welcome, for all who dwell in these hills have had at some time or another some cause to be grateful to him.

I gather from their conversation that many do indeed regard him as a wizard, sorcerer, and soothsayer. Their rude minds see no evil in this. Dwelling outside the Christian nation, witchcraft and warlockry are meaningless terms to them. Mr Macgregor informs me that Malecky himself dismisses all such claims, and they are made by others on his behalf.

Alas I am not comforted, but am reminded of William

Munro's observations, and recognise the ancient pattern of Malecky's activities. Banished from the Lowlands he has taken root among these wild hills.

☆

Sawney first saw the dragoons through his glass. Some distance they were frae us then. But I remember very weel him putting doun the glass and turning tae mysel and Jock Elliot and saying,

-Heaven maun save us now, for we are quite outmatched on earth.

They were in greater numbers than we had ever previously encountered, and our condition was poor, and haeving skirmished a bit recently we had very little powder and shot. Jock Elliot himself then looked through the glass and said,

-Sae naething o their numbers for the present, they'll ken soon enough.

Sawney grew a bit sharp at that and telt him that he was in command and saw little sense in sic temporary deceptions, gien that they maun fight in the end.

We were on a bit ridge wae our backs tae a small bit wood whaur we had slept the previous night, and surrounded as we were by naked hills there was nae better position tae which we could flee. Sawney kenning that the dragoons had seen us drew our ain men up on the ridge, which, if the numbers had been mair even wad hae been a fair enough position. The horse he hid in the wood, and he telt them awe plainly that this was likely tae be the toughest fight they had sae far fought, but if they stood firm there was a chance, but if they ran awa there was nane. Kilbracken said that the Lord wad surely reveal himsel in our midst.

Tae this Sawney said naething in reply, but set about briskly preparing our position, instructing us how tae erect what defences we could tae hamper the horses. That done, we drew oursels as best we could intae the wood hiding our ain horse out o sight in the trees.

Awe could now see the dragoons, and it was clear tae

awe that they were in nae mood for parleying, and the number o them sent even Kilbracken praying mair fiercely than at any previous time. Prayers that were interrupted by their captain crying on us tae surrender in the king's name and tae his mercy. Weel we kent what that mercy wad be, and Sawney cried back that the Lord had not brought them tae this ring tae dance tae a false king's pipe.

At that the captain just lowered his sword and on they cam at a brisk trot, wheeling tae fire their guns. Their first volley did little damage, but we could not answer it as we should hae. That nae doubt gied them some confidence, and on they cam at a gallop thinking tae outflank us on baith sides. Only when they were awe but on us did Sawney gie the order tae let fly wae our ane volley. It knocked many frae their saddles, but still they cam on, crashing against the rude defences which we had built, and weel placed on higher ground the pikes checked them in a maist desperate and furious fight, but on they cam again, their minds bent on the fact that they maun soon owerhelm us.

At this deidly turn Sawney hit them in the flank wae our hidden horse, which mightily surprised them, for our horse fought like men demented, and in perfect order cutting their way intae the midst o the dragoons and out again, tae regroup and charge ance mair. Sawney set sic an example that day o cutting men frae the saddle that nane o the enemy could be found tae stand against him, and whaurever he appeared in the fight they wad scatter before him, and some in desperation tried tae shoot him and hit their ain comrades, and for a time it seemed that a miracle wad indeed happen and our poor horse wad drive them back.

It was not tae be. They had hunted for us lang I dinna doubt, and they had another troop in reserve, and now it cam on crashing against the pikes, some tae be flung frae their saddles when their horses tripped on the traps we had set for them, ithers splintering pike shafts wae their ain bodies, themsels incensed and blude mad wae the stubbornness o what they had nae doubt thought o as a poor opposition.

Twa or three I piked mysel, and ane I dirked as he lay on the ground before he could rise tae his feet. But anither cam at me wae sic force that his sword slashed the heid off my pike, leaving me wae a weapon o nae mair use than a broomstick, and he wad certainly hae killed me had not Jock Elliot cut him doun frae the rear.

-Save yersels, he shouted tae awe the women and the bairns, and tae any that could get free. But for many that could nae lan-ger be done, encircled and outflanked on awe sides, and some sodgers already in pursuit o them that had ran intae the wood.

I louped upon my ain horse at that point, in time tae see Jock Elliot killed, and I fired my last ball at the man wha had killed him, but I ken not whether I hit him or whether I did not.

There was naething tae be done. Kilbracken himsel I saw killed while lustily calling on Heaven for assistance. Sawney I saw wae what remained o our horse in the centre o a wild and unequal fight, jumping his horse and laying about him like a man in pursuit o death, but I could neither reach him or call out tae him.

It was then I saw a bairn, running it kent not whaur, and I scooped it up and threw it ower my saddle and rade frae the field while it was still possible tae dae sae.

I kent very quickly that there was twa horse pursuing me. Ance clear o the fight I drew in my horse slowly, that being the last thing in the warld they wad expect, and they, thinking they were gaining, and seeing that I was a woman, and nae doubt thinking that it wad be wasteful tae just kill me, put spurs tae their ain beasts.

The first ane tae draw alangside I cut at wae my sword splitting his jaws apart sae that the teeth flew frae his heid as he fell. The second, wha was a bit behind cam on at full gallop, but wae my ain horse half turned I dug my heels in and took him in the flank wae sic force that his ain beast went doun, and he thrown frae its back. Before he could regain his feet I rade my horse ower him, killing him wae my sword.

Nae mair cam. The fight itsel was now ower. I telt the bairn tae cling tightly tae the horse and galloped frae that place as hard as I could, skirting the bit wood in which a bludy pursuit was on.

Frae a distance, and some time later, the bairn, wha was

401

a girl o around eight or nine, and mysel watched the sodgers ride awa. When the last o them was out o sight we rade back through the wood.

Awe was quiet now, as silent as Heaven itsel the place now seemed. Some had been cut doun as they ran, some as if Satan himsel had been at wark on them. Ane woman I kent very weel I found thrust on tae a pike heid, anither lay, her belly filleted wae a sword cut, and her bairn not yet born lay beside her.

I looked at the bairn that was wae me, for she had said nae word at awe since the time I had snatched her. But now she wad neither wait for me in some hidden place, or dae ought else but cling tae the horses back, and I kent that I maun get off the beast and search the place tae see if there was any still living.

Whiles we gaed, and whiles we stopped. Many we found deid, many had been thrown doun and bulled like cows. Ithers we found hanging frae trees. Ane I found alive and naked crawling on the ground, but she could not speak tae me, and for awe I could find nae deidly wound upon her she deed in my airms very shortly.

I kent on that day, that neither Heaven nor Hell ruled on earth, but steel and guns decided the affairs o people whether for right or whether for wrang, and I cursed Heaven for awe these folk, and why, it cared as little for a curse as it did for a prayer. And I remember very clearly that a great fear took me ower in that silent place, for bird and beast and awe things natural had fled frae it, that the warld itsel was nae mair than a Godless, witless, roaring beast o a thing.

We cam at last tae the place whaur the fight had been. I sat doun for a time amang the deid, kenning nae langer what I should dae, or why I was not deid. I looked up at the bairn, Kate was her name, which I kent, for still she wad say nae word at awe, and I could not tell what she could comprehend and what she could not, and baith things it seemed tae me wad serve her naething but ill.

It was about then, or some time later, I ken not truly, when I saw Sawney's horse standing amang the trees like something out o a dream. When he saw me he let out a call,

but he cam not tae me as he aye wad hae done, and when I
went ower tae him I could see that he was sarely wounded
and could dae nae mair than stand.

-Whaur is yer maister? I asked him, and I think even if he
had been a creature o speech he could not hae replied. But a
bit frae him I found Sawney lying on his front, his sword
still in his hand. Near by him lay a sodger, for the dragoons, themsels maybe anxious tae be awa frae that place,
had been careless about their ain deid.

I bent ower him, he was bludie frae his bonnet tae his
boots, and tae my een certainly deid, when awe at ance, for
he had lain very still, he turned his heid and opened his een.

I ken not what I thought then for I canna recall that time
in words, but it might weel hae been that he just stared at
me, and I at him, and there was nae words at awe said, and
his een just closed again. I touched his cheek, neither kenning if what I had seen was true or false, and ance mair he
opened his een.

-Lord save us awe, he said.

-Weel, I telt him, still hardly kenning if I was speaking
tae a deid man or a living. -He has done a very poor job o
that, for ye are the second that I hae found wae any breath
at awe in them, and I ken not how that can be, that ither
deed o grief and despair.

For a time he was very silent as if his ain mind was a far
awa thing, and then he said,

-Are they awe deid?

-Awe that I hae found, o them that fell in the fight, and
them that lie in the wood. Whaur are ye hurt, and are ye tae
shortly tae dee?

-I canna move at awe Agnes, my horse went doun, and
whether I was shot or cut I canna tell. I shot ane man wha
was coming tae finish the wark, but I ken nae mair.

I found wounds in plenty on him, but the main ane was a
sword-cut that had unstrung the hams o his legs in a way
that was beyond any skill o man or nature tae mend, and I
telt him that live he might but he wad never walk or sit on a
horse again. Whether he heard my words, or whether they
made any sense tae him I ken not, for awe he said in reply
was,

403

-They fought weel, as weel as any ever fought.

-Och weel enough, weel enough, but the piper is deid and the dance is ower.

-I ken not why we should be alive, are ye no hurt at awe?

-Naething serious, I picked up the bairn and rade awa.

I ken not truly how lang I sat there wae Sawney's heid in my lap. The bairn still wad not cam doun frae the horse's back, trusting mair in it than any human thing. And perhaps it was that we were awe silent, wondering in our different ways why we were not amang the deid, or whaur the souls o the deid now were, whether in Heaven or Hell? I mind very clearly thinking that they were maist likely in nae place at awe, but were just deid.

At some point, I ken not when, but out o the trees cam this ither bairn, a lad of about eleven or twelve, and behind him anither younger ane, and for ane lang minute they just looked at us like things wha's senses had been reived frae their bodies.

-Are there any mair o ye? I asked the auldest ane. He didna answer, but then mair cam unbidden frae places whaur they had been hiding, the auldest being about twelve. At the sight o them Sawney himsel raised his heid, tears in his een.

-We're no awe deid, the Lord has preserved some.

-Their wits and their legs mair like, I said, for I wad nae langer hae it that the Lord did ought. But gently I took them awe intae my airms, and I kent that they had wandered in the wood, and had seen awe that was tae be seen there, and the mark o it was in awe their faces, and the warld that had been their warld, was now nae langer a warld but a place o blude and chaos, and any talk o the blessings o God in sic a warld seemed itsel like a blasphemy against sense.

I gaithered them up, and wae their help I lifted Sawney on tae the bit cart that was still there. And sae we left that place travelling in the deid o night, and we met nane tae ask us whaur we were ganging, and on the fourth night we cam tae Steenie's cave, and here I telt them we should bide forever and aye, and nae harm should come tae us let the warld gang on as it pleased, it wad be for us neither a place tae remember or tae speak about.

☆

August 1699.
I feel I am looking into a despair beyond despair, which sears my soul and which my mind cannot grasp. The figures from my dream constantly appear to me, whether from memory, or in new dreams, or in my waking hours, it is no longer possible for me to distinguish, but they appear in different garbs and in different forms. The spectre, for I cannot give it the name of a man, mounted on a horse of fire, I often think to be Malecky himself, and the woman who rides by his side I know to be Agnes Douglas.

In some visions she is naked, in others she is clad in black armour, and in yet others she is so enshrouded in a grey plaid that I can only guess that it is her from the way her eyes seek me out.

None of this I can any longer be sure of. I think of Andrew Gilmore's father and his neighbours going up to bury the dead of that bloody muirland brawl, and I do not know how their souls stood it. Did some cry upon Heaven for vengeance, while others dug up their weapons and prepared to fight, with Heaven's help or without it? I think of honest gentle Andrew Gilmore, at that time a mere youth, unsheathing the sword that Sawney Bain had given him. I look over the mountains at the endless storm that pounds them. It has been three days now, and I imagine that God has sent this storm on purpose, that I may have time to compose myself before coming face to face with Steven Malecky. I read over the last unequivocal letter that Mathius Pringle had written to his poor Wattie:

'I confess Wattie, that in the midst of all our trials I had not thought that the last earthly sight mine eyes would behold was the sight of English heretics and sectaries tramping the land unopposed, which is unprecedented in our history. But in this hour that is a trivial thing brought about by our own sins and omissions and lack of faith, an instruction in how poor is our earthly vision. It will pass Wattie, when we are worthy of its passing, when this most stubborn and recalcitrant of people

405

learn to be guided by His word and His word alone, and not by what their weak judgement deems as warldly necessity.

We had the imp of ruin in our grasp, and we allowed him, to this day I do not know how, to escape that grasp. That story you know well enough, and it will serve some purpose if it arms you against the foolish notion that Satan is easily beaten, which many weak people hold to out of cowardice.

It is a great lesson Wattie, that Sawney Bain, who was, as you know, the instrument whereby we apprehended Malecky, did after all his backsliding and confusion, have grace con-ferred on him in such a manner that he alone had the courage to point his sword at ane who was hardly less than Satan himself, and say, tak him if ye hae the courage.

Having thus at the end done his duty he was subsequently killed at the battle of Dunbar, joyful and ignorant, for we were at fault not he, that Malecky in the confusion after Dunbar, slipped ance again from our grasp.

I cannot believe Wattie, anything other than that he is still at large and Israel will not be restored to us until he is finally struck down.

So I charge you with this Wattie, that when you hear aught of him, and be assured that you will, for he is not ane to ever be slack when mischief is afoot, you are to seek him out and destroy him. Any means that come to hand are permissible, for subterfuge, poison, treachery and deceit, are his own true weapons and he must be met with them.

You are not a soldierly man Wattie, which is not to be regretted, it will save you from rash and foolish acts for he is uncommonly skillful with his weapons, but against Christian resolution he has no defence. As you know, Mr Dalyrimple of Aberdeen drove him from his sight with a flick of his hand, despite Malecky's drawn sword, which was of less use to him than if he had wielded a feather in his hand. And when I myself arrested him in Edinburgh he made no attempt, well armed and well mounted as he was, to either fight or flee.

Seek him out Wattie, and let the Lord guide your hand, which He will do, and see to it that you neither hesitate or falter in the obeying of that guidance.'

☆

Nane ever deed in our cave, which Sawney said was a miracle, and a sign of the Lord's gude will. And whiles it seemed tae me that it could hardly be ither than a miracle, for mysel wha had ance thought never tae hae bairns, now had them wae as much ease as I had previously avoided them. As indeed did awe ithers when they cam tae their proper age. Nor did any o these bairns dee when they were born, or when they were bairns, which had never been heard of before, nor could hae been thought possible.

The strings in Sawney legs did not heal, which, he declared, was in nae way because sic a miracle could not happen, but was the Lord minding us o the warld outside and awe its warks, which He had abandoned tae the chaos o its ain passions, and wad hae us abandon tae. But o this cave He had made anither Eden, and it was His will that we should bide there and multiply till the appointed hour when He wad call us forth. And was not the proof o this the fact that neither death nor famine nor pestilence visited us, forbye we kent very weel that they raged mightily in Chaos.

I minded very weel how they had raged, and how they still raged, but the bairns we had brought tae the cave minded very little, and it may be that in time they minded naething at awe. I ken not, Sawney wad indeed strive for an explanation, for sic was his nature and had aye been, and it might weel be that his brain at last becam addled wae sic striving, and his memory o things nae mair than a whig-maleerie flitting between Heaven and Hell and visiting despair upon the route.

I canna say truly. Whiles he wad say nae word at awe for days and nights, but wad converse only wae his Bible, and sic angels and spirits that he said visited him, forbye they were never witnessed by mysel or any ither, and his speech tae them, for he spoke lang, was in nae tongue that he had previously kent, neither the Lawland or the Hielan, or the Swedish or the German.

At ither times he was a maist cheerful man, dinging doctrine, and catechism, and psalms, intae the bairn's heids, sae that awe becam maist proficient.

The darkest times cam when nae angels visited him, and he could tak nae pleasure in our company, or his ain, and even his Bible it seemed, was small comfort tae him then. But these times wad pass, signified by some sign or ither he wad receive frae Jesus, or frae some angel wha's name he kent, for in time he kent half the Heavenly host by name.

For mysel I troubled my heid very little wae sic matters, but wad think lang on the road that we had ganged, wild and far awa as it now seemed, and whether this place was a blessed place, or a place o despair, or whether it was a beginning or an end, I ken not.

☆

On the fourth day the rains had stopped. The minister was once again in the saddle riding behind Roderick Dhu, through narrower defiles than any they had previously encountered. The Highlander's manner, the minister observed, was cheerful, almost gay, hailing everyone they met, and they in turn hailing him. He is happy, the minister thought, that he is nearly home and at the end of his task.

Towards the late afternoon they passed through a dark and awesome glen whose granite slopes towering on either side seemed to the minister to divide time itself. As they reached the furthest point the landscape broadened out into a rich green valley surrounded by mountains. Cottages now appeared, and from the doorway of each, tartan-clad figures saluted them, Roderick Dhu, who now rode alongside the minister, answering each by name.

'My people are a mite curious Sir, for which I apologise.'

'Am I that much of a curiosity?'

'I hae lang sent word ahead Sir in order that we should be properly received, and nae doubt that word has got about. . . And why, there is my kinsman Neil Roy himself.'

The minister watched as a stalwart man of about forty rode towards them, mounted on a tolerably good horse, his dress that of a high ranking Highlander. He appeared to be alone and without arms. When he drew alongside them he doffed his bonnet and bowed slightly.

'Ye are welcome Sir, in Macgregor's country.'

The minister returned the bow. He saw features in which guile, good nature, and pride were equally mixed, a savage mountain chieftain with the name of an outlaw and the manners of an archaic king. The minister's companion he embraced in an extravagant fashion, addressing him in his own language so that the minister had no idea what passed between them. When he turned to the minister again an extraordinary candour had taken over his features.

'Sir,' said he. 'I hae sad news for ye which will be ill tae bear after sae lang a journey, but your sadness is shared by us awe.'

The minister glanced quickly from the chieftain to Roderick Dhu. It seemed to him that his features had also changed.

'Mr Malecky is deid, Sir. He deed suddenly and quietly twa nights ago.'

The minister closed his eyes. He felt his head reel. For a time that seemed endless he felt in danger of falling from his horse. When he opened his eyes Neil Roy's arm was steadying him, his gaze penetrating his. Robbed of pride it now seemed a dissembling thing.

'Come Sir, he was a very auld man.'

The minister closed his eyes again, a sensation between laughter and pain burst in his bowels and rose to engorge his soul.

'Is your hurt then sae great? Even when ye did not ken Mr Malecky?'

With an effort the minister recovered himself. Both Roderick Dhu and Neil Roy were now regarding him with expressions which he could not decipher. A short distance away a woman waited with three children. Vaguely he realised that they were Roderick Dhu's wife and family. The man was saddened and anxious to be gone. He was waiting to be thanked? He was waiting to be dismissed? The minister did not know, from every doorway and vantage point in the glen tartan-clad figures watched him, beneath the cool perplexity of their gaze he felt their hatred. He felt Neil Roy's voice breaking it.

'Ride with me a bit Sir, ye will of course while ye are here, bide in my house.'

The minister steadied himself. He said goodbye to Roderick and thanked him for his services. The Highlander bowed slightly, the expression on his face as aloof as when the minister had first met him. The chieftain touched his arm.

409

'Come Sir, I think ye are in need of some refreshment.'

The minister rode alongside Neil Roy through the village. He felt the clanspeople's eyes on him, now no longer merely curious, but fiercely probing his very existence.

'The people are generally sad Sir . . .'

The minister's senses reduced the chieftain's words to a prattling sound. This fellow, he thought, can see that I am moved, but he can have no idea of the consternation that I feel.'

'But why Sir? Death is the end for awe, and in its appointed hour will not be jouked, and indeed Steenie was not uncheerful at the prospect. He looked quietly at me and declared, 'Why Neil Roy, I fear Catriona was right, and I will not get tae meet this minister wha is sae anxious tae meet me.' And he bade us awe gude-night as if he was quite sensible of his condition, and was nae mair afraid of it than he was of any ither thing.'

'Catriona?'

'My mither's sister Sir, and Mr Malecky's wife. Amang us she has the reputation of haeving the sight, which has been demonstrated true on many occasions, and she had said that Steenie could send for the black man as he pleased, but he wad not meet him.'

'By the black man she meant myself?'

'Weel I think she could mean nae ither.'

The minister felt his whole being shudder. He glanced at the clansman and it seemed to him that Neil Roy returned his look with one of such shrewd penetration, that the minister, though it had been impressed upon him that the laws of Highland hospitality were inviolable, felt suddenly afraid of him.

'She was merely describing your clothes Sir, which are of course nae mair than those of your calling.'

The minister sighed. In his own parish the Black Man was a peasant name for the Devil. Whether Neil Roy was aware of that the minister could not tell. The Highlander drew up at the door of a house which by the standards of the Highlands was rather a fine one, and politely indicated to the minister that he should dismount. The minister did so, mastering an apprehension that his legs would no longer bear his weight.

He was greeted at the doorway by a fair, handsome woman who was Neil Roy's wife. The greeting was cold the minister thought, and the woman quickly excused herself.

410

'She has reason tae be grateful tae Steenie and deeply laments his passing. But come ye are welcome, and sit yourself doun.'

He ushered the minister to a seat beside a good fire. He poured whisky from a flask into two glasses and handed the minister one. For once the minister was grateful for the drink, it enabled him to be quiet and plead his weariness.

His eyes travelled round the room taking in the barbaric weapons which hung from the walls amid the lengths of tartan which passed for draperies, the rough furniture with the occasional fine piece. It was the best house he had been in since coming to the Highlands. On the floor above he could hear the sounds of the woman moving about. He had, he thought, felt many conflicting things when he had resolved to make the journey here with Roderick Dhu, but a Christian purpose over-ruled them all. Now he felt like a foolish man being tolerated by an Amalekite chieftain.

'It is strange is it not, that ye should come awe this way, and sic a thing happen at sic a time?'

'God calls us all in his own time.'

'Aye indeed sae Sir.'

The minister hesitated, aware of Neil Roy's gently questing eyes.

'As God has decreed that Mr Malecky and I are not to meet, would it be right, or indeed proper, that I should speak to his wife?'

The Highlander's features broke into an open smile, which would have re-assured the minister, were it not for the fact that he no longer trusted the man.

'Och Sir, whether it be right or proper I ken not. Are there rules in sic matters? What I dae ken is that Catriona has asked that ye gang tae see her, and she is not a woman that likes tae be denied.'

They had anticipated, it seemed, a request that had been slowly forming itself in his head. The minister's brain besieged with suspicion, could make nothing reasonable out of that.

'Then gladly I will go and see her.'

'Tomorrow Sir, I will gie ye a guide wha will tak ye tae her, tae the house on the hill whaur she and Mr Malecky lived.'

For a moment Neil Roy appeared to hesitate.

'I ken not what your business was wae Mr Malecky, Sir, and I trust ye will pardon me for speaking plainly. He was a man Sir, that awe true hearted folk that kent him, loved him, and, as is generally the case many false hearted folk hated him. I was against him sending for ye, I mean nae offence, my mother's sister said that it was an ill thing and ill would come of it. That aside, it was Mr Malecky himself wha insisted on it. But as he is now deid, and if it is no great secret, I wad like tae ken your business wae him.'

'I had some news of friends of his, who are themselves both now dead, but all three were originally of the parish of which I am now pastor.

Neil Roy rose to his feet. The minister noticed with some satisfaction the irritation on his brow.

'Weel Sir I will trouble ye nae mair on that point, and nae doubt ye are tired. Ye shall eat and then ye can rest. While ye are in my house Sir, think o it as your ain.'

'I am grateful Sir.'

'I wad say the same tae any wandering beggar wha cam tae my door, sae I can surely say it tae a friend of Steenie Malecky's.'

August 24th 1699.

I feel as if I am in a wilderness of lies. At supper the chieftain and his family were courtesy itself, and yet I feel they hate me. That I may be misjudging them I am aware, but I strongly suspect that they, and all the people of this tribe think that I am responsible for Malecky's death. I cannot be sure, but given the ravings of her they regard as a prophetess, I cannot think it unlikely.

I have prayed long and hard tonight for a meaning to all of this, and if there is one, and I must believe there is one, it escapes me. Indeed it is as if the meaning that I sought has turned to a thing of dust as I was about to grasp it.

I have considered all my actions. I have reflected on the strange irony that if it had not been for the rains I might have confronted Malecky on his deathbed. Indeed I have considered that I may have been mistaken about Malecky himself, for these rude people do seem to hold him in extraordinary high regard.

412

That is of course not a new or unusual thing, and I cannot forget the pitiful case of Helen Melville, or all that has passed, or the blasphemies, sacrileges, and sorceries, attributed to him. And yet, I believe I did not entirely discount the possibility that I might have found an entirely different man – but to find none at all . . .

I do not expect to sleep much tonight. I stand by the window of what I believe is the best room in the house and look down into the valley. The Children of the Mist, these people style themselves, and indeed it is easy to fancy that the mist itself has conjured them up and will as easily dissipate them, for they seem to my eyes to belong to no earthly time.

That this is a fancy I well understand, for their fierce and bloody reputation seems to be a well attested thing. Indeed Mr Gilmarten in his book gives this particular clan a special mention as unregenerate renegades. They of course see themselves in quite a different light as a much persecuted and wronged people. Whatever the truth of the matter is, that they bear their lot with a stoical, indeed to a Christian mind, insufferable pride, can hardly be denied them.

Tomorrow I must climb a hill to meet Malecky's widow, this prophetess of theirs. I wonder at that, did the wretched man always choose to live on the tops of hills, and is the country to have yet another Steenie's Hill? I wonder too, what I shall meet with in this prophetess. She is a very old woman now, but that she is indeed the savage Catriona of the Mist, intimate friend of Agnes Douglas, is no longer in any doubt, and indeed thinking of her in ungodly alliance with Malecky I quake in my soul for these people.

☆

'Here is the man wha will guide ye tae Catriona.'

The minister looked at a short, sturdy, bearded Highlander. Lachlan Oig was his name and Neil Roy had vouched for him as a reliable man. To the minister's eyes he looked like a grinning ruffian. The chieftain handed the reins of a Highland pony to the minister.

'It will be a handier beast for the climb, and your ain fine horse could dae wae a rest. I hae instructed Lachlan tae tak ye

413

there and bide until ye choose tae return.'

The minister thanked him and mounted the pony. Lachlan preferred to travel on foot, trotting effortlessly at the minister's side.

For a time the journey was easy until they left the glen and started to climb steeply up the mountainside, Lachlan directing the minister with a combination of gestures and cries, which dimly he realised, the clansman thought was comprehensible English.

The minister, following Neil Roy's advice, allowed the pony to pick its own way, quickly appreciating that it was an extraordinarily sure-footed animal. His guide trotted ahead, leaping like a cat over every impediment. In such a fashion they wound their way higher and higher up the mountain. When the minister looked back, the glen and all it contained had receded behind a blanket of mist. When they were almost at the top of the pass, Lachlan stopped, and pointing with his arm he gesticulated towards a ridge high above them.

'Catriona's dugs.'

The minister looked up. There outlined against the sky stood two large hounds of the kind the minister was now accustomed to. First one and then the other started a long deep-throated baying, and now alongside them stood the figure of a woman. The minister could hardly make her out, but she waved to them and called out in her own tongue, which Lachlan answered. For a few minutes the minister felt himself the ignorant subject of their wild and incomprehensible dialogue. He looked at Lachlan's long dirk. How simply, and without the slightest possibility that the world outside the glen would ever hear of it, she could order the Highlander to kill him.

Lachlan turned to face him, his uncouth bearded face pitted faintly with the small pox. He grinned like some mountain demon.

'Ye Sir . . .'

The minister watched him struggling for words. He pointed once again to the woman.

'Catriona . . ! She calls ye . . .'

The minister understood that he was to go up alone. Lachlan by a number of gesticulations appeared to imply that he would wait at the foot of the crag. As well as he could, he thanked the man, and nudged the pony forward on the last part of the precipitous climb. On once turning he saw Lachlan running like a deer down the mountainside.

When he reached the top of the crag the two hounds investigated him briefly, and then at a word from their mistress they loped silent as wolves to her side. She sat enthroned on a finely carved chair in front of a neat well constructed cottage.

The woman herself was an ancient crone with snow-white hair. For a moment she simply stared at the minister, then with the aid of a staff she drew herself upright in the chair, throwing back her plaid.

'Good-day madam.'

She nodded her head slowly.

'Ye hae cam ower late for him ye sought.'

'So I have heard.'

'Hae ye nae condolences tae offer tae ane that has been sae newly widowed?

For a moment it seemed to the minister that her voice contained its own echo.

'I . . .'

'Say nae mair Sir, ere ye damn yer soul wae falseness, for I canna believe that ye regret his passing ower much.'

'I deeply regret not meeting him.'

'There was never any fear o that Sir. I telt him lang ago that ane day a man in black clothes wad cam riding North tae seek him, but wad be disappointed in his seeking. The loun just laughed. But as ye see Sir, why even the cleverest man on earth can be a damn fool in some things.'

The minister neither knew how to deport himself or reply. For a space of time there was a heavy silence in which the woman seemed to slip away, and then once more her voice rang out.

'Bide not ower lang amang my people . . . Oh they will not harm ye, think ye not that, but they ken Catriona's words, and ye hae cam, and they hae lost a friend. Nane is tae blame for it, it was time he was awa.'

Suddenly she stood up. Even as an old woman she was tall and straight and hardly seemed to need the support of the staff. For a moment the minister felt himself inexplicably over-awed.

It was as if she dictated to the air of the place.

'Now Sir, why hae ye cam, and think weel before ye answer, for ye are ower much o a freshwater man tae carry me wae some bairn's tale.'

'I have some news of old friends of his.'

The old woman smiled. Astonished, the minister felt his cheeks go red. She bent down to stroke the neck of the hound.

'Why Bran, he thinks that Catriona o the Mist is naught but a girl.'

She straightened herself up, her eyes once more scrutinising him impassively.

'Why Sir, are ye sae fond o him and his friends that ye wad travel frae the far South-West tae the Hielans? For if ye are sae fond ye are the first o the black-coated gentry tae feel sae kindly. Why Sir, the lave o them wad be reiving the earth tae find his corpse and think their een blest at the sight o it.'

The woman's voice now rang in his ears shrill as a predatory bird's.

'To be plain, he was named as a warlock, and was believed to be such by all who had Christian knowledge of these matters.'

The woman smiled again. The minister felt his chest tighten. Her smile like a hideous scar yawned mockingly.

'Why, even in my own parish there is a young woman that he bewitched and seduced, a mere child.'

'Weel Sir, ye are a brave man, and nae doubt but what ye say is true, though bewitched is maybe an ower strang word, for the lassie was willing enough, and minds him fondly enough . . . Or dae ye Sir, mean tae imply that force was used?

'He took advantage of her.'

The woman thumped the ground fiercely with her staff.

'Nae mair Sir, nae mair, I hae kent the man lang and will not hae him damned in his grave. The lassie, I ken, has nae mair than kind thoughts for a kindly auld man, and if some ither words hae cam tae her lips, then some damned carrion craw that kens not a true heart has put them there.'

'I forbid you to speak like that.'

'Forbid Sir! Why Bran, it wad seem our black-coated gentlemen kens not truly why he cam, or truly whaur he is.'

'There is a God in Heaven, old woman.'

'Nae doubt there maun be, for his servants lie like a pestilence upon the earth . . . That was Steenie's opinion, for mysel I care as little for the gudeman in Heaven as I dae for the false-hearted that in his name wad rule the earth.'

'You are blaspheming, old woman, I tremble for you.'

The woman stamped her staff on the ground.

'Tremble as ye please.'

The minister felt an awful tremor run through his body. He strove to contain it, when suddenly staring into the grey caverns of the woman's eyes, he realised that she was quite blind. For a moment this knowledge overwhelmed his senses.

'I beg your pardon, but such blasphemies compel me to protest. But I realise that living as you do you have been denied any proper religious instruction.'

'Ye hated him, and ye wad hae burned him, if ye could but hae caught him. But aye he jouked ye, aye he was swifter tae escape than ye were tae grasp, but aye like wolves ye took up the scent. And now ye hae cam and he, he has jouked ye again, fairly and for aye.

'Warlock ye cried him! Sorcerer and witchifier, and ye ken not how he laughed at sic nonsense, aye and dreamed o a day, that maybe itsel was but a dream, when sic things that sae bedevil the minds o people, wad become like dust under their feet.'

The minister felt his anger rising. Old, blind, and ignorant, she might be, but the devil dwelt within her, as he was now convinced the Devil had indeed dwelt within Malecky. It was his duty to fight that Devil.

'I also bring you news of Alexander Bain and Agnes Douglas.'

'Agnes Dhu, but she is lang deid, and Sawney tae. I ken awe this weel, why dae ye think it should be news tae me?'

'Do you know how they died?'

'Hinged and burned!'

'How do you know this?'

'How is it not tae be kent? Dae ye not ken how far and wide yer deeds are written? Are ye deaf tae awe but the thunder o yer ain tongues? Why Agnes Dhu hersel has telt me awe that I need tae ken. Like a dark wind she comes tae me frae far beyond the mountains, and I ken her by the beat of her heart, which I ken very weel, as I ken very weel why ye hae cam sae far intae the country o the True People. Tae seek out Steenie Malecky, aye

417

and tae find out if any answer lay in him, aye, and maybe tae kill that answer if ye had found it, forbye I dinna think ye wad hae succeeded in that. But awe these things were in yer mind, raddling it day and night. Weel Sir, now ye hae cam, and ye hae found him tae be but mouldering dust like awe deid things, and only mad, auld Catriona o the Mist tae feed ye Hielan rant, and aiblins that will counter that which is in yer soul and aiblins it will not.'

Suddenly she stretched her staff out and gave the minister a rough thrust in the chest. He staggered back a few paces, astounded.

'What say ye Sir? Wad ye murder me tae? Ye hae a pistol I dinna doubt, and I hae ane tae, and sall meet ye at ten paces if sic is yer wish, and then an end will be put tae the last o yer torments.'

'I have no thought or wish to murder anyone, least of all you.'

'Nae heart for the deed mair like.'

'You are mad.'

'Och there is little doubt o that. And ye nae doubt are a very clear headed man, and a minister o the Reformed Kirk that is now a power in the land. Not the power that it ance dreamed it wad be, begging now its leave tae preach frae an earthly king, wha is nae doubt blithe tae see it break its rods on the backs o a sare-ridden people, that it in its gude sense kens will never rise again.'

'I do not understand you.'

'It matters little if ye understand me, tis yersel ye maun understand, and it is plain tae me that ye dae not that.'

'I think I understand myself quite well enough.'

'Come Sir, enough o this protestation o what a sane man ye are, ere ye drive yersel mad ere ye gang hame. For already I see in ye enough ranting and stamping tae boil the blude o maist men, as ye boiled the blude o Agnes Dhu, and ye wad boil the blude o Helen Melville tae gin ye had the chance.'

'What Devil makes you say that?'

'What Deevil? Och Sir, but ye are a bairn, for did ye not rage and rant and storm at her, flinging her frae ye wae harsh words? And did not yer heart rage against her mair fiercely than yer words? When it may be that yer true desire was tae dae nae mair than fling yersel upon her, but awe yer een could see was Steenie Malecky's arms about her. Och Sir, tis sae plain tae see, that I wha hae nae living een in my heid can see it.'

'How can you dare? I have my duties, and for one such as yourself to impute such blasphemies . . .'

Catriona raised her staff. For a moment she stood poised, and then with a swift and confident movement she advanced upon him. She was now very close. He did not know if she knew how close. He could not move away. He knew that if he took one backward step it would be tantamount to flight. He felt her breath caress his cheek as if it had become a sense that replaced her sight.

'Madam . . .'

'I am nae madam, I am Catriona o the Mist, wha could if she chose, snap her fingers and hae ye killit.'

'I was told, I have your chief's word that, I am in no danger.'

'Why Sir, there are wolves in these mountains are there not, are the people tae bear the blame if ane should mak a meal o your soft flesh?'

'I think that most unlikely.'

'Why Sir, if Catriona o the Mist is of service at awe tae her people, it is tae warn them of unlikely things, aye and maybe even impossible things . . .'

'I fail to comprehend you. That your people think of you as a prophetess I am well aware . . .'

'But ye Sir, hae a reason and an understanding far aboun sic things. '

'I do not mean to offend you.'

'Och minister ye are indeed but a freshwater man. I can feel the ground Sir, trembling beneath yer feet, the heart trembling in yer breast. Baith things are wiser in their fears than yer words are brave in their pride. For there is a dark road before ye alang which ye sall gang whether ye will or no, and it will lead ye tae a place that is not presently kent, and may weel be nae place at awe, and then again it may weel be a place that is very real for awe that, and it may be that it will be a place o joy, and it may be that it will be a place o sadness, and it may be that ye sall not hae the power tae tell ane frae the ither, and yer heart will be untrue tae yer senses, and yer senses untrue tae yer heart, and the ane will love them that ye scorn, and the ither will scorn them that ye love, and och but I pity ye, for I see a great wolf beast on that dark road, and whether it is leading ye on, or whether it is hunting ye doun, I ken not.'

'Please desist . . .'

'It is a road alang which many afore ye hae ganged, wae white steel in their hands, weel busked in the armour o their choice, and wae Godly slogans on their lips that wracked the ear o Heaven, and awe the answer they got at the finish, I hae brought ye tae the ring and now ye maun dance!'

The minister felt his reason disintegrating, something unspeakable was swelling inside the woman. He tried to cover his eyes, he tried to move away. but with a movement that was barely perceptible Catriona was always with him, an expression in her blind eyes more malevolent than anything the minister had previously encountered, asleep or awake. Suddenly it was as if he was faced with a dreadful metamorphosis,

> Had we twa been upon the green,
> And never an ee atween,
> I wat I wad hae had ye Flesh and Fell,
> But yer soul sall gang we me.

'Why Sir, if ye retreat any further I fear ye will put Lachlan tae the trouble o carrying ye hame.'

The minister looked round. He was dangerously near the edge of the precipice, and yet with relentless pressure she thrust him back. He felt a savage desire to simply fling her aside, and yet he knew it was an impossible thing to do, neither his strength or his nerves were equal to the task. Catriona seemed to possess both an ephemeral lightness and an impossible solidity. Once again her hideous countenance metamorphosed before his eyes, passing through a battlefield of rage and torment.

Suddenly he knew there was nothing imaginary about his danger. The temptation to thrust him over the edge was seething like a fury in the woman's breast, and yet still he could make no move to defend himself. Her body, burning with a Satanic heat, pressed itself hard against his. Slowly she raised her staff high in the air above his head and let out a hideous yell in her own language, and then as slowly as she had raised the staff she grounded it.

The collision as it struck the earth was more awful to the minister's ears than his senses could explain. It was as if these same senses, along with his reason, had ceased to serve him in any way that he could comprehend. Transfixed, he watched the slow movement of her head towards him and felt the soft flesh of her lips caressing his.

'When these people that hae been for the present dinged doun, rise again, as ane day they surely will, it sall not be for King or Kirk or God in Heaven that they rise, and they will ask nae leave o ony.'

She took a few paces backwards, her sightless gaze never leaving the minister's.

'Now Sir, I wha had ye fairly, as ye ken in yer heart, hae fairly gien ye quarter, and I hae telt ye awe that ye wish tae ken, sae now tak yersel frae this place and trouble me nae mair.'

Slowly she turned her back on him and started to stalk her way back to the cottage. The minister watched her go, suddenly reduced to an old blind woman with a staff. He now felt a strange inexplicable desire to call her back, and yet, as powerless as he had been to resist her, he was now powerless to call her name. He simply watched her go, her plaid thrown back, and her great mane of white hair cascading over her back.

He started to walk after her, and yet the impossibility of catching her, or calling to her, or making her turn back, was now quite clear in his mind. Without any further acknowledgement of him she closed her cottage door behind her, and the two hounds moved without any outward show of menace to block any attempt he might make to follow her.

For a moment he stood still, his eyes surveying the impossible place and the impossible landscape that surrounded it, before he turned and walked back to where his pony stood. He took up the reins, realising with a sudden sharp anguish that he did not trust himself to mount it or ride it. He started to pick his way down from the crag on foot, allowing it to follow him. At the bottom he found Lachlan calmly smoking his pipe. He turned his head, his eyes glinting cheerfully.

'She is well?'

The minister had no idea whether Lachlan meant this as a

question or a statement. He had no idea how long the man had been sitting there, or if he had observed anything at all. Coolly he took the reins of the pony and gestured to the minister to mount.

This the minister now did, and for a moment it appeared as if Lachlan was reluctant to release the bridle, as if he was aware that the sturdy horseman who had ridden up the mountain was a very different man from the frail rider who was coming down it.

☆

August 27th. 1699.
The chieftain has offered to guide me from his glen as far as the Highland Line. This he does out of a laudable concern for my safety, and a fervent wish to see me depart from his domain. Alas, my own desire to be gone, is greater than his to see me go, nor have I any desire for his company, but I must accept it, or risk wandering in these mountains forever.

As we rode through the village from each cottage the clanspeople came to their doors, as if to re-assure themselves that I was leaving. I know I judge them harshly, but I cannot see them otherwise than as a race of warlike children over whom Malecky's malign spirit lies. Nor can I rid my mind of the feeling that they are all privy to a dark conspiracy, and that I have been lured to this place to be the victim of a Satanic prank hatched out by a hideous mountain witch.

Before we left the glen Roderick Dhu stepped forward surrounded by his family. He doffed his bonnet in his customary extravagant fashion.

'Fare ye weel Sir, I hope ye will mind Roderick Dhu and his people in your prayers.'

I thanked him once again for his services, and blessed each of his family in turn. He thanked me for this with much feeling, being quite ignorant of the fact that while I administered the blessing my soul was quaking for him and all his people.

At the entrance to the pass I turned and looked for the last time on that gentle valley guarded by its mountains and its mist. I will never come here again, nor will I ever be able to erase the memory of this place from my mind.

They rode silently in single file. The minister felt no desire to break it. Often the minister would entirely forget his companion's existence. At other times he would stare covertly at the broad back in front of him. He rode his horse with his feet dangling free of the stirrups in the careless, indolent Highland manner. A Lord of creation, the minister thought bitterly, securely and unshakeably astride the complacent beast of his own pride.

In these moments the minister felt an anger akin to a blasphemous hatred for all things human raging like a torrent through his mind. He wanted to thrust the man from his horse and order him to pray for forgiveness, as he had wanted to wring the neck of their blind prophetess.

When on occasion Neil Roy turned his head as if assuring himself that his guest was still with him, the minister had seen himself reflected in the dissembling mirror of his countenance as a ridiculous thing, a shambling cleric stumbling helplessly in a heathen wilderness, owing his survival to savages who were too ignorant to be afraid.

When the road was wider Neil Roy held his mount back a few paces so that he was now riding alongside the minister.

'You're an unco silent man Sir.'

'I apologise, but I have much on my mind.'

For a time the chieftain again fell in with the minister's mood, and then as if suddenly tiring of it, he said:

'I wad hae liked it if ye had visited us in a happier time, for we can be a blithe enough people tae our friends. But this curse of outlawry, which was lifted on account of our loyal service, has ance again been visited on us by the usurper William of Orange. And again Sir, it is as it has been for near a hundred years, that only our swords and wits defend us that bear a name mair royal than any that ever cam out of Holland.'

'To my mind it would seem an unwise and unkind decree.'

'Ye call it unwise and unkind, but ithers Sir, call it great and good and just that we should be hunted day and night, murdered if they could but find the means, doun tae the last bairn, and they wad see the warld as a happier place if nane young or auld of our name walked upon it. Tis strange is it not, that sic a great hatred should be borne by sae few?'

'I agree that it seems to me excessive to visit it from generation to generation.'

Neil Roy fell silent, coldly silent the minister thought. He could do little about it, his own mind was a turbulence, and he confessed to himself he did not know what could or should be done with this tribe of intractable heathens, and if he was undoubtedly a better chief to his people than Doig was laird to his tenants, that seemed to only further complicate the question.

It was some time before Neil Roy spoke again.

'I think Sir, and pardon me if I am wrang, but my mother's sister has much affected ye.'

The minister felt sharply irritated. He had put up, out of necessity, with this man's company, his silent scrutiny, his veiled questions, and now he was trying to inquire into the state of his soul.

'She aye has that effect Sir, in wha ever gangs near her. I hae kent her awe my life, and still I canna say that I ken her truly. And times I think that the power that has been wae her awe her life, tae ken men's thoughts and deeds, lang afore they themsels thought them, or thought tae dae them, rises at times tae near owerwhelm her, sae that the words she utters are their ain maisters, and she but the mistress o their birth. And yet, I ken, as awe the people ken, that words which appear tae be nonsense when she first speaks them, hae a sense o their ain which is in time revealed. We ken this, but still I wad not hae ye troubled ower much on her behalf.'

The minister looked at him. He found the man's words impudent, but whether Neil Roy meant them to be compassionate or mocking he could not tell.

'I am a minister of the gospel Sir. If my heart is troubled at finding pagan superstition in a Christian land then I believe it is justified in being so. But believe me, I have faith in a power which is sufficient to prevent me being affected.'

For a moment the minister could see that Neil Roy was actually angry. There was, he thought, a discreditable satisfaction in that.

'Aye weel Sir, I'll say nae mair.'

'I did not mean to offend you.'

424

'I think I am mysel the best judge of when I am offended.'

'If I might speak plainly . . ?'

'As plainly as ye please Sir, which is the only way tae my mind an honest man should speak.'

'I cannot believe otherwise than that your people would benefit greatly from the building of a kirk, and the installing there of a good and Christian man who speaks your own language.'

'Ye may be richt Sir, ye may be richt, but I ken not whaur sic a man is tae be found, and tae be plain mysel, we hae had a pickle in the past, and a pickle kirks tae, but little good we ever got o them. But ye are mistaken Sir if ye think that I, or my clan, are enemies of true religion, or indeed of education. Why Mr Malecky himsel undertook tae act as dominie, and if he had little inclination for preaching nane could deny that he was a very learned man . . .'

'Mr Malecky?'

'Aye indeed Sir. Why he had hardly returned tae us a six month when he gaes tae my forebear and says, Patrick Roy, for that was his name, this warld is a changing place, and the bairns o the Gregorach maun learn mair than their swords, they maun learn their letters tae.

'Weel, for that purpose a school was built, and Maister Malecky wad impart awe that he kent tae awe that wad learn it, and wad ding reason intae heids wae great persistence, which I ken very weel haeving mysel sat at his feet when a bairn.'

The minister felt his heart crushed. He rode in silence, his mind burdened by more weight than he felt it could bear. If Neil Roy noticed anything of this he gave no indication of it. He reasons, the minister thought, that if I have come such a long way to meet Malecky I will welcome a conversation about him.

'I still think that if you now sought the services of a Godly man and made him welcome, it would be to your great spiritual benefit, and perhaps even earthly advantage.'

'Weel Sir, if ye ken sic a man, and he is willing, then nae doubt he will be made welcome. But ye maun tell sic a man, that he wad be dwelling amang the wild Gregorach that hae been put tae the horn a hundred years, and are beset by enemies on awe sides, as weel as king and state.'

The minister felt the brazen challenge in the chieftain's words. He felt his heart sickening under the awful truth, that it mattered very little to him what happened to them, and perhaps it no longer mattered what happened to anyone in this land. He felt less for them than Marten Gilmarten, who at least desired to civilise them, forcibly if need be. Did he truly know that he would find a race of prideful heathens dominated by a blaspheming witch, and having learnt the rudiments of learning from a confirmed atheist, warlock, and political renegade?

The minister eventually parted from Neil Roy at a point which the chieftain declared was already beyond the Highland Line.

'Afore ye lies the Sheriffmuir, and if ye keep tae the road across it, and ride briskly, ye should be in Stirling afore the night.'

The minister shook hands with him before they parted. Fifty yards away from him he turned. The Highlander was still stationary on the ridge where he had left him.

Neil Roy, seeing the minister turn, raised his right hand in salute before turning his horse down the other side of the ridge. For a moment the minister imagined him, this friend, intimate, and student of Steven Malecky, sitting indolently aloft his horse allowing it to pick its own way and its own route down from the ridge, his mind picking over the enigma of his strange guest. He would be content that hospitality had been satisfied, honour had been satisfied, and that he personally had seen to all of these things as a chieftain should.

And yet, the minister thought bitterly, if he knew but a tenth of my true feelings, he might well think me stark mad.

The minister turned to face the broad desolate expanse of the Sheriffmuir, bounded to the South by the naked rampart of the Ochil Hills. He felt his soul disintegrating within him. He had dragged it in pursuit of a past which had gaped like a bloody wound. In search of a meaning he had entered at Heaven's command a festering darkness, which had now vomited him forth into this desert, where as far as the eye could see, nothing moved or lived, and Neil of the Mist's assurance that if he followed the road he would reach civilisation by nightfall, merely the final act of a Satanic prank. The minister

426

felt suddenly afraid.

As he rode, this fear turned into an inexplicable terror which seized hold of his will. The night, as if in confirmation of his fear, descended about him, and a hurricane, it now seemed to him, tore across that darkening plain, and dreadful things without beginning, end or meaning raged within it.

He dug his heels hard into his horse. The animal, unused to such treatment, plunged into a gallop, and despite the hooves drumming in his ears the minister felt like an inert thing borne on the back of a storm. He heard himself cry out to Heaven and his own voice burst about his ears, hurled back at him from a void of darkness within which fearful shadows raged. A troop of horses now thundered noiselessly to his right, and a regiment of foot marched to his left. Above them all flew the great Saltire of the Covenant.

The minister sank low in the saddle. He could feel the plunging equine fear between his legs, and all around him the thunderous roar of the twenty-third psalm mingled with the boom of cannon. He looked to the right and the horsemen unsheathed their swords, and the banner rose into the air as if it was no longer fixed to any earthly standard but flew like a living thing over the heads of the soldiers, as if the very elements themselves were surging forward with a Christian battle-cry howling in the wind. Overwhelming the horsemen, overwhelming him, riding knee to knee in a storm of flesh and steel, their banner snapping and cracking like a serpent, and riding high on the crest of that serpent the naked figure of the Douglas woman, a white sword spinning in her hand.

On the road ahead an army of foot appeared, and the sound of musketry cracked in his ears, and like some terrible motion that was of the night itself, the pike-heads rose to meet them, and their shafts splintered against the horse, and the riders flew from their saddles, and the minister heard a cry like a wolf howling in the wind, and faces he knew rose to meet him, and others reeled back soundlessly on their heels, their spears lancing the sky like darkness piercing darkness, and the banner that flew in that darkness was now itself black, and its emblem a naked human figure swinging from a gibbet, and ridden still by its wild rider it plunged in the sky and the earth roared fire at her command.

The minister felt his head split apart, his entrails steam from his bowels. Steel hard points pierced his eyes, slashing blades unstrung his limbs, and the swarming hands of human beasts tore his flesh from his bones, and wolves with one eye red and the other eye golden, raced across the plain, answering his howls with howls of their own.

☆

The minister opened his eyes. The night still heaved about him, but as he looked it seemed to miraculously calm itself, the light of the moon once again casting itself about the hills with a natural glow. He felt neither warm nor cold, the grass beneath him neither wet nor dry. Indeed he could not be sure that the bed upon which he lay was natural grass. Nor could he be sure that the world into which he stared, despite its seeming ordinariness, was any world at all.

His horse stood over him. It seemed to the minister that its sides still heaved and its flesh still trembled, and its moist eyes wept tears of bestial perplexity.

Whether it was then, or some time later, the minister could never be sure, but suddenly he became aware of the distant sound of the pipes. He could not tell how far away they were, or in which direction they were moving, but the air they played was familiar to him, and he believed he had often heard it played in Trig. His memory was not sufficient to give the air a name, but the instrument he felt sure was not the great pipes of the Highlands but the small pipes of the Border.

The minister raised his head. He could see nothing. The music seemed to flit from muirland to mountain, to change direction and cadence, as if some swift, moving element of the night was the musician. He heard himself groaning. He laid his head in his hands. He prayed that whoever played these pipes would appear, and would be a Christian man.

As the minister prayed, his horse let out a sudden piercing whinny, and before the prayer ended the music had stopped, as abruptly as if it had never existed. The silence that followed reduced everything in the minister's mind to an imagined thing until it was broken by a human voice.

'Why Sir, ye hae taen a fall hae ye not?'

The minister tried to turn his head and failed. The voice appeared to change its direction.

'Steady now Sir, steady, ye ken nocht but there might be a bone broke.'

Painfully he turned his head, and there towering over him the minister could see quite clearly in the moonlight, the figure of a one-legged man.

'Are you the piper whom I hear playing?'

'Aye, aye, that wad be me, tae keep my spirits up and the fairies in a gude humour.'

The minister could at first make nothing of the man's features, so shrouded were they in darkness, but he appeared to be dressed in a soldier's greatcoat, and from his belt a short sword dangled. These accoutrements, along with his peg leg, gave him an appearance of extraordinary decrepitude. With some agility he bent over the minister and struck a flint. The minister could see the man's face now, an ancient, grey crevasse to which an unkempt beard clung, and on top of which a blue bonnet sat.

'I prayed that you would find me.'

'Weel yer prayers hae been answered Sir. Which is no a thing that awe men can claim, for the Lord answers some and no ithers, and nae doubt has his ain gude reasons, and kens whether the heart o the prayer be a true heart or a false, better than the supplicant himsel. But bide still Sir, ye micht weel hae broke a bone or twa, and I hae been a sodger and hae some small skill in these matters.'

The minister felt the man's hands running over his body with gentle certain movements. No earthly thing he felt had ever re-assured him as these hands did.

'Try tae move yer richt leg Sir.'

His voice too sounded kind, the minister surrendered himself to its instructions, his right leg moved, and then his left leg, and all his limbs likewise.

'I think ye hae had the stuffing knocked out of ye baith top and bottom, but the Lord be thankit, naething mair than that.'

'I think I was barely conscious until your pipes woke me.'

'Weel, the Lord be praised Sir. I heard ye cry out, and then I heard yer horse, begging yer pardon nae doubt for throwing ye frae its back.'

'I was riding him rather too hard. I wanted to reach Stirling tonight.'

'Stirling, Sir? Och yer weel off the road tae Stirling. Why Sir, yer weel off ony road at awe. Mysel was on that road and but for the grace of God micht weel hae ganged richt past ye. But now Sir, forbye I can find nae bones broke, my advice is no tae be ower hasty in yer movements. Dis yer heid hurt?'

'It does indeed.'

'Och weel, after sic a dunt that's only natural. But now Sir I hae some very gude whisky, purchased but recently frae a Hielanman in exchange for ane o his Protestant Majesty's pistols gien me while I was a sodger. I, deeming it better tae be fortified within than armed without, and the Hielanman, being a Hielanman, nae doubt thought the clear opposite, and wha kens, but the Lord guided my judgement then, foretelling in that hour what was tae come tae pass in this.'

'Your faith does you credit.'

'Nae credit tae me, wha's life has been a maist indifferent ane whaur Godliness is concerned. But much credit tae my faither wha was a very Godly man, and my mither wha was blessit aboun awe woman that I hae met since, for as awe men o sense ken Sir, a mither's breast is the pleasantest hillside upon which a man can recline this side o Heaven.'

The minister could sit up now. The piper thrust the flask of whisky into his hands.

'Tak as deep a drink as ye please Sir.'

'How do I look?'

'Like a man Sir, that has been thrown arse ower heid frae a horse. Aye, and I dinna doubt, thocht the blessit hour o his salvation had arrived, but has woken up tae find that the troop marches on, and the land ower which it marches is an earthly ane, and even lesser blessings are worth some thanksgien. I ken the feeling very weel Sir, haeving been a sodgerly man, but ye Sir, wha I can plainly see tae be a scholarly gentlemen, are maybe a stranger tae it.'

The whisky cleared the minister's head. He quickly realised that the one-legged man who had towered over him at first appearance, was slightly less than middle height, and was indeed an ancient, ragged wreckage of a soldier.

'I am very grateful to you friend. Indeed I would like to

430

know your name.'

'My name Sir, is something of an embarrassment, gien the lie as it dis tae every aspect o my nature, and denying in its very utterance the Godly hopes o my blessit parents. Through nae fault o their ain Sir, they haeving nae power tae foretell the future, or the reproaches that it wad raise in my ain heart, as weel as laughter in the mouths o the ignorant. But they caed me Samuel Free Frae Sin Gilfinnan, and if ye hae ocht o mercy about ye Sir, I will be addressed and answer briskly tae Sam Gilfinnan.'

For a moment the whisky affected the minister in such a way that it seemed to him that the small man was hardly anything more than a sprite of the hills babbling incoherent nonsense.

'I think your father laid a heavy burden on your back.'

'Aye, that he did Sir, that he did. Little kenning at the time o my nativity, that it wad neither be as broad or upright as his ain. But that it seems has aye been the nature o the warld, as the poet Homer tells us. Are ye versed in the Greek tongue? I doubt not but ye are, and nae doubt ken the bit better than mysel, but Homer tells us wae great perspicacity, that few men are as gude as their faithers, but maist are worse. Which tae my mind maun mean that for the last twa or three thousand years and mair, the warld, and the quality o the folk in it, hae been ganging steadily doun a steep hill, which is getting steeper and steeper awe the time.

'Aye Sir, and while I am far frae a learned man, I canna help but wonder that when the great day o judgement dawns, the Lord will bend doun and pick up the bits that remain and think that these were very different folk frae the anes he planted in the bonny garden o Eden, and bade them be happy there. And doubtless they were happy, until that day cam tae pass in which they scunnered him and he had tae drive them out. Aye and forbye they hae hammered on the door wae swords, spears, and guns. this hundred years past and mair, I think he is little inclined tae let them in again, and sae we maun mak dae wae the wilderness, and whatever graces, mercies, trials, and divisions, he chooses tae put amang us . . .'

The soldier stopped. For one endless moment the minister had felt as if he was listening to the prattling of a lunatic, conjuring up a parody of doctrine out of a brain of dust, and simultaneously scattering it to the earth.

'I like tae meet a learned man ance in a while, for ye could weel hae been a loun. Forbye if that had been the case Sam Gilfinnan wad hae gien as freely o his whisky and his humble skill, seeing that tae his mind there are nae real divisions amang men, except atween the true and the false, and if ye ken ocht about the warld ye ken that has very little tae dae wae rank or education.

'But a learned man in this wild place, why it is maist surprising, maist near a miracle, and maist providential that I should hae cam by, and as I dinna think ye are quite ready tae move yet, and as Sam Gilfinnan is not the man tae desert ye, I think that a warm nicht, gude whisky, and learned conversation maun be our solace. And if that should grow tiresome, why a bit tune on the pipes will keep our spirits up. For I Sir, ken tunes frae awe pairts o Scotland, for I hae been in awe pairts, and can converse wae the Hielanman in the Hielan tongue, and the Lawland man in the lawland, and can play a Hielan rant as weel as a Whiggamore ane, and can play auld sangs as weel as the greatly inferior anes o the present day, sangs being much like men in that respect.

'Aye indeed Sir, I can play ony rant o nonsense that a man can sing. Sangs tae mak him weep, and ithers tae mak him draw his sword, and yet ithers tae mak lassies dance and fling their gowns in the air, and bless an auld man wae a blink o that in which he ance gloried. For that is my trade now Sir, wha was ance a weel turned out, twa legged sodger in General Mackay's regiment, raised tae defend the honour and doubtful title of his Protestant Majesty, William of Orange, and which as awe folk ken, was cut tae pieces at the place caed Killiekrankie, which the Hielanmen ca Rinrory.

'And wha can say Sir, wha can say, maybe they should indeed hae the naming o it, for in awe fairness they won the day, for awe that it brought little gude either tae them or tae King James. For as ye nae doubt ken, that day also saw the end of Claverhouse o bludie memory, shot deid in his victorious pride by a Christian man wae a silver bullet in his gun, which is the richt and proper way tae deal wae warlocks. And now he sits at the richt hand o Satan, his maister, drinking boiling goat's piss, which he thinks tae be fairer than ony wine o

France. And that Sir is, tae my mind, a very gude example of the Lord's mercy and justice.

'But awe that forbye Sir, even a gude Protestant monarch like Dutch Willie has but little patience wae a ane-legged sodger, nae doubt reasoning that haeving been shamefully defeated in his service he ought tae be honourably deid. Sae now I maun mak my living as my strength and skill on the pipes will allow.'

'Indeed so Sir.'

'And now Sir, as I hae telt ye, and nae doubt, for which I trust ye'll pardon me, deafened ye a bit, wae my name, place, and pairts o my story, what micht yer ain be, or are ye just a bit gentleman wha graces the earth wae his presence alane.'

The minister's head ached. Gilfinnan's features danced before his eyes as if they had become inextricably enmeshed in the turmoil of the night, and his own imagination.

He turned his head aside. He has been kind, he thought, and he knows no other way. When he looked again at the piper, his eyes appeared like two bright flames darting forth from a skull of granite. Relentless in their malignancy they seemed, proclaiming that their owner was more than just a garrulous old man. The minister's reason fought the apparition until it seemed to him that the combat numbed his brain, but Gilfinnan's eyes twinkled merrily now, and his hands reached out to gently grasp his shoulders.

'I think Sir, that ye are no quite as weel as ye imagine. Whisky is fine medicine, but of a necessity deludes the senses.'

The minister again looked into the piper's face. Samuel Free From Sin Gilfinnan's countenance now shone with tenderness and affection.

'I am a minister of the Reformed Kirk.'

The radiance of Gilfinnan's features seemed to increase with each word the minister spoke.

'Weel is this not an uncovenanted mercy? And am I not indeed a blessed man? Tae be, after sae mony ill deeds and blasphemies, wild and Godless rantings, tae be here, at maybe the very extremity of my earthly life, tae be allowed tae be of service tae ane o the Lord's chosen? Now wad ye not think minister, that a man sic as mysel, can, without ony hint o pride, but in the greatest humbleness that he is capable o, think o

433

himsel as blessit by this encounter? Even tae blessing the horse
that threw ye, and thinking that it couldna hae done itherwise
than by the Lord's command, tae gie his servant, wha has aye
in his heart loved him, though no perhaps wae the outward
show o the Pharisee, a chance tae be of some service tae him ere
he looked upon his face?'

The piper's voice as he spoke took on the cadence of an
incantation.

'I think Sir, that it was very provident that you came along
when you did, but I think you should moderate your language
somewhat.'

'Aye indeed minister, aye indeed, the rebuke is weel deserved and humbly received. But I beg tae think Sir, that the
Lord will forgie the ecstasy of a man that afore this blessit
nicht, had a soul that he could only believe was beyond awe redemption.'

'I do not believe that we are ever beyond hope.'

'Och I can see in ye minister, a truly mild and forbearing
man, but ye ken not the wild and desperate paths that I hae
travelled. Aye and when green eyed temptation glowered like
a cat in the heather, did not Sam Fettered Tae Sin Gilfinnan cast
his plaid frae off his back and his breeks frae off his bum? Och
minister, a bairn could number the times he didna, and the Deil
couldna number the times he did. And when drunkards drank
and roared and sang, did I not roar and drink the faremaist?
And when blasphemers blasphemed, did I not tak the prece-
dence? And when men o earthly reason sang their song o death,
did I not blow up my pipes and play a fine tune tae their
singing? And yet, and yet, even Sam Gilfinnan it seems may yet
reside amang the blessit . . .'

'Oh come Sir, I cannot think you are as bad as all that.'

'Och mony wad say worse. Some wad declare that if their
horse had thrown them upon the Sherramuir at midnight, they
wad raither hae been clapped in clay than restored by Sam
Gilfinnan.'

'Then they would be foolish men.'

'Aye, nae doubt, nae doubt, the history o man has aye been
a great dream of glory and a tempest o foolishness. And he has
aye dreamt the first and let himsel be whisked awa by the
second, and aiblins he will rise again and aiblins he will not.'

'I'm not sure I follow you or get your meaning.'

'Och I'm not sure I get it mysel, and nae doubt it has nae meaning at awe if sic a learned person as yersel can see nae sense in it.'

To the minister's eyes it seemed then that the piper's face underwent another transformation, becoming a thing of depthless guile which the minister could neither look upon or deflect, until it chose to give way. This it did with a sudden merry laugh, leaping onto his single leg with a nimble jump.

'Why minister I could spend a year in discourse wae ye, but tis near morning, and nae doubt but ye wad like tae be on yer way if yer strength will haud. But if it will not, Sam Gilfinnan sall bide wae ye as a gude sodger by a hurt friend.'

'No, I think I am quite recovered now, I ache, but that is all.'

'Then let us ride. And if ye will permit me, then I wha ken every earthly track there is, for awe I am fell ignorant o spiritual anes, sall guide ye out o these bit hills.'

The piper helped the minister to his feet. For a full minute he stood and stared out at the landscape around him. He watched the dawn cracking over the naked darkness of the hills, which bore no sign of the tumult of the night before. He turned to his companion. In the morning light, Samuel Free From Sin Gilfinnan looked every undersized inch a splendid ruffian in the last stages of decrepitude. He watched as he hobbled over to his horse, swinging himself with extraordinary dexterity into the saddle. The steed, the minister thought, perfectly matched his master's age and station.

The minister mounted his own horse.

'A fiery beast nae doubt,' Gilfinnan said.

'He has never thrown me before.'

The piper nodded quietly and sagely. It was as if this information only further confirmed the providentiality of the occasion in his mind.

'Now Sir, I can tak ye tae auld Stirling toun, whaur I ken whaur a bit breakfast can be had, and there I can leave ye. But if ye hae a mind tae gang on I can tak ye ower the Forth and put ye on the best road.'

'I think breakfast is my first consideration.'

'Then I ken just the place Sir, decently kept by a bonny widow wife and her dochter, whaur ony friend o Sam Gilfinnan's will aye be welcome.'

The piper, still deep it seemed to the minister in his outlandish ecstasy was as good as his promise. He led the minister down from the hills, allowed him to buy them breakfast, and regaled their hosts with the repeated story of the lost sheep found, as he now termed the incident on the muir.

When he finally parted from the minister on the South side of the Forth it was with much prolonged farewells.

'Och Sir, I wad hae liked fine tae hae accompanied ye, for mony are the burdens that lie heavy on my heart, untelt, aye and I fear, except tae a man o yer great and forbearing piety untellable, for they wad mortify the heart and ears o the lave o gude folk. But frae that blessit hour, and that blessit spot upon the Sherramuir, Samuel Fettered Tae Sin Gilfinnan, resolved tae free himsel o these fetters.

'I canna promise that he will aye succeed on every occasion, for I see a fierce and deidly contest ahead, and whether the pike-line o his soul will stand firm against every charge I ken not, but that it will endeavour tae dae sae I hereby solemnly promise. Aye and when the pike-line wavers, and the musketeers wad run awa, I will mind yer words upon the muir, and bind them tae me like a corselet o steel, and the memory o our blessit meeting will be like untae a troop o Godly horse tae the rescue o ane sinful man. For is it not weel kent that unsupported foot canna stand for lang against horse? But that yer prayers and blessings and Godly words will empty the saddles o temptation and ding doun the horses o lust, strive and ficht though they nae doubt will, I canna in my hairt doubt, and they will mak o this ancient carcass o mine, a battlefield, tae the Lord's glory and thine ain . . .'

'Mr Gilfinnan, I assure you . . .'

'A rebuke, minister and a timely ane. Och minister, I wish that ye were aye on hand tae administer sic timely rebukes. For och I ken that Sam Gilfinnan's pride is a dark and wicked thing, steering him tae heights far aboun onything that he's worthy o, and proving it in the end by casting him doun tae grovel in the dust like a beast.'

'Will you stay in Stirling?'

'Och I ken not minister. Nae doubt I sall bide a bit, and play a bit tune. But I sall not bide ower lang for a toun is a temptful place, and it may be, wha kens, we sall meet again.'

'I do intend to hurry South swiftly. I have been too long away from my parish.'

'Och a blessit place that parish maun be, like an earthly vision o the Kingdom o Heaven itsel, and ye maun ken how I honour the Godly spirit o duty that is in ye, that maks ye hurry tae tak yer place at its heid and set an example tae laggard, laird and loun. And whether we sall meet again, or whether we sall not, is in the Lord's hands like awe things. If it is his will, then nae doubt it sall be sae, and if it is not the Lord's will, then I bid thee gude day and fare weel, and when I say my prayers aye will I mind o ye.'

The minister looked steadily at him. A terrible jester he seemed to be then, an aimless, feckless, loudmouthed rogue. For a moment he remembered the granite countenance of the previous night. He dismissed that as an apparition conjured up by the feverish state of his mind. He smiled kindly, confessing to himself a desire to the point of despair to be free of this loquacious Samaritan.

At last he watched him shamble off on his ancient horse, shrilly whistling the twenty-third psalm.

'If he avoids temptation for a day, it will be a miracle,' the minister said quietly, as he watched him disappear into the warren of the town. No sooner had he said these words, and with the crescendo of Gilfinnan's voice still ringing in his ears, the minister felt utterly miserable at his own lack of compassion. It could have gone very hard with him in the hills if he had not met the one-legged piper. Gilfinnan was hardly to blame for the state of the minister's senses, or the fact that his sudden appearance had made him briefly appear like an apparition from Hell on a night of such apparitions, the worst night of the minister's life.

☆

It was four days since the minister had left Stirling. The misery he had felt when parting from the piper had remained with him. The apparitions which had pitched him from the saddle now tore at the sinews of his mind to a degree that only relentless prayer could quell.

As he rode, he watched the grey clad figures in their fields. Within the memory of the oldest and the youngest, thousands had been killed in battles, thousands more by plagues and famines, and still they were there, their bodies braced against the weather, their minds braced against their history, as if that was just another of the elements against which they struggled.

They were unknowable, the minister thought. The idea that in the time he had spent at Trig he had somehow got to know them, seemed to him now wholly fallacious. They were unknown even to themselves. The knowledge they had of themselves had been taught to them, and deep in their souls, that which had been taught, had, against all the aims of their teachers, mingled with and awoken, fierce passions and hungry desires, dreams that would drown the earth itself.

Now they stood huddled in their plaids, a people created in God's image, and for whom God occupied no higher place in their minds than their own impossible desires. They had borne Christ the Lamb as their tribal God to the battlefield of tigers. They had martyred themselves to build what they imagined as God's Kingdom on earth, and they had presumed to dictate to God, what that Kingdom should be, and who should dwell in it.

The minister thought, as he often thought, of that last vicious muirland brawl. One of the many whose memory sang gloriously in their minds, eclipsing all that they had been taught.

'These people, wha hae been for the present, dinged doun, sall ane day rise again, and ask nae leave of Kirk or King or God in Heaven.'

In his reason, once he was free of her, the minister had discounted her words as being those of a deranged and vengeful woman.

Looking at the people now, saluting him as he rode past them, he was gripped by a pervasive fear that he could not tell. Did the shattered dreams still slumber there, like the weapons he knew lay hidden in their barns? Or were they now indifferent to all that had once moved them, sheepishly obedient to the authorities set over them?

'They must be taught obedience, respect, and industry,' Gilmarten had written. 'They are mostly strangers to the first *and second of these virtues, and because of the times they have lived through, have almost forgotten the third, and as a consequence, famine, pestilence, and riot, plague the commonwealth.'*

Marten Gilmarten wrote, and Sir John Doig's vast and ruddy countenance beamed upon him. The future belonged to them, and they embraced it and each other, with gratitude and prayer. And yet, the minister thought, one of Neil Roy's bare-rumped clansmen, might well think his lot preferable living in spiritual darkness, than a tenant farmer in Trig living under a Christian laird and his minister.

There was reason now, he thought, for that awful, silent invulnerability of Alexander Bain. That heart that had sought, that hand which at the Kirk's command had betrayed a friend, those eyes that had glittered with such stubborn challenge to all authority, had yielded long ago, and his soul had been devoured by the wolf of time, in whose belly it lay, and which he, in his ignorance, had mistaken for the bowels of Christ.

He looked up at the sky. Rain had been falling lightly on his face for the last hour. At first he had hardly noticed it. At the first peal of distant thunder his eyes anxiously scanned the landscape. There was now neither sign of human being, or of human habitation. The cattle stood bunched under the shelter of a clump of trees, their bodies quietly waiting. A few birds still flew, urgently seeking shelter.

It would have been customary for him on such a journey to spend the nights in the houses of his fellow clergymen. This the minister did not do, preferring instead to stop at wayside inns, rising early in the morning and continuing on his way. That morning he had been told by his host that a storm was to be expected.

At the third peal of thunder he pulled his cloak over his head and urged his horse forward into a fast canter. The storm was almost over his head when the minister noticed a hut slightly off the road, smoke rising from the gap in the roof that served as a chimney. In his haste to reach it the minister was almost upon it before he heard the sound of music coming from within.

The minister pulled up his horse. In the doorway stood the one-legged piper.

439

'Why minister, tis ye is it not?'

For a full minute, with the storm thundering over his head, the minister was too astonished to answer. Gilfinnan was now dancing before his eyes, his greatcoat flapping like the pinions of a gigantic bird whisked there by the winds of the storm itself. His hands reached for the bridle of the minister's horse.

'Mr Gilfinnan, how fortunate . . .'

'Fortunate Sir, aye, aye, tae ye it is nae mair than fortunate. But for mysel Sir, why I canna but think that my auld een are blessit, and my spirit reborn. For och, mony a lang and lonely nicht has Fettered Tae Sin Gilfinnan spent since last we met, wrestling wae the spirit o his sinful flesh, a task for which he has neither the skill o learning nor the Grace o God. And mony's the day I wad say tae mysel, if only ance again ye could meet that Godly man ye met upon the Sherramuir, then ye wad ken, that sinful man as ye are, the Lord has aye his een upon ye. And tae see ye now Sir, a shining licht tae awe men, but mair, o muckle mair than that tae Sam Gilfinnan.'

'I am pleased to see you, Mr Gilfinnan.'

'Aye I trust that ye are. But whether ye are, or whether ye are not, the Lord has appointed it tae be thus, and we canna jouk his commands. But cam awa intae this bit biggin, for if this storm that's brewing is tae my mind, not yet the flood, it will in a minute or twa mak us unco wet.'

Helplessly, it felt to the minister, neither the piper, nor his logic, could be evaded. Inwardly sighing, his grateful memories of the man eclipsed by his all too real presence, he allowed Gilfinnan to lead his horse into the hut. It was entirely bare except for a fine fire which roared in the hearth, and two logs which served as seats.

'Light doun minister, light doun and warm yersel.'

The minister dismounted. A flagon of whisky sitting on the floor set him to wondering if Gilfinnan was ever actually sober.

'I hae a bit modest refreshment minister, which a singing playing man maun aye hae.'

'Mr Gilfinnan, I am pleased to meet you again, and I am happy to wait out the storm with you, but I beg of you to moderate your language. It is excessive to the point of being unseemly.'

'Ye are richt Sir, maist richt, and yer point is weel made, and even an ignorant sodger loun like me kens very weel that he can blaspheme without kenning it, sae lang has he spent amang sinful discourse. But frae now till I draw my last breath, my tongue sall moderate itsel as best it can. But why minister, a man wha feels sic joy in his hairt at yer presence, and is in himsel a simple man, kens nae ither way tae express his joy, apart frae joyful language.'

'Enough Sir, I am content that I perceive you to be joyful.'

'Aye minister, ye hae a gude hairt, which has a richt tae be contented. But Sam Gilfinnan minister, och Sir, I ken not at awe how tae tell it, for I maun wring my hands and weep tears at the very thought o awe the resolutions that he made, and awe that has befallen him since he pairted wae yer Godly company, and how awe things fell out the clear opposite o what he had resolved.'

'Mr Gilfinnan, what has befallen you, you look as I left you?'

The piper slowly raised his bowed head, and to the beseiged mind of the minister it was as if it was again fixed in the transient malevolence that he had imagined on the Sheriffmuir. His brain reeled in his skull, as if it was once more in the grip of a greater storm than the one that was now crashing about the hut.

'Och minister, the appearance o awe things in this warld is a maist deceptive thing, sae lang has it been held in thrall by the maister o lies himsel. And it is not a proud boast, but uttered in the full knowledge o his wretched and fallen condition, that the appearance o Sam Gilfinnan is the maist deceptive appearance of awe.'

The man's remarks were so apt, that for a moment the minister felt as if his reason, and every sense his body possessed, had been violently overthrown and now lay prostrate at Gilfinnan's feet. In that same moment the vision passed, Gilfinnan's eyes now shone with kindness. Indeed he seemed cleaner, with his beard neatly clipped, than at their first meeting.

'The Lord knows the truth in all things, and in all men.'

'Aye indeed Sir, and therein lies the fear and trembling which grips at the hairts o awe men, and maks some long for life and fear death, and ithers long for death and fear life.'

Gilfinnan bent down and threw some logs on the fire. When he looked up again his face was as contrite as a mischievous dog's.

'Och, sit ye doun minister, sit ye doun, I ken very weel that it canna be itherwise than that ye maun think o me as the maist wretched, the maist faltering, the maist infirm o purpose pilgrim that ever yer een beheld. And I canna believe that sic a sight can be a joy tae yer een, nae mair than it wad bring joy tae the een of my reverent mither and faither should they be alive tae behold it, which by God's mercy they are not, though nae doubt, frae his bosom they look doun in sorrow.'

'Sir, Mr Gilfinnan . . .'

'Comfort me nae mair Sir, till ye ken what ye comfortest, for that ye are a merciful man and a tender-hairted man I hae ample proof. But there is a time minister for tenderness, and there is a time for sternness, and sae be not ower hasty tae gie quarter till ye ken what it is tae be, for awe that Samuel Fettered Tae Sin craves quarter, he kens very weel in his hairt that he is maist unworthy o it . . .'

The minister was silent now. It was as if the churnings of Samuel Gilfinnan's soul was like the churning of the world itself, the endless whine of misbegotten and unloved children.

He thought again of Andrew Gilmore's father and his neighbour's, burying the dead in that ghastly wood. Had they looked at Heaven and thought a curse, that unlike Agnes Douglas they had dared not utter? If she had not parted so hastily with the children and the wounded Sawney Bain, they would have been found and joyfully succoured, and the horror of the cave would never have come to pass.

The minister closed his eyes. When he opened them he almost expected Gilfinnan to have disappeared. He was still there, his face glowing, shifting, being reborn, or crumbling through time? The minister could no longer tell or care.

'Och minister, tae see ye, against awe my protests tae the contrary, tae see ye deep in prayer for the soul of Sam Gilfinnan, crying in the Lord's ear that there was gude yet tae be found in the soul o that pestilential man. For I couldna help but hear ye Sir, and hear my name repeated, ower and ower as ye pleaded. Och Sir, humbled dae I feel, sae unworthy tae sit at yer feet, that had it not been for that bit storm I wad hae fled this place, coward as I am, I hae some vestiges of sodgerly honour and proper behaviour left.'

For a moment the minister was astonished. If he had prayed, he had been entirely unaware of it.

'Oh come, Sir . . .'

'My ain unworthyness minister, my ain unworthyness, why Sir, ye ken not, but haeving heard ye pray I maun tell awe. After awe the Godly discourse that we had, and at which my auld hairt leapt wae sic joy, that nicht upon the Sherramuir, whaur aiblins ye flung yersel frae yer ain horse at great risk o life and limb, tae be the blessit instrument o my salvation . . .'

'Enough Mr Gilfinnan, that is nonsense.'

'Na, na Sir, stop me not now, when ye hae set a course ye maun steer it. Ye ken Sir, yon gude fine inn whaur we had breakfast, which was a gude enough breakfast in a warldly way, but was as naething tae the feast my spirit had tae sit at the same table as yersel. And ye left me Sir, upon the bridge at Stirling, a man fortified and resolved, and proud tae think himsel reborn.

'Weel, that man held true minister, armoured as he felt himsel tae be, sae that nane could fix a petard tae his soul, but wae the Lord's help he dashed it awa. And sae he did, for ane hale day, singing and dancing as his profession is, for the gude folk o Stirling, and only partaking in the moderate refreshment that a singing man maun aye hae. And then evening cam, and still he held out . . .

'But, och ye maun ken minister, dae ye mind that gude woman and her dochter, wha managed the place in which we breakfasted, Janet Blane was her name, och weel she minded ye, and thocht her inn blessit by yer presence?'

'I do remember her . . .'

'Weel minister, ye maun ken her circumstances, and I mean this as nae kind o extenuation, or ony attempt tae jouk what canna be jouked. But ye could weel see that she was a very fine and wholesome woman, and no unhandsome for her time in life. But, she kens very weel, that she is past the age when young men come a courting, and ony that wad pretend sic affections, hae but ane eye on her, and anither on a very profitable inn, whaur they might rest their feet till judgement day, and never be short o whisky or ale.

'Sae, tae awe sic folk she taks a broomstick and sweeps them tae the door. But Sir, she kens, that for awe his sins, Sam Gilfinnan is not that kind o man, the sin o avarice being the ane, maybe the only ane, that has never found a place within his hairt. And minister, ye maun ken, that when nicht comes doun and darkness presses in thick, at that time aboun awe ithers, a human body kens that it is but a thing o clay and dust intae which Heaven has breathed a bit o life. Which is why we aye say our prayers at bed-time, armouring oursels against sic thoughts. While at the same time we ken very weel that the best o armour aye has a bit chink in it, intae which whiles a serpent crawls, and awe folk ken the comfort tae be had frae anither human body as poor and lost as yersel.

'Why minister, Janet Blane has lang kent that comfort, and as a consequence misses it now, and what better man than I? Sae I reasoned in my faithlessness, wha had been a great friend and comrade o her man in the days gone by, and held him in my airms as he deed, mortally wounded by a musketball. Aye, and at that time just afore he passed awa, he made me promise that I should aye keep my een upon Janet and see that she cam tae nae hairm.

'And now she, trusting in my weel kent lack o avarice, and my honour as a silent man, wad tak me tae her bosom for sic comfort and companionship that human bodies aye crave in their hours o weakness. And it seemed tae me then, beseiged wae earthly reason, that it was not the kind o offer an honourable man should refuse . . .'

The minister tried to interrupt. Gilfinnan held up his hand.

'Na, na Sir, I hae set out tae tell awe, and awe sall ye hear. For I canna say, and aiblins I wad like tae say, and maybe it wad appear a lesser sin tae say, that I steered mysel tae her bed out o companionship and friendship. But it canna be said, minister, for lust Sir, lust gripped my flesh and raged there, aye and was raging still in the morning, aye and the next nicht tae. And while it raged, och I prayed, aye and I made Janet pray, that my een micht ance again be blest by yer Godly presence, which explains the extremity and the extravagance o my joy, on which ye richtly rebuked me, tae see ye cam riding doun the road, and I thocht, though stern wad be yer necessary strictures awe micht not yet be lost. Och Sir, like an angel o the Lord tae a soul adrift ye were minister.'

'Fornication is always a sin.'

'I ken, minister, I ken . . .'

'More than that I will not judge.'

The minister could not bear to look at Gilfinnan's face. It seemed to grow older and harder and still as death.

'Weel minister, sic a great joy I tak in yer forbearing words, and the assurance that awe might not be lost, and through yer prayers Sam Gilfinnan may, despite awe, reside amang the blessit.'

The minister did not know whether he felt revulsion, fear, or pity. Why indeed, he wondered, were they saved for so long? Preserved by an anarchic and wayward fortune, or chance? The Devil hardly had the real power to so direct events on earth. Was murder and cannibalism merely a condition into which they had degenerated?

He looked at Gilfinnan. An unbearable malevolence shone from every aspect of his features. The fellow, his wretched confession over, was now inordinately cheerful, inordinately considerate, inordinately flattering, a vile and detestable jester who held the fragments of the minister's soul in his hands.

'I hae a proposition tae mak tae ye Sir. Tae my mind it seems ye hae but a poor mind for the routes of this warld, forbye ye hae a great and profound ane for the ways o the spirit. And as Sam Gilfinnan is the clear opposite o yersel, why, minister I sall, if ye will permit me, accompany ye, which will be an exchange, for awe that it wad be blasphemy tae call it an equal ane, tae compare my earthly services wae yer divine instruction.'

This man would not leave him, the minister thought. It was not by chance that he had found him on the muir, nor chance that he had met him here, nor was this proposal a sudden or spontaneous gesture. This man was temptation and despair, born in a place devoid of light or reason.

The minister looked again at the piper. His eyes now seemed vast and loving things, islands of tranquillity, citadels of peace and wisdom. The minister loved him, and longed to be loved by him in turn. And then noiselessly as a shadow falling the seemingly impregnable towers of love collapsed into frenzied phalanxes of steel. The world of God had died in the savage years through which he had lived. In that small, dark wood the meaning of everything that had been human was stripped and violated and butchered, and the world that now remained was an arbitrary comedy, a cruel jest in a wilderness of lies.

The minister felt himself giving way to a harsh and vicious hatred. To think that because these people had imagined that God existed in their own image, and had followed that image to their own destruction, they would in the future think they could live without God at all.

'Ye do not appear tae be ower weel minister, maybe yer fall has left ye mair affected than ye think, which is anither gude reason why I should gang wae ye, haeving, as I dae, some humble skill in medicine.'

'Mr Gilfinnan, I thank you very much for your kind and Christian offer, but I am quite recovered, and I think I will travel on my way alone.'

The minister's words, against his conscious will were uttered like a challenge. Gilfinnan merely bowed his head.

'As ye please Sir, Samuel Gilfinnan is not the kind o man tae thrust himsel upon ony that dinna desire his company.'

'I mean no offence.'

'Och Sir, nane has been taen. How could a plain speaking man like mysel tak offence at plain and honest speaking? I ken very weel that my ain unworthyness and sinfulness mak o me a doubtful companion for ane sic as yersel.'

'I did not mean that Sir, it is my custom to travel alone, I find it pleasant.'

'Indeed sae Sir, I understand that weel enough. Tis my custom on occasion when rich gentlemen fling themsels frae their horse's back tae lie at my feet, tae rifle their pockets in the likelihood o finding a bit sillar.'

'Mr Gilfinnan please, you do yourself and me an injury.'

'Say nae mair Sir, say nae mair, dunts and injuries baith gien and taen, hae been my trade, and nae doubt I sall live till ane proves fatal.'

The piper sprang on to his leg and stump and dragged his horse out of the hut. With an extraordinary suppleness for one so old and infirm he leapt on to its back. Once mounted he blew up his pipes, and turning in the saddle he saluted the minister with an extravagant doff of his blue bonnet.

'Weel awa minister, weel awa, bid awe in the Godly parish o Trig a richt gude day frae Sam Gilfinnan.'

The minister longed to call him back. With a cruel slowness the figure of the piper and his ancient horse receded. Once he was on the road and out of sight the minister strained his ears to catch the sound of the pipes, the air continuing to ring in his head long after it had materially faded.

The minister felt utterly alone, more alone than he could have imagined it possible for a Christian to be. His eyes roved round the wretched hut, settling on the dying embers of the fire.

He left the hut when he realised consciously that he was waiting for the impossible Samaritan to return. It was almost evening now, the smell of the rain-soaked fields assailed his nostrils. As he rode he watched the crows flapping heavily down to reap the bounty of the refreshed fields. Corbie crows was how the Scots referred to their clergy when they were out of humour with them. Would that now be the title on Gilfinnan's lips? He observed the large strutting carrion birds bitterly and pressed his horse forward into the night.

☆

The minister rode all through the night. By noon the next day he was once again in the Border Hills. His agitated mind strove to find some satisfaction in covering so much ground. This dissipated early in the afternoon when he encountered a small army of itinerants. To the minister's eyes they appeared more wretched than any he had previously seen. As he rode past them their eyes scrutinised him from some veiled hinterland of the spirit in which decay and despair, lived and breathed and walked.

In Marten Gilmarten's book he had read:

'As for the hosts of vagabonds, beggars, and broken men that at present infest our countryside, they, and their multitudinous and unsanctified familes, are like a plague of locusts on a field of wheat. They should be split up and sold by the state, maintaining as far as possible, if they are not too numerous, the families that already exist among them, into the service of

447

Christian people, who in return for their labour, will undertake to feed and clothe them, and see to it that they attend kirk and regulate their lives decently.

'The benefits of this would be manifold. The country would be rid of a section of its population who through idleness, pride, and prodigality, and in some cases, misfortune and infirmity, have become a pestilence upon the Commonwealth. They live outside the discipline of the Kirk and the laws of the State, wandering without purpose in the more barren parts of our land. They are a detriment to Christian morals, fornication, incest, drunkenness, and other abominations too horrible to mention, flourish among them.

'At the present time, they reive everything and produce nothing. Putting them to work, putting before their eyes a Christian example and seeing that they observe it, will, at the very least, remove this sore from the countryside and increase the nation's wealth.

'That some sternness will be needed to carry out this policy I do not deny. Severity of punishment must discipline the flesh that the mind has abandoned, and as these people are at present not fit to mingle with Christians in worship, I advocate special services for them, and special enclosures within which they must dwell. For those who rebel against these strictures I advocate severe punishment for a first offence, for second or persistent offenders, deportation is probably the only cure.

'If any should object that I am advocating selling my own countrymen into slavery. I reply, are they not slaves already? Are not their spirits enslaved by their idleness and the bestial passions that are the result of it? Are not their minds enslaved to their bellies? '

The minister's eyes could not meet theirs. When by accident they met, the wanderers lowered their heads. Still he felt their judgement lie heavier on him than if they had displayed the insolence and violence that Gilmarten accused them of.

By the evening the minister was lost. He knew he had taken some foolish turning when suddenly he came once more upon the wanderers, who had been travelling in the opposite direction, camped for the night. He reflected that he could not even be sure that they were the same ones, to such a similarity did their state reduce them. And yet, it was as if they knew, and indeed were amused at their knowledge, and waited for him to ask for their assistance.

This time the minister rode slowly up to them. In the half-light of the evening, their poverty partially concealed, their outlandishness strangely seemed to increase. One man in late middle-age with a barbarous growth of beard, detached himself from the rest and strode towards him. He carried a large staff across his shoulder. As he approached the minister, he, as if suddenly conscious of the threat contained in it, lowered it from his shoulder to the more peaceful position of being an aid to walking.

'Gude-evening, yer honour.'

The man was older than the minister had at first thought, and if his clothes were mere rags, his voice was civil.

'Good evening to you. I beg your pardon, but I fear I have lost my way. I am travelling to the town of Trig.'

The man pointed with his staff in the direction in which the minister was actually riding, as if he had not fully understood the question. The expression on his face was neither friendly nor unfriendly, just a face, the minister thought, that now saw its place as a denizen of another world. He thought of the clan that had once inhabited the cave. They would have dragged him from his horse. This man merely stood with seemingly ageless patience waiting to be commanded.

The minister started to once again explain his situation.

'Are you certain that I am now on the correct road?'

The man appeared to smile faintly as if the notion that he could be wrong in this was quite preposterous to him. He was about to explain further when his words were interrupted by the sudden and startling re-appearance of one whom the minister had every rational reason for believing he would never see again.

'Mr Gilfinnan . . .'

Mounted on his ancient horse, impossible, the minister thought, that it could have covered such a distance in so short a time, the one-legged piper seemed to just emerge out of the multitude, gently prodding the beast forward.

'Och tis yersel, minister. Why is this not providence itsel which has brought this tae pass? That I wha pairted frae ye wae

449

harsh and prideful words, which Sir, I hae regretted, and which hae been the cause o mony bitter tears. Och minister, ken ye not how, when the foolish pride and arrogance o my heart, had finally fled the field o this wretched and defiled carcass, and the craws o remorse and repentence did tear at its entrails, why did I not bid them tear on? That I wha had been sae blessit, and thocht mysel redeemed by yer presence and yer counsel, should hae cast them baith frae me in sic a fashion, why it surpasseth understanding. And och minister, tae now set my een upon ye ance again, and if my een dae not deceive me, for keen as ye ken they are in awe earthly things, for awe they are utterly blindit tae things spiritual, I think yer present situation is ane in which I can ance again be o some service, small service, but I ask nae mair . . .'

The minister felt his mind succumb to the impossible. This man, who could travel at a speed bordering on the miraculous, would never leave him.

'Samuel Gilfinnan, is it really you?'

'Och minister tis nane ither, and whether ye were brocht, or whether ye socht, I ken not, but I canna believe itherwise than that I am trebly blest by the sight o ye. As are awe my poor friends in this pitiful place, wha hae languished lang in the wilderness driven out o hame and land tae range wae the beasts o the hills.

'Och Sir, cast yer een about ye. Hae ye ever seen in ony place on earth, folk mair pitiful than these? Each wae a fierce tale tae tell o oppression, sorrow, suffering, pride, and wickedness. Why the poor bairns that are born intae this place think that these are the total o awe the earth contains. But now ye hae cam tae them Sir, and nae doubt it seems tae their een a near miracle. Why, I can see it like a shining licht in awe their faces, even tae that ancient loun that stands by ye his mouth agape, and in the hairts o awe this congregation.'

With a wave of his hand the piper seemed to sweep aside whatever words the minister was preparing to utter. He turned to the itinerants, his voice ringing in the minister's ears, now a loud braying, utterly lunatic thing.

'Harken tae me, ye Christless crew o a foundering ark. Afore ye stands a man, wha's Godliness, Sirs, has made him a shining licht upon the earth. A man wha has toiled and prayed michtily

450

for the sin-sodden soul o Sam Gilfinnan. Wha threw himself frae off his ain horse, at the mortal risk of his ain neck, tae check Sam Gilfinnan's heidlang gallop tae perdition. And even, and even, when I in the pride and vanity o my hairt cast him frae me, he is naething daunted, but maun ride day and nicht, sparing neither himsel nor his gude horse, tae seek me out whaur ere I might be. And is it not fitting? Och is it not mair than fitting? Is it not a miracle nigh equal tae ony in the Bible, that in his seeking he should come upon an army o folk auld and young, and bairns not yet born, that are my kind friends, and near as sinful as myself, tae be the blessing and salvation o us awe?

'Sae let us mak a pulpit, for I ken this man, and I ken weel the strength o the Lord that is in him, for think ye not that the Lord wad send some freshwater man tae wrestle for the soul o Sam Gilfinnan. And forbye the fact that he has ridden hard through wild hills and mirk nichts tae be amang us, he asks neither for food nor drink, but only for a place frae which he can speak. We hae sic a place sae let us mak it ready.'

To the minister it was as if a thunderclap had rent his senses. Gilfinnan seized the bridle of his horse and seemed to hurl both it and the minister into the midst of the multitude where a host of hands plucked him from the saddle and whirled him through the air. When he once again found himself upright he was standing on top of a cart.

In the minutes it took for the minister's head to clear, absolute horror was replaced with absolute rage. He heard himself bellowing at them, his words disintegrating amidst the beast-like howling that surrounded him. They cried upon him for a sermon, they cried upon him for a preaching, some fired ancient guns in the air, some danced with demoniac indecency, some, it seemed to him, strove to overturn the cart and tear him to pieces.

Suddenly Gilfinnan was beside him on the cart his wooden stump drumming fiendishly on the bottom. The minister felt himself sink to his knees and the piper, gently but firmly, dragging him to his feet.

'Ye maun preach Sir, itherwise I canna answer for yer mortal self.'

The minister stared at him, as so often he had stared at him

451

before. So ancient and frail he looked, that in any physical contest the minister felt he could have knocked him down with ease, but at that moment his limbs hardly bore him upright.

'Who are you . . ? And what is the meaning of this?'

Gilfinnan's eyes, blazed now, it seemed to the minister, with an insight and passion which he had never encountered before. It was as if the metamorphosis which had so shocked him upon the Sheriffmuir had now become a Satanic totality which had transformed everything about him.

'Why Sir, wad ye deceive me? Hae ye not een in yer heid as true in sense as my ain which hae led me tae ye, and ye tae me? And dae they not tell ye that there afore them is a gude and Godly congregation? And Sir, is it tae matter that few hae a hale shirt upon their backs or shoes upon their feet? Why Sir, in this congregation there are folk wha hae marched for the Covenant when the great o the land wad abandon it, aye and ding it doun. There are folk here wha hae been cut tae pieces in its service, standing against twice and thrice their number. Folk wha hae been harried frae their hames, wha hae held them that they loved in their airms as they deed, and hae seen the ruination o awe that they ance held dear, but they counted that as naething when they heard the great drum o Heaven sounding aboun their heids, and saw the great banner o Heaven unfurled in the sky, assuring them o a paradise on earth and eternal salvation ance they had dinged doun the enemies o God and true religion.

'Och a hard road they travelled through mony a mirk dark nicht, wading through rivers o blude, hearing the roaring o the michty in their lugs. And hae awe their sufferings brocht them tae nocht but this, that a freshwater halfling preacher man will not say a word o Grace in their lugs? Forbye these lugs hunger for his words fiercer than a wolf in Winter hungers for meat? Na, na Sir, it surely canna be, and if it be, then Sam Gilfinnan will save ye nae mair.'

The man's whole countenance was to the minister's eyes like a thing on fire, his body held upright by a mad and malevolent will. The minister looked at his audience. It was dark now and they were almost silent. Some had lit torches in the lights of which their faces shone. The minister found himself staring into each gaunt countenance, and then in an instant they all merged into one ravaged visage which seemed to belong to neither age, sex, or time, but was still a furious human thing.

The minister was silent. He knew there was no possible way he could articulate any words at all. At any moment he felt his legs and senses would fail him and the enormity of this Heathen night would devour him. A world passed away it seemed to him in the time it took before they realised he would say nothing, and it was then that an awful rumble rose as from one throat and forward they surged towards him. The minister felt the cart give a sickening lurch as he was thrown from its back.

When he opened his eyes it was as if the itinerants had entirely forgotten him, and were now engaged in a savage carousal to the music of Gilfinnan's pipes. High, wild and shrill, the music tore through the night, and through the minister's soul, shrieking across the hills in a tumult of hydra-headed sound. Within that tumult the obscenity of the dancers reached an insane delirium, some casting their rags from off their backs, others hurling themselves to the ground in furious drunken couplings, for if they had neither food nor clothes, drink they had in plenty. Gilfinnan stood on the barrel drumming on it with his wooden leg, thundering out obscene peasant ballads and bawdy adaptations from the psalms.

The minister lay in the heather where he had fallen when he had been pitched from the cart. His head ached. His eyes like things that scarcely belonged to him delved into the shadows. Not ten feet from where he lay a couple writhed savagely on the ground, to be joined by another and another, fleshless ghosts hurling themselves through darkness, as if their skeletal frames were the instrument, and the earth, heaving to their music, itself the barbaric musician.

In one corner between two carts the minister saw two men fighting, their swords locked in silent combat as if they were utterly alone, united in a terrible antagonism. Equal they seemed at first, their fight a thing of eternity, until one with a strength that seemed suddenly relentless, started to drive the other back until he could retreat no further, and could merely with a desperate and failing strength ward off the other's blows. The fight, the minister eyes now told him, could only have one end, for their was little doubt about the mortal intentions of either, when suddenly there rang out the sharp crack of a pistol.

For a second both the tumult and the duel appeared to shudder in the midst of their exertions. Gilfinnan thundered on the barrel with his wooden leg, for it was he who had fired the shot.

'Ye hae fairly beat him,' he cried out. 'Now fairly gie him quarter.'

A pregnant hush fell on all the revellers. The victorious combatant his sword raised high above his head looked around him in consternation.

'Damn ye awe,' he cried. 'Ye hae yer ain business, we hae ours.'

The minister was certain that he would finish the stroke when once more the piper's voice rang out.

'Ye'll maybe not hae heard much o Sam Gilfinnan, but ye'll not hae heard that he ever missed his mark at this range.'

The piper's arm with the levelled pistol at its end, appeared to the minister's eyes to stretch over an infinity of time and space until at last the man sheathed his sword. In that instant Gilfinnan fired his pistol in the air, struck up again with his pipes, and as if commanded by a fiendish sign from Hell the uproar recommenced.

The minister laid his head in his hands. From where he lay it was as if the world, the night, and the people themselves, had become one great black shuddering mass. He noticed then, almost as if it was a thing outside himself, that he too was half naked, clad only in his shirt. He noticed it, but his mind could not contain it. His nakedness, like everything else his mind tried to concentrate on, disintegrated at the touch of his reason, into a myriad of whirling fragments that were related only to the tempest that kept them in motion. He looked up and saw a woman crawling through the night towards him.

He could see her quite clearly. She was almost naked except for the rags of a grey plaid that clung to her sides like the tattered skin of a beast. He could not tell her age. He could not tell anything about her appearance, except that it existed, and appeared to be moving towards him, an undulating mass of flesh, flesh which seemed to decay and be reborn as it moved. She rose above him now a towering pillar, gleaming white in the moonlight, swinging his breeches round her head.

'Why minister hae I no yer breeks awa? Ken ye not them? Why see ye not how their raven colour maks them tae flee through the air.'

She hurled them high into the sky. It seemed to the minister that they did for a second turn into a great black bird wheeling above him. The woman with a leap stood astride him. She tipped her head back and took a mouthful from a flagon of ale. Taking it from her lips she flung herself upon him.

'Why Sir, yer breeks hae taen tae the air, and yer flesh it seems wad follow. Och, eager I feel it tae be, eager tae be at the mowing, och, eager I ken it is, as eager as I feel it tae be, and atween my legs I hae that which its eagerness may transgress, an weep tears o joy for its transgression.'

For an eternity it seemed to the minister that his mind was transfixed by a fiendish heat which emanated from the woman's mouth along with her words. As her lips closed about his he summoned all his remaining strength and thrust her aside. In that same moment she retaliated by grasping his hair and twisting his head round towards her. Her voice hissed in his ear.

'Why Sir, ken ye not that I hae a dungeon dark and deep whaur ye may rest yer heid and weep. Och, tis a place not far frae here, and watered lang wae mony a tear.'

Suddenly she released him, and leaping to her feet she picked up his fallen breeches, and whirling them round her head, she launched her body into a furious gyration.

> Here lies a Godly man that winna mow,
> That winna show a carline how,
> Forbye he has cast his breeks tae the wind,
> And telt his een they maun be blund.'

To the minister's senses it was as if the hideous shape and the hideous noise tyrannised over the elements. As if the cave itself had erupted from Hell summoned by the drumming of Gilfinnan's wooden leg and the rant of his pipes. For a second time the woman was crawling towards him, her eyes pools of impossible darkness, her voice purring like a great cat's.

'For now we are alane upon the green, and nane sall come

us atween, and I sall hae thee Flesh and Fell.'

The woman was now a real thing, now a phantasmagoria of the night, crawling through an infinitude of space. He could neither take his eyes off her, or turn them upwards to the space that rolled above the leaden hills.

All of a sudden, the tumult ceased, and all, it seemed to him, was floating in silence, and he himself was floating on a great cloud of balmy silence.

Through that silence he could see the woman quite clearly. All her motions and actions had abrubtly changed. She was on her feet, and she was trying to drag him to his feet.

'Rin Sir, ye maun rin for yer life!'

And then she was no more. The music had ceased and they were all fleeing the place. The minister felt their legs rushing past him and leaping over him. There was no mistaking their urgency.

The minister could barely find the power to move. Slowly he turned his head in the opposite direction, his mind functioning now at the behest of a limp and shattered curiosity. There, standing on the brow of a hill, outlined against the sky, stood what the minister perceived to be the gigantic figure of a man. Round his head in slow curves he swung an awesome two-handed sword. At every motion the great engine made, it was as if Heaven itself parted to let it pass.

For a time the figure simply stood. Then with a roar which seemed to exceed anything the night had so far produced, he charged down the hill into the glen his great sword hewing vigorously at anything in his path. All had fled, but this neither checked nor quelled the fury of his onslaught. The terrible blade rose and fell with a rapidity which deceived the minister's vision.

He closed his eyes. In the darkness he heard his soul groaning under the weight of a deranged mind and impotent body. Piercing that darkness there was yet another voice, a voice that the minister loathed, and now knew very well.

'Jedidiah! Jedidiah! Ken ye not me?'

The minister felt his mind finally disintegrating. He forced his eyes to open and he saw the one-legged piper hurl himself forward with demoniac agility, almost under the arc of the great cleaving blade.

456

'Jedidiah! Tis Sam Gilfinnan wha tells ye that awe hae fled afore ye, and ye hae the field, and tis an unseemly rage that vents Godly anger on a briar bush when the enemies o the Lord hae been put tae rout.'

An age seemed to pass before the sword ceased its motions, coming to rest on the giant's shoulder. Gilfinnan, his head barely reaching the man's chest, grasped his arm.

'Why Jedidiah in the nick o time hae ye cam. I speak not for mysel, wha is weel kent as a worthless man o nae account. But ower behind yon briar bush, stretched out on the green, lies a Christian man taen by this Satan's host, stripped o his duds and near done tae death, and wad hae been had not the Lord commanded ye, for I ken nae ither that could hae done it, tae be up and daen. And weel hae ye been daen, but ye maun cam Sir and I will show him tae ye, and ye maun put awa that muckle sword lest ye raise ony mair apprehensions in his heart.'

Barely conscious, the minister was aware of them walking towards him, aware that he was once more the subject of the piper's words.

'See, here he lies, Jedidiah, a very Godly man, ye hae my word on it. Set upon as ye can see, mocked, beaten, stripped o his raiment, and tempted maist wickedly, tae sic a degree that he has near lost his life in resistance, and nae doubt wad hae had ye not cam alang, at Heaven's command, tae be his salvation. But now Sir, ye maun lift him up, which is aboun my power, and we sall tak him hame.'

The giant stooped. The minister felt himself being grasped and swung aloft as if he was no more than a child. He heard Gilfinnan's admonishing voice.

'Gentle ye muckle loun, the Christian man may weel be unconscious, which tae be plain, is nae surprise tae me, but he is still lang for this warld. I will bring alang his gude horse, which is itsel a maist blessit beast, and by a miracle hasna been stolen awa.

The minister heard Gilfinnan's words. He opened his eyes and beheld an outlandish, hirsute countenance, devoid of any human expression or sign of intelligence. He fainted, yet still he could hear the piper's voice, a prattling, dissembling thing which inhabited a place far away from him. The place he was

457

in was a place of silent shadows. He lay prone in that place, and one by one the shadows drew alongside him. He no longer doubted the identity of any.

The first he acknowledged was Sawney Bain himself. He appeared as the minister had only read of him, a tall stalwart soldier, his hand on his sword hilt, his Bible in his saddle-bags, his eyes alive with desire.

He watched as the face seemed to move through a century of bloody years, each one slowly drawing its own scars, until the minister was confronted with an ancient maned head whose blue eyes shone placidly in confusion and defeat, and whose hands clasped about the long stem of a pipe.

The minister remembered very clearly buying that pipe. He had chosen it with care, as if it was in some way an instrument that would unlock the man's soul. Now it seemed curious to him that he should have thought so, and strange that he should have been so angry when it had not succeeded. Even stranger that he could have imagined that anything coherent could have been revealed by that torn and mutilated carcass of history. He was justified in his silence.

The blue eyes shone gently out of the darkness.

'When first I engaged in this business, this end was not what I had in mind at awe.'

☆

When the minister awoke he was lying on a pallet covered in straw inside a hut.

At first his eyes could not adjust to the gloom, and then they picked out the figure of Gilfinnan sitting in the shadows. The piper was quietly drawing on his pipe, apparently unaware that the minister was awake. That he was a true fiend, was, the minister recalled, his last conscious thought concerning him. An imp of lies and evil straight from the Hinterland of Hell, and so unreal had he become that the minister was astonished to find him still inhabiting the earth.

He glanced through the open door of the hut. There too sat the impossible giant, his beard resting on his chest, his blue bonnet clamped firmly on his head. His weapons lay beside him, the great sword embedded in the ground, and a long spear within easy reach of his grasp.

He did not appear to be asleep. Occasionally his head would turn, first to the left and then to the right, his eyes scanning the night. There was nothing casual about these movements, if anything disturbed his vision his hand would clasp the shaft of the spear, only releasing it when whatever had attracted him no longer did so.

The minister closed his eyes again. When he opened them Gilfinnan was staring down at him. For a moment the minister's eyes traced every line of that villainous, deceitful, countenance.

'You are a true fiend,' he said.

'Och, minister could I be onything else?'

'Leave me in peace, I will not be tormented by you further.'

'Och, minister, in an earthly way'o speaking, peace is not an easy thing tae come by.'

'In the name of God I command you to depart from me.'

'Hush minister, tak not the name o God lichtly in this place, Jedidiah micht tak it wrang, and madman he micht be, but he's a muckle huge ane.'

Gilfinnan's slightly anxious glance towards the giant surprised the minister. He was, despite everything, almost amused.

'As you will not in charity, leave me in peace, and I cannot at present make you, at least, if you are capable of any truth at all, tell me who he is, and what is this place you have brought me to.'

The piper's voice was suddenly very low and quiet.

'Why Sir, this is the poor biggin of Jedidiah Gilhazie, a man wha is as far aboun awe men in Godliness as he is aboun them in height. But a word o warning in yer ear, minister. He kens not richtly wha ye are, for awe I hae assured him o yer saintliness, an assurance which for the time he is inclined tae accept. But dinna dispute wae him on ony matter o religion, and aye agree wae him should he seek tae question ye on ony point o doctrine. For should ye dispute wae him in ony way, he micht just tak tae thinking that ye hae cam frae the Deil tae destroy him. And minister, he is in maist things a gentle man, but a fell dangerous ane when confronted by ony o that host that he calls the Lord's enemies, and his brain Sir, is a damned unchancy organ when it is set the task o precise discrimination.

Why only last nicht ye saw him mistaking poor wandering folk for a regiment o Hell coming tae kill him.'

'Mad he might be, but I can fully understand his error.'

'Aye weel, nae doubt ye can minister, being a man o sic great penetration. But maybe ye should learn tae look mair kindly on folk wha hae suffered lang and much wae but little recompense in the past, and likely tae hae less in the future.'

'I will not be mocked or scolded by you, even when you seem to believe that I am in your power. If this Jedidiah is such a devout if peculiar Christian, I wonder that he tolerates your company, or accepts your assurance on anything.'

'Och minister, I am nae doubt, and nae doubt deserve tae be, a worthless man in yer een. But that forbye I am weel enough thocht o by some. And in truth, ye ken but little o what ye speak, and indeed, very little o yon man wha guards the door, wha if his brains are as addled as ye think, and I hae nae doubt but they are, has his ain reasons for being sae.'

'You have not told me who he is.'

'Och minister, tae ken wha he is now, ye maun ken wha he was then, and that is a lang lang time ago, for he is a fair bit aulder than ye micht think. Indeed a man o reason micht weel think his age is as unnatural as his size. But if ye will permit me, and for a time at least, cease yer rebukes and railings. That I deserve them I dinna dispute, but I hae also been o some service tae ye, I will tell ye his story as I mind it.'

Gilfinnan drew heavily on his pipe. The minister turned his head away.

'Och weel Sir, if ye dinna care tae hear it, Sam Gilfinnan is no the kind o man tae inflict his words on them that dinna want tae hear them.'

'You are a dissembler, Mr Gilfinnan, but tell me his story.'

'Weel, weel, I gied ye fair warning when first we met, that I was not a saintly man, but a lang lost sheep wha had found his shepherd. A bit turnabout frae the tale in the Bible I grant ye.'

The minister glanced through the door of the hut. The dawn was starting to break and the giant appeared to be sleeping.

'Tell me his story, Mr Gilfinnan, or be silent.'

'Weel minister, as ye hae expressly commandit me. It took place a lang time ago, lang afore my time, for as I hae telt ye, he is a fair bit aulder than ye micht think. But there was this bit priest wha wad gang on a pilgrimage. I ken not exactly tae what place he wad gang on this pilgrimage, but nae doubt it was a very holy ane. He was o the Roman Church this man, sturdy and weel fleshed, mounted on a gude horse, and in his ain branch o doctrine a great disputer.

'Now he had been alane on the road for some days, I ken not exactly how mony, when he met this minister o the Reformed Kirk wha was likewise ganging on a pilgrimage, and was likewise a very stern man o his doctrine. Weel, as ye can nae doubt imagine, a great dispute arose atween them, which they baith resolved tae their ain satisfaction, each haeving sae fairly bested the ither that they becam gude friends and wad continue the journey side by side disputing fiercely awe the while.

'Some days they spent in this fashion, pleasantly enough nae doubt, when they were joined by anither preaching, pilgriming man. Now this third man was a Bishop o the Episcopal persuasion, which he declared he could champion chapter and verse wae ony man on earth. Weel Sir, ye can weel imagine the three cornered battle that now took place, truth dinging doun heresy, heresy dinging doun truth, till exhaustion in its mercy conquered awe. But the upshot o the meeting was that he wad ride along wae them, which they accepted, for after awe, despite the holy purpose, it was a gey wearisome journey, and the company o learned, if misguided men, wad nae doubt mak it a mair cheerful ane.

'Now they travelled some days and some miles in each ither's company, dinging each ither's brains wae Latin, Greek and Hebrew, chapter and verse, and never tiring o the business. Then ane bricht morning, weel breakfasted, and warming themsels up for the gude ficht, they were joined by a fourth man, wha at first sicht, gied them some justifiable cause for concern.

'This fourth man ye see, was riding a gude horse and was very weel armed, wae a gude sword and a spear, twa or three guns, and a steel bonnet on his heid, and looking, every lang inch o him, like a man wha kent the use o these things. But awe that forbye, he bade them gude morning in a very civil and Christian manner, and announced that he tae was ganging on pilgrimage, haeving, as he himsel confessed, spent awe his previous life as a wild Border reiver, he now felt some penance was due.

'Now ane and awe, they were a bit uneasy about this. Not that they ony langer expected ony danger frae him. But it was plain tae their een that he was nae mair than an ill-bred Border loun wae a bad conscience, and hardly fit company for Godly and learned gentlemen.

'Sae a great dispute arose on the question, till the minister o the Reformed Kirk, wha was a very canny man, offered tae question the weir-man closer and report back tae them. This they agreed on, and this he did, and in time he reported back that it was his firm belief that this meeting was not a chance thing but was a great act o Providence. For he argued, was not the road an unchancy place, and mony a wild bit o it through which they still had tae pass? And was it not possible that the Lord himsel had sent this gude man o his hands tae be their guardian, which was further evidenced by the man's humble and respectful manner? He kens his place, this minister declared, and I hae nae doubt but that he kens how tae keep it.

'This, they awe declared, was a wise and Christian proposal, and ane o some significance, it being the first point o agreement that they had hit upon since first they had met. And sae, wae a bit nod in his direction they indicated tae the weir-man that he micht gang wae them.

'Sae on their way they rade , disputing as fiercely as ever they had, the Border clansman bringing up the rear. Whether he paid ony attention tae their disputes, or whether he did not, I canna say, and nae doubt he thocht them far aboun his heid. They, for the maist part, clean forgot him, only calling him tae attention ance in a while when a part o the road aheid seemed a bit dangerous tae them.

'Now naething untoward befell them for a week or mair, until ane evening, marching briskly through a dark auld glen, there awe at ance in front o them, was a sicht that nane had ever seen afore, and few wad wish tae see again. Richt in front o their een was a monstrous man in black armour, mounted on a great black horse wae ane ee golden and the ither ane blude red. And ower his back was a great twa-handed sword, and in his hand a great twa-pronged lance, and he waved his lance in sic a way that a bairn could tell that this was nae earthly creature, but that forbye, he wanted a word. That word was, for ye can be sure they were silent men now, that Satan had risen frae Hell in rebellion against God himsel, as ance lang ago he had done.

'That time, as awe Christian folk ken, his army had been routed frae the field and cast doun frae Heaven. But that, the monstrous man declared, shaking his spear a bit, wasna the case this day, for the pikeline o the Lord had been broken, and their horse cut tae pieces and driven frae the ficht, and only the citadel o Heaven itsel still held out bravely, forbye it couldna be expected tae hold out much langer, it haeving been breached already in mony places.

'He spoke these words maist calmly, but as ye can weel imagine, our gude pilgrims were thrown intae some confusion, trembling and fear, and kent not at awe what tae dae. It was then that the angel, for sic he was, raised his right hand tae quiet them, and went on tae tell them, in a simpering kind o voice ill-suited tae his martial appearance, that for awe the great battles that were being presently fought in Heaven, little wad change on earth. Satan, he declared, wad hae as much need o gude and learned men tae serve him as ever God had, and he bade them desist frae their causeless panic, for he had not come tae kill them, but tae offer them new positions, much like their auld, but under a kindlier maister.

'This it seems michtily re-assured them, and if they shed a bit tear at first, they were cheerful enough shortly. Awe except for the weir-man, wha, forbye he had observed awe that had taen place, had said nae word himsel, and now he just turned his horse around and set off doun the road at a brisk pace.

'The angel, seeing this, flew after him crying that he needna flee awa sae swiftly, for the Deil had as much need o gude fichting men as ever God had, and nae doubt there wad be a captaincy in it for him. At this the clansman turned sharply about and shook his spear in the angel's face, and declared that he had fought in mony battles whaur a brave stand had turned a rout intae a victory, and betide him weel or betide him woe, he wad gang and lend a hand in this ane, and put himsel under the Lord's command, and wae his ain spear point raised, he dared the angel tae bar his way.

'Weel Sir, there he sits, Jedidiah Gilhazie, armed wae the

sword he took frae the Angel o Hell in single ficht, waiting for the Lord tae command him, and kenning, that when that time comes, the Lord kens whaur tae find him. But for the present he kens very weel that Satan's legions are awe about him, and when on a mirk nicht they should seek tae owerwhelm him, he is naething laith tae gang forth tae meet them point and edge, and put the muckle cowards tae flight.

'Sae now ye ken minister, and if his brains hae become somewhat addled wae waiting, and if whiles, like last nicht, he mistakes honest folk for the Deil's host, weel we maun be forbearing about that, and canny folk just mak allowances, and on occasion, gude use o their legs.'

The minister was silent. He felt his heart sink under the weight of the story, and the presence of the glowering giant at the door.

'A wearisome tale Mr Gilfinnan, do you really believe such things?'

'I had the story frae my faither, and he frae his faither afore him, and the living proof o it is afore my een. And indeed, if tale it is I hae telt ye, I ken nane that can clap a sensible history in its place. Och minister, ye hae ridden far and wide and found but little I think, and nae doubt Jedidiah is the last o them that wad strike a blow in God's cause.'

'The last, Mr Gilfinnan? I think not.'

'Weel Sir, and here I speak plainly tae ye. It is my belief that when the people rise again, it will not be for Kirk or King that they rise, nor yet for God in Heaven. For tae my mind the time o these things is ower, and they are deid in folk's hairts, forbye the fact that as yet they ken it not.

'Aye Sir, tae my mind when the people tak up arms again, as ane day they surely will, they sall dae sae in a new cause, which will be their ain cause, and awe these things which are at present baith feared and worshipped will be as ane against them.'

Gilfinnan's features were set now in a way that the minister had never seen before, gone was the sacriligious jester, gone was the Bacchic piper, gone too was the demoniac apparition. He appeared now as a creature utterly beyond the minister's power to either admonish or rebuke. He remembered the prophetess in the Highlands. The meaning of her words, indeed the words themselves, were almost identical to Gilfinnan's. To the minister's mind it was as if the world itself had broken free from its axis, and nothing that had previously stood there would stand much longer. Catriona's other words ranged freely in his brain, as if his mind had no longer any power to quell them.

' *Och but I pity ye, for I see a great wolf beast on that dark road, and whether it is hunting ye doun or whether it is leading ye on, I ken not.*'

He looked at the piper, vulpine jaws it now seemed to him gripped the stem of his pipe.

'Who are you?'

'Ane that kens ye weel enough, and awe that hae ganged afore ye.'

'Answer me plainly.'

'Dis it matter wha I am Sir? I am not o yer time. Why, I am nae mair than a loun ye met upon the Sherramuir. Ye seek for answers Sir when they are awe about ye. Ye seek for reasons when there are nane tae gie. Ye seek tae justify yersel when Marten Gilmarten wad justify ye a thousand times, and a few days in Edinburgh wae yer een open wad confirm that he is not a foolish man. And nae doubt ye think that Jedidiah Gilhazie is nae mair than a mad loun wha kens not his place or time, and ye reflect not at awe on the meaning o awe the things that hae brought him tae this pass, and nae doubt ye wad like this warld tae be a kind and Godly place full o Christian folk, each contented in their station.'

The minister closed his eyes.

'*There is a dark road afore ye alang which ye sall gang whether ye will or no, and it will lead ye tae a place that is not presently kent, and may weel be nae place at awe, and then again it may weel be a place that is very real for awe that, and it may weel be that it will be a place o joy and it may weel be that it will be place o sadness, and it may be that ye will not be able tae tell ane frae the ither, and it may be that yer heart will be untrue tae yer senses and yer senses untrue tae yer heart, and the ane will scorn them that ye love, and the ither will love them that ye scorn . . .*'

There was nothing that he could imagine now, nothing that his reason could grasp. The world into which he plunged was

465

a turmoil, void of substance or sense. A subterranean cave which had once been a dark forest in which there had once been the shape of trees, and into the shelter of these trees people had fled, to be hunted down by the blood-mad soldiery of a Christian king. And when they had ridden away the forest became a many chambered tomb in which the dead lived and breathed and spoke. In time they had emerged, their naked bodies swarming forth from their darkness into a moonless night.

'It fell about this nicht that we wad gang hunting. I lay in my position wae Nancy by my side as was our custom. It was a warm summer nicht o the kind we favoured. No sae dark that we could not see our marks, but ower dark for the folk o Chaos tae see us.

'Alang the road cam some o these folk, and rich enough they nae doubt were, for they rade in a fine bit carriage wae a gude horse tae pull it, and by their carriage rade an armed man.

'It was sensible tae shoot the armed man first, for we could not see properly what was in the carriage, sae Patrick directed that Nancy, mysel, and Colin, should awe train our guns on him. This we did, and when they drew alangside, woof, bang! and out o the saddle he fell, and the man that drove the coach fell wae him, forbye I ken not wha shot him. Then the horse fell tae and awe was silence, nane appearing frae within the carriage.

'At first we waited, and then Patrick ran up tae it, and Nancy and mysel ran up tae it. And in it, looking out at us maist strangely, was a carline a bit aulder than mysel but no much, and dressed in fine claes.

'She didna move, or mak ony sound at awe, but just looked at us, and the way she looked it seemed tae me that forbye nane had hairmed her she was hersel near deid.

'That she was not we soon kent, for she let out a fell scream as Jean, or it might hae been Catriona, I canna mind, raised her pistol tae shoot her, for we liked not tae linger ower sic business, but tae dae it quickly, which was mair kind.

'That nicht a thing fell out which had never afore happened. Patrick knocked up the gun and said that he wad tak

466

the carline alive, and wae his ain gun he dared ony tae check him.

'This was against awe that we kent, and awe that we had previously agreed. For had not mither aye telt us that the only folk that we could bring alive intae our cave were bairns wha could learn tae be like us?

'But that nicht nane dared countermand Patrick. For a lang time afore that nicht Patrick had grown mair and mair factious wae wanting tae be chief, and wad aye seek tae build a party o support around him, and Patrick being the largest and strangest o us awe, and the leader in awe our enterprises, it was a fell lot easier tae be wae him than against him.

'Awe this mither had watched. But getting very auld now she could dae little tae check him. And faither just said that Patrick had a proud and ambitious hairt, and the Lord aye laid up ruin for sic folk. That nicht he himsel picked up the carline in his airms. I ken nocht o what she thought when he did this, for she didna struggle but just made unco queer sounds as she lay ower his shoulder, sounds like what an animal wad mak, wae her een sometimes open and sometimes shut. And when they were open they were like twa great stars which shone in her heid. Nancy took me by the airm, and I could feel her pressing it very close, and nae doubt the carline had seen them that had been wae her lying deid, and a terrible noise o struggling and yelling she put up sae that Patrick could hardly hold her, and baith Colin and Elijah cried out tae stop this Godless behaviour and shoot her properly.

'Awe Patrick did in reply tae that was tae ance mair raise his ain gun, and he said he wad dae as he pleased and nane should try and stop him. Ithers did as they were telt, but Nancy pulled me awa and we ran back intae the cave, and she said that she thocht something terrible wad happen this nicht.

'And sae it cam tae pass, for when mither wha was sitting in her usual place saw that this carline was still alive her een blazed wae an awful rage sic as I had never before witnessed. Patrick had put the carline doun on the ground beside him, and I mind weel how she just sat there, her een it seemed hardly daring tae look at us awe.

467

'I had never seen ane o the Chaos folk sae close and sae alive afore, apart frae bairns, which are different, but her skin was whiter than ony skin that I had ever seen, and her een now just straining tae be out o her heid. And then mither yelled at Patrick for being a blackguard and an ill-born bastard, and demanding tae ken what the meaning o his behaviour was. Faither said naething, but his face was like the sky in Winter, or like untae the Lord himsel in his anger. But he said naething, and we awe just watched, and Patrick said that he wanted her, and wanted her alive, and ony that hairmed her wad hae him tae answer tae. And then he drew his sword, and wae it in ane hand and his gun in the ither, he demanded that ony that wad dispute wae him should dae it now.

'He looked around the cave as he said this, and tae avoid his een I looked at the carline, but I could tell naething o her thoughts, and maybe there was nane tae tell, but she was weel covered up, as awe the Chaos folk are, tae hide their shame.

'I ken not clearly what happened next, but awe at ance, out o this confused silence, mither had a gun in each hand sae fast that nane o us saw frae whence they cam, but baith o them were levelled at Patrick, and mither, auld as she was, we weel kent wad not miss at that distance. She cried Patrick a fornicator and a blackguard, and mony ither things she cried him, saying that she wad hae nae violations or fornications in her house, and nae son o hers wad behave in sic a cruel way, ither than he killed her first.

'Patrick stood like ane that had lost the power tae move or speak, when awe at ance the carline let out an eldritch scream, and Patrick tried tae strike the guns frae mither's hands wae his sword, and mither shot the guns, ane ball fleeing out intae the sea, but the ither hit Patrick square on his brow and he deed straight awa.

'Mither just looked at him then, and I ken not at awe what was in her heid. But awe she said was that he was the first tae dee in the cave and she doubted not but that he had damned us awe. She looked ower at the carline wha looked as if her hairt had gaed clean out o her breast at the sound o the gun. But mither smiled kindly on her, and then she commandit in a voice that nane dared dispute wae that she should be set free.

'That was done, and whether she counted it as a blessing or whether she did not, I canna tell, for there was nae sign on her face that I could read.

'That nicht there was neither laughing or rejoicing in our cave. We buried Patrick doun by the sea's edge, and faither reading frae his Bible said that what had happened was the herald o the end, and mither went doun tae the sea and washed hersel and said naething mair.'

The minister opened his eyes. Gilfinnan was bending over him, his countenance a thing of infinite malice.

'Why minister, I thocht ye had near passed awa.'

'What is to become of me?'

'Och minister, I sall bide wae ye, and will not leave ye or desert ye until ye are in a safe and peaceful place, and aiblins there is nae sic place, and I sall bide wae ye forever and aye.'

☆

The minister knew nothing of the time which intervened. When he regained consciousness he was lying in a bed in a pleasant room.

He had, he thought, been in it before, but a vast chasm seemed to divide his memory from the present. At the mouth of that chasm stood Sawney Bain, and by his side, Agnes Douglas. Both were quite familiar to him now and he recognised them instantly. On their right stood a decayed giant and a one-legged man. They belonged to an ancient furious tale in which people had raised God as their standard and had defied order, authority, and history, and marched in rebellion against them all. A rebellion which a blind Highland prophetess and a drunken piper had both declared would have no end.

As the minister watched, another man appeared at Agnes Douglas's side, mounted on a fine black horse and wearing a Highland plaid. The minister remembered Mathius Pringle's first description, 'He was a subtle, clever, clean looking man,' and he knew that he was at last looking at Steven Malecky.

All the figures, unaware it appeared to the minister, of his presence, faded as the door of the room opened. Through it walked a woman with a shawl drawn over her head. She walked over to the bed and stared down at him. He felt her eyes scrutinising him, piercing him, seeking out the estranged thing that had become his soul.

'Helen, you are Helen Melville are you not?'

She took off her shawl and shook her red hair free.

'Why minister, I could hardly be ony ither could I?'

'How did I come to be here?'

'Ye were brought minister, by a man wha bade me tak care o ye seeing that ye were ill, and he telt me not tae let ye gang out till ye were weel, he telt me ye had taen a bad fall frae yer horse.'

'Who was that man?'

The woman smiled. To the minister's eyes her smile became as one with the chasm, peopled, it now appeared, with vast multitudes.

'Just a kindly auld man o little account.'

'That does not properly answer my question, do you know his name?'

She did not reply. The minister, once again, felt his senses begin to fail him. The chasm broadened out into a vast midnight plain surrounded by terrible mountains.

'Is Martha here?'

'Martha is deid Sir, some three weeks back, sae I am alane now.'

'I would have liked to have attended at her burial.'

'Och but ye hae been awa minister, far awa, and Martha had her ain Cameronian folk tae pray for her.'

The plain was endless, dwarfing the multitudes that inhabited it. Malecky alone stood out, an ancient shiltron spear now rested on his shoulder. The minister felt her hands cradling his head.

'May God rest her soul.'

'Aye minister, nae doubt but he owes her that.'

The minister wanted to reply but no words came. Silently she drew his head against her breasts.

'Ye are weak minister, weak as a bairn, and hae been raving twa or three nichts.'

The minister opened his eyes. The woman appeared to him

470

as a naked thing borne on a cloud of air.

'How is my parish?'

'Och Trig is fine, but the laird is deid.'

'Sir John Doig dead? How can that be?'

I only ken the story at second hand, but it seems some speech he made in Parliament michtily angered the common folk o Edinburgh, and they set upon his carriage in a mob, owerturning it. As a consequence o this they say he broke his neck.'

The minister saw the laird's vast corpse stretched out on the plain, crows pecking his eyes. The spear that he now knew belonged to Malecky was embedded in the ground at his head. His senses now accepted the sight with extraordinary equanimity.

'May God have mercy on his soul. How are they taking it in Trig?'

'Maist cheerfully, forbye they hae some apprehensions as tae the next Doig that is on his way, for it seems that there is nae end tae the breed.'

She looked at him. She was smiling broadly, amused at her own wit. He stared at the naked expanse of her neck and shoulders. Her eyes shone brilliantly back at him. She looked calm and self-assured, and outside any authority that he could wield.

'I demand to know who brought me here?'

'Och, minister, I wad hae thocht ye wad hae done wae demanding.'

'If you will not tell me leave me in peace.'

Gently she replaced his head on the pillow. She pulled the shawl once more over her shoulders, rose to her feet and turned slowly away from him. Something, he no longer knew what, howled from within him.

'I demand to know, was he a one-legged man?'

She appeared to take an age to leave him. The minister's eyes followed every swaying line of her body as she walked. When she reached the door, she turned and smiled at him.

'He was only an auld wandering man o Martha and mysel's acquaintance, wha kent this place was near Trig and thocht tae dae ye a service.'

THE END

471